FIVE SUNS PRESS

First published by Five Suns Press (USA) 2023

Copyright © Z. Thirteen, 2023

First edition 2023

ISBN 979-8-9889106-1-9 (hc.)

ISBN 979-8-9889106-0-2 (pbk.)

Featuring contributions by L. Rachel

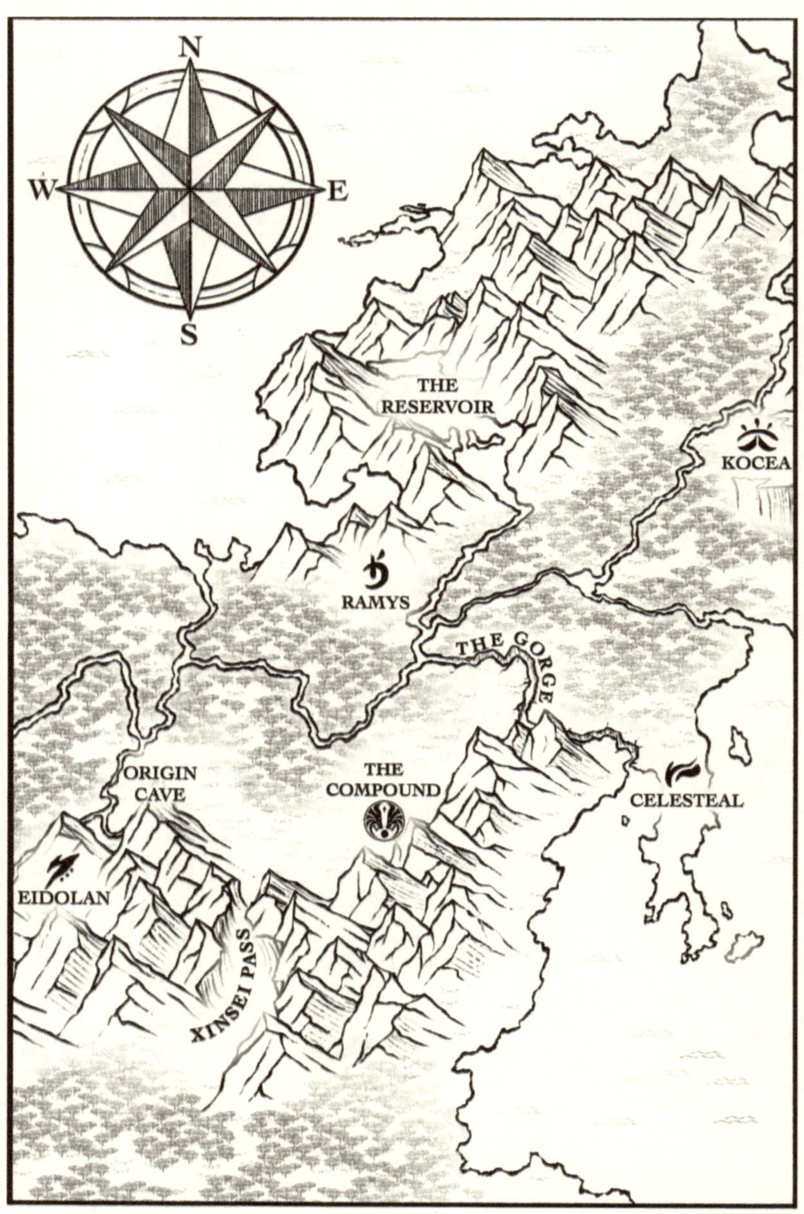

N
W
E
S
THE RESERVOIR
KOCEA
RAMYS
THE GORGE
ORIGIN CAVE
THE COMPOUND
CELESTEAL
EIDOLAN
XINSEI PASS

ISTHMUS

Z. THIRTEEN

Five Suns Press

CONTENTS

1. INCHOATE — 1

2. AUGUR — 18

3. DIATRIBE — 45

4. COVENANT — 73

5. ABYSS — 95

6. CATACLYSM — 120

7. RESPITE — 146

8. LAZARUS — 170

9. PROPHECY — 195

10. GENESIS — 217

11. APHELION — 238

12. SABBATH — 262

13. EXODUS — 285

14. PERIHELION — 301

15. TREMOR — 324

16. SODOM — 352

17. WRAITH — 379

18. PULSE — 410

19. PRODIGAL 430

20. REPENTANCE 456

GLOSSARY 478

ISTHMUS

I
INCHOATE

The drum of pounding feet against fertile soil bounced between the trees, the only thing familiar now.

Power rippled beneath his skin as he raced through the jungle and his broad chest heaved with desperation. Low-hanging branches ripped his flesh raw as he tore through the brush, thick muscles stinging with every stride. Four long legs carried him far and fast, and steam poured from his nostrils as he left his pursuer far behind. He threw back his head and howled, a triumphant whoop coming from deep within his gut as he laughed.

Kodokuna's celebration was cut short as his foot caught on a rock jutting out of the soil, and he flew forward. The chase was over before his massive weight even hit the ground.

In seconds, his pursuer was upon him. With a guttural roar that shook the forest itself, a heavy figure soared overhead and landed hard on top of him. He found himself face to face with a maw full of gruesome yellowed teeth, the fangs encrusted in gold.

"You're faster than you look, old man." He choked on his words as his throat was pinned in a vice-like hold.

"*Wait!* I'm sorry, Rataan-Leih," he wheezed through the brown-furred ghaengste's strong grip. "This time, I—"

"This time is the last time, you insufferable fool. The Ramys clan will not tolerate insolent rogues marking our borders and harassing the scouts." Rataan-Leih snarled, his gilded claws unsheathing. "You were exiled out of mercy, *hona'dei*, you are lucky we didn't just kill you."

Kodokuna winced at the pressure digging into his neck.

"I have nowhere else to go!"

Rataan raked his claws against the skin of Kodokuna's throat, lacerating the vulnerable flesh with a splatter of black blood.

"The patience of the lunai has run out, Kodokuna. If I catch you on Ramys land again, I will rip you apart."

Kodokuna cried out and writhed, agony tearing through his neck. Rataan released the hold on his jugular and stepped off, scowling down at him.

"Get up, boy."

Kodokuna reluctantly obeyed and hoisted his oversized body out of the dirt, still heaving from the chase. He forced himself to look up at the familiar figure before him, hard golden eyes and a scarlet mane cropped into a proud arc along the older man's neck.

"Your mother's death broke your only blood tie to the clan; you have nothing left here," Rataan continued coldly. "You are a man now, not a child. Take your exile with grace and leave this land or you will learn the true fate of an outsider."

Kodokuna stepped closer to the older ghaengste, his previous fear suddenly falling away.

"Take my exile with *grace?*" His breath caught and his nose twitched as he tried to calm himself.

"You've never left the clan, you don't know what it's like to be alone out here—" His voice cracked as anger turned into frantic pleading. "You know I'm as good as dead."

Rataan lifted his bearded chin and glared down his jagged snout at the other man. His words came out as harsh and merciless as the look in his eyes.

"Do not tell me what I know, learn what you do not. Yes, the *weak* will die, but the strong survive because Matka spares those of Her children worth sparing. Ask yourself, boy, are you worthy?"

...

"Damn it!" Kodokuna whipped his tail back and forth as he paced through the trees. He was young, too young to have accurately judged how many times the lunai would tolerate him trespassing to flirt with the clan scouts. He was large, larger than his kin by a gargantuan proportion. He shook the ground when he walked, he towered above crowds despite his adolescence. And he was strong; far too strong for the clan to consider him a harmless nuisance. To them, he had become a threat. That much was clear, he didn't once entertain the possibility that Rataan might be bluffing. The old kaunek-leih was many, many things, but he was not one to bluff. There was no doubt in Kodokuna's mind that if he didn't leave the area soon, he'd be killed. And yet, he couldn't will himself to move from where Rataan had abandoned him.

"I'm going to die out here," he croaked in tired acceptance to no one but the still air. The young ghaengste let himself drop to the cool soil with a huff.

"Old bastard..." he whispered under his breath as he carefully touched the wound on his throat. Pulling his palm back, he cringed at the oily black liquid staining his paw pad. He shook his head, as if to refuse the pain, then slowly lowered to the ground and set his mighty head on his arm. A stubborn anger twitched behind his tense brow as he fought the heaviness of his tired eyelids. Maybe he was daring Rataan to come back, to make good on his word. Oh, how it would enrage the old commander to find the giant rogue laying right where he'd left him; how much it would haunt him to be so disobeyed and so unfeared. The thought satisfied Kodokuna just enough to momentarily ease his plagued mind.

A single crimson feather lazily floated down through the trees, dancing in the cool jungle air. It quietly found respite on the moist ground as he surrendered to the lull of a weary slumber.

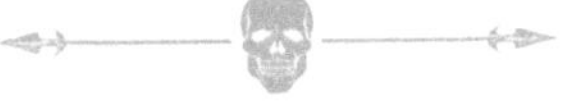

"Come on, people, let's get a fucking move on!"

A voice like thunder boomed through the storage hangar as the crew scrambled to collect their luggage. Captain Short barked orders at his subordinate soldiers and derogatory words of impatient encouragement at the rest of the personnel.

"Go. Go! Go!"

He followed close behind the last few stragglers down the ramp, nearly stepping on the backs of their heels as he herded them like cattle. Two other men in camouflage uniforms snickered in the background as they watched their superior officer terrorize the med team lagging behind.

Following a sharp look from the captain and a quick, shrill whistle, they halted their cackling and slowly lowered the storage unit's gigantic door. They marched down the ramp to follow the rest of the crew.

The congregation passed through another towering airlocked doorway, and the dim glow of the passage gave way to glaring lights and wide, stark-white halls. An echoing clash rang from behind them as the solid steel doors locked shut, and the crew of the Remus-Romulus Expedition Program stood crowded together, staring ahead, their luggage in hand. Before them laid the open expanse of the compound, its fluorescent-lit common room sprawling with doorways to hallways that would undoubtedly take time to scout through. The twenty-six warm bodies on board Expedition Remus took in the first glimpse of their new lives for the next four years. A life of endless unknowns on an unexplored planet — an entire world for them to be the first to discover. Researchers, medical staff, and military personnel, all the best in their fields, prepared to be the first humans to settle on Dwarf Planet 7355264Z. The pioneers of a new era of human life.

"I guess they're just going to stare all day, then." The captain's voice broke through the silence like a gunshot and made several of his crewmates jolt. "Master Sergeant Fischer, you're in charge of barrack A. Master Sergeant Mendoza, barrack B. Crawford, you're with me. Understood?"

He was met by an equally loud cacophony of 'yes sirs' and 'yes captains' as his subordinates split into groups and scattered to fulfill the respective duties they'd been briefed on prior. The research and medical teams headed straight for the living quarters.

Doctor Sherri Daniels was far from the only person aboard who was already irritated by the captain's raucous voice, but she may have been the one least distracted by it. The young botanist had too many racing thoughts and daydreams for the glorified soldier's premature tyranny to derail her focus. That and part of her was just a little too thankful for the fire he'd lit under her crewmates' asses. She felt she might explode if they waited even a second longer to get started, and she headed through the corridor at a rushed march. Sherri was quite possibly the only human on this new planet who truly and genuinely wanted to be there.

Sure, they were all there for a reason. They all said yes, they all answered the call. For some, it was a once-in-a-lifetime opportunity they just couldn't dare refuse. Some were motivated by fame and glory. Most were bought by the promise of a planet-sized paycheck. But Sherri Daniels was there to *be there*. She might as well have been working her entire life to catch an opportunity like this; her entire career, at least. She would be the first botanist in human history to study alien life. Her top priority was getting off base and out into the new world.

"When are we getting out there again?" Sherri asked no one in particular as she walked through the dormitory hall among several of her new coworkers. The eagerness lacing her voice gave away that she already knew the answer but simply wanted to hear it from someone else.

"Mission briefing calls for four full weeks of observation before we're permitted to make first contact," an extremely tall and slim man answered from her right, then he glanced down at her.

"But I'm guessing you already knew that, considering you spent the entire trip going over the briefing files. We haven't officially been introduced." He extended his hand for a cordial shake. "Doctor Marshall Novak."

Sherri gave him a firm handshake and a curt smile.

"Just gauging how likely everyone else is to actually adhere to that timeline. Doctor Sherri Daniels."

She already knew of Doctor Novak, and more significantly, she knew of his achievements in nuclear chemistry and rocket science. He struck her as more casual and personable than she'd expected. By most accounts, he was described as an arrogant prick and worse. Despite not meeting him in person before take-off, she'd recognized the sleek glasses, sharp features, and neat brown hair fading to gray. Handsome but not strikingly so. He was vastly taller in real life than he looked in pictures, however, and she already resented having to crane her neck to meet his eye.

"Glad to be working with you, Doctor Daniels." Doctor Novak nodded as he released her hand and continued walking with a confident but slightly uneven saunter. Sherri broke off from him and the rest of the group as she spotted her room number.

"You as well, Doctor. I'll see you around." She gave a polite wave to the rest of her coworkers with whom she had yet to exchange introductions before unlocking her door and rushing inside. She flung her bags on the closest of the two beds and wasted no time unpacking as quickly as possible. There was no schedule to be fulfilled on arrival day beyond moving in and configuring all of the compound's functions, but Sherri's personal itinerary was far from empty. She was still unsure how likely it was that she'd remain confined to the cramped white halls for the full observation period, but she'd be damned if she didn't investigate every single facet of her new home and neighbors in the meantime.

It was beckoned by the scent of blood.

Stalking along the jungle canopy's sheltered branches, it scanned the foliage below with a steady eye for the source of the smell. It was faint, not enough blood to emanate from carrion, but plenty to suggest an imminent meal. A thick mist that clung to the skin sat stagnant among the broad leaves, carrying with it cold whispers of hunger. Droplets of morning dew glinted through the dimness, refracting yellow and blue ribbons of light that pierced the canopy above. It crept along a vast winding branch toward the scent of the blood; the source was just ahead now. Gracefully slipping through a tangled curtain of vines, it looked down over a clearing in the trees and gazed upon the bloody vessel.

The beast below was unlike anything it had seen before.

A ghaengste of the forest, impossibly large — monstrous. He lay limp on the mossy ground, but even in his relaxed state, there was a dangerous rippling of sturdy musculature beneath his faintly twitching skin that gave proof of life. His smooth fur was a dusty tan, the scales trailing down his spine a dull brown, and hints of olive painted stripes down his flank. The same green color trailed down his neck and long tail in an unruly mane, growing darker at the roots. Brutish teeth hanging slightly below his lip made a ferocious addition to his outlandish appearance. Perhaps he was dying, as the ghastly cuts on his throat, shallow breaths, and growing pool of black blood might suggest. But despite his weakness and wounds, the beast was no prey, and the stranger felt like anything but his predator. Still, the titan below was maimed and unsuspecting. The stranger soundlessly crawled to a lower branch to get a closer look, calculating how fast it would have to move to tear the remainder of his throat out before being detected.

As if he heard its thoughts and smelled its intentions, the beast's dark, beady eyes snapped open, double pupils contracted.

...

Kodokuna awoke to the feeling of being watched, but the dark jungle around him revealed no company. He supposed it was the judgmental eyes of the Great Mother Herself watching him through the faintly glowing bark of the trees and the cold soil beneath him. There was not a place on the treacherous planet where he'd felt sheltered from Her gaze. Not a place on Matka where one could be alone. He'd been taught as a child to be grateful for his home on Her flesh and Her stewardship of ghaengstekind, but deep down, life on Matka had always felt far from a blessing.

He peeled his massive weight off the cool forest floor with a strangled grunt, pain ripping through his neck as his wound stretched open with the movement. His chest was now dyed black, and he grew lightheaded as he realized how much blood he'd lost. He pondered whether Rataan-Leih had intended for him to bleed out or simply wanted to injure him severely enough for something else to come along and finish the job. Kodokuna knew all too well that he'd need to bandage his wound, and he knew he should have done it hours ago before the sweet scent of his weakness had time to waft through the hungry woods. Yet he still hesitated, lingering in the clearing. He was sure Matka would seal his fate any minute now. Most likely another hungry rogue like himself would come to claim and cannibalize him, or a particularly bold pack of kru'vaii would finish him off. Perhaps Rataan would come back and do the honors himself. The commander's ironic words rose in the back of Kodokuna's mind, and he nearly laughed.

"Matka spares those of Her children worth sparing... reihggus shit. Matka put us here to watch us kill and eat each other, and She laughs while we do it." Kodokuna spoke boldly to himself, loud enough for any lurking enemies to hear. Part of him wanted to be heard; part of him wanted a fight. Maybe most of him did.

"The Mother hates me just as much as the lunai do. Damn Her." He dragged his feet through the soil, beginning to trudge along aimlessly. He chuckled and shook his head as if he finally understood the punchline to some bad joke.

"Damn you!" he called out into the jungle, tilting his chin in the air to amplify his youthful voice. "You hear me, Great Mother? Damn you, and damn the lunai

too. I'd rather be a *dead hona'dei* than alive and answering to those pompous monarch pussies."

A low growl rose in his torn throat with a fiery sting as he recalled the commander's cold threats.

"And damn you, Rataan! Damn you most of all, *you self-important son of a—*"

"Who is Rataan?"

Kodokuna's stomach seemed to drop right out of his gut as every muscle in his body locked up in terror. He spun around in a circle, eyes wide and hearts slamming against the inside of his ribcage as he scanned the tree line for the source of the words. He saw nothing, smelled nothing. But the mysterious voice kept echoing in his head, feminine and eerie and dangerous. For a moment he was frozen, and he grew dizzy as a chilling thought invaded his mind.

"...*Matka?*" he whispered so quietly it was barely audible, his voice cracking as his mouth grew dry.

"Who is Matka?"

The voice seemed to reverberate from the surrounding trees themselves, as if it were the fog speaking to him.

Kodokuna slowed his racing thoughts and glanced around the clearing again, his shoulders slightly slumping as fear gave way to confusion.

"What?" His brows furrowed and he leaned down to peek underneath a shrub in front of him. "Show yourself."

"Look up."

Kodokuna gradually scanned upward into the canopy's shadowed abyss. His gaze found its mark, partially obstructed by the shady leaves but pale and ghostly against the darkness.

The stranger perched perfectly still on a high branch, staring down at him with a chilling gaze like a specter of death. Its fur was a sickly shade of white and from lean shoulders hung massive blood-red feathered wings. Most of its head and neck were obstructed by a wild, matted mess of garnet curls. Only one crystalline eye was visible through the tangled mane, and it glowed like piercing ice as it stared straight through him.

It was a ghaengste, like him, but a winged sky dweller instead of one of his own kin. He'd never met a sky dweller before, but he'd heard countless wretched tales of their bloodlust and savagery. He knew there was only one way this would end, the same way it had every other time in history their kinds crossed paths.

"Let's make this quick," he said in his surest tone, squaring his stance and cursing his voice's shredded hoarseness.

The pale stranger dropped weightlessly to a lower branch, her form now entirely illuminated by the beams of light penetrating the tree cover. She slowly cocked her head to one side, her unblinking eye not leaving Kodokuna's face for even a second. His chest clenched.

She was bigger than he thought they'd be; of course not nearly his size, but her long wings gave an intimidating extra bulk to her silhouette. His eyes landed on something that disturbed him above all else. From her skull sprouted too many horns — two distinct sets. One pair curved down below her ears with the sharp ends curling out, and another wicked-looking pair spiraled far above her head. She was mutated; the deformity was a harrowing sign of impure blood and a bad omen. His horrified realization was cut short when the ghoulish stranger spoke again.

"You are in a hurry?"

Her voice was monotone and soft, with the tone of a whisper yet the volume of a song. It was somehow even more harrowing now that he could see the maw from which it came.

"I have plans after I kill and eat you," Kodokuna replied, not completely sure where that came from. He hoped it sounded frightening, but calling up into the trees was straining his throat.

"Bleeding to death?" the stranger responded without a hint of emotion or any inflection at all in her echoing voice. He cursed under his breath at his ruse being so quickly discovered.

"Yeah."

"You wish to use your final strength to kill me?" Her head slowly tilted in the other direction, and Kodokuna began to wish he could kill her just to force her to blink.

"I've never slain one of your kind before. Why not?" He silently begged himself to keep his mouth shut. Just this once. He was used to intimidating others with his sheer size alone, but his words gave away his inexperience. The stranger simply flicked her tail.

"We are not the same kind?"

This time her steady voice sang a different ominous melody. Her face remained blank and unwavering, but her tone held something less stoic. Curiosity, perhaps. Her words seared an ache in Kodokuna's chest that he could not identify nor explain, but it made the hair on his shoulders stand on end. Confusion clouded his mind, then horror, then disgust.

"Do I look like I have feathers on my ass to you? My people are *nothing* like your kind," he snapped. The sky dweller before him finally broke her unwavering eye contact as her gaze wandered down to her long hanging tail. She seemed to be noticing for the first time that it did indeed have feathers on the end. She looked back into his eyes.

"What am I?"

"A wind-humper."

"Oh."

Kodokuna nodded almost sympathetically, then cleared his throat, immediately regretting it as pain sliced through his wound.

"Look, I've had a long day here, feathers. Come down here and fight a good fight, or flutter off somewhere else and leave me be. I won't tell anyone if you don't."

The winged ghaengste's tail swayed back and forth carelessly, her posture relaxed and unfearing. She remained silent for so long that Kodokuna began to think the exchange was over.

"You wish to be alone?" she finally spoke.

"...It's an alternative to death, I guess." He sighed, realizing for the first time that he might prefer the latter option. Perhaps he kept coming back to the clan for a reason beyond rebellion and adolescent hubris. Maybe he was hoping they'd either accept him back within the walls or simply kill him. He wasn't sure if he cared which.

"You are hungry?" the stranger asked, abruptly shaking him from his thoughts.

"Sorry?"

"That is why you wish to kill me?" she clarified. Kodokuna stared up at her, his brows creased.

"I don't *wish* to kill you. It's not personal, it just... is. And you're a little too lean to make a good meal, anyway," he explained, though he sounded unsure even to himself. Unsure of why he was bothering to stick around and explain his motivations to the strange winged beast. And a mutant, at that; he half-expected the planet to open below his feet and swallow them both just for speaking to one another.

"You do not wish to be alone, but you do not wish to kill me." She sounded out each word as if weighing its meaning.

"I think I'll just leave while you contemplate that." Kodokuna began to back away.

"Do not do either."

"You're not all there in the skull, are you?" He stared up at the sky woman, wondering how her wretched species could have such a villainous reputation if they were all this clueless.

"Join me."

Kodokuna coughed, certain he'd heard her wrong.

"What did you just say?"

"I wish to join together."

That time her words were clear as day, echoing off the trees and seemingly straight into the pit of his weak stomach. Kodokuna began rethinking many things, but most of all why he'd attempted to communicate with the forsaken creature in the first place. He managed to force out coherent words.

"Why the hell would you want to do something like that?" He stared up at her in bewilderment, not yet able to even fully comprehend her sacrilegious proposal.

"You are very strange to look at," she stated matter of factly, "and very large."

"Thanks."

"I think if you were with me, I would not get attacked often."

"Probably true."

"I think if I were with you, you would not get scratched often." She gave him a look he might have described as smug. "I can fly."

"Also true, but you seem to have forgotten," Kodokuna interjected. "Your kind eats my people's children. And my people take any opportunity to slaughter your kind. Joining you would be almost as heinous as befriending an ocean dweller; it's unnatural."

The stranger seemed to ponder that for a moment.

"I have never eaten a child," she replied, "and you have never killed one of me. That is what you said."

"Never too late."

"Join me," she repeated. Kodokuna stared up at her, his eyes narrowed, considering whether or not he might be hallucinating.

"You realize we would be killed for something like that, yes? Whether found by your kind or mine, or anything in between, we'd be executed for heresy. Or just for fun," he exclaimed in exasperation and glanced over his shoulder, increasingly nervous about talking to her for this long.

"We are more likely to be killed alone," the stranger said. Kodokuna hesitated.

She was right, and he knew it. She was a sky dweller, and she was clearly completely insane, but she was unequivocally right about that one fact. A lone ghaengste was a dead one, and apart, it was only a matter of time before the Mother delivered them that truth in blood. Maybe not today. Maybe not tomorrow. But there was no such thing as being truly alone on Matka, for the lonesome died.

If it was not this strange sky ghaengste, it was no one. The other forest dwellers saw him as a threat, a looming danger. Given his current weakness, they would kill him as soon as they got the chance. But this peculiar winged woman was unafraid of him, for better or for worse, and that was perhaps the closest thing Kodokuna would ever get to companionship. His fate was decided right alongside his exile — he would either be eaten by the dangers of his planet or eaten alive by his own loneliness. All at once, he realized which end terrified him more. His answer came without his mind's permission.

"Fine."

He regretted it as soon as it left his lips, but whether for fear of solitude or will to live, he could not bring himself to take it back. The stranger dropped from her perch, landing soundlessly on the damp ground before him.

"I said fine," he said quickly, taking a step back. The sky dweller looked up at him instead of down upon him for the first time, lifting her chin to meet his gaze. Her visible eye shined bright with a dangerous new twinkle. He swallowed hard.

"Am I Rataan?" she whispered, her voice somehow quieter when she was close to him.

"What?" Kodokuna got the feeling he'd made a horrible mistake. "No?"

"Who is Rataan?"

"The kaunek-leih. From the Ramys clan." He turned and began to walk, having been reminded of the commander's violent promises. "Let's get far away from him before I change my mind about this whole heresy idea, yeah?"

The woman followed, and he could feel her watching the side of his face intently.

"Who am I?" she asked.

Kodokuna let out a long, heavy sigh.

"That is a great question; who *are* you? Do you have a name?"

"No. You have a name?"

"My name is Kodokuna. Friends call m— you can call me Kodo." He glanced back at her briefly, then hastily looked forward upon confirming that she was still staring at him.

"I can have one?"

"One what?"

"A name."

Kodo stopped walking and looked down at her, thinking on that for a short while.

"Leida. Your name is Leida," he concluded with a satisfied nod.

"Why?" Leida asked. Kodo turned and shrugged as he walked on, more life in his pace than he'd had in some time.

"It means 'to fly,'" he answered simply.

"Because I can fly?"

"Because you can fly." He looked down at her with the smallest of smiles — and he could have sworn the corner of her mouth hinted at one in return.

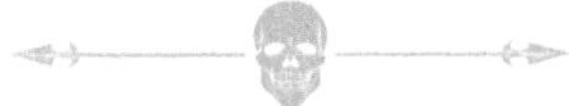

0540 Central Standard Earth Time — RREP Day After Arrival

Sherri had been awake and showered for nearly an hour. Now she waited alone in the commons for the bright compound lighting to kick on at 0550 as it was programmed to do each morning. In the meantime, she drank her coffee at the kitchen bar and took notes in her journal by the faint glow of the after-hours night lights. She'd already found the compound to be most peaceful in its resting state, when the halls weren't so glaringly white and the generators were powered down to a faint, contented hum.

As she tightened her unruly ponytail, the thick blonde curls already fighting free from the elastic first thing in the morning, she caught sight of a pulsing ripple in her coffee mug. The dark liquid's surface bounced almost hypnotically, and a new figure entering the room gave away the source. Captain Short marched into the kitchen, his heavy gait shaking the floor beneath his boots.

He carried a large crate labeled 'MEALS, READY-TO-EAT.' As he heaved the cumbersome container onto the counter with a grunt and began unpacking it, the compound lighting system kicked on and illuminated the vast room as if on cue.

"Morning," he said.

"Good morning," Sherri replied as she picked up one of the MRE bags. Based on the comically complex diagrams on the back of the package, she concluded that 'ready-to-eat' was beyond misleading. In fact, the word 'meals' itself seemed inaccurate. Her curiosity satiated, she returned the package to the pile the captain was counting out and went back to taking notes in her journal. She'd already filled up page after page with details of her new station, including most of the compound's interesting parts and a brief list of the names and descriptions of her new coworkers.

"I didn't know you squints still used paper, I keep seeing you with those tablet things," the captain observed, glancing down at Sherri's leather-bound notebook. Sherri narrowed her eyes at him studiously.

"Squints," she parroted slowly as if confirming she'd heard him correctly.

"Yeah, squints. Academic types." Captain Short turned back to his task, apparently with no intention to elaborate further. Sherri took the opportunity to examine him closely for the first time; he and the rest of the Remus militia were not among the names she was familiar with prior to boarding the mission.

Captain Short was well-kept in every way, from his neat goatee to the wrinkle-free camouflage uniform he clearly wore with pride. Large but not tall, his commanding presence filled the quiet room. The only flaw in his otherwise pristine appearance was a streak of gray in one of his dark eyes and a jagged scar trailing down his cheek beneath it. There was a cautious, intelligent focus in the mismatched eyes that was mismatched with his brazen demeanor. It made Sherri wonder how much of his behavior was simply an act for his subordinate soldiers. She abruptly turned back to her journal to continue her notes without another word, letting the captain guess whether he'd offended her or if she was just that unfriendly.

The awkward quiet of the commons was soon obliterated by a methodical booming that sounded distinctly reminiscent of a drumline. The drumbeat evolved into the marching of boots as the rest of the militia entered the kitchen in a neat cluster, and Sherri's attention was once again stolen from her notes as she watched the spectacle. The soldiers organized in an assembly line through the kitchen as if it were their hundredth day of the routine and not their first. Captain Short tossed MREs down the line like meat scraps to junkyard dogs. Each individual in uniform caught their breakfast package and in rhythmic succession barked out a well-timed 'thank you, captain.'

The scene struck Sherri as a performance, like something out of a very boring and very stiff circus. It fascinated her nonetheless, and she considered that observing and cataloging the humans around her might be enough entertainment to keep from getting cabin fever. For now.

A welcome outlier from the newness of everything sat down beside her.

"Doctor Daniels," the man greeted with an enthusiastic English accent, "I didn't get the chance to say hello yesterday. It's been quite a while, hasn't it? Haven't seen you since —"

"Since the microecology convention last year, yeah." Sherri grinned and gave him an eager handshake. "It's good to see you again, Giovanni."

She'd recognized the handsome, tan geologist with the neat mustache immediately; Giovanni Rosenquest was a hard character to forget.

"The professor is here too, right? You know I have yet to meet him? I've been dying to hear the other perspective of your archaeological exploits, maybe minus some of the embellishments," Sherri teased, gently tapping his arm with her elbow. Giovanni chuckled and shook his head.

"I've never embellished a thing in my life, love." He gave her a subtle wink before pouring his coffee. "But yes, my brother is around here somewhere. Couldn't tell you why, he begged me not to accept the position. Then when he couldn't talk me out of it, he joined me. Just can't let me have all the glory, I guess — there he is. Harrison! Over here, mate."

A man who looked nearly identical to Giovanni, only taller and significantly older, approached. Sherri stood up to greet him.

"Doctor Rosenquest, it's a pleasure. Doctor Sherri Daniels." She offered a hand, which he shook firmly.

"The pleasure is all mine, Doctor Daniels. Your Amazonian field guides have spared Gio and me from some rather unfortunate botanical mishaps on more than one expedition," he said with a warm smile, though his eyes looked tired behind his round glasses.

"And your publications on the Awá people saved my ass once or twice in my own field assignments," Sherri replied with a laugh, sitting down again. Harrison took the spot on the opposite side of Giovanni, using his younger brother's shoulder as a support to lower himself onto the seat. They began discussing the length of the observatory period over their coffee as the rest of the common room filled with the remainder of the research team and medical staff.

"Have you all gone to look out the windows yet? It's unbelievable," Doctor Novak interjected as he emerged from the large glass doors of Laboratory A. Almost every head in the vast room perked up slightly, and the chattering voices quieted.

"Windows?" Sherri and the brothers said at the same time. Marshall nodded.

"In hallway Delta. The vestibule connecting the terrosphere is almost entirely acrylic. The reinforcement shell system was still on from transport, but I turned it off so we —"

The other research team members were already wiping their mouths and getting up from their seats.

"Do you have access to the compound blueprints?" Sherri asked in a rush of curiosity as she marched past him.

"Of course I do, I helped design this place."

"I want a copy." She pointed a finger at him as she walked backwards toward the lab doors. Doctor Novak hesitated before nearly being crushed as the Rosenquest brothers shoved past him on either side. Several of the soldiers seated for breakfast looked up at the captain with subtle pleading eyes until he dismissed them with a wave of his hand.

"Go."

...

A group began to form in the clear hallway, and before long, the wide space along the acrylic panels filled with bodies. Despite the crowd, no one said a word. No one shuffled, no one coughed. There was complete and total stillness, like the collective crew and the compound as one all held their breaths in awe at the sight before them.

They looked out over a vast meadow surrounded by a thick jungle, obscured by fog at its farthest reach. The crest of mountains rose far in the distance, framing the view like a royal crown. Brilliant light bathed the atmosphere in turquoise and haloed the peaks, and a gigantic planet loomed over the horizon. The planet took up nearly a fourth of the visible sky, and emerging from behind it, a glaring yellow sun reared in triumphant glory. Lower, a smaller blue sun climbed above the silhouette of the mountain range and into the void of stars. There was not a single cloud in the morning sky, only a clear twinkling expanse of the heavens painted by the suns with hues of gold and jade.

The entire scene sat still as if timid in their gaze, yet faintly swayed with a gentle pulse. Lazy, rhythmic waves rippled back and forth through the grass, much more like breath than wind. As the planet inhaled with life, the crew found their own breath once again.

They were hypnotized, encaptured by it. The sight before them gave new meaning to the word 'human;' it no longer held the power it once did. It was alien here, distant and endlessly small, and so, so far from home. They were stripped of everything they knew and could define before the present moment — reborn into infancy, nameless and bare. The shallow breaths they finally took were not the same as before; they were the first desperate gulps of air outside the safe haven of the womb. Quickened heartbeats reverberated through every warm body in the room and pulsed with the change of the world before them as their new reality settled in.

A new era of human life.

2
AUGUR

"That's new..." Sherri spoke in almost a whisper, staring out the window at a fallen tree.

It had been ripped from the ground at the roots, only the crater from where it had once been anchored was several yards away from its final resting place at the base of the fence. She studied the scene intently, comparing it to all the sketches of the window view she had drawn throughout week one. There was no doubt — the tree had been standing the day prior.

Exhilaration grew in her chest as she noted the odd characteristics of the tree's roots: they were a fairly bright shade of aquamarine that stood out against the rest of the specimen's dark, rich, nearly black bark. The root system was tangled together, twisted in a maze-like jumble that looked almost geometric. The tree was close, only just outside the tall holographic electric fence that surrounded the outer wall of the compound. A small crowd began to form around Sherri, but she hardly noticed them. Flipping to a fresh page in her journal, she began sketching the tree, silently thanking her sharp vision as she caught a peripheral glimpse of Doctor Novak frantically cleaning his glasses with his tie.

"What the hell could have caused that? Some sort of geyser?" he asked.

"Maybe. I need to get a better look at those roots. Where's Rosenquest?" Sherri looked around. This was their first real observation on the planet, which automatically made it the most important experience of her career thus far. Possibly the most important experience of humanity as a whole — or maybe she was high on grandeur, and it was just a fallen tree.

"Right here." Marshall gestured to the tan, thin, older man behind him who shook his head knowingly.

"No, Gio. Where's Giovanni? I need our geologist," Sherri clarified, quickly becoming exasperated with the brothers' shared name. Fortunately, Giovanni entered the room on cue.

"Oh. What the hell?" he said plainly upon seeing the source of all the commotion.

"That's what I said," Marshall mused, clearly entertained by their overexcitement at a simple tree.

"I'm thinking gas deposit, minor explosion. Thoughts?" Sherri asked, only tearing her eyes from her journal for fleeting seconds.

"No, the roots are in perfect condition," Giovanni answered. "A gas deposit with enough built-up pressure to launch an entire tree out of the ground would be more likely to destroy it, or at least severely damage it. And I can guarantee that crater would be a hell of a lot bigger."

The group quieted as they stared out the window, cocking their heads back and forth as if looking at it from different angles might solve the mystery. Marshall was the first to break the extended thoughtful silence.

"Well, I'm just an astrophysicist, so what the hell do I know." He put his hands on his hips. "But that looks like it was physically ripped from the ground and thrown."

There was another pause before the eldest Rosenquest interrupted the creative images surely growing from such an idea.

"Maybe some sort of weather event," Harrison quickly suggested, "A storm, perhaps. Bridgeland?"

He turned to the short, round meteorologist to his left. Doctor Carl Bridgeland was already swiping through the weather data from the night before on a handheld tablet.

"Nothing interesting on the barometer or the anemometer," Carl replied as he shook his head. "Not so much as a light rain, even."

There was another shared silence as the familiar hum of uncertainty reverberated. Sherri furiously scribbled notes, recording every single idea that crossed her mind, no matter how outlandish or fleeting. Gradually, the group thinned as each researcher exhausted their knowledge and gave up, clearing out to go find something else to do.

Within the hour, Sherri sat there alone, cross-legged, studying the tree. As if staring at it hard enough might make it speak to her, tell her what had happened to it. The shadow of a cloud passed overhead, briefly bathing the tree in darkness before swimming across the plains and out of sight. She recorded that it must be windy; the shadow had traveled relatively fast.

Her train of thought stopped dead, as did her pencil. Slowly, she raised her eyes and studied the atmosphere. There was not a cloud in the sky.

She stood up to look closer, moving back and forth along the panes to get every single angle possible. She hadn't seen one cloud since she'd been staring out that window all hours of the day for the past week. The sky was perfectly clear, a calm ocean of aquamarine glistening with its ever-present stars.

Sherri pressed herself against the glass, searching desperately for anything that resembled condensation in the atmosphere. *What the hell was that?*

Maybe it was just her imagination, her overly strained eyes, or a larger native insectoid. Earlier in the rover stage of the RREP, there had been recordings of birdsong-like noises, sparking heavy suspicion that there was a species slightly more complex than the observed insects. Something bird-adjacent that was responsible for the sounds. So far it had remained unconfirmed, but Sherri told herself that it must be related to the shadow. She took a deep breath and decided she needed a break. Maybe they were already going a little mad with anticipation at barely a week in.

...

The Remus militia had quickly settled into indifference at their new station. The enlisted soldiers had dragged a table and chairs into the barracks to play poker; the currency they gambled with ranged from cash to condoms, cigarettes, and contraband alcohol. The captain wasn't present for their debauchery, of course, but he knew how they entertained themselves. They weren't quite as quick to hide their off-duty activities as they thought, but he let them have their fun. So long as it kept them occupied and out of trouble.

The small unit he'd been assigned was made up of individuals from a variety of ranks, branches, and backgrounds — so far none of which had particularly impressed him. Captain Short himself was contracted by the Army, as were most of the other twelve soldiers. Some belonged to the Navy, a couple of Air Force, and one single Marine with a crazy eye and a mean streak. But the captain had already made it clear that the specific branches they came from meant nothing to him. Here, they were the Remus militia, and the nation they served was the Remus-Romulus Expedition Program. But that didn't stop them from making each other miserable.

Corporal Keenan stumbled out of the barracks doors, thrown rather, just as Master Sergeant Mendoza was walking in.

"I think she likes me," Keenan chuckled hysterically to Mendoza as he clumsily collided with the older man's shoulder, then backed away with a splatter of saliva on his grinning face. Blood oozed from his nose and mouth.

"Wipe your face and lay off the whiskey, Marine," the sergeant scolded as he righted himself, shaking his head as he continued through the doors. The dim room greeted him with loud music and laughter, and he wasted no time making his way to the poker table. He lowered himself into the seat beside a tall graying woman with a vicious scowl on her face and blood smeared on the knuckles of her right hand.

"What did he say this time?" Mendoza asked quietly as she dealt him his cards.

"Nothing worth repeating," Master Sergeant Fischer growled through the side of her mouth. She was infamous for her cold demeanor and quick temper, but Corporal Keenan's lewd comments would have pushed anyone to their limits.

"Well, try not to kill him just yet." Mendoza sighed as he pulled a pack of cigarettes from his pocket.

"Don't want to kill him." Fischer clenched her jaw. "I want to cut his fucking balls off and hang them from a string around his neck."

"Who says you don't know how to have fun?" Mendoza offered a half smile and nudged the other sergeant with his shoulder. She gave no reaction, but the air around her seemed to boil just a little less. Master Sergeant Mendoza had a way of reassuring the most troubled of souls and remedying the most hopeless of situations, and he'd quickly become the self-appointed peacekeeper of the RREP militia. The others had begun calling him 'Mama' or simply 'Ma' for his soft nature and constant concern for how they were doing. He was too humble to label himself an honorable man, but his comrades would have done it for him. Mendoza set a cigarette between his lips and lit it as the game picked up.

"You know those'll kill ya, boss," a younger man with his patrol cap on backward mused as he reached over to take one from Mendoza's pack. He put it between his teeth and leaned forward.

"Don't let Crawford see you with your cap on like that, Greene," Mendoza warned as he lit the cigarette in the other man's mouth, "And shave for once, will you?"

Corporal Greene frowned and rubbed the growing stubble on his chin, but he was interrupted as the man beside him let out a long whistle and pushed his cash into the center of the table.

"All in," Sergeant Krei said, looking around the table with a challenging smirk. There was a tense silence as the other players gulped from their cups and studied their cards. One of the chairs was empty, its usual soldier absent from the game.

Captain Short had already taken full advantage of the compound gym, where he could usually find some momentary peace while his subordinates gambled in the barracks. Solitude was a fleeting privilege in the prison they now called home.

"You need a spotter, Captain?" a juvenile-sounding voice asked from the doorway. Short glanced up from beneath the bar he was bench pressing, chuckling as he looked over the lithe young man and his perpetually lively eyes. Private Zheng was stronger than he looked, sure, but the plates on the bar must have been four times his weight.

"Sure, kid, I could use a spot," Short humored him. Whether he admitted it or not, he didn't mind the private's company too much — it was the one thing familiar to him on the entire planet. Private Zheng was the only recruit Captain Short had known prior to the RREP; Zheng operated under his squadron in Iran. It had been Short who saw the kid's potential and recommended him for the mission.

"Sick of poker already?" he asked as Zheng put his hands on the bar to support it.

"I'm not much of a gambler. Or a drinker," the private replied with a sheepish look, and Short was reminded of just how young the boy was.

"Give it a few years," he assured as he began his sets again and Zheng dutifully assisted.

"You still giddy about outer space, Private?" Short continued with a grunt, lifting the weight above his breast.

"Yes, Captain," Zheng responded, a persistent smile tugging at the corners of his mouth. "Grunts on the ground to astronauts across the galaxy, huh? Who would've thought. And the view isn't bad, either."

The smile took over his face and he grinned at the wall, no doubt seeing pictures in his mind of alien landscapes and gleaming stars. Short let out a breathy laugh.

"We're still grunts, boy, don't you forget it. Just grunts away from home. Brought along to protect the research assets from each other, I guess. There ain't nothing up here but us."

Zheng cocked his head at that.

"How can you be so sure?" the private asked. "Even mission control wasn't *sure*. That's why we're here, isn't it?"

The captain shook his head.

"We're here for insurance, that's all. If there was anything other than bugs and bushes out here, we would've seen it by now," Short answered offhandedly. Zheng nodded in silence, though Short could see from the twinkle in his eyes that he was daydreaming about something far more wondrous.

As the conversation quieted and he continued his sets, Short couldn't help but pray his words remained true. He prayed he hadn't made a mistake recommending the kid for the expedition, but deep down, a crushing doubt weighed on him. As soon as he'd seen the list of heavy munitions sent with them, something felt wrong. The overstocked armory across the hall haunted and mocked him. Over and over, it asked him the one question he didn't have an answer to. *For what? For what? For what?* His gut filled with more dread every minute, and for now all he could do was shove it down and pray. He willed himself to have faith in the mission, and faith in their command.

Kodo padded steadily through the foliage, savoring the environment in a way he rarely allowed himself to. In spite of the perpetual Matkan chill, the suns shined gleefully and pierced the tree cover with beams of welcome warmth. Vibrant light illuminated curling ferns and the tiny waterfalls that constantly trickled from tree taps. The entire jungle sparkled and glimmered enough that it might strain the eye, and faint chatters and whistles echoed among the branches. Despite his careless pace, his new companion fought desperately to keep up. It seemed unnatural for a sky dweller to be bound to the vulnerable soil, far from the protection of trees and sky. Leida jogged to match his natural speed.

"Kodo?"

"Yes?"

"You can say my name again?"

The tall young man sighed and looked down at Leida, who was looking back up at him with an intensity he thought he might never get used to.

"Leida," he said plainly. He couldn't quite tell if it satisfied her or not, but she hurried ahead of him to take the lead. Her wings shifted on her back as she tread on, as if dissatisfied with their temporary retirement.

"Hey, you hungry? I'm hungry," Kodo called to her.

"You have said that already."

"Well, you didn't get the hint the first time."

She paused for a moment.

"We will first find somewhere to rest for the night, then we hunt. You can hunt?" Leida asked.

"I'm only the best hunter the Ramys clan ever had and lost. Kicked out, whatever," Kodo cockily replied, though his stomach raged at the idea of waiting even a moment longer for relief.

"With your wound," Leida clarified.

"Oh. Yeah, sure I can," he said with what he could only hope sounded like conviction as they began walking again.

Leida abruptly took flight. As she launched herself into the air, Kodo desperately called out to her, left to wonder if he'd already annoyed her into leaving him. In seconds, she was out of sight.

Before he had time to mourn their underwhelming and short-lived friendship, Leida reappeared as suddenly as she'd fled. She swooped back through the trees and gracefully dove to the ground in front of him.

"There is a good spot near the creek that way" — she gestured with her wing in a direction to the north of them — "well guarded."

Kodo stared dumbfounded but followed her when she began walking in the designated direction.

They arrived at a secluded clearing protected by thick trees and a small brook. But Leida's muscles remained tense as she timidly stalked over to the runoff creek that wound through the foliage, and spent minutes just sniffing and studying the water before finally taking a drink. The scars that littered her flank whispered of the dangers that lurked beneath the surface of Matka's lifeblood. Leida's skin twitched and rippled constantly beneath her white fur as if she were about to take off running at any moment, and her ears flicked at every tiny disturbance.

Kodo observed her seemingly perpetual discomfort as he gingerly approached to quench his own thirst. He noted the many ugly, pink marks carved into her pelt and the way her feet clenched and unclenched every few seconds, as if unsure whether or not to stay anchored to the planet. His eyes wandered to her protruding ribs, then her wild matted mane, and finally rested on her double pair of horns.

"You were alone before because... you're a mutant?" he asked quietly, frightened of both the subject itself and the weight it might carry. She glanced at him from the corner of her eye, then lowered herself to the bank, gazing at her distorted reflection in the water.

"I have more horns than you..." Leida observed slowly and thoughtfully. "I suppose that is it. I was left alone when I was small." There was no sadness in her cold tone, only contemplation. Kodo continued watching her closely.

"Mutated children... like you... they're bad omens. It's why they're cast out." He recited what he'd heard many times, though he cringed when he realized the implications of his statement. Leida either didn't notice his impudence or didn't care. She looked unphased, hanging onto his words.

"Not that — well, you can't be that much of a curse; we haven't been struck by lightning *yet*..." Kodo let out a sheepish chuckle that quickly faded into an awkward silence. His eyes gravitated back to the scars covering his companion's body, and he wondered how she'd possibly survived for this long on her own.

Most like her never made it past childhood; most starved to death, helpless and scared, abandoned by a cold Mother. He could imagine it all too well. Leida searched his face in her particular way that made him feel like she was peering directly into his skull through his eye sockets.

"The ones who left me... Why not kill me if they did not wish for me to survive? As you wanted to," she asked.

Kodo let out a small exhale as he recalled what he'd been told as a child.

"We don't kill our young, it is against natural law to destroy what Matka gives us. That's why we banish and exile those that are impure or tainted. We let Matka reclaim them; they are Hers, not ours," he explained gently.

"This name you say... who is it?" Leida asked. There was an innocence in her piercing eye, but it glowed so ardently that Kodo couldn't force himself to hold her stare. For a moment, his anger at the Great Mother rose in his chest again, hot and desperate. The fury of a young man forsaken in a world that abandoned and rejected him. But the feeling of Leida's icy gaze against the side of his face cooled the heat of rage, and the sensation washed him in familiarity. A watchful eye, a perpetual chill, a never-ending presence. Matka had returned to him through the eerie presence of the woman beside him, and as he forced himself to meet her eye, he finally allowed himself to accept the truth that had been clouded by pain. Matka never left him at all. She'd answered his call.

Kodo took a steady breath, his shoulders falling slack as the anger lifted from them. He looked down at the creek and slowly dipped his paw into the water. Scooping it back out, he let the water run off his pad and between his clawed fingers.

"This is Matka," he said, suddenly wistful with remembrance. He looked to Leida, finding the strength to return her eternal stare.

"Matka is our Mother, She is the one who created us. Feeds us. This is the water of Her womb." He grabbed a heap of wet soil and felt it in his clutch before releasing it, watching it fall to the ground. "And this is Her flesh. Her spirit lives within the planet, it courses through us with every breath we take."

He firmly placed his palm on his chest, feeling the powerful beat of three war drums within.

"It is Her divine Motherhood that makes our hearts beat, and She paints the paths of the people with Her own blood." His words came to him as naturally as the flowing creek, and with them the reignition of something he'd once lost.

Kodo spoke with a passion previously unknown to him, and Leida stared at him with a look of wonder and fascination.

"She created... me too?" she said, her tone cautious.

"Yes. Matka created you, and then when your people gave you back to Her, She chose to keep you in the world of the living. Maybe She has plans for you." His demeanor was genuine for the first time since they'd met, and his voice was soft. Leida fell silent, her gaze still trained on his face as she timidly laid her palm on her chest as he had his own.

She felt the music in her rib cage in a way she had never noticed before, even and heavy and deliberate. Strong with blood and life, not fear and hunger. She breathed in a deep, grateful breath of air that felt foreign in her lungs, or perhaps just forgotten. The words the man beside her spoke were alien to her; she could not trust or distrust them. She knew nothing of people or spirits, she knew nothing of Mother. But she had begun to know the forest dweller Kodokuna, and for the moment, that was enough. Leida opened her mouth to say something, but at first no sound came out. When it finally did, she didn't ask the questions of existence and unknowns that hummed at her. Instead, she settled on the one thing she did know.

"You are hungry?"

"Finally." Kodo grinned and jumped to his feet.

Shortly after setting off to hunt, the two young ghaengste found they made an indomitable team. Leida was right — their combined strengths made them a force like no other on their hostile planet. With her agility and speed in the air, she could spot prey from miles away and drive it to a clearing where Kodo lay in wait. And despite his wounded throat, his sheer brawn allowed him to take down prey large enough to feed them both for days.

For the first time, Leida was not aimlessly fighting to survive. And for the first time, Kodo had somewhere he belonged. Beside her, he walked as the suns set on the horizon and they wandered back to their camp. Kodo carried the corpse of a large adult hyyecut, a hardy furred herbivore, on his back. The cool air clouded around them with the heat of their panting breath and they walked leisurely, a privilege neither of them had known before. Upon reaching the campsite, the temperature began to drop rapidly.

Leida glanced over at Kodo as he shoved the slain animal off his shoulders, her attention caught by the yelp he emitted when he strained the wound on his neck.

"I can help you..." she offered as she shredded the carcass into chunks with her razor-sharp talons, but her voice came out hesitant and wary. She'd already seen what the giant was capable of with a crippling injury, and she wasn't sure she wanted to behold him at full strength. He laughed off her comment.

"I'll pass on those eunuch-makers of yours coming anywhere near me. I think I've had my fill of being mutilated for a while. And you don't look like much of a caito," Kodo retorted.

"What is this?"

"A healer. A good one."

Leida thought for a moment, toying with the idea in her head.

"I am a good healer. But I will not mind if your throat falls out of that hole while you sleep." She shrugged and continued butchering the hyyecut meat. Kodo swallowed, then flinched as he did it.

"Well... I suppose it's a win-win, then," he mused in a sheepish tone. "Either you fix me, or you kill me and it's not my problem anymore."

The brutish ghaengste gave his companion a timid look and hesitantly lifted his chin to expose his throat to her. Leida approached, studying the wound for a moment.

"I will not kill you," she said, then began plucking specific vegetation as she searched their surroundings. Kodo appeared more interested in stealing frantic bites of the carcass as his stomach emitted a desperate grumble.

Leida returned to him with a small collection of herbs, then chewed and spit them into her palm. She cautiously reached out and tilted Kodo's chin to the side, having to stand up on her back haunches to reach. Then she smeared the herb mixture into his scabbed-over wound while he sat rigid and still as a statue, aside from the pulse racing in his neck and his eyes tracking her talons.

"Stay," she ordered. Kodo did as told, and she approached a nearby tree to scratch off the outer bark with sharp claws. After scraping deep enough, she peeled off a smooth, membrane-like material that coated the tree's core. She carefully tore off a length of the material she hoped was large enough and brought the slimy green sheet back to Kodo. As she began to lay the natural bandage over his wound, Kodo quietly spoke up.

"How do you know how to do this?" He cringed as the cool wet herbs took effect.

"I am quiet. I watch," was all she replied. Kodo observed her with a contemplative look for a moment.

"I was never taught how to heal, I'm just..." He paused. "I was just a hunter. If we got hurt, we went to the caita for care. And I guess I never paid enough attention to pick anything up."

He lifted his bearded chin higher as Leida smoothed out the membrane on his gashes, coaxing the mixture to bind to his skin.

"Kodo?"

"Hm?"

"Why are you with them no longer? Your people." She glanced up at his face as she finished the poultice, slowly removing her hands from his neck. Kodo's stomach growled in response.

"That's a story for another day, feathers. Let's eat," he replied as he eagerly snatched the severed leg of the hyyecut, tearing into it viciously. Leida watched him for a moment, then found her own piece of flesh to fill her empty stomach. They settled in side by side as the dark jungle brightened with the illumination of glowing foliage around them and bright stars above. They ate carelessly and ravenously as the forest filled with the sounds of Kodo's obnoxious laughter at his own jokes, and Leida tried far too hard to get them.

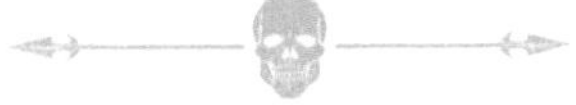

Over the course of week two, more trees in view of the glass hallway ended up on the ground. Some were ripped entirely out of the dirt and strewn away, others simply broken in half. There were a few leading theories, but nothing provable or remotely satisfying to the puzzled research team. Days passed and they grew desensitized to the mysterious happenings beyond the fence. It became all too casual when someone discovered that another tree was down or another ghost cloud had crossed overhead. They all began to acknowledge that sooner rather than later they would need to go out and investigate. They needed samples, data, and numbers. They needed more than a view through a window.

A slow morning brought the research team sprawled about on couches in the commons for a group brainstorm. They debated and discoursed, running through the scientific process over and over while lounging in overly lax positions and eating instant noodles out of Styrofoam cups.

"What about the bird calls? We haven't beaten that dead horse in…" Marshall glanced at his watch. "Almost five minutes." He laid on a couch he was far too tall for, his feet hanging off the end.

Sherri let out a drawn-out sigh and tugged on the roots of her frizzy hair.

"Can we refrain from calling them 'bird calls,' please. We have no real evidence that it's even emitted by an animal. Or any evidence at all, actually. But I'm favoring some sort of powerful, localized twisters ripping the trees out of the ground — Bridgeland? What's the word?" she asked from her spot on the floor beside Giovanni.

"Tornado, cyclone, or vortex," Carl said, not looking up from his notes. Sherri affectionately smacked his knee with a throw pillow.

"I meant what do you *think*, smart guy."

Carl looked up with a start, finally seeming to join the others in the room.

"Oh. I guess it's possible there could be wind vortexes forming small enough not to register on the sensors. Seems unlikely, considering the geographic position of the compound and the recorded wind speeds."

"Or," Doctor Oliver Doyle piped up with a foreboding look, "There is a sinister, eldritch monster lurking on this planet that fucks trees."

The room groaned in unison at the sarcastic oceanographer, whose expertise had proven so far irrelevant to the issue at hand.

"Doyle, tap in or get out," Sherri jabbed.

"Just saying, it's as likely a theory as anything else at this point," he retorted.

"Let's start with the mundane and work our way up to the fantastical and eldritch, shall we?" Harrison interjected with a huff.

The discourse died out once again, the scientists chewing on their individual ideas of the mundane and fantastical. An uneasy air filled the space around them as none could deny that unfortunately, Doyle was right. As much as the mission briefings were wrapped up in a government-sealed ribbon and written in enough empty complexity to mimic completeness, they didn't know enough about this planet to count anything out. They didn't know anything with certainty at all.

"We shouldn't be here," a quiet voice suddenly rose from the silence. "They tried to warn us." Doctor Roger Myles spoke in almost a whisper, the ecologist's voice shaky as if he regretted using it.

"What are you talking about, Myles?" Sherri scoffed. "We were practically begged to do this. I was, at least."

"They told us about what this planet did to those involved with the prep stage." Roger shook his head. "The rover team. The drone team."

Now the entire group eyeballed Roger. Marshall took his glasses off his forehead and slid them back down onto the bridge of his nose.

"Yeah, a lot of people quit," he said, but his tone hinted at uncertainty.

"They didn't quit," Roger insisted. He hesitated, his gaze lowering, "They cracked under the pressure. Began hearing things in the recordings, seeing things on the monitors. Things that weren't there. They were paranoid, convinced something was out here, toying with them through the rovers. They had to be let go because they couldn't handle it."

"You don't know that, it's all just rumor," Carl argued.

The room grew tense. Roger's claims were the deep fear that lurked in them all, whether they admitted it or not. The fear that there was something dangerous out there with them, something bigger than insects. No matter how vague the odds, no matter how many conferences and briefings assured them of the planet's desolation, they would never escape the possibility that 7355264Z was hiding something. The possibility that they'd missed something, and that they would pay for it dearly.

Roger looked around at all the eyes on him, his tired face tight with concern.

"I've worked on this project a long time, I knew them. Some were friends," he explained. "It was years ago now that they sent the first rover. It was damaged upon landing, battered by the rough terrain with only the camera and power system intact. Stationary but always recording. The rover team had to watch the feed from that camera for years. It never caught anything definitive, just occasional movement and noise. They said it looked so much like Earth, too much like Earth, so similar your mind couldn't understand why it felt so wrong. And the footage taken at night recorded horrible shrieks and wails — and clicks, god, they said the clicking alone was so repetitive and deliberate it would make you lose track of time and space. Like us, they never saw evidence of life beyond insects. But shortly before they sent Remus... the rover was destroyed."

He faltered now, fear rampant in his beady eyes.

"In the footage, it appeared to be... crushed. They tried to tell mission control that something was out here, that they had to push back the Wolf One launch, but they were just put on leave. They sent us anyway."

Silence clouded the huge white chamber as the ecologist's story settled in the air. The possibility of complex life was a known variable outlined in the mission documentation, sure, but up until that point, it had been discussed as an unlikely afterthought. Simply something they couldn't yet disprove. But the planet already seemed more promising than they'd ever hoped, too promising. Too perfect.

"Well I, for one, call bullshit," Marshall said, breaking the silence. "It sounds to me like the rover team couldn't handle that their project was an anticlimactic failure, and anyone might go insane staring at the same stretch of landscape for too long. Hell, clearly we all are. Why don't you go take five, Myles?"

Roger solemnly looked into his eyes for a moment, then stood up and walked away. The room was heavy with thought as each researcher sat quietly with the faint unease of an unknown and ever-nearing future.

Leida welcomed the morning like an old friend. The night had been her greatest foe for as long as she could remember, the time of day when she finally had to sleep, forced to surrender herself to vulnerability. She hated it, never resting for more than an hour or so at a time. Sleeping on the ground beside Kodo was different, though she hadn't decided if it was better or worse. Warmer, at least.

"Kodo?" she interrupted him from singing as they packed up their primitive camp.

"Leida," Kodo said her name as if he regretted giving it to her.

"I still do not understand," she began.

"I need something more specific, feathers."

"You say it is bad to kill the spawn of this... Matka. Yes?" Leida ruminated on each word as she said it, watching the ground as they headed through the jungle.

"Sure."

"But you say I, too, am the spawn of this Matka." She furrowed her brows beneath her tangled mop of hair.

"Yes."

"So why do you try to kill me?" She looked up from her feet to catch his eye. Kodo huffed out a long sigh.

"The word is *did*. I'm done trying to kill you, remember?" he explained. "And I already told you all of this. *I* tried to kill you because you're a sky dweller, my natural enemy. The only reason your people didn't kill you when you were a kid is that they were *your* people. And you were, you know, a kid."

Leida considered that for a moment, staring at him as he dodged her gaze.

"I do not see this difference," she finally said.

"*Wings*, Leida, you have *wings!*" Kodo groaned. "What do you mean, you don't see the difference?"

Leida's eyes slightly narrowed.

"Your people... they are very scared of wings," she tried.

"Yes — no! No, it's..." Kodo groaned as if struggling to dig through his memories, but his hesitation held a nagging doubt.

"It's what we have to do to survive, Leida. The planet just isn't big enough for all of us. The mountain dwellers kill your kind, your kind kills my kind, my kind kills the ocean dwellers. And when we can't find others to kill, we kill each other. That's who we are, that's how it's always been. Welcome to Matka."

He trudged ahead in silence as Leida lagged behind, once again focused on her own thoughts. Kodo made distinctions between their kinds, things she'd never had the luxury to notice or care about. He saw sky dweller, forest dweller, other. She saw *me, you,* or *enemy.* Leida attempted to translate the forest man's words into something she understood, only she wasn't quite sure there was a language they had in common. They lived on the same planet but came from different worlds. He spoke of nations and wars, people and spirits. To her, it was all the same. Shelter or danger. Food or hunger. Chase or chased. She grasped at any tongue they might share, and settled on the only one she knew for certain — sight.

"But it has not always been this way," she began, "I have seen it."

"Do you listen to me at all?"

"You are wrong. I have seen pictures."

"It's like speaking to a rock."

"In a cave."

"Pictures in a cave —" he scoffed, but Leida interrupted him.

"*I speak* but *you* do not listen." She abruptly stopped walking, and he halted in suit. She forced herself to fill the momentary silence despite her quiet nature.

"I have seen carvings in a cave, years before this. I took shelter from a storm in an old cave, very old, in the southern mountains. There were pictures on the wall. A story, but a different story than the one you tell me now. You lie."

Kodo now stared at her silently, a cautious look in his dark eyes. Leida's sudden boldness surprised her too, but she continued.

"It told the story of you — of your kind," she explained faster, pushing the words out before she had a chance to stumble or he had a chance to question them. "And me — the winged ones. And it showed the finned ones, and the furred ones. But they were not fighting, they walked together. Like us. It was not like you said. But... the pictures changed. Something happened, I do not know what, and they started killing each other. All of them, hunting each other, like they do now. But they did not before. The things you tell me are wrong."

Kodo watched her with furrowed brows and a fleeting gaze. Leida could tell he didn't believe her, or refused to try. She felt she was running out of words; her throat was dry after saying more than she had in all her years of life. She wasn't sure why she cared so much to understand the young man before her and be understood by him. But up until that point she'd had nothing, nothing until he'd given her a name.

Leida. To fly.

She made him say it out loud over and over, and repeat the meaning because it was all she possessed. Perhaps she wanted more. More names, more meanings, and more possessions. Maybe if she could show him all she'd seen and never understood, he could explain it. Maybe she could finally ask the questions she'd never had the privilege of asking. But Kodo didn't seem to have any more answers for her.

He stared at her in silence for such a long time that she gave up and continued walking.

"Leida," he finally said, "wait."

She stopped and turned back around, watching him expectantly.

"Why... are you telling me this now?" he asked. There was a hurt in his eyes she didn't recognize.

"I tell you because I have seen but I do not understand," Leida said simply. "You can understand but you have not seen."

Kodo nodded slowly, his gaze searching through the wild curls obstructing her face.

He was beginning to understand that she didn't recognize the weight of what she'd told him. To her, a cave was just a cave, and a story was just a story. She spoke as if it were something he'd forgotten that she wanted him to remember. To him, her words were a cold betrayal, the static before the storm. Most of him didn't believe her, and the part that did wanted more than anything not to. The story of their people he'd been told from birth was one of nature and eternity. Matka was the Mother of war, there was no natural state of peace on Her body. Her cannibal children fought because it moved their blood and beat their hearts. She did not make their world hostile for lack of love, but for it. The infinite war of the ghaengste was the flesh that fed them, their blood the rain to water their world.

The story Leida told was meaningless.

If what she'd seen was true, the races warred not because peace was impossible, but because they'd lost it and didn't want it back. He didn't believe it; how could he? He was as much a beast as the rest of them, he felt the hunger of Matka within himself. Perhaps he hadn't killed one of Leida's kind, but he'd tasted enough blood in his young life that it didn't make a difference. He'd consumed the flesh of the others and of his own. He'd been taught for as long as he could remember to fear the enemies of his kind, to hate the vermin that infected their planet and threatened their people. To defend the forest and ravage the rest. The trial of Matka, kill or be killed. Kill or be killed. *Kill or be killed.* That was the way of their world.

Yet he stood before his most dangerous natural adversary, the scourge of the sky. He'd failed to kill her. And now she was the only creature on the forsaken planet he could dare to call friend after being exiled by his own kin. The only person who had shown him anything resembling care since...

Since his mother died.

Memories flooded back through the wall he'd built to keep them contained. Her warm voice telling him he was perfect just the way he was, regardless of his towering size or his deviance or his bloodline. He began to realize that the one whose words meant the most to him never spoke of the unbreakable law. His mother never fed him lessons of monsters that lurked in the skies, the oceans, the mountains. She told him of beauty in their world, of truth and kinship. And deep down, he recalled the sadness in her eyes while she watched her only son be taught violence as gospel. Deep down, he was not born with bloodlust, it did not come naturally to him. It had to be forced down his throat and then it spread through his gut like a sickness. It wasn't nature nor eternity. And maybe it wasn't the truth he'd thought it was.

"Show me."

Sherri had nothing to go on and everything on the table. Doctor Myles's words echoed in her head over and over.

They were convinced something was out here.

Something out here.

She shoved the idea into the depths of her mind and pulled a sheet over it. She'd always been called a dreamer, and she'd never minded it much. Dreams were fruitful, and so far, they'd done her well. But speculation, speculation was the enemy of discovery.

The fact was, they had no evidence that pointed to the existence of life any more complex than plants and insects on 7355264Z. Sure, the simple existence of said life implied the presence of other entities in the ecosystem, but the findings from the rover and drone stages revealed a world at an early stage of evolution. A world ruled by microorganisms, decomposers, and flora. A world ripe for the taking.

Sherri had immense respect for Doctor Myles, a seasoned researcher and one of the leading theorists in extraterrestrial biology. She'd been looking forward to working closely with him on the ecological projects of 7355264Z. But even the sharpest of scientists and the strongest of men were often shaken by the unknown, and they were about as deep in the unknown as man had ever gone. The observational period would end in two more weeks, and then the real work would begin. The agony of speculation and the constraints of the unknown would fall away, and they'd finally discover the truth of this new planet.

"Does anyone have a Bunsen burner I can borrow?" Sherri called out to the room as she scribbled agricultural plans in her notebook.

"I want her back by nine," a voice Sherri recognized as Doctor Novak's answered as a Bunsen burner was set beside her journal.

"You got it. Hey, and thanks for those blueprints I asked for." She flipped her notes closed and began screwing the gas hose to the burner.

"Sure, but let's keep mission control in blissful ignorance about that, yeah?" Novak patted his palm against the table once before rolling his chair back across the aisle to his own station. Sherri laughed through her nose.

"What are they going to do, fire you? One hell of a cab fare for your replacement." She lit the Bunsen burner, but looked up to offer him a reassuring wink. "Our little secret."

...

Captain Short had a bad feeling. He could no longer ignore the turmoil among the research assets following the strange occurrences outside the window. Most of the other soldiers seemed oblivious or unbothered by the scientific development, and he intended to keep it that way. The captain himself, however, could not afford the luxury of ignorance. If the researchers were worried, he was worried. Unfortunately, that meant he would have to involve himself in business he really did not care to be involved in. As he infiltrated their territory, he felt the disconcerting urge to prepare himself.

The lab in itself was an alien world to him, and he couldn't have been farther outside his element. Like the rest of the compound, the large, glaringly-white room had high ceilings and cold air. Scientific instruments he couldn't have begun to identify covered the long counters that sprawled across the vast room. Some workspaces were clean and organized, others looked like they'd experienced a devastating natural disaster. All the scientific personnel were working hastily, writing notes, and doing minor experiments. Short was surprised they were already finding so much to do.

"Can I help you?" demanded a stern feminine voice, and Short looked down to see Doctor Sherri Daniels staring up at him with a pinched expression. After a quick glance around, he came to the conclusion that he was in the middle of her station, standing amongst the strewn-about papers, equipment, and what seemed like hundreds of potted plants. And dirt. So much dirt. He wondered how she maneuvered through the unkempt jungle even when he wasn't in her way.

"Hope so. Your little science fair here needs to keep me in the loop. On anything pertinent, anyway; I don't care about your flowers," Short explained casually. With each passing second that he stood there, the resident botanist seemed to become increasingly furious at the intrusion. Doctor Daniels scoffed, releasing a chuckle that sounded anything but cheerful.

"*We* need to keep *you* in the loop? On what?" She laughed in his face. "I don't answer to you, Hoss, and you sure as hell don't give me orders. Why don't you go do your job, and I'll do mine."

Captain Short's jaw clenched. Of course, it couldn't just be easy.

"This *is* my job, Doc, because they sent us up here with enough munitions to destabilize a small country and I want to know what the hell they're for. Considering mission control sees me and my men as prepackaged meat, I'm guessing you might have been briefed a little more than I was," he argued, her attitude quickly wearing through his patience. Doctor Daniels sucked on her teeth.

"Whatever mission control did or did not disclose to you is their business, and I can't blame them. Good day and goodbye," she hissed back, now crossing her arms and standing close to him.

"Don't bullshit me, sweetheart. Are we alone out here or not?" Short demanded; he had been done with this conversation minutes ago. Doctor Daniels stepped even closer to him so abruptly he thought she might actually attack him. Instead, she just leaned up close to his face.

"Do *not* call me sweetheart, you son of a—" She exhaled sharply, seeming to think better of her next word. "*Obviously* we're not alone, you've seen the insects. We've known there was life on this planet since long before Wolf One touched down. You want me to spell it out for you?"

"You know god damn well what I mean," he snapped. "Are there any threats?"

The botanist pursed her lips, brown eyes flaring with rage.

"*We. Don't. Know.* You'll figure it out with the rest of us when we go out there and you either piss yourself or you don't! Now get the fuck out of my lab."

He marched past her before giving himself the chance to react, nearly shouldering her on his way out but purposely missing her by a hair. Daniels didn't move or flinch, though the eyes of the entire lab were now trained on the two of them. Short supposed the answer she gave was as good as he was going to get, although he made a mental note to avoid the crazy lady scientist no matter what further questions he may have. He found himself praying, for hardly the first time, that this mission would not take a turn for the worse.

Kodo was beginning to doubt that Leida had any idea where they were going, but then he saw them. Peeking through a break in the trees and crowned against the brilliant sparkling sky, a snow-capped mountain range painted the horizon. The peaks were archaic and magnificent, unlike anything Kodo had ever seen. They made the mammoth trees of his homeland look like newborn sprouts, and for the first time, he considered Leida lucky to have seen the beauty hidden at Matka's reaches. He usually resented it — the chaos and the violence of their harsh world. But as he stared up at the ridge in the distance, where the land met the endless heavens and kissed the gleaming suns, he was washed in appreciation for the planet. He'd always been warned to stay away from the mountains, for there were monsters hidden within the dismal wasteland. He'd never even been far enough south to see them. But now he gazed upon the haloed peaks in the foggy distance, and they sang of peaceful stillness.

"You really believe you can find this specific cave again?" Kodo asked. "I think mountains have a lot of caves, no? And that's a lot of mountains."

Leida nodded once.

"Yes. It is there."

She pointed to the tallest point in the mountain range, and Kodo frowned down at her. She looked up at him, glancing over his large body, as if discovering for the first time that he lacked wings.

"Oh," she said.

Leida stopped walking and sat down, seeming to consider the urgency of their pilgrimage. Kodo also halted, watching his companion and awaiting her conclusion.

"It is a long journey. We will be camping for more nights," she stated. Kodo affectionately pushed her with his shoulder as he walked past. Even at his gentlest, she slightly stumbled.

"You know what? I can think of worse journeys and worse company." He smirked playfully and waved his thick tail back and forth. He trotted in a circle around her, bouncing from foot to foot as if he were dancing. Leida watched him with a puzzled expression and opened her mouth to say something.

Before she could, Kodo swept her feet out from under her with his tail. She fell but immediately rolled back up onto her feet into a stance that was ready to launch her forward and attack. Her hackles raised, and she stared into his eyes as fear briefly washed over her own. Guilt invaded him and his ears dropped against his head.

"I'm sorry, Leida, I was just playing. You okay?" Kodo timidly approached her with his head lowered in a non-threatening posture, and Leida slowly began to relax.

"Playing...?" she echoed, eyeing him up and down.

"Yeah, playing. I wasn't trying to hurt you," he said softly but kept his distance. Leida stood up straighter and cocked her head from one side and then to the other. Then the woman's pale face twisted into a chilling snarl with dagger-like fangs bared, and she launched herself at him.

Kodo tumbled to the ground with a gasp of terror, cut short as the air left his lungs. He did nothing but wait for his entrails to be ripped from his gut and for the coldness of death to claim him. Only it never came, and he opened his eyes to see Leida's proud face peering down at him.

"Do not worry, I am just playing," the strange woman said as she gave his chest a stiff pat, and Kodo threw back his head in laughter. He rolled out from under her, jumping to his feet. She leaped on his back, wrapping her paws around his neck and ferociously biting his ear.

"Ow," he laughed through a yelp and fell to the ground, rolling over on top of her. They clumsily wrestled down the slope while tangled in one another, tumbling to the bottom of the rise where it met the bank of a creek. As they rose from the forest floor, Leida still nipping at his tail too rambunctiously, Kodo noticed her white coat had begun to turn green with grass stains.

"Green's a good color on you, feathers," he teased, shaking out his tousled mane. "If I didn't know any better, I'd think you were a forest dweller like me."

"But I have wings," she corrected him with a smug gleam, but her face dropped as the wind blew. Both ghaengste raised their noses to the air, identifying the scent at the same time — ocean dweller.

"It's upstream," Kodo whispered, seeing in Leida's contracted pupils that she'd come to the same conclusion. They sank to the ground and soundlessly crept forward into the bushes. Kodo found himself a little impressed at his own ability to move with stealth despite his brutish size, but the feeling was cut short as he stepped on a stick, snapping it instantly. They both stopped dead at the sudden sound, and Kodo quietly cursed at himself. Through their frozen silence, a splashing noise arose from the babbling of the river.

Past the bushes, a ghaengste sat peacefully on the river bank catching fish. The telltale bluish fins on her tail and back gave away her race — an ocean dweller. The duo watched as the sleek brown figure skillfully caught a dark serpentine animal with her claws and nonchalantly stalked further onto the embankment to lounge on the grass. The beaded blonde locks of hair cascading down her face swayed as she stretched lazily. She was still upwind of the two observers, completely unaware of their presence.

"Are we going to kill her?" Kodo murmured next to Leida's ear.

"No, Kodo," she replied in a whispered hiss. He shrugged innocently.

"We should bring it," Leida said after observing for a moment longer. Kodo almost choked but calmed at the sight of Leida's harsh gaze warning him to keep quiet.

"*Why?*" he whispered back.

"It can swim. We are strong together but the water is a danger to us. We could change this," she explained, and in her expression, he could see memories of lost battles. She stared at his face in a way that made him wonder if she had figured out he could not both make eye contact with her and will himself to say no.

"Ocean dwellers are *not* very useful. And she'll swim away, Leida, we can't," he pleaded. Leida shook her head.

"I will approach because you are too frightening."

Before Kodo could reason with her, Leida quietly padded out of the brush. She neared the new ghaengste.

"Hello," she said from behind the stranger. Her imitation of a friendly tone was cold and dead at best, and Kodo resisted the urge to slap his palm over his face. The ocean dweller froze, then slowly turned to look at the other ghaengste in the clearing. She immediately dropped the fish from her mouth and scrambled as fast as her short legs would carry her back to the water's edge.

Leida took flight and swooped over the water, almost as if she couldn't stop herself, and snatched the smaller ghaengste out of the river before she could dive. The other woman spat and fought, desperately writhing and forcing Leida to drop her back onto the grass. Leida landed in between her and the water, blocking the most obvious path with her outstretched wings.

"I thought you didn't want to kill her!" Kodo exclaimed as he breached the shrubbery, paying the comparatively tiny ghaengste between them no mind. The stranger turned to him and, now surrounded, began savagely snarling.

"Begone, you repulsive, vile creatures, so help me, Mother! I am royalty of the Celesteal clan — a princess! I'll be missed! Do you want a war? Because that is exactly what you'll get if you harm a single hair of mine! You will be hunted, found, *skinned*, and *butchered; your children too!*" The aquatic woman roared viciously at them, spinning around frantically to watch them both.

"We're not of the clans, it'd be no war of ours," Kodo retorted with a dry laugh, raising his brow in surprise at the little beast.

"We do not wish to hurt you," Leida spoke up in what could have been an attempt to sound gentle.

"*Of course* you don't, only that tends to be an inevitable part of being eaten alive. Find an easier meal, *inbreds.*" The stranger spat her words like venom and she turned to make another run for the water. Leida stepped in her path.

"Please, stay," Leida said, but the hysterical ocean dweller just continued her rageful raving.

"You'll have to kill me! But you had better do it quick, because the full forces of the Celesteal clan will be here *any second* to castrate you and *skewer your heads ON SPITS!*" she bellowed. Kodo and Leida exchanged dubious glances.

"Sure, Your Highness. How about we all calm down and talk for a moment to buy time until your 'army' shows up, yeah? You're a long way from home," he said, and Leida nodded as if she thought that was a very clever thing to say.

The stranger looked between them with wild eyes, but she had no way to escape. She took a deep, forced breath and lifted her chin.

"Fine. Go on, do tell how you're going to cook my meat and wear my scales as jewelry. I'm *quite sure* I've heard worse from better foes," she hissed coldly. Kodo peered at Leida through the corner of his eye, as he still hadn't figured out what it was they wanted from the ocean dweller.

"We have joined for strength," Leida explained, "because he is very large, and I can fly. You swim, we do not. If you joined us, we would be stronger as three."

Kodo rushed to fill the tense silence left by his companion's bluntness.

"She's taking me to a cave that supposedly proves our kinds used to coexist," he added, gesturing with his chin at Leida. "And we're also not *completely* stupid so we know you aren't royalty. Judging by your beads and paint, I'd guess you're just a scout. So what do you have to lose if you leave Celesteal behind?"

He watched her widened eyes closely, not quite sure why he suddenly cared what this stranger did. He supposed he just wanted to believe that he was better off outside of clan life, and someone leaving it by choice would prove that to him. The stranger stared between the two renegades with a horrified look.

"You are insane."

"We seek the same thing that you do. To survive," Leida replied calmly.

"The next time you meet one of our kinds, they will not come in peace," she continued. "Maybe you will kill them, maybe they will kill you. But now you have a choice. We give you a choice."

Kodo softened as he shared a brief look with Leida, feeling a deep gratitude for the strange woman from the sky. The one creature on this planet who had offered him a choice. The ocean dweller before them blinked in silence, her bright orange eyes dissecting their promises and intentions.

They might have made sense if it wasn't a clear attempt to lure her away from the safety of the water so they could cannibalize her. A choice in their brutal world, to reject the bloodshed and seek peace in solitude, it was a paradise unattainable for a people as vicious as the children of Matka. It was too good to be true.

"A tribe of a forest, a sky, and an ocean dweller. Natural enemies coexisting. You expect me to believe this nonsense?" She scoffed. "It's wrong, it's heresy. It's impossible."

"Yes," the sky woman answered. "Do you have a name?"

There was a long pause as she thought about the consequences of her answer. She sighed.

"Alvi. My name is Alvi."

"Come with us, Alvi," the forest man said gently. "Don't die in the name of the clans and their endless battles. Everyone always does, sooner or later. You and I both know that."

It was true, Alvi wouldn't dare deny it. She'd lost more friends and sisters than she could count to territorial disputes and forest raids. But the Celesteal clan was her home, and the ocean dwellers were her people. They couldn't guarantee her safety, but these two outsiders certainly couldn't either.

"What will you do to me if I refuse?" she asked, cursing the timidness in her voice.

"Nothing," the sky dweller answered. Alvi searched the other woman's half-obscured face for truth, but she wasn't sure she knew what that looked like.

They waited a moment longer, then the winged ghaengste walked past Alvi to climb back up the hill.

"Come, Kodo," she called back gently. "We should leave now."

The forest giant stole one more glance at Alvi before following after his companion.

Then Alvi stood alone in the clearing, tense as her racing hearts attempted to slow. The strange outsiders had left her, apparently to go live in freedom and heresy. She could hardly even imagine it, a life outside of a clan. A life where she wasn't a part of something larger, fighting battles over conflicts she didn't understand. Where days passed without fallen comrades, and coming of age didn't mean picking up arms. Where she wasn't scout or hunter or warrior. A life where she was just Alvi. It was a childish dream, one it was time to grow out of. Safe clan walls were a blessing, one she knew she should be old and wise enough to hold on to each day she could. Because that day, she was part of something larger. That day, the Celesteal clan needed their scout, and she had duties to attend to back home.

But that day, she wasn't quite old or wise enough.

Damn.

"Wait! I'm coming!" Alvi cried as she took off up the hill, sprinting as fast as her stout legs would carry her.

3
DIATRIBE

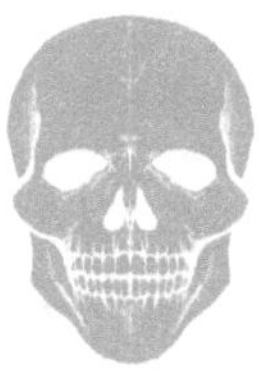

At first, the disoriented man didn't know where he was, only that it smelled of antiseptic and steel.

Then the gentle snoring of his younger brother brought him back to his new reality. Harrison lifted his head from the pillow and forced his eyes open to find the other form in the darkness. Giovanni slept soundly in the bed across from his in the small room, but just the sight of his chest rising and falling with each breath gave Harrison some minuscule comfort. They'd been there three weeks now and it never seemed to get more familiar. How did he end up here? He sighed and scratched his stubbled face as he rose to a sitting position, his eyes wandering back to the other man who was fast asleep. Of course, the answer was the same as all the other messes he'd gotten himself into again and again — Gio.

He would do anything for his brother, follow him to the ends of the universe to keep him safe. And this time, he really had. He thought back to all their previous adventures, dangerous archaeological digs and long expeditions that seemed so very pedestrian now. The time he'd spent away from his wife, the distance that grew like a tumor in the marriage. Harrison twisted the wedding band on his finger and his chest ached. It had been nearly two years since they separated, but he clung to the ring as naively and as stubbornly as he clung to hope.

The clock on his nightstand read 0323. As if attempting to run away from the thoughts in his head, Harrison stood up and quietly shuffled out of the room. He had no destination in mind, only to be anywhere other than in bed, staring at the back of his eyelids in rotten silence. He ended up in front of the windows.

The clear acrylic hallway, their only view of the outside world. He leaned against the far wall and gazed out over the dark valley. It was beautiful and absolutely petrifying. Harrison had seen some of the most remote and magnificent parts of their home planet, from the Amazon rainforest to the Alps. And yet the only thing he could compare the sight before him to was the open sea. Graceful and serene, violent and merciless. Standing on Planet 7355264Z was akin to standing on a boat in the middle of the ocean, the entire world at his fingertips and the whole weight of it threatening to drag him under in the very next breath. It was everything and he was nothing, and yet in his infinitesimal nothingness, he became Atlas holding up the heavens.

Harrison admired the stars in the sky, the only source of light illuminating the moonless planet. Even the stars somehow looked unearthly, too dense and too bright, but they made him feel closer to home. They seemed to freckle the entire world as if they were falling out of the sky and littering the trees beyond the plains with specks of the celestial. Squinting into the distance, it abruptly dawned on him that there were, in fact, stars in the forest. He realized for the first time that he'd left his glasses on his bedside table as he studied the fuzzy glowing lights past the tree line. They didn't twinkle like stars, but seemed to hover lazily on the horizon.

He reluctantly tore his eyes from the view and jogged back to his room. Snatching his round spectacles off the bedside table, he faltered and his stomach felt empty as he caught sight of the clock once again. 0437. He'd already been up for an hour?

He shook off the confusion and rushed out of the room, fumbling to put his glasses on over his protruding nose as he stumbled through the dark halls. His heart beat to the rushed tune of the compound's faintly whirring generators and his pace picked up with a sense of urgency. When he found himself back in front of the windows with newfound eyesight, his brows furrowed and his pulse quickened enough that he felt it in his ears as he searched.

The lights were gone.

...

"How many?" Marshall was only half involved in the conversation, the other half of his mind buried in the chemical analysis notes on his portable tablet.

"Well, I didn't count them because I didn't assume they would be gone in a moment. A handful," Harrison explained.

"Fireflies."

"Doubtful, they were stationary. But I'll ask Myles and Daniels about it."

The two men found seats at one of the large round tables as the soldiers completed their morning routine of filing in while Captain Short tossed them prepackaged meals. A few minutes later, Sherri and Giovanni joined them at the table they'd seemed to designate for themselves and the rest of the research team. The busy, brightly lit common room was reminiscent of a school cafeteria organized into cliques during meal times. The rest of the seats at the research table were promptly filled by Doyle, Carl, and Roger. Marshall took the opportunity to speak before Harrison could.

"Rosenquest — sorry, *Doctor* Rosenquest — saw glowing orbs out the window this morning. Or something." Marshall cast a teasing look across the table at the younger, less educated Rosenquest. Giovanni scowled, but Harrison loudly cleared his throat before the other brother could jab back.

"Thank you, Doctor Novak, I too possess the gift of speech." The older man glared at Marshall. "But yes, I woke up around three-thirty this morning and saw some strange lights out the window. In the tree line, definitely not a reflection." He paused to sip his coffee.

"Maybe a dozen, they were significant enough to see from across the plain — do we have a measurement on that distance yet? Anyway, they weren't terribly bright. Glowing as opposed to illuminating."

"Were they moving?" Sherri asked as she nodded along.

"No, still from what I could tell. Novak says insects, but there was no flickering either," Harrison replied. Sherri briefly quieted in thought.

"Gio, would you get a distance estimate for the tree line using the satellite imagery we have?" She turned to the geologist, who glanced up at her over his English muffin.

"Sure."

"I think insects are a decent start; maybe they were resting on the trees. What do you think, Myles?" She turned to her other side where Roger was seated. Beads of sweat had already begun to form on the ecologist's forehead, and for a moment he just watched his breakfast plate in silence. Then he finally seemed to notice his peers staring at him.

"It's possible," he said quietly. Sherri's face pinched in a dissatisfied look, and the table fell silent once again.

"Just be straight with us, Myles," Marshall said shortly. "Do you think there's something out here? Something we don't know about? Complex, animated, dangerous, whatever you want to call it."

Roger looked solemn, an unsettling reaction from an ecologist at the prospect of newly discovered life. He scratched his scraggly gray beard.

"They thought there was something out here. The prep team, they were good scientists. They were smart, they were dedicated, this expedition was the shining achievement of their careers. Of their lives." His voice grew hoarse, his dark face gaunt and forlorn. "And mission control didn't listen to them, said they weren't mentally fit. I didn't either. Maybe they weren't fit, maybe it did break them. But being here now... I believe them. Something doesn't feel right," he said in a hushed tone. Several people spoke at once.

"I don't believe it, we haven't *seen* any evidence."

"Technically that's not true."

"Yeah, right."

"It's not impossible."

"We better fucking hope it is!"

"There's no point in arguing about it now," Sherri said, raising her voice over the debate. "The fact of the matter is we don't *know* anything about this planet for certain. We have numbers, images, and theories, that's it. And we won't have anything definitive until we can collect samples."

"No, what we *have* is an advanced ecosystem theoretically capable of hosting complex life, and a useless, paranoid ecologist," Doyle snapped, glaring at Roger.

"Shut up, Doyle," Sherri shot back. The oceanographer opened his mouth, but both Rosenquest brothers on either side of him gave a simultaneous glare that caused him to snap it shut. Sherri sighed and gave Roger a look she hoped appeared reassuring.

"We'll figure it out."

Gradually, the discourse quieted as they continued eating their breakfast. Sherri stared down into her cereal bowl as she zoned out, ideas and possibilities flooding her mind. *We'll figure it out.* They only had one more week left of the observational period. One more week, and they'd get all the answers they needed. They'd collect samples, photos, and first-person accounts. In one more week, their boots would touch soil, they'd have fresh air in their lungs, and they would finally be able to do what they were there to do.

Her thoughts were interrupted by a timid intrusion. One of the nurses was calling out, attempting to get someone's attention.

"Excuse me, excuse me! There's something wrong with the fence... it's not turned on."

"How did you know she was not a princess?"

"The lunai-vaus of Celesteal can't bear children. I overheard the caita of my old clan mention it."

"Clan?" Alvi's shrill voice made them both jolt. "Tell me you don't mean..."

Kodo released a long sigh.

"Ramys, yeah. Relax, I'm not exactly on good terms with them. I'm exiled," he explained casually. Alvi scowled up at him with a brow raised.

"Who did you have to kill to get kicked out of the *Ramys clan?*" she demanded. "Are you some kind of war criminal? Although I hear Ramys crowns war criminals lunai."

The forest man glared down at her through the corner of his eye, and she put some distance between them. After a moment of hesitation, he answered.

"No one knew my father, my mother was an outsider, and they didn't take kindly to me growing so much bigger and uglier than the others. The lunai didn't want my bloodline muddying the pool, and clearly I'm too irresistible, so they threw me out and threatened to kill me if I ever came back..." He paused.

"I also may have exchanged some 'uncivilized' words with a guard. And a blow or two. But he started it."

Alvi stared hard at the back of Kodo's head. After a few more paces, she cleared her throat.

"And the mutant?"

"She was ditched as a kid, doesn't remember much," he answered, glancing at Leida as if to ask for confirmation, which she gave in the form of a subtle nod. Alvi fell silent behind them, her pace slowing to a shuffle. Wondering if it was too late to turn around and run back to where she'd come from.

Alvi studied the four horns curling out from the sky woman's skull in different directions. She'd never heard of a ghaengste carrying the sinister omen of a mutation and living to adulthood. She shuddered to imagine where Leida may have come from.

Still, the giant terrified her more. She'd seen more forest dwellers than she wished she had, each more monstrous and bloodthirsty than the last. They all paled in comparison to Kodo. She was sure he was heads taller than any of his kin and must have had the strength of ten. The ground quivered beneath her with every step he took, and she feared it might buckle under his weight and fall away at any moment. She took note of the bandage on his throat, saying a silent prayer that she never met the creature responsible for wounding such a beast.

As they walked through the jungle in silence, Alvi observing the two most terrifying ghaengste she'd met so far, she struggled to imagine what lay in her future. She knew the future that awaited her back home. Friends, family, community. The hunt, the war. A home and relative safety. There was nothing wrong with it; it was an honorable fate. A life served for the good of the Celesteal clan was a life well spent. But she had no idea what lay ahead for her away from her homeland. She had *no idea*. Just the thought of that fulfilled her more than anything else she'd experienced in her young life. And so, she didn't turn back.

A thunderous cry shattered the still air like glass, and Alvi was violently ripped from her thoughts. A forest dweller burst forth from the foliage in front of them, eyes wild and frantic. Alvi used the uproar to duck unnoticed behind a log, and the newcomer's focus found Leida first.

The much larger ghaengste flew at Leida, gaping maw aimed straight for her throat. Leida was quicker and more agile. She ducked out of the path of attack in a blur of white movement. Kodo grabbed the attacker by the neck with a guttural growl and slammed her so hard onto the ground it created a shockwave that nearly threw even him off balance. The pinned ghaengste stopped struggling, sputtering for air, and Kodo's eyes widened as he stared down at her.

"*Foolish boy*, what are you doing!?" the stranger hissed. Kodo let some weight off the older ghaengste, a strong, seasoned hunter from the Ramys clan. He wouldn't have described her as a friend by any means, but he knew her well.

"Jarao... go home, leave us be," he pleaded, but the woman below him roared over his soft words and her face twisted with repulsion.

"*Us?* You and this creature? They were all right about you, giant, you *are an abomination*," Jarao spat and clawed at his wrist. "The lunai will hear of this!"

His chest clenched, and his ear twitched at the distinct sound of Leida's long talons unsheathing from her paws. He knew as well as she did, maybe better than she did, that this woman could not leave alive.

Shit. You couldn't just go home.

He didn't want to do it. Beneath his claws was a ghaengste he had known for his entire life. Though she had never once shown him anything resembling compassion; she'd looked at him as if he were an outsider just like everyone else. She had not mourned for his mother, just as the rest of them did not. But she was his own kind. His fellow hunter. His kin.

Kodo squeezed his eyes shut, and he could hear Jarao quietly release her held breath. Then he reared and slammed his gigantic paws down on the woman beneath him with unimaginable force. Her chest caved in and her neck broke with a deafening *crack*. His breath quivered and his eyes stung with guilt.

"You killed her... from your own clan..." Alvi whispered, he hadn't noticed her creep out from the bushes. Leida sheathed her claws once more. For a moment, Kodo stood frozen with his eyes closed, unwilling to open them.

"Ramys isn't my clan. Not anymore." He finally opened his eyes, gazing down at the corpse below him in exhaustion. "They're not my kin any more than they are yours."

Leida walked past slowly, stepping away from the mangled body.

"We must keep moving," she announced. Kodo forced himself to walk on but glanced back at Alvi. The small woman looked between his tired eyes, then back at the body of the dead Ramys huntress. She followed after him.

The companions kept going, finally breaching the thick jungle once and for all.

...

"The yield was successful, but one of my hunters never made it back."

A tall dark ghaengste stood in front of the throne, proud, yet he did not make eye contact with the king who sat atop it.

"I ask permission to send a search party. Jarao is not one to wander off." His stoic voice echoed against the tanned hide of the vast tent, his amber eyes twinkling with firelight.

The lunai-vaus rose from his lying position, sitting up on the platform covered in furs that served as his seat. His fur was rich and dusky like the man's before him, outlined in black striping, and scarred windows rimmed by decorative circlets were cut into his cheeks. Gigantic black fangs hung down far past his chin. Torchlight danced off the glimmering metallic paint and leather armor that adorned his body. His eyes met those of the subordinate below him.

"You fret prematurely, Sirrah-Jel. The feeding will begin soon, and the suns are already fading." The ruler spoke in a low voice that matched his harsh appearance. "I will relay the lost sister's absence to the edge scouts, so they may keep an eye out. That is all."

Sirrah's face pinched into a scowl, but he quickly hid it with a bow of his head.

"Yes, my lord," he replied, turning to dismiss himself. The king on the platform called to him.

"You will find her on the hunt tomorrow morning, little brother, whether the Mother has claimed her or not." His gritty voice echoed with power through the chamber, but his tone was soft. Sirrah nodded but did not turn around to face his leader.

"Matka have mercy on you, Vaus-Levah," he called back in a much less pleasant tone, his farewell laced with frustration.

"You as well, Sirrah-Jel," Levah said dismissively. He laid back down on his throne pedestal and watched his younger brother leave the grand tent.

Shortly after Sirrah-Jel's exit, the long heavy curtains hanging from the tent entrance flapped open once again. This time an armored woman entered with a purposeful stride, toned musculature clear under her white fur. Her pale mane was braided back against her neck, and the saber-like fangs jutting down past her chin were yellowed and chipped from age and battle.

"Levah," she announced sternly.

"Erro," Levah replied affectionately.

"The Mother has picked up a parasite." Erro climbed up the stairs to stand before him, and he gently rubbed his face against hers in greeting. She kept speaking without pause.

"The edge scouts have spotted a sky vessel grounded in the valley to the south. There has been no movement so far, but I have ordered them to keep eyes on it."

"Have Visaan and Avias been informed?"

"Yes, it was they who discouraged me from commanding an exploratory raid. Though I've yet to be convinced not to." Erro climbed atop her throne beside Levah's, one of four on the platform. The king offered her a carafe of ale from beside his seat, which she took gratefully.

"More fugitives sent to death?" he suggested.

"No, the structure is fortified. I'm told some sort of light barrier surrounded it. It does not sound terribly dangerous, but they came with defenses nonetheless," Erro responded, taking a swig of ale.

"Visaan suggests we should leave them for the bandits. With any luck, they might lure the Gutfyres away from our borders with the promise of an easy meal. Avias agrees," she continued, dissatisfaction lacing her hoarse voice.

"Ah, our good-natured counterparts are no fun," Levah cooed. "There could be valuable materials in that vessel, and I can see that you're itching for a fight, my queen."

The woman beside him finally broke her stoic demeanor, a hint of a smile cracking the edge of her frown.

"Yes, I crave nothing more than to leave this forsaken throne and see bloodshed once again," Erro mused. "And yes, our better halves have grown boring with age."

The queen sighed, releasing the stubborn tension from her shoulders.

"But they are right in this matter. We shall leave the trespassers for the Mother to claim in Her own time."

The other lunai allowed a look of disappointment to cross his face, but it quickly waned. His desire to exterminate the intruders was born of selfish gluttony, and he would not claim it was by necessity. Because it did not matter whether they ordered the eradication of the parasites, if they threw them to the mercy of the Gutfyre bandits, or if they simply left them to the elements. The mysterious outsiders would meet their end one way or another, and it would be the same ending that Matka destined for every other soul that dared trespass on Her flesh. Swift, brutal, and just.

It didn't take an expert to confirm that the electric border fence was down. In fact, the glowing blue light barrier was gone entirely. In its place stood an arc of useless metal spokes resembling utility poles. After a concise investigation by Doctor Novak, they concluded that the fence command CPU routed to the control room had been damaged during landing. Fortunately, there was a secondary control panel. Unfortunately, it was outside.

Sherri immediately volunteered to activate the fence from the outdoor panel. As she headed for the front door, she could already taste the fresh air, and barely heard the protests of her peers. Even if it was just for a moment, just long enough to reset the fence, she couldn't pass up the opportunity for a premature introduction to the outside world. She mentally repeated the lock code for the door, which she'd already memorized, and her heart raced in anticipation.

Someone grabbed her arm as she reached for the keypad. Instinctively, Sherri flipped around and snatched her arm away as she raised her other hand in defense. She stopped as she found herself face to face with the captain, mere inches apart, his hard gaze staring into hers daringly.

"Don't put your fucking hands on me," Sherri hissed through tightly clenched teeth, but her raised hand found its way back down by her side.

"You're not going out there, squint," Captain Short ordered.

"*Bite me*, gun, I'm turning on the fence." She shrugged her coat on as she attempted to continue on her path. Sherri practically lurched to type in the code, but her finger met a meaty hand rather than a keypad.

"I think we got off on the wrong foot," the captain tried with his hand covering the panel, a patronizing cadence in his blunt tone.

"You wouldn't know the right foot if it kicked you in the ass," Sherri retorted. "Move your hand."

"Not happening. Get out of the way," Short replied. Sherri narrowed her eyes in irritation, and for a moment she considered spitting at him. She glanced back to his hand on the control panel, unbudging, and then the many eyes staring at them throughout the hall. With a sharp huff, she spun around and shoved past him back the way she came. The captain's booming yell echoed through the compound as she stormed off and slammed open the doors to the lab.

"Taylor!" Captain Short barked, shaking his head after the retreating botanist. A private with a buzzcut and spirited blue eyes jumped to attention.

"Yes, Captain," the young man barked back, and Short clapped him on the shoulder so hard he stumbled forward.

"Congratulations, son, you'll be the first boot to make contact with planet 7 3..." He pushed Private Taylor toward the door. "The panel's on the wall just outside, can't miss it. Key code is 182114. Get it done and get your ass back in here. Roger?"

Private Taylor nodded once with another overeager 'yes, Captain,' and a crooked smile invaded the young man's freckled face after being dismissed.

...

After a brief fright with the fence malfunction, the compound quickly settled back into its normal routine. The research team ran tests with the little evidence they had, hardly speaking to each other. Doctor Novak busied himself with the atmospheric composition of 7355264Z, having checked out one of the portable respirators to study and cross examine with his hypotheses. The atmosphere on the dwarf planet was strikingly similar to that of Earth, but the air contained amounts of barium that would be lethal for a human to breathe unaided. To avoid any side effects and maintain healthy blood oxygen levels, they were instructed to utilize their respirators once every six hours when exposed to the outside air. The equipment resembled a venturi mask with a short hose connected to a small tank, and a hook for attaching to a backpack or belt. Marshall found himself half hoping to share a drink with the inventor of the system and half wishing he'd thought of it first.

"Any idea where Daniels ran off to?" He spoke to the room as he admired the device in his hands. He'd been about to ask their youngest teammate a question before noticing that she was not at her usual station scribbling away in her journal.

"Where do you think?" Giovanni answered from deep within his own studies.

"Probably in the rafters, hunched over a mangled voodoo doll of the captain," Doyle added offhandedly.

Sherri was not, in fact, plotting morbid revenge on Captain Short, though she would've liked to be. Instead, she blew off steam by chipping away at the laborious task of assembling the terrosphere for planting.

A specialized greenhouse, the terrosphere formed a vast dome of honeycomb-like paneling designed to regulate the solar energy absorbed from the several suns of Planet 7355264Z. The dome had been calibrated to mimic the solar conditions of Earth, and Sherri was cleared to begin the agricultural project, perhaps the most important experiment of the entire expedition. The adventure, the exploration, the danger, it was all beyond thrilling and glorious. But they weren't sent for glory, they were sent to assess the viability of 7355264Z as a possible site for human colonization. A possible site for home.

Earth wouldn't be able to support humanity for much longer; that was clear. Each passing year they further outgrew their native planet and strained its resources even thinner. The idea of leaving it behind for good gave Sherri a dizzy feeling; it was something she knew was inevitable but dearly hoped she wouldn't live to see. Now they were racing against a ticking clock to find a replacement, and 7355264Z was the strongest candidate in the history of the Salvation Initiative so far. And whether it proved viable or not, Sherri was a part of leading the way to ensure the future of her species. She wore that honor like the sail of a ship.

In order to determine if 7355264Z could sustain civilization, they had to start from the very beginning: agriculture. And what a beautiful thing it was, the soil and the seeds that would sow a rebirth for the human race. Sherri considered that future as she prepared the sod plots for planting, humming contently to herself. Heaving the oversized fertilizer bags exhausted her stress from earlier in the day, and measuring the dimensions of each crop quieted her busy mind. It was the closest thing she would get to home, toiling amongst the dirt and the saplings, and it was close enough.

"Need any help?" a voice rang out behind her. Sherri jumped up with a start and nearly clutched her chest, spinning around and quickly crossing her arms in an attempt to look nonchalant.

"Doctor Novak, I didn't — hear you come in." Her alarm turned to a gentle scolding. "You know, normally one announces their presence when they come up on someone from behind."

"I just did." Marshall smirked. Sherri gave him an unenthused look.

"Earlier would be appreciated. Scissors." She pointed at a pair sitting on an overturned pot next to him, and he handed them to her in silence. She took them and began to cut open a large sack of soil.

"Are you just here to help me pour dirt, or was there something else?"

"Ah." Marshall finally seemed to remember why he'd come. "I was wondering if you had a hypothesis as to how the native vegetation utilizes the barium content in the air, if at all," he explained, back to his pragmatic demeanor.

"I need samples," Sherri began, unable to hide the impatience in her voice. "But they obviously have some function to process it, no telling if it has any particular adaptational value. So far, I've operated under the assumption that it plays a role in their photosynthetic equivalent, maybe comparative to Earth's own. But right now, assumptions are all we've got."

Marshall nodded along as he watched, looking very intrigued by her process of distributing dirt and cordoning off sections.

"You seem to have a problem with assumptions," he noted. Sherri swiped some soil off her legs as she walked past him to grab a spade.

"I'm a field scientist, not a theorist. No offense —"

"None taken."

She returned to her current section and began carefully tilling the plot.

"I'm just ready to get out there. To see, and touch, and taste." She smiled through the grime covering her face, passion rising in her once again. "To put all our theories and our assumptions to the heat and see what catches fire."

The trip through the plains and along the runoff beck went by quickly and uneventfully. The suns were warm, the ground soft and flat, and Alvi could swim in the stream when her feet grew tired. There were few enemies to worry about as they'd left Ramys land behind a day ago and the open horizon made it impossible to be taken off guard. Only when the terrain began to slope upward did potential foes become the least of the trio's perils. As peaceful meadows transformed into unforgiving rock paths, their heaving breaths echoed far down the treacherous drops, bouncing off stone walls and singing cautionary hymns.

"This journey is easier to fly," Leida said as she glanced down at the cuts and scrapes on her pads.

"Not helpful," Kodo grumbled. After a moment of silence, Leida halted.

"Where is Alvi?"

"*Shit*, I *told* you she'd fall —" Kodo scrambled to the edge of the trail, peeking over. A pebble hit him in the back of the head with a sharp clack.

"I'm right where you left me. *Halfwits*," Alvi hissed through heavy gasps as she struggled to navigate the rocky terrain, left behind by her larger companions when the brook gave way to upland waterfalls she could no longer swim in. She rushed to catch up as Leida had already resumed walking, but Kodo followed for only a few steps before stopping again. Sighing, the mighty beast lowered himself to the ground in a crouch.

"Get on."

"What?"

"Before I change my mind."

Alvi snapped out of her hesitation and eagerly climbed on top of Kodo's back. She settled in comfortably as he stood up and continued; the gigantic ghaengste hardly seemed to notice the added weight. They walked in silence for a few more road switchbacks and Alvi found herself entranced by the height from her new view. Sitting atop Kodo's broad shoulders was like riding on the hump of an ancient reihggus, looking down over the rest of the world. It was an invulnerability she'd never thought possible, and it filled her with both fear and gratitude.

"I do my best to avoid being up close and personal with forest dwellers, but even so," she began, "You've got to be twice as big as any I've seen."

"I get that a lot," Kodo replied.

"And definitely twice as wide. You know, back in Celesteal we call your kind 'ijgras' — driftwood. Shaped like sticks and always showing up where you're not meant to b—"

"Got it, Alvi."

Leida walked ahead of them and gave no indication she'd been listening to the conversation. Alvi glanced down over Kodo's shoulder.

"Why are you such a freak of nature, anyway?" she started again.

"Just... growing more than others, I guess," he mumbled. Alvi scrunched her nose in disbelief.

"Grow*ing*? You're not still growing."

"I'm five suns old. Still growing."

Alvi blinked in horror.

"You're just a kid!" she exclaimed. "The Ramys lunai aren't terribly smart, are they? One would think they'd want a monster like you *in* their army when he matures. Not against it."

The giant below her fell quiet for a moment, and she thought she might have seen the side of his face flinch.

There was that word again, 'monster.' Despite still being in his adolescence, Kodo's towering form and monstrous appearance had often resulted in being treated as a much older man. While he was grown enough to be on his own and developed in most ways beyond height, he was rarely given the same tutelage as others his age. He just hoped the women he traveled with now would not think less of him for his youth and obnoxious size.

"I'm not a *kid*. Just still growing," he huffed. "And the lunai aren't stupid, they just don't care where I end up. I was never going to be a Ramys warrior either way; they never had me trained to fight."

Alvi scoffed.

"I saw what you did to that huntress. They didn't have to."

Kodo didn't have a response to that, nor any snide jokes to distract from the hurt in his reticence.

"But," Alvi broke the extended pause, "I'm... glad you were there, big guy. I don't know if I could have talked myself out of that one alone."

He glanced back at her with a small nod; and Leida, who had been mute for many minutes, finally spoke up.

"You are very dangerous, Kodo," the winged woman said without turning back. "It is terrifying."

Kodo's ears fell to the sides of his head in disheartenment.

"And I am very glad for it."

Alvi laughed from atop his back. His tense face slowly softened, and he lifted his head a little higher. He was dangerous, and he was terrifying, and those things would undoubtedly haunt him for his entire life. But Leida, in all her cold-blooded enigma, was glad for it — an emotion he hadn't even suspected she was capable of. And for the moment, that gave him a pride he'd never experienced before.

The air thinned as they rose in altitude, and they quieted as they were forced to focus on their breathing. Kodo's lungs burned alongside his muscles and the temperature dropped rapidly when the wind began beating against them, yet he smiled to himself as he tread onward up the mountain. For the first time in all his life of being a giant, a monster, and an abomination, he may have found the only two ghaengste on the planet stranger than him.

…

They could no longer see more than a few feet in front of them. Floods of white, treacherous white, and sharp stone made up the flesh of the mountain. The winds whipped and cut at the three figures savagely, as if warning them to turn back and never return. They'd been traveling for days now, and if it were an option to turn back around, they most certainly would have. But now the icy hell had them trapped in its clutches, the storm an impenetrable fog. Their only hope was to climb on and get above it.

The snow's haze clouded their eyesight and ice crusted onto their noses and mouths, but Leida's tightly folded wings acted as a scarlet flag to guide her companions. Behind her, Kodo trudged on, fighting through the snowdrifts and driving his shoulders forward against the vicious gusts. Alvi clung desperately to his back; the cold so intense her brown fur had grown a silvery white sheen over top of it, and the woven tendrils of her blonde mane were pinned back against her neck in the wind.

Suddenly, their precious red feather beacon disappeared as the blizzard seemed to swallow Leida whole. Her friends screamed for her to no avail, the words ripped right out of their mouths and lost in the howling wind. They suffocated helplessly in the freezing air, panic setting in, but Kodo fought on. He kicked faster through the heaps of snow, legs churning, frantically searching the wretched whiteness for any sign of Leida.

And then it was over.

Like a snuffed fire, the storm ceased. All fell silent. Slowly, Kodo and Alvi rose from their hunched positions, bracing against gusts that no longer existed, and looked around. A voice called out to their backs.

"Here."

They spotted Leida behind them, crimson feathers like rubies against the snow, standing still in the sudden calm like a ghost. She shivered in the cold, steam pouring out of her nostrils as she caught her breath. They shook off the snow as they joined back together.

The scene left behind by the blizzard froze over, completely still, tranquil after the tumult of the storm. And yet the quiet was worse. Now they could see what appeared to be miles of snow and nothingness in every direction. No wind, no noise. Nothing at all. It was as if the air absorbed every breath, every step. Even swallowed time itself.

"Leida... where are we?" Alvi sat straight up on top of Kodo's back. She scanned the vast empty horizon for the peak they had been headed toward for so long.

"Did we get lost in the storm?" Kodo asked, now looking around the desolate plain as well.

"No. We are close," Leida assured them and started walking once again. Kodo followed, though he glanced backward to exchange a look of concern with Alvi. But they kept on, following the winged woman, beginning to grow uncertain of what it was they truly sought in the perilous wasteland. Leida wanted answers to questions she didn't have the words to ask, and Kodo supposed it was simple truth that he desired. Alvi just hoped they found shelter soon.

"Have I told you two about the time I took on the bandit outlaw Maijako single-handedly and won?" Kodo disturbed the silence.

"You did, actually," Alvi quickly interrupted. "And telling us again won't make it any more believable."

The forest man scoffed.

"Leida believes m—"

Kodo was slammed to the ground, hit hard by something with the strength of a boulder and the force of an avalanche. An explosion of snow shot in every direction and Alvi was thrown clear, disappearing under the white powder.

"Kodo!" Leida cried out, searching through the upheaval of churned snow as savage growls and the sickening crack of teeth against teeth echoed across the white expanse. Before Leida or Alvi could find him through the blinding chaos, Kodo ended up on top.

He hadn't figured out what hit him until he was pelted in the face by a ferocious roar from the creature beneath his paws. The monstrous bellow was so deafening it stabbed through his eardrums like a spearhead, splatters of saliva showering his face. As the noise echoed across the landscape, Kodo found himself looking down into the crazed garnet eyes of a young man, jaws bared. But the man looked wild, fur long and pale, his beard thick and untamed.

A mountain ghaengste.

Kodo's bewilderment at the sight of the fabled beast only lasted for a moment, but it was long enough. The mountain man lurched forward and headbutted him with an excruciating *crack*. Brawny horns collided with Kodo's skull as a spray of blood littered the snow, and for a moment, he couldn't see. The stranger took the opportunity to kick Kodo square in the chest, crushing the air out of his lungs all at once. Kodo was thrown into the snow once again, and a mortifying thought rose in his mind.

This asshole might be stronger than me.

Kodo sputtered for air, scrambling to his feet as the stranger charged. The mountain man was cut down just short of his next attack as something slashed into him from above like an asteroid. A storm of ebony drops rained down upon the snow and the mountain ghaengste cried out, holding his wide paw over a gash across his face. Leida rolled onto her feet in front of Kodo, snarling at the assailant.

The wooly beast threw his head back and another long, ear-splitting roar erupted from his gaping maw. Proud and dreadful like the trumpets of war, it reverberated across the open tundra and bounced off the surrounding mountain peaks. Kodo had recovered his footing, and a different feeling now rose in his gut as he faced his first worthy rival. A challenge. He charged, and the two men clashed once again.

Just as Leida ran to his side, Alvi's frantic cry rang out above the chaos.

"The paint!" the ocean woman yelled, and Leida stopped her approach in confusion.

"Look at the paint, he's not alone!" Alvi screamed even louder, and horror twisted in Kodo's stomach as her words sank in.

Kodo found himself looking down over the pale attacker just long enough to confirm: his light gray fur was decorated in tribal amethyst paint and jewelry made of bones. This ghaengste belonged to a clan. And he'd just called them.

"Kodo!" Now both women screamed over the growling and roaring and tearing of flesh. *"We have to go!"*

At first, Kodo couldn't urge himself to abandon the brawl, but the terror in his companions' voices overpowered his ego. He released his opponent and took off, trudging after the others through the thick snow. His long, powerful legs sunk straight through the powdery substance, the speed he normally possessed stolen away by the confining landscape. Alvi disappeared under the heaps entirely, her movement achieved by leaping a few strides at a time, but she wasn't fast enough. The bulky mountain ghaengste chased after them with effortless grace. He gained on them quickly as wide paws carried him atop the sleet.

Kodo realized this was not a fight all three of them could flee. He stopped, shortly followed by Leida as she noticed him break away.

"Take Alvi!" Kodo called to her. "I'll catch up!"

Leida shook her head and began to turn back to fight alongside him. Then their eyes met, and his plea rang out without even opening his mouth.

Trust me.

Leida grabbed Alvi out of the deep snow and launched into the clear sky, her vast wings carrying them away with a single beat.

Kodo spun around to meet the charging adversary. They collided once again, the mountain man's claws slicing into his flesh and heavy paws beating him further into the snow. Kodo didn't know how long he had until enemy reinforcements arrived, but after meeting the strength of the beast he fought now, he knew he wouldn't survive being outnumbered. That fact was confirmed as he took another crushing blow to his chest, then his side. He had to end it while he still had a chance. To hell with the pain.

Kodo stood on his hind legs, reaching a colossal height, and then launched downward with his massive body's entire weight. His already bloodied skull smashed into the other man's. Agony rang through his eardrums and shot through his eye sockets like lightning. The shockwave seemed to make the snow's surface vibrate across the entire valley and shake their very bones. Now, the heads of both men were smeared and splattered with hot black blood, and colorful spots blurred Kodo's vision. He ignored it, not waiting for the warm wetness to turn cold before he reared back and again slammed his skull into the other ghaengste's. The sound of moist, heavy clacking would have sickened him if he had the chance to think about it before he rammed again. Again, and again, and again, a deep inky color soaked across the pure white snow and his rival was no longer coherent enough to even pull away. Kodo reeled back again, then smashed his head into the shorter man's once more. This time the collision was so violent blood began to drip from all four of his nostrils, and the vibration rang through each and every one of his teeth.

The gray beast fell to the ground, still.

Kodo allowed himself no time to focus on the searing ache in his skull before scrambling through the snow after his friends. But as he took his first shaky step in the direction Leida had flown, the entire planet began to tremble and pulse beneath him, and he was nearly thrown to the ground. A herculean crack exploded somewhere behind him, followed by a deep rumbling. He looked back, first at the bloodied man in the snow, and then at the monstrosity in the distance.

Like a rageful god, an all-consuming ocean of snow and ice raced toward him down the slope.

Shit.

At first, Kodo's legs wouldn't obey his frantic pleas to move, and he could only watch as the avalanche ate everything on its warpath toward him. The blinding tundra was now blackened in its infinite shadow. He managed to start clambering backward as it seemed to grow more desperate, hungry even — no, *starving.* The vibrations traveled up his legs, straight through the bone as if it might rip him apart piece by piece. As he finally tore his eyes from the petrifying sight, they caught something that made his hearts sink into his gut.

The man in the snow, his side gently rising and falling. He was alive.

Oh, you bastard.

Kodo ignited then, his muscles kicking into action. Before he could stop himself, he was sliding through the snow back toward the catastrophe. His paws slipped around in the icy slush as he heaved the bulky gray beast onto his back, still unconscious. Then he launched himself across the drift with a desperation he'd never felt in his young life, yet it was as familiar as his own name. He no longer had to fight against the deep snow; he soared on top of it with the swiftness and the hunger of the avalanche itself. Matka quivered beneath his feet but they did not waver. He charged through the icy wasteland with the kind of speed that stung his eyes and burned his lungs. The kind of speed that had saved his life every time before and surely would again. The kind of speed that challenged him, beckoned him, commanded him to do what he was born to do.

He ran.

Lab A's frosted glass doors slammed open so hard it was a miracle they didn't shatter. Captain Short barged into the room, his brown skin nearly turning red with rage as the deafening bang echoed through the compound.

"One of you motherfuckers is going to tell me what's out there, *right now,*" he bellowed.

"We don't know —!" Doctor Daniels began to yell back in frustration, the only one bold enough, but he cut her off.

"What did this!?" he roared and flung something onto her desk, sending papers and instruments scattering in every direction. She opened her mouth to lambaste his recklessness, but choked on her words as her eyes settled on the object he'd thrown. On her desk sat a camouflage green patrol cap.

Now dyed crimson with fresh blood.

Sherri only stared, wide-eyed and speechless, her mouth dry.

"One of my men is *dead.*" The captain looked around at each of the researchers. "'We don't know' ain't good enough."

"Captain, we want answers as much as you do," Harrison spoke up, his voice slow and cautious. "But we don't have them yet. I'm sorry."

Short just stared at him with a cold fury in his eyes, his nostrils flaring with each hard breath. He snatched the cap off the desk.

"No one goes outside!" he boomed as he shoved through the doorway. For several moments, everyone sat in silent shock, not daring to move a muscle. Then Sherri stood up and hastily wiped the blood smear off her desk before heading to the exit.

"Where are you going?" Roger asked in a hush, as if scared the captain might hear.

"We need that hat, it's evidence," she said but stopped at the door. Her colleagues stared at her disapprovingly.

"Look, we have to clear out anyway for resterilization," Sherri added shortly, "Since that moron decided to parade a fucking biohazard around in here."

"Give him a minute, Daniels, for your own sake," Giovanni countered. Harrison abruptly rose from his desk, putting a hand on Gio's shoulder to guide him up as well.

"Let's go have a coffee break while the lab resterilizes, then regroup to discuss this with clearer heads. Yeah?" the elder Rosenquest suggested, looking around the room solemnly but pausing on Sherri as if to plead she not do anything rash. She cleared her throat and nodded, gesturing to the door as the rest of the men stood to join her.

"Let's go then."

...

The ever-present hum of the generators seemed quieter, as if a chilling shadow had been cast over the entire compound. It haunted each and every member of the Remus crew, causing their skin to prickle and their hair to stand on end. They had all been well briefed on the dangers of the expedition, sure; as soon as they stepped foot on the shuttle, they'd agreed to risk their lives. But being willing to face death was an entirely different thing than feeling it whisper in their ears.

Everything had changed.

They had no body, no confirmation, but the captain didn't need a body. He knew it in his gut, in his mind — the soldier was dead. Not a single shot fired, not even his rifle left in the grass.

Short ran through the morning's events over and over. Sergeant Crawford informing him that Taylor hadn't come to check in, and then that feeling, that awful feeling. Like being punched in the chest. Grabbing his rifle and rushing out of the safety of their metal walls into the open valley. He knew as soon as he saw that the fence was still off. He'd been through enough battlefields, lost enough comrades to know what it meant when the mission was left unfinished.

A man died trying.

"We can't confirm death."

"Bullshit, the blood quantity on the hat alone is probably enough to confirm death."

"We'd know that for sure if we *had* the hat."

The research team argued back in the lab, which had just been unsealed after completing its self-contained ethylene oxide sterilization cycle.

"There are alternative possibilities to expiration, that's all I'm saying," Sherri insisted.

"*'Expiration,'*" Carl critically echoed her insensitive word choice. "You're all heart, Daniels."

"She's right, though," Giovanni added with a shrug. "There's no body. For all we know, the man just wandered off. Maybe he hit his head, got confused."

Doyle scoffed.

"Your theory is that he ran into the wall, smashed his skull open, and then fled in a daze. Maybe stick to rocks, kid," the older man mocked. Harrison was in the middle of defending his brother's insinuation when a new voice interrupted.

"For fuck's sake, who cares whether or not he's dead?" Marshall exclaimed. "We clearly have more pressing matters at hand here. Such as, I don't know, the quickly increasing possibility that something dangerous is out there."

The room quieted at hearing what they'd all been too afraid to say out loud. Whether they could confirm the soldier's fate or not, the likelihood of complex life had just skyrocketed in the worst way possible.

"Well, before we make a claim that bold, we need to check the perimeter cameras. We *have* cameras, do we not?" Sherri spoke up, though the hair on her arms prickled at the idea of what they might see on the recording.

"They have yet to be configured because they'll need to be accessed from the fence. Meaning outside," Marshall explained. Doyle slowly spun his chair around to face the astrophysicist.

"Novak, you're in charge of the compound operations, correct?" Doyle questioned.

"Yes."

"Then the camera setup is your responsibility."

"Well, yes —"

"And the fence — the *malfunctioning* fence, might I remind you — is also under your department. Is anyone else seeing a pattern?" Doyle said accusingly.

"I don't like your fucking tone, Doyle." Marshall suddenly sat up in his chair. "In case you've forgotten, we haven't been permitted to do outdoor testing and maintenance yet. Oh, right, and before today we had no reason to believe we were in danger, and therefore had no reason to worry about the damn fence! So I suggest you rethink your implication that this is *my* fuck up."

"Stop!" Roger exclaimed, startling the others out of their argument.

"It doesn't matter!" the old man continued, his eyes bloodshot like he might've been fighting back tears. "We're not alone, there is *something out there*. It killed that man; we all know it. Don't you see that? Nothing else matters anymore."

Roger's grainy voice faltered and his dark eyes fluttered around the room. He was right, but the others wouldn't dare admit it. Life and death, the two indomitable truths, rendered everything in between obsolete. If the planet beneath them revealed the presence of real life and real death, it would become the only thing at all. Beyond discovery, beyond knowledge, beyond conquest.

"You're wrong," Sherri said after a pause. "If there is complex life on this planet, everything matters that much more. Danger aside, we could be making history in more ways than we ever thought possible."

She chewed on her lip for a moment.

"But it won't do us any good to cower now." She continued. "Next week marks the end of the observational period, and then we'll be free to survey and explore."

From across the aisle, Marshall laughed and shook his head.

"Did you miss all the yelling and screaming? The captain just said no one goes out," he reminded her. Sherri released a dry scoff.

"Captain of who? Not me, that's for god damn sure."

When he was a child, Kodo had been warned never to try to outrun a falling tree. Gravity would always win a footrace. Instead, he was taught to outsmart the tree and run sideways. Gravity would never win a battle of wits.

Gravity will never win a battle of wits.

The avalanche was much, much larger than a falling tree, but he hoped and prayed it was just as witless. As he tore horizontally along the slope with the mountain man thrown over his back, the flood of snow rushing closer by the second, the vibration was so violent his vision blurred and his teeth chattered. He could see nothing but snow and hear nothing but rumbling. Still, he ran.

Even when the looming shadow whizzed right past his haunches, ice nipping his tail, he continued to run. Even when his vision cleared and his teeth ceased chattering, he continued to run. It wasn't until he could hear the tumultuous rumbling begin to soften with distance that he allowed himself to slow and finally look back.

The calamity had been left far behind, and the colossal sheet of ice and snow flooded down the mountain right past him. It was a horrible sight, such power and violence, and he hoped he never saw anything like it again. He ignored the banging pain in his head and the beating terror in his chest as he continued in the direction Leida had flown. A crushing hopelessness suddenly weighed down on his shoulders, or perhaps it was the brawny man he carried, as he became pungently aware of his separation. He was now alone in the snowy hellscape, disoriented and far away from his only companions.

Then, like the outreached hand of the heavens, a beacon. As Kodo raised his face to the cold air, he spotted his scarlet flag, peeking clear as day over a ridge on the peak in front of him.

Leida.

He trudged to the incline's base, making a mental note never to forget the dangers of the snow itself and the creatures that lurked beneath it. As he began his ascent, the adrenaline dissipated and weakness gradually invaded each muscle and bone in his body. Kodo was strong, but this new beast tested the very way he defined strength. He'd known pain in his young life, pain and fear and failure. But he'd never known weakness. It terrified him.

He blinked inky blood out of his eyes as it steadily trickled down his forehead. With each passing minute, the unconscious beast he carried across his shoulders grew heavier and heavier. The mountain man was smaller than Kodo in stature, but fuller bodied in both muscle and fat than any ghaengste he'd ever seen before. The fur that covered his body was wooly, and it kept Kodo's back warm and sheltered from the slicing winds.

His muscles stung against the hulking weight, and yet he never stopped to ask himself why he was still carrying the man.

"Kodo."

A familiar voice pulled him out of his thoughts, and he looked up to see Leida perched on a boulder, watching him closely.

"We found the cave," she said, her tone cold as usual, but at that moment it was the most joyous sound ever to touch his ears. A relieved grin spread across his face, and her head cocked to the side as she looked past him at the man on his back.

"You brought it," she observed.

"There was…" Kodo released a heavy exhale, unsure where to begin. "I'll tell you all about it later."

Leida seemed to think that answer was more than enough, hopping down from her boulder to approach the limp form with caution. She sniffed his gently heaving belly.

"He lives…"

Kodo nodded timidly.

"He can see as well." Leida turned away. "Alvi waits."

She walked up the slope, leading Kodo and his unconscious load up the mountain to discover the truths they'd chased so far.

Upon breaching an icy ledge that was impossibly high in the atmosphere, they were greeted by the vast mouth of a cave. They entered to see Alvi facing away from them, sitting and staring at the back wall in silence.

The dim cavern was larger inside than seemed possible looking in, and the blinding glow from the outside world reflected off the crystalline stone in fragmented shards of sunlight. Intricate carvings and paintings adorned the walls. At first, Kodo could only do the same as Alvi — stare. Slowly, he eased the man he was carrying onto the stone floor, unable to tear his eyes from the scene around him. He walked deeper into the cave, shuffling to the center as his sight adjusted in the darkness. As he turned around in a circle, attempting to behold the entire chamber, he was faced with a sight like none he'd ever seen. The carvings covered every single inch of the giant hollow, like tattoos on the flesh of a frozen deity. Images and scripts were chipped into the rock with pristine skill, but the lined edges cracked and crumbled with age. Kodo's shallow breaths grew faster as he searched for some rhyme to the scrawled world before him, somewhere to start. Then he completed his astounded circle and found himself turned back to the mouth of the cave. Chiseled proudly over the archaic portal, the beginning.

It was Matka.

The planet Herself, haloed by all five of Her brilliant seasonal suns. The stone was stained with ink and faded by the passing of more time than the young ghaengste could fathom. Ceruleans and olives and golds and rusts all blended together to paint the ancient map of their home. Stars and nebulas framed the area, carved deep into the stone. Written in the ghaengste tongue, right below the planet, was one word:

MOTHER

Kodo slowly stepped to his right, following the trail of stars that led from Matka. They guided him to four carved figures arranged in a circle. The geometric simplicity of the lines that formed them made it difficult at first to discern what they were. Then Kodo recognized the familiar angular skulls, the horns on their heads and backs, the double-lobed ears. They were ghaengste. One had wings like Leida — a sky dweller. Another had fins like Alvi — an ocean dweller. The other two were a forest dweller like himself, and a wide scruffy one he assumed to be a mountain dweller. They stood together proudly in a rounded formation like the four secondary suns had crowned the carving of Matka.

Kodo slowly walked around the curved wall of the grotto, coming so close that he could reach out and touch the cool, smooth stone. Leida was right; the carvings told a story. The petroglyphs depicted ghaengste of all races, not only coexisting but consorting. They hunted for each other, fought against and alongside one another. They warred and allied, thieved and fed, but they shared the land beneath them and the blood within them. A deep, splitting agony rose inside Kodo's stomach. He read the stories on the wall, unable to look away, and yet he felt it was never meant for his paltry eyes. It was bright and blinding and searingly painful, like staring into the suns. Images of children of all different races playing together, entire families subsisting with one another in tribes and clans. It was glorious, and he'd never felt so unworthy and so yearning. He wasn't sure if he believed that it was possible, or if he ever could. But as he continued to read the story inscribed on the walls, the harsh truth forced its way through his weary eyes whether he welcomed it or not.

As Kodo began seeing pictures of heartbreak, betrayal, and slaughter, he knew deep in his chest that this story was true. The downfall of their people began as all things did: for love. He read inscriptions telling of a forbidden love affair, a broken treaty, and the hatred that spread like a virus through the people. The nations picked sides against one another as their concord descended into chaos, and then they chose no sides at all. They chose war itself, against everything and for nothing. As he neared the other side of the cave, the vibrant paint hues faded into dripping darkness. The wall became smeared and splattered with so much black pigment that Kodo swallowed in dread; he could only hope it was just paint. The etchings showed the families that used to live in harmony ripping each other limb from limb, their treaties shredded right along with their flesh. Children that played together slain in battles they were not yet old enough to fight in. Those that tried to flee and coexist in secret hunted, cut down in cold blood. Rebel uniters beheaded and paraded on spears as a warning to those who dared fraternize with the enemy. The images on the stone wall told of a torn and divided people retreating to their four corners of the world. Isolated and afraid, savagely fighting to protect the only land they could now call home. Kodo's eyes stung as he stared in horror at the hideous, broken images gouged into the dark side of the cavern. He finally stepped to the right once again, weakly, and found himself back in front of the cave's mouth. He stood before Matka, suspended over the gleaming sunlight breaking in from the outside world.

Kodo read the inscription once again, but this time it meant something different. It rang through his head as a sorrowful whisper, a cry for mercy so old and so weak it almost meant nothing at all.

MOTHER

4
COVENANT

Shit, his head hurt.

He cracked his eyelids open, only to frantically squeeze them shut again as the bright light seared painfully through his skull like a red-hot iron. He could hear a voice nearby. No, several.

"What about the living carpet?"

"Hey..."

"Do you have the strength to carry him down?"

"Do I have to?"

"Hey."

"What, Alvi?"

"He's waking up."

Damn it. He tried to lift his head and force one eye open, weakly pushing his body away from the blurred figures. The floor was cold as ice, and he choked on the thick ancient dust.

"Get... away from me, I'll..." His head fell back onto the ground without his permission, his eyes rolling back in their sockets. The splitting headache and the throbbing in his ears muffled every noise. *Mother, make it stop*. He emitted a long, garbled groan as he silently begged to black out again.

"Great, Kodo, you gave him brain damage," accused a shrill feminine voice with a thick, unfamiliar accent.

"Oh, how *dare I*. Last time I ever save your ass."

That voice was familiar. Young, masculine. Insolent. It came back all at once, and his hearts pounded in his chest. He sat up abruptly with a violent coughing fit.

"You!" he snarled. "You're the one who bashed my head in, you son of a bitch." He winced and coughed again, desperately trying to open his eyes and face the giant who had overpowered him. A new woman's voice entered the mix.

"You attacked us." The breathy words were cold but not vindictive, and their owner held something cool against his head. The more he blinked, the more the shapes came into view. The outlandish trio he had faced the day before. At least, he hoped it was only the day before. How could he ever forget the mutated sky dweller, the loud little ocean dweller, and the single largest ghaengste he'd ever seen in his life? A horrible sight, they were. He cleared his throat, attempting to shove down his pain.

"Who are you, what do you want with me?" he demanded despite the world spinning around him. The gentle-voiced sky woman sat in front of him.

"I am Leida, he is Kodo, she is Alvi. Do you have a name?" she said. He forced himself to face them, sitting up straighter.

"I am Rykr, son of Vaus-Ramaala," he declared as powerfully as his dry throat could muster, his pride emanating throughout the grotto. Leida looked behind her at Alvi and Kodo.

"Who is this Vosramala?" she asked. Rykr blinked at the other two strangers.

"She's serious?"

"Vaus-Ramaala is the sole king of the Eidolan clan. This is his son, apparently," Kodo whispered to Leida.

"Ah." She nodded.

It was only then that Rykr focused on his surroundings, confusion growing as he studied the carved walls.

"Where am I?" he asked, shakily rising from his slumped position on the stone floor. The trio looked between one another.

"It is a story," Leida said slowly. "One you may wish to know."

Rykr at first only watched her suspiciously, unwilling to turn his back on the strangers. It wasn't until he looked closer at the inscriptions painting the cavern that he softened, and he cautiously approached the wall.

"We should leave him for a moment," Alvi whispered, and her companions followed her out, leaving Rykr alone in the origin cave.

...

"He's been in there for a while. You think he ran off?" Kodo asked with increasing unease, looking over to the mouth of the cave.

"There is only one entrance," Leida replied.

"Maybe he dropped dead because Kodo smashed his brain into a fine paste," Alvi piped up.

"Will you let it go?"

"Not a chance."

A gray figure came trudging out of the mouth of the cave. The hefty ghaengste seemed to be headed straight down the mountain and fast, but Kodo stepped in his path.

"Get out of my way. I don't want to go another round with you, but I gladly will if you don't *move*," he snapped. Kodo didn't move.

"Relax, little guy."

Rykr flew at him, toppling his massive weight to the ground. They rolled around in the snow, both nearly sailing off the cliff's edge several times as they wrestled.

An agonizing screech filled the freezing air and echoed across the mountain range. The brawling men separated as they threw themselves away from the searing noise and covered their burning ears.

Leida removed her sharp talons from the boulder behind her and the echoing squeal ceased. Kodo rose from the snow first, rapidly shaking his head and sneezing in an attempt to release the pressure from his ears.

"Pussy," Kodo whispered under his breath. Rykr snorted out a cloud of vapor.

"Watch it, dickhead," he snapped.

Leida looked down at Alvi, who was climbing on top of Leida's feathered tail to separate herself from the cold snow, then at Kodo, then at the angry prince.

"You are very sturdy," she noted. "Most would not survive against a thing like Kodo."

Kodo glanced over at her, unsure whether to take offense or not, then shrugged it off as a compliment.

"He's a big bastard, that's for sure," Rykr scoffed. "But no match for a trained Eidolan warrior."

Kodo's face twisted in protest and he opened his mouth to remind the mountain man of his barely intact skull, but Leida interrupted.

"You could join us," she suggested. "We would be stronger with you."

Rykr blinked in shock, and he looked around at the ghaengste before him as if only now registering that they were comrades.

"Who is 'we?'" he exclaimed. "What is this? Some sort of... blasphemous cult?"

Alvi burst into laughter, only to be quickly silenced by a look from Leida.

"No," the sky woman answered. "We are a tribe."

She said it as if she were tasting the words as they came out, trying them on like a new garment. Her declaration struck Kodo as something only she would be bold enough to name, and only because she never did understand the weight it carried. It filled him with pride.

"Do you have a death wish?" Rykr gawked at them with eyes wide. "I shouldn't even be speaking with you; you're traitors, renegades. You should leave this land. Now."

Alvi's brows creased as her face dropped its previous amusement.

"How can you say that after what you've just seen?" she demanded, "Did you even bother to read the story of your — of *our* Mother? It was not always this way! We may be traitors to the clans, but not to Matka. This is not Her will."

"You know *nothing*," Rykr snapped back. "Nothing of me, of my clan."

Alvi stared at him with stubborn judgment in her amber eyes, and he scowled down at her. Kodo nudged the ocean woman's shoulder.

"He's not coming, Al, he's not like us. He's got a throne and a crown waiting for him back at home. Why would he choose to be an outcast when in a few years he'll be king?" He looked to Leida as he explained, and she nodded hesitantly. They'd come to see what they needed to see — the truth. What they did with that truth was their choice, and theirs alone. Rykr had the same choice to make for himself. The trio began to prepare for the journey back down the ridge when the mountain man spoke again in his gravelly voice.

"There is no... throne waiting." Rykr let out an abrupt breath, flinching as if the words had forced their way out painfully. "I'm not going to be king."

The three renegades paused, all eyes studying the young prince. He didn't look back at them; instead, he gazed out over the majestic mountains around and below them. His home. His land. A deep longing rose in his throat, but his lip curled in anger.

"My father passed me up as his heir. My sister too. He's chosen new blood to rule our people after him," he finally admitted. "I'm no more lunai than the three of you."

Rykr had only gotten the news a day ago now, and the wound was still fresh enough to ache and torture him. It had been why he was alone out in the tundra when he met the strange rogues; he needed to clear his head. Only now his head was the furthest thing from clear, pounding with so many questions and conflicts that he could hardly breathe. He craved ignorant bliss and longed to be who he was a day ago. A young prince whose only concern was preparing to be king. Now he was trapped between his loyalty to his clan, the betrayal of his father, and the story of their very people changing before his eyes.

"Maybe it's time for a new story," Alvi said gently, and Rykr couldn't stop himself from glancing back at the outsiders. Kodo lifted the ocean girl onto his back, then looked to Leida expectantly. She gestured for them to continue back down the peak but studied the mountain prince for a moment longer.

"Are you coming?" she called.

Slowly, reluctantly, almost as if there was a spear at his back, Rykr followed.

The captain thrust into her firm and slow, his hips pushing into hers with a heavy rhythm. He rolled his tongue over her soft breasts, her swollen nipples, and then up the center of her chest. His hungry lips traced along her skin, following the gentle curve of her throat until they were face to face. His icy gaze stripped her down to her core as he pushed deeper inside her.

"*Shit,*" Sergeant Fischer hissed under her breath, pressing her nose into Captain Short's temple as he sucked on her neck and bit the edge of her jaw. His rough hands ran along the sensitive flesh at her waist and stomach, her skin tingling and burning beneath his grasp. Sweat coated their quivering bodies and the smell of sex hung in the air around them, their shadows dancing along the wall in the dim lamplight. The captain slammed himself into her again and again. The sergeant grabbed a handful of the sheets in her fist, her other hand clawing into his bicep. A low gasp escaped her throat as he throbbed inside her. She squeezed her eyes shut tight and tilted her chin to the ceiling, grinding her hips up into his desperately.

"Look at me, Sergeant," Short ordered and grabbed her chin in his calloused fingers to face her back toward him. Her eyes lingered on his for just one starving moment before rolling back in ecstasy as he thrust firmly inside her again.

Her brows tensed in something between stinging pain and consuming euphoria, her entire body writhing and prickling with heat and pleasure. The captain grabbed her hips, wrapping her leg around his waist in order to cram his entire length inside her. He groaned and huffed yearningly, inhaling her scent, her breath, her desperate moans. She dug her short nails into the muscles of his back and shoulders as he nearly knocked the breath from her lungs with every insatiable union. Their gasps and groans filled the air around them, the creaking bed frame a metronome in the choir. Fischer let out a strangled cry and shoved herself up into the captain's warm body, squeezing her legs around him like a vice and cursing them for shaking. She panted and embraced him as every pulsing inch of him stretched her further open.

After the captain's rough, vigorous thrusts had intensified so much that the bed was no longer creaking but banging against the wall, he finally pushed himself into Sergeant Fischer as deeply as she could take him. His breath caught. He clenched his teeth, releasing a long guttural groan as he came. He rested there for a moment, catching his breath with his eyes closed. Then he gingerly pulled out of her.

Short leaned down to meet her lips for a kiss, but he was stopped by a finger pressed to his eager mouth.

"You know the rules, Captain — no kissing," she corrected him with a crooked smirk. Short pulled his face away from her scolding finger but conceded with an abashed nod, rolling over to her side.

"Forgot," he said casually, reaching over the side of the bed to grab a cigarette out of the pack on the nightstand. He fell onto the firm mattress as he set the cigarette in his mouth and lit it, but he'd only managed half of a drag before it was plucked from his lips. Fischer set it between her teeth and took a long puff as she sat up and checked the time on her watch.

"You're pushing it, you know," he teasingly warned as he crossed his arms behind his head, looking over her face and bare chest.

"Yeah, you are too," Fischer said with dry amusement as she put the cigarette back in his mouth and climbed over his bulky form off the bed.

"Same time tomorrow?" she called over as she began collecting her clothes off the laminate floor and dressing herself, the captain's eyes watching her every movement.

Short nodded as he released a long exhale of smoke from his nose.

"Yes ma'am," he replied through the cigarette as he sat up as well, scratching his chest lazily as she left the room.

Short snapped his head to one side, then the other, cracking his stiff neck with a groan. He sat on the edge of the bed, smoking in silence for what seemed like forever, thinking about everything and nothing at all. As he stared at the wall, he lost the battle to the image wrestling for the front of his mind. The bloodied cap, the untouched button. Eager young eyes, gone without a trace. Not even a body to bring home to his mother. The captain flinched at the thought, then sighed and rubbed his hands over his face as he shoved down the plaguing guilt. He stood up to get dressed.

...

"So what now?"

This may have been the one situation they weren't briefed on. They'd lost the first of twenty-six warm bodies aboard, his end still unconfirmed, and they had no clue what was responsible. They'd seen nothing, and that was somehow infinitely worse than seeing anything at all, no matter how horrifying.

"Well, first thing's first — we need to send a transmission to Houston and update mission control about what's going on," Carl began. "God knows what we'll tell them, though."

Sherri nodded along, her feet propped up on her desk.

"Let's draft that message as a group when we've got some actual theories to present, otherwise mission control won't take us seriously," she added. "It's not like there's any real rush; it'll take days to get there anyway. Do we have any data yet from the hat?"

"Captain Short only gave us a clipping from the inseam to work with," Marshall answered. "Didn't want us destroying the only thing left of the invisible boy, I guess. So far we know the kid's blood type, which we already had on file, and a whole lot of nothing else."

A few sighs broke throughout the lab, and Sherri shook her head.

"Have we completely ruled out foul play yet?" Giovanni piped up. Doyle turned to Harrison.

"Doctor Rosenquest, I respect you highly as a scholar, I want you to know that." The oceanographer's face reddened. "But if your air-headed little brother says one more stupid fucking—"

"Oh, *fuck off*, Doyle," Giovanni snapped.

"Watch yourself, Doctor Doyle." Harrison gave Doyle a threatening glare, then swatted Gio on the shoulder. "Both of you."

"You can put them all on the table and measure *after* I've left the room," Sherri interrupted impatiently. "But right now, we have more important things to discuss. Gio's not wrong, we should check the cameras in hallway Alpha to make absolutely sure no one followed Private Taylor outside."

"*Thank* you," Giovanni huffed.

"But," she continued, "it seems awfully early for folks to be resorting to homicide, so we need to seriously discuss the alternatives. Most importantly, what we should be looking for when we go out to survey. We only have one more day of observation, then we're cleared to make contact."

"Now hold on," Carl interjected. "Maybe we should postpone the first survey. I mean, we can't justify knowingly going out there if there are any suspected threats... right?"

Sherri scoffed, not missing a beat.

"Are you joking, Bridgeland? That's why we're here! We all knew the risks when we signed the papers. You're a coward if you try to back out now."

"No, actually, we did not know the risks when we signed the damn papers," Doyle argued. "We were all briefed on the predictable dangers of space travel, but aliens? Hell no, no one was prepared for this. It's not worth the possible loss of life."

"It's our job!" Sherri exclaimed.

"I'm with Daniels on this one," Giovanni added. "We're not here on vacation; we can't cower inside this shoebox for the next four years. And I don't know about you all, but I just don't like you blokes that much. I'll take my chances with the locals."

Sherri gave Giovanni a grateful look, and he nodded.

"Well, I'm not going," Carl said stubbornly. "I'm a meteorologist. I don't need to *see* the weather to analyze it. I have instruments for that."

"Compromise, kids." Marshall interrupted the bickering. "Everyone should be responsible for their own research. If Daniels and Rosenquest want to go out and collect plants and rocks to their hearts' content, that's their prerogative. As for those of us with disciplines that don't require field work, we can stay inside. Problem solved."

They all seemed to agree with the solution, some more enthusiastically than others. Harrison was spinning his ring nervously and glancing around the room. Roger had a look like a man sitting in the electric chair.

"I say we have a talk with the captain about making sure there are always guns available to play escort, just in case," Harrison suggested, clearing his throat and giving his younger brother a look that said *please, don't do anything stupid.* Doyle snorted.

"Good luck 'talking' to the captain about anything. He's not going to let anyone else outside after he sent that kid to his death."

Rykr looked behind him after almost every step. As they climbed down the mountain, his hearts pounded and lurched. He didn't know if he was doing the right thing, or what he was doing at all. But he knew that right now, he wanted to be anywhere other than home. So why did he keep looking back? Why did he hate the thought of his family presuming him dead?

Part of him thought he'd return one day soon, or maybe not so soon, and his father would realize his mistake. The other part of him hated the notion of ever returning. He knew nothing other than his land, his people, his responsibilities. He'd spent his entire young life buried underneath the ice and snow. All for nothing.

"Hey Rykr, how tall are you?" Kodo called ahead to him, having been whispering back and forth with Alvi. Something about how large and beastly mountain dwellers were rumored to be, though Rykr got the sense neither of them had any idea what his people were truly like.

"Excuse me?"

"How tall are you?" Kodo repeated. "You know, compared to the rest of your kind. I thought mountain dwellers would be bigger."

"I'm... taller than most of my people, I suppose," Rykr muttered back.

"You owe me five coins," Alvi said smugly to Kodo.

"I don't even have one coin."

Rykr did his best to ignore the incessant chatter, gritting his teeth as he prayed for a moment of silence. Or for at least one of his new companions to fall off the edge of the slim mountain trail, whichever came first.

"It gets steeper after this. We should rest for the night on that ledge up there," he said through his teeth, gesturing to an outcropping ahead. Kodo began to protest, but fortunately Leida was already heading to the ledge in question.

They climbed onto the jutting shelf one by one, finding it sheltered by the encapsulating mountain. As Kodo, Alvi, and Leida settled in close together for warmth, Rykr quickly made his way to the very edge of their outcropping. He looked out over the peaks below them, capped in snow and bathed in the vibrant sunset. They rose from a thick fog that hid something he'd only heard stories of: the warm, fertile land of their planet. Somewhere down there was an entire world he'd never seen. Fear bit at the inside of his throat. The mountains themselves bred him, the ice ran through his veins, and the wind gave him his every breath. As much as he tried to swallow it, he could not overcome the uncertainty of the unknown. Slowly, he breathed the icy air into his lungs, savoring the burn and wondering how the air would taste below. After a while of hesitation, he forced himself to join the others.

"What is being royalty like?" Alvi spoke up as she studied him intently. She appeared to have a specific fixation on his thick beard.

"It's fine," he replied, scooting slightly farther away from her.

"This... 'new blood,'" Kodo began. "The ghaengste that's supposed to rule Eidolan after your father. They bigger than you?" he asked.

"No, not... really. What do you care?" Rykr's nose scrunched in irritation.

"Just wondering why you didn't make the cut, that's all." Kodo raised his palms in surrender. Alvi batted him in the side of the head.

"Don't be rude, ijgra."

"It was just a question!"

Rykr sighed and shook his head.

"He... is a strong warrior, my father's heir," he finally admitted. His companions watched him curiously, halting their bickering.

"A good man. Jonn-Leih is his name. An outsider to our clan, but I love him like a brother."

A deep pain made Rykr's voice falter, and an even deeper confusion.

"And he loves me like his own. That is why… I don't want him to see me like this, this angry with him. Because he will be a great king, a better one than I would be, and I hate it. But I do not hate him. I don't want him to think I do."

His words came out hoarse, and he fought the urge to hang his head in shame. Kodo watched him with wide, focused brown eyes.

"Your people, they seem…" Kodo seemed to be struggling to find the right word. "Honorable. My people, they kill each other for their thrones. Friends, lovers, even brothers."

Rykr softened just slightly, his stubbornness falling away as he pondered what he'd known honor to be. Alvi broke the thoughtful silence.

"Does all that hair on your lip get caught in your mouth?" she asked as she reached out to touch the scruffy fur on Rykr's snout. He yanked his head away and a low growl built in his throat.

"No, I trim it. Why can't you ocean dwellers walk by yourselves?" he shot back. She rolled her eyes.

"We can walk just fine, but I'm too valuable to waste my time *walking*," she explained in a patronizing trill. Kodo let out a loud and obnoxious guffaw.

"Her legs are too short to keep up," the forest man said with a laugh. Alvi glared at him, then wasted no time giving a detailed lesson on the natural advantages of the ocean people and their apparently impressive kingdoms. Kodo took the opportunity to spin his own tales of mighty forest warriors, though there was no telling how much was true. And Rykr felt just a little less homesick as he told his new companions more about the honorable history of the mountain clans.

Leida flicked her tail as she listened to their stories of kings and clans, all so foreign to her. She thought back to the carvings on the origin cave's wall, each line and figure in its ancient story. She could remember images of the things they called thrones and kingdoms, warriors and royalty. And yet, no matter how hard she tried, she could not recall a picture of the thing Rykr had called 'love.'

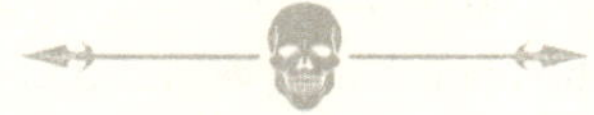

Sherri found Captain Short in hallway Delta looking out the wall of windows. He was staring at the tree line on the horizon, jaw clenched tightly as it had been every other time she'd seen him. She approached casually, ignoring the warnings from her colleagues that she was likely the last to have any luck forming a rapport with him.

"Beautiful, isn't it?" she said as she joined him, putting on her best imitation of someone more agreeable. He didn't look away from the acrylic portal to the outside world, his arms crossed tightly over his chest.

"Sure," was all he replied, his tone quieter than she'd grown used to. But even at its lowest, his powerful voice was strong and orderly.

"Are you looking for whatever took Private Taylor?" Sherri asked, glancing up at him in an attempt to catch any physical hints that might show what he was thinking. He said nothing, did nothing. Sherri had to use all her self control not to roll her eyes at the robot of a man. After quickly exhausting all the attempts she was willing to make at small talk, she got to the point.

"Okay, look. I know you're reluctant for anyone else to go outside after what happened, but we can't do our jobs without field work. My team requests that we meet in the middle and you spare some of your people for us as escorts on the first survey. Just in case," she explained, now facing him. He turned to face her as well, cold eyes boring into hers.

"You need samples, yes?"

"Correct."

"So you and the rest of the geek squad stay put, make us a list, and I'll send some errand boys out to get what you need," he countered. Sherri huffed and shook her head.

"That's not how this works, dude. We need to *see* the world with our own eyes. Your guns don't have the trained expertise to identify and catalog valuable environmental factors." She fought to maintain her patience but couldn't help the frustration at having to explain *her* job to *him*. He stared down at her, seemingly grinding his teeth, and Sherri anticipated him saying something stupid just to be a pain in the ass.

"I'll agree to your terms if and *only* if you tell me right now, no bullshit, what you think we're going to find out there," he demanded. She stood up a little straighter, suddenly taking him seriously.

"Based on the data we've gathered, our group consensus, and my professional opinion," Sherri quickly answered, "I don't think we'll find much more than vegetation and insects. Not yet. I believe there might be something out there more complex, and yes, possibly dangerous. But what we know right now implies that our alleged mystery caller is small enough to hide and is extremely elusive. My team concurs. No bullshit."

The captain scratched his neat goatee, and Sherri found herself surprised that he was human enough to experience an itch. After a moment of silent deliberation, he nodded.

"Fine. You want to go on any field trips, I chaperone. Deal?"

Sherri let out a heavy breath.

"Deal."

...

"We are cleared for launch tomorrow, gentlemen." Sherri sauntered into the lab, a new determination in her gait.

"We make first contact in the morning. And we'll be escorted by the best bodyguards 7355264Z has to offer, so you big babies can rest your weary minds." She made her way back to her desk, high-fiving Giovanni as she passed his chair.

"And so the real work begins," Harrison said wistfully, though his weathered face had even more worry on it than usual. The other men around the room displayed varying degrees of excitement, anticipation, and dismay at the impending adventure. Roger sat in silence at his station in the corner, staring down at his desk.

"Let's just hope that Short and the rest of the cavalry don't do anything stupid or compromising," Sherri added as she sat at her station in the back corner of the lab. That thought stuck with her for a moment, and she could only hope that the presence of the brazen soldiers didn't sway the results of their first survey. She shrugged off the faint feeling of dread and turned back to the equation she'd been working on for days. In order to kill time before the end of their prison sentence, she'd been attempting to work out the possible density of the plant life on 7355264Z, using only the basic knowledge they had of the air density. It was a feat that somewhere in her mind she knew was impossible, but she'd always had a hard time grasping the concept of 'impossible.' She sighed and aggressively scratched out her work as she hit a dead end.

"Hey, Novak," Sherri called across the aisle, "I need a chemist."

"I happen to be one." Marshall rolled his chair over to her. "And an astrophysicist. And an —"

"Save it for the resume, slick," she said, cutting him off as she flicked through the disorganized pages of her journal. After a moment, she settled on a page full of nearly incoherent scribblings with a chemical compound circled in red in the lower corner. She pointed at the series of letters and numbers with her pencil.

"The tests from the hat sample were largely inconclusive, but we got a hit on whatever this is — trace elements of carbon, hydrogen, nitrogen, oxygen. Some sort of alkaloid. Thoughts?"

Marshall leaned over her to get a closer look. She'd noticed that he seemed to have a habit of choosing to get closer, rather than just taking whatever he wanted to look at. Her thoughts wandered to the pleasant smell of his crisp lab coat.

"What laundry detergent do you use? It smells great."

"This is familiar... Confirm with Myles, but it looks strikingly congruent to some kind of batrachotoxin," Marshall said as he tapped her journal with the pen he normally kept behind his ear, ignoring her question. Sherri blinked twice, her eyebrows raising.

"You mean what, like a neurotoxin?"

"Exactly."

"It has to be some sort of venom." Sherri's eyes grew wide. "This is fantastic!"

She didn't bother to hide the childish grin on her face as she abruptly stood up to collect her notes and update the rest of the team.

"I'm sorry, *what?* The soldier was eaten by something that produces a neurotoxic steroidal venom. We might as well kill ourselves now, it'll be less painful." Doyle paced back and forth in front of his lab station and stroked his dark mustache.

"It'd be easier to kill each other." Marshall shrugged, then snapped his fingers as if he'd had an epiphany. "I know, we'll pick partners. I call Harrison."

Harrison perked up in alarm as Sherri huffed.

"You people are impossible!" she exclaimed, "This is a *good* thing, guys, it's the first real piece of evidence we have! And you have to admit, it's pretty incredible."

"We shouldn't have come..." Roger, who had been staring into blank space for the entire conversation thus far, whispered. Sherri's mouth dropped into a frown. Doyle stopped his pacing and shook his head accusingly at the older man.

"Grow the fuck up, Myles. We get it, we're all going to die. Is that what you want to hear?" Doyle snapped, but a deep English-accented voice rang out at such a commanding tone it was hardly recognizable.

"Sit down, Doyle. You're not helping anything by being an ass," Harrison barked with a harshness no one had heard from him prior; even his brother blinked in surprise. Doyle took a seat, almost involuntarily.

"Look, at least we've got a start," Harrison said with a sigh. "We know something, which is a hell of a lot better than nothing, yeah?" He looked around at his peers despite visibly shrinking at the sudden attention. The others in the room gently shuffled with sighs, shrugs, and nods, and Sherri gave him a grateful look. No matter their excitement or their terror, or anything in between, the next morning they would make history. Whether it be heaven, hell, or high water, a new frontier waited for them outside of those steel doors.

A call filled the air like thick fog, whole and all-encompassing. A deep, vibrating howl that flooded the atmosphere with music; a song that trailed up and down in depth and pitch. Like an underwater orchestra, thousands of different instruments came together to sing with infinite voices in one choir. It permeated up through the trunks of the jungle trees and then rose into the sky on a high note. Over and over it sang, the planet itself buzzing and echoing with the triumphant melody. He finished his song.

His mane and beard were grayed with age but he was well-muscled, strong, and he stood tall with his head lifted into the wind. His tawny fur was littered with scars that told of the man's grizzled history. The marks of a warrior.

The marks of a king.

He began the descent from his cliff overlook, savoring the humid breeze and sweet smell of morning. His tail swayed as the armor and jewelry adorning his form jingled and clanked in a gentle percussion harmony. Water dripping from leaf to leaf made steady joyous taps to the beat of his footsteps as the jungle came to life. He observed the colorful insects that buzzed between the trees to welcome the awakening. When the old man breached the tree line, pride swelled inside him as he gazed upon his kingdom. Laid out before him was a vast clearing, giant archaic trees surrounding it with rope bridges and treehuts strung between their branches.

He watched in humble belonging as his people filed in and out of their homes, working among their neighbors and pulling carts of food and furs. Children ran and played carelessly across his path, and their parents bowed their heads to him in honor as they chased after their young. Finally, the king's eyes settled on the ghaengste he sought most. A smile spread across his face as a sleek woman, pelt the color of copper and naked of armor, approached him with a sway in her step and a sparkle in her eyes.

"I heard you singing for me, Visaan." She smiled and rubbed her head under his chin, then circled around him and caressed his face with her soft maned tail.

"You know I have to make you fall in love with me all over again each morning, my queen. Is it working?" Visaan cooed as he groomed the fur on her nape with his long tongue.

"Just as every other morning," she sang, her voice breathy and gentle like a summer breeze. She wrapped her arms around his neck to hang on him lazily as he whispered something in her ear that made her smirk and begin to purr. Someone whistled sharply.

"Visaan, Avias," called the tall man who approached them. "Terribly sorry to interrupt, but your presence is requested in the lunai hall."

"Right at this moment?" Avias asked with a sour impatience lacing her voice.

"Erro beckons us," Levah replied, shrugging as if that were explanation enough. It held true, as the other two lunai glanced at each other and paused their affections to follow him.

The three rulers walked purposefully through a vast royal tent, treading on the dirt floor hidden beneath a long knitted rug. The tree trunk pillars lining the walkway held torches that threw faint green light, glimmering against the various jewelry they all wore proudly. They approached Erro, the seasoned queen sitting tall upon one of the four cushioned platforms on a raised stage.

"The missing huntress was found dead," she announced as her compeers approached.

"Gutfyres?" Visaan asked with his teeth clamped together. Erro shook her head, her nostrils flaring in rage.

"No. She was left on her back, neck snapped in half and her chest caved in. None of her belongings were missing."

Avias's mouth fell open and Visaan's face dropped. Levah remained stoic, yet his eyes held a stare filled with guilt.

"No gutter I know of would kill a ghaengste in such a way or leave without her coin; nor were the remains fed on beyond scavenging. Jarao was not hunted or robbed, she was murdered." Erro continued coldly; her face twitched as she fought back a snarl. Levah did not bother hiding his own fangs.

"Pointlessly *crushed* and left for us to find," the dark man bellowed "She was dive-bombed. The sky dwellers must be sending some sort of sick message."

A raucous voice rang out from the shadows, echoing through the long hall.

"I've only known of one ghaengste strong enough to commit such violence, and it was no sky dweller."

A man with a neatly cut crimson mane stepped out from the shadows, golden eyes glowing from beneath his helmet. All four lunai turned to face him.

"You were not beckoned, Rataan-Leih," Visaan called across the palatial tent.

"What is he speaking of?" Avias demanded, looking between her fellow lunai with furrowed brows.

"The giant." Erro sighed and shook her head. "He was troublesome, no doubt, but I hardly think he would enact revenge for his exile on a fellow hunter. You always did hold resentment toward him, commander; don't think it went unnoticed by us."

"That boy is long dead by now, Rataan," Levah added. "Strength alone cannot compensate for a lack of sense."

Rataan approached the lunai with an even stride, his expression foreboding.

"I hold no contempt for the giant, but we all knew what he was capable of. We all knew he was a danger to the clan. I only worry it is worse than we thought." Rataan made his way to the throne platform, lowering his nose to the rug in a reverent bow.

"He posed a danger to our bloodlines and our reputation," Visaan interjected as Rataan rose. "But he was no murderer."

"Desperation can taint even the purest of us." Rataan lifted his chin to gaze up at the lunai.

"He was bold, my lords, bold and angry," Rataan continued, "I should know, it took me many weeks to drive him out of our land. I believe his rebellious insolence alone is reason enough to suspect him, but his monstrous strength cannot be ignored. If he is still alive, the tunahk-dahn will find him. All I ask is to bring him in for a trial. "

"He was barely more than a child, Rataan," Avias snapped harshly. "Our answer is no."

The commander flinched at the queen's tone, but he lowered his chin with a nod.

"I apologize for my haste, my lords. I trust you understand that I wish only to serve your grace and protect our people."

He bowed once again, concern painting his hardened face. Then he turned to dismiss himself, marching back the way he came.

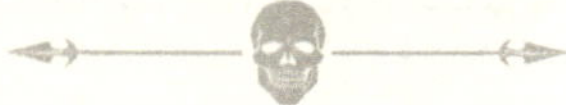

The anticipation spread throughout Sherri's chest, then stomach; the only thing she could compare it to was the effects of the G-forces on launch day. The sheer power that drove her body had felt like it might rip her apart, but instead, it carried her into the heavens. And yet even that experience didn't compare to the emotions that swelled inside her now.

They had been on Planet 7355264Z for the full observational month now, and it felt simultaneously like it had been years and only days. Finally, today, they would enter its true vessel. They would breathe in its air, they would feel its soil beneath the soles of their shoes. They would touch it, taste it, and learn the secrets it had been hiding from them since they dared throw themselves to its mercy. Sherri had been awake for hours already, and she'd spent every second preparing for their departure. Now it was rousing time for the rest of the crew, and she found herself physically unable to keep still. She paced around the kitchen area, following Giovanni as he collected his breakfast.

"What do you think it'll smell like?" she gushed. Gio paused in contemplation.

"Cinnamon and sandalwood," he cooed, "I hope."

Sherri shook her head, though she couldn't wipe the smile from her face.

"Humor me." She playfully pushed his arm, then hopped up to sit on the counter beside where he was buttering his toast.

"We've only seen one tiny, static sliver of this planet, and now we're finally going to discover what all it has to offer. We're so close, Gio, so damn close, can you believe it?" Sherri exclaimed. Giovanni laughed as he glanced up at her.

"To be honest with you, Daniels, I don't know that I'll believe it until I see it." He took a bite of his toast. "Doesn't feel quite real yet, does it?"

A low voice interrupted their musings, and Giovanni silently mouthed 'here we go.'

"Gio, could I speak with you in private?" Harrison asked, approaching his brother and offering a forced smile to the woman sitting on the counter. Sherri began quietly inching away as Giovanni let out an exasperated sigh.

"Let's get it over with now, shall we? Don't do anything stupid, don't take unnecessary risks, don't seduce the locals; have I missed anything? Beyond the fact that I'm thirty and not thirteen, that is."

Harrison crossed his arms and his mouth twitched.

"No, I think you've covered it," he grumbled. He retreated, but not without giving his younger brother's shoulder a firm squeeze. Gio and Sherri returned to their reverie, quickly falling back into a discussion about the climate of 7355264Z.

Harrison took a deep breath as he walked, briefly whispering a quiet prayer to himself. He reached inside the collar of his shirt, feeling the cold metal of the small Star of David that hung from a chain against his chest.

"That's the second time I've seen you pray just this morning."

Harrison glanced up to see Marshall leaning against the wall, watching him.

"Big day ahead," he replied simply. The taller man chuckled.

"That's one way of putting it. If you're that worried, why not stay inside? Skip the deadly part?" Marshall challenged, crossing his arms.

"And miss all the action? Wouldn't dream of it. What about you, Novak, are you coming?" Harrison asked.

"Hell no, I like my life, thank you very much," Marshall laughed. Harrison just shook his head and offered a weak smile. Marshall Novak wasn't the kind of scientist who valued discovery over his own life, and perhaps Harrison envied him for it. He glanced around the vast room as the rest of the crew organized into those anxiously awaiting their first steps into the outside world and those who were spectating. There was more energy in the compound than he'd ever seen before. It seemed every single soul aboard was in the commons chatting amongst themselves. He watched Sherri and Gio excitedly bounce ideas off one another, Roger and Doyle sitting silently nearby and taking deep breaths. The group of soldiers selected to escort them hovered around the commons, shoving each other and joking. Captain Short stood in the middle of it all, looking over some paperwork as a bright-eyed young man appeared to be telling him a story. As Harrison observed the deep furrow in the captain's brows and the juvenile grin on the face of the soldier beside him, he felt the urge to pray again for what was out of his control. Instead, he focused on the one thing he did have complete control of. He took another deep breath.

...

"T-minus-five till departure, folks," Captain Short called through the room. Most of the crew had congregated in the vestibule leading to the front door, dubbed hallway Alpha, even the ones who had no intention of stepping outside. The vast, cold common room was suddenly unbearably dense and hot. The survey team stood around and sat on benches lining the walls, the research team checking their backpacks, and the soldiers loading their weapons. The captain shoved through the crowd as he made his way to the front, knocking one of the hyperventilating researchers right into Corporal Keenan. Doctor Myles desperately attempted to right himself, still unable to catch his breath.

"Who the fuck let you in here, old-timer?" Keenan bellowed as he grinned at the panicking old man. "You having an asthma attack?" He cackled in the gray-haired man's face. Roger backed up out of the marine's way with a stumble.

"Worry about yourself," he said to the looming brute of a man, clearing his throat and desperately clawing for composure. Keenan began to snarl a morbid threat, but he was cut off by a sharp yell.

"*Fall in!*" Captain Short called so loud the compound itself seemed to quiver around them, and every soldier frantically jumped to their feet and organized into two lines facing the exit.

The captain had made his way to the very front, standing before the vast steel door. He grabbed the edge of a bench that several scientists were sitting on, pulling it, and them, closer so he could step on top of it. Now above the crowd, he clapped his hands once, looking around at the men and women below him. His soldiers dutifully stood up straighter, and Sherri roughly shoved between them to get to the exit.

"Showtime," Short said, clearing his throat.

"As we know by now, there is a potential enemy outside this door. We don't know what we're walking into, or how dangerous it could be," he called out over the crowd, all eyes on him.

"But if I hear any of you motherfuckers crying, it ain't gonna be what's out there you have to worry about," he continued, his voice raising as he spoke. "So keep your rifles cocked, your balls in hand, and shoot anything that looks like an alien. Aim to kill."

Keenan barked out a deafening, guttural, *"Oo-rah!"*

Sherri glared up at the captain accusingly.

"Are you an idiot?" she spat. "If you go out there and start shooting at everything, you're going to get us all fucking killed."

Short hopped down from his pedestal with a grunt as he slung his rifle over his shoulder.

"In case you forgot, my job is knowing which things to shoot and shooting them. I've got it covered," he said and grabbed the loose end of his rifle strap in his teeth, biting down and yanking to tighten it.

"Your job is to hold a gun and look tough, not compromise this entire operation." Sherri huffed as she tightened her own backpack straps, then took a few hearty sips from her canteen.

They faced the door.

"My guns, my operation. Should hell break loose, bullets will fly, I promise you that," Short said with a sneer as he typed the code into the keypad on the wall. The door began emitting a shallow whirring sound.

"You're disgusting, you know that? You make me sick," Sherri shot back. A clanging sound echoed from inside the door, indicating that the outside layer had opened. It began whirring again.

"Oh yeah? You'd get along great with my ex-wife. I mean, best friends," Short replied. Another clang and the whirring started again. He chewed on the inside of his mouth.

"Maybe I'll give her a call," Sherri retorted under her breath. Whether it was the internal structure of the door or the heartbeats of the people filling the hallway, it seemed to pulse with a distinct *bu-bump, bu-bump, bu-bump.*

A series of metallic clicks sounded from within the whirring mechanism.

The captain exhaled heavily, watching his reflection in the steel door. Sherri stood tall beside him, also staring straight ahead, and they both fell silent. The whirring stopped.

"Here we go."

A blinding light flooded into the hall as the doors slid open.

5
ABYSS

With Rykr leading the pack, they made quicker progress down the mountain. He knew the shortcuts and the easiest routes, turning a several-day trip into one. As the group breached the world below the fog, they witnessed the full glory of the vast planet stretching before them.

Rykr had to stop for a moment and catch his breath as he saw the color green for the first time. Organic, alive, it was different from his homeland in every conceivable way. The cold, hard stone made way for lush grass and rich soil, trees sprouting into view as they walked along the beck. High in the atmosphere, they could see miles ahead out over the open plains. A soft expanse of lively green, welcoming and joyous like the Great Mother's own arms outstretched in embrace. The world before them was warm and inviting, and yet it seemed only possible to know its truth when they were far from the clutches of civilization. Far from the bloodshed.

"Could we stop for a moment?" Rykr asked. He hid it well, but his chest felt stuffed with overwhelm.

"We just stopped," Leida replied, walking past him.

Rykr cleared his throat but kept on. He wasn't ready, but maybe he never would be. It felt wholly foreign, the land that birthed his new companions. As if they were from different planets. Before his reluctant consorts, he'd encountered few ghaengste that were not his kind. He'd heard stories of the ones that lurked above and below, but even the storytellers of his youth did not seem to know much about the other races of Matka. He'd been comfortable in his closed community, so far from enemies and their planet's conflicts. Today, he abandoned the comfort of his safe haven and confronted the unknown.

"I don't know why I'm the only one that ever seems to care, but where are we going?" Alvi asked, her tail swaying gently back and forth on Kodo's back as she sunned herself in the rising light.

"Somewhere warm, I hope," Kodo piped up.

"Somewhere safe," Leida answered. Rykr's face twisted into a scowl.

"You people don't even have a destination? Perfect," the mountain man grumbled, internally debating whether it was too late to turn back.

"We should head east toward the coast for warmth and safety," Alvi quickly suggested. "We can catch the river at the fork in the tree line, it'll take us straight there."

"You think that's a good idea?" Kodo glanced back at her. "That would take us back past Ramys land and straight into Celesteal territory. I don't know about you three, but I don't like the idea of getting caught in that frontline."

"Well, we can't stay out here in the plains. This is sky dweller hunting ground," Alvi countered, stretching lazily across Kodo's back.

"Some tribe," Rykr huffed, increasingly regretting his rash decisions.

"It's new!" Alvi exclaimed in defense.

"Rykr is right," Leida interjected, and Rykr glanced around in confusion before replying.

"...About what?"

"We are not a very good tribe. We must find others," she continued. Kodo padded ahead to catch up with her.

"Then maybe Alvi's right, and we should follow the river to pick up some more ocean dwellers. They don't seem too picky," the tall man offered.

"What does *that* mean?" Alvi hissed.

"Nothing."

Leida interrupted just as Alvi unsheathed her claws.

"It would be good to have more that do not attract attention." Leida nodded. "And Alvi's people do not seem to want to attack us as much as the others."

"We might have luck with the rogues that hang around the river," Alvi reluctantly conceded, putting her claws away. "I wouldn't mind having one of my own kind around to talk to. Assuming they're desperate enough to tag along with you fools, that is."

"Like you?" Kodo chuckled, looking awfully pleased with himself for producing a valuable idea.

"Watch yourself."

"We will go to the river to search for rogues," Leida confirmed with a nod, her head slightly raising from its normally low posture. As they walked, her steps became less tentative, her muscles less tense.

To Leida, there had only ever been survival and solitude. But now, among her growing group of allies, the world around her seemed to exist in a less savage way. Her feet staying anchored to the ground below her had felt so chillingly vulnerable at first, and yet now it represented something to her — something bold and solid. It was new, this sense of security. These people she now called 'friends.' The simple pace of her heartbeats was slower and more sure of itself than she'd ever experienced, and that alone was something she cherished with every passing second.

"So we are seeking out vagabonds with nothing to lose," Rykr clarified with a skeptical look as they kept on down the trail.

"Yes," Leida replied.

Rykr made a pinched face, as if comparing himself to that description.

"And then what? We recruit whoever will listen?" he asked.

"Yes," Leida answered again.

"And what about when the local clans catch our scents?"

"We evade them."

"And when we can't evade them anymore?"

Leida was silent for a moment, and a foreboding static filled the air.

"That's what Kodo's for," Alvi said, breaking the silence and patting the large man below her on the shoulder. He looked up in confusion, clearly having tuned out a while ago, and the others chuckled at his obliviousness.

As the suns grew hotter, they descended from the last foot of the mountain into the open valley, leaving behind the rocky titans for good. The steep hills flattened to the even expanse of the plains, and the beck's rapids calmed to a gentle stream. They followed the water under the open sky, across the fields of green. The sound of their laughter and bickering echoed out over the rolling plains and led the way through the valley before them.

...

Rataan had a poisoned feeling in his gut.

It was not a physical sickness that ailed the kaunek-leih, it was a feeling of dread he hadn't been able to shake for a while now. He wouldn't go as far as to say an assassination attempt hadn't crossed his mind, but he'd grown quite sure that the feeling in his stomach was not born from venom or elixir. It was one of pure instinct, the very same instincts that had protected his people since he was chosen for his position. He wore the trust bestowed upon him by the lunai as a sacred blessing, and he used it as a fearsome lance to guard his nation. His leaders trusted him to serve them, serve their clan, and that he would do until he drew his last breath. And they trusted his instincts when he advised them to cast out the rebellious young giant.

The commander trekked through the jungle, deep in thought. He often chose to wander the edge of the Ramys territory, much like a mere scout, just to keep an eye on their borders. Some might have thought it a lowly way for such a distinguished authority figure to spend his precious time, but he considered it a great honor. Rataan's duty was to take charge of the nation's forces, train their warriors, and protect their land. He saw no more honorable way to serve his mission than on the ground, outside of their walls, standing between his beloved people and any enemy that dared to threaten them. This time, however, he sought something specific in his scouting. Only he wasn't quite sure what. A sign, perhaps.

If he was lucky, he'd find the skeleton of a gigantic young forest dweller. It wasn't that he hated Kodokuna; his leaders thought him vengeful, but that wasn't it. He had no hate for the boy, no, he had children of his own to protect. It was that he loved his clan enough, he loved his people enough, to transcend hate. He would do anything to ensure the lasting security of the Ramys clan and the lunai he served. Anything.

Rataan stumbled.

He was distracted, unusual for him. He had stepped in a divot in the ground, and he made a low growl of frustration as he lifted his foot from the dirt. His irritation dropped to horror as his eyes wandered down.

His foot had planted into a gigantic paw print, at least twice the size of his own. It was several days old, he would have guessed. Because it had been left when the world was muddy and damp, no smells remained in the area, but Rataan didn't need a scent to identify the source. He knew only one man large enough to create such a monstrous track — the giant.

It wasn't much, but enough to indicate that Kodokuna had still been in the area when the huntress was killed. Rataan immediately began to search the area for any more evidence when something caught his eye. Another set of prints. They were small and light; they'd hardly made an indention in the ground but were clear as day to Rataan's keen eye. The size indicated a small woman or a young ghaengste; they were far too small to belong to Jarao. It meant that Kodokuna was not only alive and well, but he was no longer alone. The spiked ridge of hair on Rataan's shoulders bristled with the realization, the same way it always stood on end when he could sense a storm coming.

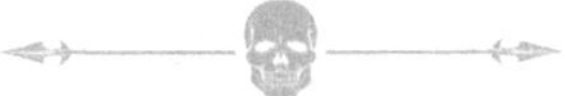

The grass was still green, the sky more or less still blue. But the planet felt alien in every sense of the word, like they'd breached the bounds of somewhere they should never be. As if they were breaking some universal rule.

The suns glared so blindingly they could feel a gentle burn on their skin, but the climate was cool. The gigantic planet in the starry cloudless sky loomed overhead, staring them down as if it were judging their worth. The atmosphere felt impossibly vast, empty, and the air tasted like ice. They could hear no noise and feel no breeze, yet the lush grass of the valley slowly swayed back and forth like it was underwater rather than in dry air. The landscape was rich and colorful yet desolate and barren, a world that seemed like it should be crawling with life but wasn't. Something about it felt apocalyptic, as if it were once the cherished home of a people long gone. It was so placid they might have believed it was only a picture, not a real landscape, until their boots met the soft fertile ground.

It began.

For what seemed like forever, no one said a word. One by one, the survey team stepped out of the confining safety of cool metal, sterile oxygen, and fluorescent bulbs into the glory of the all-seeing suns and the endless sky. The heavens were like a calm ocean suspended above them as if one might have expected to see their reflection if they looked hard enough. The silence seemed to swallow the faint hum of breathing, footsteps, and the familiar beating of hearts. For the moment, they were awestruck children. They turned in circles, looking around, eyes wide in callow wonder.

Sherri nearly fell to her knees but slowly squatted instead. Her legs were weak and as she inhaled a quivering breath, she was now a newborn fawn, baptized in the cold new air outside the warmth of utero. Another breath and she found strength in her limbs again.

Pulling a sample collection bag out of her pack, Sherri gently grasped a clump of soft grass. She coaxed the roots out of the moist dirt as carefully as she might handle a precious artifact. In her humble hands, she now held something so incredible that one human couldn't dare comprehend it through words alone. A small sob attempted to rise in her throat as she felt the urge to weep. Not from fear, not from sorrow, but at the indescribable beauty in her clutch. The soil of a new world. The soil of their salvation.

"Fischer, Greene, Keenan, Krei, Sanchez, Torres, Zheng, myself, and squints two-through-six. Thirteen, people, remember that number. Stay close, eyes up. Got it?" the captain called out.

"Let's move."

Even Captain Short had paused to gawk at his surroundings, but he wasted no more time before taking control of the situation. They began their trek across the expansive valley slowly and cautiously, the soldiers immediately taking formation around the researchers. The scientists peered around in dumbfounded astonishment, fruitlessly attempting to comprehend the magnitude of the sight around them. The guns remained focused on every horizon, the open plain a prime position to be caught vulnerable.

"Pick up the pace," Captain Short ordered, gesturing ahead with his rifle. Sherri kneeled to the ground in response, scooping a small blue shrub out of the ground with a trowel. She placed the plant into a cup-like container, screwing a clear dome on top of it and then pressing a button to begin the air filtering process. After taking a moment to study it, she tucked it in her backpack and stood up. She found herself eye to eye with the captain, a warning look in his stern gaze.

"Keep up," he said, escorting her back to the center of the formation she'd wandered out of. She didn't even argue with him or explain the importance of taking their time; she was completely and utterly captured by the environment around them.

"Trippy..." Corporal Greene muttered as he walked, staring up at the planet over the horizon. It resembled Earth with its blue oceans and green landmasses, yet there was something frightfully uncanny about the swirling clouds hugging its atmosphere.

"I've seen parts of Florida that look 'bout the same," Keenan chortled back, casually giving the magazine in his rifle a couple of hard smacks to check its security. He was given a few skeptical looks in response, but no one challenged him. Instead, they fell back into the hypnotization of their surroundings. Even Keenan shut his mouth as they stepped through a sea of wildflowers. At least, that's all they could think to call the tall plants with petals that resembled hundreds of translucent insect wings trailing down a central stalk. Sherri gently reached her hands out, allowing the frail plants to stroke her fingertips as she walked. She admired them as they swayed and rattled with the group's movement.

"Is anyone getting the feeling that we're being watched?" Doyle asked after they'd made it halfway across the meadow.

"No..." Roger replied, terror invading his dark eyes.

"Me neither. Where is this supposed threat we were so worried about?" Doyle spoke again, turning around in a circle and peering at the grass as he walked. They hadn't seen any fauna at all, not so much as flies in the air or worms in the ground. Their theories were vague at best, but they knew the planet contained life. The only question was to what degree.

"We still don't know for sure that we have anything to be worried about." Sherri shrugged. "But the suns are high, and our voices have already carried through the plain. If there's anything out here, it's laying low right about now," she explained as she watched the sky, then narrowed her eyes. She could have sworn something moved past the smaller sun, blocking it out and making it blink from her sight for just a moment. She put her open hand over her brow to shield her eyes, scanning to get a clearer look.

"Keep moving, ma'am," a soldier she hadn't talked to before, Torres, said as he guided her forward. It took her a moment to tear her gaze from the sky, but slowly she began walking with him. Then she pushed ahead to the front of the group.

Beside her, Harrison took the respirator off the hook of his pack strap, putting it over his face and breathing deeply for a few seconds.

"I'm just saying" — Doyle glanced at Roger with a cruel smirk — "we suspect *some* sort of venomous animal is out here, do we not? Keep an eye out."

"Hence why we're surrounded by eight M15s," Harrison added. "Relax, gentlemen."

He gave Roger a reassuring look and patted him on the shoulder.

"Not to mention, an animal as elusive as the one we're expecting would be extremely unlikely to come barreling out at us in the open," Sherri interjected, stopping again to pick up a stone and hand it to Giovanni as she studied the ground.

"Yeah, no shit." Doyle pointed ahead. "We're coming up on that tree line awfully fast."

Sherri looked up. Indeed, the dark trees on the horizon were growing rapidly. Growing too much, it seemed.

"Hey, I'm no botanist," Private Zheng piped up, "but don't those trees look kind of... big?"

The entire team looked ahead now. Sherri stretched out an arm and held her thumb over the horizon, closing one eye to gauge the distance. The private was right; they were still about a mile away from the forest and the trees appeared vastly larger than they should have been. Sherri took out her camera and snapped a picture.

"The size of redwoods, maybe bigger," she said in barely contained amazement, picking up her pace.

"Doesn't megaflora usually imply the existence of megafauna?" Zheng asked with an eager gleam in his eye.

"Um — ma'am," he quickly corrected himself, clearing his throat. Sherri gave a gentle laugh at his excitement and the fact that the youngest soldier appeared to have more intelligence than all his peers combined.

"It can, yeah," she said with a smile, her exhilaration growing by the second as she made her way to the very front of the group beside the captain. He roughly rubbed the side of his face.

"I miss Tehran," he muttered, and Sergeant Fischer chuckled from beside him. Keenan let out an obnoxious whoop from the back of the congregation.

"*Whew,* I don't know about you boys, but I'm ready to shoot at fucking *something.* Gettin' twitchy back here, Captain."

"Shut your mouth and keep those twitches to yourself, Corporal," Short snapped without turning around.

Sherri's face twisted in disgust and she glared between the captain and the corporal.

"You better hope you can keep your dogs under control, Short. Because if your people lose their cool, we could end up in a shit load of trouble we didn't have to be in," she hissed up at him, then abruptly stopped to pick up a twig.

"I've got no god damn problem controlling my people, Doctor. I suggest you worry about controlling *yourself,*" he growled through his teeth. She huffed and put the twig in a sample collection bag.

"I'm not the one threatening to poach our research subjects."

"Do your job, Doc. Mine doesn't suit you."

"*I am.* My job is to learn about this planet. Part of that is apparently making sure you haven't destroyed it before I've gotten the chance."

"Don't you have flowers to pick or something, woman?"

"Excuse me?" Sherri spat.

"I said, *don't you have —*"

He fell silent as all went dark. They looked away from each other and slowly upward into the canopy of the trees looming ahead of them. They'd walked right into the vast inky shadows. The trees were bigger than redwoods, much bigger, and they now blacked out the suns. The rest of the group stopped behind them, also going quiet and staring up in awe. They were ants compared to the gargantuan trees, minuscule and utterly insignificant. The shadows consumed them and the jungle towered over them like the gates of the underworld. Sherri's eyes widened in something between reverence, terror, and complete surrender. Slowly, she began to walk toward the colossal pillars —

Into the darkness.

The renegades had followed the stream past the tree line, where its gentle current wound through the foliage and cut through the steep hills. Rykr stared up at the magnificent trees as the group's pace slowed to an amble. He'd never seen anything like them, something so tall and ancient yet so alive. In their own way, they reminded him of the peaks of his home. The still air of the jungle felt thicker in his lungs, and even in broad daylight, the world below the canopy was so dark he found himself squinting to see. He silently wondered if any of his people had been this far from the mountain before, or if perhaps he was the first.

"I've got another one," Kodo interrupted his thoughts, choking back a laugh.

"How do you measure a reihggus's hump?" he continued slyly as his companions attempted to ignore him. After a few moments of being persistently nudged, Rykr caved with a sigh.

"How?"

"Lift your tail," Kodo cackled, barely letting Rykr finish. Alvi slapped him hard in the back of the head.

"You're a *child*," she scolded. Kodo lifted his head and grinned in response.

"Hey, I'm all man, baby." He winked, and Alvi feigned an exaggerated gagging noise.

"The *size* of a man, maybe," Rykr grumbled.

"Bigger than the average man."

"Oh shut up, everyone knows the taller the ghaengste the smaller the —"

"Stop," Leida said quietly, halting as she stared straight ahead.

"Do you smell it?"

Alvi lifted her nose to the wind, then froze as she inhaled. Her eyes grew wide. "Blood."

Leida cautiously began stalking in the direction of the scent, the others hesitantly following her. No one said a word. They crept along, and the noxious, metallic stench of blood — so much blood — grew so potent that it stung their heaving nostrils. As they tread nearer, another smell filled the still air: ocean ghaengste. They climbed a steep hill, and as they approached the crest, they could detect the source of the repugnant odor of death on just the other side.

A writhing serpent of thick black smoke rose from the far side of the ridge, a haunted beacon daring them to face its vessel. By then they could sense that there was no life in the area, not even the buzz of insects to join their racing hearts. The Great Mother Herself seemed dormant, as if She were hiding from Her creations and holding Her ragged breath.

Leida reached the top of the hill and stopped dead in her tracks. Rykr followed, his normally stoic face flinching as he came to a rest beside her. Kodo took his time slowly walking up the hill, dragging his feet and gritting his teeth in anticipation. Finally, he breached the summit and sick horror washed over him.

The woman on his back let out a cry of agony like she'd been stabbed through her hearts.

Mutilated bodies lay strewn across the ground beside the riverbank. The grass was soaked black, the soil turned to dark mud, and the rushing water thick and murky as it was polluted by seeping blood.

A camp of ocean dwellers, torn limb from limb and dead so long they were cold. Not hunted, not battled, but slaughtered. Their shredded remains littered the clearing like the drowned aftermath of a raging flood. Step by step, the young renegades weakly made their way down the hill. The air was thick and hazy with smoke; it made time and space feel sluggish. Frail plumes climbed from quenched campfires and clawed their way into the air as if desperately struggling to escape the horrors of the site.

The companions stepped carefully through the smog around gooey pools of tar-black blood and milky purple organs spilled in the dirt, seeping from the corpses' torn bellies. It seemed to be a small family tribe not unlike their own, but they struggled to match every limb to a carcass. A severed head stood impaled on a pike in the center of the chaos, bulging eyes wide in frozen terror, mouth agape and still oozing ropy blackened saliva.

Alvi climbed down from Kodo's back; she could say nothing as her gaze met the pale lifeless eyes of the head on the spear. She stared at the dead woman's face, captured in eternal anguish, wondering in silent despair who this had been. Maybe the leader, maybe a warrior, maybe a mother.

Leida gingerly stepped over a deadened fire pit as she sniffed around for any hint of survivors. She knew already that there were none, but she approached the dilapidated tent anyway and peered inside the frayed door flaps. Leida stayed there for a moment, staring inside the hut without making a sound, without any reaction at all. She didn't move, didn't breathe.

Rykr stopped beside her, then hesitantly looked into the entrance as well. He immediately ripped his head away from the cloth doorway and lurched to the side as he retched onto the grass, convulsing as he emptied the contents of his stomach.

Within the tent was an atrocity unlike anything Rykr had ever seen. The remains of children and infants. It was impossible to tell how many due to the mangling of the corpses. Their bodies were ripped to nothing but child-sized limbs, blood-soaked blankets, a broken doll. The smoke that eerily billowed through the campsite and the nauseating stench of bloody entrails combined in the air to taste unbearably toxic and rotten. The world was silent for the slain family, silent except for the low hum of the planet Herself weeping.

Tears stung Alvi's eyes and fell down her cheeks as she began to emit a long, low whine from deep in her throat.

Kodo hadn't moved since they'd entered the site of the slaughter; he stood still in the midst of it all. Paralyzed. His senses were blurry, his stomach hollow and twisted. He scanned the area, fruitlessly attempting to count the number of the dead. His gaze halted on a tree with something smeared in blood on its trunk.

Not smeared, written.

A symbol painted in oily black, a curve with a vertical line dragged through the top and a mark beside it. The sigil of the Ramys clan. It was then that Kodo's hearts, his stomach, and his soul caught up with his eyes. Bile clawed up into his throat but he swallowed it. All at once he understood, his tired mind finally managing to comprehend the cruelty before him. This was a routine culling; the Ramys leaders saw this abhorrent act as 'cleaning the banks.' The very clan that reared him, the people he was raised with. His people. Barbarians. Savages. Monsters.

Like him.

"Rykr... what are you doing?" Alvi suddenly spoke, her voice shaking, as she noticed the stocky man's rushed movement despite her misty vision.

He was dragging the mauled remains into a line in front of the hut, his jaw clenched in rage but his eyes dull and weak. One by one, he arranged the slain ghaengste next to each other as best he could. He pulled the severed head from the pike and set her beside a body of the same color.

"Rykr, stop it, don't touch them." Alvi wept hopelessly, her voice trembling. "Leave them be."

Rykr didn't respond. He marched to a fallen tree and snapped off two large branches, then shoved them into the ground on either side of the corpses. They crossed at the tops, forming an inward angle over the fallen ghaengste. Kodo, Leida, and Alvi could only watch their friend in silence. Rykr tore off the necklace of fossil and stone that hung from his neck, his lip curled in anguish. He hung the pendant from the wooden triangle's crossed junction. It formed a shrine, like the ones the mountain people made for their own fallen. But Rykr wasn't done. He snatched a sooty log from over the fire and dug it into the soft, blood-soaked soil in front of the grave. Then he dragged it around to mark lines and curves in the hardening mud. He was writing.

Alvi found the strength to stand and approach the hastily-made creation. Her weary gaze wandered to the writing on the ground.

"Iesu'talei..." she read aloud quietly, her voice ragged and out of breath.

They stood in silence for a moment, all gathering to stare at the site.

"I do not understand," Leida said. She didn't recognize the Matkan word of the old tongue. Alvi didn't take her eyes from the shrine, but her voice had regained some of its previous clarity when she answered.

"Justice."

Rykr struck at the marked tree with a vicious snarl, slicing his claws through the bloody Ramys symbol.

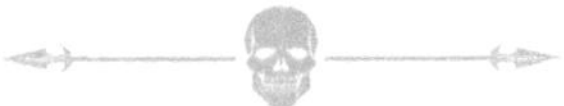

The jungle stretched upward to an unfathomable height, the canopy trapping them in a dark cage. Precious beams of light cut through gaps in the leaves like lances of fire, seeping all the way to the ground. They could hear various noises now, but it gave them no comfort; it was even more mysterious than silence. There was distant humming, buzzing, and the occasional whoop or warble, but none of it familiar. They could see no source of the sounds. Whatever wonders spoke to them were hidden well out of sight, behind them, or in the corners of their eyes. As if whenever they attempted to gaze upon the orator, it was swallowed up by the leaves. Or perhaps the noise was coming from the forest itself, whispering to them through the bark of the trees, which appeared to have a slight glow in the dark haze.

The blue of the tree roots traveled further up the trunks into slight pulses of turquoise light that dissipated before they hit the center of the tree. Giant vines dangled from the branches like outstretched limbs, some so long they nearly touched the soil. Collections of vines stretched between the trees and tangled together with the moss, forming hammocks and chandeliers far above the forest floor. When they walked through rare rays of sun, the heat was almost painful compared to the cold air of the darkness around them.

"Daniels, are you seeing this?" Giovanni beckoned, the first one to speak in what seemed like an eternity. Seconds, minutes, hours? The botanist rose from the spot where she'd been kneeling, studying an exposed root that curled up into an arc taller than her head. She pocketed the samples she'd taken from the bioluminescent green bark and approached him, then paused and cocked her head.

There was a hole in one of the trees, and from it, a small stream trickled down along the trunk.

"Sap?" Gio suggested, looking enthralled by the seemingly endless flow of liquid before them. Sherri rushed to take a collection tube out of her backpack, carefully holding it under the stream.

"Looks like water. Lots of it..." she noted, watching the tube fill with perfectly clear fluid, then glancing up the trunk for any hint at the source. She screwed the top on the tube and put it away, brows furrowed in thought.

As they continued hiking along, they noticed more and more of the tree waterfalls. In fact, almost every tree in the jungle had at least one. They listened to the sounds of the dripping and trickling, and when someone had something to say, they said it quietly — as if 7355264Z itself might be eavesdropping. Playful sparkles of light reflected and danced off the cascades, and the twinkling glow lit the way as they continued deeper into the forest. They entranced Sherri, drawing her closer to the trees and their infinite taps.

She hoisted herself up onto a low branch to get a better look at one.

"Hm." Sherri studied it, pulling out her journal to take notes as she assessed the anomaly. Her peers gradually began clustering around her. Harrison called from somewhere below.

"Please be careful up there, Doctor Daniels, we don't know what that —"

Sherri dipped her hand beneath the small shower, letting it wash her palm and run through her fingers.

"Is..." Harrison finished with a sigh as his brother snickered beside him. Sherri smirked to herself as she reached into the side pocket of her backpack and pulled out a flashlight.

"Hey, Myles," she called down to the congregation as she clicked on the light. "Do these look like they were made by animals to you?"

She aimed the flashlight into the wide hole, scanning around for a moment.

"I hope not."

Sherri murmured about his unhelpfulness without taking her focus off the task at hand. Then she bent over and stuck nearly her entire arm and head into the gap in the bark.

"I've seen this movie before, watch — something's gonna grab her whole damn arm and yank her in." Corporal Greene snickered to the man next to him, snapping his teeth and growling for effect.

"Hey, I'm just enjoying the view." Sergeant Krei chuckled back as Sherri peeked out at the disturbance behind her.

Something grabbed the back of the soldiers' packs, and both men gasped in terror. The captain yanked them away from the commotion, dragging them apart from the group around the tree. Then he roughly pushed them aside.

"Go stand over there and keep watch. Useless fucking creeps," Short barked as the two soldiers stumbled away.

Sherri shrugged off the distraction and turned back to the tree. As she searched for clues inside the hole, she grew even more intrigued.

"The entire thing is hollow, like a cactus," she called out, her voice echoing throughout the massive chasm inside the tree. She removed her head from the gap.

"It looks like the water drains down from above, flowing along the inner walls of the trunk. The holes must be a kind of drainage system so the roots don't get flooded," Sherri explained as she snapped some pictures of the inside of the tree, then scribbled down some notes in her journal.

"I wonder if there's a basin up there..." She looked up, craning her neck all the way back in order to faintly see the top of the giant tree. This one appeared around as tall as a cell tower if she had to guess, but the trees seemed to vary greatly in size. She was already planning when and how she might get the chance to climb up there when the captain interrupted her thoughts. He was making a habit of that.

"Alright, get down here. Let's keep moving," Short called up to her. Sherri did an exaggeratedly low impression of his nagging voice under her breath but began to climb down. Her descent required some maneuvering between several branches and roots, but she eventually made her way back to solid ground. She rejoined the team after hopping down, casually saying something to Harrison about 'lightening up.'

A buzzing sound grew in volume rapidly. All eyes shot up to spot a single, bird-sized insect lazily flying across their path. It was shiny and iridescent, reflecting between green, magenta, and blue, making it impossible to tell its true color. It appeared to have six distinct wings, but it could have just been its flight pattern playing tricks on their eyes. It looked like a giant flying spider more than anything else, or perhaps a beetle with a fat body and several long legs trailing beneath it. The team observed in cautious silence, and Sherri took a picture with her camera.

"Maybe that's what ate Private what's-his-face. Sorry, what-*was*-his-face." Keenan chuckled, then aimed his rifle at the creature and closed one eye as his cheek rested on the stock. Before he could switch the safety off, Captain Short shoved the gun's muzzle toward the ground and grabbed Keenan by his shirt.

"Don't test me, motherfucker," Short growled in the marine's face through his teeth. Keenan just raised his free hand in surrender, feigning a look of innocence.

"Sorry, Captain."

Short shoved the larger man backward.

"We don't waste rounds on roaches," the captain barked loud enough for everyone to hear but turned and kept walking forward. "Let's go."

He whistled to call back the loitering crew members, and every soul prepared to trek deeper into the abyss.

"Where's Krei?" Corporal Greene asked as he rejoined the congregation in preparation to move on. The captain slowly blinked at him, and Greene backed up a few steps.

"What the hell did you just say? He was with *you!*" Short snarled.

"I — uh, I had to take a leak, and he said he was gonna go back to the group, and I didn't — I'm sorry, Captain, I *really* had to go..." the corporal rushed to explain in a sheepish whine, squeezing his eyes shut as if bracing to be hit. The captain exploded.

"You split up so you could take a *fucking piss!?*" he roared, and Greene flinched, apologizing again as Sherri butted in.

"Are you out of your mind? Keep it down!" she hissed. "If any specimens were around, they're gone now."

Captain Short exhaled hard through his nose, his upper lip twitching.

"We've got bigger problems right now, Doc," he snapped as he pushed past her.

"No more wandering, is that clear?" he yelled as he looked around the group, briefly pausing on Greene with an accusing glare.

"Move out!" he ordered and turned to continue on their route.

The rest of the team hesitated.

"We're not even going to look for him?" Roger spoke up timidly. The captain kept walking but called behind him.

"Sergeant Krei will head back to the compound if he's still alive."

No one had said a single word since they'd left the site of the massacre. They walked with a cloud of despair hanging over them, and the jungle around them had grown silent and soulless. They couldn't feel the eerie, ever-present eyes of the Mother watching them, or the buzzing static of the forest's spirit. They were alone and abandoned.

Leida stared ahead, deep in thought. She couldn't figure out what she felt, if anything. Empty, maybe, like something vital had been removed.

Rykr's anger pulsed through the entire jungle. He was disgusted and furious, and deep down in the pit of his gut, he was petrified. He didn't know those ghaengste. They were outsiders to him, strangers from a world he was warned never to seek. But even they had families. Even they had children. And they were destroyed, annihilated without mercy or thought. He had never smelled something so foul or seen so much blood. His eyes burned with rage.

Alvi wanted to go home. This time it hadn't been her friends, it wasn't her family, it wasn't her. But it could have been. She considered leaping down from Kodo's back and running, running as fast as her legs would take her, back to the inner walls of Celesteal. Back to the ocean. But she feared if she stepped down onto solid ground, she might again feel the thick pooling blood of her people soaking her fur black and drowning her alive.

Kodo's world was caving in around him as everything he'd been told was proven right in front of his eyes. He wanted to crawl out of his skin and hide away, he wanted to be anyone else and no one at all. He was born from monsters, reared by monsters, and yet he was the most monstrous of them all. The unholy demons that tore that poor family apart and left them for the scavengers feared *him*, hated *him*, because he was even more barbaric than they. He was the beast of all beasts.

"I'm sorry," Kodo said, almost so quietly it was inaudible, the first one to speak. Alvi remained frozen atop his shoulder, not even her tail swaying as it normally did.

"What are you sorry for? You didn't do it," Alvi answered, her tone dry and empty.

"My people did."

There was a moment of quiet as they shuffled along.

"Someone has to pay," Rykr snapped from ahead, shattering the tense silence. He turned around to face Kodo with a vindictive glare.

"Maybe *your blood* should shed in wake of theirs. It's the same blood of their killers, it'll do just fine," the mountain man snarled, his lip curling over his bared teeth. His jaws snapped together, hungry for vengeance. Kodo stopped walking but not to defend himself. His dark eyes stared blankly at Rykr, numb, almost as if he wanted to be punished.

Leida appeared between them, her long white fangs gleaming inches from Rykr's face.

"You will not touch him," she warned, her voice even and quiet but her words a promise as true as a blade to his throat.

"He is one of those *fucking savages*," Rykr spat. "He would commit the very same if he hadn't been exiled. If he wasn't a *hona'dei*."

Kodo's ears dropped to the sides of his head and his face flinched.

"You are no better," Leida said slowly, her chin raising to better meet Rykr's gaze.

"*What did you say?*" Rykr roared. "I would never murder innocent children, my people would never do something so disgusting, so shameful."

His bloodshot eyes glowed in fury, and Leida stared between them with a cutting intensity.

"I have seen what your kind is capable of, I have seen the blood they have shed," she hissed, "And Kodo's, and Alvi's, and mine. You are no more innocent."

Rykr's nostrils flared and heaved thick steam. Then his eyes softened and fell from hers for just a moment, wandering over the vicious pink scars cut along her body. They carved words that told a story of boundless journeys and bloody battles. The anger stubbornly returned to his face.

"He came from that clan," he growled.

"And now he is here," Alvi snapped from atop Kodo's back, startling them. "It doesn't matter where he came from, or who he would be if he was still there. The Ramys clan is as much his enemy as they are ours. I don't *care* whose blood runs through his veins; that makes him one of us."

Rykr stared up at her and faltered. Kodo's shoulders slowly slumped beneath her, and he squeezed his eyes shut. Whether it was in tearful gratitude, or whether he just couldn't bear to look at his friends any longer, it wasn't clear.

"I want..." Rykr winced as if bitten by his own mind. "I want blood, I want justice. I want them to pay for what they did."

Rykr's eyes, normally so much older than his years, suddenly looked hopeless and frightened. Kodo's head was hung in shame, and Leida kept hearing that word echoing in her head, over and over. *Justice.* Alvi spoke again, a small flame flickering in her amber eyes as she gazed at the ground.

"They will." Her voice was worn from weeping, but there was faith wrapped in its tatters.

"The Mother always pays blood with blood."

...

"There are enemies outside of these walls, warriors. Do you know what that means?"

Rataan-Leih paced back and forth in front of eleven armored ghaengste lined up side by side. His heavy armor clanked and he looked over their faces as he walked, searching their gleaming eyes.

"It means you are *not welcome here!*" the commander suddenly bellowed. "Drinking, fucking, growing *weak* and fat as you indulge in the safety of the clan."

Rataan halted in front of a man that towered over him, brown fur rippling with powerful musculature. He stepped toward the brute, raising his face so close that their noses nearly touched.

"Who are you?" Rataan snarled.

"*Faro-Dahn!*" the warrior roared on cue. "Tunahk-dahn of clan Ramys. Undefeated."

Rataan stepped to the side, finding himself eye to eye with a pale, lithe woman.

"Who are you?" he barked from deep within his gut.

"*Io-Dahn!*" she called out. "Tunahk-dahn of clan Ramys. Unshaken."

The commander took another sidestep, now in front of a woman who looked identical to the other beyond a patch over one of her eyes.

"Who are you?" he hissed in her face.

"*Iago-Dahn!*" she boomed like thunder. "Tunahk-dahn of clan Ramys. Unbowed."

Rataan walked a few more paces, seeming to have made his point. Then he lurched back to the line, baring his teeth in the face of a red-furred man who was missing a leg, a wooden replica in its place.

"*Who are you?*" Rataan roared.

"*Mahrz-Dahn!*" the red man roared back. "Tunahk-dahn of clan Ramys. Unchained."

The commander casually stepped back to view all eleven of them, finally satisfied.

"So you have not forgotten that you are the most elite and revered warriors of the Ramys clan!" he cried out, "Then *why* are you still here? There are Gutfyres stalking our borders, robbing our shipments and caravans. There are ocean dwellers polluting our waterways with their filth, stealing our fish. There is a murderer afoot, responsible for killing an innocent hunter. *GO!*"

The warriors broke formation, scrambling to collect their weapons and tighten their armor.

"And keep your eyes out for the exiled giant! I want to know of any sightings immediately," Rataan added as they prepared to depart.

They hadn't seen any movement since the insect, which had come and passed hours ago. There was still no sign of Sergeant Krei, and the captain could only hope he'd gone back to the compound. Maybe they'd return to find him cowering, having run away, and Short would yell at him and punish him with laundry duty, but he'd be okay.

Something deep within Short told him that wasn't how the day would end. He was a man who listened to his gut, and this time it was twisting and doing backflips, trying to get his attention.

"How are we looking back there?" he called to the researchers behind him. "Got what we need for the day?"

Doctor Daniels laughed as she pushed past him in the formation.

"What we need is to explore and catalog every component of this planet," she replied. "It might take a while. Four years, to be precise."

A vine so long it seemed infinite stole her attention, hanging so low it brushed the ground. She flicked open a pruning knife and began to cut off the very end.

"Come on, Doc, you've got more samples than you can carry. What more do you want?" Short huffed in exasperation.

"A pilsner, if you've got one," she replied as she bagged the vine cutting. "If not, a little patience will do."

The captain shook his head, beginning to wonder if she truly woke up every morning plotting creative new ways to be a pain in his ass.

The botanist had already veered off to join the Rosenquest brothers as they probed beneath logs and stones beside a small stream weaving through the trees like a snake. The perfectly clear water carried little opalescent flecks on its surface.

"Don't take up all your sample space, folks," Doctor Doyle called out to the group, beckoning their attention to an ethereal sight upstream.

The creek met a larger cascade traveling down from a mossy ridge. It formed a magical web of trickling waterfalls, twinkling as a shower of sun pierced through a gap in the trees and illuminated the water. Scattered specks of refracting sunlight glittered and danced across the surrounding trees; the entire jungle was suddenly exploding with glowing color. The waterfalls leapt into a crystal-clear pool, the surface gently shimmering as it rippled. The reflective pollen settled across the clear water to give it a pearly sheen. A swarm of small, colorful insects fluttered across the pool's surface as if welcoming the crew into their world. Like the garden of Eden was opening its doors and beckoning them inside.

"Wow…" Giovanni broke the silence with a laugh, then playfully smacked Harrison's arm as if to make sure he was looking. He jogged ahead to the water where Daniels kneeled. The two of them got to work, laughing and chatting as they bagged rocks, soil, and aquatic foliage. Doyle busied himself with collecting water samples and performing ph tests, while Harrison sat beside him and sifted through the creek bed for shells and fossils. Even Doctor Myles, who had been silently cowering for almost the entire day, couldn't seem to keep his shoulders from relaxing.

"Maybe this is really it," the ecologist said in quiet disbelief. "Insects, vegetation, water, and sunlight. The perfect formula for a new home."

He shared a brief look with Doctor Daniels, a soft smile on her face.

Captain Short wasn't convinced. He kept looking back into the water after ordering his men to diligently watch the forest around the area. He'd never been particularly scientifically inclined, and he wouldn't claim to know much about any jungle that wasn't concrete. But he was beginning to think the entire planet was far, far too empty. They knew there was life — they'd seen the insects with their own eyes. And yet, there was not a single visible organism in the water. No fish, no tadpoles, nothing. Not even flies swarming around. Something about it chilled him to his core. He'd been stationed in the sands of the Middle East for years prior to this expedition, and he could swear the desert felt worlds more alive than this vacant planet. The more he sat with the feeling in his stomach, the surer he was that there was something deeply unholy about the ground he stood on.

"Finish up what you're doing and then we're heading back," he called out to the researchers. "This place is giving me the creeps."

"Gio, be a dear and go hold his hand," Doctor Daniels said with her eyes glued to her open journal.

She was sketching a large flower that floated on top of the water. Its petals were a glassy, translucent yellow-green, almost as if it were plastic. It appeared to be anchored to the bed by several frilly tendrils, like jellyfish tentacles, swaying and dancing in the current. Giovanni began to protest, but the captain beat him to it.

"You're not as funny as you think you are, Daniels, you know that?" Short retorted. "Get up, let's go."

"I'm not done," she shot back, biting her lip as she scribbled in her journal.

"Take a damn picture," he snapped. She ignored him.

Giovanni nudged the botanist with his elbow as the rest of the survey team packed up to leave.

"There's always tomorrow." He chuckled, and Sherri shook her head with a smile.

"There's always today!" she exclaimed but took out her camera to snap a picture of the flower. Then she put her materials away and zipped her backpack with a wistful sigh. She looked over the creek, the shimmering stones, and the moss that adorned them as if saying a reluctant goodbye.

When Sherri finally stood up from the bank and began walking back toward the group, she took her time admiring the jungle around them, the thick ferns and the colorful flowering plants. She stopped for a moment to listen to the music of humming, buzzing, whoops and warbles, and a steady clicking.

"Come on, greenthumb!" Doyle called back to her, and she jogged to catch up.

...

The longer they walked, the darker and quieter the jungle became. The doors to their garden of Eden began to shut, and they were left out in the cold once again. They saw no more occasional insects, they could no longer hear the gentle babbling of the brook behind them, and yet the forest felt anything but lonely. It seemed the trees themselves were staring at them, like if they looked close enough, the swirling bark would open to reveal thousands of accusing eyes. The canopy created a black cloak like the shadow of a giant, and for a while the atmosphere was so silent it seemed to be a vacuum that sucked the very breath from their lungs. Until the birdsong.

It was quiet at first, a nearly undetectable whistling tune. Then it grew louder and more deliberate, like a flute or a piccolo. Gentle and lulling, it stroked their weary ears and warmed their clammy skin with its soft embrace. Everyone scanned the trees for the creature that might be singing to them, but no one said a word. Captain Short clicked his rifle off safety.

"What are you doing?" Sherri whispered from beside him. She glanced down at Short's weapon suspiciously, then back up.

"Just being prepared. Keep walking."

She wasn't sure if something really did feel wrong, or if his paranoia was getting to her. But suddenly Sherri couldn't fend off the tingling feeling of static electricity in the jungle air, like a storm was coming. Except there was not a cloud in the sky.

She shook off the stiffness and walked faster, determined not to let her imagination run wild. The pleasant birdsong seemed to have died out now. Perhaps the singer had moved on.

Sherri continued taking pictures of odd moss formations and interesting plants as they walked. The whole world was incomparable to anything she'd seen before, and every step she took in it invigorated her. The tension melted from her shoulders as she hurried ahead to examine a puddle. Sherri began sifting around for any signs of small organisms and bagging samples from the unique plants in the pool. A bright fiery colored flower caught her eye, shaped like a feather with long curling tendrils for petals. Something else flickered in her vision. She leaned down, looking closer into the water.

The glowing orbs. She recalled Doctor Rosenquest's account from weeks ago about lights in the darkness. Only they looked tiny in the water. She couldn't imagine how he would have seen them from across the plains. When a ripple disturbed the pool's surface, she realized they were only a reflection. Slowly, painfully slowly, Sherri began to stand up.

She almost didn't see it, it was so still.

The glowing orbs came into focus first. Eyes. And they were staring right through Sherri's own, staring deep inside her soul.

Even dwarfed by the towering trees, it must have been over ten feet tall. At first, she couldn't determine what she was looking at, only that there was a dark figure in the shadowed vines. It was imposing, long-legged, and a whip-like tail trailed behind it, brushing the ground. It stood completely still, but Sherri couldn't concentrate enough to tell what exactly it looked like; she was captured in its gaze. She could make out spines or horns growing out of its body. From its head, from its back, maybe everywhere. Two distinct pairs of nostrils on its snout flared with hot breath; that was the only part of it that moved. Steam poured from its nose as it heaved, disturbing the image of the statuesque beast. And it was a beast; that was the only name she could give it.

Her eyes fought to focus, and she could make out its long, thick neck. It was gaunt and skeletal under its dark skin, no, it was bulging with thick muscle — she couldn't tell. As Sherri's heart pounded viciously, her vision blurred with each frantic pulse of blood through her body. The eyes, the eyes were all she could keep in focus.

She could hear the shuffling of the rest of the group as they approached her from behind. Her chest clenched and her knees threatened to buckle. She tensed every muscle, keeping her eyes locked on the creature, though she wasn't sure she could tear them away if she tried. Finally, she managed to utter two shaky words as her team caught up with her.

"Don't... move..."

6
CATACLYSM

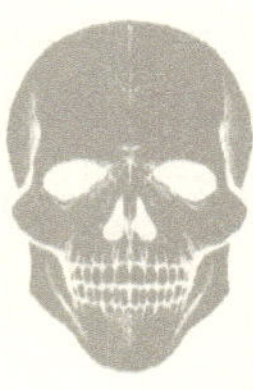

For a moment, it was like the planet stopped spinning entirely. Nothing moved, nothing breathed, everything frozen in time.

If only it had lasted.

A sound halfway between a freight train and a rocket launch ripped apart the silence and shattered the still air to pieces.

Sherri's ears popped and went quiet as blood began dripping from them, then something shoved her hard to the side as shots rained upon the raging beast. She scrambled to her feet in time to see a universe of bullets embed themselves into the monster as it reared on its hind legs to reach a massive towering height and unhinged its lower jaw. The entire planet shook but all Sherri could hear was ringing.

The world was slow and heavy. She was being yanked by the arm through the dense trees, her muscles barely receiving the signal in time to start running. Looking around, she could make out Harrison, Doyle, Giovanni, and Roger also sprinting through the trees, pulled by soldiers.

Sherri stumbled over a log but didn't hit the ground. Her head spun as the soldier gripped her arm and towed her along until her boots once again found the dirt below her. The atmosphere was still blurry as the pressure in her ears built and built and built as if she were drowning underwater. Then a stabbing pang shot through her ear canals as they finally cleared and allowed the catastrophic noise to invade her skull.

She instantly missed the silence.

The tumultuous chaos of the beast was indescribably loud, even as they covered ground in retreat. Its echo tore through the trees like the explosion of a nuclear warhead, and the entire jungle trembled as if the sky were going to collapse on top of them at any moment. Roger tripped and hit the dirt, falling free from the grip of the soldier dragging him. Sherri's soldier abruptly let go of her arm and she saw his face as he flipped around — the young unshaven one. He grabbed the old man by the shirt and forced him onto his feet.

"Go! Keep going!" Corporal Greene screamed at her as he dragged the stumbling man along. Sherri didn't waste another second. She took off running as fast as she could, faster than she'd ever thought possible. Sharp branches sliced and cut her muddy flesh but she couldn't feel a thing.

She burst through the thick jungle into the open plains. The blazing sunlight blinded her for a moment but she tore through the sea of grass anyway. Her boots dug into the ground as she ran, and the monster wailed and shrieked behind her. She didn't dare look back. The *ratatatatatat* of high-powered artillery cracked through the air, and for a split second, she hoped they weren't killing the animal. The thought was sucked away as another roar burst from the trees, closer — so much closer — and there was not a shred of pain in the calamitous bellow. It was a rageful torrent, the shockwave sending vibrations up through her teeth and she feared the colossal sound would shred her entire body apart into displaced atoms. Sherri ran on, legs churning with all they had and heart desperately pumping every ounce of blood in her veins. Stiff waist-high grass whipped her bare skin raw but she focused only on the compound, still seemingly miles across the field. Figures reached the fence's border — the soldiers and her peers, except for Greene and Roger who she could only hope were somewhere close behind her.

Another monstrous howl boomed through the air closer yet. The noise shook the ground so violently it threatened to collapse, kicking Sherri's legs out from under her and sending her tumbling through the dirt and mud until she rolled to a hard stop. She frantically scrambled to find her footing, sliding in the damp grass as the sound of voices filled the air. Two more soldiers raced toward her through the meadow, yelling at her.

"Get up! GO!" Sergeant Fischer screamed, hurtling over a fallen log with Corporal Keenan sprinting on her heels. Sherri managed to plant her boots into the dirt and she launched herself up, tearing toward the compound yet again. She only made it a few more strides before there was a deafening boom and what felt like an earthquake or a violent eruption. She was launched off her feet once more, her body thrown through the air. She landed yards away, the breath knocked from her lungs and soil exploding around her. Sherri skidded to a violent halt as the planet continued shaking and lurching every few seconds. As she got to her hands and knees, she realized she had landed within the border of the electric fence — a fact which held no comfort as it was turned off. The yelling of soldiers and the distinct voices of the Rosenquest brothers came from within the doorway.

"Daniels! Come on!" they cried to her, but she couldn't focus on what they were saying as she finally bore witness to the scene in the plains.

Halfway across the meadow, the beast was rearing and slamming its mammoth feet into the planet over and over again. The ground shook so hard with each collision that Sherri couldn't get up no matter how hard she fought to rise. The monster raged and thrashed and screamed, its hideous jaws open impossibly wide and gushing bright scarlet blood. Fischer and Keenan tumbled ungracefully to the ground next to Sherri, managing to reach the fence. Greene and Roger frantically clambered nearer, Greene carrying nearly the older man's entire weight with their arms hitched over one another's shoulders. Further away, Captain Short was covering them and occupying the beast by unloading magazine after magazine into its hide, though the bullets seemed to have no effect other than enraging and distracting the vicious behemoth.

The ground stopped quaking abruptly. The monster halted its pounding and thrashing, then slowly tilted its head to one side as deafening gunfire was replaced with a pathetic clicking. Short started running.

Greene and Roger made it inside the border, the old man clutching his chest and panting heavily. The young soldier began dragging the scientist into the building as the men inside helped him. A desperate screaming drew their eyes up to see Captain Short sprinting for the compound as fast as his legs would take him. The colossal beast galloped after him, gaping maw frothing red, beady eyes glaring hungrily, shaking the planet with every step.

"Turn it on!" Short screamed. "TURN ON THE FUCKING FENCE!"

For a moment no one moved, maybe in shock, or maybe hoping their hesitation would allow him time to make it. They were ripped from their hopes as he cried out again.

"What the fuck are you waiting for!?" he bellowed, speeding up as the monstrous creature behind him shrieked again.

Sherri fought through her stupor and lurched for the keypad. She punched in the code as fast as her trembling fingers could manage, then slammed her palm against the button.

A faintly bluish wall of light started crawling between the fence posts. Starting from the back of the compound, it gradually arced into a semicircle as it connected the points formed by the tall conduction poles. A loud buzzing noise was emitted as both ends spread nearer, approaching a closing point.

Short ran faster. The pursuing beast snapped at the air behind him with its dreadful jaws, revealing gigantic, pointed black teeth. The wall began to slide together into a solid border.

Short dove and narrowly slipped through the slim opening as the two ends of the wall met with a flash of light and a sharp crackling. The monster skidded to a halt in front of the barrier. It glared at them through the translucent blue light, eyes bulging wildly, its four separate pupils dilated into crosses and darting around. It unhinged its cavernous maw and released a haunting, guttural scream as thick gobs of frothing saliva pelted the fence and vaporized with angry hisses. Then it turned and left, long tail thrashing as it bounded away.

The captain stared at the retreating beast through the fence with wide eyes and chest heaving, patting from his torso down to his legs as if to make sure his body remained intact. He let his head fall back and hit the dirt.

A brilliant light shone over the horizon, streaming over the leafy treetops like a golden halo. As the twin suns crested the jungle canopy, Leida took in a long inhale, as if breathing in the cold light. The view from the very tallest trees in the jungle might as well have been the view from atop the world, looking down over the planet from space. The raw suns were pure and blinding without the atmosphere to contain them, and the ever-present stars were brighter above the fog in the lower sky. It was a view meant only for Matka Herself, a sacred sight Leida was unworthy of. And yet it felt like home to her, or at least as close as she could ever hope to get. She took one more gracious breath of the thin stagnant air. Then she leaped.

She sliced through the canopy like a white comet shooting down through the atmosphere with a trail of red flames. Dust exploded from a shockwave around her when she landed.

"Show off," Kodo muttered.

"What did you see?" Alvi asked.

"We should cross the river and follow the southern bend. We are too far north. Too close to the Ramys border," Leida reported.

"Too close?" Rykr growled. "We should be hunting those bastards, not avoiding them."

Kodo's face grew serious, his normally soft gaze foreboding.

"You're not from around here, Rykr, you don't understand," he explained. "Ramys owns this land. The region lives under their claw. They're well-trained, well-fed, and well-armed. The only threats to their forces are the Gutfyre bandits, and we better hope we don't run into them either. Rogues, tribes, everyone else, well..."

He flinched as if stung by the memories behind his eyes.

"We wouldn't stand a chance. Forget it."

A scowl crossed Rykr's face and his tail thrashed as he turned away.

"So what, then, we run?" he snarled. "Live in fear, stick to the shadows? That's no life. That's no honor."

Alvi hopped down from Kodo's back and approached Rykr, peering around his broad shoulder.

"Kodo is right," she said gently. "We're no match for Ramys. They have hunted my people, attempted to drive my home clan back into the ocean for hundreds of suns. They're strong and bloodthirsty. But we'll grow stronger, like Leida said; we'll find more like us. We won't live in fear forever."

She glanced back at Leida, who nodded in confirmation. Kodo spoke up again.

"Exiles like me, mutants like Leida. Outcasts, refugees, Mother knows this world is full of 'em. Why not join them?" Kodo said hopefully, the warmth returning to his eyes. Rykr turned back to his companions, his brow still stubbornly furrowed with doubt.

"And how do you three propose we get them to join a sorry sight like us?" he asked. "Unless Kodo's going to knock out and kidnap every damn drifter on the continent."

"That was *once*," Kodo grumbled.

"Once is plenty," Alvi cracked. Leida flicked her tail, standing up to prepare to move on from their resting place.

"They will join us for the same reason we have joined each other," she said as she beckoned them along. "It was not always this way. It does not have to be this way."

They walked on, making their way steadily to the river, guided by the winding web of tiny trickling creeks and Alvi's natural magnetism toward the water. Leida was silent as they trekked, as usual, but this time she had a faint bothersome feeling that nagged at her like a fly in her ear. Her eyes darted between the trail ahead of them and the trees in the distance. Her wings shifted on her back as she couldn't help the feeling that something was watching them. She kept her eyes open, listening to the sounds of the forest rather than the chattering of her companions.

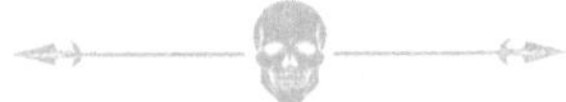

The compound was in chaos.

The crew members all crowded into the commons, babbling in frantic terror and desperate confusion. The captain felt like he was frozen in place and there was a hurricane raging around him. He watched the homebound crew interrogate those who had seen the outside, the medical staff rushing to check vitals and treat injuries, including the old man's dislocated knee. A nurse with nearly white blonde hair appeared in front of him.

"Excuse me, sir, you need those wounds treated right now. Please come with me," she said, gently taking him by the arm to lead him away. *What wounds?*

Short looked down to see several wooden splinters and other shrapnel embedded in his arm and chest; he didn't remember an explosion. Then an image flickered in his mind: the monster hitting a tree with its long, powerful tail, toppling it with a sickening crack. He shook his head to clear the memory and reluctantly allowed the woman in scrubs to tow him along.

"Ma'am?" He finally spoke. "Did Sergeant Krei make it back? We lost him while we were out there."

The nurse gestured for him to sit down on a hospital bed after reaching the med bay and glanced over at an aged doctor with a yellow tie. The doctor shook his head sympathetically, and the nurse turned back to Short.

"I'm sorry, Captain, no one came back before the rest of you..." she said tenderly as she began to carefully cut off his shirt. He nodded, watching her blankly as she worked. Then he tensed and looked up. His gaze searched around the med bay and through the floor-length windows that opened out to the commons.

Greene, Keenan, Sanchez, Fischer, squint one, two, three, four, five.

He sat up straighter, eyes scanning around wildly as he looked through the glass.

Where's Zheng?

He remembered ordering him to take one of the research assets and go. He saw the researcher, but not Private Zheng. His chest clenched and he rose from his seated position.

The young private emerged from the walk-in freezer carrying a tray of ice. Short's shoulders relaxed as a timid voice rose through the bustling noise. *Captain?*

"Captain? Are you still with me?"

He shook himself out of his stupor, looking back to the blonde nurse; her name tag said 'McNeil.'

"Sorry, I'm here," he said with a sigh, allowing her to guide him back to a seated position. Nurse McNeil gave him a look of concern but continued tending to his wounds.

Captain Short silently counted heads again — eleven. Krei was most likely dead. Torres was definitely dead; Short had seen the beast tear him in half with his own eyes. The sting of cold alcohol washing his chest sparked him back to reality like the shock of a defibrillator, and he finally caught up with all the ways his world had just changed.

What the fuck was that thing?

...

Sherri had barely even gotten through the door before she pulled out her journal and hastily sketched the creature while the memories were fresh. Disorientation and adrenaline blurred her mind, and she grew frustrated as she began to lose images of what the damn thing looked like. She knew it was big, really big, but she couldn't hang on to any details. All she could remember — what she couldn't forget — were the eyes. Bright, blinding, glowing in the dim forest atmosphere. Not reflecting, glowing. Each eye had two pupils, but they weren't round or ovoid or slitted. They were crosses, like the steeple on a church. She drew each fragment to the best of her ability. A familiar voice spoke and she jolted as she was brought back from her recollection.

"You should go get checked out in the med bay." Doctor Novak stood beside the couch she sat on. Even though she had just seen him that morning, it felt like it had been years.

"I'm fine." Sherri waved him off, desperately scribbling down every fleeting visual she could pull from her mind. She almost felt she could cry as her memory failed more and more, the pictures leaking through the cracks of her mind like flowing sand. Her scrawlings became less like a beastly animal and more like violent abstract scribbles of the terror it had left inside her. Marshall slightly leaned over her to glance at the journal, then at her.

"That's what you saw?"

Sherri nodded.

"Do you think that's what killed the soldier?"

She chewed her lip as she often did when drawing.

"Maybe. It was huge but quiet. It ambushed us. It's possible it could have managed to sneak up on the soldier before he could fire a shot, but who knows," she explained, still fixated on the sketch. "An ecosystem supporting life that big, that advanced... It has to eat. There's more out there, more that we haven't seen."

There was a tense silence as that thought settled in the air. Marshall seemed to be intensely focused on her drawing. Her hand trembled as she added some shading to one of her sketches of the creature; its face was beginning to resemble some sort of grotesque, demonic bull. She remembered to add a second set of flared nostrils, plumes of steam pouring out of them. Marshall exhaled.

"Guess you're not going out there again, then?"

"The hell I won't," she argued. "This is only the beginning, Novak, we've barely scratched the surface. We need to get back out there as soon as everyone's back on their feet."

The tall man just stared at her, blinking, until she turned back to her sketching.

"You're crazy," he said; she ignored him. She'd been called crazy so many times in her life that it held no meaning to her. After scribbling a few more vague notes and adding some final touches, she snapped her journal closed. Sherri got up and headed for the lab. The clamor was beginning to die down.

"Where are the brothers?" she called as she walked, her question answered as she spotted Giovanni wave to her from the bar.

"Gio," she beckoned. "Come on, we have samples to sort."

Giovanni weakly clapped his older brother on the shoulder and rose to follow her while Harrison stayed behind to catch his breath for a moment longer.

"Wait." The captain's voice stopped Gio, but Sherri continued on her path for the lab doorway.

"Doctor Daniels," he boomed. "We need to talk about the clusterfuck that just took place out there."

She gritted her teeth and stopped mid-reach for the door handle.

"Have a seat," Short commanded.

Sherri released a heavy huff and turned, coming to sit at a nearby table with her lips pursed in impatience. She got the feeling the captain would have nothing of value to contribute to this conversation. Short walked to the front of the room, now wearing a clean shirt identical to the one he had on previously, with several bandages visible on his arms.

"Sergeant Krei is dead," he began, "Sergeant Torres is dead. There is at least one big fucking cat thing out there. They are lethal, ugly, mean motherfuckers, and our weapons seem to do only minor damage.

"Our situation has officially gone from unfortunate to knee-deep in hot shit. No one goes back out there unless I say otherwise."

"We startled it! One botched encounter can't derail the timeline of the expedition," Sherri argued, rising from her seat. "Mission control needs us out there learning about these things, learning how to coexist with them. This isn't your call to make, Short."

She stared at him in challenge, biting the inside of her cheek. The captain stared back, his arms crossed and nostrils flared.

"I don't give a damn who startled what or what you want to learn about, Doctor. There is an enemy outside of that door that will kill us if we give it the chance. That makes it my call."

"We're not here to hide, we're here to research. If you'll excuse me, I have work to do instead of listening to you bitch and whine like a fucking coward." She turned and stormed into the lab, double doors slamming behind her.

Rataan had caught a scent. At first, he thought he'd detected a whiff of the giant. But it became muddled the longer he followed it. As he walked along, the words of the lunai echoed loudly in his head.

He was barely more than a child, Rataan. Our answer is no.

And they were right. His leaders were strong, wise, proud ghaengste, and he respected them with every fiber of his being. But more importantly, Rataan *loved* them. With all three of his hearts and the full extent of his soul, he loved his lunai and he loved the people of his clan. And because of that, he had to foresee the destruction capable by mere children when they could not. He had to protect them against the threats they were too compassionate to crush. The boy who towered above them all, the outsider who would never truly be one of their people. Kodokuna's mother had brought him to Ramys as an infant but he was not a Ramys ghaengste, he did not accept their ways or serve their leaders. He was headstrong, bold, and impudent. He was not only a danger to their bloodlines and the reputations of their guards, as the lunai thought, he was a danger to their very power. Even with his youth, he was stronger than any other man. Even Rataan. Even the lunai.

And that could not be allowed.

Rataan knew what the giant was capable of, he always had. And he knew that the giant murdered that huntress, but the lunai didn't. Not yet. He had to show them, one way or another; if that meant bringing the boy to his knees before them and ripping a confession straight from his throat, so be it.

He was pulled from his thoughts by the faint sound of voices, miles away yet his ear twitched at every tone. He froze and listened, but he couldn't make out the words. His pace sped up to a rushed stalk, his steps silent but hungry. The echo of the voices bounced between the trees, carrying straight to him as he followed the scent he'd been tracking. As it grew more potent, he could now identify the stench of the giant without a shadow of a doubt. But there were other smells infecting and tainting it, chillingly alien and yet vaguely familiar. With a vertical leap, he scaled the distance between the ground and a low-hanging branch, heaving his sturdy body up the tree.

Rataan barely had to climb any higher before he saw the giant, standing nearly as tall as the lower tree cover. The dusty hide tinged with olive striping gave him away, though not as much as his mammoth size. But something strange perched on his back, and Rataan crept out further onto the branch to get a better view. His blood ran cold.

There was an ocean dweller riding on the giant's shoulder; its short stature and blue fins unmistakable. The commander's mouth dropped open, but he choked on his horror as another creature came into view through the broad leaves. Walking in front of the giant was a slim, white ghaengste, massive scarlet wings folded by its sides. A sky dweller. Rage boiled over in Rataan's stomach as an insidious story played out before him. The giant was fraternizing with the enemies of the Ramys clan, no doubt feeding them information and weaknesses that could bring the downfall of the nation. Perhaps the dead hunter found him out, or he attempted to recruit his previous cohort as an internal spy, and she was killed for refusing. It was all so obvious now. The cowardly giant would never have made it on his own. He had no honor or shame; he would go running to whatever tyrants would feed his starving belly. Rataan's hearts pounded through his chest as all his fears, his instincts, his desperate pleas were realized. Then his eyes widened with an inconceivable dread as a fourth figure became clear through the tree canopy. A long-furred ghaengste, stout and broad, its coat the color of slate and snow. Rataan could watch no longer. He launched himself from the branch and hit the ground running. He tore through the trees back to the clan.

...

"Faro-Dahn!" Rataan roared as he passed by the brutish warrior outside the wall. "The twins are stationed at Krajfell camp. Go fetch them and meet me. Quickly, son!"

The brawny man nodded without a word, sliding his helmet on and taking off in a dead sprint northbound. Rataan slammed through the clan gates and shoved aside a passing vendor as he marched through the bustling courtyard.

The commander burst through the entrance of the lunai chamber, the tent flaps blowing wildly behind him as his voice echoed in the long room.

"My lords," Rataan heaved. "I have spotted the giant, fraternizing with —"

He stumbled on his words for a split second, realizing that what he had to tell them would sound like insanity. Even he could hardly fathom what he'd witnessed.

"He walked alongside a water dweller, a sky dweller, and..." — His brows furrowed, pleading with the lunai to believe the unbelievable — "a mountain dweller here beyond the snow. I believe them to be plotting against us; there is no other explanation for their union."

The leaders before him erupted in discourse, varying from the gentle scolding of Avias to Erro's sharp yell.

"This has gone on *far* too long, Rataan-Leih. You are growing delusional with misplaced hatred," Erro spat, rising from her throne.

"You disobey direct orders, commander, and now this? We told you to leave that boy alone!" Levah barked.

"*Enough*," Visaan bellowed.

"Let our kaunek present his claim before you call him a liar and a lunatic," the eldest king growled, receiving affronted looks from his counterparts. Rataan stood up straighter, nodding in gratitude.

"Punish me however you so choose and I will bear it with bleeding pride, but first let me prove that I am not mad, that I am no liar. Let me bring you the giant to be tried for his crimes and the heads of his savage conspirators," the commander urged with a determined scowl.

The lunai exchanged glances, as if silently debating. Simultaneously, they all seemed to find that there was more to lose in ignorance than a fruitless pursuit.

"Fine," Erro ordered, "bring us the giant and proof of his alleged treason."

Rataan bowed his head once before turning and rushing out of the vast tent, grabbing a spear on his way that had been leaning against the wall.

"*Faro-Dahn! Io-Dahn! Iago-Dahn!*" he roared as he marched toward the entrance gates of the village. The three warriors fell in step beside him, armor shuffling and eyes alight with hunger.

"We have heads to reap."

...

The suns were still high in the sky, but the jungle felt colder than usual. The river had grown from a calm flow to a writhing and thrashing serpent, attempting to claw its way up onto the banks as spray jumped out of the water and turned into a thick mist. The renegades had been following the southern leg of the channel for most of the day, and the farther they got from the Ramys territory, the more they relaxed. For once all four ghaengste were silent, ambling along the water's edge and allowing the exhaustion from the days prior to weigh on their shoulders. Alvi was asleep, peacefully lounging across Kodo's back as her tail gently swayed against his side, and the others finally began to let their guard down as well.

"Kodokuna!" A powerful, grainy voice echoed through the trees, seeming to come from all around them at once.

"The young giant, always so feared."

It rang out and pierced the air clear as day. Alvi searched around wildly as she awoke with a start.

"Not so frightening now, are you, boy?"

It was closer now, right behind them. Leida's head flipped around first. She didn't remember when she'd stopped checking behind them every few seconds, but they would pay for it now. A low growl formed in Rykr's throat as he realized that this was not a social visit. Kodo turned around slowly; he would recognize that voice anywhere. There stood Rataan-Leih, a vicious gleam in his fiery golden eyes.

"You've lowered yourself to the rest of the *scum* of this planet, I see," the old commander spat, studying each of Kodo's companions with repulsion.

The renegades stepped closer together, all facing the proud armored ghaengste.

"Alright, from the top."

Doctors Novak and Bridgeland listened from their desks as the survey team recollected the journey and iced their bruises — with the exception of Roger, who was laid up in the med bay with a dislocated knee and undoubtedly endless new fears. Sherri was getting a splitting headache from attempting to recount the day's events over and over. Thinking all the way back to that bustling early morning made her sickeningly dizzy.

"We left the compound and hiked across the plain," Sherri began with an exhale. "It was impressive at the time, but there wasn't much to see in comparison to the jungle."

"The suns make it feel warm, really warm, even though the temperature stayed a cool ten," Giovanni added. "What is that, fifty Fahrenheit?"

"We're Americans, not idiots. Celsius will do just fine," Marshall muttered. Giovanni lifted his hands in surrender.

"Anyway," Sherri took over, "past the tree line, it's all temperate rainforest, at least by earthly classifications. Cool, humid, huge towering trees and dense leafy foliage. Oh, and the trees are hollow with drainage holes that seem to constantly release water. I don't know all the specifics yet but I have some theories if —"

"The insect?" Gio interrupted.

"Right, then we saw the insect. Just one at first, maybe the size of a pigeon, but we didn't get close. It hovered like a dragonfly, looked more like a long-legged beetle or an arachnid." She found herself struggling not to stumble over her words.

"We reached a forked creek," Giovanni jumped in, "and we saw a small swarm of different insects but they moved too fast to get a good look. I got some great sediment samples, and Harrison found some truly fantastic fossils and shells of some sort, almost akin to ammonoids and brachiopods."

"I took plenty of water samples, if anyone cares," Doyle interjected.

"Then the captain insisted we head back," Giovanni continued, "and Daniels got ahead —"

Sherri cut in to finish the story.

"I got ahead of the group, and then I... saw it, but it was so shadowed I couldn't make out much. At first, it just stared at me, completely still. I guess it got spooked when the rest of the team caught up..." She trailed off, still trying to wrap her head around the fact that she'd just had a close encounter with a real, complex, flesh-and-blood extraterrestrial lifeform. She pondered the idea that this could all be some sort of vivid fever dream, and maybe they all were, as the room had fallen silent.

"Daniels, can you hear alright?" Marshall said with his brows furrowed as he stared at the dried blood still painted down her cheek. Sherri came to the conclusion that this definitely wasn't a dream as she suddenly felt a very real aching in her ears.

"Yes, I'm fine," she said quickly, trying not to flinch as she became abruptly disturbed by the high-pitched ringing she'd been ignoring that entire time. She pulled herself from the distraction of the incessant ringing, turning back to the lab equipment currently testing her samples.

"I suggest we get that message for mission control drafted sooner than later. They need to know about this," she said, changing the subject as she looked through a microscope at one of her vine cuttings.

"And it couldn't hurt to mention Short's attempt to hijack this entire expedition," she added after a pause.

"You know, the captain has a point," Harrison said gently. "It would be wise of us to step back and study all we have so far before we go rushing back out there. We don't know what we're getting into."

Sherri scrawled down some notes in her journal, her jaw tensed.

"We won't know what we're getting into until we go find out." She looked up from her sample. "This isn't the time to pull back. It's time to get smarter and get to work."

...

The captain repeated the day's events over and over, picking apart his memories in an attempt to pinpoint the beast's weakness. It had to have one. And he was sure somewhere deep in his mind, he'd subconsciously noticed it. He paced up and down hallway Echo, the corridor where the armory was located. That damn armory, stocked to the brim with explosives and munitions, always mocking him. For the past four weeks, it had whispered in his ear, *For what? For what? For what?*

Short wasn't naïve; he knew they would have to go back outside the safety of the compound and once again face the horrors that hid among the trees. As much as he wished they could pack up and call off the expedition, that was never an option. They'd come to prove that 7355264Z could sustain human civilization, and now that they were already there, they weren't allowed to abandon ship unless they proved it couldn't. And Doctor Daniels, in all her stubborn obsession, was right. One botched encounter confirmed nothing. They'd come too far; the planet was already too promising. Hell, it almost looked like Earth. But it certainly didn't feel like Earth. It smelled and tasted different in every way. The land itself emitted the hatred and hunger of a breathing, bleeding life. But it was close enough that there was no turning back. Close enough that they couldn't leave the mission uncompleted. Now the echoing voice of the full armory sang a different tune in his head. Challenging him. Testing him. Waiting for him to make the call.

Now what? Now what? Now what?

"What do you want, Rataan-Leih?" Kodo put on a face he could only hope looked brave. He had allies now, and they outnumbered the kaunek-leih. And yet that gave him no more confidence than standing alone against the weathered commander. The older man looked between the renegades, lingering on Rykr for a moment.

"I'm impressed, you even managed to lure one of the savages out of the snow," Rataan said, staring into the mountain man's eyes. Rykr let out a loud growl, snapping his teeth together so hard it made a sound like rolling thunder.

"*Watch your mouth*, old man," Rykr snarled, but Alvi gave him a look that silenced him. The ocean woman stood with the rest of them after climbing off Kodo. Rataan slowly began to laugh, looking around as if he were waiting for someone to explain the joke.

"Tell me, hona'dei, what is this?" Anger flashed in the commander's eyes as he chuckled. "Some sort of pathetic rebellion against the Ramys nation, a coup? What could you possibly hope to gain from associating with these *creatures*? What did they offer you?"

Kodo's brows furrowed at the dangerous accusations coming from the man before him, and he shook his head.

"The only thing they offered me is company. Let us be. We don't want any more to do with your clan than you want to do with us."

The smile fell from Rataan's maw, his amusement burning away to rage.

"And that is worth taking an innocent hunter's *life?*" His lip curled over fangs coated in gold and filed into razor-sharp points. He did not wait for a response before continuing.

"By the law of the Ramys clan, in the name of the Great Mother, you will be tried for murder and treason and the rest of them will die where they stand," he bellowed, his voice growing louder as he spoke. Kodo's chest clenched in horror, and his companions stepped closer beside him.

Two identical women stepped out from the trees behind Rataan. They were armored, with long golden swords strapped to their sides. One of them had an eye patch and a hellish grin, but both had scarlet paint swiped across their faces — the mark of the tunahk-dahn.

Kodo bared his teeth as he realized they had no choice but to fight their way out. He knew all too well how dangerous the tunahk warriors were; he remembered watching them train night and day when he was a child. With his companions beside him, however, maybe they had a chance. Something in Rataan's gleaming eyes made him falter.

"You thought I would waste the sisters' time with you, boy?" the commander scoffed.

"Io, Iago, you take care of the *vermin*," he commanded in a prideful belt. Then Rataan's shoulders began to relax.

"The giant is all yours, Faro."

Kodo's stomach dropped as a hulking ghaengste lumbered out of the trees, his battle-hardened hide covering brawn as thick and dense as logs. The massive man was also marked with red paint across his eyes and he wore a thick helmet. Though not as large as Kodo, Faro-Dahn was rippled with musculature and trained to kill. He stepped out from behind Rataan, his gigantic black teeth showing through a cocky smirk. Then he charged, a guttural roar like a volcanic eruption bursting from his open jaws.

Faro rammed Kodo into the ground just as the twins lurched at the other three rebels. Iago, the woman with the eyepatch, turned straight for Alvi.

Rykr stepped between them and snarled at the attacking tunahk, but Iago only snickered.

"You mountain savages are so primitive, you don't even have the weaponry to stand a chance," she hissed with a villainous smile.

"The mountain people don't need blades, I'll crush you with my bare jaws," Rykr roared and lunged at the lean woman.

Iago dodged his blow, drawing her sword from its sheath and swinging it with her jaws.

Rykr barely yanked his head back in time. The tip of the sword shaved off the end of his beard, narrowly missing his throat. He backed up, snarling as Alvi slipped into the river behind him.

Leida had taken flight, dipping and barrel rolling as she dodged Io's sword strikes, occasionally getting a blow in from behind. She was fast, but she had never gone up against opponents so well-trained and well-armed. With each passing blow, she became more aware that they were bested. She glanced over at Kodo, hoping for a promising sight. There was no such promise to be found.

Faro had beaten the giant to the ground, and a dagger lay buried up to the hilt in Kodo's bruised shoulder. He groaned through desperate heaves, black blood seeping from his maw as he winced. His massive weight was an anchor that kept him from rising against Faro's deathly grip. His brute strength was no match for the warrior's skill.

Leida was only distracted for a moment, but that was enough. Io leaped high into the air, biting down on the end of Leida's tail, and slamming her into the ground.

Iago had pinned Rykr at the edge of the river with her foot driving down on his throat and her sword aimed at his face. He growled and stared into her one eye, too proud to look away even as he waited for the sword to plunge through the center of his skull.

Just as Iago reared back to slam her blade through Rykr's forehead, something launched out of the angry river and crashed into her like a breaking wave.

Alvi's fangs latched deep into Iago's throat, and her momentum sent them both tumbling backward. She bit down hard, driving her teeth in until she could hear the other woman's trachea begin to splinter and crumble. Iago thrashed, choking as gobs of inky blood retched from her gaping mouth.

Colossal jaws clamped down on the back of Alvi's neck. She was violently ripped from her target and slammed against a tree with enough force that her bones emitted a deafening crack.

"Alvi!" Kodo cried out, lying beaten on the ground, helpless to stop the scene before him. Faro let out a deep, hoarse chuckle as he turned back to the young giant, leaving the ocean woman in a crumpled heap. Leida and Rykr were barely holding on against the sisters, and their fighting grew weaker at the sight of Alvi's limp body. A satisfied grin unfurled across Rataan's face as he watched.

Faro began stalking back to Kodo, his heavy steps shaking the ground, gazing pridefully down at the tears forming in the young man's eyes and the dagger in his flesh. Kodo didn't look at him, only at his fallen friend.

"It must be a good season for us," Faro snarled.

"Just the other day we got to slaughter a whole family of those *river-rats.*"

Kodo's gaze snapped back to Faro. Something had changed in his pitiful expression; his tearful brown eyes were now blackened with blind rage.

Kodo lurched up from the ground and toppled the mighty warrior with one strike. Faro rolled to his side and began to rise but was immediately slammed back into the dirt so hard the breath was crushed from his ribcage. Kodo turned, biting onto the hilt of the dagger still embedded in his shoulder. He ripped it out of his flesh and threw it to the ground, ignoring the stringy spray of black blood that exploded from the wound. His beady gaze was dark and thunderous, absent of every shred of its previous fear. The surrounding fighting had stopped. Now every ghaengste on the river bank stared in terror at the new beast born before their eyes.

Kodo reared, towering above the lower tree cover. He opened his jaws and belted out a savage, barbaric war cry that shook the jungle and deafened the ears of any unfortunate enough to be in its vicinity. Faro had regained his footing and lunged for him, but Kodo dove downward with his snarling maw agape. His jaws engulfed Faro's entire head and he bit down straight through the helmet; it split in half and fell to the ground. Kodo's claws drove into the warrior's throat as he held him at his mercy, his fangs crushing through flesh and bone and brain. The air crackled with the sharp sound of Faro's skull shattering under the starving fury of Kodo's monstrous teeth, hot blood spilling down his chin and bathing his heaving chest.

Kodo jerked his neck to the side, effortlessly flinging Faro away by his collapsed and gushing head. He let out another beastly shriek, bloody teeth bared, and approached the fallen warrior again as Faro attempted to rise despite his brain bulging through a cavity in his crumbling skull. Kodo reared once more, this time to crush Faro's spine.

"Enough,"

Rataan bellowed, and Kodo froze before delivering his final blow. All fell silent.

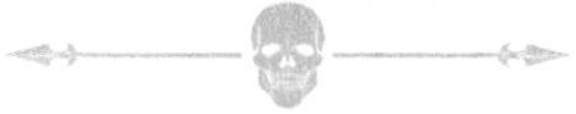

Mornings were the most monotonous. The lights flicked on at the same time, the coffee machines began brewing at the same time. It made the days feel blurry and indefinite. Though perhaps the automated schedule wasn't to blame; perhaps there was something wrong with the planet itself. The crew followed Earth time, and Planet 7355264Z's day seemed eerily close to twenty-four hours. Almost as if the planet's suns were attempting to mimic Earth's own. But even if the hours of daylight roughly matched their earthly clocks, time seemed to disobey the laws of reality. It was in subtle ways, ways that made them think they were just too tired to notice the minutes go by. But days seemed like years, nights felt like mere seconds. And mornings passed vaguely, leaving the crew feeling as though they were stuck in a recurring dream. The morning after the first survey, however, every soul on board was suddenly grateful for the monotony. The dreamlike haze half convinced them the previous day's horrors hadn't happened at all.

"Ma," Captain Short said as he walked through the kitchen, passing the soldiers sitting at the bar. Master Sergeant Mendoza looked up from his breakfast.

"What can I do for you, boss?" the sergeant said in his signature overly casual manner that always seemed too charming to be disrespectful.

"You took inventory of the armory, yes?"

"Yes, sir."

The captain leaned against the counter.

"How many grenades?" he asked, and the other soldiers quieted as they ate, listening. Mendoza cleared his throat.

"Six-thousand frags, three-thousand chems, two-thousand non-lethals, and eight-hundred illuminates. Give or take."

"Give or take?" The captain raised an eyebrow.

"Give, as in you asked for some and I gave them. Take, as in you took 'em," Mendoza said with a soft gleam in his warm gaze. Short shook his head at the older man.

"Don't get smart with me, Sergeant," he warned. "It's all logged?"

"Yes sir," Mendoza confirmed.

"Thank you, Ma," Short said with an exaggerated patronizing tone as he walked away.

"You're welcome, boss," Mendoza sang after him.

Sherri had poured her cereal as slowly as physically possible while she listened in on the conversation from across the kitchen. After its conclusion, she quickly made her way to her designated table with the rest of the research team.

"Short is already developing a sinister plot to destroy all life on this planet," she said as she sat down in between Giovanni and Marshall.

"That's kind of his job, haven't you ever seen a science fiction movie?" Marshall replied.

"You mean yelling at him about peace, love, and coexistence hasn't worked?" Giovanni added. "What was it you called him?"

"She called him a whiny bitch," Marshall recalled with a cackle. Sherri fought back a smile as she shoved Gio's arm.

"You're an asshole. Both of you." She pointed an accusing finger at Marshall as if to ensure he didn't escape her lighthearted scolding. They chuckled some more as she took a bite of her cereal, then she gestured across the table at Harrison with her spoon.

"What about you, Rosenquest One; do you think I'm unjustified in my dissent too?" she asked, remembering to cover her mouth as she chewed. Harrison looked over his round glasses, pulled from the book he was reading.

"Unjustified? No, not at all." Harrison paused. "...But if I did think so, I wouldn't have the stones to tell you."

The men around the table fell into more laughter, and Sherri couldn't help but chuckle under her breath as well. It felt good, laughing and teasing again, and for a moment it was like they were back on Earth living their previous simple, ignorant lives. As the amusement died down and they slowly returned to their breakfast, the memories began to seep back, and Sherri remembered what she'd actually wanted to talk about.

"Speaking of Short's diabolical plans," she began. "I know we're all still recovering, but we have to form our own plan to achieve a different outcome next time we encounter the natives. For one, we need to be going out in smaller, quieter groups."

Doyle scoffed, shaking his head.

"Yeah, I have an idea for a different outcome — we don't have another encounter," he retorted. Sherri sighed impatiently.

"Come on, Doyle. You know as well as I do that's not how this works."

"Sure it is," he argued. "In case you haven't noticed, mission control isn't *up here* with us. They're shit out of luck if they want to start firing folks."

"They'd probably withhold payment if we stopped working," Carl spoke up, sounding as if he'd already given that idea much thought. "Maybe even file a lawsuit if we really pissed them off."

Sherri gestured at Carl to second his counterargument.

"Well, let's catch our breath for a bit and then revisit this conversation when Myles gets discharged from the infirmary," Harrison interjected. "I visited him earlier this morning. Doctor Cuthbert says they want to hold him a little longer for observation, but he's alright."

There were a few nods as they went back to their meals. Sherri finished her breakfast as quickly as possible, then stood up from the table and stretched her shoulder.

"While you boys are taking your sweet time eating, I think I'll get to work."

"Breakfast is the most important meal of the day, you know," Carl replied matter of factly. Doyle smirked.

"Every meal is the most important for you, Bridgeland." He snickered, targeting the meteorologist's weight for hardly the first time. Carl grumbled under his breath, something about unoriginality. Marshall took a bite of his toast and nodded to Doyle across the table.

"You've got egg in your mustache," he remarked, and Doyle quickly wiped at his mouth as the other men laughed.

As she left, Sherri could hear the men behind her chatting and eating, the event of the prior day no doubt subsiding from the forefronts of their minds. And as she entered the lab once again, she found herself wondering if it would ever leave hers.

...

As the captain made his way back to the barracks after breakfast, the sound of a deafening crash and an all too familiar voice screaming profanities erupted from behind the doors. Short burst into the room to the sight of Corporal Keenan attempting to strangle Corporal Greene on the poker table and just about succeeding.

Short wrapped his arm around Keenan's neck and yanked him backward with all his weight. Several other men rushed in to help hold Keenan back as the marine continued viciously snarling like a rabid dog. Comrades on the other side of the barracks restrained the other corporal as he struggled to jump back into the fight. Short stood in front of Keenan and grabbed him by the front of his shirt to yank him down to eye level.

"*Keenan!*" the captain screamed in his face and tightened his grip on his shirt.

"Shut up and settle down, Corporal, or so help me *God...*" he snarled, matching the ferocity of his subordinate. Finally, Keenan was calm enough to form words.

"That little *cocksucker* swung on me first, Captain," Keenan spat through the saliva hanging from his lip, a wildness in his bloodshot eyes.

"FUCK you, jarhead! He was talking shit on Krei, Captain," Greene bellowed and lunged against the tight grip of his peers. *"It wasn't my fault!"*

"I've heard enough, I don't give a damn who started it," Captain Short barked over both men. "Now you two morons get to spend the rest of the day together, doing push-ups side by fucking side. You can eat your dinner on the floor," he snapped and started to walk away. Then he hesitated as he heard no movement from the two young corporals behind him.

"*Now!*" the captain roared, startling both men into immediately dropping to the floor. They began their punishment, and Short shook his head as he picked up the overturned chairs strewn across the room. Something caught his eye while he pushed them back in their places, and guilt bored a void into his stomach. He read the words carved into the wooden poker table:

WAIT FOR US
Private First Class Jack Taylor
Sergeant Joseph Krei
Sergeant First Class José Torres

"*Kill him, Kodo,*" Rykr snarled from where he stood, Iago's sword aimed at his throat once more. She was weakened, wheezing and gargling on blood from her collapsed trachea, but neither of them knew if she would be quick enough to deliver the final blow before he could make a move. Neither were ready to find out.

Leida and Io were now both on their feet but in a vicious stalemate. Leida wouldn't dare look away from her opponent long enough to glance at the state of the fight around them, but her ears swiveled at every noise and movement made by her companions.

Kodo stood completely still, staring down at the warrior bleeding out at his feet. Perhaps the sound of Rataan's voice alone captured him, wrapped the chains of the Ramys clan back around his neck and held him in place. Faro was somehow managing to drag himself up out of the dirt.

"Kill him!" Rykr roared again as every ghaengste in the clearing awaited the next moments.

A pathetic, almost inaudible groaning sounded from behind them, and Leida's eyes widened.

"Alvi lives," she hissed to her friends, backing away from her opponent slowly, step by step. The vengeful fire in Rykr's eyes abruptly quenched at the realization, and he began inching away from Iago, following Leida's lead.

"Kodo," Leida said as if reaching out under the black torrent that drowned the young giant, beckoning him to take her hand. Rataan still appeared as calm as the ancient trees surrounding them, but he readied his spear.

Kodo's bloody lip twitched in hunger as he looked over the downed warrior, half-dead yet forcing himself to rise on crushed bones and shredded flesh. Then the young giant's hard eyes weakened all at once, and he released a heavy gasp of breath. He backed away from Faro, stepping between Rykr and Leida where they'd separated from the sisters. Io and Iago watched Rataan with complete focus, awaiting his command.

Rataan gazed down at Faro's bloodied, trembling form. The great warrior now stood on his feet once again and attempted to raise his head, but it twitched uncontrollably to the side every few seconds and one of his eyes was dangling free from its socket by the nerve. The commander gave his order.

"Tunahk," Rataan barked, staring deep into Kodo's eyes with disdain.

"Move out. The suns are setting."

The Ramys warriors looked to their commander in shock. Iago opened her mouth to protest, then shut it as Rataan gave her a cold, warning glare. Slowly, Faro and the sisters broke from their defensive positions and returned to Rataan's sides.

Rykr rushed to Alvi and crouched by her limp body, his shoulders dropping with relief when he saw her flank weakly rising and falling with breath.

"We will meet again soon, giant!" Rataan called. "And when we do, I will no longer have the patience to take you alive. I will bring your head to the lunai as a trophy alongside the rest of these savages."

He walked back into the trees, the tunahk hesitantly turning away as well. Iago was the last to leave as she took the time to shoot a condemning snarl in the direction of the rebels. Then she limped after the others.

...

Rataan dragged Faro into the lunai chamber, shoving the battered man to the foot of the thrones. Faro nearly fell to the ground, weakened and bloodied, but managed to regain his balance and shakily bowed to his leaders. The speechless lunai looked over the warrior's wounds, his body littered with broken bones and the side of his skull caved in as if it had been beaten with a rock. Blood oozed onto the floor from a gaping hole in the side of his head, and one of his horns was snapped off entirely. It was nearly impossible to determine what was exposed muscle and what was brain matter. The fact that he remained conscious at all was a miracle from the Mother.

"This is what the giant is capable of," Rataan spat with hatred.

"The twins are with the caita now; Iago's throat is badly wounded," he continued, stepping toward the stage.

"It is worse than we thought, my lords. The giant and his group of enemy conspirators are dangerous and depraved. They must be destroyed."

"It is true then, this plot against our clan?" Vaus-Levah asked, more to the wounded warrior than to the commander.

"The giant was with one of each enemy nation, my lords," Faro panted, his voice slurred.

"They were untrained and disorganized, but we were — we didn't —"

The warrior coughed through the blood gushing up his throat and out of his mouth, and Vaus-Avias rushed off her perch to approach him.

"Quiet, son, lean down," she said gently as she came to stand before him, dwarfed by his hulking size. Faro obeyed, bowing his head to her. She began to tenderly clean the wounds on his head and the blood off his face.

Rataan stepped to the base of the platform, looking up at his leaders with fire in his eyes.

"My lunai, in all the years I have served you loyally, it has been my honor to crush your foes and protect our people. And I will do so until the very last breath the Mother breathes through me. These renegades are dangerous, and their rebellion cannot be ignored. We cannot let this threat grow. We must kill it in its infancy."

His gaze was pleading and impassioned, his voice hoarse. Avias looked up at her fellow leaders on their thrones, pain in her eyes as she tended the warrior's wounds. Then she turned to the kaunek-leih that stood before them all.

"Find them."

7
RESPITE

They were no longer just drifters. They were now fugitives for resurrecting the very thing their people had sworn to destroy: unity. The natural state, thrown out of balance by lifetimes of war, and yet they bonded together against all odds. No matter what they called themselves — allies, companions, a tribe — it was a fate they'd chosen of their own free will, and yet it was inescapable all the same.

But they were tired. It was starting to seem that the Great Mother wasn't listening after all. She didn't hear their cries, or see their cause. Perhaps they hadn't seen Her since before the river camp, the slaughtered family. Maybe She was hiding, ashamed of the atrocities occurring on Her flesh, the guts of innocents soaking into Her cold fur. Or maybe She'd accepted the sins of Her cannibal children, and She didn't care how they lived and how they died.

A faint groan floated down from Kodo's back. Leida stopped and turned around, standing up to peer at the injured woman.

"Alvi?"

"Hngh... what happened?"

"You were thrown into a tree."

Rykr nudged her away to give Alvi back the space she had invaded.

"Try not to talk or move, Al; you broke a few ribs. But you'll be fine," Rykr explained, downplaying her injuries and shooting Leida a look that warned her not to correct him. Alvi let out a small whimper but said nothing else.

"We must find safety as soon as possible." Leida continued on their course. "We will not survive another ambush."

They were already retreating from the forest, headed back to the mountains to hide away; they knew that was the only place so remote and treacherous not even the Ramys clan would dare seek them. As the snowy peaks rose in the distance, hurrying them along, Rykr stared at them with a yearning gaze.

"Rykr, we must stay far away from your people on the road," Leida said as they walked.

"I understand," he replied.

"You must navigate us so we avoid them." She glanced over his face curiously, noticing the sadness painting his features. He nodded dutifully but his longing eyes remained trained on his homeland.

"We'll need to head east of the Xinsei pass, instead of the west." He jutted his chin toward a dark rift in the mountains that divided the range in half.

"But I've never been to that region before... I don't know what we'll find," he continued, eyeing the rapidly growing peaks as they pushed on. Leida couldn't get her legs to move fast enough.

Her chest felt heavy with a feeling she couldn't identify, but it hurt. Fear, perhaps. Not fear of death; Leida did not know enough about death to fear it. It was simply something she felt driven to avoid until she could avoid it no longer; the end of her story had no more meaning to her than the beginning. No, it was the fear that true safety did not exist on their planet. The fear that maybe what they chased had lived once before, its time now past, and it would never live again. Maybe their world had not always been this way, but perhaps now the bloodshed was the only thing that fed it. A bloodshed Leida herself knew nothing of, yet even she, a born rogue, could not escape it. The plague that infected their brothers and sisters and ravaged Matka's skin. She wasn't sure when she'd been consumed into its hungry belly, or if she could ever possibly gnaw her way back out of it. She supposed it all began with the origin cave in the mountains, and then it had erupted into an unstoppable forest fire when she met the giant boy who taught her about their world.

He'd hardly said a single word since the Ramys ambush, and part of Leida wondered if he was even the same boy she'd met in the jungle. The boy who'd given her a name.

Leida led her broken and bloodied tribe out of the jungle, one of them nearly dead. They could feel the forest air clawing at their heels as they trudged onward, whispering needle-sharp threats that pricked at their ears and necks. The cold damp clutches of the trees and the eyes hidden in their bark held onto the rebels with a hungry desperation, as if they were the last chance for eons at a meal.

As they left the massive trees behind for good, they gazed up at the dark rift in the peaks, vast and broken. To the west of the chasm, the peaks were high and white and the rays of sunlight created a halo that glowed around the blinding snow. The east side of the pass was engulfed in shadow; it was frigid and still and hidden by fog. After hesitating for a moment, and remembering the savage, starving clutches of the forest behind them, the rebels tread eastward.

...

"What did it look like?"

"I don't know, fat and hairy. Let it go, Mahrz."

Two ghaengste patrolled the forest, both marked in reddish paint and dressed in armor. The pale woman had a bandage around her neck, her voice a quiet gravelly whistle, and her expression clearly held disdain even under her eyepatch. Her ear twitched in annoyance, and the red-furred man beside her continued asking questions as they walked. The sunbeams cutting through the tree cover warmed their backs but could not mellow the woman's sharp temper.

"That's quite the story," Mahrz continued. "A real *mountain dweller*, the thing of legends. And you fought it? Must have been rough." He looked ahead as he walked, not noticing his companion's fury until it was too late.

Iago headbutted him in the side of the face, his vision growing blurry as her horns made contact with his skull.

"*No shit,* it was rough, we lost. Faro can't think, I can't speak, and Io looks like she's been finely chopped up for hajva soup. Will you shut your fucking trap already?" she wheezed in a grating whisper.

The man winced and growled, quickly putting space between them in case she lashed out again.

"Easy, Iago. You know I didn't mean anything by it," he snapped but softened as he limped faster to keep pace with her. He dodged her tail as it thrashed and studied her face as if calculating his next move.

"You three will heal fast, and we'll finish it next time. You were outnumbered; there's nothing to be ashamed of," he continued reassuringly. Iago's tense shoulders seemed to think of relaxing, but her face contorted into a scowl once again.

"Next time, I'll rip them apart piece by fucking piece, mark my words. Rataan-Leih never should have —"

"Never should have what?"

Rataan stalked out from behind a tree, his sharp voice still echoing through the dark forest. His stern golden eyes cut straight through the young warriors' skin, chilling their bones.

"Never should have trusted you to get the job done?"

He walked closer, looking them up and down. Iago's face twitched as she strained to hold her tongue, but she erupted before Mahrz could stop her.

"Fat lot of help *you* were, Rataan-Leih," the woman spat despite her impaired voice. "It's no one's fault but your own for expecting us to take down a fucking giant *and* his gaggle of —"

Rataan roared in fury, getting so close to her face she could smell the blood of his last meal on his breath.

"Hold your tongue, girl, lest you want it cut out like your eye. If you ever speak to me like that again, I will throw you out of the tunahk order without a second thought, and you will be a common *fucking scout* for the rest of your miserable life. Is that clear?" he snarled. She didn't flinch despite the saliva showering her face.

"Yes, commander," Iago said, nostrils flared.

Mahrz stared ahead silently, standing tall beside his temperamental comrade. Rataan glanced at the red man's stoic face for a moment, but then he turned away.

"I thought so."

The kaunek-leih didn't say another word as he walked on, though the young duo followed obediently. Both had been warriors under Rataan's order since they were children, and they knew all too well what awaited them back in the clan grounds after failing an objective. Training.

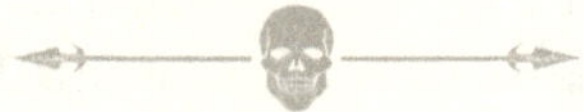

It should have been unsettling, how pitch black and stagnant the compound was first thing in the morning. But the quiet stillness apart from the few faint glows emanating from the appliances and machinery was, for the most part, serene instead of eerie. Perhaps it was the contrast — the last bit of silence before the waking of the crew brought an unmistakable, overwhelming chaos. The compound unfailingly woke itself at 0550 every morning. Like a living creature, its eyes would snap open as every fluorescent bulb flicked on and the whirring of its generators breathed life into the twisting halls. But before it woke up, all was quiet. Sherri was one of the few that got to enjoy those moments of solace.

Flipping on the light switch in the locker room was an unwelcome pain, and she blinked as she adjusted to its glare. The anticipation of a hot shower quickly remedied her aching eyes. Sherri wasted no time in turning the knob all the way to hot and undressing, then stepping under the water before it had time to heat all the way. That was the other benefit to waking up at such an excessively early hour — getting to shower privately, a luxury she savored every single morning.

However, as she attempted to massage the conditioner through her tangled curls, she suddenly got the sense that she wasn't alone. She could swear it sounded like there were two showers turned on instead of one. Upon listening closer, she determined it was just her imagination and continued her shower unbothered. The hot water beat onto her tan skin, soothing her sore muscles. As droplets beaded on her eyelashes and her shoulders relaxed with the heat and pressure of the water, she allowed her heavy eyelids to close.

Two glowing orbs.

Four pupils.

Crosses.

That godforsaken sound.

Sherri's eyes snapped open and her muscles jolted with the urge to cover her ears. Again, she could hear the horrible, blood-curdling shriek — no, rumbling roar. It was every voice together, the highest and lowest pitches her ears could comprehend all at once. It still banged around the inside of her head like the frantic ringing of a bell, and she feared it always would.

She sighed and studied the grout in between the shower tiles for a moment, slowly rubbing her palms over her stomach, her ribs, her chest, her arms. Bringing herself back to her body. Back to the present.

Sherri cleared her throat and turned off the showerhead. Wrapping herself loosely in a towel, she hummed quietly as she wrung out the exceedingly thick hair she was always battling with. Then she opened the door to the stall and stepped out, still distracted by her locks that seemed to double in stubbornness every day.

She smacked right into something. Hard.

The inertia threw her backward and she slipped, her towel nearly falling off. She managed to catch it close to her chest just as something else caught her by the arms. Blinking once, twice, Sherri found herself face to face with an angel. A tattoo of an angel, that is, on the left pectoral muscle of a broad wet chest. A silver dog tag dangled from a ball chain against the brown skin. More interestingly, a silver hoop was pierced through each nipple.

Sherri slowly looked up, her eyes finally resting on the captain's stern face. Despite the deep crinkle in between his heavy eyebrows and the permanent scowl, he looked more dumbfounded than upset. His hands remained firmly grasping her biceps as if he didn't trust her to support her own weight. Sherri managed to regain her bearings as the awkwardness set in, an alarming tension for a woman who was seldom acquainted with the feeling of shame.

"Hi."

Hi? She wasn't quite sure what else to say; *unhand me,* maybe? Though she didn't feel manhandled by him, at least not this time. He wasn't entirely unwarranted in grabbing her, Sherri was pretty sure she would have fallen straight on her ass if he hadn't. Captain Short stared back down at her, his narrowed eyes looked tired.

"Hi..." was all he said.

Short also became increasingly aware of not only the awkward feeling, but the fact that they were both mostly naked and definitely closer than two professional acquaintances would generally be in a locker room.

"You can let me go now..." Doctor Daniels cleared her throat. She glanced up from his chest to his face, then down to his towel, and back up to his face.

"Oh. Sorry. Yeah." Short slowly released his grip on her arms. He allowed his hands to rest on his hips, tightening the towel around his hips just to be safe. His eyes drifted over the woman before him, who was stiffly adjusting her own towel around her curvaceous figure, inadvertently causing it to ride up and expose more of her full thighs. Her curly hair was far longer when wet; it cascaded over her shoulders and revealed more of her face than it normally did. Short felt his skin growing hot in embarrassment. Or maybe not embarrassment, but he didn't have any intentions of exploring whatever unfortunate feelings might be rising in his stomach and —

"Nice piercings," the botanist said, breaking the tense silence and taking another look at his normally hidden jewelry.

"Okay, I'm going to leave now." Short nodded and sidestepped to walk around her as she also stepped to that side. She cleared her throat as she accidentally blocked his path, stepping to the other side in order to keep walking — just as he stepped in front of her.

"Oh."

"Oops —"

They cut each other off once more.

"Stop." She stiffly patted his bicep twice in farewell, then rushed to scoot past his wide form. He caught a glimpse of her reddened face before she quickly turned away from him, already speed-walking away to grab her things and leave.

"What the fuck?" Short said quietly to the empty room, shaking his head as he collected his clothes.

As the rebels tread onward, the mountains on the horizon seemed to flee farther out of reach. The valley was endless and quiet, and it became harder and harder to tell where the land met the sky.

They traveled slower now, suspended in the middle of the meadow as if they were walking in place. Every now and then a small animal would skitter through the grass and disturb the gentle swaying of the plants around them, but everything would fall back into its hypnotizing harmony almost as suddenly as it was disturbed.

"We will camp here," Leida announced, stopping abruptly. "There is no shelter to be found."

She was gazing ahead at the two suns, which were seemingly in a race to hide behind the distant peaks.

"Finally. I'll go hunt," Kodo said, gently setting Alvi on the ground with Rykr's help before stretching once, then breaking into a sprint. Rykr and Leida watched their young companion as his giant form grew smaller in the distance.

"Should one of us go with him?" Rykr asked.

"No. We must stay here with Alvi." Leida looked toward the ocean woman who was curled into a fetal position on the ground. She hadn't spoken since the Ramys ambush, and it seemed more was crushed than only her ribs.

As Leida started a fire, Alvi silently watched a flower in front of her face as it swayed back and forth, back and forth. She allowed her head to rest on the ground in defeat. For once, she didn't want to lay there. She wanted to get up, move, tease the others, laugh and tell stories. Instead she just closed her eyes in a desperate attempt to fall asleep.

Her face twitched and tensed at the memory that played behind her shut eyes. The image of the massacred family was burned into the backs of her eyelids even though it seemed like so much had happened since then. She'd experienced death before in her young life, more than she ever wished she had. But something was different now. Perhaps it had just been too many lives that she'd witnessed waste away, or this time she'd wandered too far from home. She didn't know if she'd ever be able to close her eyes again without seeing the hecatomb of her people, so instead, she focused on every single movement Leida made. Collecting sticks and dry shrubbery, placing them methodically into a pyramid formation, taking larger logs from Rykr as he brought them to her. Alvi hung on to every intimate detail in an attempt to busy her troubled mind.

The fire sparked to life weakly at first, then began to grow.

"Alvi."

She looked up from the flames to see Leida approaching, that ice-blue stare boring into her. It had always made Alvi a little uneasy, but she lifted her head to acknowledge the other woman.

"Your bandages must be replaced," Leida said, sitting down beside her and dropping a rolled up leaf on the ground between them. It fell open, revealing medicinal herbs and moistened bandages. Alvi glanced up at Leida with a growing hesitance. She'd been unconscious when her wounds were originally dressed. The idea of being touched and feeling every moment of it made her hearts jolt, her chest tightening uncomfortably. She was tired of being in pain, tired of being scared, and the thought of any more sickened her. She glanced down at herself. Her entire torso was looped tightly in pale strips, but they were stained black with blood.

"Alvi."

She looked back to Leida.

"I would not hurt you..." Leida lowered herself closer to Alvi's height without breaking her fervent eye contact.

"We are friends. I would not hurt you," Leida said quietly as she lay beside her companion, studying her closely. Her eerie voice was soothing in its own way.

"You'll be gentle?" Alvi asked reluctantly. Leida nodded, ever so slightly scooting nearer.

"I have very gentle hands." She showed Alvi her paw, palm side up, her pink pads exposed. A smile suddenly grew across Alvi's weary face.

"You are amused?" the sky woman asked. Alvi weakly giggled, then winced as pain flared through her rib cage.

"Ow — yeah," she said, still quiet, but a small smile persisted. "Your pads are so smooth and pink, like a baby's."

Alvi touched Leida's open palm, and it twitched as if it was thinking of retreating. But it remained open, allowing Alvi to feel its surprising softness.

"I have only begun to travel on foot," Leida explained, retracting her paw. Alvi nodded, watching what the other woman was doing closely. She allowed herself to find comfort in her steady hands as she worked, and she took deep breaths in preparation. Leida began removing the bandages from her torso, and Alvi flinched, not in pain but at the anticipation of it.

"I hurt you?" Leida asked, a cautious curiosity on her face. Alvi forced herself to relax, sighing and shaking her head.

"No, I'm okay. Thank you, Leida."

Alvi breathed deeply, repeating that first phrase in her head. She was okay. Bruised, battered, a wanted fugitive, and more terrified than she'd ever been in her entire life, but she was alive. And that in itself was a great stroke of luck in their angry world. She tasted the air as it went in and out of her mouth, savored every beat of all three hearts in her chest. She was alive, and that was so much more than their planet promised to most. Alvi swore never to take it for granted again — not for herself, but for her brothers and sisters who were not lucky enough to be spared.

While Leida tenderly treated her friend's ghastly wounds, she began to feel that nagging fear again. Laying her ginger palms on Alvi's side, feeling the heartbeats beneath her skin, Leida finally understood the fear.

For the first time, Leida could feel the pain of others. She could feel in her own hearts the heaviness of her friends' hearts. She couldn't help but resent it. She discovered more and more with each passing second that having something meant having something to lose. It terrified her in a raw and guttural way that she'd never felt before. She could feel Alvi's sorrow, drowning her like a slow flood. She could feel Rykr's anger, threatening to suffocate him like a racing avalanche.

Her eyes darted around, her ear twitching in unrest as she noticed a presence was missing. Kodo was out hunting, and for some reason, his absence was what hurt the most. She could not feel him drowning or suffocating — she never had. His hearts were strong and mighty and young; they washed her like a cool spring breeze, unburdened by the horrors that plagued the others. Her chest ached with the innocent hope that he would come back soon and teach her of the Great Mother, or tell her silly stories. She hoped the tiredness that hung over the campsite would not touch him as it had the others. Most of all, she hoped he would come back the same Kodo he was when she'd met him.

Giovanni had finally dragged Sherri out of the lab to do what she was really there to do instead of agonizing over classifying the native. It was a necessary hijacking, whether she admitted it or not.

Advanced technology meeting the grace of nature — the terrosphere was a sight to behold. As Sherri and Gio entered the gigantic dome, warm humid air bathed them in fresh comfort compared to the cool sterile halls of the rest of the compound. The sunlight filtering through the honeycomb textured glass brought a welcoming gleam as it reflected off the leaves and tile. A large portion remained empty, though a cordoned-off section bloomed with native Earth crops: corn, potatoes, even an apple tree. The rest of the area housed several outlandish sprouting shrubs, native specimens that Sherri had planted in rectangular plots.

"You know the rules — no idle hands."

A heavy terracotta pot containing something blue and feathery was thrust into Giovanni's arms.

"What the hell am I holding?" Gio asked incredulously. A plant, apparently. It hung over the sides of the pot, its soft barb-covered tendrils dangling freely.

"I'm calling it a moth fern for now. But hey, maybe I'll name it after you if you prove useful," Sherri said as she searched through her equipment. "You know what? The leaves even look a little like your mustache. How about 'Pilosum Giovanni Labrum'?"

"I'm going to assume that translates to 'Giovanni, the gorgeous and brilliant,'" he said with a smug smile.

"Someone's been brushing up on his Latin," Sherri teased as she grabbed a trowel, picked a plot, and began digging. Gio had just begun to wander off and explore when the botanist's voice called him back.

"Hey, did you ever get around to figuring out if you could reverse-engineer those humus samples we took?" Sherri called over as she reached out, and he promptly handed her the planter he'd been holding.

"You'll be the first to know," Gio replied distractedly, leaning his head all the way back as he studied the pattern on the vast dome ceiling.

"Gloves, please." Sherri extended a hand, and he brought her a pair of gloves sitting nearby.

Giovanni watched her plant the moth fern while he enjoyed the warm, filtered sunlight. As it shined on his tanned face, he closed his eyes and imagined he was on a tropical beach somewhere, surrounded by cold cocktails and topless women. It almost felt like home.

...

Feeling her knees sink in the dirt as her hands worked on something more natural to them than writing or drawing was distinctly sobering for Sherri. She finished planting the moth fern promptly, getting up and wiping her hands on her shorts. After taking a istment to admire her work and give the plant a few quiet remarks of affectionate praise, she turned to leave. Giovanni, however, was nowhere to be found.

"Gio?"

No sign. She began making her way down the path into the thicker plotting of trees and plants.

"Giooo!" she called, peering through the foliage. Something tapped her shoulder.

"You're it!" Gio exclaimed childishly, then took off in the opposite direction.

"Cheat!" Sherri cried out and tore after him through the surrounding leaves and vines.

She knew the layout of the terrosphere like it was the back of her hand — she'd plotted it herself, after all. Using her home advantage to cut him off, Sherri rounded a blind spot and ducked under Gio's arm to tap his side as she ran past.

"Gotcha!"

"Damn!" He turned on his heel and chased after her.

She laughed as she slid across the tile and jumped over garden plots, maneuvering through the shrubbery with haste. Glancing behind her, she realized that her friend was much faster than she'd given him credit for and was gaining quickly. She sped up.

An electric pain shot through her ankle, coursing up her calf.

"Ow! *Shit* —" Sherri tripped, falling on her hands and knees and skidding on the tile. Before she had time to register what had happened, Giovanni was kneeling beside her.

"Hey, you alright? Oh."

Gio's gaze was trained on her ankle. Sherri looked down as well, her eyes widening as she realized that her entire ankle was swollen and purple.

"I don't know what happened..." she started, trailing off as Gio put her arm around his shoulder and lifted her up.

"Come on, let's get you to the med bay, yeah?"

Nothing cleared Kodo's head quite like hunting did. It was simple, raw, instinctual. The silence calmed him, the chase fueled him, and the kill fed him. Where some used spears and traps, Kodo had always used his natural-born claws and teeth. It made him feel connected to the world around him and the life of the prey between his jaws, the blood that ran down his chin and fertilized the soil he stood on.

He headed back to camp with the carcass of a mature kru'vaii tossed over his shoulders. The creature was a proud animal, old and magnificent, her twilight-colored hide glimmering beneath the setting suns. Her lifeblood bathed his heaving sides and mixed with his own beneath the bandage on his shoulder. She would feed him and his friends a nurturing meal they so desperately needed, and gift them the strength she'd been growing for all her many years of life. He silently thanked her as he approached the rebel camp.

Leida perked up as he neared the fire.

"Very good, Kodo," she praised him in a monotone voice and helped heave the slain carnivore from his back.

"She's a big one too," he bragged.

"Don't push it, kid," Rykr grumbled as he began butchering the meat. Kodo swatted Rykr in the side of the head with his proudly waving tail as he passed. The other man snapped around to land a bite, but he seemed to let it go as Kodo went to check on Alvi.

Without a word, he set a small piece of meat he'd saved beside the wounded woman. Alvi didn't take it, but she opened her eyes and glanced up at him with a grateful look. He left it with her in case she changed her mind, then returned to the fire to rest his tired muscles.

"Ryk," Kodo said as he sat down beside Leida, no longer able to stand the silence. "How come you don't know what's on the other side of the mountain pass? I thought you rock-eaters were all over the place up there."

Rykr shot him a glare after the term 'rock-eater' but paused. He quietly touched the blunt end of his beard where it had been trimmed by the blade of a sword, and for a moment his face twitched into a scowl. Then he shook it off and refocused, finally answering Kodo's question.

"Not really." He cleared his throat.

"Eidolan is the only real clan of the southern range. The rest of the ghaengste that call those mountains home are rogues or family tribes. But we don't journey to the other side of the pass. It's a wasteland..." He trailed off, his brow tensed, and he watched the campfire's embers flit away. Kodo glanced at Leida through the fallen silence, wondering if she, too, noticed the unease in their friend's stare.

...

After a well-needed meal, the rebels allowed the soothing music of the night to lull them to sleep. Alvi wasn't able to eat much, still weak from her injuries, but she eventually fell into a fitful slumber. Rykr, they had all discovered, could sleep anywhere and through anything. In no time at all, his snoring mixed with the crackling of the fire as their campsite hummed with the sounds of rest.

Kodo, however, tossed and turned. He was plenty exhausted, maybe more than he'd ever been before. The soreness and the tiredness that had built over the past few days hit him all at once like a landslide, and yet sleep would not take him. His bruised muscles and fractured bones haunted him, the stab wound deep in his shoulder a persistent agony that kept dragging him back to his battle with Faro-Dahn. He flinched as it played over in his head. The mightiest tunahk-dahn, as strong as a god and as merciless as a lightning strike. Kodo couldn't close his eyes without seeing the man's swollen brain bursting out of his shattered skull, his eyeball attached by meaty nerves while it hung from his head. Kodo should have been proud of defeating the great warrior, and maybe at one point not so long ago, he would have been. But he wasn't proud of his victory; it didn't feel like a victory at all. He was lost and terrified, of himself and of the world around him. Of what it had turned him into. Three words had been bouncing around in his head for days now, no matter how desperately he tried to tune them out: *beast of beasts.*

After what felt like half the night flying by while he sighed and rolled around, he sat up to see where Leida was.

The winged woman was sitting a ways away from the fire, so still he wouldn't have seen her if it weren't for her stark coloring. She was looking up at the stars. Kodo lazily rose to join her, approaching as quietly as he could so as not to wake Alvi.

"Leida?" he whispered. She looked over at him, her visible eye settling on his face. He couldn't read her gaze, he never could, but he hoped it was the look of an eye resting on an old friend.

"Yes," she whispered, though hardly any quieter than she naturally spoke.

"You can't sleep?" Kodo asked, sitting down close beside her much smaller form. Leida looked back up to the stars.

"No. I have many questions."

Kodo nodded in understanding, but he let out a small sigh. He had never asked many questions until she came along, and her never-ending questions had turned his simple existence upside down and inside out.

"Like what?" he replied. He wanted nothing more than to give her the answers she was searching for so desperately, but he got the hopeless feeling he didn't have them.

"This man, from the clan," Leida began. "He called us 'rebellion.' Is that what we are?"

She looked up at him, and Kodo couldn't tell how she felt about that notion. He chewed on the inside of his mouth and nodded ever so slightly.

"I think so. I don't know if we had any choice in it."

Leida seemed to accept that answer with neither satisfaction nor aversion. They fell back into thoughtful silence for a while longer.

"Do you think we will live?" she asked him. Kodo softened as he glanced down at her, then he looked up at the starry sky as if that was where he might find the answer.

"I don't know, feathers..." He exhaled. "But whether we live or die, I'd rather do it as a heretic, a fugitive, and a rebel than all by myself."

He felt Leida watching the side of his face, in the way he usually tried to ignore, but this time he looked down to meet her eye. Her gaze hovered over his like she was searching for something she'd lost.

"I would too," she said as she seemed to find what she was looking for. Kodo gently smiled at her, and he could swear the corners of her mouth curled into the smallest smile as well.

"It's sprained."

Doctor Maeda blew out a long, disenchanted sigh as he wrote something down on his clipboard.

"But I didn't land on it wrong or anything," Sherri replied. "I only fell because it started hurting."

She looked up at Giovanni, who was standing close beside her with his arms crossed. The young doctor — he hardly looked old enough to be out of med school — spoke again.

"Because it isn't a new injury. You've been walking on a sprained ankle for at least a week and only noticed it today. Are you taking narcotics?" Doctor Maeda handed her an ice pack from the freezer and strode across the room to rummage in one of the cabinets. Sherri blinked at his back.

"Sorry? Are you... asking me if I'm on drugs? If I brought drugs with me to space. To do."

Sherri raised her eyebrows in disbelief, and Gio stifled a laugh. Doctor Maeda didn't seem the least bit amused and began bandaging her foot tightly after returning from the cabinet.

"Yes, that's what I'm asking."

"No, I am not on narcotics."

The doctor pulled a loose hair from her ponytail and turned away, and Sherri laughed incredulously.

"Are you drug testing me?"

"Would you have a problem with that?"

"No." She shook her head. "Knock yourself out."

Giovanni turned away as if to avoid bursting into hysterical laughter, and Sherri pinched him in the side. A dark-haired nurse dropped a pill and a paper cup of water onto the side tray so forcefully that most of the water splashed out of the cup.

"You're in shock," Doctor Maeda abruptly said as he dug a surgical boot out of a closet. "Correction, you were in shock, which you are just now coming out of."

"Shock? I'm not in shock," Sherri scoffed.

"That's what I just said, you *were* in shock. McNeil, get her a blanket."

Sherri shook her head again, beginning to try to stand up.

"I don't need a fu—"

A new nurse, this one blonde, was already wrapping a heavy blanket around her shoulders. Sherri couldn't lie to herself, the warm pressure felt good against the cold air of the med bay. But a shock blanket? *Really?* Of all that had happened on the expedition so far, this day was shaping up to be the worst of it. In the morning, she'd run headfirst and bare-assed into Captain Short, and now she was being publicly humiliated by a child with a medical license. Perfect.

She flinched as Doctor Maeda firmly strapped a braced boot onto her foot.

"You went out with the group that got attacked, correct?" he asked.

"Correct." She sighed impatiently.

"You've been in trauma shock for a week, which means your organs have not been getting enough blood and oxygen," Doctor Maeda explained. "You need to rest and avoid strenuous activity. Next time everyone *else* is getting checked, you might consider also coming in. I'm giving you painkillers for the ankle. Keep the boot on for four weeks; you'll be fine."

He took a breath and walked away. Sherri was left with a bruised ego at being patronized so harshly, especially by a man who appeared years younger than her. She shrugged the blanket away and hopped off the hospital bed before Giovanni could help her, then snatched the bottle of pills that had been left for her as they exited the med bay.

"If I ever get injured, remind me to wait until a nicer doctor is available." Gio whistled sharply, slowing his pace so Sherri could keep up with him.

"This is humiliating. How am I supposed to work?" Sherri exclaimed, gesturing downward. Gio chuckled.

"Well, you're *not* supposed to, that's the whole point."

"Come on, Gio, I can't just lay around and be useless. We'll have to cut down on spontaneous games of tag, that's all."

She nudged him with her elbow, and he shook his head with a half-smile on his face.

"Shame."

"Have you had enough?"

Rataan's savage growl thundered through the courtyard, receiving nothing in return but a strangled choke.

"I SAID, HAVE YOU HAD ENOUGH?" he roared in the ear of the man beneath him. More choking. Ten warriors watched in agony, not by choice, but by order. They were not grateful to be spared Rataan-Leih's rage; every one of them would have happily thrown themselves at his feet in place of their brother. They felt nothing but heartbreak as the commander's heavy foot drove down into his throat.

"He can't breathe, commander!" a pleading voice broke out.

Rataan's head snapped up as he searched for the protestor. A tall man, fur red and mane black. One of his back legs was replaced by a prosthetic of wood and sinew, bound to his scarred thigh by a leather strap. Rataan's jaws wrenched open and released an ear-splitting noise that ended in a rattling vibration.

"Oh, you know better, Mahrz-Dahn," the commander hissed. He stepped off of Faro-Dahn, who immediately began hacking and sputtering for air. Rataan's chin slightly cocked to one side as he approached.

"Our strongest warrior, that is what he was supposed to be. Undefeated. And yet the only reason he still breathes today is that he was spared. You *dare defend him?*" He snapped his teeth together, twitching in anger as he stalked toward

Mahrz. The younger man swallowed but stared forward as his downed peer attempted to rise.

"You dare call him brother? Once so mighty, so promising, now..." — Rataan glared down at Mahrz's wooden leg — "a cripple."

Rataan flipped around and rushed at the warrior on the ground, who was still desperately trying to breathe. He tackled him and ripped his helmet off in a rage. He threw it to the ground, then grabbed the other man by the hair and yanked him up for the others to see. The warriors cringed, some even looking away.

Faro-Dahn's skin had begun to heal but his skull was hideously deformed. The side of his head was caved in like a sinkhole, and he lacked a horn, an eye, and an ear on the concave side. He was ruined, the light in his remaining eye dim and wrought with shame, and half of his face was now formed from bubbling scar tissue. His jaw hung open on one side, unable to close, his teeth and the scales on his forehead crumbling apart. The once mighty man's grotesque and destroyed appearance reflected that of a rotting log, crushed and falling in on itself. It was a testament to the power of the jaws that condemned him, and the shame that they chose not to kill him.

Rataan let go of his neck, and Faro crumpled.

"Do you claim this man as your brother?" Rataan bellowed at his warriors. He was met by a collective trumpet of confirmations, 'yes, commander,' as the tunahk claimed their felled comrade with sorrowful but stubborn pride. The commander stared deep into each and every eye before him, the eyes of the tunahk-dahn. Then he nodded, his jaw tense.

"So be it," he said. "But no warriors of mine will whine and wallow in defeat."

Faro was weakly rising, shaking after hours of sparring and abuse.

"Your defeated brother now serves as a reminder of the foe you stand against," Rataan bellowed. "Look at what he's become, warriors, meet his eye. But allow his failure to become the fire in your belly, because there is no time for rest. A storm is coming, tunahk, and if you are not prepared..."

He scowled at Faro in disgust.

"You will be crushed."

...

Rykr lifted his heavy head lazily, squinting to find his companions in the dramatic morning light. Alvi lay close to him, curled up in her new natural position. Despite being fast asleep, the young woman looked far from peaceful. Her muscles were tense, her face gaunt, and hair untamed. She was almost unrecognizable from the loud little ocean dweller Rykr had first met.

"Leida. Kodo." He approached the two familiar figures lying beside one another farther from the campfire. Leida shot up abruptly, and Kodo slowly stirred. Rykr cleared his throat as their eyes met his.

"Let's finish off the carcass from last night, then move on. We don't want to be out in the open like this in broad daylight," he continued, looking back and forth between them.

"Did you two... get any sleep last night?" he asked with a raised brow. Kodo stretched his long back with an over-exaggerated yawn, his toothy maw gaping so wide it seemed it could swallow planets.

"Not really," the forest man said, his voice croaky. Leida, on the other hand, was already up and steadily approaching the campsite. Then she stopped, looking ahead.

Alvi was awake and sitting up for the first time in days. Her back was to them as she faced the sunrise. The others shared lingering glances before silently walking up to join her.

"Alvi?" Kodo was the first to speak, his head cocked. Alvi only flicked her ear in response. After a second of hesitation, he closed the distance between them and sat next to her. They were silent for a long time, watching the horizon give birth to two suns, the golden one leading the way and its bluish twin slowly chasing after it.

"My mother once told me something about the sunrise..." Kodo said quietly as his tail swayed across the grass, "...but I'm not too sure I remember it exactly."

"I think she said, 'The suns rise on those with meaning'..." He paused as if coaxing the memory from the crevices of his mind.

"And I said, 'but mama, I thought the suns rose every day, and everyone could see them.'

"She just smiled at me and said, 'That's right, Kodokuna.'"

Kodo laughed softly as they watched the suns float into the morning sky together.

"Maybe there's some kind of meaning in all of this. Maybe it's not for nothing," he finished.

Rykr joined them and stiffly came to rest on Alvi's other side. He almost didn't notice Leida timidly follow and sit beside him. Her whispery voice seemed to merge with the silence when she spoke.

"I know..." Leida began, "I know that it would be easier to be with your own kind. To be with your own people."

The words made Rykr's chest tighten, but when he met her gaze, the coldness of her stare wasn't quite as frigid as it usually felt.

"But I am glad you are here instead." Leida glanced away from him and down at her feet as if to rest her eyes. With a deep inhale, she looked back at him. Then at Kodo, and finally Alvi.

"This rebellion, it can be shelter for those like us. You... you are my shelter," she finished. Alvi's tearful gaze finally fell from the horizon and found refuge in the faces of her small tribe.

Their shelter was now all they had. They were rebels, fugitives for daring to find solace in one another from a world fed by their peril. They were hunted for the sin of taking refuge from the war that ravaged their planet to the bone. Their heads still ached with the screams of gutted souls, not just of the family at the river camp, but of generations stripped to nothing but piles of bodies under the soil they stood on now.

The water Alvi swam in ran thick and black with the blood of her ancestors, drained by war.

The mountains that Rykr was born from echoed loud with the lost voices of those that came before him, frozen in time.

The trees of Kodo's homeland grew from the flesh of slain forest warriors, their lives cut short in battle.

The wind that carried Leida into the world was birthed from the wing beats of her predecessors, their feathers torn and frayed.

They were all products of the same eternal war. They didn't ask for it, nor did the rest of their kind, but they had a choice. The choice that every single one of them had — to rebel.

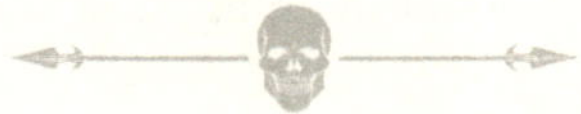

"Hey, you two." Doctor Rosenquest fell in step with Marshall and Doyle on the way to dinner as they discussed the day's discoveries, or more accurately, the lack thereof. The other two scientists looked at him expectantly.

"I don't know if you've heard yet, but Doctor Daniels sprained her ankle and is walking with a boot. I thought I'd let you know ahead of time and suggest you both resist the inevitable teasing. She seems a bit sore about it," Harrison warned. Doyle burst out laughing.

"Oh, isn't that just poetic? The ankle weight of the lab now has a literal ankle weight." He chortled, receiving a harsh look from Harrison.

Marshall at first said nothing, and hardly even seemed to have heard the exchange. When he spoke, the other two men almost didn't realize he was talking to them.

"Are you saying that because you're intimidated by the fact that she's a woman, or because you're jealous that she's over five feet tall?"

Doyle stopped walking abruptly, but quickly resumed at a more urgent pace once he realized Marshall had no plans of slowing down. He rushed to catch up, practically jogging on his much shorter legs.

"Excuse me? *I'm 5'6!*" he shouted indignantly.

"Calm down, Doyle," Harrison said, desperately biting back a laugh.

"Doctor Daniels is about the least professional person I've ever worked with," Doyle continued furiously, craning his neck to look up at Marshall. "And you should be ashamed of yourself, shrinking low enough to kiss her ass in order to get some tail. It's *pathetic.*"

Marshall finally stopped, and Doyle nearly ran into him. The tallest man began cackling, wiping an imaginary tear from his eye.

"Oh *you* want to talk about *shrinking!?*" Marshall howled, and Doyle looked as though he might hit him. Harrison put a hand in between them.

"You think you're real smart, huh, Novak? Not so fucking smart considering you can't even come up with an original insult. Yes, I am *short —*"

"I was referring to your shrinking hairline."

"You son of a bitch!"

Doyle's fist nearly made direct contact with Marshall's gut as he made no attempt to move, but Harrison grabbed the stout man just in time. Doyle stopped struggling, huffing in anger. Then, just as Harrison eased his grip, Doyle lurched forward again.

And again, to no avail. Harrison was stronger than Doyle or Marshall expected, catching the oceanologist with little effort. Marshall seemed cool and unbothered as usual, but he was no longer laughing.

"Who was it you were saying was unprofessional, Doctor Doyle? Last I checked, Daniels hasn't attempted to physically attack anyone yet. Grow up."

Marshall left the other two, heading for dinner in the commons.

"Why don't you take a breather, Doyle." Harrison released Doyle from his grip, cautiously in case he had to catch him again. Doyle was still red-faced, and he aggressively stroked his thick mustache back into its usual shape.

"Sure," he grumbled, storming off without another word.

"You must like her."

Marshall rolled his eyes at the wall. He just wanted to eat.

"Daniels and I are not having sex," he called behind him.

"That's not what I suggested," Harrison said with a warm smile as he caught up. Marshall glanced down at him. Why was he so interested all of a sudden?

"I defend my colleague from a bogus jab, so I must be in love with her!" he exclaimed, then shook his head. Harrison chuckled, which gave Marshall a weird feeling for a reason he couldn't identify.

"No," Harrison began, an amused smirk still on his face, "The fact that *you* defended anyone, instead of joining in on the bullying, seems to mean you hold a certain fondness."

Marshall sighed. He was getting awfully tired of Harrison's special kind of patronization, the kind he always seemed to wrap up in the illusion of genuine care. He tightened his tie.

"Thank you, truly, for your theory, Doctor Rosenquest. I don't know what I'd do without your expertise on my personal motivations. Can we eat now?"

To Marshall's dismay, Harrison was still smiling. He'd been looking forward to the satisfaction of seeing Harrison's face drop at the rejection of friendly banter.

"Sounds good to me," the older man said and put an arm around Marshall's shoulders as they walked into the commons. Marshall came to the conclusion he'd have to do worse if he wanted any peace and quiet from his colleagues.

...

"Man, I'm not one to complain about a check, but I didn't sign up for aliens."

Corporal Greene sat sprawled on the couch, a toothpick sitting in a wide gap between his lower teeth. They had no command, no mission. Well, that wasn't entirely true. According to Captain Short, they were under direct orders to 'stay out of motherfucking trouble for once.'

"Actually, you did."

Private Zheng hardly looked up from the little machine he had disassembled and strewn across the coffee table.

"You say something, Private?" Greene roughly set his feet on the table, making Zheng flinch and carefully reposition the bits and pieces of hardware covering the surface.

"Oh — uh, yeah." Zheng finally noticed the corporal now staring at him blankly. "You said you didn't sign up for aliens, but technically you did. The contract we signed specifically outlined the possibility and probability of life encounters. Clause twelve, I think? Also, they're not actually aliens because we're on their planet, and by definition an alien is something... not... native..." He trailed off as his comrade scowled at him.

"Private Zheng?"

"Yes, Corporal."

"Shut up, Zheng."

"Yes, Corporal."

Zheng looked back down at his work and continued carefully examining the inside of the machine.

"What's that?" a quiet voice peeped from nearby. Private Carnahan sat in a chair next to Zheng but leaned out of it almost completely, looking over his shoulder. Their large brown eyes were trained on the device on the table. Despite already being well acquainted, Zheng wasn't sure the two of them had ever had a conversation.

"It's a robot vacuum. I'm recalibrating it. Trying, anyway. It keeps spinning around and slamming into the walls," Zheng explained, scooting over slightly to put some space between him and his peer. Carnahan studied the machine closely.

"Do you think the polarity of this planet is affecting the directional sensors?" they suggested. Zheng raised his eyebrows.

"Yeah, that's what I was thinking too... Hey, do you want to help me? I could use another set of hands," he asked hopefully. Carnahan looked skeptical for a moment, chewing on their lower lip as they considered the offer.

"Sure," they finally said, climbing over the arm of the couch to sit next to him.

"Have you ever worked on robotics before?" Zheng asked as he handed them the vacuum's user manual.

"Yeah, I was on my high school's robotics team," they replied offhandedly as they read through the troubleshooting section. A smile spread across Zheng's face.

"Cool. Me too."

The two sat in predominant silence, largely only speaking when they needed to communicate instructions. The other soldiers around them came and went, paying the privates little mind as they toiled with the small machine. Zheng couldn't help feeling grateful for the busy quietness between them, and for the moment, the entire compound was just a little less lonely.

8

LAZARUS

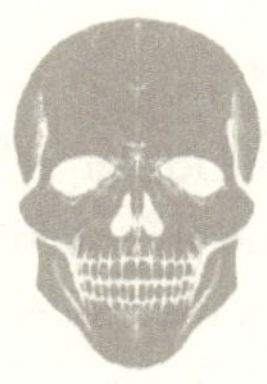

One casualty has been confirmed. Two more are highly suspected.

Planet 7355264Z contains threats we did not foresee and were not prepared for. Survey 1 was attacked by a hostile specimen estimated upwards of ten feet tall. The firearms issued to armed crew members did not de-escalate the assault. We must conclude that this planet is no longer a prime candidate for the Salvation Initiative. To continue the expedition as planned is highly inadvisable, and the Remus crew requests clearance to abort.

<u>*Wolf One to Mission Control:*</u>

Houston, please send help.

[message via Dr. Myles, Roger- RREP ecologist, head of biology]

...

The commons were busy, and the compound seemed louder than it should have been while housing only twenty-three people. Most of the crew milled around eating lunch, watching TV, playing board games, or just chatting amongst each other. They certainly had no shortage of things to talk about.

Sherri sat in silence, scribbling away in her journal as usual. She'd done hardly anything but work for weeks. She could barely remember when she'd last gotten up to eat or drink, or if she'd even gone to bed last night.

The coffee table was now littered with pieces of paper, crumpled and folded and tossed aside. They all held scrawled images of the same thing — the beast.

Hundreds, varying from charcoal drawings to watercolor paintings. It was the same creature encapsulated in the page every time but it looked different in each one. In some, it resembled a big cat, a Pit Bull Terrier, or some twisted cross between the two. In others, it could have been some kind of carnivorous equine or bovine. In every drawing, regardless of the varying details, the monster was grotesque and dark. Sherri had gotten unfortunately skilled at depicting its haunting eyes and double pupils. So skilled, in fact, she couldn't help but get the feeling those eyes were watching her.

"Getting closer?"

"Hm?" She looked up from her journal with a subtle jolt.

Marshall was lounging on the loveseat and eating from a bag of chips, watching as she drew.

"Are you getting closer? To accurately depicting the native specimen, I mean."

Sherri thought about that, studying the pages strewn across the surface in front of her.

"Nope," she concluded, continuing her current sketch as she blew a loose curl out of her face. Marshall closed the bag of chips, then whistled. Sherri looked up and he tossed the bag to her over the table, which she caught gratefully and reopened.

"I think we should schedule the second survey for next week after I get this damn boot off," she said as she popped a chip in her mouth. "You coming?"

Marshall choked on his own saliva, then laughed.

"Is that supposed to be a joke?"

"No."

"Weren't three people just killed?"

Sherri closed her journal; she'd had enough of the haunting charcoal eyes boring into her through the paper.

"No. One person disappeared, one person was killed, and another disappeared before that. As unfortunate as it is, we don't have enough data yet to accurately assess the severity of the danger we're in," she said, looking over his face as he shook his head at her and released a long exhale.

"Ice cold, Daniels."

"Oh, don't give me that bullshit, Novak." She began to gather up her drawings and materials. "I haven't seen you shed any tears over the lost lives either. Personally, I'd like to do my job and do it well so their deaths aren't in vain. That means getting back out there as soon as possible."

Marshall studied her but conceded with a shrug.

"Well, good luck with that. I'll pass. And something tells me Captain Short won't see things in the same light as you."

"Short can see things however he wants to see them, but he can't stop this expedition in its tracks." she said, already marching back to the lab.

Sherri's hypothesis was simple.

If the life on Planet 7355264Z was at all similar to Earth's, which they had to assume it was for their human expertise to have any merit at all on this mission, the indigenous animals were not inherently hostile. The most basic rule of animal behavior dictated that specimens would react in flight, freeze, or fight. Applying that logic to their first native encounter painted a simple picture — the specimen encountered one small human, it froze. It encountered an entire group of larger humans, it saw them as a threat, it fought.

The theory was as straightforward as any. The only way to prove it, however, would be to interact with the natives alone. Or at the very least, limiting survey teams to only two or three individuals. Which directly contradicted the strict 'buddy system' they had implemented with their staunch militia protectors, who had done little more than hunt bugs and wander off.

She would've liked to consult with Doctor Myles; he *was* the head of biology and theoretically had more experience in animal behavior, but he was avoiding work at all costs. In fact, they'd hardly been able to get him out of his room since the first survey. Part of Sherri was hurt that she'd been left with so much responsibility and so little guidance from her senior scientist. Roger seemed to deliberately hide from her in order to be spared her latest theories and postulations. She supposed it was better in the long run that she didn't have to rely on the squirrely ecologist for anything. Besides, she had some field experience in animal biology, despite her primary discipline being botany.

Just as she got up and started down the hall, debating whether she should make a last-ditch effort to call on Roger, she noticed someone coming out of a room the crew rarely used.

The control room.

Interesting. More interesting yet was the man who came clear of the doorway. Doctor Roger Myles himself.

The research team had been discussing the transmission they would send back to mission control regarding the attack, but they weren't finished drafting. It seemed, however, that their ecologist may have jumped the gun. Sherri said nothing as he walked past, but she looked him over suspiciously. He didn't meet her gaze.

The stone giants looming over the lower world represented something to them now. They were treacherous, cold, and unshakable. The rebels approached the mountain range not like an old friend, but like the altar of a god that had blessed them once before, and they sought her grace again.

Alvi was still weak, her movement restricted by her broken bones, but her spirits had begun to rise back to their normal height as she slowly recovered. Granted, her way of expressing it was through constant complaint.

"Didn't we just leave this shithole?" she grumbled, perched on Kodo's back in her usual spot. She watched the peaks around them as they climbed; the depth of the incline was subtle, but when she turned around, the view of the land below them was growing hazy. The air was gradually getting thinner, though Alvi had hardly noticed. Her specialized lungs could hold enough air for hours. Kodo, however, was panting like he'd run a mile.

"I forgot how hard it was to breathe up here..." he whined, his tongue hanging out of his mouth as he huffed.

"Quit complaining and save your breath. We haven't even reached where the air *really* starts getting thin," Rykr mocked.

"Thin air isn't the problem, it's freezing your fins off," Alvi groaned.

"Maybe if all your fins freeze off, you'll be able to pass for the world's stubbiest forest dweller!" Rykr called behind him with a mean cackle; being back in his natural environment seemed to have emboldened his jokes.

"You're an *oaf*, you know that?" Alvi hissed.

"Better an oaf than a gimp."

"Hey, feathers." Kodo trotted up beside Leida, Alvi turning around on his back to continue her argument with Rykr.

"Yes," Leida replied.

"You know, if you get cold, you can just stick by me for warmth," he said in what could have been an attempt at sounding cool and nonchalant. Leida cocked her head.

"I am not sensitive to the cold, do not worry. I can just wrap my wings around myself. See?" She unfurled her wings from her back and pulled them close around her, forming a shield of warmth. The satisfied smirk dropped from Kodo's face, but he shrugged.

"Oh, good," he replied, walking along. Alvi and Rykr quietly snickered behind him.

"What are you laughing at?" the forest man sneered.

"You've got a lot to learn, kid." Rykr shook his head. Kodo rolled his eyes but said nothing.

As they rounded the side of a tall cliff, the trail tightly hugging the mountain walls, a daunting and incredible sight came into view.

Ahead of them, a giant crevice cut the mountain range straight in half, the suns' light unable to penetrate the gap. Two different worlds on either ridge, an abysmal void between them.

The Xinsei pass.

The rebels stopped for a moment, taking it in. The path they'd been trekking on so far had been rocky and rough, but it was nothing compared to the journey that lay before them. The peaks sliced through the foggy sky and jutted straight up into the heavens. Now they would climb stone as sharp as blades, and the ice would form a deadly frozen sheen. The snow would begin to fall soon, as they'd long passed the point where the trees stopped growing. Now the only way was up. They had no idea what lay on the eastern rim of the pass, not even Rykr, but they prepared themselves to find out.

...

"The tunahk-dahn are prepared to depart, my lords. They will split up into two bodies and scour the region for the rebel fugitives."

Rataan stood tall and proud, looking into the souls of his leaders with both burning love and visceral fury.

"They will bring you the heads of three savages and the giant traitor to be tried for his crimes against the Ramys nation."

"Very well," Vaus-Visaan said stoically, though his wise gaze hinted at more judgment than his words. The younger, quieter king, Vaus-Levah, said nothing, but his lip twitched in eager hunger for the heads he was promised. Vaus-Avias looked over the commander critically.

"Is Faro-Dahn well enough for this?" she asked. Rataan cleared his throat.

"Faro-Dahn is one with the tunahk order, born with lightning in his blood. He will fight alongside his brothers and sisters, and follow his sworn oath to victory..."

His eyes wandered to the silent queen, Vaus-Erro.

"Or he will fight alongside his brothers and sisters and die a warrior's death."

Avias nodded and stayed silent, glancing at her fellow queen and kings on the thrones beside her.

To the surprise of her three counterparts, Erro suddenly bowed her mighty head.

"I have faith in the tunahk to destroy this threat and serve our people, as their order has sworn to do since its birth," she called in a powerful voice, *"La'al maixay."*

Rataan bowed back, his nose brushing the rug as he lowered his head in respect.

"La'al maijex."

Driven by the desperation to squeeze whatever information they could out of their limited samples, the research team in laboratory A ran tests in quiet focus. At least, quiet except for snapping at each other when someone took too long at a particular machine.

"Come on, Bridgeland, you type like my ninety-eight-year-old bubbe," the oceanographer spat, rushing the anxious man in front of him. Carl just continued battling with the moisture analyzer, then he groaned and began to backspace as he mistyped.

"For fuck's sake!" Doyle exclaimed. Just as he began to muscle Carl to the side, Harrison appeared at the meteorologist's defense.

"It confuses me too," Harrison gently said as he helped Carl figure out the experiment, giving Doyle a threatening glare before he could interrupt. Carl accepted the help with a flustered huff.

As the three men wrestled with the equipment, Sherri desperately attempted to ignore their bickering. She was getting agonizingly restless; her sprained ankle was a prison for someone who normally never sat still. As she worked on fleshing out her notes, profiling the native specimen, theorizing where it might fit into their earthly methods of classification, it occurred to her that she hadn't actually gotten a good look at it. It had been standing right in front of her, sure, but shadowed in complete darkness. By the time it came out into the daylight, she'd made a significant effort *not* to look back at it — having been preoccupied with running for her life. Some of her neighbors, she recalled, had come face-to-face with it. She stood up from her chair and abruptly left the lab.

The smell of alcohol and cigarette smoke burned her nostrils as she turned into the hall. *Jesus Christ, are they smoking in here?*

Sherri cringed in disgust at the thought of their precious oxygen being tainted by cigarette smoke. As she headed to the large double doors at the end of the hall, a door to her right opened. She couldn't be less surprised at the figure that lumbered out, though the sight of him still filled her with the feeling one gets when there's a traffic stop on their commute to work.

"Hey there, Captain," she greeted him with dread.

Captain Short looked down at her, his arms crossed.

"You lost?" he grunted.

"I wish," she muttered. "I'm here to talk. Amicably, if that's alright with you."

She said it as if he were a spirited child she was persuading to put his pants on.

"About what?"

"Which of your soldiers got the best look at the native we encountered?" she asked quickly, already eager to complete the conversation.

"Torres."

"Perfect, where can I find him?"

"Digested and recycled out in the jungle."

Sherri couldn't stop the expression on her face from falling weak.

"He's the one that got bitten in half and swallowed," Short continued slowly with his eyes narrowed, as if studying her for a reaction. His voice was stoic as always, but there was a subtle pain in his stare. Sherri sighed.

"Oh."

She rubbed the back of her neck, pausing. She didn't know the man; she couldn't even conjure an image of him in her head. Still, the terrible fact that someone had died in order to protect her left a bitter taste in her mouth. The research efforts were the top priority of the RREP, she understood that better than anyone, and yet it made her stomach turn that the guns were so willing to give their lives for a cause that wasn't even really theirs. The captain had said it better than she could when they first arrived on the planet — mission control saw the militia as prepackaged meat.

"Okay. Who else got close?"

Short was silent for a moment; he didn't appear satisfied with her response.

"Me. Corporal Keenan. Master Sergeant Fischer," he finally said. Sherri nodded once.

"Alright, I'll be conducting eyewitness interviews with all three of you. You can wait. Where do I find the other two?"

The captain's jaw clenched. He seemed even more irritated than usual, and this time Sherri wasn't sure if it was something she'd said or if he genuinely just hated looking at her face that much. She didn't particularly care either way.

He nodded at the double doors, loud voices and music emanating from behind them — the barracks.

"Keenan is the big motherfucker with the lazy eye. Fischer's the tall angry woman. You'll know them when you see them."

"Got it. Thanks," she said as she wrote something down in her journal, then veered around him to head for the doors.

Even Rykr, born from the stone of the mountains themselves, could feel that this part of the range had no kinship with him. It was foreign and it did not take well to outsiders. The air here was painfully thin and frozen; it cut the inside of his throat like a sharpened blade. He began to grow uneasy, recalling what his father had told him of what lay east of the Xinsei pass.

We do not go there, Rykr. That land does not belong to us, the king had told him when he was a curious child.

Why? he'd asked. *Are we not welcome to all parts of Matka?*

He remembered a distinct, unidentifiable look in his father's eye. He almost could have mistaken it for nostalgia.

Sometimes the Great Mother must protect us, boy, for not all of Her creations are a blessing.

As Rykr thought back on his father's words, the warnings he'd kept from his friends, he wondered if he'd made a grave mistake leading them here.

"Maybe we should turn back, Leida," he called as the wind picked up.

"No. We must find somewhere to hide," she replied, her voice barely audible over the howling wind. They continued on; it was not the white oblivion they'd grown to expect, but a dark gray swirl of stormy billows.

Alvi shot up from her huddled position on Kodo's back, staring into the distance.

"Alvi, lay down. What are you doing?" Leida hissed. Alvi watched the horizon, unblinking.

"I saw something."

"...What?" Kodo asked.

"A figure, over there," Alvi answered, eyes still locked on a spot far away in the snow. She was shaking violently, but she didn't appear to notice. Her muscles were rigid and her voice strong with focus.

"No, you didn't," Rykr said firmly. "You can't even see that far ahead in the snow. Lay back down."

Slowly, Alvi let her eyes fall from the horizon. She gingerly curled up in her original spot between Kodo's shoulders, and they tread onward. Rykr trudged ahead to meet up with Leida.

"She's delusional," he whispered quietly to her. Leida only nodded. Rykr studied her face, searching for a hint of emotion, but he found none.

"She's still weak. We should prepare ourselves for the worst."

Leida just nodded again. Rykr spent another moment looking over her face, hoping it might tell him what she was thinking. He gave up, falling behind once again.

...

"We must stop before it gets darker."

Leida raised her voice above the wind as it pelted into her with a cold sting. She searched around for any sign of shelter, but the flurries of thick snow were getting worse. A clump of snow hit her hard in the back. She flipped around, dodging another spray of the white powder.

Rykr was turned away from them, digging into the snow and kicking up billows of sleet. The others watched as he dug; his large, wide paws were perfect for shoveling huge quantities of snow. In only a few minutes, he was completely submerged. Just as Leida crawled to the edge and peered inside, Rykr's head popped out, nose to nose with her.

"If we squeeze, even Kodo might fit," he said, ducking back into the hole. Leida and Kodo exchanged a quick glance before Kodo gently took Alvi from his back and set her in the burrow.

Leida entered as Rykr helped Alvi settle in, her frail body finally able to relax without the wind beating against her.

A distressed yelp beckoned their attention to Kodo, who was struggling to squeeze his mammoth form into the hollow. He gave a forced smile as he spotted them watching the ordeal.

"Maybe I should just stay outside," he suggested with a sheepish chuckle, stuck halfway through the slim opening.

Leida shook her head, and quickly bit down on Kodo's horn before he could recoil. She pulled with all her might. The giant's torso came loose and his back end popped into the den as both ghaengste stumbled. Despite Alvi and Rykr's laughter, Kodo wasted no time flopping down beside Leida, stretching out and taking up most of the den. Leida tensed at the lack of space between them, but as the huge man's body heat filled the burrow, none could complain about how cramped it had gotten.

The amusement at Kodo's grueling struggle quickly waned as the howling of the wind outside their shelter filled the den with unease. The haunting darkness of the storm above made them jolt and tense at every noise as it rumbled the snow around them.

Rykr couldn't bear to keep quiet any longer.

"I've heard stories…" he timidly began, "from the elders in my clan."

He felt the gazes of his companions studying him, and he couldn't shake the feeling that he might have done something terribly wrong. Deathly wrong.

"They're only ghost stories, I know. I didn't say anything before because I didn't want to scare you, I —" He sighed. "I didn't want you to think I was scared."

He desperately tried to sound assured, but his voice wavered. Alvi looked him over, her bright eyes wide and brows furrowed.

"What stories, Rykr?"

Rykr hesitated, closing his eyes for a moment.

"The spirit of the mountains…" He spoke in a hush. "They say…

"They say he was once the most bloodthirsty warrior who ever walked the planet. He would skin his enemies alive, and their screams of agony could be heard echoing across the furthest peaks of the mountain range. He wore their decapitated skulls as helms, the scalps still half attached. During the many years of his bloody reign, every flake of snow on the mountains was not pure and white as we know it. It was black."

The other rebels watched him in silence, but he did not meet their eyes.

"When his barbaric rampage finally ended, his life cut loose from this plane, the Mother punished him for his sins. She punished him for massacring Her children and polluting Her flesh with his gluttony for death. She refused him peace and condemned him to wander this very wasteland for eternity… as a skeleton of his former body. Now a long-dead corpse, he does not wear the empty skulls of his enemies. He wears his own."

He finally looked around at his companions, though he wasn't yet ready to face them. He was born from the chill, immune to the bite of the frost, and yet at that moment he was freezing cold. They were silent for what felt like forever.

"*Just* a skeleton?" Kodo abruptly asked. "How does it stay together? Or… move, if it doesn't have muscles."

Rykr just blinked at him, then opened his mouth to say something before being interrupted by Alvi bursting into a fit of laughter.

"Ouch" she laughed, clutching her healing ribs, "I'll take my chances with the bone man over our living, breathing enemies."

Even Leida looked slightly amused at the observation.

"I do not think we will meet any ghosts, Rykr," she said reassuringly, and he offered a shy smile. Their amusement comforted him instead of shaming him, and he was able to relax for the first time in days. He allowed himself to laugh a little too, relieved to admit his fears. Finally calm enough to get some rest, he yawned and set his head down to sleep. It felt like it had been years since he felt the soft embrace of slumber.

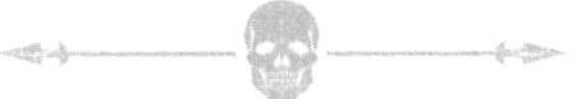

The barracks' doors swung open. One man snatched a bottle of whiskey off the table to stow it under his seat while the others scrambled to stand up from their chairs. A bald, dark-skinned man took a deep inhale, puffing out his chest.

"Officer on —!" He stopped his cry abruptly as his eyes met the intruder.

Sherri blinked up at him as his shoulders fell and his hands relaxed from their balled-up position. He waved off his peers, and they gradually resumed whatever they'd been doing before the false alarm. The hazy air filled again with laughing, arguing, rock music, and cigarette smoke. Most of the soldiers turned back to an intense game of poker being played over a haphazard pile of cash, a gold watch, a few packets of instant noodles, and what appeared to be a pair of women's underwear.

"Can I help you, ma'am?" the bald man asked. Sherri began to answer, but quickly stepped aside as a soldier leaned back in his chair to get closer to her — the one who stowed the bottle.

"I got somethin' I can help you with," he purred, licking his lips like a hungry dog and looking over her slowly. His eyes were bloodshot and inflamed. One of them, the pupil so large it nearly took up the entire iris, kept twitching as it failed to keep up with the movement of the other. Short was right — she'd know him when she saw him.

Sherri's nose scrunched in disgust.

"Are you Keenan?" she asked coldly. He grinned, revealing large, tobacco-stained teeth.

"You can call me whatever you want, baby doll." He started to stand up, but the dark soldier from before put a firm hand on his shoulder to stop him. Sherri noted that the name tape on the first man's coat read 'CRAWFORD.'

"He's Corporal Keenan. What do you need?" Crawford interjected, his tone businesslike. Sherri cleared her throat.

"My name is Doctor Daniels; I'm here to ask him some questions about the recent native encounter. He'll have to leave the game," she explained. Keenan once again began to get up.

"Sure thing, sugar, we can go somewhere mor—"

"No. Sit down. Your colleagues may remember more than you do."

Corporal Keenan slowly lowered himself back down into his chair. He tracked her with his eyes as she flipped her notes open.

"I heard you may have gotten a close look at the specimen that attacked. Is that accurate?"

"So you're one of them scientists, huh? You married?" He set a fresh cigarette between his teeth and lit it.

"I asked if you got a good look."

He met her gaze, then smirked as if he knew something no one else did.

"Yeah, I got a pretty good look at the bastard when I shot it in the fucking face."

He let out a loud, hoarse chortle like he was reminiscing with an old friend. The abrupt noise appeared to startle some of the surrounding soldiers. Sherri remained looking down on him sternly.

"And what happened when you did that?"

"The fuck do you think happened? It went ape-shit. Ripped that slow son of a bitch, Torres, head from head. Pulled trees out of the ground and threw 'em at us."

Sherri scribbled along in her journal, focused as he spoke.

"And the — what did you say?" Her pencil stopped, and she looked up from the paper. The corporal was straddling his chair backward now, his arms crossed over the back of it, staring at her blankly.

"You hard of hearing or something? I said it ate Torres, and then when it finished tearing his ass up, it tore up the rest of the fucking jungle."

Sherri's heart rate spiked, her skin prickling as she snapped her journal closed.

Sherri barged into the lab.

"The trees! We haven't revisited the fallen trees in *weeks!*" she raved, quickly gaining the attention of everyone in the room. "We were so damn caught up with the glory and the danger of discovering the native specimen that we never even bothered to relate it back to what we already knew."

"What the hell are you on about now, Daniels?" Doyle exclaimed.

"The natives downed the trees!" Sherri laughed as if it were obvious. "Maybe they were marking their territory or reacting to the light from the fence, I don't know."

"How could you possibly —"

"I interviewed one of the guns," she continued. "He said when they were shooting at the native in the jungle, it started uprooting entire trees and throwing them."

"Doctor —"

"Presumably as a defense, but it could be a repeated natural behavior. There must have been one of that species — maybe even that very same individual — coming right up outside the fence. And the vanishing soldier!"

"Doctor Daniels."

Sherri finally halted her explanation, seeming for the first time to notice her colleagues all staring at her. Her eyes landed on Doctor Novak, who was sitting on his desk with a dubious expression on his face.

"What?" she asked, short of breath.

"Slow down," he said. "How can you be so sure? I think we would have noticed that."

Sherri huffed in exasperation, her mind moving so fast she struggled to keep up with her words.

"I'm *not* sure, that's why we need to go check the trees. If there are dental impressions, that will prove the theory and give us real, tangible data on this thing."

The men around her looked at each other until one of them spoke up.

"*No,*" Roger said firmly. Sherri was surprised he was even in the lab today, much less speaking out loud.

"We barely survived last time," he continued, "And if the natives are responsible for the tree anomaly, they could be..." His face tensed with visible terror and he exhaled shakily.

"It could be close."

Sherri put her hands on her hips, briefly searching Roger's beady eyes.

"There's an uprooted tree just outside the fence. It would be close to safety, we'd have eyes in all directions."

"You're in a boot, Daniels," Giovanni argued.

"Better idea," Marshall piped up. "We have the guns drag the tree inside the fence, then we examine it."

He raised his hands out as if inviting his colleagues to agree with him.

"That would leave them awfully exposed." Harrison frowned. "The trees in the plains are far smaller than the ones in the jungle, but they'd still have their hands full. They wouldn't be able to defend themselves."

"The closest tree is dead," Sherri quickly exclaimed, clapping her hands together once. "It'll be light."

Gio jumped up to follow her as she headed out of the lab.

Eleven figures soared through the trees. The clanking of their armor, the chiming of their blades, and the fire of determination filled the air of the jungle. Their feet pounded into the forest floor with the same rhythm as their beating hearts — the drumming of the hunt. The red figure in the front of the pack had a gait different from the others; it was hard and ungraceful yet it carried him faster than any of his comrades

He leaped over a fallen log, lunging through the cutting winds like a bird of prey. His feet slammed hard onto the ground as his fellow warriors followed him, one of them breaking out of formation. She launched herself away from the soil, meeting the solid trunk of a tree, then vaulted off the side and soared through the air.

Iago hit the ground running next to Mahrz.

"I'll find them first; you realize that, don't you?" She smirked, though her quiet whistling voice was barely audible through her panting. Mahrz shook his head and laughed.

"Keep dreaming, sister."

"The only difference between dream and truth is keeping your eye open, my friend."

"Ah, quit flirting, you cocky fools," said Io from behind them. "We're approaching the tree line. It'll soon be time to split," she finished, eyeing the two of them with a half smile. Mahrz's face quickly resumed its normally stoic position, and he nodded, looking forward once again. Iago ran even harder, kicking up clouds of dust. Mahrz sprinted to keep pace with her, their comrades behind them charging on as the entire group tore through the final stretch. When they broke through the trees into glaring sunlight and out from the protection of the forest, they slowed.

The warriors looked around at one another, heaving and panting, as they each gradually came to a stop. Mahrz trotted to the front of the congregation, lifting his chin high and thrashing his long tail around him.

"Lih-Dahn! Kjell-Dahn! Raiz-Dahn! Sahga-Dahn! Faro-Dahn!" he belted, throwing his head back and releasing a spirited war cry to rally his companions. Five ghaengste met him, tossing open their mighty jaws and joining in his cry. Iago leaped a few paces in the other direction, then stood tall on her hind legs.

"Kei-Dahn! Teihnan-Dahn! Garja-Dahn! Io-Dahn!" she bellowed straight through her tattered voice. She laughed and let out a guttural roar as four more ghaengste joined her savage song.

Then the two groups of warriors turned, galloping away from one another to the east and the west. The hunt began.

...

"Get up, lazy ass." Rykr kicked Kodo in the behind, the younger man's head shooting up from its place set on his paw.

A gentle stream of golden light flooded in through the entrance of their makeshift snow den, beckoning them out into the open world. Leida emerged first.

The light was so blinding it was painful, and the world was quiet. A thick haze remained floating through the atmosphere in white billows, obscuring the horizon, but it was stagnant compared to before. As Leida searched above the fog, she realized they were now trapped in a jagged, daunting cage of mountain peaks. Tall towers of stone surrounded them and cast stretching shadows across their path, closing them in.

"Which way did we come from?" Alvi asked weakly.

"I don't know..." Rykr muttered as he shuffled through the snow.

Leida scanned the area, turning around as she and her companions searched for a trail. There was no view of the planet below. Only ice, snow, and the dark pillars that kept them from the rest of the world. The suns were imprisoned behind the peaks, their warmth chained far away. The few rays of light that penetrated the stone walls cast excruciatingly bright stripes across the range, creating ribbons of golden fire on the snow. The wind whispered through the pillars of rock far above them and created a constant humming sound. Like a giant moaning in pain, deep and endless.

Leida's sharp eye rested on a single gap in the rocky walls — a small void cut into the stone, but it seemed to emit a faint blue glow. She searched the sky for the smaller sun, but the blue star was nowhere to be found, trapped outside of the mountainous cell. She looked back to the crevice. It whistled softly, beckoning her with its lulling song. The whistling sounded timid and far, far away, yet close enough to ring loudly inside her head. It called to her, drawing her ever closer, calling her name. Not Leida; no, it didn't say the name given to her by her friend. It called her something else, something long forgotten.

Refuge.

"This way."

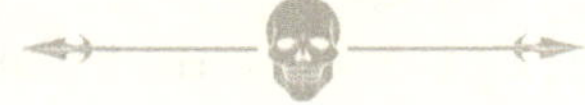

"Short."

Here we go.

"Squints," Short acknowledged Doctor Daniels and her sidekick with a nod. He stood at the bar having a cup of coffee — black — in the middle of the afternoon. The compound had been particularly exhausting lately, and he already foresaw needing another cup after this interaction played out.

"How many of your people would it take to lift and carry a dead tree, say, hawthorn sized?" the botanist said.

Captain Short just stared tiredly, taking a moment to wonder if he'd heard the words coming out of her mouth correctly. She began again.

"We—"

"I have no clue how big a hawthorn tree is, Doc, and I *really* don't like where this is going. But... four." He took a long sip from his mug.

"Four..."

"Four men. Including myself."

Daniels shrugged at Giovanni, who just shrugged back.

"Okay, cool," she said. "I need you to bring the closest log inside the fence so my team can study it. And your men need to wear gloves."

Short narrowed his eyes at her chipper expression.

"And explain to me *why* this is worth putting four lives at risk?" He leaned against the counter.

"Because the data would be highly valuable and the risk would be minimal," she answered all too quickly.

"You and I have different definitions of minimal," he replied. "Where I come from, it means 'not very much.'"

Daniels puffed out her cheeks and let out an exaggerated sigh.

"Have you ever seen one of the natives — anything, actually — aside from insects in the surrounding plains?" she asked, matching his patronizing tone.

"Not aside from when that motherf—"

"Exactly. Do you know what that means?"

"We've been—"

"The animals you're so afraid of are forest predators. Meaning, not likely to come gallivanting out of the trees and across an open plain to slaughter four sweaty humans that it wouldn't even see as an hors d'oeuvre. Not to mention, even if one did, you would have *more* than enough time to get back in the fence to safety. Case in point, minimal ris—"

"*I get it,*" the captain snapped.

"But you can't prove any of that, can you?" he continued. "Shit, you people can't *prove* anything yet. Am I wrong in assuming that?"

"No, but we had a deal."

"That's too bad. I'm not risking perfectly good lives because your tree-hugger ass is getting an itch."

The botanist looked so angry Short thought she might spontaneously combust, conveniently freeing him from her reign of terror. Giovanni timidly went to touch her arm. Then she appeared to calm all at once, put up a hand, and took a deep breath.

"Fine." Her shoulders relaxed. "I'll just go out there by myself, entirely exposed, and spend the hours that I need to thoroughly examine what I need to examine. I'll see you lovely gentlemen later."

She smiled sweetly as Giovanni muttered something indignant under his breath about being included in her condescension. She began to walk away.

"Don't play with me, Doctor, you won't," Short barked. She flipped around and stared into his eyes.

"*Watch me,*" Daniels spat. Then she turned back around, marching off toward the lab. Giovanni chased after her.

"Daniels! That boot hinders your movement too much, you can't go out there," he pleaded. She didn't even bother slowing down.

"Don't tell me what I can and can't do, Rosenquest. If you have a problem with me going by myself, then grow some balls and come with me."

Captain Short observed the two scientists from his spot in the kitchen. She was bluffing, she had to be. Supposedly, the woman was a highly educated scholar, or so he'd heard. She couldn't possibly be stupid enough to run out into a deadly alien world unarmed and unprotected.

But there she was. She was wearing a backpack and heading for the door.

She wouldn't.

She began to type in the code as Giovanni appeared beside her.

She was.

"Keenan! Crawford! Mendoza! Move it!" Short roared, his bellow ringing throughout the compound like an alarm. Three men scrambled to meet him in less than a second, as if they'd materialized from thin air. The captain snatched his rifle from Sergeant Mendoza as it was handed to him.

"We're moving a tree. Come on," he growled, already marching to the door. He shoved past Doctor Daniels as it opened, immediately stepping into the sunlight.

"I can't believe you're actually getting them to do this."

Sherri was only half listening to Giovanni as she watched the soldiers from the doorway. The captain was typing in the code to turn off the fence, and his chosen three comrades were offhandedly chatting amongst each other. The tall slender man, Crawford, was surprisingly soft-spoken when he wasn't calling out a command. He glanced over at Short every few seconds as if anxiously awaiting an order. He spoke with a handsome older man Sherri wasn't acquainted with yet, with neat graying hair and kind eyes. He had a calm, genuine demeanor, and she could swear she heard the others calling him 'Ma.' The large one with the eye deformity and the close-cropped hair, Keenan, appeared at least slightly intoxicated. He gave her an uneasy feeling; it seemed that even his brothers-in-arms were uncomfortable around him.

"Gentlemen," she called out as the fence began to slowly disappear. The soldiers looked up at her, and she lifted a box of sterile latex gloves.

"Put these on. Don't touch anything with your bare skin if you can help it," she said, tossing the box to the man closest to her, the stocky man with a face too handsome for a soldier. He thanked her after catching the box, then took gloves out for himself and passed it along to the others.

The fence was now gone, and the wall of turquoise light had disappeared with a formation of tall spokes left in its place.

"Alright, boys," Captain Short barked. "In and out."

A small chorus of 'yes sir's belted back. Short turned around, pointing an accusing finger at the two researchers standing in the doorway.

"You see anything out there — I don't care what it is — if it's not human... turn on the fence. Now *stay,* "he ordered, then turned to walk with his men.

"He's such a drama queen," Sherri said, crossing her arms and observing as the soldiers approached the barrier. Giovanni stifled a laugh and nudged her with his elbow.

"Takes one to know one. What's with your whole vendetta against the military anyway?"

"I'm a pacifist and an anti-imperialist. Guess you couldn't relate to that, huh? Good ol' chap." She said the last part in a poorly executed English accent, poking his ribs with a playful grin. Gio gasped indignantly.

"If you're a pacifist, I'm a red, white, and blue-blooded American." He poked her back, then abruptly wrapped an arm around her waist to lift her up and pretend to throw her. Sherri emitted a humiliating yelp as she struggled.

"Will you two shut the fuck up!?" the captain bellowed from outside the fence, and Gio quickly set Sherri back down. She swatted him in the arm and awkwardly readjusted her shirt as her face burned red.

They watched in scolded silence as Captain Short and his men approached the tree and found places around it to post themselves. The four soldiers dug their hands under the log's bulk and lifted with their legs on the count of three. After the log broke free from the dirt, they made their way inside the fence. They moved the load with ease, or perhaps the fear of lurking enemies motivated their pace. The end of the tree crossed the barrier.

"Turn it on," Short called once the group was within the conduction posts, and Giovanni quickly typed in the code. The light began to crawl its way around the arc, forming a solid wall as it closed them in. Everyone let out a breath. The captain and his men set the tree down and their shoulders relaxed.

Sherri hopped out from the doorway and onto the grass, her sights set on the task at hand, but her attention was grabbed by Giovanni clearing his throat. She glanced over, and he subtly gestured with his head to the captain, who was heading inside.

"Hey, Short," she called out. He turned to look at her, already scowling as if bracing for physical pain.

"Thanks," she said. The captain nodded but promptly turned to leave after ordering Crawford to stay behind and supervise. Sherri jogged over to the tree, eagerly setting her backpack down and putting her gloves on.

"Go get the rest of the team," she called over to Gio. "We've got work to do."

The rest of the research team filed out of the compound, and even Doctor Novak joined them.

It was brighter than he could have imagined. Colorful, open, and tranquil.

But it felt wrong. The idea that he was breathing alien air made Marshall feel tainted and nauseatingly homesick. After looking around for a moment, he hesitantly approached the tree with the others to take his own trace samples. He slowly lowered himself to the ground, kneeling with a pained grunt. While this planet's gravity was functionally the same as Earth's, he could swear it was harder on his knees. Or maybe he was just getting old.

Doctor Daniels leaned down so her face nearly touched the grass; she was searching the underside of the tree.

"Hey, help me roll this over," she said to her colleagues, sitting up and planting her hands firmly on the face of the tree trunk. The Rosenquest brothers positioned themselves on either side of the log, then helped her guide it over and steady it to rest with the bottom side up. Everyone fell silent for a moment as all eyes rested on the newly uncovered side.

"There they are."

Deep, vicious gashes were carved into the tree's bark. Teeth marks.

Marshall attempted to ignore the harrowing extent of the damage as the team began taking samples and measurements. Each tooth must have been the size of a butcher knife. He suddenly had vertigo.

"This is fantastic," Sherri exclaimed as she worked hastily. "These must be teeming with data. We could get information on diet, anatomy — maybe even DNA if we're lucky."

Marshall was wondering what evolutionary feat had completely removed the botanist's self-preservation instinct when his hand intercepted something at the equipment tray. Upon glancing down, he realized he and Doctor Daniels had touched hands while reaching for the same pair of forceps.

Marshall could have sworn he saw a tiny smile teasing at her lips, and he subtly winked as their eyes met. She quickly turned her attention back to the subject in front of her as a gentle flush crossed her cheeks. She'd retracted her hand without grabbing what she needed.

"They're all yours, go ahead," Marshall said with a smirk. Sherri didn't move.

"Daniels?" he asked, gently reaching over to touch her arm. She looked back at him.

"Yeah?"

"I said you could have... can you hear alright?" His face dropped to concern. Sherri's did too.

"I said I was fine."

He took off his gloves and cupped her cheek, tilting her head to face him. Sherri blinked up at him.

"What are you doing —" He covered her left ear firmly with his palm and looked between her eyes.

"Can you hear me?"

Sherri's eyes widened and she felt a lump form in her throat. She stared at his mouth, watching it move as no sound came out.

She couldn't hear anything.

They walked through a parted sea of cerulean ice, waves raging up around them and frozen into eternal crystal. It glittered and crackled and dripped, creating a living atmosphere separate from the cold death of the rest of the mountain range. Wind whistled through the canyon like the instrument of the planet itself, flooding through shapes carved in the ice and creating a soulful song.

A howl joined the symphony, drawn out and chilling, loud and sorrowful.

"What was that?" Alvi gasped, sitting up on top of Kodo's back.

"The wind," Rykr said. "That kind of thing happens up here."

They tread on through the canyon at a careful pace, the blue of the ice like a fallen sky beneath them. It was beautiful, but beautiful in the way that the sea recedes before a tsunami. Drawing souls closer with its playful gleam only to swallow them alive once they'd come too far to escape. The rebels' reflections walked alongside them on walls of smooth ice, guiding their way.

Leida took a moment to observe the mirror images painted on the glassy surface; she couldn't remember ever seeing a clear image of herself. Before she knew it, she was veering off from the group, approaching her twin trapped in the ice. She cocked her head to the side, studying the mess of long matted curls that consumed her form and the sky-blue eye peeking through, peering back at her.

There was something else in the reflection far behind her. Leida barely had time to register the figure staring at her in the still ice before she flipped around, a snarl bursting forth from her jaws as she prepared to strike.

Nothing.

"Leida..." Alvi said, her hoarse voice wavering.

Leida slowly came back to her senses, like waking up from a deep slumber. The snarl melted from her face and her posture straightened. She was still staring at the spot she'd expected to see the figure.

"There was something," she stated. Her companions looked at one another, perfectly still. The wind seemed to have changed direction.

"We must leave," Leida said abruptly.

"Keep moving," she urged as she walked between her friends to reclaim the lead.

There was a shadow in the corner of her eye. It followed her, and when she threw her gaze to catch the blurry figure, it wasn't there. It was still in her peripheral vision, never getting closer or farther away. They moved quicker. Her head snapped to the side as something whispered in her ear. No, just the wind. Just the wind.

Another howl rang out.

Louder.

Closer.

A deep rumble of lonely agony, like a monster chained under the crust of the planet itself, crying out and demanding to be released. It reverberated from all around them, through the ice and the stone and the core of the mountains. Kodo's ears were tense and rigid as the song gradually died out.

"Rykr?" he whispered, his eyes trained on the back of the mountain man's head. Rykr slowly looked at his companions, his face frozen in guilt and shame.

"That wasn't the wind..."

The stoic mountain man's eyes contained something Leida had hoped never to see in them — terror.

"Move. We must move." Her hearts raced as she began ushering her friends. The signal that drew her to this place was a siren's song — it tricked her and lured her in. It was no refuge, it was not the oasis she had thought. It was the end. She couldn't remember which way they'd come from or how long they'd been there, and suddenly she couldn't remember anything from before the blue frost.

They began to rush, and then they were running.

Another howl, so loud it might as well have been right behind them or deep inside of them.

"*Go!*" Rykr cried, and they tore and scratched desperately across the ice as fast as it would allow them to; the tsunami had arrived. Leida didn't dare look back. The bite of a frigid shadow lunged at their heels and she could swear the walls were closing in. They slid through a curve in the canyon, and her stomach sank.

A dead end. They all skidded to a stop, Kodo nearly crashing into the wall of ice as he slid ahead. Alvi leaped from his back to save herself from the impact, but it never came. They looked around frantically for a way out, then froze as another howl filled the air. It was hoarse, guttural, and impossibly loud. It ripped and cracked through their ear canals like lightning, so cold it was burning hot. When it finally faded to a stop, the rebels' eyes wandered upward. A jagged stone outcropping towered above the walls of ice, shrouded in mist, and upon it...

The skeleton of a ghaengste.

Their hearts pounded, their ragged breaths caught.

It stared at them, its hollow eye sockets judging their worth.

Then yellow suns exploded into gleaming light from inside its skull.

The fog cleared, and the beast was revealed.

An old man, fur as thick and black as oblivion itself. His body was marked in white that surrounded his face and painted down his legs and ribs like exposed bones. Around his sockets was deep black, terrible gaping black, and his eyes glowed a bright feral yellow that cut the rebels down into helpless children. The dark horns jutting out from the sides of his head were monstrous and curved, and gigantic saber-like fangs hung far past his bearded chin. The mark of the lunai.

The wind quieted its raging as if to bow at his feet; it wouldn't dare speak over him. His gaze traced over the ghaengste before him, searching so deep inside them they could feel it like a sharp blade exploring inside their rib cages. Then his haunting eyes landed on the giant young man of the forest. When the skeleton ghaengste opened his mouth, the air froze over, commanded by his word. His voice came out in an archaic whisper that rumbled through the essence of the mountains, old as time itself.

"Kodokuna."

9

PROPHECY

No wind. No sound at all.

Bu-bump, bu-bump.

Just cold, still air and eyes of yellow fire boring into his soul.

Bu-bump, bu-bump, bu-bump.

They knew him.

Bu-bump, bu-bump, bu-bump, bu-bump.

They knew him better than he knew himself. They sliced him open and dissected him, they recognized each fiber of his soul. They remembered him.

They knew his name.

Kodo was frozen aside from the desperate beating of his hearts; with each passing second, he feared they might explode in his chest. The hair on the back of his shoulders stood on end as he stared into the glowing eyes of the skeleton ghaengste. He was drowning; everything was slow and heavy, he couldn't breathe.

"Who are you?" Leida demanded, but her voice sounded muffled to Kodo, his own pulse so loud he could barely hear. The skeleton ghaengste looked down on them like a king on his throne, but Leida stood as tall and imposing as a usurper.

The stranger lifted his chin and his hoarse whisper echoed down the icy canyon like the wind itself.

"Thank you, Mother."

The rebels glanced at one another, except for Leida, who kept her gaze focused on the man perched above them.

"How do you know his name?" she demanded, her voice louder now. Alvi and Rykr came to rest on either side of her. Kodo remained frozen behind them, his companions a wall between him and the old man.

The skeleton ghaengste gracefully fell from his perch, his massive feet slamming into the cerulean ice as a spider web of cracks shot in every direction beneath him. The canyon faltered and shook under his weight. Even larger and more robust than Rykr, he would dwarf most other mountain dwellers. His eyes raised and traced over the ghaengste before him. They studied Leida first, then the wounded and weakened ocean woman quivering beside her. The stranger's gaze made its way to Rykr. He seemed to hesitate on the younger mountain dweller, and for a moment, his eyes nearly looked pitiful.

His voice came out powerfully this time, as if he were calling out into the unknown expanse of the afterlife.

"It has been a long time, my son."

Kodo found his breath again, but it came out in a ragged, shaky heave as he realized the stranger was no longer looking at Rykr.

He was looking at him.

The skeleton man stepped forward, and Kodo could only watch. He begged himself to move, speak, do something. But his words wouldn't come out; they tangled together at the back of his throat and refused to budge.

"Not another step," Rykr barked, and Leida's wings spread out from her sides to guard the other rebels. The old beast didn't seem to be listening, his gaze remained on Kodo.

It was different than anything he'd seen before. The cadmium fire of the stranger's eyes was as deep as an ocean and as sharp as a sword. There were no questions, only answers. It read Kodo in a way he could not read himself. It told him a story he could not yet comprehend.

"I will not ask again," Leida slowly hissed. "Who are you?"

The skeleton man's all-consuming tone boomed through the icy canyon again like the word of a god.

"*I am the Blood Prince.*" His voice, though not raised, roared with power and defiance.

"*I am the Black Revenant.*" It carried the spirit and energy of a charging army and rang out as gospel within the minds of the rebels.

"*I am Vaus-Kaishek, the Lost King.*

"*And you are my son, Kodokuna.*"

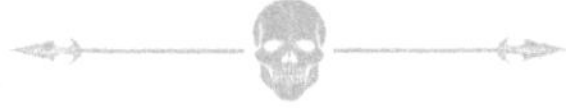

Sherri sipped her coffee as she read through a stack of lab reports. She absentmindedly rubbed her ankle, feeling where a bulky brace used to be while her peers filed into the kitchen.

"Daniels."

She startled as she finally noticed Doctor Novak leaning against the counter beside her, apparently attempting to get her attention.

"Oh, good morning," she greeted him, regaining her bearings.

"Morning. What did the doctors say?" he asked.

"What?"

"About your hearing."

Harrison stepped on the back of his shoe.

"*Watch it*, Rosenquest. You lumber around like a damn gorilla," Marshall snapped, and the other man scowled in rare impatience.

Sherri couldn't help a sigh, but then she straightened up and shook off the remnants of a fitful slumber.

"My right eardrum ruptured. They don't think I'll regain my hearing naturally, but I can get a cochlear implant back home," she explained. Marshall watched her for a moment, then nodded.

"Why?" she asked.

"Just curious." He shrugged as he took a sip of his coffee.

Gradually, the commons picked up momentum as the crew retrieved their morning cups of coffee and began to shed the weight of exhaustion.

Harrison lifted the bottom of his necktie to wipe some excess milk off Giovanni's mustache, only to be slapped away by his younger brother. Harrison raised his hands in surrender.

"Maybe you should consider wearing a tie so I don't have to use mine," he mocked, roughly pinching Gio's cheek and getting swatted again.

"How would he wear a tie?" Doyle teased. "He only buttons his shirt up to his navel."

A few laughs loosened up the surrounding scientists as they all-too-eagerly criticized Giovanni's unprofessional choice of clothing and exposed chest hair.

"Ha, ha." Gio rolled his eyes. "Tell me again, Doyle, why you're an oceanographer and not a comedian?"

"Too much sex appeal as a comedian; my wife couldn't handle the groupies," Doyle explained, and the air filled with a chorus of groans. Sherri, however, was hardly paying attention to their joshing. She was observing the men around her, one in particular catching her eye. He hadn't said anything, hadn't participated in the banter. Sweat beaded on his forehead. He made eye contact with no one.

Roger.

He had been avoiding work for weeks; he'd barely spoken to them at all. He stayed in his room most of the day, and not even Marshall seemed to know what he was doing in there, despite being his roommate. They all knew he'd been having a hard time, sure, but the rest of them had begun to bounce back from their first fatal encounter. It seemed, perhaps, his knee wasn't the only part of him that had been dislocated.

...

"Alright, let's talk tree recovery," Sherri began eagerly as she hopped on the counter while the rest of her colleagues found their seats in the lab.

"What did we learn from the dental impressions? For starters, I was able to determine that the length of the lower mandible, front teeth to back teeth, was about thirty-three centimeters. The top jaw front to back teeth is thirty-nine centimeters. Based on the pattern of the teeth indent, I feel comfortable comparing the overall bite structure to an earthly big cat. Taking those proportions into account, I've estimated the skull of this specimen is likely somewhere between sixty and eighty centimeters. Tooth length was mostly inconclusive, but my loose estimate for the front canines is, say, seventeen centimeters."

Sherri beamed, almost struggling to keep her feet from kicking back and forth childishly. She glanced around the room to revel in the discoveries with her peers. She was met with expressions ranging from anxiety to horror, and she finally noticed that they did not share her enthusiasm.

"You people are no fun. Whatever, your turn." She waved them off, then gestured at Doctor Myles as if to pass the baton. He took a breath and wiped the disturbed look from his face.

"So far nothing conclusive on the diet front. The indents were littered with organic material, but it's impossible to determine what came from the teeth themselves versus what was already on the tree." Roger spoke quickly, as if he was trying to spit out the words in fear of not saying them all.

"Did anyone measure the circumference of the tree?" Doyle piped up, sitting up a little straighter in his chair.

"I did." Sherri grabbed her journal and flipped through it. "One-hundred-and-ninety-three point two centimeters."

Doyle's brows furrowed, then he grabbed a piece of scratch paper and a calculator and began scribbling down an equation. Sherri leaned over to watch his paper, ignoring the look of irritation on his face.

"I'll take that as my turn," Marshall tapped in, stealing her attention from Doyle's math.

"I was able to get minute trace samples of the gas particles left on the tree, and cross-examined that with the control air sample I took while we were out there," he began, and a twinkle formed in his eye. He leaned back in his chair, setting his feet on top of his desk.

"Does anyone remember the barium content in the air I was so curious about weeks ago?" he mused with a distinct smugness.

"Well," Marshall continued, "I discovered a presence of barium sulfate merged with the gas particles on the tree. I found this interesting, obviously, as the atmosphere contains pure barium."

He looked around the room as if he were keeping a secret.

"Now, class, who can tell me why we require respirators on this planet?"

"Get to the fucking point, Novak," Doyle snapped, briefly looking up from his calculator.

"Wrong. We need respirators because barium is *toxic*." Marshall grabbed a rubber ball off his desk and tossed it in the air, then caught it in his hand. "Who knows the difference between pure barium and barium sulfate?"

He glanced around the room.

"Barium sulfate is insoluble, for one," Sherri answered, following along impatiently.

"Precisely, Doctor Daniels," he sang, then tossed the ball to Harrison, who caught it with ease and threw it back significantly harder.

"Alright, Avogadro," Harrison said. "Care to dumb it down for the non-chemists?"

A satisfied smirk crossed Marshall's lips.

"The native specimens of this planet have a respiratory system which allows them to convert and dilute the atmosphere. They breathe in the barium-tainted air and breathe out barium sulfate. My theory is that the process is strikingly similar to our own process of cell respiration. In other words, their respiratory system is likely congruent to our own, except they're breathing in poison and converting it to its nontoxic form. Cool, right?"

His colleagues raised their eyebrows at his theory. Sherri studied Marshall's smiling mouth just a little too intently and for a little too long. With as little data as they had, it was a damn good find. What could she say?

"Nice work, Novak." She acknowledged him with a professional nod.

"Yeah, yeah, we can all stroke Novak's dick — I mean ego — later," Doyle interrupted with a sneer. "But are you sure your measurements were correct, Daniels?"

"Positive. Why?" she demanded. The oceanographer slid a piece of paper across his desk to show her.

"Because either you botched the measurements..."

Sherri picked up the paper and her eyes widened.

"Or this thing can unhinge its jaw."

The room was quiet for several moments as everyone shifted in their seats. The more of an image they got of this monster, the more Sherri realized they knew nothing about the planet they'd been sent to settle.

"That raises the question..." she slowly began, glancing up from the scrap paper in her hands. She made eye contact with Roger; the ecologist's face was frozen like a corpse.

"Why... would it need to be able to unhinge its jaw..." he whispered under his breath, his voice quivering. Harrison placed a hand on his shoulder.

"Now, there's no need to let our imaginations run wild just yet. We're scientists, not dreamers." Harrison cleared his throat. "This thing is an organism like any other, and we'll just have to treat it the same as we'd treat any back on Earth. It's an animal, not a monster. Keep your heads on your shoulders, gentlemen."

He looked around the room, and Sherri gave him a grateful look, silently thanking him for being the voice of reason. Of course, he always was. She patted her legs.

"Well, back to work I guess," she said, hopping down from the counter. Doyle scoffed.

"Come on, I don't get so much as a 'good catch, Doyle. Thanks for your work?' Unbelievable," he said and waved off his peers.

"Don't get all sentimental on me now, Doyle." Sherri mocked him with a smirk. "You know I hate you all equally."

Kodo didn't even get a chance to swallow what he'd heard before Rykr's voice rang out through the canyon.

"*Liar*. The Lost King is dead!"

"No, boy, my blood is as hot as yours," the old man bellowed back, his monstrous voice filling the icy air around them.

"I don't like this, Leida..." Alvi whispered uneasily from close by Leida's left side. Kodo looked between his friends with helpless confusion, but Rykr wouldn't meet his gaze.

"What does he speak of?" Leida asked Rykr.

"Vaus-Kaishek was my uncle," Rykr snarled. "He died long ago; this man wears his legacy as a *fucking mask!*"

His words exploded through the air so ferociously the ice seemed like it might shatter. Kodo's head spun, his thoughts trailing off and disappearing before he could finish them.

"My father?" His voice came out like a stray child's, confused and desperate for the guidance of a mother who wasn't there. Rykr snapped around to face him.

"*Shut up, Kodo,* he's not your father. He's not even one of your kind," the other man spat harshly, and Kodo flinched and quieted. It was true, he knew it was true.

"He's a fucking imposter," Rykr barked, turning back to the stranger, "And he will admit his disgrace, or he will die where he stands in the Lost King's name."

"Rykr," Leida warned from beside him, staring at the side of his face. They did not have the luxury of fighting battles for the family he'd already abandoned. All they had were fragments of an incomplete story and a stranger claiming kinship with two lost young men.

Rykr ignored her.

"One more chance," the angry young man bellowed, his claws scraping the ice. "Tell the truth, or I swear I will rip your hearts from your chest and lay them on his grave as an offering.

"Who are you!?"

The skeleton ghaengste took another step forward, his piercing eyes gleaming with hellfire. He lifted his head proudly, steam billowing from his nostrils like flames, lit by the yellow light of his gaze. He stared straight into Rykr, straight through his rage and his terror and his sorrow.

"I am Vaus-Kaishek, the Lost King of the Eidolan clan."

His words raised louder, screaming like a vicious blizzard.

"Son of Vaus-Ti'khal."

His claws unsheathed into the ice with a splitting fissure.

"Brother of Vaus-Ramaala."

His voice roared deep from the core of the mountains, the wind picking up and blowing his wild gray mane around his heavy shoulders.

"Father of Kodokuna."

Rykr's guttural bellow filled the air as he lunged.

Marshall walked down the corridor with his hands in his pockets, certainly in no rush; there was nothing to rush for. He whistled the tune to a song by the Beatles, but he couldn't quite remember which song it was, only the melody. He heard someone else turn into the hall behind him but didn't pay them any mind.

"Hey, where are you headed?"

A familiar voice called behind him; youthful, but a little raspy. Doctor Daniels fell in stride beside him and he stopped whistling.

"Storage 226, I figured I'd take a fresh look at the hat sample from the invisible man. See if we missed anything," he said, watching her.

"I came to ask if you'd gotten the results back from the atmospheric process test?" she asked.

"No, not yet. I'll let you know when I do." Marshall paused. "Was that it?"

Sherri looked up at him, her chin subtly cocked to one side.

"No, not quite. What had you so interested in my hearing this morning?"

Marshall stopped walking, looking down into Sherri's eyes. He crossed his arms loosely across his chest and leaned back against the wall of the corridor.

"I told you, I was curious. I need to know which side of you to stand on."

"Uh-huh... and what's with that snotty little look on your face?"

Marshall smirked coyly.

"Because you didn't come to ask about the test results."

Sherri raised her eyebrow with an indignant look.

"And what makes you say that, Sherlock?"

"Because you know when I started the test, and you know the results wouldn't quite have developed yet."

Her face fell into the look of someone who'd been caught red handed and was deciding how to talk her way out of it. She shrugged off his observation.

"And why do *you* deduce I came to find you?" she asked, and Marshall chewed on his lower lip.

"Because you like me, and you want me to admit that I asked about your hearing out of concern for your wellbeing."

"Well, did you?"

"No, I needed to know which side of you to stand on."

Sherri rolled her eyes but failed to stifle a small chuckle.

"You're a cocky bastard, Novak, that's for sure," she scolded, placing her hands on her hips and shaking her head.

"Guilty as charged."

Marshall reached out to her, gently grabbing the hem of her white lab coat. He'd noticed she was wearing it out of the lab, for once. She must have left in a rush. He gently tugged her closer, slowly drawing her toward him. She gave him a daring look, as if silently asking him what he'd do next. Being so close, she had to crane her neck in order to look at his face.

"I see the way you look at me, you know," he whispered as he studied the freckles sprinkled across her nose and cheeks. Sherri's hand rested on his tie, and her normally devious brown eyes were suddenly curious and girlish.

"How do I look at you?" she whispered back, and he could feel himself getting lost in her gaze. *Those damn doe eyes.*

He regained his focus and leaned down slowly, glancing down at her shapely lips.

"Like you want me."

A nearly undetectable smile tugged at the corners of her rosy mouth. She leaned up on the tips of her toes, nearly bringing her lips to his, but stopping just before they touched. She looked deeply into his eyes.

"Well... do you want me?" she asked gently, her tone laced with a hint of innocence. Marshall's voice came out in a breathy whisper.

"Yes."

Sherri's face twisted into a malicious smirk, her doe eyes becoming that of a sly fox.

"I thought you just wanted to know which side of me to stand on," she mocked in an exaggerated coy tone, but she cut herself off with a laugh as she broke character. She reached up and flicked him under the chin, then popped off the tips of her toes with a smug grin. Her coat fell from his weak grasp as she stepped away. Marshall could only look at the ground, shaking his head and biting back an embarrassed smile. For once, he was speechless.

Sherri began to back away with her amusement painfully clear on her face, tightening her ponytail as she headed back to where she'd come from.

"Let me know if you find anything on the cap, okay? Oh, and your test results should be back by now." She glanced down at her watch and chuckled again in her usual cocky way, then turned and trotted off, leaving Marshall alone with his bruised ego.

The skeleton ghaengste ducked past Rykr's open jaws, then headbutted him under the chin so hard his teeth snapped together with an aching crack. Another blow came from his massive horns and Rykr skidded across the ice, his claws screeching against the cold frost. Leida appeared at his side but she glared at him with impatience. The violence had shaken Kodo out of his frozen stupor, and he rushed to Rykr's other side as he pushed Alvi behind him to protect her.

The stranger stared at them with a haunting, ghostly calmness. He wrenched open his maw and belted out a barbaric cry that deafened them and vibrated their bones. The canyon shook and cracked, like a living beast awoken from a slumber it never should have been raised from.

Leida took flight and dove for his neck but he dodged again, rolling over onto his shoulder and onto his feet, anchoring himself to the icy ground. Just as he rose, Rykr lurched. Rykr's fangs were seconds from burying themselves in the old man's throat, but the skeleton ghaengste rammed his wide horns and threw Rykr into the wall of ice. It cracked violently beneath his weight as he tumbled to the ground. Leida attacked from above, but instead of her claws goring into fur and flesh, they hit solid ice as the stranger disappeared into a gap in the canyon wall they hadn't seen before. He vanished into the deep blue, and Kodo slid to Rykr's side to help him up.

"You okay?" he asked, recoiling as Rykr jumped to his feet.

"I'm fine," he growled, shoving past Kodo and heading straight for the slim crevice.

"Rykr," Leida urged. "We do not have time for this. Leave him."

She headed for Alvi, who was shivering and panting from being on her feet in her still weakened state. The wounded woman shook her head and waved Leida off, forcing her hunched posture straight.

"If you want to leave, then leave," Rykr snapped, still marching after the stranger as blood dripped from his mouth.

"Why do you care?" Kodo exclaimed. "You left your clan. Whose honor are you defending?"

Rykr flipped around and bared his teeth at Kodo, his sharp eyes bloodshot.

"You don't know the first thing about honor," he spat. "Just go. This isn't your fight."

"But he knew —"

"I said get lost."

Rykr turned and disappeared into the crevice after the skeleton ghaengste, leaving his companions behind. They looked between one another after he left, their eyes showing their hurt and confusion. Then Kodo shook his head and ran after Rykr first, followed by Leida and Alvi.

They found themselves in a closed tunnel made of ice that was such a vibrant blue it painted everything within it cyan. Their breath plumed out of their nostrils in glowing turquoise clouds, and it seemed the tunnel itself was producing a slight hum. The skeleton ghaengste was nowhere to be seen.

"What are you doing here?" Rykr whispered as Alvi snaked between his legs.

"Same as you," she whispered back through chattering teeth. "Getting ourselves killed."

Rykr shook his head and drove forward through the winding tunnel, his companions reluctantly following.

"Who are you really, old man?" he called out, his voice bouncing between every wall and curve of the glowing passageway.

Kodo had to hunch over to squeeze through the tight cavern. He kept glancing at Rykr's face, looking for answers he knew the other man didn't have. He still didn't know how the skeleton ghaengste knew his name, or why he'd make up such outlandish lies like claiming a son of a different race. He opened his mouth to suggest to Rykr that they were simply chasing an old madman who was spouting confused nonsense, but he was interrupted by a deep voice. The even rumble sounded throughout the chamber, seemingly coming from within the walls of ice.

"I am Kaishek, the Lost King."

The haunting echo surrounded them. Rykr's face twisted in rage and he trudged onward through the tunnel.

The passage opened to a labyrinth of paths, blindingly blue like an ocean and sparkling like a galaxy of stars. The rebels turned in circles, overwhelmed by the ethereal scenery.

"I ruled the Eidolan clan with my brother for many strong years, before our nation was ravaged by famine and plague."

The voice of the skeleton ghaengste vibrated the ice around them; their entire world buzzed with words from the man they couldn't see.

"The plague took our children from us, and the famine took our elders."

They searched the surrounding area, but the source of the voice remained hidden. Alvi stood still, her ears perked as she listened.

"This way," she whispered, creeping down a side tunnel as the voice reverberated around them, and her friends followed close behind. Rykr's hearts began to beat so hard his companions could feel it through the ice below them.

"My brother, Ramaala, had two sons born in the midst of the tragedy. Twins."

Rykr's eyes widened, his jaw clenched.

"The plague took one of the infant boys. The other lived."

The rebels all looked to Rykr, his stubborn face falling weak in acceptance.

"My brother…" he whispered, his voice wavering. The tone rang through the cavern again as a tear threatened to fall from Rykr's eye.

"I had no choice but to leave our homeland in my brother's care while I ventured down from the mountains to seek food for my people."

Alvi's head snapped to the side as she locked onto the voice, and she ushered her companions down another passage.

"But I found more than just new herds in the grazing lands, I found more than I sought," the voice echoed louder. *"I found a woman."*

The hive of tunnels was suddenly alive with energy, as if it had its own chilling heartbeat. They were close. The voice grew louder, defiant and forceful.

"A forest woman."

The ice whistled a haunting tune, accompanying the low voice that clamored stubbornly through its caverns.

"And despite the ferocity with which I fought my own hearts, I fell in love with her."

The voice was right next to them, all around them now, and they hesitated as the passage opened to a wider grotto.

"Iva."

Kodo stopped in his tracks.

For a moment he forgot how to breathe the icy air into his lungs; his blood seemed to freeze in his veins. He thought he'd never hear that name again.

Mama…

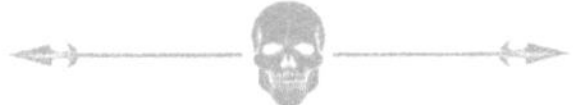

Master Sergeant Fischer cleaned her spotless rifle in silence, precious silence; the barracks were empty during physical training drills and that was the closest she'd ever get to heaven. Her serenity was stolen away as the doors swung open.

"I said I've got it, Ma."

Captain Short and Master Sergeant Mendoza walked side by side into the barracks. They studied a clipboard held between them; Mendoza seemed to be teaching the captain about the layout of the fitness scorecards.

"Who's supervising PT?" Fischer called over as she looked between them.

"I am," the captain answered without looking up from the clipboard, rubbing his close-cut goatee with his knuckle.

"You?" She shared a skeptical glance with Mendoza, who had already begun to fold his laundry in the corner.

"Yeah, me," Captain Short said with a defensive edge to his tone. "You're doing inventory. I'll send someone to assist."

Fischer went back to polishing her rifle like a priceless gem, but she nodded offhandedly.

"How about Sanchez?"

"Sure."

The captain was already heading in the direction of the gym. Fischer shook her head as both she and Mendoza watched him leave.

"What's with him?" she asked when she was sure he was out of earshot. The other master sergeant shrugged as he sorted towels.

"I think he just wants to be more involved with the unit," Mendoza replied. "It's good for him. He's been taking things hard, after Krei and Torres. And Taylor."

"Sentimental one, ain't he?" Fischer scoffed. Mendoza laughed in the jolly way he always did, quietly but from deep in his belly.

"Let's keep that between us, ah?" he said, still smiling as a short, stocky woman with a long brown ponytail leaned in past the doorway.

"Captain said you needed a hand with inventory?" Sergeant Sanchez asked, tapping the door frame with an expectant look. Fischer nodded and packed up her rifle, motioning for Sanchez to follow as she headed toward the armory. She dodged Mendoza's warm, knowing gaze as they left.

As soon as the armory door shut, their mouths met hungrily and desperately, starved for the taste of one another. Fischer had to lean down to meet the shorter woman's lips, grasping her jaw with eager fingers. Sanchez pushed up into the kiss, blindly fumbling to get Fischer's belt undone as they huffed and panted in one another's breath. Their lips parted just long enough for Fischer to peel the tank top off Sanchez's tan skin, but she had no time to admire the sight before a hand snaked down her undone pants, firmly grasping the crotch of her underwear. Electricity shot through the depths of Fischer's belly and she squeezed her eyes shut for a moment. She breathed slowly as Sanchez sucked at her neck and massaged her clit through soaked fabric.

"Don't leave hickeys," Fischer breathed, her hoarse voice missing some of its normal sharpness. Sanchez wrapped her arm around the Master Sergeant's neck, pulling her closer down to playfully nip at her earlobe.

"Why, scared the captain will see?" she teased. "Thought you were a gambler, Fischer."

Fischer shook her head and pulled Sanchez closer into their embrace.

"Not a gambler, hon, I'm house. I've got no stake," she replied, holding onto Sanchez's face to catch her lips for another deep kiss. Their mouths danced together, locked in each other's clutch for another moment, until Sanchez pulled away.

"House always has the most at stake, don't you forget it," she challenged with a sly grin, resting the tip of her tongue between her teeth. Fischer shook her head chidingly and kissed the other sergeant again, harder, to end the dreadful scourge of speaking. The kiss didn't last long, but the conversation didn't resume either as Sanchez took to a knee. Fischer leaned her head back and her shoulders relaxed at the anticipation of relief.

Fischer released a long, hissing sigh as Sanchez's tongue finally found its way between her slick labia for a firm lick. As the other woman's warm mouth massaged her, the intensity following the guidance of her huffing and moaning, a tingling buzz traveled over every inch of her fair skin. She hung onto the pulsations of rippling energy that shuddered through her core and out through her limbs, rolling her hips with the rhythm of Sanchez's tongue. Her abdomen became hot and sore as heat traveled through every sensitive muscle, and the gasping breaths of both soldiers filled the unwelcoming armory with a rare moment of heavenly escape.

...

Marshall was rarely one of the first back in the lab after lunch, but something about the invisible man's cap was calling to him. They must have gone over it fifty times by now, but every once in a while, it seemed that last ditch fifty-first time was all it took. He was surprised to see an unlikely colleague back in the lab early as well — Doctor Myles. Had he even been at lunch? Marshall couldn't remember. No matter, he quickly sat down at his desk to prepare a slide for the cap sample and take another look under the microscope.

He set his glasses to the side and closed one eye to look through the microscope lens. Cotton fibers, dead blood cells, a close-cut hair. Obvious, useless, boring.

Marshall jolted as someone whispered in his ear. No, not in his ear; from across the room. Was it whispering or breathing? He lifted his head and put his glasses back on, peering at the other man in the lab.

Roger was at his workstation, facing away from him and whispering. To himself it seemed, maybe silently rambling or babbling. Marshall watched and listened for a moment, but he couldn't pick out any coherent words.

"Myles."

The man jumped in his seat, nearly knocking several things off his desk. He turned around, and Marshall studied his clammy face.

"...You okay?" Marshall asked. Roger nodded vigorously.

"I'm fine," he said with a chuckle, wiping the sweat off his brow and abruptly getting up to step out of the room. Marshall watched him leave, then shook his head and turned back to his work. As he studied the dead soldier's blood cells once again, Roger's words bounced around in his mind.

We shouldn't be here... they tried to warn us...

Don't you see?

Nothing else matters anymore.

Marshall shook off the eerie words as the rest of the research team entered after lunch. He watched as they milled around and went back to their stations, like airplanes on autopilot. He paused on Doyle, disgust crossing his face as he witnessed the oceanographer shove an entire half of a tuna sandwich in his mouth. Without taking his eyes off Doyle's grotesque eating habits, he rolled his chair across the aisle to Sherri's station as she sat down.

"Notice anything weird about Myles lately?" he whispered next to Sherri's good ear as his gaze wandered to the door where the ecologist reentered with a fresh cup of coffee. She glanced up, observing Roger as he made his way to his own station.

"Weirder than usual?" she whispered back.

"Yes."

"I hardly see him at all these days," she muttered with a sigh. "Though I did notice something last week that I wanted to talk about, but I haven't had the chance. Think you can keep him distracted for a few minutes?"

A mischievous smirk crawled across Marshall's face.

"I've got some ideas."

"Kodo?"

The rebels now all stared at their youngest companion, who had halted behind them with his face washed in horror.

"That was my mother's name..." Kodo whispered so quietly it was barely audible.

The godlike voice boomed through the tunnels again, this time as a deafening roar. It made Kodo's teeth chatter and his muscles tense.

"I was discovered with her by my comrades, and I was to be brought back to my own kingdom as a prisoner. A blasphemer and a traitor."

It wasn't the same woman, it couldn't be. But there was something about the way the strange man said her name, like it came from all three of his hearts at once. It echoed through Kodo's ears so loud it hurt; he wanted nothing more than to scream. Only a shaky exhale came out.

"Before I was taken to be tried, Iva gave birth to a single son."

The words shot through his hearts like lightning.

"My son."

Tension pulsed throughout the tunnels, rolling through Kodo's body on a bloody crusade as it filled every inch of him with terror. His companions now stared at him with expressions of disbelief. Even Rykr did not protest, the anger and denial drained from his face.

"No..." Kodo whispered, but it was lost to the ice in the tunnels.

The story of the skeleton ghaengste crashed over him and forced him to heed its call, accept its truth, hear its name.

"She named him Kodokuna. Wanderer."

When the voice came again, it was no longer thundering through the mountain. It was calm and close behind them; the roaring petered out to a soft hum.

"She said one day he would wander across the gap between our worlds and unite our family." The skeleton ghaengste stood at the end of the tunnel as still as a statue, watching them.

The young giant quivered in horror and sorrow. He understood. Finally, devastatingly, he understood.

Beast of beasts.

He was the enemy of their world. The symbol of what could not be. He had spent his entire life desperate to understand why his people did not claim him, why he never belonged. He knew now that they were never his people.

He did not have a people. He did not have a place. They could all see it in his eyes, and smell it in his tainted flesh. He was the spawn of an unholy union that haunted their very existence, towering over them in the form of the monstrous behemoth that grew like an infection alongside their people.

The very blood that ran through his veins was impure.

The Lost King stepped toward the rebels.

"Stay away from me," Kodo snarled, but his voice cracked as he turned away. Leida stood between Kodo and the old man.

"What do you want with him?" she asked.

"I want him to know." Kaishek's voice still filled the cavern, but its harsh edge had softened. The gentle rumbling of a storm from inside a sheltered cave, it reverberated through the ice. He paused for a moment, looking over the four young ghaengste. Four torn worlds, brought back together by the Great Mother.

"To know that I'm an abomination?" Kodo hissed, "To know that I'm a dirty mongrel? A halfbreed?"

The flame in the old man's burning eyes grew warm and still.

"To know that you are where you are supposed to be," Kaishek answered. "Standing alongside the people of the other worlds as allies, not enemies. Wandering across the gap."

The four rebels hesitated but stood close beside one another, the savagery of their world close on their heels, and an uncertain future just out of their reach. Kaishek nodded at them, his gaze lingering on Alvi.

"Your friend from the sea is hurt," he observed gently. "She needs food and warmth. Please, come."

The old man turned his back on them, walking away through the tunnel. A warm green light flickered at the other end, seeming to have only just appeared. The rebels looked between one another in uncertainty. Kodo's face was weak, ashamed, and terrified, a child cast aside without a home. Rykr's jaw was clenched in a pain he bore silently, and a confusion he couldn't shake. Leida looked to Alvi, who quivered violently as she struggled to remain on her feet, her eyes heavy in aching exhaustion.

Leida turned, leading her companions after the mysterious Lost King.

Giovanni whistled as he finished his preliminary notes, then got up from his seat. He resumed his jovial whistling along the way to the refrigerated storage unit across the hall, and all the way back into lab A. He carried a tray of cataloged soil and sediment samples, not in any particular rush as he headed to his station.

His foot caught on something.

Giovanni stumbled and dropped the tray. Sample jars sprawled in all directions, shattering as plumes of dirt showered the ground and everything else in the vicinity. He looked around wildly for what he'd tripped over, then froze.

A foot jutted out from behind the desk next to him, and when his eyes wandered upwards to find the face of the person it belonged to, his rage boiled over.

"Novak, you bloody moron!" he snapped, quickly kneeling to assess the destruction.

Doctor Novak feigned an innocent look.

"I'm sorry, Rosenquest, I should have been paying closer attention to where I rested my legs." Marshall shook his head in exaggerated guilt. "But we should start cleaning this up, yeah? By now sediment microparticles are filling the air, and we have no idea what breathing this stuff in could do."

Giovanni was already heading to where they kept the broom and dustpan, a furious scowl on his face as he snatched it off the wall.

Everyone else now watched the ordeal, and Sherri glanced around in alarm until she noticed one important detail as the scene unfolded. She spotted Roger, nervously pinned against the wall in order to get as far from the alien substance as possible. Marshall abruptly erupted into a coughing fit, and Sherri caught on to the charade. *One hell of a distraction.*

She covered her face with her arm and also began faking a harsh cough. The two received confused looks from Doyle, Carl, and Harrison, and Giovanni was too busy sweeping to pay any mind. Sherri felt a pang of guilt watching him; she hadn't intended for there to be casualties.

"I'll just go get some water while you clean that up." Roger wheezed, his voice hoarse and his face pinched as he rushed out of the room. Sherri and Marshall's coughing turned to laughter after he left, and Marshall slid his chair over to offer a high five which Sherri reluctantly returned. He had gotten the job done, after all.

The four other men in the room stared at them, appearing completely lost.

"Shit, why didn't anyone tell me it was 'terrorize Roger day'?" Doyle exclaimed. "I didn't get the email!"

"We needed him out of here so we could talk," Marshall explained. "Rosenquest, quit sweeping."

"Uh, there could be some actual health concerns if I don—"

"It's standard potting soil from the terrosphere, it won't hurt us. Your samples are safe, I switched them out."

"Oh."

Giovanni looked slightly impressed and returned to his desk to sit back down.

"What do we need to talk about that doesn't include Roger?" Gio asked. Sherri took over.

"Roger."

She got up from her chair to come closer to the congregation, leaning back against Doyle's table.

"Last week I saw him coming out of the control room looking guilty. I suspected he'd sent a message to mission control without consulting us, so I took a look through the log but found nothing. I still think he did it but covered his tracks. He knew damn well we'd decided to draft that transmission as a group; we're not going to function up here if we can't make decisions as a team."

"Well, we can't prove that just because he looked guilty." Harrison said.

"I'd say that's the least of our problems. Earlier, I heard him rambling incoherently to himself like something out of a horror movie," Marshall remarked from his seat as he tossed a rubber ball around.

"Sounds like a healthy way to de-stress to me," Doyle replied.

"This is serious," Sherri argued. "If Roger really is struggling to hold it together, we could have some major problems. We don't have a qualified psychiatric professional up here. The only mental health resource mission control sent with us is that damn yoga breathing DVD." She huffed in frustration.

"I thought the breathing DVD was a nice touch," Harrison interjected with a timid shrug. They all looked at him as if he'd said something in Latin until Carl broke the awkward silence.

"Look, obviously Roger is having trouble dealing with the pressure. We all are. I say we just call him back in here and talk to him like grown-ups."

"And say what, exactly?" Marshall butted in. "'We think you're losing it, buddy, maybe you should take some time off and —' oh wait, *he can't!* Maybe that's his problem."

"Maybe that's whose problem?" a quiet voice called out from the doorway, and the rest of the research team turned around. There stood Roger, clutching a cup of water and tapping it anxiously. The other scientists looked between one another. Harrison cleared his throat as Giovanni started sweeping again.

"Ah, have a seat, Doctor Myles." Harrison gestured to the ecologist's station. "We wanted to talk to you about how you've been feeling and how we can help. We're a bit worried, mate."

Roger slowly shuffled to his seat, watching closely as Giovanni finished cleaning up.

"We know you sent that transmission to Houston without including us. What the hell?" Sherri couldn't hold her tongue, receiving shocked glares from her colleagues. Roger's eyes widened.

"I just — it was urgent, and you..." Roger blinked hard, shaking his head. "It's urgent, don't you people see that? We can't just sit around drafting! We need to act, we need *help.*"

"...Okay, I'm sorry." Sherri exhaled gently, biting the inside of her mouth. "But we need to talk about these things as a —"

"There's nothing to talk about," Roger exclaimed, his voice cracking.

"We're trapped here with those — those monsters, and god knows what else. What the hell do we have to talk about? It's already over." His eyes began to get misty and bloodshot, his breathing heavier as he loosened his tie.

"Have a drink, mate," Harrison softly suggested. "Let's all calm down for a moment. How can we help?"

Sherri glanced uneasily around the lab; all eyes were on Roger.

"I don't need a *drink,*" Roger snapped. "You can't help, no one can. They don't care about us. I need to — I just need real air, I want to go home," he rambled, rubbing the back of his neck and bouncing his shaky knee.

"Breathe, Roger, take a deep breath," Harrison said in a soothing voice, and went to place a tentative hand on Roger's shoulder. Roger jolted away.

"Don't touch me, don't tell me to —" he spat, trailing off as he stood up from his chair.

Harrison stepped away, raising his hands in surrender and quietly apologizing.

"I can't breathe in here," Roger muttered, abruptly shoving his way out the door. The rest of the team sat in silence after he left.

Sherri let out the breath she'd been holding and pushed her stubborn curls out of her face. She rubbed her eyes, already racking her brain for anything else that might offer a solution.

"That went well." Doyle was the first to break the quiet tension.

"Shut the fuck up," Marshall whispered.

"Excuse me?"

"Doyle, shut the fuck up. Do you hear that?"

Sherri watched the quizzical faces of the men around her, frustration rising in her throat. They clearly heard something, but she didn't. She firmly pressed her palm over her deaf ear in a vain attempt to muffle a ringing that wasn't there. Squeezing her eyes shut tight, she desperately tried to focus on only her good ear. There it was — a faint whirring sound.

She could hear it.

A faint whirring sound and then a deep clang.

Her chair clattered over on its side as she tore out of the room.

IO
GENESIS

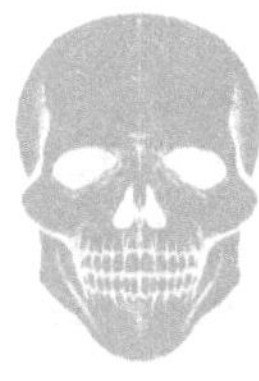

Sherri slammed through the lab doors, her heart pounding as she sprinted through the corridor.

"Roger!" she cried, begging him to hear her. Begging him to stop. Begging for her ear to be deceiving her. Her pleas were ignored as she rounded the corner, and her heart dropped into her stomach.

The exit door was open, a brilliant light illuminating the entryway. In the distance, there was no blue wall stretched between the fence poles. The barrier had been turned off.

"ROGER!" she screamed, lurching through the open door. She was yanked back by the arm before her feet even met the grass beneath the stoop.

"Ma'am, get back from the door," barked the soldier who'd grabbed her, Master Sergeant Fischer. Sherri thrashed against the other woman's strong hold.

"My colleague is out there in the middle of an episode, *get the fuck off me,"* she snapped, but Fischer only dragged her away from the open portal. Captain Short came barreling past, slamming a magazine into his rifle as he shoved through the doorway.

"Hold her, we'll get him. *Keenan!*"

Sherri fought the urge to struggle more — spit, kick, do something. A sickened feeling poisoned her stomach and her heart raced. The feeling got worse as a large man with familiar deformed eyes jogged through the door. He tossed his cap off his head and onto the grass, letting out an enthusiastic cry.

"*Woooohooo,* we gonna kill us some aliens, Captain? Been dyin' to watch one of those fuckers go down. Where's the basketcase?" He whooped again, leaping a couple of steps ahead to land next to the captain like an overeager child.

Sherri could only watch in silent horror.

"Shut it, Corporal, I've got a mind to use you as bait," Short snapped as he searched the area. "*Doctor!* Get back here, man, it's not safe!"

They spotted him standing halfway across the meadow and facing away from them, his shoulders slack. The captain and the corporal marched through the brush cautiously, watching their surroundings with a close eye but keeping one on the scientist all times. He was completely relaxed, too relaxed, almost swaying with the breeze. Short whistled quietly through the side of his mouth, gesturing to the tree line to signal Keenan to watch it.

The air was cold with an incomprehensible dread.

"Doctor," Captain Short called. "I need you to start walking over here, can you do that for me?"

The old man didn't move. He appeared to be staring at the horizon, almost as if watching a movie.

"Doctor?"

The breeze sung whispers of warning, the tall grass fluttered and rattled ominous threats. Static filled the air like before a lightning strike, yet there was not a cloud in the sky. The tension kept building, nearing a breaking point, but the lightning didn't come. All remained still.

"Get over here, motherfucker!" Short barked through the eerie silence.

Roger seemed to start regaining awareness, his muscles began to come back to life, the tips of his fingers gently twitched.

Slowly, so slowly Short had to bite back another yell, the old man began to turn around. When his eyes landed on them, they looked bloodshot and tired. Not frightened, not sorrowful. Just exhausted. Like there was nothing left in him, his body empty where it stood.

"Come on," Short whispered under his breath, and Keenan readied his weapon.

Roger's shoulders were slumped, his expression blank. His gaze lazily traced over the meadow, his brows slightly furrowed as if he didn't know where he was and didn't particularly care.

"Come on, brother, *let's go,*" Short called out again more pleadingly, locking eyes with the old scientist. Slowly, hesitantly, the man took one shuffling step forward.

"Captain. Ten o'clock," Keenan said, aiming his rifle through the trees.

Two glowing dots. Completely still, shrouded in the darkness of the jungle.

"Move!" Short bellowed. Keenan's gaze remained trained through his scope.

"Out of range."

"Doctor!"

Roger finally seemed to come back to life, the light in his eyes rekindling all at once as he began to move.

Gunfire exploded through the meadow and Short grabbed a grenade off his belt, but Roger was in the creature's jaws before his second step even met the grass.

The native yanked Roger up and bit down; a thick spray of blood and a guttural scream of agony ripped from his throat and split through the still air. Roger thrashed, his shrieks gurgling and sputtering through the blood that filled his lungs and squirted from his mouth. The beast effortlessly tossed him in the sky, then caught him as its massive teeth drove through his chest and collapsed his ribcage like a rotten egg. His hellish cries were cut short, ending in the long squeal of a pig at slaughter. Then he went limp, his head and mangled limbs swinging back and forth weakly. Waterfalls of bright red blood and ropes of entrails steadily poured from the beast's giant maw, and it watched the two men in the meadow as it bit down again. Roger's bones were audibly crushed to shards as the life seeped out of him, along with the gooey scarlet blood flowing from his gaping eyes, his flared nostrils, his open mouth. Faint cries echoed behind them from the compound, hopeless and impossibly far away.

Like an insect underfoot, he was gone.

"You gonna use that grenade, there, Captain?" Keenan asked, backing away at a hurried pace as he rushed to reload his weapon. Short raised the grenade to his face, biting off the pin and spitting it out.

"Move. Move it," Short ordered as he reared back and hurled the grenade. It landed neatly at the native's front paws. Short grabbed Keenan by the back of the shirt and dragged him along as both men stumbled backward, unable to rip their eyes from the scene. The native looked curiously down at the projectile between its feet, the mutilated mass of blood, flesh, and organs that used to be Roger still in its jaws.

The explosion erupted through the field like a giant gunshot, sending the beast sprawling away and sliding across the grass. Short and Keenan both rolled to the ground, guarding their heads as shrapnel whizzed overhead and pelted the grass near their feet.

After the shockwave settled, Keenan immediately sat up, looking over the carnage.

"Eat that, bitch." The marine chuckled maniacally as the captain heaved himself to his feet. Short swiped off some of the dirt that covered his clothes, then rubbed the back of his neck. It was over as quickly as it had begun. Another battle lost, another life gone in the blink of an eye.

"Fuck," he hissed through clenched teeth as Keenan rose to his feet beside him.

"FUUUCK!" he roared at the planet, reeling back and kicking a clump of soil across the sprawling plain. He rested his hands on his hips, watching his boots in defeat. A faint cry.

No, several.

"Look!"

"Behind you!"

"Run!"

Keenan and Short's eyes met in exhausted horror.

Both men turned to see the monster roll onto its feet, stumbling for a second, then it shook its mighty head and thrashed its tail. It was singed and blackened but did not appear discouraged as it raised its devilish gaze to meet theirs, stained lip peeling back to bare jagged hooked teeth.

"Go. Go. Go go go *go go go GO!*"

The two men took off across the field, their boots tearing up the ground beneath them as they sprinted as fast as their burning legs could carry them. They struggled to keep their footing as the planet shook with giant footsteps.

"THE FENCE! NOW!" Short cried, heaving as he ran for the compound. Keenan passed him on his much longer legs, cackling as he ran.

"Hahahaha come and get it you son of a — SHIT!"

A shrieking roar consumed the air right behind them. They ran harder, closing in on the fence as the familiar turquoise light trailed between the conduction poles.

They passed through the gap in the wall of light with time to spare — too much. Keenan turned around with his weapon ready, but the captain grabbed him by his shirt, yanking him toward the congregation within the door as they screamed and rambled over each other.

The beast closed in, the walls inching together too slowly.

Short hurtled through the open doorway, dragging the other soldier with him. He lurched for the keypad to punch in the code as the others desperately tripped over one another as far into the compound walls as possible. All except for one.

Sherri stood just within the door, staring through the portal as it began to shut.

The native had skidded to a halt just short of the closing barrier. It sniffed at the light of the fence instead of attempting to squeeze through the gap. Right before the compound's steel door shut, Sherri caught a glimpse of the native swatting a small rock with its tail, watching intently as it flew into the electrified hologram and vaporized.

The door finally locked shut in her face with a clang, eliminating her view of the outside world. Sherri's voice came out in a hoarse whisper.

"They're intelligent..."

The rebels saw no other choice but to follow the old man through the winding tunnels and hope he had more answers for them. Hope he might stitch closed the holes he'd ripped in their known world.

The tunnel opened to a hollow of stone and ice, glowing with a vibrant green from the fire in the center of the cave. As soon as they stepped through the opening, they were met with the intoxicating smell of cooking meat and a warmth that seemed impossible among the ice.

Dried herbs hung from the ceiling, a hearty meal roasted over the fire. Various furs and skins padded the floor, and the inside was larger than they expected;

even Kodo could almost stand up straight. Scrapings and paintings decorated the rock wall with scenes of blizzards and kings. Soft hues of blue and green dimly illuminated the atmosphere, the emerald flames casting a gentle light. The rebels hadn't eaten much more than small game Rykr was able to sniff out under the ice, but even that was limited. Their stomachs ached and they stared wistfully at the meat cooking over the fire.

Kaishek took the meat off the fire before it was even cooked through and ripped it into chunks. He silently tossed sizable pieces in front of each of his guests, then sat on a pile of furs and looked around at the young ghaengste before him.

"Eat."

They began savagely digging into the food without further invitation, Alvi shoving between Kodo's legs to grab the haunch of an unrecognizable creature. They finished their meals with the haste of rabid beasts, and Kaishek watched each ghaengste in the strange group closely.

"I don't buy it." Alvi finally broke the cave's silence, apparently energized after a hot meal. "That Kodo's a halfbreed."

All eyes turned toward her; she was sitting close next to Kodo and staring at Kaishek over the fire.

"You claim to be his father..." she continued, squinting as if in thought. Kaishek nodded.

"Yes."

"And your brother is the lunai-vaus of the Eidolan clan."

"Yes."

"Rykr's father..."

"Yes."

Alvi looked at Kodo, then at Rykr, then back and forth a few more times.

"Then... they're cousins."

Kodo and Rykr glanced at one another with pinched faces, somewhere between disgust and disbelief.

"Yes," Kaishek answered, stubbornly holding onto his patience. Alvi stared at the two young men for a moment longer, then lowered her voice to a hush.

"... Are you sure? Sorry, Kodo, I'm sure your mother was—"

"I am sure," Kaishek snapped. Alvi quickly shut her mouth and turned back to the remnants of her meal. There was a long, tense pause as Kodo stared into the flames with his brows tightly furrowed, his eyes glazed over with confusion. Kaishek studied each and every feature he had inherited from his mother.

"Kodokuna."

Kodo twitched, startled. His eyes darted up across the fire.

"Where is... your mother, boy?" Kaishek asked, but his normally powerful voice came out smaller, older, and hesitant.

The cave grew deathly silent. Even the fire seemed to stop crackling, and the look in Kodo's eyes made Kaishek's ears drop to the sides of his head. He didn't need to hear the words that came from the young man's mouth. By the time they finally did, his hearts were already dead in his chest.

"She... died. Not long ago," Kodo admitted quietly.

Kaishek's eyes squeezed shut, and his jaw clenched tight in agony. When he opened his eyes again, the burning flame in his gut was gone, only smoke in its place. He lifted his head and released a long exhale, nodding.

"That is why you've left the Ramys clan?" he mustered. Kodo nodded.

"... Sort of. They exiled me after... I never really belonged there, I guess." He looked at his feet in shame. Kaishek watched him for a moment longer, then looked at the others.

"You are not alone anymore, I see."

Kodo glanced up from the ground. He almost looked surprised to see his companions, as if he'd expected them to be long gone and had been afraid to check. He nodded hesitantly, his eyes still lingering on their faces as his shoulders relaxed. Kaishek took a longer look at the two young women, one from the sky and one from the sea.

"And what are you two called?" He barely had the chance to finish his question when the sky dweller answered in a husky whisper.

"I am Leida," she said as if she'd been waiting for someone to ask. The ocean dweller shook her head at her strange friend with a smile.

"My name is Alvi," she added, "I'm from Celesteal originally, but I suppose heresy was more exciting. Or so it seemed at the time."

Leida spoke again before Kaishek could respond.

"We are a tribe," the sky woman clarified. Kaishek blinked in surprise, glancing around at his guests.

"A refugee tribe?" His voice was soft with disbelief, but the words brought some breath back into his lungs. Leida nodded.

"Well, only now, we seem to have begun a rebellion against the Ramys clan," Alvi explained. "At first, we were just seeking out an old cave. It had carvings that told the story of our people from a long, long time ago. A time when we coexisted — it's true. Then Kodo stole Rykr from his family."

Rykr rolled his eyes and began to protest, but Alvi continued her story.

"We set out to find more like us and saw... some terrible things along the way. We found trouble with Ramys and ended up wanted fugitives. Then we fled up here because the Ramys tunahk-dahn are hunting us, and we figured not even they are insane enough to follow us up to this wasteland." She sighed as she finished, shifting uncomfortably and touching the bandage on her torso.

"It sounds like you four have been on quite the journey," Kaishek said, looking over the rebels. Their young eyes were hardened and tired, their flesh tattered and bruised. Alvi seemed out of breath after her retelling, taking a moment to rest. Rykr's horns, fangs, and claws were chipped and cracked, most likely from more battles than years lived. Leida's lean muscles were strong, but her form was gaunt and underweight, her feathers frayed. Kaishek's eyes wandered to the giant gnarled scars carved across Kodo's throat.

"Yeah, well, this journey's going nowhere fast," the forest man said dryly as he watched the fire. "They'll kill us if they catch us again. We're no match for the tunahk."

Alvi leaned her head against his shoulder, and all four of the rebels seemed to slump in exhaustion. They watched the fire crackle and dance as if they might never feel warmth again after it was quenched.

"No," Kaishek said, "You are not."

Memories from the darkest part of his mind flared up. Bloody stories of barbarians and soldiers. The Ramys tunahk-dahn had been called the greatest force on the planet, dating back generations before his own time. His powerful jaw clenched.

"Not yet."

The rebels perked up, just slightly, as they all looked to the elder ghaengste. His gaze rested on the old, worn weapon in the corner. A double-headed axe made from raw metal and hardened fossil. One head of the blade was white bone, the cutting edges laid with sharpened steel. The other side of the blade was black bone, a horrible crack gauged through it up to the silver blade. The leather-wrapped handle was worn with teeth marks from the fangs of a younger man, a warrior like no other — the Black Revenant. Kaishek said a silent prayer to the stone below his feet and the weapon of his youth.

Lend me the spirit I once had, Mother.

Awaken the blood inside of my veins, Mother.

Give my descendants the strength of my ancestors, Mother.

"I will train you."

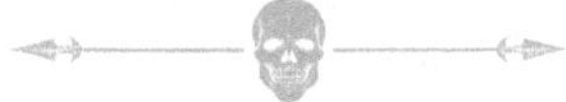

The crew stood there in silence long after the doors were safely shut. The image would be forever burned into their minds: the blood and flesh dripping from the creature's jaws, the limbs and intestines hanging past its chin. Roger's deafening shrieks and moans, the life leaving his eyes as they watched helplessly.

Slowly, the congregation became aware of their surroundings and began to wander away from the door. The soldiers cleared away first.

Sherri's legs shook with weakness, and she cursed herself for it. She found herself praying to a god she didn't believe in that she didn't look as terrified as she felt. Roger was dead. They didn't even have a body for his husband to bury. Her stomach twisted into knots and she desperately choked down the urge to vomit right there in the corridor.

"Let's go sit down." Harrison was the first to speak, his voice soft and his eyes dull. Sherri cleared her throat and nodded, allowing herself to be led as Harrison herded the rest of the research team to the commons.

They quietly found their seats on the couches and chairs, just sitting there for a while.

"Well," Doyle exhaled, his voice a little hoarser than usual. "Congratulations, Daniels."

All eyes turned to him; Sherri's face pinched with confusion and disgust.

"You've just been promoted to head of biology."

The other scientists glared at him; his eyes and his tone hid something deeper than his cynicism. But he was right, and it hit Sherri all at once. She was the biologist now. It was on her. The thought made her sick.

"Not now, Doyle," she snapped, shaking her head and desperately attempting to clear her mind of the atrocity she'd seen only minutes before. Or had it been hours? Harrison held up a hand to quiet his colleagues and cleared his throat.

"Alright, that's enough. We need to send word to mission control. So they can... notify his family," he said like he was out of breath. He kept glancing across the coffee table at Giovanni; the younger man hadn't said a word. He just looked down at the ground like he was deep in thought. Marshall spoke from where he leaned against the wall with his hands in his pockets.

"Is it too soon to ask for volunteers to move his stuff out of our dorm? He was my roommate." He looked up. He was met with several headshakes and scowls, and Sherri scrunched her nose in repulsion.

"Yeah, too soon, Novak. Maybe let it sit for a second before you switch the conversation back to yourself. Fucking asshole," she spat. He opened his mouth to say something, but she didn't give him the chance as she stood up abruptly.

"What happened to Roger is on us, I hope you all know that. We knew he was scared, we knew he was struggling. But we made a joke of him instead of helping, and now he's *dead*."

She looked around at her colleagues with her brows tightly knit, her teeth gritted as fury rose in her throat.

"Don't you put that on us. Don't you put that on our shoulders, Daniels," Doyle snapped. "Myles was killed by that thing out there, not us. Myles drove himself insane, not us. His blood is not on our fucking hands," he finished with a glare. Sherri's face grew hot.

"No, Doyle, it is. We had every opportunity to help, or at least *try*, and if you can't get your head out of your ass long enough to see —"

"Oh, for God's sake, *enough* with your moral superiority, woman!"

"Fuck you!" Sherri exclaimed. "He was our friend, and we cared more about our own egos than we cared about his well being. The least we can do is own up to it. Fuck all of you."

She gave them all a vindictive glare as she stormed out of the room, leaving them behind in silence.

Sherri ended up in the terrosphere.

She didn't even remember how long she'd been there, but suddenly she was sitting on the ground among the sprouting shrubs and crops. Hiding like a stubborn child, her knees pulled up to her chest, her arms crossed on top of them.

Get up, Daniels.

Grow up, Daniels.

Her legs didn't obey her, and before she could stop them, tears began falling down her cheeks. Her throat was clogged with stifled sobs, her chest filled with shame. She wanted to scream, not in sadness, not in fear, but in rage. Rage at herself, not at her peers. Her forehead fell forward to rest on her crossed arms as the guilt smashed into her all at once; flooding through a broken dam, it began to drown her. The vicious words she'd spat at her teammates echoed in her head.

He was our friend, and we cared more about our own egos than we cared about his well being.

She corrected them in her mind, and within seconds, she was shaking and breathing in small, jerky heaves.

He was my friend, and I cared more about my own ego than I cared about his well being.

He was my friend.

Her silent tears turned to choked weeping as she thought about all the things she never got a chance to learn from him. All the things she'd imagined they would discover together as a team. She'd been so frustrated with his cowardice; she hated him for throwing in the towel and leaving her all alone. She needed him, and so she'd pushed him away and cast him aside. His sorrowful voice crying out *nothing matters anymore* haunted her mind. And she'd been too damn selfish and too damn prideful to tell him what he really needed to remember.

They mattered, what they were doing there mattered.

He mattered.

Maybe if she'd said the right thing, he'd still be alive. Maybe if she didn't push him so hard. Now all she could see when she closed her eyes was his bloodshot gaze in his final moments, terrified and knowing. His limp body hanging out of the native's mouth, bathed in so much blood he was barely recognizable as human. His final shriek, the way it choked and cracked and died out. She'd hear it for the rest of her life.

It rang through her head over and over again as she sobbed hopelessly to herself, no one around to hear but the soil and the sprouts.

...

A fire raged inside Short's chest and all he could do was get as far away from his soldiers as possible. They couldn't see him like this, they couldn't see him shaken. His fists begged for something to hit, his lungs burned with the yell he was holding in. Then he was shoving open the door to the armory. What was he looking for? He didn't know. He supposed he was just there to let it mock him some more. To taunt him with more questions he didn't have the answers to, and more problems he didn't have solutions for. The names of more people he couldn't save.

He looked around at the gun lockers lining the wall. The massive government-labeled crates full of ammunition, grenades, and field equipment. The entire expedition, the heaps of munitions and crates of heavy artillery had haunted him. The amount of weaponry they'd been sent with had warned him and filled him with dread. Now it wasn't enough. Now it poisoned his gut with more dread and infected his head with more questions, but no longer because they'd been sent with more weapons than he knew what to do with. Now, there was not one thing in that damn arsenal they knew could protect them from the enemies outside of their walls. Now, there wasn't one thing that even seemed likely to. He erupted and punched the locker nearest to him. The metal made a horrible clang as his fist collided with it, leaving behind an ugly dent. He huffed and shook out his hand.

The armory taunted him once again, its fateful questions echoing off the mesh lockers and steel walls.

How long? How long? How long?

"I still..." Rykr's gruff voice echoed in the cavern. "I still don't understand."

The crackling fire filled the air with a sleepy warmth, but it did little to soothe the heaviness that hung over the den. Kaishek nodded, his weathered face genuine.

"We rarely do."

Rykr's expression contorted into anger, a growl forming in his throat.

"What does that mean? I don't understand *you*. You're... alive? Banished? My father... my father told me..." He hung his head and the stubborn scowl melted from his face. Tired defeat took its place.

"What did he tell you, boy?" his uncle asked with a pitiful tone.

The other three rebels were now listening as well, watching Rykr, and he wished they would look anywhere else. He longed for them to leave him be, to abandon him with his shame and his rage. He was angry, but he was always angry. This time was different. This time he'd grown rash, defiant, and selfish.

"My father told me you died before I was born. That you died a heroic death, driving the Ahsuei bandits from our land. A warrior's death..."

Rykr squeezed his eyes shut for a moment as the stories of his youth played over in his head. The stories he'd learned by and lived by, his family's very history.

"Ramaala lied," Kaishek said plainly. Rykr flinched as if he'd been licked by the flames of the bonfire. If he couldn't trust in his father, his king, he didn't know what or who else there was to trust. He'd been betrayed by the man he cared for most, the man he'd done everything for. The man he wanted to be. His spiraling thoughts were interrupted once again by his uncle's low voice.

"He lied to protect you," Kaishek continued, "To protect his clan from the truth. To protect them from me."

Rykr's brows remained firmly scrunched together, his body tense. Before he could manage a response, he rose and stormed through the back entrance of the cave, shoving between Kodo and Leida on his way out.

As the chill air filled his lungs, he could breathe again. The warmth of the den had been suffocating him, and all he wanted was to burrow under the snow and hide away.

"Rykr?"

He'd grown so familiar with the feminine pitch that came from someone he'd only known for a short while.

"Go back inside, Al."

The ocean woman didn't leave. Instead, she marched through the thick snow to sit beside him.

"Hey fluffy," she said, bumping his shoulder with hers. "Want to know something?"

Rykr released an exasperated huff and watched the hot breath pour from his nostrils, then disappear.

"No, but I bet you're going to tell me anyway," he replied.

"Everyone lies. Especially parents. Children can't understand some things, so it's only right to lie to them." She shrugged. Rykr glared down at her.

"Was that supposed to make me feel better? No offense, tide pool, but I don't think you get it," he grumbled. Alvi just chuckled.

"My father has many, many children. Probably more than he can count. When I was a girl, being the pest that I was, I asked him who his favorite was." She fell into more gentle laughter. "You know what he said?"

"What?"

"He said I was." Alvi broke into a grin, her amber eyes gleaming brightly through their exhaustion. She seemed to shed some of the ache from her shoulders, even if just for a moment.

"What a load of shit, right? It wasn't until later that I realized he probably didn't even remember my name, but at the time it made me feel loved."

She looked over the whiteness before them, the gentle snowflakes riding on the breeze.

"He didn't have to lie; he could have just told me to piss off and run along. But he didn't want to disappoint me. I'm grateful for that."

Rykr let out a slow breath and closed his eyes for a moment, savoring the icy breeze. He felt the petite woman next to him shivering against his flank and opened his eyes to glance down at her. Her bandages would need to be changed soon; a spotting of black blood was soaking through. He could tell from her shallow breaths that she was in pain, but her posture was tall and proud.

"Come on, let's go back inside," he said, rising from the snow to re-enter through the back entrance of the Lost King's den. Alvi stopped him.

"Rykr."

He looked back down, glancing over her with concern that she might have hurt herself. She just walked past him back to the den but spoke sternly as she did.

"You've been an ass to Kodo, you know that?"

"Yeah, I know."

He followed after her and held the entrance curtain aside as they returned to the warmth of the cave.

As they came back into the cavern, Alvi found a seat to rest among the furs and pelts without another word, and Rykr could feel all eyes on him. He was grateful when Kaishek finally spoke, as it drew the attention away.

"Your father is not a perfect man, Rykr, but he cares for his people. For his family. My treason was a betrayal to our legacy, a wound on the throne itself. He had to protect his kingdom from the shame of my crime, the only way he knew how.

"To bury it," the old man finished.

Rykr nodded slowly, his ears gently twitching. His anger, his sorrow, his stubbornness, and selfishness began to depart from over top of what truly bothered him. He missed them. He missed his family and his home. He missed his juvenile dreams and ideas of what his future held. His sheltered world had been shattered more suddenly than he could adapt, and he still hadn't figured out who he'd be when it was all over and done with. He didn't even know who to try to be anymore. He found his own seat, making his way to a pile of furs close beside Kodo. The young giant hadn't said much since he'd been told of his lineage, but his silence alone seemed telling enough. As Rykr sat down to rest his weary form, he knocked the side of his horn against Kodo's, so gently it could have been an accident.

"I'm sorry, brother."

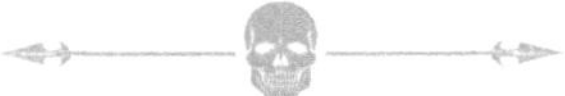

The only thing that lay between them and certain demise was an electric fence.

They'd lost four lives.

They were outmatched. Unprepared. Vulnerable.

And yet, Sherri wasn't ready to give up. Not even close. With every horrific circumstance, with every coming hurdle, came a new question to answer. A new puzzle to solve. A reminder of what they were doing, and why they were there — discovery. For a moment, Sherri began to wonder if maybe she was losing it too.

Unprepared, outmatched, vulnerable.

But she could still see through it. Through the hopelessness of their station, through the sorrow of their losses, through the nightmares and the cold sweats. She could still see the next leap for mankind, and she still believed that they could make it. But something had to change.

They already knew what didn't work. Large groups were walking targets. The M15s did little more than distract the natives, and the grenades merely stunned them. Given a stationary target in an open landscape, they would attack. It had taken four lives to learn those lessons. Sherri had no intention of losing any more, nor repeating any mistakes. And now they had strong evidence that the natives were intelligent, or at least capable of reasoning and problem-solving. Sherri saw it with her own eyes — that thing calculated the risk of crossing the barrier of the fence and chose against it. She had to get back out there and learn more. It was her job alone now, no one else would do it. In order to safely observe the natives, they had to go minimal contact, minimal disturbance. They had to be quick, quiet, and small.

Sherri was going in alone.

"Doctor Daniels?"

Torn from her thoughts, she looked up from her journal at Doctor Rosenquest standing in the doorway.

"Yes?" she called back to him quieter than she intended, then cleared her throat

"We've received word from mission control. I told them to wait for you, but —"

Sherri was already jumping up and slipping past him through the doorway. Harrison clumsily stumbled out of her way, then turned and followed.

The rest of the crew was already gathered in the commons, loitering and sitting around. Standing at the counter in front of the congregation, Doctor Novak read from a tablet.

"The concerns of RREP Wolf One have been received and weighed. In a response transmission, provide the name and details of the confirmed casualty for next of kin notification.

Clearance to abort prematurely has been denied, and a decision has been made to advance the timeline of the program in response to the new developments. Research on the native fauna of 7355264Z will take precedence over all other Remus functions. Begin collecting formal reports as soon as possible, including samples and photographs. In light of the recent completion of "Salvation" Shuttle II, phase two of the Remus-Romulus expedition plan will commence ahead of schedule.

Advancement Romulus: Wolf Two will soon launch from Canaveral to join Wolf One carrying militia reinforcements, resupplies, and return fuel.

Mission Control to Wolf One:

We thank you for your service to your nations and planet.

[message via Houston NASA Mission Control Center, RREP support terminal]"

There was a moment of silence before the room erupted.

"So we're bent and fucked," Marshall finished.

"Not necessarily, we just have to stay alive until reinforcements arrive," Giovanni argued, raising his voice over the murmurs of concern.

"And how do you suggest we do that?" Doyle scoffed. "Did you miss the vaguely threatening part where they told us to stay put and get our happy asses back to work? They just stripped us of our right to cower. They dug our graves."

The captain shoved through the crowd and snatched the tablet out of Marshall's hands.

"Motherfuckers," Short whispered as he scanned the message for himself. "They're only going to inform Torres's family. God damn it."

"Technically the only *confirmed* casualty is Doctor Myles." Marshall shrugged. "He's the only one who had reliable witnesses —"

"I suggest you think long and fucking hard about the next thing you say to me," Short snapped with a glaring threat in his eyes. Harrison pulled Marshall away by the tie before he could open his mouth again.

Sherri took the tablet from Captain Short, who made no attempt to hold on to it as he was already trudging away. She scrolled up and down the screen, reading the message over and over again. She had to do something, and do it quickly, before the rest of her friends and colleagues went marching out into the abyss to get themselves killed. She shoved the tablet in Giovanni's hands and rushed away.

"Where are you going?" the geologist called after her.

"Didn't you hear them? Research," she called back.

Sherri yanked her desk drawer open, pulling out all her drawings depicting variations of the same beast made with charcoal, ink, and paint. She flipped her journal open to her notes on the native. Spreading everything out in front of her, she stepped back so she could get a wider view of the papers.

Eyes on the front of its head, they're predators.

Pointed teeth, carnivorous.

Horns and spines, built for defense.

No, they're elusive and agile, built for offense. Both?

She huffed, pushing her frontmost curls behind her ears and tightening her ponytail.

Long legs, two sets of nostrils. Built to run. Pursuit predator.

No, it ambushed us — ambush predator. Adapted for two environments?

She stepped toward the desk, nodding. Bracing herself with her hands planted firmly on the table, her eyes wandered around each page of notes and sketches. Her loose concepts of its body were horse-like, galloping and leaping.

Can't outrun it.

She hesitated, sorting through her memories.

But Short did, it took a moment to get up to speed — it's heavy.

Anything that large uses a huge amount of energy to move. Use its size against it.

She chewed on her lip for a moment.

It took us by surprise each time. It's opportunistic. So don't be an easy meal.

Don't be an easy meal.

Sherri took a deep breath and began sweeping the drawings back into the desk drawer. She put her journal in her backpack, then a few objects from her field equipment cabinet: a water filter, a folded-up tarp, a sheathed machete.

They were here to do research. Nothing would stop her from doing that. But they had to get smarter. *She* had to get smarter. No more mistakes, no more casualties. She took a quick look around the empty lab. Then she grabbed an aerosol can of air freshener off the counter and a butane lighter from Novak's station and tossed both objects in her bag.

Just don't be an easy meal.

Kodo had never been formally trained in much of anything. In the Ramys clan, they'd simply thrown him into a hunting party and said 'watch and learn, kid.' Of course, he'd naturally excelled at hunting and most other things that required speed and brute force. But now, Kaishek prepared to train them in combat, apparently convinced he could make them into a force to rival the Ramys tunahk-dahn. The idea sickened Kodo, and he couldn't begin to figure out why.

He grew increasingly nervous as they prepared to depart from the cave's warmth, and Kaishek strapped a villainous-looking axe onto his back.

"That's quite the axe you've got there," Alvi said curiously as she studied the weapon; it was nearly as large as her, scarred and stained by years of battle. Kaishek nodded.

"This is Y'xara. It holds the wrath of my ancestors within its blades, so they may fight alongside me until the day I join them," the old man explained wistfully. Leida stood up on her haunches, peering intently at the weapon on his back as if searching for the aforementioned ancestors in the scratches on the bone and the reflection of the metal plating.

"Inside of it?" she asked skeptically.

"In its very marrow," Kaishek replied. "The white blade is my mother's scapula, the black blade my father's."

Leida nodded in understanding, seemingly satisfied with his simple explanation.

"Now it's a real family reunion." Alvi teasingly grinned up at Rykr. "Say hi to grandma and grandpa, Ryk."

"I wish you'd let that one-eyed freak from Ramys kill me," Rykr grumbled under his breath and shoved her away.

"The blood of great warriors runs through your veins, boy. The blood of war itself," Kaishek said proudly as he passed Rykr, ignoring the young man's previous remark.

"It runs within both of you," the old king continued as he nodded warmly at Kodo, then passed through the back exit flap. Kodo's ears twitched sheepishly, but he reluctantly followed after his father.

"About that." He cleared his throat. "This... training idea, I'm uh — I'm not much of a warrior."

Alvi's laugh sounded from behind them as the rest of the rebels emerged from the grotto.

"Tell that to the tunahk missing half his head," the ocean woman cackled unhelpfully.

Kodo flinched, the images returning to his mind: the mauled warrior, the crushed huntress. The river camp, not destroyed by his jaws, and yet he felt just as responsible. Maybe he'd just stopped being able to tell the difference in the blood. To him, it was all just black.

Kaishek looked over Kodo's doubtful face for a moment with furrowed brows. Then he abruptly turned to continue his way up the ridge, calling behind him,

"Aye, I'll make a warrior out of you yet, boy."

Kodo sighed but kept walking. Leida fell in step beside him, lagging behind the rest of the group with her old friend.

"You are frightened?" she asked quietly, studying the side of his face. Kodo thought about it for a moment, watching his breath seep from his nostrils.

"Yeah. Are you?" he replied.

"No. Of what?" She cocked her head. Kodo thought longer before replying.

"Me, I guess. Of what I am. Of what I've done." He flinched at hearing the words out loud, and he gritted his teeth as he awaited her answer.

"I think I still do not understand the importance of what is what, and what is done," Leida explained thoughtfully. "I think you are just Kodo."

Kodo looked down at her, at her gaze boring into his, at her mystery and indifference. He softened, his shoulders relaxing as he walked alongside her, the woman from the sky who never could see the gaps between them.

"I'm glad I met you, feathers," he said gently, like he was realizing it for the first time. Leida just shrugged.

They crested the ridge, climbing up to a flat expanse of solid stone gently flaked in snow. From atop, it looked like an island floating in the sky — nothing but white fog and blue sky surrounding it. Oblivion below in all directions.

Kodo lifted his head to the wind, letting it blow in his face and imagining it whisking away the doubts that plagued him. Leida sniffed the ground for a moment, then looked ahead at Kaishek. She observed him for a moment as he scanned the area.

"Kaishek," she called.

"What do you have to say, girl?" Kaishek said as he marched into the center of the stone flat, still turned away from them but his loud voice projected clearly. Leida followed behind him.

"My name is Leida," she said as if she were answering a question.

"You say you will teach us to fight like the Ramys warriors. But they fight with armor and blades. We do not," she observed, her voice steady as she stared intently at the back of his head. He glanced back at the young woman.

"That, *Leida,*" he said her name from deep in his chest, "is half true. Eventually, you will need weapons."

He turned around to face the young rebels as he pulled his axe from the sheath on his back.

"But you are wrong that you lack blades." He tossed the axe to the side; it scraped viciously against the stone plane and spit forth angry sparks.

"The Great Mother provides us with the most important weapons of all. Swords, daggers, axes; they are useful tools, but they do not make a warrior. We are meant to taste the blood we spill, not waste it on the metal of a blade. If we allow ourselves to forget the natural state of war, we will soon after forget the cost of war. Claws, horns, fangs, and the hearts in our chests — that is what makes a warrior.

"You have not yet known the perversion of the blade. That is good. I will first teach you to master the weapons the Mother gave you at birth. You will learn to respect the flesh you inhabit, so you may gain respect for the flesh you destroy. A blade does not feel the life leave a man's hearts. Your fangs feel every fragment of his soul passing on. This forces us to choose wisely which of the Great Mother's children we take from Her. Only then should you learn to fight with a forged weapon."

The rebels listened closely as he spoke, and the Lost King nodded once, his fiery yellow eyes glowing with the resurgence of something long gone.

"Let's begin."

II
APHELION

Rykr slid across the icy stone, skidding to a halt as he rolled to his feet. He panted heavily but his legs remained strong under his hefty weight.

"Getting tired, old man?" he huffed through labored breaths. The ghaengste before him threw back his head and laughed a deep, hearty rumble.

"We haven't even begun," Kaishek responded.

Rykr lurched, aiming for Kaishek's throat. His jaws didn't have the chance to meet flesh before his opponent's horns made contact with his skull. The impact left his vision blurry, and just as he recovered, he was grabbed by the scruff of his neck. Kaishek heaved him upwards so forcefully that all four of his feet left the surface below him, then he was slammed down into the stone ground. Rykr's skull throbbed and he breathed hard as his body sluggishly thrashed, trying to will itself up.

"Not bad, boy, not bad," his uncle said, helping him to his feet and guiding him off the training pad.

"Leida," Kaishek called out. "Shall we?"

Leida watched Rykr stomp off the stone platform as she rose to meet the old man. When she came to a halt close in front of Kaishek, she had to crane her neck to meet his gaze.

"You got it, feathers!" Kodo whooped enthusiastically, and Alvi covered her eyes.

Leida searched the Lost King's face, and she found him harder to read than any riddle or proverb. But she didn't need to know the thoughts behind his mysterious shroud; he already spoke clearly in the only native tongue she'd ever known: body language.

She detected the tiniest twitch of his shoulder from the corner of her eye, and by the time he lunged forward, she'd already ducked away. Carried by his immense inertia, he stumbled slightly and looked back at her with a gleaming smirk. She kept him in her keen sight, then abruptly took flight and struck down.

Kaishek rolled to the side just as Leida's claws collided with the stone he'd been standing on milliseconds prior, and searing sparks spit wildly from where her talons gouged into the mountain. She nearly dodged a blow from his powerful tail as it whipped toward her; she was quick, much quicker than him. Where she lacked training, she made up for it in agility and an unbreakable vigilance gained by years of harsh survival. His eyes tracked her as she soared in the air around him, stalking him like a predator on the hunt. Waiting for an opening.

For a split second, he lost track of her, but a split second was all she needed. Leida dove.

But as soon as she caught sight of his eyes, she knew she'd made a grave mistake.

The Lost King spun around and rose, reaching a terrifying height. With one powerful strike, he batted her into the ground like a shooting star hurtling to its explosive demise. She cried out as she collided with the hard stone, her wings crumpling around her.

Her friends gasped, though she could hardly hear them through the ringing in her ears. A hiss built in her throat, and she was on her feet again despite the dizziness.

"You *lie*," she hissed, scowling at the old man. A smug expression sat comfortably on Kaishek's weathered face.

"Did I?" he mused. She did not find the humor that he did in the situation. Her lips curled back from her hooklike fangs, and a rattling sound seethed through her teeth.

"You turned your back on me. But you were only pretending. You lie." She spoke slowly, piecing it together with agitation lacing her normally placid voice.

"Put your teeth away, girl."

"Leida," she snapped venomously.

"Leida." His voice was no gentler than normal, but his eyes were calm. "I did not lie to you; I used your vigilance against you. I feigned distraction as a strategy."

Leida huffed in frustration but sat back on her haunches.

"That is the same as lying," she insisted.

"High stakes cause for low blows, Leida," Kaishek explained patiently. "All is fair in war, even deceit. You must learn the strokes of battle beyond the physical."

Leida turned to walk back to her spectating companions. She couldn't recall anyone telling her that she 'must' do anything, and it stuck at her like a thorn in her foot.

"And we will need to cut your hair," the old man added. "It obstructs your vision."

She flipped around and snapped her jaws just short of Kaishek's face.

"You will not touch it," she whispered with stinging poison. Kaishek's eyes widened, so subtle it was barely discernible.

"So be it, but it will hold you back," he warned. She shook her head, but turned around to trot back to the other three.

"It has not before and it will not now."

Marshall observed in silence as Corporal Greene opened and closed the fridge door, cocking his head back and forth like an animal exercising its limited critical thought. Then, after a moment of deliberating, the soldier landed a sharp kick to the side of the refrigerator.

"Hey, Captain," Greene called behind him, setting a toothpick in the offset gap of his lower teeth, "the fridge is out."

Captain Short got up from his barstool with a groan.

"Do I look like a handyman to you, Corporal?" he asked, approaching the scene.

"No, sir."

"Then what are you bitching at me for?" The captain pushed the younger man to the side in order to repeat the opening and closing ritual for himself. Marshall found a twisted sort of amusement in watching their dilemma, at least until he remembered that the fridge was a shared appliance. Spoiled food in their closed-off compound was a problem they hadn't prepared for, and one he really didn't want to encounter.

"Pull it out," he said as he joined them.

"Sorry?" Short gave him a suspicious glare.

"I said, pull it out from the wall. Or do you just maintain those muscles for our enjoyment?" Marshall mocked listlessly. He'd barely finished his sentence when the captain grunted and grabbed either side of the heavy appliance, leaning it back toward his chest and pulling it out. The metal fridge squealed against the ground as he dragged it, then banged like a bomb had gone off when he ungracefully let it settle back on the floor. Everyone in the room jolted at the commotion, but Marshall simply motioned for Short to get out of his way after fetching a toolbox.

He quickly got to work on the fridge, and even as the commons began to fill with breakfast-time patrons, he was largely ignored. He didn't mind, instead feeling uncharacteristically at peace as he busied himself with the menial task.

"Ha, three PhDs and you're the one on your knees fixing the fridge," a familiarly smug English accent snickered behind him.

"First of all, Giovanni, I have *four* PhDs," Marshall replied without looking up from his work. "Maybe you'd be able to count if you'd gone to university."

"We both went to Stanford, you ass."

"Apparently not for long enough."

"Do you wake up every morning with the intention to be a pompous cunt?"

"No, I wake up every morning with the intention to be a doctor."

"Where's Daniels?" Harrison interrupted, giving his brother a loud clap on the shoulder before he could jab back. It seemed the two youngest research team members were never far apart.

"Right here," Sherri answered as she walked into the kitchen and sat on the barstool beside Gio. He looked down at her with his cheek set on his fist.

"Plans for today?" he asked.

"Nothing special, maybe a nap." She shrugged. She was eyeing Marshall, who was pretty attractive when he was making himself useful and keeping his mouth shut. He appeared completely focused on fixing the fridge — surprising, considering he rarely did anything that might benefit anyone other than himself. Sherri gave her head a slight shake, tearing her gaze from where he kneeled on the floor, and reminded herself of his usual arrogant, self-centered, insensitive attitude. She started getting herself worked up as she remembered the way he'd reacted to Roger's death.

"Since when do you nap?" Giovanni said, sharing a look with his brother on the other side of her. She took a sip of her coffee and glanced up innocently at her friend.

"Been a stressful few days, hasn't it? Maybe you should take one too," she replied quietly with a weak shrug, and Giovanni looked ashamed for asking. Sherri had been hit harder by Roger's death than she liked to admit, and they were all shaken up after what they'd seen. Gio gave her a reassuring nudge with his shoulder.

"Maybe they disappeared into thin air, *poof*."

The sharp tip of an angry tail swatted the old king's cheek.

"This is no time for *jokes*, Visaan," Erro snarled at the grizzled man.

"If you had it your way, there would be no time for jokes at all," Visaan crooned. "Why are you so bothered, anyway? You said you trusted the tunahk-dahn."

"I do trust the tunahk," Erro replied. "But I have a dreadful feeling this will not end with only the heads of four rebels. I fear it will grow into something more."

The pale queen aimlessly walked around the room, her brows furrowed in thought.

"You speak like Rataan. You really believe he is right about this?" Levah spoke from where he'd been silently cleaning his armor.

"Rataan may be bellicose at times, but that is why we've trusted him to protect our people. He has never led us wrong as our kaunek-leih, and he never led me wrong when we served in the tunahk together. I trust his instincts," Erro explained. She didn't deny that the commander could be paranoid, but in this instance, she did not consider it unwarranted. For the first time in recorded history, a group of all four races was seen consorting. It was only natural to fear the end of times. Erro wandered to the far wall, halting in front of a line of tapestries. She studied the intricate stitched patterns and images of great warriors.

"Visaan," she beckoned, suddenly calmer.

"Aye," Visaan responded as he appeared beside her.

"You mentioned an ocean dweller residing with one of our kind once," she continued.

"And when did I mention this?" The old king raised a brow as she glanced up at him from the corner of her eye.

"After an entire barrel of imported malaavi root ale."

He nodded with a knowing smirk.

"Ah, I remember now. Yes, a merchant I traveled with once told me of working alongside a man of the sea. Said he collected valuable stones and shells from the river bed for her to sell. In return, she protected him and gave him a cut. The arrangement ended suddenly and violently, of course; he fancied theft over trade as all rivermen do. That is the story she gave me, anyway. Tales were her favorite thing to barter, not all of them true."

Erro nodded along, hanging onto each of her fellow lunai's words. The fire that burned inside Rataan's chest was hot and unyielding; it consumed every breath he took and grew through his heart. Slowly, Erro's hearts, too, began glowing with weak embers.

...

"Come on, then, boy."

Kodo swallowed hard, watching the old man stretch his muscles and crack his worn joints. The Lost King. His lost father. He still wasn't even sure what that meant.

"We haven't got all day," Kaishek called again, his rumbling voice firm. Rykr pushed Kodo to the center of the stone flat.

"Go on, brother."

Kodo ended up chest to chest with the Lost King, somehow feeling dwarfed by the other man despite being heads taller.

"I don't want to do this," he muttered, stubbornly breaking eye contact and taking a step back.

"Speak up," Kaishek growled. Kodo's ears pinned to the sides of his head in shame.

"I don't want to do this," he snapped, "I don't want to spar, I don't want to fight. I don't *want* to be like the tunahk, or to be like you — I don't even know you."

Kaishek's brows furrowed, his eyes hard and challenging as he stared down at Kodo. Then he turned away from the other man, seeming to give up on him.

Just as Kodo let out a sigh of relief, the rest of the air was slammed from his lungs as he was whipped off his feet by a powerful tail. He landed hard; the massive force shook the ground and challenged the mountains themselves.

"Get up, boy," Kaishek barked. Kodo just groaned from where he lay on the ground.

"Get up!" the Lost King roared again.

"Bite me." Kodo grimaced defiantly.

The old man snarled and lurched. Kodo squeezed his eyes shut, bracing himself for pain. Kaishek's jaws clamped around Kodo's horn and yanked, forcing his massive weight up off the cold ground. Kodo had just begun to rise when the pressure was released.

A flash of white blurred his vision, then red. A spatter of hot liquid landed on his nose.

Leida stood between him and the Lost King, bristling. An ugly gash cut right across the bridge of old man's snout; black blood bubbled and leaked into his flaring nostrils.

"Leave him be," Leida hissed, her wings outstretched in front of Kodo.

"He must learn to fight," Kaishek bellowed, his nose twitching as blood dribbled past his bearded chin.

"He knows how to fight," the winged woman snarled back, taking a step forward.

"He cowers like a *child* at the first sign of pain!" the old man snapped. Leida's claws unsheathed and a vicious growl rumbled from within her.

"I do not."

Kaishek's sharp eyes narrowed, and the thick fur on his shoulders raised on end. He lunged, a barbaric roar booming through the gigantic fangs that thrust past his jaw.

Then shadow swallowed the daylight.

The Lost King's claws did not cut into skin, his saber fangs did not bury into flesh. Instead, a solid wall now stood between him and the sky woman, a broad chest heaving with ragged breath. Slowly, his gaze traveled upward. He craned his neck, staring into the steaming, heaving nostrils of a man so large he blocked out the suns. A smile spread across Kaishek's lips.

"There you are..."

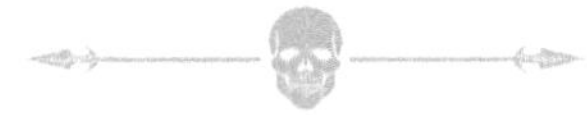

Sherri had no intention to take a nap.

She tied the laces of her boots in anticipation. The crew had begun to settle down in the weeks after the initial botched survey, and the tension in the air had started to dissipate. There had been more chatter, fraternization, and the spirit of the expedition had started to heal.

Then all at once, it had been stripped away and thrown back at them. The loss of Roger shook the compound, and the message from mission control spit in their faces.

But it had to be worth something. The lives lost, the damage they'd all undoubtedly carry for the rest of their lives; it couldn't be for nothing. As long as they were on the planet, Sherri had to do her job. This time, however, she was going to do it right. The hardships of humanity, both trivial and exponential, left her mind as it shifted gear.

Sherri quietly turned the corner into hallway Alpha, already having announced that she was going to take a nap and leaving her peers in the lab. The loud music, obnoxious laughter, and cigarette smoke emanating from the barracks had given her the green light. Her backpack was stocked with all the field equipment she could fit inside it, and the coast was clear. She went for it.

She quietly slinked toward the compound's looming exit, the giant metal door staring back at her in challenge.

Almost there.

She held her bag tight to her back to avoid the items inside clanking or shuffling.

Almost.

Someone stepped in front of her, her path blocked by tightly crossed arms and that familiar perpetual scowl. Sherri halted and clenched her jaw in frustration; she nearly released a childish whine as she longingly gazed over his shoulder at the door. *So close.*

"Funny seeing you here," she said. It was her own fault; she should have known he would smell any sign of productivity from miles away. Captain Short was eyeing her backpack.

"Where are you headed this morning, she-squint?" he asked accusingly, his voice still raspy so early in the morning. She slipped under his arm with a spin.

"Thought I might hit the mall," she cooed. She'd made it to the keypad.

"We had a deal."

"That's too bad," Sherri spat his own words back at him as she rushed to type in the code. She almost thought she'd get away with it. Maybe he'd just give up.

"Fischer, Keenan, Sanchez, Greene!" Short belted, and Sherri groaned.

The summoned soldiers appeared in haste, awaiting orders, and several of her colleagues turned the corner as well. Sherri gritted her teeth even tighter as she watched what seemed like the entire crew hijack her solitary survey. *There goes the plan.*

She could only observe helplessly as the team scrambled to prepare while the door whirred and clicked. She caught sight of Doctor Novak casually leaning against the wall in the background, just watching.

"You coming too?" she called out to him sarcastically. She already knew the answer, but his cowardly self-importance almost gave her a slight twisted comfort.

"It's your hill, you die on it," he called back, clicking his tongue.

…

As Captain Short loaded his rifle, he could feel the malevolent eyes of Doctor Daniels boring into him like burning coals. He wasn't quite sure what had her so pissed off this time, but he made a point not to waste energy trying to understand her motivations. He didn't care how much she resented him, so long as she didn't get in the way of his damn job. That seemed to be her goal, after all, or at least complete anarchy was. But nothing had ever stopped Short from completing his objective before, and he sincerely doubted the temperamental little botanist would be the first to succeed. No matter how hard she tried to run off and get herself killed, his orders were to keep her and the other research assets alive. He'd failed once, and he wouldn't let it happen again. This time, it'd take the devil itself rising out of hell to stop him. The heavy weight of grenades in his ALICE pack affirmed that conclusion.

The doors opened once again, and it was just like the first time.

Blinding sunlight. Crisp air. The stillness of a photograph.

Unearthly.

But time passed differently now. It went too fast, like someone had pressed a fast-forward button. Their first survey had seemed like it was in slow motion, even during the attack, but now everything felt frantic and rushed. Captain Short knew the eerie nature of the planet was finally getting to him. He couldn't trust it, and that was the worst part. He couldn't even rely on the ground beneath his boots, the air he breathed into his lungs.

He shook his head as Doctor Daniels darted around taking samples in the sea of grass.

"Can you stand still while I take a headcount? God damn," he said. She didn't look up from the shrub she was examining.

"Already got one; six guns, three researchers. Can you do that math in your head or do you need —"

"Got it, shit — six guns? I only called four." The captain flipped around to identify the extra head, only to see Private Zheng standing right behind him, looking up at him sheepishly.

"The fuck are you doing out here, Private? I didn't call you," Short barked down at the young man, his nostrils flaring. Zheng swallowed hard.

"I'm sorry, Captain, I thought you did. I must have thought you said my name when you said..." — he looked around at the others — "...Fischer."

"Zheng, Fischer, kinda — kind of similar..." Zheng gave an innocent smile, sweat beading on his forehead. Short leaned down close to the private's face.

"Don't let it happen again," he growled, then rushed away to keep an eye on the frolicking botanist.

Sherri slowly marched through the grass, taking in her surroundings with arms outstretched, letting the tall blades stroke her fingers. The sky gleamed in triumph, suns both yellow and blue bathing the planet's surface in light. Everything appeared to be glowing, releasing a golden haze that was carried on into the mist, blurring the horizon. She'd never get used to the cloudless sky and magnificent planet looming past its atmosphere.

Then her eyes landed on a spot of mutilated ground in the distance, a shredded patch of blackened terrain. The blast mark. The spot of Roger's death. The awe was sucked from Sherri's chest and replaced with rotten, gangrene dread. She looked around at the landscape, her colleagues and friends, the planet stalking them in the distant sky.

Open air. Large group.

The horrors of the truth settled in. There were dangerous predators on this planet capable of devastating carnage. They knew next to nothing about them at this point, but Sherri had just enough data to leave no room for hubris. If caught vulnerable like last time, people would die.

This was not the plan.

"What happened to your nap?" Giovanni asked from beside her, jolting her from her spiraling thoughts.

"Couldn't sleep. You know me." She gave a nervous chuckle, then quickly turned to the rest of the congregation.

"Hey, let's make this quick," she called out to the others. "I just need a couple of fresh specimens."

Kaishek stared up into the young giant's dark eyes with a challenging smirk on his bloodied face.

"Hit me."

The words had barely left the old man's mouth before he was head-butted in the face so hard his vision went blurry and his skull rattled. The deep cracking sound of the collision made all three spectators wince in vicarious pain.

"I should've warned him about the head, huh? Kid's got a hell of a skull," Rykr said to Alvi through a grimace. Leida reluctantly returned to the other rebels as Kodo went tumbling past them.

Kaishek let out a heavy snort as he blinked hard to clear his spinning vision. Kodo was already on his feet. A hearty laugh exploded from the old mountain ghaengste as he shook out his thick mane.

"Come on!" he bellowed, rearing onto his hind legs.

They collided.

Kodo's hearts slammed around in his chest like they were trying to break free from the prison of his rib cage.

He caught a powerful blow sent by a thick tail under his chin, his jaws snapping together with a splitting thud. He noticed something white fall from his open mouth as he was struck again, this time in the stomach. Bile rose in his throat but he swallowed it.

He felt no pain — that was what haunted him.

Not soreness in his muscles, not the biting cold, not even fatigue. His mind conjured no thoughts at all, not of fear nor anger. He knew only the adrenaline that flooded hot through his veins, and the desperation that billowed like smoke from his maw.

His fangs met flesh, and he clamped down hard on the thick skin and dense fur of Kaishek's mighty neck. He met eyes of furious yellow, but only for a split second as he heaved the bulky older man right over his head, gracelessly falling over backward as he slammed his opponent into the ground. The mountain itself shook with the thunderous force, loose stones rattling off the cliff face and falling into oblivion below.

The Lost King groaned as he dragged himself to his feet. The midnight black fur coating his body was slick with sweat, and his sides pumped in, out, in, and out as he panted. The fire in his eyes grew brighter by the second, but Kodo lay still.

"It is true, you are strong," Kaishek's hoarse voice called in its eternal boom as he looked down on Kodo, still slumped on the stone.

"But you hide from your strength. You fear it."

His father's tone was not harsh, his words not sharp, but they cut Kodo.

He didn't want to be strong anymore.

He used to take pride in it, wearing his strength like the paint of a warrior. It was all he had. The others hated him for it, feared him for it, but not so long ago, part of him had always hoped one day they would learn to embrace it. Maybe one day they'd see him as a virtue, not a threat. He knew now that would never happen. His strength was not something to be proud of or revered; it was a crime against nature Herself, and everyone had always known it except for him. He knew now, the shame it carried.

"Because it's an abomination. Like the rest of me," Kodo snapped as he rolled onto his feet, spitting a gob of blood onto the stone below him. Kaishek's brows furrowed, a dubious laugh falling from his lips.

"What nonsense do you speak of, boy? Your strength is a blessing."

"It's a curse," Kodo spat, "That *you* gave me. What were you thinking? What was —"

He paused, flinching as he recalled the way the Ramys clan had ostracized his mother. All because of her giant bastard son.

"Is this what you wanted?" Kodo scowled in shame and disgust. "To create a fucking monster?"

He turned away, beginning to trudge off the stone platform, dodging the concerned gazes of his companions as he passed them.

"Kodokuna," Kaishek called after him. He ignored him.

"Son."

Kodo turned around, baring his bloody teeth with a low growl.

"Leave me alone. You don't even know me."

"*I know you,*" Kaishek growled back stubbornly. "I know you because I know your mother. She lives in your eyes, I still see her. Soft like the soil, unyielding like the trees. She was no monster. She raised no monster. You have nothing to fear, boy, because she did not fear you. She did not cower."

Kodo couldn't help softening as memories of his mother washed the blood from his claws and the sickness from his stomach. It was true, his mother did not love him despite his deviance; she loved him *for* his deviance. He was a breathing symbol of the world she so desperately dreamed of. As her nearly forgotten words resounded in his head, he understood them for the very first time.

You are the greatest thing I could have done for this cruel world, Kodokuna.

He squeezed his eyes shut, and his chest clenched.

My wanderer.

When she'd looked into his eyes, she did not see a monster. She saw a piece of the man she had loved, a piece of the future they'd been stripped of. She saw a better life.

Kodo let out a slow breath, finally managing to look at his father again. His friends.

"Come." Kaishek gently beckoned, beginning the trek back to the den. "You all did very well today. You'll be warriors in no time."

"Isn't it amazing?"

Private Zheng was involuntarily spinning in circles, trying to take everything in. The permanent stars and the bright suns. The giant planet overhead that stared down at them, a constant reminder that they weren't on Earth anymore. How could they forget? Someone pushed his head down from its craned position, tearing his eyes from the sky.

"Eyes forward, not up, kid. Isn't what amazing?"

Zheng glanced up at Corporal Greene, unable to wipe the small smile from his face.

"This, all of it. The discovery of another planet sustaining advanced life, the future of extraterrestrial colonization and diplomacy. And we get to be a part of it — you and me, two soldiers. You don't think that's amazing?"

The corporal chuckled.

"Sure, I guess. 'Course, we're here as alien fodder, so."

Zheng frowned.

"Either way, we're here. Even if we didn't make it home, we'd have done something revolutionary for our world, and we'd have seen more than most people could even dream of. I think that makes it worth it."

Greene scoffed.

"Well, I hate to break it to you, kid, but some things are just better than discovery and diplomacy. Like pus— oh, shit—" He stumbled as he stepped into a hole, barely catching himself on the private's shoulder to keep from toppling to the ground. Zheng stopped in surprise, grabbing hold of the other man's arm to steady him.

"You okay, man? Oh. Shit."

Both soldiers stared at the ground below Greene, his foot lodged in a deep crater in the soil with four smaller divots above it.

A gigantic footprint.

"Excuse me? Doctor Daniels?"

Sherri was carefully, oh so carefully, digging a small spidery shrub out of the dirt. Its delicate roots clung to the soil, stubbornly threatening to tear at any abrupt movement.

"Juuuust a second," she called back, not taking her eyes off the task at hand. She gingerly grappled with the fragile roots, coaxing them to let go of their anchor. Finally, she won the miniature battle and the shrub surrendered, allowing itself to be uprooted and stored in a collection pot. Sherri stood up, turning to face the others.

"Who called m— oh my god, don't move." She rushed over to the man who currently had one foot directly in the middle of a deep pawprint. She cursed under her breath as the others jogged over.

"What's your name?" she asked, wiping her hands on her shorts.

"Corporal Greene," the soldier replied.

"Okay, Corporal Greene, I need you to lift your boot directly up at the same angle it went down, do you understand? We need to minimize the damage as much as possible. That means no shaking, jolting, or twisting your foot," she explained quickly, taking his arm and putting it over her shoulders to help bear his weight. "Straight up and out."

Greene shook his head with a sigh as Zheng firmly grabbed hold of his other arm to help guide him. Sherri nodded.

"Okay. Lift."

The corporal slowly lifted his boot as the people on either side of him guided his weight before his foot came completely dislodged, and he stepped free from the crater. For what seemed like forever, the entire congregation just stood and gawked at the massive indent. It looked almost like the pawprint of a big cat, only splayed out and nearly as wide as a car tire. Sherri kicked into gear.

"Stand back, please, give us some space," she said as she gently ushered the guns away.

"Game plan?" Giovanni said as he and his brother appeared on either side of her.

"Do you two think it's possible to dig up the whole section of soil and transport it back to the lab for preservation?" Sherri asked, dropping her backpack to the ground and rummaging through it.

The two archaeologists looked at one another, then back at the track. Harrison grabbed a tape measure out of his bag, then kneeled to measure the perimeter around the footprint. He shook his head.

"No, not without excavating the whole area."

Sherri sighed, resting her hands on her hips.

"Photos, samples, plaster cast, mark the area. We'll just have to hope it survives the night. Cool?" She looked up at the men, who were already getting the necessary tools from their packs.

Harrison nodded once.

"Yes, ma'am."

Giovanni tossed a package of dry plaster in the air and caught it in the opposite hand.

"You got it."

...

"Squints."

The captain didn't even look up from his watch as he barked at the scientists, his hand on his belt as he waited.

"Gun," a sarcastic voice replied as Doctor Daniels dusted off the plaster cast and prepared it for extraction. Short contemplated the equivalent nickname she'd dubbed him and his comrades for a moment and came to the conclusion that it had a ring to it.

"How long?" he asked as he plucked a toothpick out of Corporal Greene's fingers right before the corporal put it in his mouth. He set it between his own teeth as Greene watched helplessly.

Doctor Daniels remained focused on her task while she and the Rosenquest brothers began to wiggle the cast free from the soil.

"How long are you going to bitch?" she called back.

"How long are you going to play with dirt," he retorted.

"Five more minutes. Unless you've got twenty bucks, then we can move some ass," she said as the cast started to budge. The brothers quietly argued about how they'd split the money for a moment before Sherri shushed them and the form broke free. Even Short passed on delivering another comment as he watched the delicate process of the cast being flipped over, then set into a large plastic tray by all three sets of gloved hands. As Harrison packed it in with foam rolls and snapped the lid on, Giovanni began marking the area with stone cairns. Everyone's breath slowly let out.

"You gonna go quietly or will I have to drag your ass inside?" Captain Short broke the silence as Doctor Daniels stood up and dusted off her knees.

"I forgot my sneakers so I'm not exactly prepared to run from you. We could box, though."

"Oh, she's got jokes." Short rolled his eyes and shook his head.

"We can go. I've got what I need." Sherri said with a shrug.

"What was that?"

"I said," — she looked up at him and exaggeratedly slowed down her voice — "We-can-go, I've-got-what-I-need."

Short narrowed his eyes.

"The fuck are you up to?"

"Going inside, you want to come?"

The captain glared down at the woman before him, dissecting her with his eyes in a desperate attempt to figure out what unholy force might cause her to make something easy for him. He slowly leaned in, so close to her face their eyelashes almost touched.

"I'm watching you, Doc, you hear me? You're up to something, and you can play dumb and innocent all you want, but you ain't fooling nobody. Make one wrong move, I'm there," he said in a voice so low it was edging on a whisper. She stared right back.

"I like that cologne on you," Sherri replied smugly. With that, she turned away from his accusatory gaze.

The group finished packing up their supplies and began the short hike back to the compound.

"Hey!"

Kaishek had already begun leading the rebels back down the mountain path, but the shrill voice made him turn back around.

Alvi swallowed, briefly filled with regret as she was faced with the skeleton ghaengste's grizzled visage. He'd looked short and stout next to Kodo, but as he towered over her, she was reminded of just how mammoth a beast he was in his own right.

"What?" His voice was even and dry, but it boomed across the mountain range with boundless power.

"Where are you going?" Alvi demanded, clearing her throat.

"We are going to eat, to rest."

"Already? You *forced* Kodo to spar, and he didn't even need it." Alvi scoffed. "What about me?"

"Hm? What about you?" Kaishek asked.

Alvi marched closer, glaring up into the old man's skull-marked face.

"*What* about *me?*" Her sharp teeth bared in rage.

"Where is my training, my lesson, my sparring match? You don't think I'm worth your precious damn time out here in *exile,* old man? You don't think I'm capable because I'm small? Because I'm an ocean dweller!?" she spat viciously, her ears pinned back against her head as she hissed.

Kaishek blinked, studying her snarling face and glaring fangs. He looked calm, as he always did, but his head cocked in curiosity.

"Alvi," he began, "you are not yet at full strength. But even when you are, I will not train you as I would a larger ghaengste."

"You arrogant son of a whore, *how dare you —*"

"But that is not because you are any less capable of a warrior."

Alvi bit her tongue as the Lost King explained.

"Your strengths are not in size, like Kodo, or weight, like Rykr, or speed, like Leida. I will not put you against an opponent that towers over you and expect you to thrive in brute combat. I expect you to play by your own strengths, not mine. Do you understand?"

The ocean woman looked Kaishek up and down critically, but the fire in her stomach began to quench. She knew, of course, that physical strength was not her greatest asset. But it was a shock to hear that the old brute of a mountain ghaengste might know there was any other kind of value. She allowed herself to calm, the shame in her chest falling away.

"Then what do you want from me?" she asked, her voice slow and suspicious.

A soft, knowing glimmer formed in Kaishek's wise gaze. He leaned down so he could be at her eye level. Her entire skull was not much bigger than his snout, but she watched him boldly and expectantly.

"Surprise me," the old man said with a gentle wink. Alvi considered that for a moment, studying him. Then she simply continued on their original path.

"Sure, grandpa," she replied dryly as she walked past him.

...

What is taking them so long?

Rataan snarled at the empty air, the hair on the back of his shoulders bristling in rage as his muscles twitched and his mind raced.

The tunahk should have found them by now, they could not have gotten far.

A deep rumble began in his chest, like an earthquake ready to split the ground beneath him. The vibration continued through him, spreading into his burning throat.

Then it ceased and he whipped around as someone entered the tent.

"Sirrah-Jel," he greeted with a nod, his voice even and warm as if rapt to see an old friend. The darker, younger man nodded back in respect. Rataan wandered nonchalantly to a table nearby, his posture now relaxed.

"Have you heard any word from the tunahk?" the commander asked offhandedly. He aimlessly adjusted a bottle on the table, sliding it to a different position. Sirrah slowly shook his head, eyeing Rataan's face.

"No, Rataan-Leih, I apologize. I came to report signs of Gutfyres in the western hunting grounds — corpses strung from trees again. I ask if you have any warriors to spare that can accompany my hunting parties."

Rataan's face dropped and his expression grew cold as his eyes came to rest on Sirrah.

"My warriors have greater concerns than some straggling gutters. Take a few guards and combine the parties to double their numbers." Rataan dismissively turned back around.

"My hunters are on edge after —"

"Then they won't allow themselves to be caught vulnerable," Rataan spat. "Tell them if they encounter any gutters, spear their heads to the trees as a warning to any others. Is that clear enough?" He jutted his chin toward the door. "Leave."

Sirrah turned with a growl, but he didn't loiter another second before exiting the way he came.

Rataan paced alone with the rage in his belly once again, his claws scraping the floorboards as he tread back and forth, back and forth. The room seemed to vibrate around him, the air thick and heavy and humid. Something was coming, he could feel it as clearly as if the Great Mother had told him Herself. But now all he could do was wait for Her to give him another sign.

Whirrrrr

clang

Marshall's chest ached in a way it hardly ever did. Something buzzed past his sternum, pressure built as his heart rate increased. That sound.

Whirrrrr

clang

He knew what it was, of course. The inner mechanisms of the door working as the airlocked seal broke. But it wasn't the door itself that gave him the odd chest pain, it was what would follow. Inside the compound, they were safe. Ignorant. But as soon as that door finished opening, the rug of ignorance would be yanked out from under their feet. He'd swallowed that reality with relative ease before. But sure enough, images of bloodied colleagues barely conscious as they flooded into the corridor filled his head, and his chest kept hurting. Who wouldn't make it inside today? He closed his eyes and pressed two fingers against the artery in his neck, focusing on his rapid pulse.

Whirrrrr

click click click

He held his breath, still sitting in his desk chair. Listening from the isolation of the lab. He awaited the calls for medical help, the gasps of air, that dreaded headcount.

Nothing.

His eyes opened, and he stood as his curiosity got the best of him. Creeping to the lab door, he took a deep breath as he prepared to enter the commons.

He opened the door and immediately collided with something slightly below his chest level. His eyes widened in unbecoming terror for just a second as he looked down.

"Jeez, Novak, you okay? You look like you've seen a ghost."

He blinked as he found himself staring down into curious brown eyes. The pressure in his chest released.

"In my defense, I'm looking right at one. Aren't you supposed to be mincemeat?" He exhaled as he studied Sherri's face, which appeared completely intact. She began to scoot past him.

"Ha ha, very cute. Move please, we have a cart to wheel in."

"Oh."

Marshall stepped to the side as Sherri marched into the lab, followed by both Rosenquest brothers wheeling in a cart, a large tray atop it.

"What's in the tray?" Marshall asked cautiously.

"If you wanted to know so bad, maybe you should have come," Sherri said with a shrug as she helped guide the tray onto a clean table.

"Why's that? I could just wait here with Doyle and Bridgeland, dick in hand, while you three stooges get yourselves killed doing grad-student work." Marshall leaned against a table with his arms crossed, watching her smugly. Sherri narrowed her eyes.

"Hm... whose dick was in whose hand?"

Marshall opened his mouth to deliver a clever rebuttal, but she didn't give him the chance, pushing past him once again. He found himself wondering if she was deliberately failing to maneuver around him, an obnoxiously large obstacle. He didn't get the thought out in time before she interrupted him.

"If you have nothing valuable to add, at least make yourself useful and come help me get the molding supplies to reconstruct the foot. Clay is heavy."

"The... foot?"

Sherri was already walking away without a word. Marshall sighed, debated on not following, and then subsequently jogged after her.

Doctor Novak fell in step beside her as she headed for the supply closet. After a moment of silent walking, Sherri spoke up.

"So what's your problem?"

"Sorry?"

"You've been especially insufferable, insensitive, and generally antagonistic lately," she explained. "Normally I don't care, but ever since Roger, you've been an even bigger prick."

There was another brief pause as Marshall seemed to think about that, looking down at her from the corner of his eye.

"Care to elaborate?"

"Well, for starters, treating those of us who choose to go out in the field and do our *jobs* as inferior and stupid."

She looked up at him now, his sharp face contemplative.

"Ah, maybe it just peeves me when perfectly good scientists risk their valuable lives for unnecessary glory," he countered nonchalantly. Sherri stopped in front of the storage closet and turned to fully face him.

"You know it's not unnecessary. You know damn well we're just doing what we're here to do. If you think Roger's life was so valuable, then why are you acting like it means nothing that he's dead?" she snapped, her face growing warm as she couldn't stop the anger rising up through her chest. Their friend was dead and Marshall still couldn't drop the above-it-all act. He shook his head.

"What? I'm —"

"No, you know what? Save it. You self-serving, self-important asshole —"

"H—"

"You don't get to sit inside tinkering with kitchen appliances like a pussy while the *real* researchers do *real* research and then pretend we're making unnecessary sacrifices, judging us from up on your high horse like some *holier-than-thou old fuck —*"

"Hey!" Marshall barked, his light brown eyes growing sharp and stern, "Watch your fucking mouth; if anyone on this planet is an arrogant, self-righteous egomaniac, it is you."

"Oh, that's really rich, Novak, you want to call me arrogant?" She laughed in disbelief. "At least I give half a shit about other *human lives!*"

"Give it a rest, will you?" Marshall spat back. "I may not have the moral high ground, but at least I'm honest about it! This might shock you, Daniels, but while maybe *your* world revolves around you, this one doesn't!"

"You're *unbelievable!*"

"You're *fucking unbearable.*"

She didn't even get the chance to lean up before he grabbed her face firmly and smashed his lips into hers, meeting her halfway.

Marshall's normally graceful fingers grasped her jaw roughly, and Sherri wrapped her arms around his neck as she deepened the embrace. He rolled to the side, pulling her along with him away from the corridor wall and pushing open the heavy storage room door with his back as they stumbled inside.

Marshall's breath hitched through their kiss as Sherri's hands grasped at the hair at the nape of his neck, and he moved his mouth from her lips to her chin, then her throat. She hopped up to fold her legs around his hips, her heart racing.

He wrapped his arms around her waist to support her weight with his large hands; he was strong for his slender build and Sherri realized just how longing she had been. She began to count in her head how long it had been since she'd last had sex, but the hot tickling sensation of Marshall sucking on her neck cleared all thoughts from her weary mind. All but one.

"Fuck me, Novak," she breathed next to his ear through a contented moan.

She could feel a smirk cross Marshall's lips as they trailed back up her jaw and his nose brushed her ear. Her back met the nearest wall and he closed the gap between them, the hard buckle of his belt pressing into her soft stomach.

"That's better," he huffed as their eager mouths met again. Sherri hummed into the deepening kiss and she felt his crotch become firmer against her as his hips grinded into hers, pinning her against the wall. His rhythm kindled a growing flame in her hungry gut and a buzzing inside her dampened underwear.

Marshall's long fingers found the hem of her top and he broke the kiss as he lifted her shirt, revealing more of her skin as she pulled at his tie. Sherri began to protest when he set her back on her feet, but it became a delighted chuckle as he undid her shorts and slowly kneeled before her. She gasped in premature pleasure as he yanked her bottoms past her hips and down her thighs, freeing her full curves.

He guided her pillowy thigh to rest on his shoulder, wasting no time as he pushed his face between her legs. Sherri's breath caught as he tongued her throbbing labia and two of his fingers slipped deep inside her. She found herself tugging firmly at his soft hair as his skillful fingers and hungry tongue inched her closer and closer. Heat, lust, and sweat traveled along her skin as her choked moans accompanied the clink of his belt unbuckling.

Marshall pushed his free hand down the front of his pants to stroke himself to the maddening music of her praiseful gasps and breaths. His erection twitched and tried to fight free from his zipper as he finally felt Sherri's cum coat his fingers and fill his starving mouth. A cry of ecstasy sang from her ragged throat as every muscle in her body clenched and burned and quivered at his touch.

"Shit, Novak, maybe I was wrong about the self-serving part," Sherri panted and let out a dazed laugh.

"Don't kid yourself, honey," he teased, smirking up at her as he dragged his tongue across the moist flesh of her inner thigh. "It doesn't get any more self-serving than this."

He rose back to his towering height with a stifled grunt, then pushed her back against the wall and studied her full figure in wolfish hunger. Sherri unbuttoned his shirt, running her hand down his chest and stomach eagerly as her gaze climbed to his eyes.

"Then serve me now," she whispered, grabbing hold of the band of his open pants and firmly pulling him closer by the stiff fabric. She slowly tugged his fly further open, releasing his throbbing shaft as it bounced out from his zipper.

"My pleasure," he growled as he lifted her again, rushing to wrap her legs around his waist and paint her neck and collarbones with kisses. A soft gasp escaped Sherri's lips as the head nestled into her hot flesh. Marshall let out a long, hoarse groan before tossing her further up on his hips to guide the rest of his length into her. She clutched at his open shirt as he began to thrust yearningly, savoring the wetness and warmth of her hole.

Their bodies moved as one fluid animal and the cramped room filled with a saturated fog of desperation, tension, and release.

The storage shelves were shaking now, Sherri grabbing hold of one nearby as Marshall slammed her against the wall. Sweat coated their bodies and amplified the slapping of his hips against hers, their weary breaths and moans joining the tumult of the stuffy closet.

Sherri cried out and raked her nails down Marshall's back, causing him to jolt as he pushed into her in the final moments of their tryst. His back muscles clenched beneath her fingers and he buried himself within her once more. She sighed with pleasure as she felt him release, letting out one final moan as she let her head fall into the crook of his neck.

"I needed that," she sighed contentedly as she ran her fingers through his hair. Marshall was still too busy panting and gasping to immediately reply.

"And they say you can't play nice with others," he finally huffed with a cocky, worn-out smirk, his head falling to rest against hers. Sherri gently slapped the side of his cheek with a scolding smile.

"Who says?" she said with a laugh, finding herself unable to be bothered by the fact that this was the very same egotistical, unbearable Doctor Novak from before. For a moment, she didn't care about his selfish attitude or inappropriate wisecracks, she didn't care about much at all. For a moment, she wasn't a doomed scientist on a hostile planet with the fate of her kind on her shoulders.

For a moment, she was just a human.

12
SABBATH

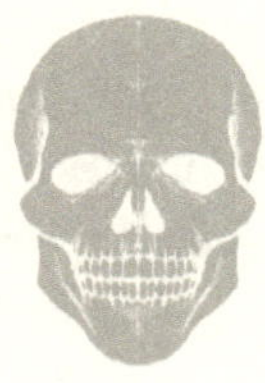

"Is it just me, or will this be a regular thing?"

Sherri laughed at the boldness of the man beside her and stretched her arms upward, letting them rest against the headboard in satisfaction as her bare chest rose and fell.

"Don't get cocky on me, slick." She smirked up at him and lightly pinched the tip of his chin. Marshall looked over her tanned face admiringly, supporting his weight on his elbow as he lay next to her on the bed.

"Me? Cocky? Never," he teased as his fingers traced the soft skin of her stomach, leaving tingling bumps in their wake. He leaned down close to her lips, his long nose brushing against hers as he watched her. Sherri took in how he looked without his glasses, noting the youthfulness of his features. It contrasted with his gray-streaked hair, which was messy for once, and if she hadn't looked through his file, she might not have been able to guess how old he was.

"What, you can't see me without your glasses?" she goaded as he hovered nearer to her. Marshall smirked, biting at his lower lip.

"No, care to get closer?" he cooed.

"Nope," Sherri taunted with a smile as she rolled out from under him and began to climb out of the bed. He playfully swatted her naked behind then laid his head back down on the pillow, and she giggled energetically as she redressed to make her journey to the locker room.

"Ice cold." Marshall winced, shaking his head.

"Always." Sherri finished dressing, then gave him a quick, rough kiss on the cheek before scampering out of the room.

...

Sherri entered the kitchen with wet hair and an enthusiastic skip in her step.

"Gooood morning, Gio," she greeted her friend, stealing a freeze-dried grape from his fingers and popping it in her mouth, then ruffling his hair as she walked past. Giovanni pulled his head away to indignantly readjust his slicked-back hair but smiled as he plucked another grape off the plate.

"Mornin'," he replied. "Slept in late? You've usually been up for hours by the time we come out."

"I was awake, just not up. Early meditation," she explained nonchalantly.

"Meditation, hm? Something you can bond with Harrison about, then. I woke up to him sitting on the floor the other morning, facing me with his eyes closed. About passed out from fright; I thought he was bloody possessed."

Giovanni snickered even after earning a swat to the back of his head from his older brother walking past. The brothers teased back and forth while the rest of the research team filed in for breakfast, but Sherri interrupted their bickering.

"Gio, have you taken a look at the soil scrapings from the footprint yet?"

"It's the first thing on my to-do list —"

"Corporal, *please!*"

At first glance, what appeared to be a drunken bull came barreling through the kitchen. Carl barely made it out of the way in time to avoid being trampled by the massive shirtless man that came charging through.

"*Whewww*, is this your girlfriend, maggot? She's pretty cute, huh?" Corporal Keenan howled, holding up a picture frame as a much smaller man trailed close behind.

"Give me my picture back, Keenan. Please," Private Zheng pleaded as he followed along, getting red in the face but keeping control of his voice. Keenan cackled and held the frame far out of his reach.

"What, you don't want to share? Stingy little son of a *bitch*," the corporal sneered, baring his teeth in Zheng's face. The private didn't flinch, and Keenan growled like an animal, his nose twitching as if he were about to bite.

"Come on, kid, take it. Give me a reason to rip your head off with my *fucking teeth*," the marine taunted. "Why don't you grow some fucking balls for that pretty girl of yours to —"

"I'm not going to take it from you, Corporal. Just give it back," Zheng said slowly. His jaw clenched and grinded in his mouth, as if he were fighting to hold back a threat he couldn't promise.

"Five."

A loud voice thundered from across the room.

"Four."

Both Keenan and Zheng looked around wildly, simultaneously spotting the captain in the doorway. His face was twitching with the barely-contained rage of a hurricane.

"Three."

"Heyy, Cap, I was just playin' around—"

Keenan's skull was slammed into the counter so hard his teeth audibly snapped together in his mouth. His cheek was pinned firmly against the cold surface by a vice grip on the back of his neck.

"Two one," Short growled and twisted the marine's muscular arm behind his back so roughly the bystanders feared a seemingly inevitable crack, then snatched the frame out of his hand. He handed the picture to Zheng, who took it quickly and without a word.

"You picked the *wrong* day to start shit, motherfucker, know why?" the captain spit, his voice on the edge of a roar.

"Wh—"

"Because I'm running on no god damn sleep, and your ugly fucking face is looking like a *picture-perfect place* for *MY FUCKING BOOT!*" he screamed in Keenan's ear, the pinned man's face contorting into a grimace as the bellow rang through the room.

Sherri glanced at Marshall, who had a similar 'oops' expression on his face. The rest of the crew stood around frozen, staring at the violent spectacle before them in rattled silence.

The captain released the larger soldier, stepping back and wiping his mouth with the back of his hand. His tired eyes were wild and stormy, the silver streak glaring against the redness of his bloodshot sclera.

"Do us both a favor and don't let me see you for the rest of the day, Corporal," he spat, roughly shoving Keenan away. The marine finally showed some ounce of sense and stumbled out of the area without a word. Sherri decided it was in her best interest to look innocent and eat her breakfast as she could feel the captain's sharp eyes searching the area. They rested on Marshall, who was unfortunately far too arrogant to play dumb.

"You," Short snapped. Marshall glanced up briefly from balancing a spoon on the rim of his empty coffee mug.

"Who, me?"

Captain Short's fist planted on the counter in front of the scientist with a heavy thunk. The spoon fell into the mug.

"You're in the room next to mine. 2C?" Short asked slowly, his nostrils flaring. Marshall made a face at the fallen spoon.

"Guilty."

"Next time, keep. It. *Down*," the captain hissed.

The two men stared at each other for a tense moment, and Harrison squeezed his eyes shut. Doyle looked like he was in the front row at the circus.

Marshall clicked his tongue.

"I'd love to help, pal, but I wasn't the noisy one." He winked smugly and stood up to leave. Sherri suddenly became extremely interested in the label on a nearby sugar packet, studying it closely.

Don't blush, don't blush, don't blush.

She felt Giovanni watching her from her left, and she could practically hear the lightbulb over his head ding as he connected the dots.

Damn.

Soft green firelight painted the walls of the cave and bathed the figures around it, warming them in emerald hues. The smell of dried herbs and dusty animal hide hung thick in the air, and the sounds of the howling, singing wind were far away and muffled.

Kodo yawned, letting his tongue stretch out of his mouth as he lowered his giant body down onto a furry pelt with an audible *fwump*. His heavy head fell to the side, leaning against Leida's shoulder. She tensed a bit, but allowed it.

Kaishek watched them in silence. The seasoned young woman, the innocent young man resting his head on her shoulder. His eyes wandered to his nephew, so stoic and angry inside. Then to the little ocean dweller whose spirit far outweighed her body. The four ghaengste before him with nothing to call their own but the new bonds between them. They carried the burden of their world, whether they knew it or not.

But the sight of them was too much. For a moment, the Lost King had to fight the urge to scare them away. To make them leave his isolated prison, to make them run far away and never return. Even as his gaze found his lost son, who shared the face of his love, something inside him wanted to fight, scream, throw him out for awakening whatever it was that stirred in the old man's hearts. It was his hearts, after all; that was what ached and churned and longed to be alone. They were ancient and scarred. They were the hearts of a warrior, and they'd frozen over long ago among ice and death.

Kaishek's weary eyes rested on the flames and he saw in them a younger man, fur black as blood against the white snow. From the moment he was born, the rare darkness of his pelt had been a mark that he was a stronger beast than his kin. He had to be stronger. Unlike the rest of the mountain people, he could not blend in with the snow. He did not have the privilege to run or hide. From birth, he was destined to fight mercilessly, savagely, and with unquenchable bloodlust.

And he did. The young man he watched in the fire killed and ravaged and wrought terror. He was a barbaric prince, he demanded the scalps of his enemies and destroyed everything in his wake. Then he was a tyrant king — he spread the flames of fear and slayed anything that stood in the way of his glory. The young man in the fire rampaged until he was soaked to the very bone with cold blood; he knew nothing of gentleness.

Until he did.

Kaishek remembered the feeling of gentleness then.

In her smile, in the sweet music of her laugh. In her soft eyes, the color of tree bark and fertile soil and potent tea. In the way she touched her head to his, the way she corrected him when he pushed back too hard. In her tail swaying as she danced, her long hair dragging through the grass and collecting leaves.

His warrior hearts had resisted her with all the raw power in their veins, and then surrendered to her with the very same. They melted in her grasp, released to her, expected neither mercy nor care. Hers was the only battle he'd ever lost, the only opponent that ever felled him.

But she was gentle with him.

And then she was taken away.

His chest clenched again with the reflex to fight the rising feelings as he refocused on the air around him. He wanted nothing of gentleness; it had already broken something inside of him that could never be recovered. Gentleness had no place in their harsh world; it was a weakness they couldn't afford. He knew nothing of the innocence inside his son, he knew nothing of how to care for it. The man in the fire wanted to destroy it like he'd destroyed everything else on his war path, treat it like an enemy and burn it to the ground. The man in the fire raged hot and furious, he did not want young ghaengste with love and innocence and hope. He wanted an army, he wanted soldiers.

He wanted blood.

Kaishek tore his eyes from the fire, and once again, they rested on his son. Kodo.

The boy's face had shed its worries and grew warm at the touch of the woman he leaned on. His head rested on her shoulder with no regard for the fact that she could move at any moment, letting him fall. He relaxed his weight into her with infinite trust. His deep, hopeful eyes glowed like a lighthouse in the darkness of his brutish form and the horrific scars carved into his throat.

The raging flames in Kaishek's chest gradually calmed, and he breathed slowly.

...

"A lonely tree,
A sea of souls.
The waning glee,
And waxing coal.
A fire that burns in rain and snow,
But what of the children?
We'll never know!"

A jubilant voice floated between the tents and huts, quiet but clear as a bell. The tone was young and full of hope, but the words it sang were tinged with a bittersweetness and the distinct feeling that the singer didn't quite understand them. It was a child's voice.

"Where did you hear that song, boy?"

The boy stopped singing, and his prancing feet halted almost too suddenly for his lanky body to follow suit. He stumbled slightly before turning around with his head tilted.

"Oh, Vaus-Erro." The young prince broke into a soothed smile, trotting up to the queen eagerly. She couldn't stop her stern face from softening as she noticed the boy seemed to have grown taller from just the day before.

"I heard Caita singing it while he bandaged the scrape on my knee. It left a scar, look." He fell back onto his rump and lifted his leg to show her. "Grisly, hm?"

"Ah, a nasty one indeed. Do you know what they say about scars, Tahro?" Erro asked with a smile, leaning in as if to tell him a secret. Tahro blinked in awe, hovering nearer and already widening his eyes at the wisdom she might share with him.

"Every body has its own story, and every scar is a page," Erro continued in a wondrous whisper. "Each scar you earn represents the writing of your tale. Remember that, Tahro, your story must be told. Even pain, even wounds. Those are the moments that determine how long your journey will grow to be.

"We all choose whether to let our battles stop the story in its tracks, or to fight for our own happy endings."

The weathered queen winked before shooing him, sending the boy on his way to continue whatever his original adventure may have been.

As Tahro's singing and prancing echoed further away through the maze of huts, the queen contemplated how much he took after his parents. He was the spitting image of Visaan, but he'd always had Avias's soft nature. The youngest prince and his brothers were more than enough for Erro's taste; she felt no need to bear children from her own womb as she already loved the boys like they were her blood.

The tunahk-dahn's training courtyard came into view as she strolled, and Erro was reminded of when her sisters were Tahro's age. Io and Iago were unlike the sweet boy in every way; but every once in a while, she caught a glimpse of their youthful spirits in his eyes.

As Vaus-Erro passed the well-worn grounds of the courtyard, fertilized by years of shed blood, she was filled with memories of kinship and battle. Of standing beside her brothers and sisters of the tunahk-dahn, slaying the clan's foes and taking new land for their nation. She recalled Rataan-Leih alongside her, when they were both young and hungry and free. Now she was queen and he was commander, both dull and honorable fates. But their hearts were that of soldiers, and they would always belong to the battlefield.

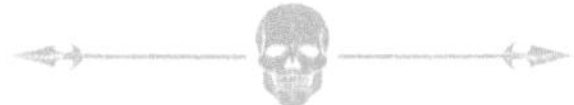

Sherri had always been relatively artistically inclined. Between nature journaling, scientific drawings, and mindless doodles, she knew her way around a sketchbook pretty well. But sculpting? She grew more frustrated by the minute. The familiar sensation of a pair of curious dark eyes boring into the side of her face didn't help either. She released a heavy sigh.

"What, Gio?"

He barely let her finish before leaning over her desk.

"You and Novak? Really?" Giovanni whispered. His station wasn't even next to hers, but Harrison's was, and he seemed to be using that as a cover for his loitering. Sherri gave him a scolding look.

"It's casual and it's none of your business. That's all I'll say about it."

"But —"

"That's all I'll say about it."

"*Novak?*"

"I need a break!" she announced loudly to the entire room, wiping clay off her hands as she stood up. A disappointed look dropped over Giovanni's face.

"You alright?" Harrison leaned back in his chair to look at her from his desk, a pen hanging from the side of his mouth.

"I'm at a standstill. I've got this pad reconstructed to a T, but I have no idea what the rest of the phalangeal structure is like. I didn't get a good look. Not to mention, there are no claw indents on this track but that doesn't fit with our classification of the species so far."

Harrison adjusted the pen between his teeth, then took it out and gestured to her with it.

"Perhaps you should conduct some more eyewitness interviews."

Sherri exhaled and nodded before reluctantly heading for the door.

"Good luck."

Luck. Sherri didn't exactly believe in luck, but she couldn't disprove it either. If it existed, however, she was praying for it as she walked into the barracks.

Old rock music blared in her ears as soon as she opened the door. Her single functional ear, rather, and Sherri became abruptly aware of her one overloaded eardrum as it was flooded with a cacophony of noise. She fought an aching dizziness while it seemed like the entire right side of her skull was brutally invaded by Metallica.

It took a moment to spot the person she sought between the smokey haze in the air and her disorientation. She eventually located the tall, aged woman with a long braid fading from gray to blonde. A cigarette hung loosely from her lower lip and she blew smoke out of her nose as she dealt cards from the head of the poker table.

"Master Sergeant Fischer?" Sherri asked from behind.

"Who's asking?" Fischer replied dryly, not looking up from her task.

"Doctor Daniels, RREP botanist." Sherri placed herself at the side of the other woman's chair, forcing her way into her line of sight. "I'm here to ask you some questions about your encounter with the native."

Fischer puffed some smoke out of the side of her mouth, then tossed the remainder of the deck in front of the man beside her.

"Ma, you're house," she said just as blandly as she said every other thing and stood up to follow Sherri. Sherri found herself surprised that the sergeant didn't put up more of a fight, and more surprised yet at just how much the other woman towered over her. She vividly recalled her previous run-ins with Fischer's might, most notably being caught and restrained by her like a powerless prey animal. Sherri stowed any remaining grudge to the best of her ability as she led the soldier out into the hallway for a more quiet interview.

Sergeant Fischer leaned against the wall and crossed her arms, watching expectantly. Sherri flipped to a fresh page in her journal, cleared her throat, and began.

"Can you tell me what you remember about the specimen's appearance, Sergeant? What did you notice, how would you describe it?"

"Big. Fast. Leggy. Long tail that'd sweep you off your feet," Fischer explained like she was giving a statement to the police but didn't intend to disclose any more information than absolutely necessary. Sherri took notes, glancing up at

Fischer's hard, dull green eyes. They had a way of distracting from the woman's otherwise attractive face, making her look years older and worlds meaner.

"And if you had to compare it to an animal from Earth, what would it be?" Sherri asked.

"A dog, I guess. Maybe a Great Dane."

Sherri cocked her head up at the soldier, following each raspy word as she scribbled in her journal.

"Would you say you got a good look at the native's feet?"

Fischer just shrugged and nodded.

"The footprint we found indicated that the natives don't have claws like most Earth predators, w—"

"They do."

Sherri's scrawling pencil stopped in its path, and she looked up at Sergeant Fischer once again.

"I'm sorry?"

"They have claws."

"The track —"

Fischer lifted the bottom of her shirt to her chest, revealing a grotesque, stitched-together gash carved through her toned midriff. A long trailing crevice was cut into her side, where the dense muscle had been ripped apart and the skin was loose and shriveled. Even weeks after the attack, a train track of hundreds of sutures sewn through the healing wound served as a ghastly reminder.

"They have claws."

Sherri blinked in shock; she didn't even remember seeing blood on Fischer's clothes the day of the incident. The adrenaline must have given her tunnel vision. She was speechless for a moment, studying the harrowing injury in awe.

Before she could think about it, Sherri gingerly reached out and grazed the soldier's tense stomach, so softly there almost wasn't contact at all. The warm skin of Fischer's belly twitched beneath her gentle fingertips, defined abdominal muscles contracting at the tenuous touch. Sherri's eyes wandered up to the stern gaze observing her closely.

"Did I hurt you?" she asked in almost a whisper, her voice more timid than she'd intended. Fischer gave a small shake of her head, still holding the hem of her shirt just above the band of her bra.

"No. Go ahead," the soldier replied, her hoarse voice stale, but her cold eyes slowly traced up and down Sherri curiously, maybe smugly. Her mouth seemed to flutter into a small, daring smirk, but just for a moment. Sherri watched the sergeant's teasing lips as she silently chewed on her own, a lengthened breath falling through her teeth. The tips of her delicate fingers dragged just slightly, almost involuntarily, down the hard lines of Fischer's stomach, her thumb barely catching the metal of the other woman's belt. Fischer's hand reached out, coming to rest on Sherri's waist.

The door to the barracks swung open, and Sherri quickly retracted her hand as her face grew hot. She began to back up as another soldier came through the doorway, and Fischer released her lifted shirt.

"Thank you, Sergeant, hope your wound heals well," Sherri said as she cleared her throat and flipped around to rush out the way she came.

Come on, Daniels, focus.

"Uncle." Rykr's voice gently disturbed the extended silence of rest and the lulling music of the fire. Kaishek was pulled from a deep ocean of thought.

"Hm?" He glanced up and across the firelight at his nephew.

"You said eventually we would learn to fight with forged weapons," Rykr continued curiously, "But we don't have any. And we don't exactly have access to clan blacksmiths or merchants, like the tunahk do."

Something deep within Kaishek ignited then, his head raising higher. He nodded slowly, then stood up as the other rebels began to pay attention.

"This is true," the old man replied, opening a chest made of woven fibers near the wall. "Your cause is young, you lack the resources of your enemies."

He pulled out a rolled-up parchment from the chest, then began to spread it out on the stone floor before the four rebels. A map.

"But this infancy is not only a hindrance. You are not yet known, and you have nothing to lose. This gives you the freedom to move quickly, boldly, and unpredictably."

Kaishek grabbed a piece of charcoal from the edge of the fire between his claws and used it to mark the map. He drew an X over an outcropping to the south in the middle of a large bay.

"To take a risk."

Alvi's bright amber eyes widened.

"Years alone in the mountains have driven you insane, Uncle."

Kaishek's gaze warned Rykr, who quickly closed his mouth before any more rash words fell out.

"Do not speak before you have listened, boy."

All eyes stared at the old man, and he continued despite their looks of confusion.

"The Celesteal clan rears the finest blacksmiths of Matka. Their metals and craftsmanship are far more advanced than anything the Ramys clan could hope to possess." He glanced at Alvi.

"You do not yet have the numbers nor the bloodlust to rival the Ramys warriors. But if you play the game right, you stand to gain superior weaponry and a fearsome ally.

"But it is up to you, Alvi. You are their kin. Only you can appeal to your home nation."

Alvi stared up at him in shock.

"You *are* insane," she exclaimed. "Vaus-Kharax would never allow a sky or mountain dweller to cross her borders, much less give them aid — and Kodo? A *forestman*? He'd be killed on sight! Do you genuinely expect me to prance back into the kingdom I *abandoned* and demand the queen arm my sacrilegious rebellion?"

The other rebels looked between one another, as if the idea didn't seem so doomed when she put it that way.

"You could talk a kru'vaii off a meat wagon," Kodo conceded with a shrug. Alvi glared at him.

"Absolutely not." She shook her head. "Look, grandpa, I appreciate the hospitality and the guidance. But we do a fine job of making enemies all by ourselves, thank you."

Kaishek's teeth gritted as his patience wore thin. His young pupils knew nothing yet of uprising or war. They didn't understand the weight that they carried; they only cared how they would make it to the next morning, the next meal. They'd never even stopped to imagine victory, or to dream of what the world stood to gain from their fight.

"There is more." Leida spoke up, staring right through his gaze with a focus like a honed blade. "What is it?"

The Lost King met her eye, and a heavy tiredness weighed on him. He remained silent for a moment longer as the rebels searched him for his intentions. He found himself searching for them as well.

"You seek to survive. You seek shelter," he finally admitted, his rumbling voice quieter than it usually knew how to be.

"But your destiny is more than that." He looked around at each of the young ghaengste. "Why harbor lost refugees when you could liberate them, secure the fates of their children? Look at yourselves. You have already achieved the impossible simply by standing alongside one another."

His voice was passionate, but it held a sorrowful, desperate plea within it.

"You are the isthmus of our kind. The bridge that crosses the gap between our rifted worlds. The vein that feeds our broken people with the healing blood of Matka. If you'll let it, if you'll answer the call... You could be so much more than refugees or rebels. You could be the beginning of a better life." Pain slowly invaded him, then his eternal pride withered to shame all at once.

It was too late for him. It was too late for his family. For his Iva.

He'd failed her. He had not been able to give her the life she dared to dream of. The world she'd been brave enough to seek, strong enough to love. And now he would never get the chance to show her the fruition of what she'd believed in so fiercely.

But he could still avail the cause of her people, guide the way of her son. He could bear his blade once again and carve the future of the planet itself in her holy name.

He had to. He would. Or he would die trying, so that he may greet her as the man she'd seen him to be, not the man he'd let himself become.

"I will train you." Kaishek repeated his oath, but now his voice held a new fury. "You will grow strong and formidable. And you will bring harmony to your people by peace or by blood, by word or by war, because that is the meaning of your union. That is the end of your journey."

The young rebels stared up at the Lost King, their shoulders heavy with the burden he'd spoken of. But he did not lay it in their hands, no, that was done long ago by a power much more divine than he. The message he gave was not a command, it was a reminder of why the drums beat in their weary chests. The rebels urged to give it back, to reject his order and to seek the furthest path from the one laid before them. But something inside them, beyond their knowing grasp, understood that it would follow them to the ends of the world. Their destiny coursed through the ground beneath their feet, and there was not a place on the planet where they would be sheltered from Her gaze.

Captain Short was nearly swiped in the face by a mess of blonde curls as a familiar figure marched past him. Doctor Daniels didn't even bother acknowledging his presence before she sped away; it seemed the troublesome botanist never walked at a pace any slower than hauling ass. He found himself contemplating how many places she could possibly have to be at on time in a stagnant place like the compound. The taste in his mouth grew sour as he wondered again, *how many places could she possibly have to be?*

Short sighed then spun on his heel to follow her. That woman had given him nothing but bad feelings and headaches ever since she'd clawed her way up from hell and into his life, and lately it had grown even worse. He passed a congregation of his soldiers occupying themselves by playing a game of darts, using a photocopy of an anonymous nude backside taped to the wall and what appeared to be syringes. The captain snatched the lewd photo off the wall and shoved it in the trash can.

"You better take those unused syringes back to wherever the hell you found them, or it won't be a paper ass getting nailed to the wall," he barked and jutted a finger at the men. They scattered in all directions, one grabbing the still-packaged syringes and sprinting them in the direction of the med bay. Short just shook his head and drove on in the direction he'd been headed.

"Stupid motherfuckers," he muttered to himself as he caught a glimpse of a curly head ducking into a heavy doorway. He sped up to catch her.

His shoulder was seconds away from colliding with the glass doors to catch her in the act of something nefarious when he registered where he was. His eyes met the plate next to the frosted glass.

LABORATORY A • MAJORA

Oh.

He took a step back, peeking through the unfrosted glass panel beside the doorway. All research team members, including Daniels, appeared to be innocently doing whatever it was they did. He let out a breath and cursed his paranoia for dragging him on a wild goose chase. After quickly glancing around to ensure no one was watching, he released the yawn he'd been holding in all day, then blinked his tired eyes as he began making his way back to the barracks. The sleep deprivation tortured him, and the aftermath of his recent failures was drowning him like thick, hot tar. He snuffed his inhibitions like an uncontrolled flame; he couldn't start doubting himself, not now. As soon as he stopped trusting himself, his comrades would too.

Keep it together, Short.

"The claws are retractable, like a feline's. That's why there are no claw indents on the track, they were retracted," Sherri explained with pride and wonder shamelessly evident in her voice. And, as per usual, the room didn't seem to share her enthusiasm. Except for loyal Giovanni, who offered a hesitant smile beside his brother who was sweating profusely.

"Oh goody!" Doyle exclaimed.

"Oh brother," Carl wheezed.

Sherri was already making her way back to her station.

"This is great, at least it's something to compare the phalangeal structure to. But damn, I wish I had pictures." Something tugged at the back of Sherri's mind. She once again pulled out everything she had so far. Journal entries, countless drawings, the plaster cast, the half-sculpted recreation. It was a start, but she'd need more. She had four years on 7355264Z to discover everything she could about its environment. She was a field scientist, for god's sake, this wasn't the kind of world she could learn about from inside a lab. No one could.

Sherri took a moment to water her potted samples; her favorite was a small specimen that resembled a patch of common grass at first glance. But the vibrant green blades were more like tendrils slowly swaying and dancing of their own accord. It moved as if it were underwater, floating with a nonexistent current. Sherri could have watched it for hours, letting it soothe and ground her like a sunset or a prayer. Caring for the simple, blissful plants was the closest thing she had to worship; it healed her in a way she could only imagine religion did for believers.

She put her hand above the swimming grass, careful not to touch its fragile blades, and watched it stretch upward as if to grab at her fingers. Then she moved her hand to the side, chuckling as it reached over eagerly, magnetized by her skin.

"That's a little creepy," Marshall's smooth voice rang out from behind her.

"I think it's magnificent," Sherri said with a smile. He approached, reaching a hand over to lean on her desk — which she quickly slapped away.

"Ow."

"This desk wobbles, don't lean on it. You could knock the plants off," she explained.

"I'm not that heavy." He laughed but put his hands in his pockets to signify his surrender.

"Heavy enough." Sherri went back to toiling and caring for the potted plants with an almost motherly contentment as Marshall watched. He stepped a bit closer.

"I've been thinking," he started.

"Handsome *and* he thinks? I don't believe it," she teased, glancing at him between cataloging her sample care regimens. Marshall shook his head, but his voice lowered as he leaned in slightly closer and a smirk whispered across his mouth.

"Oh, I'm full of surprises," he said. "If you want to stop by my room tonight, maybe we can do some private experiments."

Sherri couldn't hold back a tempted smile, but she shooed him away.

"Mhm, some of us have very real experiments to do." She sprayed him with the water in her misting bottle. "Save the flirting for outside the lab, tiger."

Marshall flinched at the sudden misting but laughed as he backed away with his hands raised.

"Alright, alright. See you at lunch."

Sherri glanced down at her watch as he retreated; it was earlier than she'd thought. The morning was young despite how long it had seemed to drag on. She still had the majority of the day at her disposal. Time was their most limited resource, and they had to hold onto whatever minutes they could as they slipped through their fingers. The seconds on her watch face ticked by with the rhythm of the gears in her head and the beat of her heart.

I have time.

She watched as Marshall headed out of the lab with the Rosenquest brothers. They were teasing him about something, but she couldn't make out what over the sound of a blender whirring in the kitchen. In fact, the blender seemed to mask all the usual sounds of camaraderie and the eternal humming of the generators. She took a moment to watch the closed door and listen to the clangor, then glanced down again at her ticking watch. *I have time.*

No more mistakes. No more casualties.

Sherri's racing heart was no longer in her chest, safely tucked behind her ribcage. It was far away, outside of the sterile lab. Outside of the safe, steel walls of the compound. Outside of the electric fence, even, out in the wilderness and the vastness of the planet's otherworldly atmosphere.

She grabbed her backpack and chased after it.

She took a mental inventory of everything in her bag, everything she might need to function and survive in the wilderness of Earth and more. How different could it be? She knew that answer all too well, and her mind wandered back to the concept of luck as she hurriedly slipped through the lab's side door. She crept into the main entryway but past the corner of the commons. She typed the code into the keypad next to the door, willing the cacophony of the kitchen to drown out the familiar clangs and whirrs of the mechanical entrance. Just for a little longer.

An intense sensation began to buzz up through her legs.

Whirrrr

clang

The buzzing rose into her stomach.

Whirrr

clang

It filled her throat, her ears, her hands and feet.

Whirrr

click click click

The door slid open and Sherri didn't even give herself the chance to stop and listen for witnesses. She stepped out and typed in the code to shut it.

clang

She released the breath she'd been holding. Turning around, her gaze went right through the translucent turquoise light between her and the great expanse of wilderness. The last defense.

Snatching the portable keypad remote off its holster next to the control panel, Sherri typed in the fence code once again. The wall of light split down the middle, and she walked through the gap, through the light, into the meadow.

Into the wild.

"How?" Leida watched the Lost King like his words were something that had followed her for many years but only just caught up with her. Whether she knew it or not, something had drawn her from isolation into the civilized world and the sins that it bore. Perhaps this was it.

Kaishek looked over each one of the rebels, his face stern.

"A peace treaty," he said, his low voice steady and sure. "Between the clans of the region. The Ramys nation wants you dead, we know that much. If they catch you now, they will kill you without ever hearing about your cause." He began to symbolize the other clans across the map. After Celesteal, the ocean dwellers, he marked the territory of Ramys, the forest dwellers. Then Eidolan, the mountain dwellers to the west. And finally, to the east, the sky dwellers of Kocea.

"But," he continued, "if you can win the support of the other three clans, and convince them to ally with the rebellion, the Ramys clan will have no choice.

"They will sign the treaty, or they will find themselves the common enemy of a united coalition like no other. Mighty as they may be, they do not stand to win that war. And they never will."

The rebels glanced between one another hesitantly. The Lost King had explained it as if it were simple.

"What makes you so sure the other clans won't kill us just as quickly as Ramys would?" Kodo asked. "In case you haven't noticed, we don't exactly look like the kind of people you want crusading through your city."

Alvi made a snide comment under her breath about the use of 'we,' but Kaishek answered Kodo's question all too quickly.

"That, boy, is why you will start with Celesteal." The old man had a satisfied twinkle forming in his eye, and the rebels couldn't quite tell if this plan was something he'd been ruminating on for many years or if he was making it up as he went.

"Because you share a mutual peril with the Celesteal nation, and there is nothing more bonding.

"The Ramys clan has victimized the ocean people for centuries; they have sworn to push Celesteal back into the sea no matter the cost. And now they seek to crush the rebellion. In order to stop the slow massacre of her people, the queen needs the same thing that you four do: Ramys to be restrained, their hold over the region released. The rebellion can offer her this future, should she arm your cause."

A darkness fell over the rebels; they'd seen firsthand the destruction of the ocean people wrought by Ramys. They would never forget the sight of the slaughtered family, and they would never forget the promise they'd made to each slain soul.

Justice.

There was a pause as they returned to the memories that had driven them so far. Alvi's ears twitched with the pleading screams of her lost kin, demanding retribution. Rykr's scowling face was twisted in vengeful rage, his anger bubbling over like magma. The icy stare of Leida's gaze carried within it unimaginable witnessed horrors and a lifetime of sleepless nights. And Kodo was still imprisoned by a shame he couldn't run from and eaten by a guilt that wasn't his to bear.

"Well," Alvi said with a sigh, the first bold enough to answer the Lost King's call. "There are worse things to die for. But —"

She pointed an accusing claw at Kaishek, narrowing her eyes.

"You have to come with us, old man."

Kaishek furrowed his heavy brows, almost laughing in disbelief. Before he could protest, the other rebels chimed in.

"Yes. You must aid us." Leida nodded decidedly.

"We're heretics, not errand boys." Kodo shrugged.

The Lost King looked between them, speechless for once. Then he glanced at Y'xara, leaned against the wall of the cave like the abandoned gravestone of a self long gone. The axe called out to him as it had many years ago, but no longer of wrath and conquest. Now it demanded a promise be kept, the time now come. It called for redemption. Kaishek let out a long, slow breath.

"Fine," he managed hoarsely.

The task that had been bestowed upon the rebels seemed a little less daunting with the new addition. Kaishek had proved to be an exceptional warrior, even in his later years, and five somehow seemed so much greater than four. Their journey had proved treacherous beyond what they ever intended, and they were certain a long path of suffering awaited them ahead. But for just a moment, while they still had the chance, they let it go. That night, they had full bellies and a warm fire, and they savored it like a sacred piece of god. That night, they forgot about the memories behind them and the road ahead of them, and they laughed and joked and told stories from their homelands. That night, they were not renegades or refugees, fugitives or rebels. They were just friends.

The Lost King watched the unruly young ghaengste chuckle and tease each other carelessly. Even Leida's blunt face had a small, stiff smile on it, and she looked more at ease than he'd thought she was capable of. Rykr tried desperately to keep hold of his grim scowl but was fighting a losing battle as he watched Alvi perform an exaggerated impression of Kodo's clumsy swagger. The giant boy himself didn't bother trying to stifle his explosive laughter, as he never did, and he looked at Leida every few seconds as if to make sure she was as amused as he was.

They were innocent, above all else. Mother knows they had blood on their hands and more battle scars than years lived, but they were as innocent as their brutal world could ever allow. Kaishek watched his young pupils and the feeling in his chest was different than last time. He didn't have quite the same urge to harden them, to thicken their skin, to callous their spirits. To turn them into an army, a force that would bring lords to their knees. As his gaze met Kodo's, back in his spot leaning against Leida's shoulder, he studied his soft eyes. He was gentle.

But there was not a hint of weakness to be found.

Kaishek had been wrong. He had let his fears and doubts convince him that Kodo's gentleness would be his downfall. That their violent world would crash over him like thundering waves, crush him before he ever grew into the man he was meant to be. But as he watched his son, he felt a deep shame for the harshness he'd forced onto him. Because the boy before him, still a boy and with all his innocence and naivety, was anything but weak. He'd judged Kodo wrong, so wrong, and he felt sick as he recalled all the ways he'd hoped to change him. To make him into a soldier. To make him hard, stoic, merciless.

Like him.

Since meeting him, Kaishek had wanted his son to be like him. He'd wanted him to be strong. But Kodo was not like him. He was gentle, and loving, and spirited. His hearts were greater than his monstrous strength. He was like his mother.

He was strong.

...

"Iago, we're looping back near the western border."

"*Thank you*, Kei, I know where the borders of my own clan are," the woman in front hissed, her voice a tattered croak.

"Why are we headed back home?" Io interjected suspiciously. Iago glared back at her.

"We're not."

"Then why are we headed this way?"

"I have a feeling."

"A feeling?"

Iago stopped walking, turning to face her comrades.

"*Yes*, I have a feeling about the western river bend. *No*, we're not going home. Any other stupid questions?" she asked with a sneer.

"Yeah," a sleek, dark-furred woman piped up listlessly. "When was the last time one of your 'feelings' actually got us anywhere but in trouble?"

Io chuckled, her normally calm eyes twinkling in impish amusement.

"*I* remember, Teihnan," she began, dodging Iago's frantic efforts to shush her. "It was when she had a *feeling* she could take down a bull reihggus by herself —"

"*Io* —" Iago warned.

"And she got thrown so high in the air, Rataan-Leih had to climb up and get her down from a tree," the other twin finished with a cackle. "Trouble, sure, but no trouble for us!"

Iago's nostrils twitched as the other tunahk giggled at the memory.

"You're awfully confident that I'm above killing my own sister, aren't you?" she growled at Io, enraged at being the twin on the receiving end of a joke. Her sister simply tapped the tip of Iago's nose with her own.

"*Very,*" Io mused and continued casually on her way.

Iago rolled her eye, marching after Io with an irritated snort, followed by the rest of their companions. Their heads were low as they inhaled the scents of the jungle, both new and old, spreading out through the brush as they searched for any sign of the rebels — dead or alive.

The fur on the back of Iago's shoulders suddenly stood on end, as did that of her twin sister beside her. The two women looked at one another.

"Stay low," Io whispered, looking forward and slowly pressing on. Iago stalked after her, motioning for the others to follow up the hill. The faint smell of death hung in the air, so subtle it was barely discernible from the foggy scent of desperation the jungle naturally emitted. The five tunahk crested the hill and slowly, one by one, came to a halt. Garja furrowed her brows.

"This..." she began.

"This is one of the ocean camps we raided..." Teihnan finished quietly from beside her, confusion clear on her face.

Iago walked forward into the dilapidated ruins, now barely distinguishable from the dirt and ash. She marched through the fallen tents and the long cold fire pits, kicking aside broken spears and half-buried pots. Her feet halted in front of a line of decaying skeletons.

"They've been honored," Iago observed in disgust after several moments of silence, studying the branches forked into a triangle above the corpses. She squinted and cocked her head at something hanging on the arc, gently swinging like a pendulum. A necklace of bone and crystal, carved with unfamiliar runes.

"By other ocean dwellers?" Kei suggested as she investigated the remains.

"No," Iago spat, "by our missing rebels."

In one swift movement, she snatched her sword from its sheath at her side, swinging it through the wooden structure's peak. The logs fell, and she plucked the fallen pendant out of the wreckage with the tip of the blade, then flung her sword into the mud with the necklace still caught to it.

Tangled in the leather cord of the pendant, a clump of thick gray fur. Mountain ghaengste.

The tunahk were silent, studying the scene before them. They stood at the site of a massacre they themselves had perpetrated, their paws on soil fertilized with blood they had spilled.

Blood that the rebels mourned.

The matter of the primitive rebel plot had been trivial; at first, this hunt had originally seemed little more than an exercise. Just something to keep them occupied in an extended time of peace. But something far, far more dangerous than they ever could have imagined was lurking on the horizon. Four fugitives of different races, banding together to bring the end of the Ramys nation; they'd thought it impossible. A fool's errand. But Faro's crushed skull and Iago's choked voice attested to something larger, and the honored site spelled something sick and infectious. Nothing was clear now, except for one small piece of knowledge that grew and spread throughout the deserted clearing, so bold they could no longer ignore it.

The rebels had bigger plans than they'd thought.

"Why?" Teihnan finally spoke through the heavy silence, her voice just slightly more engaged than its usual tone. Io answered calmly as she gazed at the ground.

"It is a threat."

The other tunahk turned to find where she stood, backed away and staring at the foot of the wrecked grave. Their eyes followed her ever-focused gaze.

Gouged deep into the ground, eternalized after the blood-soaked mud had hardened to cement, one word:

IESU'TALEI

13

EXODUS

Fog rolled over the horizon in billowing waves, shadowing the suns and bringing in a dark chill. The wind whistled in long, sorrowful cries as it echoed between the sharp mountain peaks and deep valleys. Weeks of clear skies and bright sunlight had lit the way for relentless training and steady healing, but now a storm brewed in the distance.

"Uncle."

Kaishek hesitated for a moment before tearing his eyes from the horizon, turning to look at the man who was approaching.

"We've almost finished packing, but there's a storm coming. Should we wait until it passes to begin the journey down?" Rykr asked. Kaishek shook his head, once again looking over the angry swirling sky as if it were an old friend.

"No. If the storm becomes too thick to travel in, we could lose our opportunity. We need to get ahead of it." He walked past his nephew, back toward the other rebels. His broad shoulders were tense as he shuffled through the snow, and his long tail thrashed of its own accord. Rykr followed dutifully.

"Where's Tiny going to ride?" Rykr cocked his head as they rejoined their companions, looking up at the makeshift pack strapped to Kodo, full of equipment and provisions Kaishek insisted they bring. The cargo took up most of the available length of Kodo's back, and even with his impressive strength, it was sure to slow him down.

"Right here." Kodo patted the tight spot between his shoulder blades, behind his neck. "I can handle it."

Kaishek looked between the rebels with tired eyes.

"She has been healing for weeks now. *Why*, again, can she not walk on her own four feet?" he sighed. Alvi opened her mouth, no doubt to enlighten him, but not before Rykr picked her up by the tail and tossed her into a nearby snowdrift. Her entire body disappeared into the white powder, leaving no trace of her save for a muffled hissing.

Kaishek gave Rykr a sharp look, then retrieved their shortest comrade from the deep snow, subsequently releasing a cacophony of growling and spitting and several vulgar threats. He casually walked by Rykr, tossing Alvi directly onto the younger man's head.

"Fine, you carry her."

"What?" both he and the woman draped over him exclaimed at the same time. Kaishek was already wandering away to collect his last few belongings for the journey.

"I am *not* going to be responsible for the amphibian. Leida can do it," Rykr objected.

"He smells even worse than *Kodo!*" Alvi cried.

"That's a lie and you know it."

"It's not my fault you smell like a reihggus in rut."

"Enough!" Kaishek bellowed, his harsh voice cracking across the mountaintops. Rykr immediately straightened and looked toward his uncle in alarm, and Alvi scrambled down the side of his neck to use him as a living shield.

"Uncle... are you... okay?"

Kaishek turned away from them, sitting in his usual perch above his cave. His head was hung, his posture tense and slouched, a rare sight from the proud king. With a long, low sigh, he lifted his head and studied the horizon once again, the jagged ridge that acted as the bars of his infernal prison.

"I have been imprisoned in this wasteland for many years..." he began quietly. "I do not remember the outside world. I do not remember life beyond solitude."

His gravelly voice was monotone, slow and bitter. He watched over his solemn kingdom from his icy throne. Frozen in time and space, absent of all life beyond his own. He didn't want to leave it.

He didn't want life. He didn't want breath.

He wanted to be far away from the eyes of others and the beating of hearts. To be left alone to become one with the ice, the wind, and the ghosts.

"So forgive my lack of eagerness. I never thought I would leave this hell," he finished coldly, then turned to face his young allies. They did not fear the outside world, even if perhaps they should have. And they certainly had no intention of freezing in the ice and snow and angry wind for eternity. He willed himself to believe he was one of them, or maybe just to pretend.

The Lost King leaned down and closed his jaws around the handle of his axe, half buried in the snow. His eyes fell closed for a moment as he felt the worn leather and petrified wood against his ancient fangs.

I wield you again, Y'xara.

His chest clenched as a long-broken connection sparked back to life.

As you wield me.

"But we have a storm to beat. Let's go."

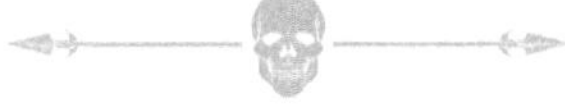

Doctor Daniels tried to compare it to something, but she couldn't. It was incomparable to anything her human eyes had ever perceived before.

It was alive and dead, all at once. It wasn't still but it didn't move, it was silent but deafeningly loud. It was both generously giving and hungrily evil.

Sherri walked deeper into the chilling belly of the jungle and all was quiet. Stagnant. She was suddenly, overwhelmingly aware of the blood in her veins and the air in her lungs. The operations of her own body echoed so loud within her skull it overpowered the gentle hum of the forest. But she marched on, breathing slowly, allowing herself to relax into the clutches of the jungle. Becoming one with the stillness.

Deeper she went.

As she trekked on, the foliage became thicker and she pulled her machete from her backpack, securing the sheath onto her belt. She swung the blade through the thick tangling of vines that blocked her path, but a feverish guilt bored through her stomach, rotten and sick like she'd hurt a dear friend. The shame brought with it a feeling of something stirring, as if she were being judged for her selfish crimes. Just slightly, like the crust was beginning to unstick from the tired eyelids of the world around her. She began to lose track of whether the faint drumming in the atmosphere was her own pulse or the natural pulse of the forest.

Her eyes landed on a broken young tree, snapped in half and partially uprooted. Like the ones around the compound fence. Sherri shoved down the nagging feelings of disgrace as she carefully cut a path to the dilapidated tree. There were faint teeth and claw marks fraying the edges of where it had been severed, and she kneeled by the roots to take scrapings of the wounded bark. From her lowered position, she could now see further ahead through the dense vegetation. She focused in the distance.

Another downed tree. This one was uprooted entirely, ripped out of the ground but leaned against a neighboring log. Even from where she crouched, Sherri could see the violent gouging made by five gigantic claws. Her eyes widened as they honed in even further through the green jungle. Another one. A third tree formed a dotted line with the first two, like stone cairns marking a beaten path.

They're trail markers.

She slowly rose from her kneeled position, putting the bagged scrapings in her backpack as she stared through the trees. More downed trees laid a path into the distance. As Sherri began to follow the trail, beckoned by its signal, the hair on the back of her neck stood on end. The frequency at which the air around her vibrated seemed to change, as if the planet's rotation had switched direction.

...

"Has anyone seen Daniels?"

Giovanni approached the rest of the research team at the coffee pot, where the other men were chatting amongst themselves while they refilled their mugs before returning to the lab.

"She wasn't in the lab, so I checked the terrosphere and she wasn't there either," he continued with a shrug. Harrison, Doyle, and Carl all glanced over at Marshall.

"What the hell are you looking at me for?" Marshall scowled. "I've been with you pricks all day. Last I saw, she was working."

"You can't find the tree hugger?" a gruff voice barked accusingly. The researchers looked to see Captain Short marching over at a fast pace.

"She's probably just napping," Carl suggested.

"What, like she was last time?" Giovanni replied. They were cut off by a booming yell that made everyone jolt.

"First GI to find Doctor Daniels in this giant motherfucking tin can gets first MRE pick at supper!" the captain roared through the halls, and every soldier in the compound scrambled in different directions. "Blonde woman, cargo shorts, attitude. *Find her!*"

"No, sir."

"I couldn't find her either, Captain."

"Not in the gym."

"Showers are empty."

"Is this one Daniels?"

With each soldier that reported in — confused, dejected, and empty-handed — the building horror inside the captain's chest flared. He knew better. He knew better than to ignore his gut, he knew better than to let another one slip through the cracks, but he had doubted himself. And now she was gone, just like that, another failure. Now he'd pay for his doubts.

Short breathed hard as he desperately sorted his racing thoughts and frantic dread. Slowly, he turned around to face the congregation of scientists.

"She's outside, isn't she?"

The men in white coats looked between one another.

"Most likely."

Short turned and marched toward hallway Alpha, the corridor that led to the one and only exit.

"You know, maybe if you were more professional and willing to compromise, she wouldn't have felt the need to go off alone." Marshall shrugged, scratching his back against the corner of the entryway.

"Fuck off, white boy, ain't nobody talking to you." Captain Short shook his head as he punched the code into the keypad. Each time before, the mechanical door of the compound had opened far too quickly, leaving no room to breathe or to prepare themselves. This time, it seemed, the inner mechanisms couldn't have worked any slower. After a painful few moments of clicking, the door slid open.

Short stepped out immediately upon seeing the luminescent fence intact. His eyes came to rest on the indented shelf beside the door that usually contained the remote keypad. Empty.

His boot collided with the metal wall with a deafening clang.

"Where do you think you're going, brother? *Get back here!*"

"The little shit couldn't have gone far…"

"Doesn't matter, he won't be getting off easy after we tell Vaus-Erro what he did."

"*Ha!* You hear that, Tahro? You better stay gone!"

The two young men turned and went back the way they came, cackling to each other as they left.

The boy finally let out his breath and slumped on the tree branch he had climbed up to. Then he shook off the leaves he had covered himself in, groaning in dread.

"Vaus-Erro's going to make me train with the tunahk for *days* for this one," Tahro sighed to himself.

"Or worse" — he shuddered — "clean their armor."

He nearly gagged at the thought. As far as he was concerned, any punishment at all would be too steep for his petty crimes. Besides, his hollow-skulled older brothers deserved to be embarrassed in front of the poor recipients of their failed courting attempts. It wasn't his fault he could talk circles around them and they didn't know the first thing about romance.

Tahro began the descent from his perch, carefully hopping from limb to limb until he landed gracefully on the ground. He silently praised himself for the soft landing, as he was still at that tall clumsy stage of boyhood. The height of his father yet thin and gangly in build, when he wasn't tripping over his oversized paws, he was knocking his head on low branches and doorways he could swear he fit under just the other day.

The boy carelessly trotted deeper into the forest. He was sure his young life would meet its premature end as soon as he went home anyway, so why not enjoy what was left of it?

A grouping of small, vibrant flowers caught his eye, and Tahro stopped to inspect them. Slipping off the brown leather pouch that always hung over his back, he began thoughtfully picking the most colorful flowers from the bunch and putting them in his bag. Then he moved on to searching for the shiniest or most pleasantly shaped rocks, also adding them to his collection. His loneliness subsided as he found himself distracted by a colorful winged insect. He followed it around for a moment.

"Hey, wait, where are you going?" Tahro called, laughing and pouncing at it. He rolled to his back playfully, batting at it with his paws in the air. It danced across his vision, illuminated by the pools of light soaking through the tree cover that glowed through its wings. Blue and yellow gleams of light dripped down through the canopy, bathing his smooth fur in warmth. The damp moss and dirt below him were cool in comparison; it chilled the emerald scales along his spine and sent a gentle jitter up through his body. He blinked up at the gargantuan trees and imagined they were the towering legs of giant ghaengste. They walked over him, massive archaic bodies sailing across the planet gracefully, no idea he was even there.

After a moment of restful daydreaming, Tahro abruptly rolled back to his feet. He shook off the damp dirt and moss, then tightened his bag against his side and broke into a graceless sprint.

The wind pushed his short blond mane back against his neck and the worries from his shoulders. Plunging through creeks and puddles, he made no attempt to dodge them as he welcomed the chilling water and splattering mud. He decided all at once that his consequences and tribulations could wait. For the time being, he was on an adventure. Colorful feathered creatures fluttered out from the trees as he passed, flapping overhead and howling wildly. He howled back at them, laughing as he tore through the underbrush. The cold breeze and dim world surrounded him in a cocoon of invulnerability; when he was alone in the arms of the Great Mother, he could do anything. He wasn't the youngest prince of the Ramys clan, he wasn't a son, or a brother, or a boy. He was one with the planet, in the natural state he was born in. He was part of the trees and the soil, the creatures that fled from beneath his eager paws and soared above his unruly hair. He was as he was meant to be.

...

The rebels were quieter than usual on the journey down. Perhaps they were drained by the grueling weeks behind them, or discouraged by the uncertain future ahead. They knew the Ramys clan awaited them, and the tunahk-dahn would be hot on their trail as soon as their scent hit warm air. Darker yet was the potent fear of the Celesteal clan. They were to walk straight into the belly of the beast and call for allyship. None of them except for Kaishek, not even Alvi, foresaw it going in their favor.

"Hey, gramps."

No reply.

"Grandpa."

Kaishek released a long, drawn-out sigh, beginning to notice the disparity in the way his new companions seemed to regard him. Grandfather, teacher, uncle. He wasn't sure which Kodo had decided on yet. Stranger, maybe.

"What, Alvi?" he grumbled.

"You said you loved Kodo's mother, no?"

"Yes."

"What's that like?"

The old man paused, walking in silence for a moment before responding.

"You will find out if you experience it," he answered.

"Well, I think I'd like to. Maybe I'll find a mate and raise a family," she mused, her tail swaying off the side of Rykr's back.

"What for?" Kodo piped up. "Almost no one in Ramys did the whole pairing thing. I don't get the point."

"That's because you have the emotional intelligence of a leaf."

"Is that a complim—"

"No. It's not so uncommon where I'm from, there are plenty of mated pairings in the Celesteal clan. We're a very romantic people," Alvi explained with a dreamy look, like she was imagining what her future wife and children might look like. Leida took the opportunity to get a word in.

"What is 'love'?" the winged woman asked blankly.

"Sex." Kodo's casual voice stopped both Rykr and Kaishek in their tracks. Alvi choked on her own gasp and erupted into a coughing fit.

"What is 's—" Leida continued obliviously.

"*No!* No. No," Kaishek loudly intervened, giving his son a threatening glare. "None of that is important right now."

The old man sighed, and for a moment considered turning around and going back the way he came.

"Keep moving." He shrugged off the temptation and continued to walk down the path. Alvi stretched her limbs and sighed to herself as the group followed.

"Sorry I said anything in the first place," she mocked. "Clearly you brutes will never have to worry about experiencing sex nor love."

Kaishek kept his teeth firmly gritted to resist inquiring if she'd included him in that snide comment, or from reminding her of the living proof of his exploits not two strides behind them.

"I'm going to assume you're referring to bird-brain and no-brain," Rykr retorted, and Alvi scoffed loudly.

"What, like *you* get any—"

A loud whistling sound, then the icy gust of something launching close over their heads. Leida slammed something into the rock wall above and then tumbled onto the trail.

Another sky ghaengste.

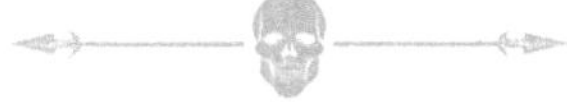

It seemed every crew member aboard, from surgeon to soldier, was gathered in the commons, listening. This was now the second time a rogue researcher had brazenly rushed out into the wilderness, and it had become an argument of whether or not it was a human rights violation to keep them monitored at all times. Most of the other scientists, of course, just wanted their botanist back.

"We have to go look for her. Now. She couldn't have gone far," Giovanni insisted.

"Daniels is an expert outdoorsman and hiker, she could be miles out by now," Harrison countered.

"What are you saying, you don't think we should go after her?"

"No, that's not at all what I mean, I just —"

"Can we skip the arguing? She's dead."

All eyes landed on Doyle, who had his arms crossed and his jaw clenched. Carl made a gasp halfway between disbelief and physical pain, and Giovanni took a step toward Doyle before Harrison grabbed his arm.

"Why don't you keep your fucking mouth shut for once, Doyle," the younger Rosenquest brother snapped in warning. Doyle shook his head, his face tense.

"We're all scientists, we're all realists. She was alone, she's most likely dead."

"You don't know that."

"Novak. You're the statistician, aren't you? I can see you doing the math in your head over there. Tell them."

Marshall had been the only one who stayed silent, leaning against the wall with a distracted expression. He scratched his chin as he seemed to study the lines of the linoleum flooring.

"I don't have enough variables or a large enough factor pool to accurately estima—"

"Oh, quit bullshitting," Doyle interrupted coldly. "You know far more about quantitative probabilities than the rest of us do, just spit it out."

Marshall finally looked over his glasses at the other men.

"My estimated statistical probability gives her about..." — he casually lifted his sleeve to check his watch — "two more hours before we should assume she's dead."

The discourse had died down, and for several agonizing moments, no one else said a word. A firm voice broke out from the front of the room.

"Two hours?" the captain called over.

"Two hours until her likelihood of survival isn't viable," Marshall called back and nodded once. Captain Short let out a long exhale as he shook his head.

"I'll take it," he said as he checked the chamber of his sidearm, then tucked it in the back of his pants as he jogged toward the armory.

"We're burning daylight, boys!"

...

It drew her closer, deeper. Like the promise of water in the desert, the promise of fire in the dark. Sherri walked onward, following the tree cairns and marking her own trail as she went. The jungle bore the secrets she so desperately longed for, and she could feel it stir more and more by the minute.

As she hiked, she listened closely to the static nothingness around her. She almost thought she might outlast it, stay just a little longer than the forest could bear to keep quiet. So she followed its call, beckoning it to her, daring it to show its true face. It couldn't hide forever.

Then, all at once, the planet awoke. A cool breeze whisked through Sherri's curly mane, the only strong sweep of wind she'd felt since her arrival. The first herald gust of a promised land.

And with it, the jungle came alive.

It stretched its weary limbs as winged creatures fluttered out of the trees and scrambled across branches. It lifted its sleepy eyelids as plumes of thousands of insects hovered out of the grass she walked through before they rose into the arching canopy. She'd crossed the invisible barrier between stagnant death and perennial resurrection all at once. The sound of chirping animals and wind whistling through holes in the trees filled her hearing ear, welcoming her back into Eden. The frozen shadows around her were suddenly moving with the swaying leaves, dancing like pools of spilled ink. The fluttering sound of unknown forms skittering through the lower shrubs joined the tune, and a methodical series of clicks tapped like the metronome of its orchestra. Like a symphony finally released from rest by its conductor, the planet showed her what it was truly made of — life.

Sherri tiptoed through the brush, attempting to take in her sudden bustling company. The world was no longer dark and cold; now it was vibrant and green and blinding. The eyes of birdlike creatures watched her curiously from the trees. She didn't dare take pictures so as not to scare them away. Something like a rabbit darted past her boot, but she could hardly make it out before it disappeared in the dense ferns and wide leaves. The jungle now cradled her in its arms, embraced her in a softness she didn't think it capable of. She heard a new sound growing in the background of the chatter; it wasn't a whoop, or a howl, or a chirp, or a click.

It was music.

A beautiful, rising song, building in intensity and volume. A nightingale, no, a thrush or a finch. There were notes of golden oriole and oriental magpie, yet it was different from them all. It was sweet like honey, tangy like lime. It was all instruments and none at all, loud and confident and deliberate, it demanded an audience. It soothed her sore ear and enveloped her in a bright lullaby.

The breeze became warm on the back of her neck. No, hot. Sticky and humid air made her curls cling to the skin behind her ears.

Sherri turned her head to the side slowly, so slowly she was hardly moving at all, staring through the corner of her eye.

Oh, fuck.

For a split second, Leida was gone; only a blur of white and red and the sound of ripping flesh remained. The other rebels could do nothing but watch as she and her target sailed off the cliff's edge, locked in a bloody embrace. Then they steadied in the air, wings beating to keep them afloat, screeching in volatile fury as talons shredded one another's skin into black ribbons. Leida battled with the other sky dweller, clear as day against the cloudless heavens and wearing light armor. A clan ghaengste.

"Leida!" Kodo cried out helplessly as he watched with the rest, confined to the rocky trail and unable to help their companion.

It was a desperate and feral kind of violence that filled any onlookers with terror, the two winged beasts shrieking wildly as they gored into each other. The other rebels rushed to her aid when Leida finally overpowered the stranger, diving and slamming them back down onto the trail with a forceful boom. Kaishek quickly stomped down on the attacker's wing and pinned his claws through it before they could rise. A pained cry fell from their maw, but it was immediately replaced by hoarse gargling as Leida dug her long talons into their gut and tore their belly wide open.

She panted hard, blackened saliva dripping from her lip as the attacker bled out at her feet. Their intestines steadily leaked out onto the ground like a nest of serpents, washing the stone around them with bile and blood.

"*Shit*, feathers, are you okay?" Kodo appeared at her side, frantically assessing the bloody gouges across her body as the other rebels searched the air around them. Leida nodded at Kodo as she caught her ragged breath.

"I don't see any more," Alvi said from where she stood atop Rykr's shoulder for a higher vantage point. "It looks like it was just a straggling Kocea scout."

"They were awfully far out here for a wingback," Rykr noted uneasily, his gaze scouring the horizon.

"They were," Kaishek said. "We should keep moving. Can you continue, Leida?"

"Yes." The sky dweller was already limping around the disemboweled corpse to continue on the path. Her companions looked between one another briefly, then followed before she could get ahead. Her fur was smeared with black blood, but her wounds looked relatively shallow, and they began to understand why the young woman was covered in so many scars.

"You know," Kaishek began as he fell in step beside her, offering a shoulder to brace herself against, "For having all that hair in your face, you don't miss much, do you?"

"I do not," Leida agreed with a small satisfaction in her eye, walking alongside the old man but refusing his help.

...

Rataan paced among the decaying corpses where his warriors had led him. The smell of rot tainted his every breath and the fires of rage boiled hot within him. He was consumed with it, his ears pinned flat against his skull and his lip curled back over his gilded fangs. The tunahk only watched, completely still as if they hoped he wouldn't notice them standing there.

"How dare they?" Rataan whispered to himself, his voice a quiet hiss. His tail whipped back and forth, and his armor clanked as he flipped around and paced the other direction.

"HOW DARE THEY?!" he roared, his lower jaw unhinging and then snapping closed so hard it might've cracked his teeth, were they not plated in protective metal. He trudged faster, kicking bones aside as his golden claws sheathed and unsheathed with each step. In, out, in, out, in, out.

"Vermin, traitors, *filthy fucking hona'dei* — they *dare* challenge the Ramys nation? The clan that reared the giant?" he snarled, a horrible rattling sound vibrating from his throat and saliva spraying from his maw.

"These disgusting wastes of the Mother's precious water deserved *worse than death!* They should be so lucky that we only culled them and the *plague* they spread on our sacred land." He ripped the linen off a fallen tent, throwing the fabric to the side to expose tiny bones and decomposing blankets.

"And the giant spits in our faces, he *honors* these pathetic creatures. He dares to threaten us for cleansing our own home."

Rataan spat the last word out like he was running out of breath. After a moment of silence, he exhaled, almost chuckling to himself.

"I knew, I always knew, didn't I? That there was something wrong with that boy. That he was dangerous, that he would disgrace us. *Didn't I?*" He paused again, a soft smile on his face as if he were the butt of a silly joke. The tunahk glanced between one another warily.

"I see now why the bastard mongrel was never truly a part of our world." His amusement quickly shifted to a still, calm tone. "I see now that he was never truly one of the forest people at all.

"He was a weak, pathetic shell of one. Like his mother."

He looked around the campsite thoughtfully for a moment.

"What do they fucking expect!?" he erupted. *"Threatening* the Ramys clan, *defacing* our territory, *disrespecting* the will of our lunai. Do they think they could ever possibly survive this fight? *I will slaughter each and every one of them, slowly and gladly!"* he shrieked, striking the rotten heap of bones with his tail and scattering the remains in the upset soil.

"BURN IT!" he screamed at the tunahk, his eyes widened and throat burning like wildfire. *"BURN IT ALL! BURN IT DOWN! RID THE GREAT MOTHER OF THIS REPULSIVE WASTE!"*

The tunahk scrambled to light their torches and throw them at the ghost of a camp. Rataan cried out once more as the grave clearing exploded into scorching green fire and poisonous black smoke.

"Call the rest of the tunahk back! The hunt is off, this storm ends where it began."

Teihnan glanced at her companions, then lifted a spiraled horn from a cord around her neck. She held it between her jaws and closed her eyes, taking a deep breath.

Teihnan-Dahn blew into the instrument, releasing a deep wail that shook the planet itself.

Oh, fuck.

She could see it in her peripheral vision, but for a moment, she refused to look at it directly. Then she did.

Sherri tore her gaze from a spot on a tree to her direct right and allowed it to drift further behind her. Hot air stung her eyes, her eyelashes fluttered.

Its massive nose was a foot behind her head. All four gaping nostrils breathed in her scent. Heaving, pulsing, dripping mucus and pouring forth vapor. A long, thin tendril reached forward and stroked her cheek; she squeezed her eyes shut tight to control her breathing. A whisker.

Inhale. Steady.

She opened her eyes again slowly, forcefully.

Exhale. Slow.

She turned her body to face it before her instincts could stop her.

It was not the devil rising out of hell. It was the face of hell itself.

Gleaming eyes stared into hers, four pupils boring into her, each shaped like a thorny crucifix. They were sickening, knowing; feral like a starving animal, but wicked in a way that only man could be.

It was so tall it had to lower its angular head down past its protruding shoulders to be level with her. At first, all she could relate it to was an archaic deity, an ancient dragon, a biblical demon.

Diamond-shaped scales ran from its forehead, all the way down its spine, but the rest of it appeared to be covered in short fur. Diabolic horns twisted out from its head, long ears with two pointed lobes below them. Matted hair grew in a shaggy mohawk from the scalp of its long neck, its rancid breath smelled of ammonia. It was a monster beyond all human comprehension. Sherri stared into its familiar haunting gaze, fighting not to be captured by it again.

It's not a dragon. It's not a demon.

What is it?

There was a machete on her belt, a makeshift blowtorch in her backpack. Neither deadly enough or accessible enough to defend herself with. She wracked her brain. They had no knowledge of this species' behavior, they had no idea where it stood in its ecosystem. But Sherri knew earthly life. She went through every lesson she'd ever learned about deterring large predators, over and over, trying to compare this creature to one she already knew. She settled on the biggest.

It's a bear.

Sherri took a deep breath.

Then she roared in the beast's face as loud as she was physically capable. She threw up her arms and released the most guttural and primal scream her body could produce. She thrashed and howled and shrieked, expelling her battle cry with every single ounce of fearsome savagery she could draw from deep within her gut.

It took a step back. Watching her. Startled.

Then it unhinged its jaws. Sherri immediately clamped both hands over her good ear, throwing herself away just as the beast's horrific cry burst forth with the force of a jet and the volume of a shotgun blast inches from where her skull had been the second before.

Not a bear. Not a bear. Not a bear.

Her body obeyed not her brain, but the adrenaline in her veins, and before she knew it, she was on her feet.

The familiar sting of branches and leaves whipped her skin raw as she tore through the jungle. She leaped over roots and sprinted between trees, the racing native close behind. Sherri didn't dare look back. She had an advantage, being small enough to duck under logs and easily slip through foliage, but it wasn't enough. Not even close. She didn't have the time to form coherent thoughts, she had no more theories to prove or hypotheses to test. She didn't have a plan, she just ran.

Then, like a ship off the coast of a deserted island, she saw it.

A burrow nestled in the crook of a tree's tangled roots, the opening far too small for the native. She had no idea how deep it went, or what might lie inside it. But it was her best shot. It was her only shot. She didn't give herself the chance to calculate the risks before she dove inside.

The beast's titanic jaws snapped down on a tree root just as Sherri tumbled into the hole. She had a single moment to take a breath as she discovered that the burrow was actually a widening tunnel that had no obvious end. She was interrupted from her realization as she was sprayed with a thick flood of dirt. Dusty soil choked her eyes, nose, and mouth.

The native was digging. Fast. Its monstrous scythe-like claws made quick work at tearing apart the roots and rocks at the entrance hole. Just as Sherri began to blindly scramble further into the hole, its gigantic head exploded through the gnarled roots and snapped at her shoelaces.

"No! Fuck!" she screamed as she clawed through the muddy burrow and kicked at the gnashing beast's nose as hard as she could. Finally catching hold of an underground root, she dragged herself across the moist soil and out of reach of the frothing jaws and biting canines as it shrieked in fury. Now with all options eliminated save for one, Sherri turned and crawled on her hands and knees further into the darkness ahead.

Deeper yet, she went.

14
PERIHELION

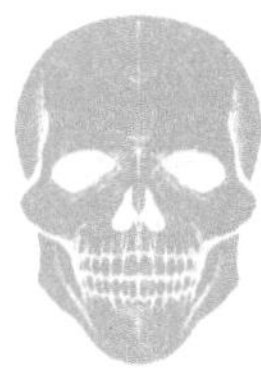

224. 225. 229? Damn —

Sherri counted each stride carefully, determined to keep track of how much ground she'd covered and how long she'd been in the dark tunnel. The burrow had widened enough that she could stand now, at least. She walked upright and aimed her flashlight at her feet as she counted steps. It seemed the native had given up on her; she could no longer hear growling or feel the vibration of digging, but she didn't intend to turn back and check.

Treading on, she searched for some sort of secondary orifice in the underground shaft. She watched out for evidence of the tunnel's mysterious tenant as she walked, though she wasn't sure she wanted to meet the architect of such a massive burrow. Her mind wandered to picturing a giant, horse-sized naked mole rat, and the image gave her a chill of disgust. It grew harder to focus on counting her steps as she paused every few seconds to check her respirator supply, her watch, and her compass. The compass had proved completely useless; the needle just spun around wildly like a pinwheel, but she kept an eye on it anyway. Not knowing which direction she was headed made the hair on her arms stand on end, and she was almost sure she could faintly see her breath through the cold darkness. The eerie tunnel was pitch black aside from the beam of her flashlight.

No, pitch black aside from the beam of her flashlight and the faint glow up ahead.

Sherri broke into a dead sprint, throwing caution to the wind and leaving it far behind in the muddy darkness. She clambered through the narrowing end of the tunnel and tossed herself out of the opening, disregarding the roots and rocks that scratched at her skin as she passed through.

She took a deep breath of the fresh air, laying on the soft soil and letting go of a little laugh, just relieved that the suns were still overhead, more or less. *That wasn't so bad.* Sherri hopped to her feet and dusted herself off, eager to get her bearings and get back to base. She had a sunset to beat, and an infinitely better image of a native to sketch out.

High ground, she needed high ground. If she could locate the mountain range, she could find the compound sitting at its foot. A nearly building-sized rock formation ahead promised a perfect vantage point. It took her a few minutes to navigate the massive boulders, but the soft moss acted as a graspable netting and her eagerness to get home drove her to the summit. As she crested the highest point, far above the forest floor, she was filled with a childlike euphoria. A breeze whisked through her wild hair as she savored the familiar feeling of freedom. Sherri celebrated her victory in solitude as she always did; it was a bittersweet memory as natural to her as the breath in her lungs.

But her mind crawled back to Roger, and she found herself wishing he'd seen the beauty of this world the way that she did. If only he'd been able to look past the danger, if only he'd been able to see what it could turn into, maybe he would still be alive. But she finally began to understand that he could never have embraced the future that she did, because he had too much to lose. The difference between Sherri and Roger was that he had something waiting for him back at home. Something better than this. She couldn't imagine it, a life dedicated to something greater than discovery. She had everything she needed right there in her body and in her backpack.

Sherri spotted the mountains on the horizon and gauged the distance with her fingers. It was far, but she could make it if she rushed. Something distracted her as she descended. She stopped on top of one of the lower boulders, listening closely.

Music.

It was different this time, a gentle twinkling lull that was full of vibrato; dynamic, willful, and hypnotic. It danced through the jungle, pulsing through the branches and tingling the tips of her ears. If the stars in the sky were to sing, it would be that heavenly melody. Sherri found herself slipping down from the boulder and starting not toward the compound, but deeper into the jungle toward the enchanting song.

No.

Turn around, Daniels.

She stopped, staring into the trees, longing to see the creature that sang such a sweet song, or perhaps it wasn't a creature at all. The music was so choral and operatic that she couldn't form an image of what in the natural world might produce it. Her curiosity battled savagely with her logic.

There's always tomorrow, as Giovanni might have said. She rushed back in the direction of the compound, fighting to ignore the tempting song that still floated through the forest around her. Then it stopped.

Sherri pondered why it might have been cut short as she entered a clearing. Then her pace slowed, her pulse quickened; the potent feeling of being watched clutched her ankles and weighed her down. Her eyes scanned the jungle but she kept urging herself slowly forward. The exhaustion of the day fell heavy on her shoulders all at once like a crashing wave, and for the first time, all she wanted to do, more than anything in the world, was go home.

She wouldn't have seen them if they weren't glowing so brightly. But as the eerie bluish light glared straight through her chilled bones, she couldn't miss the pair of eyes in the bushes ahead. Watching, waiting. Two pupils in each giant eye. Sherri began slowly backing away, her vision locked on to the stalker. Something in its sharp gaze taunted her. It knew she'd spotted it. Loud and clear, it dared her to make the first move.

Maybe she could make it back to the burrow, but she didn't have a head start. Running wasn't a good option, and yelling certainly wouldn't work. If it got close enough for her to use the machete, she was already dead. Seemingly on its own, Sherri's hand slowly crept to the side pouch of her backpack, closing around the aerosol can. The lighter was in her pocket.

The native exploded out of the brush. Sherri snatched the can and lighter from their places as it lunged.

The ground beneath her lurched, a blur of color flashed across her vision, and a tumult of bestial shrieking exploded through her skull. *What a pitiless way to die.*

As the dust cleared and her brain began to catch up with the world around her, Sherri struggled to comprehend the violent scene as reality.

Another native was now on top of the first. The blue-eyed one was fighting for its life, screaming and screeching and thrashing, but it was hopeless. Its attacker was larger, roughly the size of the first specimen they'd seen, but it was thin, maybe even underweight. It didn't seem to matter, though, because before Sherri's mind could return back to her body, the lanky native had closed its colossal jaws around the screaming victim's throat. It bit down and jerked its head to the side, the blue-eyed beast's shriek replaced by a crisp snap as its neck broke cleanly. It fell limp.

Sherri was paralyzed; her adrenaline now worked against her. Time slowed down and she took in every single detail as if it were the last image she'd ever see.

The prevailing native stared back at her with studious emerald eyes as thick black liquid oozed from its panting maw.

It was hairless, which he found strange.

Though not completely hairless. It had a big poofy mane tied back behind its head, but the rest of it had no fur. And it somehow perfectly balanced on its hind legs without a tail to support it. *Weird.*

Tahro cautiously stepped off the rogue he'd just killed; she was young like him, probably too arrogant to know better than to cross so close to the Ramys border. He bet his father would be proud of him.

"Hey, little guy, you're okay now," he quietly cooed, inching closer. He knew, of course, the mysterious animal wouldn't understand his words, but he hoped it would be calmed by his gentle tone.

Tahro leaned in to get a closer look. It was maybe the size of a young kru'vaii if kru'vaii stood on two legs. Odd looking, but it seemed harmless enough. That is, until it started breathing fire.

The two-legged creature suddenly spat a large plume of hot flame directly at his face, and he jerked his head away just in time to avoid any damage beyond a singed whisker.

"Woah! How did you do *that?*" Tahro exclaimed, his eyes widening in awe. That was new.

"What are you..." He sniffed a little closer, careful to avoid a more accurate blast of green fire. A shiny gleam caught his interest. The creature was holding some sort of metal canteen and a tiny rectangular object that smelled like... burning fuel. He made a face.

"Hey, *you* didn't make that fire... this thing did. How does it work?" He gingerly poked the metal container with his nose, but the naked creature barked and punched him hard in the face.

"Okay, okay, *sheesh*. Keep your secrets." He sneezed once and sat back on his haunches. It was an aggressive little beast, that was for sure, and far different from anything he'd seen before.

"Where's your family? Or are you the only one of your kind? I've never seen one before. I'll have to ask my father if he has, he's seen *every* kind of animal. Vaus-Erro says he's so old he's even seen the extinct ones," Tahro rambled, his voice becoming muffled as he bit down on the strap of his satchel and pulled it off his shoulder.

"Mama says he's 'seasoned,' not old, whatever that means. But I'm pretty sure he's just old. And — hey, wait, don't leave," he faltered, noticing that the creature was slowly backing away, its eyes trained on him.

"I have food, are you hungry? What do you eat? I have meat and fruit, and some flowers I just picked up."

He waved his side bag in the air slightly, hoping the strange animal would catch the scent of the snacks he'd brought along.

It hesitated, then stood up straighter. Something changed in its beady eyes as it studied him. Fear timidly subsided to what looked like disbelief, and finally, wonder.

...

As they maneuvered down the foot of the mountain, Kaishek and Rykr leading the way down the rocky incline, the rebels were silenced by the views around them and the road ahead of them. Slowly becoming aware that they were no longer safe. No longer guarded.

Alvi climbed from Kaishek's shoulder back to Rykr's after braiding the old man's dark mane off his neck, aiding his battle against the increasing heat.

"The Celesteal clan is to the east, yes?" Kaishek said as he helped her over.

"Yes, if we bank right, we'll be able to follow the cliffs all the way to the gorge. But we'll have to go north and cut through the forest before we make it the rest of the way. That's the only place where the river is shallow enough to cross," Alvi explained offhandedly as she started on Rykr's braids. Kodo shook his head.

"We can't, it's a death trap. There are Ramys patrols up and down the banks constantly looking for stray river dwellers, and the tunahk are already hunting us." Kodo argued.

"No way we get through without tipping them off." He shook his head again like a stubborn child. Alvi glanced at him, then back at Rykr's dense mane.

"Well... there is a bridge..." she said quietly, as if hoping they wouldn't hear, or at least wouldn't notice that she was the one who had said it.

"A bridge?" Kaishek raised a brow hopefully.

"Yes."

"Over the gorge."

"Yes."

"That we can cross...?" The old man squinted at her unusually hesitant demeanor. She offered a nervous shrug.

"That *I* can cross..."

"It is destroyed, isn't it?" His face dropped abruptly.

"It's not *destroyed*. It's just very, very old," Alvi clarified. "And three of four of you weigh enough to drag an island back under the sea. Individually. And the other one can fly."

She received a chorus of huffs and groans. Leida piped up.

"I can fly," the sky dweller said as a statement, quiet but sure.

"Yes, Leida, we know."

"I can fly you *across*," she finished. Rykr and Kodo looked at one another briefly, then started laughing.

"Not a chance," Rykr chortled. Leida's expression was hard to read underneath her matted curls, but it gave the impression that her patience was waning.

"I can for a short distance. I have flown over the gorge many times. There are parts small enough for you to jump and me to carry you the rest of the way." She glanced over Kodo's gigantic form.

"... Maybe not Kodo. But if I take his cargo first, he can jump by himself."

Kodo choked on his own saliva.

"Hold on," he interjected with a cough, "Your plan is: Rykr and the old man, who both outweigh you probably ten-to-one, hurl themselves off the edge of the gorge and trust you to carry their weight across the distance they can't cover. Alvi we just, I guess, fling across —"

"What?"

"And *I'm* supposed to *jump?* And clear it?"

Leida nodded affirmatively.

"You have very long legs," she said reassuringly and stiffly patted the side of his leg. Kodo looked to Kaishek for help.

The old man walked along casually, but his ears were perked back to listen. His thick black and silver mane was now tightly plaited against the back of his neck, and he seemed more relaxed because of it. He finally looked back at his companions and pleading son.

"Sounds like a plan to me." He nodded at Leida, who nodded back as if she determined that to be the correct response. Kodo could only whine hopelessly.

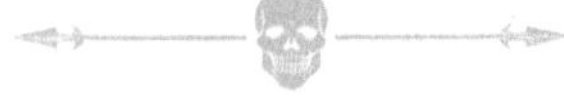

"Doctor Daniels?"

"Doctor Daniels!"

"If you can hear us, stay where you are and call out!"

The small blue sun began to fall toward the horizon, slowly at first, but it seemed to descend faster with each passing second. The search party knew they needed to return to the compound before the brighter yellow sun had the same inclination.

Captain Short checked his watch, his stomach turning at the fleeting timer. According to Doctor Novak, the runaway botanist's probability of survival was about to run out. He wasn't even entirely sure what that meant, but he knew it wasn't good. He let out a quivering sigh so quiet no one would have noticed if not for the billowing vapor of his breath.

"Time's up. We're heading back," the captain called to his team, gesturing with his pointer finger in a circular motion above him to signify that they were turning around. The group of soldiers made a few smart comments under their breath. A couple sighed in relief, but they all turned around to march back the way they came. All but one.

"We're giving up?" a young voice piped up from behind them. Short turned around and looked down at Private Zheng.

"What did you say, Private?" he barked loud enough for every other soldier to flinch and shake their heads scoldingly. The private cleared his throat.

"Are we giving up, Captain?" Zheng barked back in a voice that was distinctly deeper than he normally spoke.

"I'm not risking any more perfectly good lives chasing ghosts. That answer your question, son?" Short announced more to the entire congregation than just to Zheng. The young man nodded once dutifully.

"Yes, Captain," he said through the pain in his eyes. Short firmly pushed the shorter soldier along by the shoulder.

"We can't afford to waste time on lost causes."

They began the journey back, but the captain carved arrows into the trees with a bowie knife as they went, marking the path to the compound.

"Captain's got a soft spot for the kid, huh?" Corporal Greene whispered to the soldier beside him. Upon glancing over, he was met with Sergeant Mendoza giving him a deathly warning look.

"Oops. Sorry, Ma." He winced at his mistake.

"Captain's got a soft spot for the kid, huh?" Greene immediately whispered to the soldier on his other side. He shut his mouth once again as he looked up to see Corporal Keenan looming over him.

"Yeah, because you're all faggot Army fucks," Keenan spat through the side of his mouth with a cocky sneer. The other corporal gave him an ingenuine smile.

"You jarheads have such a way with words, you should go tell him that," Greene replied smugly without missing a beat. Then he immediately fell forward into the dirt as Keenan tripped him. He lunged up from the ground but was yanked back just before his fist collided with the marine's jaw.

"Let me go, Ma," Greene growled and struggled against Mendoza's strong grip as Keenan cackled.

"Easy, Corporal," Mendoza hissed in a low voice. "Not the time, *not the place*. You hear me?"

He slowly released Greene as the younger man's muscles relaxed and his fists unclenched, while Keenan giggled hysterically.

"You got that handled, Ma?" Captain Short called back from the front of the formation.

"Yes, sir," Mendoza called ahead as he shoved between Greene and Keenan, using his own body to separate them.

It was silent for a while as the search party made their way back through the jungle with a cloud of dread hanging over them. The vicious atmosphere of the forest haunted them, and the ticking clock of waning numbers threatened their very cause. They'd lost another life, another irreplaceable life. With each failure to protect the assets, a desperate fury inside the captain grew.

...

All at once, Sherri realized that she knew nothing. Nothing at all.

You're a field scientist, Daniels, get it together.

Go through the process.

Make observations.

What are the facts?

Tawny colored specimen, sitting seven to ten feet in front of her. It was making consistent clicks, chuffs, and moans. It sounded halfway between a lion and a gorilla, but the clicking was so deliberate and rhythmic that it was nearly indistinguishable from Morse code.

Diverse vocal range.

Its lips and muzzle were coated in inky, oily liquid from the throat of the dead specimen.

Black blood.

It was unphased and undeterred by receiving a face full of chartreuse flames.

Green fire?

It appeared relaxed, its head curiously cocked. Short, light-colored hair trailed down its neck like a horse's mane. Bright eyes, large on its head, wide and owl-like. It was strangely emotive, its face expressing clear dubiety. Its pupils were not dilated into crosses; they were ovals instead. Sherri gathered that was a good sign.

Docile. For now.

It was tall, taller than she'd fully realized, twice her height. Sherri hesitantly allowed her gaze to wander from its face to the brown object it had dropped on the ground between them.

A bag.

An oblong leather pouch with a flap secured by a loop of cord around a tooth. Trailing from it was a long strap that had gone around the native's shoulders. It looked remarkably, terrifyingly manmade. Stitched and sewn, even.

Sherri couldn't begin to identify the feeling in her chest. Whatever it was, she knew it was the result of the human world changing in ways she couldn't yet fathom. She was dizzy, and for possibly the first time in her life, she felt grossly unqualified. Sherri was just a young human botanist, what did she know about extraterrestrials? What did any of them know about new worlds? New life? They were lost, and she'd only just accepted it. So, so very lost.

The native made a new sound. A high-pitched coo, halfway between a purr and a chirp. It was a stark contrast to the low chuffs and clicks the beast had been making, which she'd assumed were investigative vocalizations.

Sherri took a deep, slow breath, watching with wide eyes as it leaned its massive head down near her face, inching ever so slowly nearer. Her fists clenched in anticipation. It showed no aggression, just a studious curiosity, and so she resisted the urge to hit it again. Its snout was still stained in sticky black blood from the giant monster she'd witnessed it slay in mere seconds. But its bright eyes were glimmering instead of glowing. They held an almost childlike wonder, as if waiting for her to tell it a story.

"What?" she whispered aloud. It was sitting only five feet in front of her now, its head dipped down to her eye level. It made another few inquisitive clicks, like it was asking her the same thing.

"Brrrrp?" It breathed a strong gust of air into her face as it sniffed her, blowing her unruly curls up over her head.

"Okay. Okay," Sherri softly crooned, straining to keep her quivering voice gentle. "Please don't bite my head off."

She inched her makeshift flamethrower back into the side pouch of her bag; her bare hands had been more effective anyway. The native seemed to notice her moving, and it made a few clicks from its throat in response. Then it nudged her chest with its snout. The force was enough to knock her over on her behind, but she immediately jumped back up and reclaimed her space by shoving the native's nose back as hard as she could.

"Hey," she barked, doing her best to channel Captain Short's commanding presence in her voice, "Don't push me."

The native cocked its head and flapped its ears around.

"Clik clik brrrap." It made a series of noises that reminded her of running her fingernail along the teeth of a comb. It lowered its mighty head a little, and its vibrant peridot eyes softened. Sherri stared at it for a moment, trying to determine what exactly was going on in its head.

Then Sherri did something she knew better than to do. But whether it was scientific curiosity, simple affection, or she just wanted to prove to herself that she could do it —

She reached out and touched the beast.

She gingerly laid her palm atop its nose, allowing her fingers to settle on the short fur of its snout. Four gaping nostrils pulsed with breath beneath her touch, surprisingly soft and velvety. Trailing up its forehead beyond her fingertips were platelike scales the size of her entire hand, a pleasant olive green that flashed with emerald iridescence when the light hit them. Its skin was warm, and its hot breath beat against her hand slowly but powerfully. Sherri stayed completely still, feeling the beast and sharing its gaze.

Once again, a song wove through the trees. The native perked up, its ears pricking at the noise. This time the music sounded less soothing. It was a stronger warbling verse that ended in a low bass rumble; it enveloped the jungle in an air of unease. Sherri slowly took her hand off the native's snout, preparing for it to jolt or run as it tensed. Its nostrils flared as it sniffed the air, and it stood up on all four feet and picked up its bag. She backed up to give it space.

The beast looked back down at her, a slight urgency in its bright eyes as all four pupils scanned the tree line individually from each other. Then it lunged.

Sherri dove, but it caught her in midair by the backpack and took off in a dead sprint.

As the tunahk entered the Ramys gates, answering the call of the horn, all eleven warriors merged back into a single vessel. They were whole once again as they came to a halt in silence, standing in a straight line before their commander.

"Tunahk-dahn," Rataan announced. "The lunai have heard our tenets."

"The rebels no longer slither in the region's shadows; they now brazenly threaten our way of life. Our land, our very home, where our young children sleep at night. The rebellion forewarns their violent return with a threat written near our borders, but we will hunt no longer. Instead, we will eagerly welcome them with the honor of the Ramys clan and every promise of a swift slaughter.

"Vaus-Erro has ordered every road and passage in and out of the kingdom to be locked down. Checkpoints and patrols will be set up along every edge of the territory until the rebels are found. When they are, they will be ended quickly and violently upon first sight. Understood?"

In sync, the warriors nodded. The commander called out orders.

"Lih-Dahn, Raiz-Dahn, and Kjell-Dahn will barricade the paths to the northern ridge, eliminating that entrance to the territory.

"Sahga-Dahn, Garja-Dahn, and Kei-Dahn will man a border check a few miles out from the main gates, where they will monitor all movement to the south.

"Teihnan-Dahn, Iago-Dahn, and Mahrz-Dahn will set up dams along the eastern bank of the river, shutting down the shallow crossing sections.

"Faro-Dahn will close off the abandoned mine to the west, and Io-Dahn will repair the rope bridge over the gorge. That will be the only passage in or out of the surrounding region, and that is where we will ambush them should they dare to use it. And if they are already inside of these borders…

"They will not be getting out alive."

Iago's gravelly voice rang out defiantly.

"Why will me and Io be separated? Restoring the bridge is not a one-ghaengste job," she argued. Io pushed her head under her sister's chin to quiet her, and Rataan's lip curled dangerously as he studied the twins.

"You will do more harm than good working on the bridge with your impaired vision," the commander spat. "Would you like to question my orders again, or shall we skip to the part where I strip you of your title?"

Iago's face twitched, but Io stomped on her foot before she spoke again.

"I understand I am better with my hands and lighter on my feet than the others. I will take the challenge alone, Rataan-Leih," Io said calmly.

"And Faro?" an unlikely voice interjected next. Mahrz's normally stoic tone was laced with concern.

"What of him?" Rataan growled, quickly growing impatient.

"Why is he to block off the mine by himself? He is still recovering," the red man continued cautiously, glancing at the largest warrior at the edge of the group, his helmet covering his mutilated head. A furious orange eye gleamed beneath the helm, a warning in its pupils.

"Or... not. He is strong," Mahrz backtracked.

"He is. Now go, the rebels have been in the wind for far too long and I smell a storm brewing in the distance," Rataan bellowed as he stepped back and lifted his chin to the warriors.

"*La'al maixay,*" he called to them, the words striking forth from deep in his chest like lightning.

"*La'al maijex,*" all eleven tunahk thundered back before separating.

Mahrz caught up with Faro before he left.

"You'll be alright, brother?" he asked in a hush as he trotted alongside him. Faro flicked his tail impatiently.

"Don't insult me, you soft bastard," Faro grumbled through the side of his broken jaw. "I didn't treat you like a damn eunuch when you lost your leg."

Mahrz paused, tilting his head back and forth as if he were weighing that point.

"Fair enough. I shall stow my pathetic, feeble sentiments and mincing concerns," Mahrz conceded with an exaggerated cadence. "Just don't take too long at the mine. I think Kjell was hoping to spar with you before dinner."

Faro glanced at the other man from the corner of his eye.

"Why, because he's no longer intimidated by my strength?" he growled. Mahrz smirked impishly.

"No, fool, because he's sweet on you." He snickered and shoved the larger brute's shoulder affectionately, then jogged off before hearing his friend's response. He headed back to his group, leaving Faro to his own journey.

The tunahk went their separate ways, though there was a magnetic tension that resisted, trying desperately to draw them back together. It reluctantly broke as the groups pursued their duties to the north, south, east, and west.

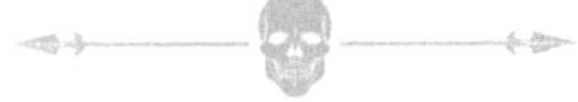

Sherri let out a blood-curdling shriek as she was swept through the jungle, too busy fighting with her backpack to curse herself for it. In a moment of triumph, she got her arms out of the straps and balled up in preparation for colliding with the hard ground and being trampled. The ground never came, nor the trampling, as she was caught around the waist. She cried out again as canines locked around her torso and incisors pressed into her ribcage. They didn't quite penetrate her skin, not yet, but that didn't stop the pain. She could only imagine it was the feeling one might experience if they were dragged behind a speeding car down a poorly cobbled road.

This is it. Damn it.

Sherri prepared for the inevitable crunch of her spine being pulverized as the native bit down, seeing Roger's violent demise in her mind again. She could only cling to the native's head, clamping her eyes closed as it leaped over logs and tore through the jungle at what she hoped was its top speed. Then the pressure lightened.

The beast loosened its jaw's crushing grasp on her and let her hold on by herself — and she did, curling her entire body around its snout and hanging on to its horns. She hesitantly opened one eye, discovering that her face was right next to its own. It wasn't looking at her, however; it focused straight ahead. For a moment, the trees whistling by and the jostling of her body seemed to slow down, and she saw more in its emerald gaze. More than a beast.

Then a guttural, monstrous roar broke through the air and shattered the momentary slowness. It didn't come from the creature carrying her, it came from behind them. Sherri finally looked back just in time to see another much, *much* larger native break straight through a dead log, closing in fast.

"Oh fuck!" she screamed and desperately tightened her grip on the beast's skull, completely forgetting any fear she had of it seconds before.

"GO!" she shrieked as if it might understand her. Their pursuer snapped at the air behind them, nearly catching the tip of the first native's tail. If her pleas hadn't lit a fire under it, that sure did. It kicked into a new gear and sprinted harder, its ears pinned to its head and its nostrils pouring out steam in a rhythmic beat as it tore through the trees. Sherri hung on with every muscle in her body, tears racing down her cheeks not from fear but from wind speed. The part of her body still in its mouth was now drenched in hot saliva and undoubtedly bruised to the bone. As she lost sight of the pursuer on the horizon, she thought for a second the ride of terror might be over.

The native leaped vertically and scaled at least a two-story height, catching hold of a massive tree. That time Sherri's scream was stifled, but only because the impact slammed the wind out of her lungs.

She opened her eyes and immediately regretted it as she saw straight down the treacherous drop, now climbing tens of feet each second. The native efficiently maneuvered straight up the trunk of the towering tree like a cat, using its claws as hooks. Sherri had never been afraid of heights before, but she supposed there was a first time for everything as she squeezed her eyes shut tight and felt bile rush up her throat.

"Don't drop me, don't drop me, don't drop me," she pleaded, her voice now on the edge of a sob. Her stomach rose into her chest as her fears were realized. Sherri was suddenly released from the native's jaws and shaken off its head. Her horrified cry was cut short as she landed unceremoniously on a hard damp surface.

Head... intact.

Arms... functional.

Legs... there.

Slowly, Sherri forced herself to open her eyes once again. The native stared straight back at her, closer than she was prepared for. She jolted and gasped despite her best attempt to stay calm. The beast blinked once, twice, all four pupils expanding and contracting rhythmically as they studied her face.

"Hello..." Sherri whispered in terror. The native sat back and unblocked her vision, now allowing her to see their surroundings. She was in... a log. A giant hollow log the size of a passenger jet. Walls of raw wood curled up and around her in a horizontal cylinder, open on both ends as light shined in through hanging sheets of moss. Sherri could do nothing but stare around the hollow — at the fungus growing through the wood, and at the native, the tops of its horns scraping against the arched wood ceiling. A violent wave of nausea hit her like a battering ram, and she felt distinctly seasick.

Seasick?

Oh no.

She identified the feeling of faintly swaying.

Oh god no.

She slowly peeled her eyes from the seemingly docile native, crawling away to peer out the nearest opening of the gigantic log.

"Oh my god."

She could see everything.

They were suspended in the jungle canopy, at least thousands of feet in the open air. She had no idea how they'd gotten that high that fast, and she considered the idea that she might have blacked out on the way. The forest floor wasn't even visible beneath the lower tree cover and thick fog. Vines as thick as oil pipelines made up a complex netting amongst the massive twisted branches and unearthly trees. The only thing she could compare it to was the view from atop a skyscraper, looking out over the world from above the clouds. Another wave of nausea hit as she realized the log was suspended by a wrapped tangling of vines like a giant's pendulum.

"Please, no. *No no no no,*" Sherri whined to herself as she gingerly tested the structure's stability by swaying her weight. It didn't appear to have an effect, but the observation gave her next to no comfort as she looked straight down through a wide gap in the wood beneath her. She desperately tried to calm her breathing, then cried out as she turned to see the alien she'd nearly forgotten about casually sitting beside her.

"*God* — damn it! What the hell are we doing up here? This whole thing could come down at any moment! Oh, you are *so fucked* this time, Daniels." Sherri covered her face with her hands. She no longer bothered controlling her voice or body language around the beast. At this point, she was either going to starve to death suspended in the air, fall to her death trying to climb down, or berate the native into eating her. All equally rough ways to go, as far as she was concerned. Something tickled her cheek.

Sherri side-eyed the creature as one of its long whiskers bumped against the side of her face. It moved and swayed of its own accord, like a tentacle. She couldn't even begin to speculate how that worked.

"You big bastards are everywhere, huh?" she thought aloud, studying the beast and electing not to think about her impending death for now. It just made a few small, unhelpful clicks.

"I've seen four different individuals just today. How are you guys so elusive? Or girls? Or neither, I guess we can't" — she glanced down between its back legs — "...Okay, well, those look strikingly male."

Sherri looked back up to his curious face, then frowned. She now had access to a docile, live specimen to study; it was exactly what she needed. But to what end? She didn't have her journal or equipment anymore. It was all still in her backpack, presumably in the dirt miles away. She didn't have her colleagues to bounce theories and conjecture off of, she didn't even have a way to give them her materials and findings after her inevitable death. What was the point of the discovery and the knowledge if she had no way of sharing it? Was it all in vain, after all?

She noticed the native steadily chirping and clicking again as if he were in the midst of his own tragic soliloquy. Listening to his strange babbling distracted her from her own thoughts, at least, and she found herself entranced by how precise and intricate his vocalizations were. She began to recognize patterns and sequences in the clicking until the chatter was replaced by a horrible, graceless retching.

Sherri stepped back to dodge a spray of saliva as he bellowed out a hoarse cough and an obnoxious barrage of gagging. She could only watch in helpless apathy; she wouldn't even have a captive audience to speak to if this animal choked to death at her feet. Perhaps she could eat him.

With one final hack, a large, heavy, thoroughly soaked object flopped to the wooden ground with a wet *plat*. Sherri blinked down at what appeared to be... her backpack.

"Oh, look at that." Sherri cringed, nudging the slimy bag with her boot.

"At least I still have my supplies," she said with a sigh. Maybe she would survive a little longer with her equipment, but she wasn't looking forward to the ordeal of searching through the wet jumble and determining how much of it had been partially digested. The native purred beside her, and Sherri looked up at him with a forced smile.

"Mhm." She nodded reassuringly. "Thanks, buddy."

She held back a gag as if it might hurt the giant monster's feelings, then put her hands on her hips as she looked down at the slimy heap.

"Shit!" She suddenly gasped, forgetting every inhibition she'd had surrounding the putrid mess. "My journal!"

Sherri fell to her knees, plunging her hand through the sticky slobber and into the bag. The native bit the other end and pulled it away, and before she could think better of it, she lunged and grabbed hold of a strap.

"No!" Sherri cried out. "Give it to me!"

She yanked at the strap with all the strength in her burning muscles, but it was ripped from her hands. She jumped up to try to catch hold of it as the native lifted it high above her head, then turned it over and shook as the contents came tumbling out. Bile-covered tools, materials, and snacks splattered to the floor, and Sherri frantically snatched up the small leather-bound book as it bounced out.

She sighed in relief as she propped it open to dry; the damage was minimal. At least her precious notes were safe. Maybe her world had been turned on its head, and maybe it was coming to an end. But she was a scientist, she was in the field, and she had her supplies back. She had no choice but to continue studying deeper and driving on until she could no longer.

Sherri looked back at the native, who was now going through her belongings, aggressively sniffing and biting every object. She huffed at the giant nuisance.

"You're kind of an asshole."

"No. Absolutely not."

"I searched all of it. This is the thinnest point."

The rebels stood at the edge of a canyon, the drop so deep they could hardly see the water below. The angry river was a savage torrent imprisoned at its depths, it roared and howled as if threatening them if they dare come nearer. The cliff face was as steep and treacherous as the fall into hell itself. Kodo stared down into the screaming flood.

"You can't make me," he said, looking across the chasm. The distance to the other rim was his body length several times over. Leida stared up at the side of his face from close beside him.

"It is not that far," she replied unhelpfully. Kodo's cargo began jostling atop his back as Kaishek roughly untied the straps and began pulling the load off.

"Okay, here we go," the old man said as he heaved the pack onto the ground.

"I'm not doing it," Kodo insisted once again.

"Take the load across in several parts, Leida, do not waste your energy," Kaishek continued as he unwrapped the supplies and divided them into smaller portions. Leida left Kodo's side to help.

"Now what was that about 'flinging'?" Alvi piped up, peering down over the ledge from between Kodo's legs. "I think I'll just take the bridge while Leida murders all three of you via coerced suicide."

"Bridge is miles upstream, you're crossing here with the rest of us," Rykr retorted as he yanked her out from underneath Kodo by her exposed tail.

"We cross together," he continued, "and if it comes to it... die together."

The mountain man shrugged, snickering smugly as Alvi squeaked.

Leida suddenly took off over the edge, a pack of items in her claws as she soared over the gap and landed gently on the other side. She dropped the cargo and leaped into the air again, gliding back to the near ledge. For her, it was barely a single wingbeat.

Kodo watched as she made the trip twice more until all their supplies sat on the other side of the gorge. He grew more nervous each time. Leida landed once again, shaking out her wings.

"I will take whoever is heaviest first," she announced.

The two mountain dwellers looked at one another, and Kaishek reached back to grab the handle of his axe. He pulled the heavy weapon out of its sheath on his back and tossed it at the ground, its blade sinking into the soil with a heavy *thunk*.

"That would be me." The Lost King nodded, as he stood nearly an entire head taller than his nephew.

"Doubt it," Alvi teased and poked Rykr's plush stomach with a prodding paw.

"You know what?" Rykr announced. "I think Al should go first."

"It was a joke!"

He clamped his jaws down on the scruff of the ocean woman's neck before she could scramble away, then lifted her in the air.

"Rykr," she pleaded. He carried her to the edge of the cliff.

"*Rykr! Rykr,* I always thought you were much more handsome than K—"

Alvi shrieked as she was launched high over the chasm, her stout body shooting across like she'd been launched from a slingshot as Rykr had grossly overestimated his throw.

"Oops."

They heard several high-pitched yelps echo out as she bounced to a halt on the other side. There was a brief moment of silence while they waited for a confirmation of her survival.

"I'm going to *make you INTO A RUG!*"

"She's fine. Your turn, Uncle." Rykr smirked as he walked away from the ledge and the vicious screaming threats on the other side blended into the background. As Kaishek cracked his neck and rolled his worn shoulders in preparation, Leida positioned herself beside the edge to act as his wings after the initial leap.

"I barely even got to know him," Kodo muttered. Rykr chuckled and elbowed the younger man's side.

They both fell silent as Kaishek took off.

The old man was unexpectedly fast, but he had to be. He charged forward with everything he had, muscles flexing and breath churning, straight to the gorge.

As soon as Kaishek was in the air, Leida's claws clutched his thick hide and her wings beat powerfully, carrying his inertia. He sank as he neared the far edge, and she bit down on the back of his neck to keep hold of him as her wings flapped harder and faster.

Kaishek's claws dug into the stone on the far edge. His feet frantically scraped against the rock face to pull himself over, and Leida groaned as she heaved his massive weight upwards with all her might. A smaller set of jaws clamped onto Kaishek's paw, and with one final pull, he lurched over the edge and landed on solid ground. Alvi and Leida released him, and all three took a moment to slump on the grass in exhaustion.

"Sorry," Alvi peeped as the old warrior assessed the deep bite to his paw and the blood soaking down his neck.

"Don't be." He nodded in appreciation. "Have you got it in you to get Rykr across?"

He looked at Leida as she spit out one of the scales from the back of his neck.

"Yes." Leida took to the air once again. She delivered the dropped axe to its owner, then swooped back to land on the near rim beside Rykr.

"Are you ready?" she asked.

"Ready for you to claw the skin off my back? Absolutely," Rykr replied dryly. Leida returned to her position by the cliff, fluttering her broad wings as if to recharge them. Rykr took a few deep breaths and positioned himself a sufficient distance away, glancing across the chasm as if to make sure that Kaishek had, in fact, made it. He started running before he could think twice.

Kodo watched as Rykr threw himself off the edge, and Leida caught hold of him and used her wings as his own. They clumsily soared over the distance, and Kaishek was there to grab Rykr by the horn and yank him the final length just as they started to sag. They'd apparently misjudged how much force they truly had as they went toppling to the ground, Alvi barely rolling out of the way in time as the duo fell over top of one another. For a moment, Leida disappeared beneath Rykr, but she pushed the bulky man off her and shook out her feathers, unharmed.

Leida lifted her wings to join Kodo where he stood alone on the other rim, but Kaishek stopped her.

"Leave him be," the old king said, then turned away from the cliff. The others did not follow him as he trekked down the hill.

"We must wait for him," Leida insisted.

"Then wait for him," Kaishek called back as he left.

Kodo paced back and forth, trying to ignore the calls from his companions as they urged him to hurry.

He stopped and looked over the canyon. He'd probably jumped farther distances on solid ground. But Kaishek and Rykr had barely made it, even with Leida's help. There was no one to help Kodo — Leida's vast wingspan would do nothing to carry his enormous form. He took a deep breath.

"It's not that far."

He accidentally focused for too long on how small his friends looked across the distance. Alvi was barely a speck.

"*Shit,* it's that far."

He shook his head, squeezing his eyes shut and wincing at the thought of being foolish enough to try to jump over the gorge. He'd never heard of anyone doing it before, and he doubted anyone ever had. The massive ravine spanned from shortly outside the tree line, through the plains, all the way to the falls, and into the bay. Most forest dwellers stayed far away from it, and any that found themselves too close rarely lived to tell the tale. He shook his head again as if trying to dissolve the fears of meeting a gruesome end. He reminded himself that if anyone could do it, it was him. Leida was right; he was built for it with long, powerful legs and lean muscles covering his body. No one was stronger, no one was faster. And no one was more foolish, that much he was sure of. He breathed hard out of his nose and looked at the deadly chasm once again, his feet shuffling in the grass. Then he tore his eyes from the drop and forced them to focus straight ahead. Straight over.

"He's not going to do it," Rykr grumbled. "And Kaishek is already down by the coast. We should just leave him."

"We *can't* leave him, who else will carry all this shit Grandpa made us bring?" Alvi kicked the pile of cargo, muttering about how the old man had left without bothering to pick any of it up. Leida shushed them as a yell sounded out from over the gorge.

"What did he say?" Alvi cocked her head. Rykr shrugged.

"I don't know, smooth? Maybe he's having a stroke."

"Move," Leida said, backing up in a hurry.

"Oh yeah, it did sound like —"

"Move!" Leida hissed and snatched Alvi out of the way by the tail, shoving Rykr as she scrambled to the side.

Kodo tore across the open plain so fast he was barely visible against the tall grass, but his mammoth form became clear as day as he launched himself off the cliff. For a brief moment, the massive beast was light and graceful, soaring through the air. He was as much a part of the sky as the colossal planet suspended above. As if he was made to be there.

The illusion of smallness and surprising grace was obliterated as the giant landed, his feet slamming into the planet like an earthquake and shaking the ground as he kept running. He threw his head back and howled triumphantly.

"Wooohooooo!" he whooped and laughed, rearing up on his tall legs as he finally skidded to a halt in the kicked-up dust. He grinned at his bewildered friends, his chest heaving with ragged breaths.

"Did you see that? Where's Dad, did he see it? Shit! He's leaving, we have to go!" the forest man rambled, yanking his friends up from their fallen positions and heaving the cargo onto his back. They quickly shook off their awe, rushing to get the packs strapped on him. Rykr plucked Alvi off the ground and threw her atop his back as they raced to meet Kaishek at the water's edge.

"Gramps! Wait!" Alvi called as they ran after the old man. Kaishek tread slowly along the white sandy beach, watching the vibrant water tapping at his paws. He halted, and Kodo barely stopped in time to avoid running straight into him.

"Why are we —" Kodo started, then trailed off as the pluming sand cleared and his question was answered.

Down the beach ahead of them, the blue breaking waves crashed against an enormous white arch protruding from the sand. Giant daggers jutted down from the top like stalactites.

The jawbone of a titan.

Cerulean banners were erected from the shallow wake on either side of the mammoth fossil, blowing proudly in the dusty gulf wind. The whistling gusts carried with them eerie sounds of rattling bones, rushing tides, and flapping tents. Distant figures stood around the arch, completely still, staring at the rebels. They were dwarfed by the mandible's size, and all armored in bone and mail. Silver weapons gleamed at their sides, and the devouring ocean lapped patiently against their ankles.

15
TREMOR

The rushing of the swift river filled the forest air, and mischievous taunts rose above it as Mahrz secured the final board of the structure.

"Even *Teihnan* finished her station before you, Mahrz, and she's incapable of moving at a speed any faster than 'half-*dead*,'" Iago sneered, leaping on top of Mahrz's construction. It was covered on top and mechanized with rolling chains, a checkpoint that every ghaengste who sought to cross the river would have to enter through. Both Iago and Teihnan had built stations of their own at different river junctions.

"Well, Teihnan also puts minimal effort into everything she does," the red warrior retorted. "In fact, so do you. Beyond cracking skulls and cleaving balls, anyway."

Iago bit onto one of the corded tassels of hair hanging from Mahrz's neck, pulling him along by it.

"Aye, I'm a woman of few true passions. Now move your ruby ass, let's see if Io needs help and then get something to eat," she said as she trotted downriver.

"Teihnan, can you keep an eye on things here while we fetch Io?" Mahrz called to the third warrior behind them as he was towed away.

"Only one."

"There's that enthusiasm."

"Whatever."

Mahrz and Iago left the dark woman behind to watch the river checkpoints as they hiked to the bridge. The embankment rose high above the water as the canal grew steeper. The torrent stretched wider, deeper, and angrier as they walked south along its lip, the bank descending from a sandy incline to a treacherous vertical drop. The pair strayed further from the edge as they traveled on into the plains; forest dwellers were not known for surefootedness.

"This is senseless." Iago's whistling voice struggled to rise over the sound of the river as they trekked along. "What was Rataan-Leih thinking when he decided to split up me and Io? And what the fuck is with him and storms lately? We won't have another wet season until the sunchaenge."

"He means it as a figure of speech," Mahrz replied as he walked, lifting his head to tentatively peek into the gorge.

"Which part?"

"The storms. I don't know why he decided to separate you from Io." He shrugged. Iago let out a heavy sigh.

"Well, I don't like it. Any of it. Have you noticed a change in him recently?" she asked as she kicked a pebble over the canyon's edge.

"Maybe. He was always a hardass, but I suppose he's been more distant from us lately. Give him time. He's only harsh because he loves us and he loves the clan. He will come back around, he always does," Mahrz reassured in a thoughtful tone. Iago seemed to think about that for a while, remaining silent for a minute. Then she perked up as she spotted a silhouette in the distance.

"There's the bridge." She gestured ahead. 'Bridge' was a generous term; it was a modest structure of rotting rope tied across the chasm, a sparing of ancient wooden boards clinging along its length. Io tiptoed along it gingerly, taking her time as she weaved extra rope around the cord already in place and secured new boards as she went. As far as they knew, no one bore witness to the bridge's original construction. All they knew for sure was that whoever originally built it had either done a very poor job or had constructed it long, long ago.

Yet there Io stood, stepping as carefully and lightly as possible over the lethal drop as she braided in more rope. It would be a several-day project; she had to work at a tediously slow pace so as not to adjust her weight too violently. She made her way to the center of the bridge, creeping from slat to slat as she worked.

"Wonder what you did to piss off Rataan-Leih, ah?" Mahrz called from the ledge behind her. "Must have been pretty bad for him to give you a shit job like this."

"Nothing," Io called back, not looking up from her work. "He's just punishing me for Iago's loud mouth because he can't tell us apart."

The twin on solid ground cackled but didn't bother yelling back a response. Iago's worn voice wouldn't carry across the vast distance like it once would have.

"Think we can help in some way?" she asked Mahrz beside her, looking around at the extra rope and wood.

"I don't see how we would," Mahrz responded with a shrug, watching the thin woman work. "Not a very bright idea for us to toss materials at her."

Io had taken off her armor and sword to shed weight, now bare except for a coiling of rope around her shoulders. All her personal items laid in a pile near where her companions stood. Iago nodded and continued flicking loose stones off the edge.

"Guess not. This is going to take eons," Iago huffed. Mahrz nodded sympathetically but didn't get the chance to reply before they heard Io call out to them.

"Iago —" Io's normally steady voice cracked in desperation, her eyes locked on the space above her. *"Iago!"*

"Io?"

"Kill it."

Io's gaze was trained on a silhouette soaring directly overhead, circling eerily in the air like a scavenger to a corpse. A sky dweller.

Iago immediately drew her sword and let out an ear-splitting shriek as Mahrz cried out to their lone companion. Io stood completely vulnerable, naked and unarmed over the deathly drop, her only support a dilapidated rope bridge.

"Io, get off the bridge. Walk to me, sister," Mahrz pleaded, but Io wouldn't dare move her gaze from the enemy above. She only inched backward, careful not to misstep but unwilling to look away. Iago screamed vulgar threats, her muted voice suddenly coming out deafening and uninhibited.

"Ha, I was hoping we'd have roasted wings tonight!" Iago roared, "Just yesterday I plucked a wind-humper so fat, it couldn't even fly! *Was that your mother?"*

Io was still working away from the center of the bridge step by step; they could barely track the flying figure through the glaring sunlight. Iago now stood on her hind legs, desperately trying to draw the enemy's attention.

"Come down here and get a taste, you gutless fucking cunt!" she roared. The figure just soared above, armor glinting against the cloudless sky.

Io kept backing up steadily, ever so slowly, her eyes trained above her as a faint sparkle fell from the heavens like a single tear. The stranger abruptly flew away in retreat as Iago screamed after it, her eye not catching the remaining twinkle in the sky.

Mahrz's sharp gaze finally trained on the falling tear and his blood ran cold.

A dagger.

"RUN!" he cried, but there was no time.

Io looked to her companions on the rim of the gorge just as the dagger met one of the precious ropes suspending the weak structure, slicing through its main support.

The entire bridge snapped in half.

"NO!!!" Iago screamed out as if her hearts had been ripped from her chest, her ragged voice tearing through her throat and screeching through the silent air. She lurched for the canyon's edge but was yanked back by the strap of her armor.

"Iago!" Mahrz yelled, holding her back with all his might. Her skull collided with his, and she shoved him away. She dove again for the cliff but was tackled to the ground.

"Stop! Sister, please," Mahrz begged, but Iago thrashed wildly and kicked at his stomach as they grappled.

"I'll fucking kill you!" she shrieked, sinking her fangs into his ear and ripping part of it off as she struggled desperately.

"Let me go! LET ME GO! I'll tear your lungs out, YOU FUCKING BASTARD!" Iago roared furiously as tears began pouring from her eye. Mahrz held her to the ground with his full weight, laying on top of her as she frantically tore into his flesh.

"I HAVE TO GET HER!" she sobbed. Her screams carried the agony of the entrails being gutted from her core, but the black blood soaking her white fur and frothing from her mouth was not her own.

"I have to get her, Mahrz! Please, please, Mahrz, I have to — I have to get her—" Her vicious snarling turned to a pathetic whining, and she cried out like an abandoned child as her fight weakened.

"She's gone, Iago, she's gone," Mahrz whispered as a tear fell from his eye onto the bloody face of the woman below him. She released a low, quiet howl of despair as she fell still, the last wail of a dying star. Something deep inside of her broke, and she finally surrendered.

The two warriors laid alone at the edge of the gorge, their quiet cries drowned out by the rage of the water below.

...

The rebels didn't have a chance to approach any further before the Celesteal guards fanned out and began marching over. The space between them was closing fast.

"What's the plan?" Rykr whispered.

"No time for a plan," Kaishek said.

"We don't have a plan?" Rykr hissed frantically, but Alvi interrupted from atop his back.

"Shut up. Let me do the talking," she said in a hush as she hopped down to the sand. "They won't care about any of you except for Kodo."

Kodo slightly lowered his head behind Leida's wings, as if it would do anything to hide his mammoth form.

"What about me?"

"Well, they'll want to kill you immediately," Alvi replied with a deep breath.

"So what do we do?" the giant urged.

"Start praying."

The armored guards halted mere strides away from where the rebels stood on the beach. All was silent for a moment aside from the crashing of waves and the whispering of wind.

Alvi took a few steps forward and cleared her throat.

"What a sight for sore eyes you all are! I love the new hair, Ephyra-Dahn. How are the kids?" she said pleasantly.

"Save it, Alvi," the woman in front barked, long ropy locs hanging from her neck. "You disappear without a trace, presumed dead, and now you lead these... *outsiders* to our borders. What explanation could you possibly have for this?"

Alvi swallowed.

"They do not pose a threat to our people. Clearly, as I stand here breathing. They wish to ally with the Celesteal nation and aid the struggle in the conflict against Ramys. These individuals are not mindless killers like the rest of their kinds, and I am prepared to vouch for them," Alvi explained, her leg jolting back to kick Rykr in the groin as she heard him open his mouth in protest. She spoke loudly over his agonized groan.

"I realize that my disappearance may lead you not to trust me, rightfully so, and I understand there are many questions left unanswered. If you'll allow us an audience with her majesty Vaus-Kharax, I will explain everything and she can decide for herself how to deal with us. Please," she finished. The warriors looked at one another dubiously.

"Watch them," Ephyra-Dahn hissed to her comrades as she gestured to the strangers sitting behind Alvi, "If one so much as sneezes, kill them all."

"Scout." Ephyra turned back to Alvi, beckoning her along. "Step aside with me."

Alvi turned to her friends with a deathly look of warning, silently mouthing something along the lines of 'do not fuck this up.' Then she rushed to walk down the coast alongside Ephyra.

The other rebels stood completely still aside from Kodo's eyes watering with the sudden intense urge to sneeze. Kaishek stared straight ahead, his eyes calmly watching a sand-colored warrior. She stared back with a scowl. Rykr's jaw clenched as he bit back the urge to pant from heat and the ache in his future descendants. And still silence came as naturally to Leida as blinking, in fact more so.

Ephyra approached once again with Alvi by her side.

"Bring the kaunek-leih," Ephyra ordered a silver warrior. "We will see what she makes of this."

The silver woman nodded dutifully and took off running back to the jawbone gates, a plume of sand kicking in her wake and blowing the entrance flags wildly.

"Twelve coins says the commander kills them where they stand and brings the queen their livers on a necklace," the sand-colored soldier snickered to her comrade beside her. The other ghaengste shook her head with a chuckle.

"And lose twelve coins? Not a chance, Ciyros."

The teasing warriors shut their mouths and shot into a straight posture, staring ahead as a cacophony of clanking bones and chiming metal rose over the rushing waves. Alvi inhaled sharply, then released a shaky exhale as she stood tall in front of her companions.

All eyes landed on a large, brawny silhouette marching across the white dunes toward them. Armor of bone and metal became clear as she approached, heavy chains hanging from her sides. Ivory fur covered her rippling muscles, and indigo paint was smeared in shapes along her flank. Her mane was shaved, leaving her completely bald.

The kaunek-leih stopped before them, lifting her head to inspect the congregation before her. Her face was exposed from beneath a helm fashioned from the skull of an ancient beast, revealing grotesque scars that curled up from the corners of her mouth in a horrific permanent ear-to-ear smile.

"Alvi," she called in a thundering growl that echoed across the sandy expanse and deafened the crashing sea.

"Smiley," Alvi greeted back, bowing her head and averting her eyes.

"You seek an audience with the lunai?"

"Yes."

"And you dare ask to present these outsiders before her throne?"

"Yes." Alvi's voice quivered, her head still bowed.

"Including the *savage?*" Smiley snarled, eyeing Kodo with bloodthirsty scarlet eyes. Alvi took another deep breath.

"Yes." The young woman finally lifted her head. "I ask only that Vaus-Kharax hear our cause. My companions are no danger here at your mercy within the Celesteal walls. Please, we want to help. I want to help."

Alvi now kept her tone from wavering, but her eyes begged pitifully. The commander's harsh gaze skinned and butchered the rebels one by one.

"I will bring you before the lunai-vaus," Smiley finally boomed, "So you may kneel before her, and she may hear you beg for your lives with her own ears."

Smiley let out a low, warbling rumble from her throat as she turned back to the gates. The tunahk surrounded the rebels in a close formation, spears readied, and drove them on into the village.

As they passed through the archaic jawbone gates, colossal teeth dangling over them like the claws of the universe, the wind seemed to freeze. The sound of the roaring ocean consumed the air, and brought with it judging eyes and accusing murmurs. They passed docks in the harbor, tents and house dunes, a market square, but all fell still in the rebels' wake.

Locals lounging on rugs and walking in from the waves watched them pass; their accusing gazes all bore into one thing.

Every single fisher, scout, warrior, and trader tracked Kodo with a guttural hunger he knew well from his days as a huntsman. For the first time in the giant's life...

He was prey.

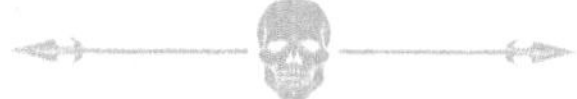

Her body was sore in ways she didn't even know were possible. As each of her limbs awoke and a hint of orange light glowed through her eyelids, she slowly became aware of the sounds around her. The lively echo of the jungle, trickling and buzzing and chirping and howling.

Sherri's eyes snapped open.

I fell asleep? How?

Her gaze darted around. She was slumped against the inside wall of the giant log, cradled in a pocket of moss. She blinked hard through the streaks of morning light, the particles of dust and dew. It seemed impossible, but her watch confirmed it — she had fallen asleep and stayed asleep through the whole night. She crawled to the edge. Looking out the open end of the suspended log, her heartbeat was gently calmed by the serene view of the trees and mist. Something clicked behind her.

Sherri turned around slowly, almost stalling, then let out a shaky exhale as she met big emerald eyes.

"You're still here," she whispered at the gigantic furry face in front of hers. The native sat on his haunches and watched her expectantly.

"You're still here," she said again, standing up in quiet disbelief. "And you didn't eat me in my sleep. This is all real."

She blinked, gnawing on the inside of her cheek as she attempted to fathom the gravity of her current situation. She was damned, there was no question, and yet she was also the luckiest human in the universe. She rubbed her hands on her pants, nodding as she accepted it all at once.

"Alright, no idle hands. If I'm going to be stranded out here, I might as well make myself useful." She sighed to herself.

"If I turn my back on you, you're not going to maul me... right?" she asked the native, studying his body language closely. He had his usual posture of docile curiosity.

"Clik."

"Fantastic."

Sherri began to walk around the cavernous wood hollow, studying the structure and keeping an eye out for any hint of a safe way down. Something along the wall of bark within a large round knot in the wood caught her interest. She stopped and looked closer.

Scrawls of symbols and shapes were carved into the surface, grouped in haphazard clusters that were nearly reminiscent of Sherri's own notes. Her foot hit something as she stepped nearer, and she glanced down. A large stone bowl lay beside her foot. It was light and thin, and it spun around after her accidental kick. In it, several flowering plants, some shiny rocks, and a few dead insects. Beside the bowl was a loose roll of some kind of textile — a blanket, or a rug. Sherri furrowed her brows at the objects.

"Do you... uh, live here...?" she called back hesitantly, as if expecting an answer. As the native shuffled nearer, Sherri began to accept that her classification of this species was all wrong. This was not any predictable predator, driven by hunger and instinct. This was an intelligent creature capable of behaviors beyond what she'd ever imagined.

"Hey, let me see your feet," she said as she turned toward him, taking a step back to get a good look at his paws.

They were wide and primitive looking, with short thick digits that sat slightly splayed. It seemed to have both a wrist joint, and a knee further up the leg.

"Hm. So how did you make all this stuff?" she asked, then paused as she noticed large claws on the inside of each foot, more like a jointed talon than a toe. *Thumbs?*

The native made a chuffing noise and sniffed her face. Then he lifted a paw and tapped her, but a gentle touch from his massive foot was enough to throw her to the ground. Sherri scrambled back to her feet as fast as she could, then firmly hit him square in the nose.

"I said *don't push me*," she snapped. "Quit it."

She almost felt bad as he recoiled in shock, but she figured she'd have to assert some sort of mutual respect with the beast if she were to have any hope of survival. Treating them like bears didn't seem to work, so she'd switched to sharks.

The native made a low warbling sound and nuzzled the side of his face against hers; she almost got the sense that he was laughing at her. Sherri accidentally broke into a delighted smile and fought the urge to scratch him behind the ears as he began purring loud enough to rival a rocket launch.

"Alright, you're *kind* of cute. But we need to set some boundaries."

She stepped back from him, moving his heavy head away from hers.

"No more shoving. You respect me, I respect you. Okay?"

He blinked at her a few times blankly, then cocked his head and made a series of clicks and chirps.

"Glad you under..." — the native appeared to get bored, wandering away to the other end of the hollow — "...stand."

Sherri sighed, taking her scheduled respirator inhalation as she watched him play with what appeared to be a bone. He flung it in the air and bounced it off the side of the log, catching it in his mouth.

She observed closely as he moved. He was far from graceful yet his form conveyed absolute power. His skull structure was angular and beastly like the rest of him, and his teeth were predatory, his sharp fangs hanging inches past his lip. She noted that the two horns sprouting from between his ears looked less like horns and more like antlers with several points. She pondered whether they might shed like a deer's and cursed herself for not knowing how to identify that possibility from only a visible inspection. She bet Roger would know.

The native's ear twitched, and a flicker of something shiny caught Sherri's eye beneath it. *An earring?*

It seemed impossible. How, and more importantly, *why* would a giant quadrupedal predator have jewelry? Sure, he apparently had uses for bags, blankets, and bowls, but those were all functional tools. Surely this beast didn't have a concept of beauty — yet there it was, a small gold hoop hanging from a hole in his earlobe. Sherri desperately longed for Doctor Rosenquest's extensive knowledge of ancient cultures; there was no doubt in her mind he'd be able to tell her exactly when, why, and how early humans developed jewelry to wear.

The stinging feeling that she was in over her head nagged at Sherri once again, and maybe a little bit of something else too.

...

It had been a largely sleepless night within the compound, something looming close in the back of the heads of every crew member. Twenty-six warm bodies had become twenty-one, and a groundbreaking adventure had become a perpetual nightmare. Their pleas were ignored by mission control, who told them, as Doyle so eloquently put it, to 'stay put and get their happy asses back to work.' A quiet air of hopelessness sat within the sterile walls in wake of Doctor Daniels's death, though not all the crew had accepted it.

"You said it yourself, she's an expert outdoorsman. She could have survived the night; we have to go."

"I just think we should be preparing ourselves for the alternative —"

"Bridgeland has to go out looking for the drone anyway, I'm going with them to look for Daniels. Are you coming or not?" Giovanni snapped loud enough that his older brother's face flinched ever so slightly. Harrison let out a shallow breath.

"Yes, I'm coming."

The captain was in the process of counting out clips and magazines to distribute when someone stopped in front of him.

"Captain Short?"

"What?" he replied, not bothering to look up at the newcomer as the English accent told him everything he needed to know.

"We've just found out one of the previously deployed weather drones is offline. Its last transmission showed that the data storage was ready for collection but the error message suggests that the signal has been interrupted —" Short cut off the rambling researcher by whistling to a nearby comrade, then handing him the counted crate of magazines.

"Pass these out, Ma." He turned back to Giovanni. "Why are you telling me all that bullshit? Do I look like that means a god damn thing to me?"

"*Because,*" the geologist continued shortly, "Doctor Bridgeland — the resident meteorologist — will have to manually collect the data. The drone in question isn't far, a few miles out, but we'll need escorts, obviously. Doctor Bridgeland, Doctor Rosenquest, and I are ready whenever your men are."

"Now?" the captain blinked as he caught on.

"Yes, now."

Short gave himself one split second to take a tired breath, then he shouted as he marched down the armory hall.

"Move it, motherfuckers, we're clocking in!"

Soldiers scrambled from the kitchen and commons to line up against the entry wall, frantically tossing the last of their breakfasts down their throats. Captain Short shoved a heavy machine gun into Corporal Keenan's chest as he returned from the armory and made his way to the front of the line.

"You're gunny, Corporal."

"Always." Keenan smirked, affectionately kissing the firearm before slinging it over his shoulder. A hefty pack was then thrown at him, which he barely caught and peeked into before securing on his back.

"Aw, you shouldn't have, Captain. I've always wanted a big ass bag of grenades."

"Shut the fuck up, Keenan. You've reached your word allowance for the day. I'm tired of hearing your voice."

"It's seven a.m."

"What did I just say?"

Keenan didn't get the chance to push his luck any further before the last series of whirrs and clangs sounded out from the door, and the hall was bathed in light as it slid open.

"Leave your cargo and weapons. *All* of it."

Leida helped free Kodo from his pack as several spearheads pointed at them from each direction. Kaishek tossed his axe onto the white sand. Smiley's sharp gaze lingered over each of the rebels.

"That is all?" she asked. Kaishek nodded.

"That is all," he replied calmly. Smiley turned to walk into the shallows. The tunahk surrounding the rebels pushed them forward as the commander charged through the wake.

"What is happening?" Leida whispered to Alvi, her quiet voice urgent.

"The entrance to the lunai chamber is below the surf. It's a short swim, you'll be fine," Alvi explained to her companions as they were driven further into the ocean.

"I cannot," Leida argued as she lifted her wings above the rising water.

"You have to."

"I cannot *swim*," Leida hissed, beginning to breathe hard and fast. She'd flown over every obstacle in her way since her wings could carry her; the depths were dangerous and she knew it well. Rare panic crawled up her throat and her gaze darted around as the cold waves grabbed at her sides and consumed her shuffling feathers. *Feathers.*

"Feathers," Kodo whispered, nudging her gently. "Get on my back and hold on. I've got you."

Leida considered flying away while her wings were still mostly dry as Smiley disappeared beneath the water ahead of them. Then Kaishek and Rykr took deep breaths before unceremoniously plunging headfirst under the waves. Alvi had already vanished. Leida finally met her friend's familiar warm gaze.

"I've got you."

She waited no longer before leaping atop Kodo's back and pinning her wings tight to her sides, squeezing her eyes shut as the water overtook them.

The ocean was a vibrant jewel around them, the sandy sea floor covered in glowing corals and schools of peculiar creatures. Rays of sunlight pierced down below the waves, and somehow the golden and turquoise light gleamed even brighter beneath the water's sparkling surface. Alvi gracefully soared through the heavy wake and the other rebels clumsily clawed at the rocks below to drive them forward through the current. They fought on, following Smiley as they were pushed by the tunahk. The ocean dwellers around them glided effortlessly toward a cave ahead, and a low rumbling sound laced with high chirps bounced through the water. They were communicating with one another in a language none of the land dwellers could understand. They were visitors in a new world. Alvi's world.

Smiley disappeared into the dark cave. Alvi followed suit, and the tunahk urged the other rebels forward with noises like thunder rolling through the surf. They wasted no time clambering through the mouth of the cramped cave, but panic set in fast as they reached a dead end. That is, until a familiar paw batted Kaishek in the head, and they looked up to see Alvi peering down at them from above the liquid surface.

One by one, they burst through a hole in a stone floor. From above, it appeared no different than a tidepool. They panted heavily, soaked to the bone, as Alvi quietly berated them to silence their heaving. The tunahk rose from the pool and shoved the rebels forward.

They were now in a vast grotto, twinkling brightly with glowing crystals and luminescent lichen on the stone walls. Pools much like the one from which they came were spread across the rocky floor. A tall platform protruded from a lagoon of faintly glowing liquid in the center of the chamber. Atop the stone tower was a draping of rugs and a woman who sat completely still. Her long aquamarine hair was in tight braids that flowed over the edge of her throne, her coat a dark umber. Her tail swayed back and forth.

Smiley stepped to the base of the pedestal, claws at the edge of the water that surrounded the queen.

"Vaus-Kharax. I bring you Alvi, the young scout who disappeared, and her outlander allies. They wish to speak with you, and I wish to hear how you will order their deaths," the brutish commander announced with a voice like a tsunami. Kharax's violet eyes did not move from where they were trained. Kodo.

For an agonizing moment, the only noise was a steady dripping and the muffled rushing of waves.

"Alvi," the queen finally said. "I hope you have brought the forest behemoth as an offering to your clan, for such a creature is worthy of a feast."

"No, my queen, he..." Alvi's normally bold demeanor broke away, leaving behind a timid young girl. "He is my friend. He is different from the rest of his kind, they —"

"No." The lunai-vaus cut her off sharply. "It is not your plea I seek, child. The barbarian shall beg for its *own* life."

Kodo's eyes widened, and he looked to Alvi. Kaishek stepped forward.

"Vaus-Kharax, you may not know who I am, but please hear —"

"Fur black as blood against the pure snow and a skull on his face, *I know who you are, Lost King.*"

The queen's voice slammed through the room like a crashing flood. It echoed off the walls and pounded straight through their humble hearts.

"*I will not* hear you, ghost, and *you will not* demand anything of me," she announced with no contempt, yet her warning choked the breath from their lungs.

"The behemoth will speak for itself. It will answer one question.

"If anyone other than the behemoth should choose to answer in its stead, these waters will run from green to black before I've even left my throne,"

Kharax explained calmly, her voice ringing deafeningly loud through the chamber. Smiley nodded at her queen, then released a sharp rattle from within her throat.

The tunahk-dahn formed around Kodo, shoving him forward at spear point. Leida snarled and unsheathed her claws, but Alvi put a hand up to stop her. Slowly, Leida stowed her claws.

Kodo stood alone before the queen.

"You only have five words to answer my question. Choose them wisely, as they will decide your fate," Kharax continued coldly. Kodo stared up at her, and he suddenly understood what it meant to be small. Weak. Even before hearing the queen's question, he got the feeling that he didn't know the answer. Her eyes bore into him with a piercing calmness as the tunahk trained their spears to his flank.

Kaishek's pleading voice rang out again.

"He's just a boy, Kharax—!"

Black blood rained upon the stone ground as Kharax's words sliced through the air like a freshly sharpened blade.

"You may have been king when I took my throne, Kaishek, but I was queen when you lost yours," she snarled across the open chamber. "You are *nothing* here, and if you speak out of turn again, I will be wearing a rare black fur coat this season. *Watch your spewing tongue* if you wish to leave this place alive."

The Lost King's tongue writhed on the ground at his feet in a puddle of tar and saliva.

Smiley's dagger pressed against his lips, and her boiling gaze begged him to open his mouth again. The old man swallowed as blood drooled from his tightly closed maw, his face calm but his yellow eyes burned in white-hot rage. Kodo breathed hard in silent horror. Kharax spoke again as the interruption died down.

"Now, *behemoth*," she continued as her eyes once again rested on Kodo.

"The forest nation has committed countless atrocities upon my people, and there has yet to come a day that I passed up an opportunity for vengeance. Outside of this chamber is a clan of hungry ghaengste. Each of them has lost sisters, mothers, and daughters to barbarians like you. They expect me to chum the water with your vile flesh, let them rip you limb from limb and feast on you for days, as I condemn the rest of your kind.

"So, behemoth, I have killed all other forest dwellers that dared near my borders, and I see no reason not to grant you the same fate. My question is simple:

"Why shouldn't I?"

The planet itself seemed to pause and bear witness to the young giant's trial. Kodo's voice echoed out without much thought at all.

"They hate me too."

All was still except for Kodo's rapid pulse, within it, a deep melancholy. The grief of a lost child in a world that had cast him away from the day he was born, and fled in fear from the day he became a man. The sorrow of a leaf without a tree, and the pain of a starving animal pleading for touch before meat.

His eyes begged for forgiveness. His hearts begged for damnation.

Vaus-Kharax softened as she studied the giant. She read him like an unfinished story, and for a moment, her own gaze held a gentle sadness. Then in an instant, it ran cold.

"Liar."

An electric tension spread through the atmosphere.

"Look at yourself," the queen spat in disgust. "You're a monster of a man, no doubt with the strength of ten. Your fangs hang down past your lip not in royalty, but in brutality. You tower over us all and I can see it in your eyes — you have blood on your claws. You are the incarnation of all your kind strives to be, of all the Ramys clan strives to be. The embodiment of *violence.*"

Leida tried to step forward but was driven back by a spear to her neck. She growled in frustration. They were helpless to change the queen's mind, all except for Kodo.

"You're right," he said, and the other rebels grimaced at his surrender.

"I am..." Kodo took a slow breath. "I am a monster. And I have more blood on my claws than I ever wanted to spill. But I am not what the Ramys clan strives for..."

He looked deep into the queen's eyes, and the truth forced its way up his throat and out of his mouth.

"I am what they fear."

The room tensed as the boldness of his words settled in the air.

"I was exiled for the same reason you want me dead. Because I am a beast among beasts. An abomination." Kodo paused for a moment, wincing as if a dagger were twisted in his gut.

"And that will haunt me for as long as I live. Even if just for the next few moments. If I am the embodiment of violence, that violence gave me no kinship with my people. But I share their blood, and maybe that means I bear their sins, too, so for what it's worth...

"I'm sorry for the sisters, and mothers, and daughters you've lost. And I hope your people find peace, whether it's with my help or by my death."

The giant bowed his head to the queen, allowing his eyes to close. A soft peace laid over his wide shoulders like the gentle water of baptism, and perhaps his apology alone was forgiveness and damnation enough. He suddenly felt more contentment than he'd known in a long, long time.

"Tell me more," the queen called out.

Sherri had never exactly considered herself the Jane Goodall type. She admired the woman's work, of course, but she vastly preferred the company of plants and fungi over that of organisms with excretory systems and vocal cords.

Yet here she was.

The native was currently in the process of spinning in circles, as if he were chasing his tail, only that didn't appear to be the objective. Sherri was pinned flat to the wall on one side of the log, desperately trying to keep all her limbs out of the range of his swinging tail. She was fairly certain a blow from any part of him would swiftly deliver her to the next plane of existence.

"*Not* intelligent, I was wrong, definitely not intelligent," she whined to herself as she dodged the tip of his tail.

Finally, he stopped spinning. He shook his head and slightly swayed for a moment, clearly experiencing vertigo. Then he wobbled to the far opening of the log and clumsily hopped out.

"*No!*" Sherri cried out and rushed to the opening, peeking over the edge to spot the beast on a giant branch a few yards down. He trotted across it recklessly, stumbling along like a young puppy as he kept balance by shifting the weight of his tail. Sherri watched in horror.

"What the hell are you doing!?" she called. She was fairly well versed in animal behavior — enough to get by, anyway. But her training had proved useless on this planet, as apparently the native species were at best extremely stupid and at worst suicidal. Sherri gasped in dismay as the native dipped off the side of the tree, very nearly falling to his death, before his tail wrapped around the branch and caught him. Now anchored upside down, he swung back and forth carelessly like a monkey or a lemur. Sherri's brows raised.

Prehensile tail.

She relaxed slightly as he seemed content with just hanging for the time being. Holding onto a root for extra security, she slowly came to sit on the open ledge with her feet dangling over. The giant beast swayed back and forth, gently batting at the insects that passed.

"You're like a colossal kitten." Sherri giggled. She recalled Captain Short calling them 'big fucking cat things,' and she guessed he wasn't entirely wrong for once. She noticed the native looking up at her, double pupils moving freely in curious green eyes.

"What...?" she asked cautiously, recognizing the look as one she'd seen in the mirror too many times to count. A dangerous idea.

The native swung side to side from his tail, and just as Sherri thought to move back from the ledge, a paw reached out and grabbed her boot.

She shrieked as she was yanked from her perch, desperately grappling to hold onto her root handle, but it was no use.

Being yanked through the jungle in the beast's deadly maw had seemed like the worst thing short of being consumed at the time, but she almost missed it as she stared straight down into the infinite misty void.

Sherri was suspended completely upside down, gently swaying above the cloudy layer of fog that lived among the trees. She breathed hard and fast from her nose, frantically searching for any branch or vine she might be able to grab hold of. A claw pierced through the side of her boot, barely missing her foot, and a whimper fell from her mouth. She'd just begun to reevaluate her spiritual beliefs when she began to rise.

Sherri sighed in relief as he pulled her up, then let out a small yelp as she slowly spun around to see his face right in front of hers.

"...Excuse me," she whispered as she gingerly reached for the hanging tip of his tail, a hairy plume on it like a giraffe's. She caught the end and heaved herself up, rushing to climb onto the branch in case he got irritated by her grabbing his tail and hurled her to her death. He didn't seem to notice the extra weight at all as she scrambled to the safety of the tree limb.

However, the momentary relief of the wide surface waned as a monstrous set of claws reached up and gouged into the wood in front of her. Then another. The native's giant face peeked over the side of the branch at her, then the loose end of his long tail shoved her off the edge and onto his stomach. Sherri groaned angrily as she mentally rehearsed her next lecture on boundaries and respect. But her temper steadily cooled as a soft vibration through the beast's furry gut soothed her; he was purring.

He hung beneath the limb like a hammock, using his claws and tail as anchors. Sherri thought it must be something he did often, as despite the stress on his muscles, he seemed completely relaxed. His curious emerald eyes peered into the canopy above them with an inquisitive sparkle. Sherri couldn't help but feel safe on his warm belly, nestled in a cradle made by his gigantic form.

Timidly, she reached forward and stroked her fingertips along the pointed rhinoceros-like horns sprouting from the bridge of his nose. All her building frustrations and qualms slowly melted away as she watched his calm face in quiet awe.

A faint flapping drew Sherri's gaze to where his rested in the leaves above, and she smiled in wonder as she noticed a group of flying creatures swirling through the canopy. They were almost batlike, but feathered and an iridescent greenish. The rays of sunlight shining through the leaves reflected off them and soaked through the fibers of their wings, framing them in twinkling halos. They chirped and crackled at one another as they soared around slightly translucent moss-covered sacks, hanging from the bottoms of the branches above. Sherri's eyes widened in adoration as she caught sight of a tiny chick peeking out from a hole in the egg sac.

Sherri and the beast swayed from the branch, and the patches of sun that escaped through the canopy warmed their skin in shimmering spots of gold and blue. The previous day had brought with it more terror and chaos than Sherri had ever experienced in her simple human life, and she had no idea what her future might bring. She was lost, far from her friends, her planet, and everything she'd ever known and loved. Any moment could be her last; in an instant, the planet could swallow her like it already had so many others. But in that moment, there was nowhere in the universe she'd rather be.

The voice Vaus-Kharax expected to hear was Kodo's, but while the one that rang out instead was much quieter, it still filled the room.

"We are the rebellion," Leida announced, stepping forward. The ocean queen's eyes came to rest on the sky dweller, her head slowly leaning to one side.

"Mutant," Kharax said plainly, as if tasting the word. Leida had no reaction; the label seemed to have no meaning for her.

"We wish to form a peace treaty. But we are hunted by the Ramys clan," Leida finished evenly. Kharax's brow raised, then, her interest piqued.

"A rebellion, aye?" she mused slowly. Leida nodded once as Kodo returned to her side, the guards having removed their spears from his flank.

"Yes," Leida replied.

"All of you? Including the ghost king?" Vaus-Kharax asked as she looked to the proud mountain man, a steady dribbling of blood still oozing from his tightly closed lips. She had never seen him in person until now, but his legend had been so great it carried down from the mountains and into the sea. His story was one of a brutal warlord, a tyrant warrior who had no mercy for outsiders; his wrath was reserved for every living thing outside of his own clan.

Yet he stood before her, in the flesh. An old man, tired and at peace. His eyes were not the rageful sunfire she'd heard so much about, but she saw deep enough through his gaze to know the truth of the legends.

The old king simply nodded, watching her with the same caution with which she studied him. It was unclear if he remained silent in respect, or because he was gagged by the blood drowning his mouth.

Kharax swayed her tail, taking in the sight of the group before her.

"A king, a mutant, a monster, and a scout," she said as she observed them, her eyes landing on Rykr last.

"And what are you supposed to be?"

The other rebels flinched simultaneously.

"I am Rykr, son of Vaus-Ramaala, prince of—" The air was pounded from the young mountain man's lungs as he hit the ground. Smiley stood over him, her claws pushing his face into the stone and a heavy chain thrown around his ankles. Rykr growled defiantly, and his companions squeezed their eyes shut.

"Let him up, Smiley," the queen said bitterly after a tense moment of silence.

"Get to the point. Tell me why you dare to enter my domain."

Alvi stepped forward and bowed her head, clearing her throat as Rykr rose with a scowl.

"We ask for your alliance, Vaus-Kharax," the ocean woman began before her insolent companions could dig their graves any further.

"We call on the clans of the region to sign a peace treaty to end the needless warring. But we are fugitives of the Ramys nation, and they pose a common enemy to us both. We seek to free all ocean people from the savage tyranny of their forces and free ourselves from their pursuit.

"The rebellion believes that peace between the nations is possible; we've proved it ourselves. But we need your help in the fight against Ramys, or they will crush us before we have any hope of completing our journey. We ask you to sign our treaty and arm our cause with Celesteal weapons. And if you do, we...

"I promise you justice for our people, by word or by war."

Alvi's tone was bolder now. It had regained some of its previous vigor, but was laced with the sorrow of loss. The queen listened patiently, and she watched the rebels in silence long after Alvi finished speaking.

Then Kharax leaped down from her pillar, landing gracefully on a trail of faintly glimmering stepping stones in the lagoon below. She traipsed across the path and onto solid ground.

"Come," she said.

Kharax led the rebels down a stairwell at the back of the chamber, a slim tunnel littered with faintly glowing specks on the walls like stars in the sky.

"You are right that we have a common enemy," the queen called behind her, "And you are right that my people have benefit to gain from your... rebellion. Whether as allies, or simply a thorn in the paw of the Ramys clan, I haven't decided."

The stairwell began spiraling down in a tight coil as it steepened, and the walls seemed to close in. A rhythmic vibration like a heartbeat sounded from within the stone, pulsating up through their feet.

"But you bold rebels seem to believe that my nation needs your aid," Kharax began again. Her tone sounded harsher as she led them, and it echoed eerily through the steep tunnel.

"Long ago, generations before mine, in a more powerful age of our history, Celesteal was ruled by three lunai.

"Vaus-Ichnai, Vaus-Kya're, and Vaus-Hestas. They were strong leaders, wise and brave. But the clan suffered. The Ramys lunai were power hungry, driven by conquest. They wanted control of the rivers and they slaughtered any ocean dwellers that stood in their way."

Kharax's normally soothing voice was a spiteful growl.

"They constructed dams to stop the migration of the fish and starve us out. But the Celesteal queens were wiser than the Ramys lunai had considered, and more ruthless than they'd ever imagined.

"Ichnai, Kya're, and Hestas voyaged beyond the river, beyond the Ramys dams, all the way to the source. To the reservoir, where the glacial pools flow down to feed the rivers, where all water of the valley is born.

"And they cut it.

"Celesteal built their own dams around the lakes of the basin, they closed off the reservoirs, they took hold of the water. Every last drop of it.

"The river ran dry, and with it, Ramys was choked of its life-giving power. The foolish forest dwellers thought they could control what was not theirs, but forgot that they, too, needed the lifeblood to survive.

"And they forgot who it rightfully belonged to."

The pulsating heartbeat in the stone walls intensified to a rhythmic banging, and it pierced their bones as they traveled deeper yet.

"The Ramys nation had no choice but to invade the reservoir, to fight to free the water, and bring the blood back to the river. And they did not intend to lose.

"They sent every single forest citizen with the strength to fight and the ability to bear a weapon; they came in hordes. They came for war."

The slim stairwell began to heat up, its pulse so intense now that the rebels began to sweat. They stepped warily as if through the veins of a giant beast, drawing ever closer to its mammoth hearts. Kharax roared over the pounding vibration.

"But Ichnai, Kya're, and Hestas beckoned them. They hailed the war. Their numbers were far smaller, and their bodies too. But the Celesteal forces welcomed the forest army that blacked out the green grass as they marched in, their masses so great their drumbeat shook the planet, and their battle cries were heard from the highest peaks of the mountains and the deepest canyons of the ocean.

"The queens held back their soldiers, they let the Ramys army take the basin unsullied.

"And then they opened the dams.

"The overflowing reservoirs ate the valley, rising up past the trees and drowning the entire basin in an all-consuming flood. Only then did the queens call the attack.

"Hundreds of forest dwellers drowned, and the few strong enough to fight the waves were dragged below and slaughtered by the Celesteal warriors. The great Ramys army was snuffed out like a weak flame. They were eaten alive by the power they sought to control, and the people within it they sought to destroy."

The stairwell began to widen now, but the heat was nearly unbearable. Rykr and Kaishek panted desperately. Kharax continued.

"That day, the reservoir became a giant lake, its water black with blood. And to this day, my people celebrate the battle of Black Lake as our greatest victory against the Ramys clan, as generations later they still have not fully recovered from their entire fighting population being annihilated. The triumph of Black Lake is the reason they have not grown strong enough to drive us out of our lands and back into the ocean."

The heartbeat was no longer one pulse, but many. Hundreds of voices merged with hundreds of synchronous bangs and the tunnel began to glow green as they descended.

"I tell you of Black Lake because there is something that you must understand," Kharax continued.

"The Ramys nation is not tyrannical because they are strong, and the Celesteal nation does not struggle because we are weak. What the forest dwellers forget, and what they must be reminded of, is that they were never stronger than us.

"And they never will be."

The queen led them out of the stairwell as it opened into a massive cavern filled with hot steam and green fire. Giant drums of chartreuse molten metals boiled and bubbled as ghaengste tugged on pulley systems to tilt the vessels and pour into molds. Ocean dwellers wearing blackened masks and wielding hammers stood in lines throughout the forge, pounding the metal into silver swords, daggers, chains, spears, armor. The tumult of a war zone filled the chamber, yet such graceful ingenuity left the rebels stunned. The grotto glowed warm with emerald flames, sparkling jewels, and shining blades. To their side, a large pool cut through the stone, the water so dark it seemed infinite, and from it, miners with faintly glowing fur emerged from the depths carrying sacks of ores.

"Welcome to the forge," Vaus-Kharax announced, vehement pride clear in her eyes as she watched the blacksmiths and craftsmen work. Alvi stepped just slightly nearer to the queen.

"Does this mean you'll aid our cause?"

Kharax turned around to face the rebels. The green fire raged around her in a brilliant halo, a sunrise beneath the sea.

"I will sign your treaty. I will give you weapons. And I will grant you my people's alliance," the ocean queen called, her voice rising above the infinite banging of the forge. "But in return I have one demand...

"Give them hell."

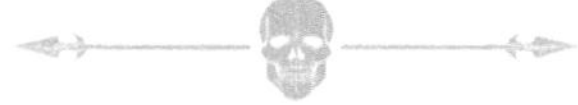

Captain Short began to accept that he'd never get used to it.

The feeling of soil beneath his boots, but the knowledge that it didn't belong to his Earth. The giant planet in the sky, looming overhead, and the faint twinkling of stars that never quite went away. The silence. The infinitely unfamiliar taste of the air.

It was no longer new to him, but it would never feel anything but foreign. He hated it.

As they traveled across the open plain, an amalgam of emotions surrounded the crew. For some, like the more brazen soldiers, it was simply another day in the office — they awaited the twisted excitement of chaos.

For others, namely Carl, it felt distinctly like walking into hell.

The coordinates of the weather drone weren't far, estimated only a mile past the tree line, if that. But that mile seemed like one mile walked infinitely closer to death. Carl had always looked down on fellow meteorologists who made a habit of chasing after storms, but getting up close and personal with tornados suddenly didn't seem like such a bad hobby. This one would be his first field survey on 7355264Z, and he hoped to god it would be his last.

"How are you holding up, Bridgeland?" Harrison gently asked from beside him as he took an inhalation from his respirator.

"How do you think?" Carl groaned.

"We'll be fine," Giovanni said, putting a hand on Carl's shoulder and playfully shaking him harder than he appreciated. The researchers tread along in the center of the group, cocooned in a surrounding formation of soldiers.

Captain Short finally seemed to notice how many scientists had tagged along on this outing, glancing back at them.

"It takes three of you geniuses to fix one weather thing?" the captain's voice barked.

"No, he's here to collect the drone data," Harrison explained and gestured at Carl. "We're here to support and catalog potential discoveries along the way," he finished, nodding at his brother beside him. Carl wouldn't admit it, but he was somewhat grateful for the presence of his teammates. Though he knew their motivations were more about searching for Daniels, or her remains, than easing his troubled mind. Captain Short scoffed, seemingly unimpressed by their ideas of 'support,' but he just looked back down at the beeping GPS in his hand and led the group in the drone's direction.

A familiar sense of danger settled in as they passed through the tree line, a dreaded feeling of cold shadows and peering eyes. The drone site wasn't far now, the beeping of the GPS grew quicker and more frantic.

"What are we looking for, Bridgeland?" Captain Short called out as he scanned the trees.

"It'll be hard to miss." Carl cleared his throat. "Imagine a big white sprinkler head. With feet planted into the ground — well, they should be, and ideally some blinking lights but we can't know for sure if it's powered on."

"Like that?" Corporal Greene spoke up and tossed a rock up into the trees, which skillfully met its mark and tapped something metal on a lower limb. The drone sat slightly cockeyed, nestled against a tree trunk and held in place by a netting of vines. The branch that supported it was at least thirty feet above the forest floor.

"*Please* don't throw rocks at it." Carl winced. Captain Short raised his eyebrows and frowned, impressed.

"Good eye and good aim, Corporal. Now go get it."

Greene looked at the captain with pleading eyes, but was met with no sympathy.

"Go."

The corporal tossed his pack and rifle to his nearest comrade and jogged off without a word.

The other soldiers watched the tree line and snickered amongst each other while Greene climbed the tree as Carl and the other researchers observed the world around them.

The spot where they stood felt a little colder than the rest of the jungle and sounded a little quieter. The already faint noises were muffled, and a subtle feeling of darkness hung over them. Carl sweat profusely. His eyes darted between the soldiers, the Rosenquest brothers who were scanning the ground for signs of Daniels, and the young man named Greene who had almost reached where the drone lay snug in the vines.

"Tie some paracord to a carabiner and toss it up to him. Bring it down on a pulley," Captain Short ordered. The soldier he'd gestured to, Sergeant Sanchez, nodded and approached the tree to help.

"Heads up, Tulsa," she called as she tossed one end of a rope up to Greene. The corporal caught it easily, then pulled a knife from his belt to cut the drone free from the vines that consumed it. He looped the cord over and under its legs, clipped it together at the top, and slowly began to lower the large device off the side of the branch. Sanchez gradually gave the rope more slack, allowing it to sink. Greene began his descent as the drone finally settled on the ground.

"Leave it there, that's a good spot." Carl cleared his throat. "I just need the data pack."

He quickly got down to the drone's level, pressing a few buttons before a tray popped open full of several cartridges. He took the first one out, pocketed it, then held a button on the machine's underside to recalibrate it. The lights kicked on as the drone glowed back to life, and Carl sighed with relief as the Rosenquest brothers watched closely.

"Okay, it's fine, the vines must have been interrupting the signal. It should be able to transmit again."

"Do we still need the physical cartridge, then?" Giovanni asked.

"Yes, recalibrating it would have wiped any data. It's a blank slate now, this cartridge is the only record of the atmospheric data within this area for the last several months," Carl explained as he stood up and Greene trotted over to the group.

"That's all?" the captain asked.

"That's all," Carl confirmed.

The group was preparing to leave when a breeze hit, and with it, a rattling noise invaded the cool forest air. The captain cautiously scanned the dark trees, holding out his hand to stop the team from moving or talking. Everyone froze as the rattling noise sounded again, a low, faint clanking and clicking to the rhythm of the whistling wind.

Captain Short looked up, just allowing his eyes to move first. Then he craned his neck to peer directly up into the trees.

Skeletons.

Human skeletons. Three of them. No, two skeletons almost intact apart from rotted away limbs, but nearby was a pelvis and a leg from a third body. They were strung up in tangled vines, falling apart as they decomposed and the mummified flesh flaked off their bones little by little. The stench of putrefied decay sat still in the fog with a forgotten promise, even far below from where they were suspended in the towering trees. Wind flooded through them while they hung and swayed, mutilated and familiar like the tapestries in a dilapidated church.

The gold and blue sunlight blended into a sickly green in the misty air as it weakly illuminated the hanging bones. Keenan was the first to speak.

"You think Krei's wallet is somewhere around here too? Fucker owed me twenty bucks."

Captain Short didn't seem to hear him, much to the rest of their dismay. He was intently studying the canopy above, then he looked over at the researchers. His cold eyes focused on Harrison.

"What do you do?" he asked firmly. Harrison hesitated before registering the question.

"I'm an… archaeologist. My specialty is in anthropology, but —"

"Are any of them women?" the captain interrupted. Harrison didn't take a second look, having already studied the skeletons thoroughly.

"No. All three appear to be young men," he said, his expression softening as he cleared his throat. "And they've been deceased a while."

Captain Short nodded, turning his head to dodge the pitiful look the aged archaeologist was giving him. There was a pause as the expectant eyes of his subordinates watched him for an order.

"Fischer," he said.

The master sergeant looked to the captain, tearing her eyes from the skeletons above.

"Yes, sir."

"Take Sanchez, Greene, and Carnahan to escort the assets back home," the captain ordered. "We're making another circle to look for Doctor Daniels. Leave the fence down but don't wait up. Roger?"

"Roger."

Greene, Sanchez, and Carnahan automatically assumed a protective formation around the researchers as Fischer began to lead them back toward the compound.

"Fischer."

"Yes, sir." She paused.

"No stops. Straight back to the compound, quick and quiet. Understood?"

"Yes, sir."

Short lingered on her eyes for a moment before waving her off. Fischer and her group headed for the tree line and back to safety.

Captain Short and the remaining soldiers marched deeper into the jungle.

16
SODOM

"What's your first name, Sergeant Fischer?"

Silence.

"Bet it's lovely." Giovanni peeked around the tall woman to catch her eyes. She kept her gaze trained forward and nudged him back behind her with the butt of her rifle.

"You'll call me Master Sergeant Fischer or ma'am," she said.

"Yes, ma'am," he replied slyly as his eyes briefly flitted over her form. Then he stumbled and yelped as his brother elbowed him hard in the ribs.

"You're an imbecile," Harrison hissed at the more spirited Rosenquest.

"Doctor Daniels is still missing, we've just discovered yet another remarkable behavior of the natives, and you can't even think with the proper head," he scolded, lowering his voice to an angry whisper at the last part. The younger brother let out a long, heavy sigh.

"Daniels will be okay, I know it. They'll find her," Giovanni insisted stubbornly. "And we'll update her on the hanging skeletons; I'm *quite* sure she'll find it riveting. You know, you could stand to think a bit less with the head on your shoulders and a bit more with the other one... Assuming you still can, anyway." A sharp slap met the side of his head.

Carl was trying and failing to ignore the brothers' bickering as he studied the daunting landscape around them. He clutched the data pack in his pocket with a clammy hand, and for hardly the first time, it didn't seem worth the risk. All of it — the data, the discovery, and the pursuit of a new world. Was it worth their lives? In the grand scale of the entire human race, it surely was. But Carl wasn't the entire human race, he was just one man. And in the moment, the rectangular drive of weather data in his pocket was just a chunk of plastic and metal and glass. Yet somehow, for some reason, he and his colleagues were readily risking their lives for it.

"Master Sergeant?" Private Carnahan spoke up hesitantly, their voice raspy as if it struggled to rise above a whisper.

"What?" Fischer huffed.

"Sanchez is gone."

Fischer abruptly halted in her tracks, and Giovanni nearly ran into her.

"What?" she hissed, flipping around. Greene and Carnahan stood on either side of the researchers, staring at the spot behind them where Sergeant Sanchez had been mere moments before.

"Fuck." Fischer flicked her weapon off safety. "Keep moving."

"But she —"

"Keep. Moving," she growled again and turned to continue forward. *Squelch.*

Sergeant Fischer stepped in something slick and wet, liquid splattering her boot, and her jaw clenched tight as her gaze wandered downward.

A spreading pool of scarlet blood drowned the surrounding soil and grass where the corpse of a woman lay mangled. Her stomach was ripped open, her organs and entrails splayed out in the mud beyond the cavernous wound. Her head was limply cocked to the side and nearly completely detached, her neck gouged open and spread so wide it rendered her half-decapitated. The artery in her flayed throat was severed; a steadily pulsing stream of blood spurted from it like a garden hose. Her brown hair was now dyed burgundy, tresses of it sticking to her cheeks and slightly parted lips. Fischer found herself touching the gnarled scarring on her own stomach as she searched Sanchez's eyes, already beginning to glaze over in death despite her face still containing the flush of life.

Without another word, Sergeant Fischer guided the researchers around the soldier's mutilated carcass as they stared, pale and silent. Corporal Greene began to kneel, reaching two fingers out to touch the dead soldier's neck, but his hand was tapped away by the muzzle of a rifle.

"She's dead. Get up," Fischer ordered, and the young man obeyed without protest. He stepped over the corpse, his eyes lingering on it, and Private Carnahan walked around. They continued on in bitter silence as Fischer urged them forward, but she knew it was only a matter of time. And she knew they weren't getting back to the compound in one piece.

She pushed on with Giovanni close behind her and the other two scientists following nearby. They traveled at a smooth, quiet jog, wary eyes scanning the surrounding area and making no sound aside from ragged breaths. Fischer's finger hovered over the trigger of her rifle.

A bright glow appeared through gaps in the trees ahead — the meadow. They rushed faster toward it, a lighthouse beacon in a dark, unforgiving ocean. Then the precious guiding light went out, blocked by a gigantic silhouette.

All at once, the forest lit up with flashes of gunfire and shook with the roars of a monster.

...

Captain Short locked eyes with Mendoza as a familiar thundering filled the jungle around them.

"*Go!*" the captain yelled as he abandoned the search for the botanist, sprinting through the trees to the source of the sound as Mendoza and Keenan followed. They charged in the direction that Fischer's group had gone, and Short began cursing himself for splitting up. He should have stayed with the squints. He shouldn't have thinned them out. He shouldn't have gone back for Daniels. *Keep running, quit thinking.*

The gritty *ratatatatat* of rifle rounds grew clearer and with it, the booming shrieks of the native.

They could now see the glowing halo of light through the trees; it beckoned them out of the jungle and into the open air. *They made it out of the jungle. They can make it. We can make it.*

The faint whisper of hope in the back of his mind was sucked away as he broke through the tree line.

An inferno of emerald and jade swirled around itself like the tattered banners waving after battle. The flames blazed hot and violent with the low, steady beating of drums and the sorrowful hums of hundreds of souls. But the bonfire's flaming banners were not a conquest flag; they were the smoldering remains of a lost war.

Io-Dahn was dead.

In one fatal swoop, one of the great Ramys tunahk-dahn was killed. The winged murderer responsible, in the wind. Perhaps a warrior on a mission, perhaps simply a scout who saw an opportunity and took it. They couldn't know.

Every ghaengste in the clan stood around the fire stack in honor and anguish. A steady song of agony rumbled from each of their ragged throats, merging together with the heavy drumming in a cried prayer to Matka.

Have mercy on our warrior, Mother.

She fights in Your army now, Mother.

Only one man did not sing in their chorus.

Rataan-Leih stared into the inferno, silent and unblinking, bearing the sting of the embers that showered his skin.

He had lost two warriors that day. Io now laid at the bottom of the river, somewhere they'd never find her, but Iago was gone too. He watched the one-eyed woman's stoic face at the vigil, lit by the empty flames of her lost sister, and he did not see his mighty young warrior. He saw an empty vessel.

Iago's eye, previously full of fire and lightning and blood, was now vacant and broken.

Io was the first tunahk of their generation to die, and she left in her wake a searing pain that her comrades had never known before. For all her years of service and all her lives taken, she had not even begun to fulfill her destiny. She was far too young.

Rataan recalled when he first received Io and Iago under his care. They'd been bred for the tunahk order, just like all others, but he'd taken them in before the rest of the warriors. They were put in his care when they had only just learned to speak, after their mother's death and Vaus-Erro's rise to the throne. It had been Erro who gave her young sisters to him; her words still echoed clearly in his head.

Yes, they'd be the youngest children to begin tunahk training. But I trust you with them, brother, and I trust you'll see that they are ready. They are strong, stronger than you or I were at their age. Iago already shows the heart of a killer, and Io has wisdom far beyond her years. Under your skilled instruction, they may just be the deadliest warriors this clan has seen yet.

It was impossible to tell them apart physically at that point. They were masters at mimicking one another, and they refused to wear any distinctive markings or apparel. But after Rataan had raised and cared for them for only a few seasons, he could tell the difference between them just by the looks in their eyes.

The twins were his sole apprentices for several long years before the other selected children were sent to him when they'd grown old enough. By that time, he knew and loved Io and Iago like daughters before he'd had his own. He was younger then, so young that he hardly remembered being full of patience for their mischief and juvenile energy. But he remembered all too well their bright eyes looking to him for guidance, the light pitter-patters of their paws chasing after him, and the chiming giggles of trouble.

The girls had been too stubborn to bond with the other nine children at first, and he recalled the many bloody fights he had to break up in the training courtyard. The day Io convinced Iago to befriend their new peers was the day Rataan finally accepted that there was only one being on the entire planet who would ever be able to sway Iago, the most spirited and rebellious of his warriors — Io.

And now she was dead. Now she was dead swiftly, suddenly, and devastatingly. Dead so many years too soon, and she took Iago with her.

Io, his unshaken warrior, had fallen from grace. And Iago, unbowed, had finally surrendered. And Faro...

Faro.

Faro-Dahn, the undefeated warrior, was overcome. He stood mutilated and sick, slowly rotting away like a walking corpse. Once so glorious, so fierce, he now exuded a contagious weakness that spread through the ranks like an infection. The third lost warrior.

Rataan had lost three of his eleven mighty children, and he could see in the eyes of the others, illuminated by the vigil fire, that he was losing them too.

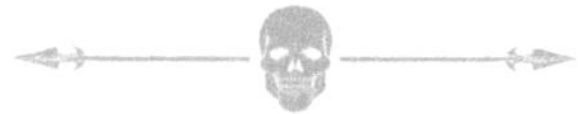

The native stood in the center of the meadow, fighting through floods of gunfire as three soldiers desperately attempted to drive it back from the researchers behind them. It stood between them and the compound, blocking their attempts to drive forward.

Captain Short ran to them with Keenan and Mendoza on his heels.

"Get its attention!" he yelled over the tumult. "Greene, Carnahan, get them past as soon as it gives you the chance!"

Short drew his weapon and began firing at the native's flank, shouting orders as Keenan and Mendoza joined him in the distraction. Fischer and the others buried rounds into its face to keep it back from the research team. A grenade exploded near its backside, and it staggered in the upheaved soil before wildly thrashing around to face the growing nuisance behind it. As soon as it turned away from the scientists, they took their chance.

Greene and Carnahan grabbed the three researchers by whatever clothing they could catch and dragged them in a dead sprint across the plains; Fischer stayed put to cover them in case the native looked back. For a second, the massive beast either didn't notice the fleeing group or didn't care. It continued lunging at the captain and his men through its disorientation, barely missing as they stumbled back out of its reach with each lurch. Greene, Carnahan, and the scientists began to make it into the clear.

A gigantic tapered tail like a tentacle lashed out and caught Carl around the torso. Harrison reached out for him, but the meteorologist was ripped away from his grasp. The native didn't even seem aware as it yanked him into the sky with the enormous serpentine appendage, Carl's terrified screams barely earning a flick of its pointed ears.

"Carl!" Harrison cried out as the coiling tail tightened, and Carl's wails started to cut into a frantic choking as the breath was squeezed from his lungs. His face began to swell and bloat like an overripe plum, his eyes bulged cherry red, and the crackling of his bones was faintly audible between savage roars and endless gunfire.

Corporal Greene aimed his rifle at the limb beneath Carl, firing into a single spot as black blood sprayed from the native's growing wound. He'd almost made a clean cut, but not soon enough. The native thrashed its tail, whipping the meteorologist's helpless body through the air and preventing Greene from making the shot. A familiar plastic cartridge soared through the air from Carl's pocket, and Giovanni ran forward to catch it, ignoring a cry of protest from his brother. Harrison caught Giovanni by the shirt and dragged him away from the flailing tail just as it tightened further around their friend. A horrible crack sounded out from the man's spine while his head rapidly engorged to an unrecognizable purple mass. Carl's eyes pushed completely out of their sockets before his entire skull exploded into nothing.

A chunky spray of blood and brain splattered both Rosenquest brothers as they fell backward in horror.

The native released a rageful scream as the tip of its tail hinged at a broken vertebra and gushed blood, then tore off and fell to the ground with Carl's headless body still in its clutches. The severed tip jolted and twitched in the grass as the furious native turned and lunged at Greene.

He dove but was caught by the leg.

"Shit! SHIT!" the corporal shrieked as he was ripped into the sky, his rifle clattering to the ground. Greene frantically pulled the knife from his belt and lurched, plunging the blade deep into the beast's face again and again, desperate to free himself. Both red and black blood showered his face and he screamed in agony as the powerful jaws clamped down tighter, snapping his tibia in half.

Fischer stared through her scope, aimed directly at the beast's face, as the captain screamed at her not to take a shot she couldn't guarantee. She took it.

A plume of black liquid and bone shards exploded from the hinge of the native's jaw, and its gigantic mouth swung open as it screeched. Greene fell to the ground with a cut-off cry, then rolled onto his shoulder as Carnahan grabbed him by the backpack and dragged him away from the flailing beast.

Keenan cackled ecstatically as his heavy machine gun littered the native's side with exploding wounds while it dodged detonating grenades thrown by Mendoza. It reared on its hind legs, releasing a guttural scream through its disfigured maw with eyes still bright istnd wild with fury. Its lower jaw only hung on by frayed skin, its pelt was stained black with gaping wounds and blast marks, but in its eyes, there was no fear. There was no desperation, there was no exhaustion. There was only rage and hunger.

"Back off it! Damn it, Keenan, BACK UP! It's not fucking going down!" Captain Short roared as they fought to keep it at bay. Even Greene went through

magazine after magazine as he fired from a slumped position on the ground, caked in soil and blood.

"We have to make another run for it. At this rate, we'll run out of fucking rounds!" Short barked at Mendoza, but they both hesitated as they caught sight of Greene's mangled leg.

"Shit," the captain hissed as he reloaded. "Okay, Fischer — *Where the fuck is Fischer!?*"

They spotted her just as she marched past Keenan, wrenching his powerful gun from his hands and slamming the butt into his stomach when he resisted.

"Fischer!" Short roared, already jogging toward her as she shoved a fresh magazine into the weapon. She walked toward the beast's backside as it turned its attention on Mendoza and Carnahan who covered the remaining two researchers.

Sergeant Fischer took off for the native in a dead sprint.

"Fischer!" Captain Short cried, then changed his course to run for the front of the beast, screaming indiscriminately at it to draw its attention.

"Cover her, god damn it!" he shouted at the others.

Fischer didn't fire, not yet. She let her comrades distract it from the front as she dodged its bloodied thrashing half-tail.

She ran closer yet, ducking her head through the kicked-up soil that plumed around her and obscured her vision in a thick haze.

She charged straight between the native's back legs and underneath it. Only then did she raise the machine gun to the sky and squeeze the trigger, holding it tight as she shot a continuous storm of ripping bullets directly into the beast's soft belly. Flesh exploded above her and black blood rained down on her like a monsoon as she marched beneath its gut toward its chest. She couldn't see through the wet mud and shredding entrails and oily liquid erupting down on her face, but she didn't need to. She fired blindly into the gushing storm above, bringing down the heavens, one foul intestine and pulsing organ at a time. The atmosphere rang loud with the violent symphony of a descent into hell, of screaming agony and burning flesh and punished sins. For once, it was not the sound of dying men and pounding boots. It was the sound of an empire falling.

It was the sound of victory.

The native reared on its hind legs, reaching its full, monstrous height. It was now torn open in an abstract ravine up to its chest, tattered insides spilling out into the dirt and exposed bones crumbling like ruins. Still, the battle raged, as Fischer aimed into the beast's gaping chest and gored a hole through its goliath hearts despite the desperate calls from her brothers in arms.

The monster slammed its colossal weight downward, crushing Sergeant Fischer where she stood in one fatal blow. Then it reared again, its gigantic claws pounding into the soldier on the ground once more, but this time it didn't stay standing.

The titan finally fell and the planet quivered beneath it.

"How is your tongue, Uncle?" Rykr asked between stealing glances at the Celesteal guards posted by the doorway. The rebels waited in a small communal chamber full of seats and rugs, under strict orders to stay put while Vaus-Kharax made an announcement to her citizens.

Kaishek let out a low sigh, his nostrils flaring. Reluctantly, he stuck out his tongue as opposed to explaining. He was now missing half of the long appendage; it ended in a sharp, flat edge where it used to have a point. A Celesteal medic had been merciful enough to cauterize it for him.

"That's not so bad. You can still taste, right?" Kodo asked curiously. Kaishek clenched his jaw, increasingly irked.

"There are more uses for a tongue," the old man murmured under his breath, but fortunately Alvi's defiant voice rang out before Kodo could inquire any further.

"You deserved it," the ocean woman interjected in an accusing tone. "Both of you."

Alvi pointed a claw at Kaishek and Rykr. The two mountain men briefly glanced at one another, then back at her with building tempers. Kaishek opened his mouth but didn't get the chance to speak.

"You two need to get ahold of yourselves. You both nearly got us killed back there," Alvi lectured firmly, her eyes sharp. "I'm getting sick of these arrogant kingly and princely attitudes of yours, because last I checked, *neither* of you currently holds those titles. Your unchecked pride puts us all in danger."

Rykr growled and stood up from his seat, but Kaishek put a hand up to stop him.

"Let her speak," the Lost King commanded. A fire built in Alvi's gaze to match the old man's.

"You asked me to appeal to my nation, to guide you through my homeland. Well, the queen doesn't care about your royal bloodline, and neither does the sea," she spat, venom lacing her words. "So you will *listen* to me if you don't want it to drown us all."

Kaishek and Alvi stared at each other for a moment in tense silence. The aged king gritted his teeth to keep from daring her to use that tone with him again. No one of Alvi's stature had spoken to him in such a manner in many years, and the last that did didn't live to tell the tale.

But she was right.

He had nearly gotten them killed. He hadn't been able to contain his hubris. He'd disrespected a queen before her throne, and he was lucky to escape with only his tongue lost. He released a slow breath, pushing the fury from his chest and letting it dissolve in the air.

"You are right," he muttered as if the words themselves scratched his throat on their way out. "I apologize."

Rykr looked to his uncle, bewildered, but a low warning growl from the old man silenced him.

"I'm sorry," Rykr breathed quietly through his fangs. Alvi hesitated for a moment, but gave a curt nod.

"Thank you," she said, then flashed a smug look at Kodo and Leida before turning away.

"And the king shall bow to a child," a gritty voice sang from the doorway.

Kaishek flipped around, his jaws snapping together barely short of the intruder's face. He found himself staring into two different colored eyes, one a glowing yellow-green and one a vibrant turquoise, both with a dusting of magenta around all four pupils. They were wild and wise and gleamed in amusement.

Kaishek stowed his teeth as Alvi bit his tail. He winced and flared his nostrils.

"You... startled me," he lied. The small ghaengste before him, neck craned to meet his gaze, chuckled even more.

"It is only a proverb, son, no need to take it so personally!" they mused. Kaishek's eye twitched in irritation at being called 'son,' but he noticed the stranger was much older than he'd realized.

They were a scrawny ghaengste, unremarkable to look at. Dull green matted curls and locs hung from their neck, longer in some places than others. Shells and small sea creatures were tangled within their hair and decorative scarifications were carved all over their dark flank. Their muzzle was grayed and wrinkled like Kaishek's own, bones pierced through their nostrils, and a small beard adorned their chin. A mischievous twinkle formed in their mismatched eyes, which were peculiar and full of secrets.

"We heard you were dead," they noted curiously, leaning up to study the Lost King's face as he slightly recoiled.

"I am not."

Alvi appeared beside Kaishek.

"Seer, these are my friends..." she said, a slight hesitancy in her voice. The old ghaengste nodded eagerly.

"Oh, how wonderful it is, to be missing, hm? And yet you are found!" They winked with a smile. Alvi gave a sheepish chuckle back.

"I heard the sea had callers from above today, but I had to see for my own," they said as they studied each stranger inquisitively. Theirs was the first pair of ocean-dwelling eyes that had looked upon the rebels with anything resembling welcomeness.

"I am Caito Anafi, though perhaps you hear of me under the more... *humorless* title of 'Medicine Seer.' Not much a fan of it myself, aye, but reputations travel farther than names, much farther, much farther. I'm sure you know this well, ah, Lost King?" They nodded to Kaishek knowingly. He did not return the sentiment.

"I was told tales of the Medicine Seer by my grandmother, that she was told by *her* grandmother. You are a few generations too young," Kaishek said with a bored scowl. Alvi cringed, but the Seer only laughed delightedly.

"Aha! I look good, ey? The ocean has secrets you know not of!" they cackled hoarsely. "Time passes slowly in the mountains, boy, very slowly, but in the depths? Not so much."

They grinned wide, revealing teeth that were unlike that of a normal ghaengste. Their jaws were lined with rows and rows of razor-sharp crooked incisors, much smaller and less uniform than they should have been. Their eyes glimmered as the land dwellers before them stared dubiously. Kaishek fought hard to cool his fiery temper so as not to offend the strange old shaman.

The giant in the back of the room cleared his throat and spoke up, in what could have been an attempt at good manners. "Uh, I'm Kodo. And this is Le—"

"I know who you are!" the Medicine Seer exclaimed enthusiastically.

"You d—"

"*You* are the fork in the road," they said as if reciting something memorized, jutting a paw that appeared to have too many fingers in Kodo's face.

"*You*," they started as they grinned up at Rykr, "You, are the gatekeeper."

They turned to Leida, her studious eye watching them blankly.

"And *you*..." They slowly cocked their head so far to the side it almost turned upside down. "You are the beginning of the end."

Leida flicked her tail.

"I am Leida," she corrected the ancient ghaengste plainly, though there was curiosity in her close gaze. The Seer paid her no mind, already having turned their attention to Alvi as they plucked a shell from their own unruly locks and tucked it behind the young woman's ear.

"You are neither here nor there," they said to her affectionately with an approving nod, then stood on their hind legs to be eye level with Kaishek. He pulled his face back as they pushed theirs nearer.

"And *you* have much to learn."

Kaishek's face twisted into a snarl, but before he could break his promise to Alvi, the outlandish shaman was already leaving the room through beaded curtains.

"The happy one will soon be here to fetch you, travelers," they called back and began singing as they left.

Captain Short knelt beside Fischer's body.

The permanent crinkles between her stern brows were gone, the squint of distaste and the ever-present wrinkle at the edge of her nose absent too. Her face was limp from exhaustion, but maybe that was the closest thing she had to heaven.

He closed her eyelids.

The master sergeant's once fair skin and hair were now stained black, crusted in soil, blood, and chunks of meat. Her chest was caved in completely, and the puncture wounds from dagger-sized claws littered her body. She looked like hell, like she'd marched through the fiery pits and never made it to the other side. The beast that lay beside her had taken the same journey. Its insides littered the grass and it had flooded the entire area with its tar-like blood. Short gritted his teeth so tight they ached as he glared at the demon's carcass, already filling the air with the pungent stench of bile and sulfur. The knowledge that the natives could be killed kept a weak flame alight in his chest, but burning brighter was the hope that they could feel pain. He hoped and pleaded that the beast had died in excruciating agony.

The captain said a quick prayer over the fallen soldier, then snapped the dog tag from the chain around her neck and pocketed it. He stood up from the mud.

"Let's go," he ordered, then turned to Corporal Greene, still slumped on the ground and breathing shallowly as Mendoza knelt beside him. "Can you walk, Corporal?"

"Sure."

"Keenan, carry him. Is everyone else on their feet? Where's Sanchez?"

"Gone too, Captain," Carnahan said as they helped heave Greene over Keenan's shoulders, despite both of the corporals' grumbled protest.

"Are you two intact?" Captain Short nodded to the two remaining researchers. He couldn't tell if they were wounded through the blood and brain matter covering them both.

"We're fine," Giovanni said hoarsely, tightly clutching the data pack as Harrison silently stared at Carl's headless corpse, still wrapped in the severed tail.

"Move," the captain said as the group started back to the compound.

...

"Mirror test: check."

Sherri chuckled shamelessly as she took notes in her journal, watching the native toss his head and dance around in front of the mirror she'd set against the wall. He gave every indication that he knew it was himself he was seeing, seemingly very satisfied by the privilege. His facial expressions showed an almost humanlike quality, Sherri could swear he was smirking. He exhibited more and more mental capability, yet his mannerisms were that of a clumsy, cocky teenager. She began to theorize that he wasn't fully mature; it would explain the lankiness in comparison to the other specimen she'd seen. Sherri scribbled another word in her current journal entry.

Adolescent?

She circled it, then closed her journal and set it aside as she stood up.

"Alright, buddy, you're off the hook. I'm running out of field tests to perform on you." She collected the signaling mirror to put it back in her bag, taking a quick look at her respirator supply.

Thus far he'd shown at least a primate-adjacent level of intelligence, but Sherri had no reason to believe her earthly benchmarks would have much accuracy for his species. She suspected that the carvings on the inside of the log were some sort of art or writing, but she was fairly sure she had no way of figuring out what they meant.

"Alright, buddy."

Sherri froze as a low voice sounded out. It had been a little while now that she'd been without human contact, but far, far too early for her to start hallucinating. Slowly, she inched around to look behind her. The native was watching her curiously, his pupils contracting larger and smaller as he studied her. She always found it unsettling when he did that, but she tried not to let on.

"Alright... buddy..." she said slowly to him.

"Al-rite bud-dee," he repeated without missing a beat. He'd even slightly parted his mouth to speak the words, his ears twitching as the noise left his throat.

"Oh my god — okay, you can parrot! Wow." Sherri scrambled to get her journal back out of her bag.

"Al-rite bud-dee," he said again, almost enthusiastically. The voice he spoke with was far from human; rather, a low garbled growl. Each syllable ended with a clicking sound, and neither his lips nor tongue moved as he said the words — it came only from his throat.

"Good job, buddy, good job. You must have a syrinx, instead of vocal cords... or maybe both? This is fantastic, do it again!" She laughed, coming over to rub the spot on his chin she'd discovered he liked.

"Goood jo-b-udee," he growled through a purr, clearly enjoying both the chin scratches and the new game. Sherri frantically opened a new page as she praised and petted him.

Ability to parrot noises
-Sound shaped by throat, not mouth
-Syrinx? Larynx? Both?
-Repeated clicking noise
-Can imitate both sounds and inflections

She scribbled down every idea she thought might be relevant. The development of speech and complexity of vocal communication was far, far from her area of expertise. Yet again, she was dragged from the comfortable bounds of botany and thrown into something absolutely unknown to her. It was daunting, it gave her whiplash, and she was sure she'd never get used to it. But god, did she love it.

"Sherri," she said, looking up at the beast before her and pointing at her chest. "*Sherrri*, can you say that?"

He cocked his head down at her, blinking as his brain seemed to work out what she was asking. She only wished she could get a look at that brain.

"*Buddy,*" he said definitively. Sherri laughed and rubbed his nose.

"No, you're buddy." She touched his chest. "I'm *Sherri*," she said clearly and touched her own.

"*She-ri,*" he rumbled, placing a click between the two syllables.

"Yes!" Sherri exclaimed, grinning as she reached up to scratch behind his ears. "Good job, buddy."

He began to get excited now, purring loudly and flapping his ears.

"*Goood j-ob She-ri.*"

"Yes!" she gasped again, hugging his massive neck. They continued to chatter back and forth, though the native seemed to attach himself to saying the word Sherri. While they made no real communicative strides, Sherri couldn't contain her eagerness at the newly opened door. They didn't quite understand each other, and maybe they never would, but in that moment, just the act of speaking was enough.

…

"Is this seat taken?"

Sherri lowered herself on the open rim of the log, sitting beside where the native lay. She allowed her legs to dangle over the edge alongside his paws, and she gently kicked her feet back and forth as she thought over the day's developments.

He seemed content and sleepy, watching over the canopy of the jungle around them. Sherri gently let her shoulder come to rest against his. She didn't fear sitting at the edge anymore, she didn't fear the void below or the massive beast lying next to her. As she looked out on the magnificent forest, she contemplated the discoveries she'd made, the things she'd seen, and the beauty of the world she and her team had feared so much. Her gaze moved from the magnitude of the view before her and found the face of her new friend. She had already learned so much from him, and yet so much more was still unknown.

But Sherri was hindered, suspended thousands of feet in the air without the lab's resources and the knowledge of her colleagues. She had gained more information than they'd ever dreamed of, but it stayed trapped in the pages of her journal and the limits of her experience. Now she was collecting evidence that they may even be able to communicate with the natives, but to what end? Every single piece she uncovered drove her deeper, and she had no idea what to do with all that she'd been given.

"I have to go home," she whispered abruptly. The native had been watching the swaying of the leaves, but he looked down at her when she spoke to him. His eyes held not understanding, but a desire to. Sherri sighed and stood up, looking at his face and cupping his giant cheeks with her hands.

"I need to go back to where I came from, buddy, so I can learn more about you. And more importantly, how to communicate with you. I can't stay with you forever. But I'll come back, I promise. Because we're friends, right? Can you say 'friends'?"

She looked into his eyes, his pupils dilating as he studied her. She knew he didn't understand her words, but she wondered if he understood the sadness of goodbye.

"Friends?" she said again, slower.

"*Fr-ends,*" he finally responded, curiously clicking as he sniffed at her face.

Once he figured out how to mimic the first sound, it was easy.

As it turned out, the little balding creature seemed to have relatively extensive language capabilities. In fact, the sounds it made were not too different from

Tahro's own mother tongue, only it seemed to vocalize at a much higher frequency than his kind did. It took a few tries, but eventually, he learned to vibrate his throat in such a way as to emit noises similar to the creature's words. Easy.

Though he still hadn't figured out what they meant.

"She'ri," he called, and it came when beckoned. He wasn't exactly sure if 'She'ri' was really its name, but that's what he'd decided to call it. However, it did seem to think that *his* name was 'Budi.'

"Good job, Budi," She'ri cooed at him softly. It seemed a little disenchanted, less bushy-tailed than it normally was. Figuratively, of course, it didn't even have a tail. Perhaps the little thing was exhausted after a long day of being taught to speak.

"No, Tahro. My name is Tahro. Can you say that?" Tahro asked, slowing his voice to a patronizing song. She'ri just stared at him, its brown eyes blinking with confusion. Tahro huffed and rolled his eyes, remembering the frequency issue.

"T—" Oh, that sound was harder. It was a new challenge to form the 'T' in a manner audible to She'ri's more primitive ears.

"T-T-T-" he clicked, experimenting with the noise in his throat. She'ri was now making chirps back, reacting to his attempts, and he fixated on the 'T' sounds in its squeaky vocalizations.

"Hey, how do you do that?" he asked. *"To? To, to to."*

That wasn't so hard, though She'ri was now watching him warily, its pulse slightly quickened. Tahro hoped he hadn't said something offensive.

"Toa- Taa- Taahro. Ha! Can you say that? *Tahro,"* he explained. She'ri cocked its head to one side, studying his face in its usual intensely quizzical way. It sort of gave Tahro the creeps when it did that.

He put his paw on his chest.

"Tahro. My name is *Tahro."* He tapped himself a few times, hoping the creature was intelligent enough to get that concept.

"Taro?" She'ri finally peeped.

"Yeah! Close enough, anyway." Tahro laughed, praising it with a soft nuzzle. She'ri nuzzled him back with its hands, but didn't seem to understand what it was being praised for. He frowned at the confusion clear on its tiny bald face.

"Look." He put his paw on his chest, patting it a few times. He was pretty sure it should know what that meant by now.

"*Tahro*. That's me," he said, enunciating as well as he could, patting his palm against his breast. Then he gently, so very gently, touched She'ri's own body with his finger. He was careful to only barely tap the little creature, so as not to trigger a violent fear response.

"*She'ri*. That's you," he finished. He could see it pause, inspecting the situation. He repeated the ritual once more, this time in reverse.

"*She'ri.*" He gingerly laid his paw on it.

"*Tahro.*" He patted himself.

A familiar look slowly lit up She'ri's speckled face, then its eyes widened in the way they always did when it finally began to understand something.

"*Taro...*" it whispered.

...

The rebels followed Smiley down yet another dark stone hallway, Kaishek glaring at the back of the commander's head but holding onto composure for the sake of their cause. He could only hope the whispers of his companions didn't reach her swiveling ears or tempt her to take another tongue.

"Al?" Rykr whispered for the second or third time.

"What?" Alvi whispered back.

"Can ocean dwellers be... male? I haven't seen one man here," Rykr asked hesitantly. Alvi's laughter cracked through the hall, but only for a moment before she stifled it.

"What? How would we reproduce?" She chuckled. Rykr huffed and shook his head, waving her off.

"Of course there are male ocean dwellers," Alvi explained in a patronizing tone. "But the Celesteal clan doesn't allow them as citizens. Any boys born here are sent to the nomadic sea tribes we ally with."

"Why?"

"We believe the natural state of the ocean is female, and so the presence of men alters the harmony of the shoal. Thus, it's traditional for the Celesteal nation to remain entirely women. Except for Oriko, of course."

"Who?"

"My father. Our breeding male. He has very good genes."

"...Lucky guy."

Kaishek quickly shushed the conversation before it went on any longer as the stone beneath their feet turned to white sand, and he was momentarily blinded by the sunlight. Stepping out of a dune and into the open air, they were on the beach once again — only no longer enclosed by the harbor and village. Now they were surrounded by a bright green ocean, the sparkling tide frothing as it met their feet. In the distance, the main coast was faintly visible, dotted with the structures and citizens of the clan grounds.

Kaishek's hair was whipped around his shoulders as Leida abruptly took flight, doing a brief circle overhead before landing back on the sandbar gracefully. She looked up at the sky as if she'd thought she might never see it again.

"No more air shows, mutant," Smiley snapped with a harsh growl. Leida said nothing, but her icy eye stared at the armored woman's face with something vaguely challenging. For just a second, her wings twitched like she might take flight again despite the warning. Kaishek shook his head at her, though he knew there was nothing any of them could do to stop her if she tried. She seemed to think better of her urges as a new voice rang out.

"Have you been hospitable to our visitors, Smiley?" Vaus-Kharax asked as she stepped out of the water, her long braids trailing behind her as she approached. A hint of amusement laced her voice as she met the commander's furious glare.

"They're alive, no?" Smiley replied with a tense jaw.

"Aye, that they are," Kharax confirmed as her gaze traced over the rebels, lingering on Kaishek for a moment. More figures rose from the sea.

Four ocean dwellers appeared in the waves and marched onto the bank, carrying between them a large ornate woven chest supported by two horizontal poles. They set it on the dry ground in the center of the sandbar, then removed the lid.

"My blacksmiths have selected a variety of weapons for you to try, rebels," Kharax announced as the craftsmen unrolled a long rug on the sand and began unpacking the chest's contents.

"My tunahk-dahn will spar with you, and you may practice with whatever arms you feel called to. The blademasters will spectate, studying your strengths, weaknesses, and inclinations in combat. They will then use these observations to design weapons tailored to your unique needs," the queen explained as the rebels admired the myriad of blades laid before them: swords, daggers, axes, spears, and more. All shared razor-like honed edges, detailed engravings, and expert craftsmanship. Leida seemed almost hypnotized, gravitating toward the reflective metals and sparkling sharpness.

"Oh, and ghost." Kharax spoke up again. "We took the liberty of repairing that ugly gash in your axe."

The smiths carefully lifted Y'xara out of the chest and set it on the ground before Kaishek, and just the sight of it washed him in relief. The axe's crack was now filled with metal, creating a silver lightning strike through the previously damaged scapula blade. The plated edges had been sharpened and polished, the entire structure reinforced. The handle had been wrapped with a fresh leather guard, the old one having been worn to nearly nothing from years of bitemarks. Kaishek blinked down at his treasured weapon, then picked it up to feel it in his jaws. It was heavier, strong and dangerous. He skillfully swung it once in a figure-eight motion, then slid it into its sheath on his back. He gave a gracious nod to the blacksmiths, then Vaus-Kharax.

"Thank you, my queen." He stiffly bowed, just slightly. Kharax gave a silent nod back as Smiley laid out a rug for her to lounge on, and the tunahk rose from the ocean to rejoin the congregation. The rebels had all now approached the array of weaponry, inspecting the arsenal curiously.

"Tunahk, help them decide," Kharax called, lowering herself to her rug to watch the exhibition. The five Celesteal warriors fanned out, drawing their weapons. The other rebels were quickly overwhelmed by the choices before them and the prowess of the warriors; Kodo forwent a weapon to impulsively headbutt one of the tunahk directly in the face.

Kaishek released a long exhale; he'd moved to sit beside Kharax and Smiley as the pandemonium unfolded. Smiley got up to move to the queen's other side, positioning herself between the two royals.

"They have a long way to go," Kaishek said to no one in particular. Smiley scoffed, but the beginning of whatever cruel comment she might have said was interrupted by a familiar trill.

"Aye, but a longer way back!" the Medicine Seer called as they joined the spectators. Smiley huffed out a sigh, but was swatted in the side by Kharax.

"Hello, Seer," Kharax greeted as the shaman bowed their head to her.

"I heard there was a show." The ancient ocean dweller snickered and dodged one of the tunahk tumbling by, inadvertently thrown by Leida as she misused a projectile weapon.

"Say, Lost King." The Medicine Seer claimed a seat beside Kaishek and glanced up at him. "Where did you find these rebels of yours?"

"They found me," he grumbled. The Seer cackled with delight.

"Ahh, another missed one found! True, most things worth losing are too, worth being found by. And those lost are more found than those not!" the shaman exclaimed. Kaishek snorted through his nose.

"Do they ever make any sense?" he muttered through the side of his mouth.

"Never." Smiley shook her head.

"Sense is bad for the liver, sits in the gut like bad fruit, it does," the Medicine Seer mused. "Will the travelers stay a while, my queen? The swells seem tolerant today, I think, no?"

Kaishek and Vaus-Kharax still watched the unruly rebels spar clumsily with the Celesteal tunahk-dahn, slowly but surely figuring out how to use the tools they'd been given. Kaishek thought he might have seen a small smile curl the edges of the queen's mouth.

"For a short while, I suppose," she conceded.

The compound hushed at the survey crew's homecoming. Men shuffled in and quietly counted heads, covered in so much grime and blood it was unclear who it all belonged to. Marshall and Doyle didn't even leave the laboratory. They could see through the glass that Carl had not returned and Sherri hadn't either. The only returning friends of theirs were the Rosenquests, clothes and skin soaked red, slumped over one another's shoulders. Giovanni looked as old as his brother.

Corporal Keenan marched straight through the commons to the med bay, dumping Corporal Greene on the nearest bed as nurses and doctors rushed to his aid. The young man kept his eyes tightly shut, as if unwilling to check if his leg was still attached below his knee.

The rest of the crew began to settle, the atmosphere around them like the still air of a battlefield under armistice.

Defeated, wounded, but over.

Marshall sat in silence until he was startled by something clattering onto his desk. He glanced down at a dirty data cartridge on the surface beside his hand.

"Can you get the weather data off of this?" Giovanni asked. Marshall slowly looked up at the younger man, briefly searching his eyes. In them, he saw all the answers to the questions in his head.

Bridgeland was dead.

So was Daniels.

"Yeah, leave it here," Marshall said and put his pen behind his ear as he spun his chair toward the computer to prepare the data files. It was then, as he was inputting the droning number sequences, that he realized he'd been clinging onto hope. He only noticed it in its absence, and like he'd been holding his breath for too long, he finally gasped in the air of reality. Sherri was dead.

He let it sink in for a moment; he sat with it thoughtfully.

They hadn't known each other long, not really. They'd only just started to have a personal relationship outside of work. Barely personal, their sexual relationship had been casual and fleeting. He briefly wondered if the feeling of loss was for her life, or for the sex. He got his answer immediately as a rush of swirling nausea flooded up his throat at even entertaining such a thought.

She was only twenty-nine. She hadn't even lived what should have been half her life. Marshall's eyes wandered to the trash bin by his desk as he felt like he might be physically sick. The shameful idea of vomiting in front of his peers prevented him from thinking about her any longer. He pushed her to the back of his mind, the dark hallway in the basement of his brain reserved for things he'd prefer to forget. He put her in the room with Roger and Carl.

...

"How're you holding up, boss?" Master Sergeant Mendoza gently asked from beside Captain Short at the bar. He discreetly offered the other man a cigarette beneath the counter, but Short rejected it with a shake of his head.

"Fine, Ma. Do me a favor and go check if my corporal gets to keep both legs, will you?" The captain waved him off dismissively. Mendoza nodded and squeezed the officer's shoulder as he left without a word. Short let his eyes fall shut for a moment, just trying to focus on his breathing.

Fischer, gone. Sanchez, gone. Both damn good soldiers. The meteorologist was gone too; he sort of liked that one. He was normal, at least compared to the other assets.

They fought so hard, they did so much damage. And still, it wasn't enough. They even killed one for the first time, and it wasn't enough.

His eyes opened as his fist pounded onto the counter, a hissing breath puffing from his flared nostrils. *Fuck.*

A sudden tapping of nearly new shoes against the linoleum sounded out, quickly getting louder. It was a foreign sound to the compound, gentler than the pounding of boots yet far from the normal slow saunter of dress shoes.

A man launched out of a doorway, sliding into the near-empty commons. One of the medical doctors, a balding man who always wore a yellow tie. He met Captain Short at the counter, panting from the run.

"You need to help—" he gasped.

"What happened?" The captain stepped around the counter urgently to read Doctor Cuthbert's eyes, and the terror in them made his stomach lurch.

"In the terrosphere — something—"

"Something *what?*"

"Something *got in!*" Doctor Cuthbert cried, tears in his eyes. Horror gripped the captain's chest.

"Is anyone still out there?" Short demanded.

"We'd gone out for some sun, but I didn't see them when I heard the crash—" Cuthbert blabbered aimlessly, barely able to form a single thought.

"WHO!?" Short roared in his face

"Nurse McNeil and Nurse Penham!"

The captain shoved him aside and sprinted down the hall.

The entire compound began booming and shaking like it might collapse in on itself.

As Short's boots pounded into the floor, the first roar shot through the halls like a nuclear warhead. He began to pray.

He slammed through the entrance of the acrylic vestibule so roughly the door frame cracked, and now he could hear the women's screams. Guttural, violent shrieking like the tortured souls of purgatory begging for mercy.

He slid into the heavy airlocked door, his shoulder colliding into it as he lurched for the keypad. Another bellow exploded out from the other side, hissing and rattling with the tumult of shattering glass. The shaking vibration was so violent that Short could hardly see the numbers as he typed them in, but he could have done it with his eyes closed. He had nearly hit the last button when he finally caught a glimpse through the small window in the door. His finger hesitated on the final digit.

Both nurses ran toward the door with everything they had, tearing through the crops and skidding across the tile. The blonde nurse, McNeil, was in front and the dark-haired one named Penham was on her heels. Behind them — demons.

The door would take thirty seconds to open.

Two natives. One erupted straight through the fruiting trees, the force shredding them to nothing but splinters. Its claws clattered and slipped around on the tiles but it tore wildly after the nurses like a feral dog to fresh meat, its frothing face curled into something like a depraved grin.

Thirty seconds they didn't have.

A larger native rammed through the terrosphere shell further away, sending glittering shards bursting in the air while it convulsed and thrashed its massive body through the opening. It didn't even seem to notice as it slashed and gored itself on the jagged edges; it only howled in rabid hunger.

Thirty seconds to open, thirty seconds to close.

Nurse McNeil made it to the towering door as the natives gained on her. She lurched for the keypad, her harrowing wails and cries echoing through the heavy steel barrier.

And the captain did something he knew he'd carry with him for the rest of his life.

His fist slammed into the large red button below the keypad before he could allow himself to hesitate.

LOCKDOWN

The door locked. The keypad shut down. The lights in the hallway glowed scarlet and an alarm blared through the speakers.

"Help! We're still here! PLEASE! SOMEONE, PLEASE!!!" McNeil shrieked, throwing herself against the window and clawing at it frantically as Penham was ripped away from the door.

Captain Short met McNeil's gaze through the window, fogged by breath and bloodied as she scratched her own nails off. Her sobs cut into his chest as she stared at him with eyes full of tears and terror and hate and grief.

"I'm sorry, I'm here. I'm with you, I'm so sorry."

The window splattered red, and McNeil's cries were cut short with a splitting gargle.

Short sank to his knees in front of the door. Something massive on the other side slammed against it over, and over, and over, pounding into the heavy steel. The captain didn't seem to notice; he kneeled before it in solemn plea with dead eyes trained on the ground.

God forgive me.

Faro-Dahn stepped through the jungle carefully, the infinite ache in his skull an ever-growing fungus. The glaring light of the sunrise between the trees seared painfully through the ghost of his missing eye and into its empty socket like a burning coal.

He was the one who did not need to tread carefully, not when he had skin as thick as armor and flesh as dense as wood. The one who tore through defenses and cut through enemies with no need for care nor thought. A power to be feared, one power unlike any other.

Except for the giant.

The giant had shown Faro that all powers were limited. That even he could be defeated.

But he was more than defeated; he was crushed. He was castrated. Constant agony sent his vision spotting with black and rendered him unconscious at times, and his mind had suffered most of all. His voice slurred and he stumbled over his words; his memory did not serve him anymore. He could not think in the clever way he once did, now trapped in the defiled head of an invalid. Not even the other tunahk truly knew the extent of how much weaker he'd become; he could not burden them with the shame of his suffering.

He no longer marched through crowds and parted seas; he tread slowly and shuffled with a permanent limp. Those who used to make way for him now expected him to apologize when he stumbled into them. The eyes that used to watch him in fear now held nothing but disgust and condemnation. He wanted no one to see him, he wished only to be a smaller man so as to hide from the hungry eyes of judgment and cannibalism.

He wished only that the giant had killed him.

A stick snapped behind him and he whipped around. Faro's hearing had been his only sense not damaged, and he relied on it now. He scanned the trees, fighting the dizziness and pain pulsing through his concave skull. A familiar man stepped out of the brush, and Faro's shoulders relaxed.

"Rataan-Leih." He bowed his head, releasing a heavy breath of relief.

"Faro-Dahn," the commander greeted. "I am glad I caught you before you snuck off again."

A sheepish look tugged at Faro's stern face as Rataan approached.

"My intention is not to sneak away, commander. I only wish to get back to my duties at the mine," Faro explained, his voice slow as he fought to get all the words out in the right order. The commander walked right past him, then stopped a few strides ahead.

"Surely your station could wait until after the morning hunt in Io-Dahn's honor. You've been so scarce lately, I was surprised to even see you at the vigil," Rataan noted thoughtfully, seeming to watch the mist settle in the distance. Faro paused for a moment.

"Io would not want us to halt our assignments to mourn. She would tell us to mourn while we work," he said plainly.

"Yes, she would." Rataan nodded, his voice bittersweet. "I am not so sure your tunahk siblings hold the same sentiment. Their sorrow consumes them."

Faro just watched his leader curiously, beginning to wonder if this was truly a social call. Rataan turned back to face him once again; the kaunek-leih looked years older than he had not long ago.

"And what about you, son? What of your sorrow?" the commander asked.

"I miss our fallen sister," Faro replied quietly, but he remained stoic. "But I will fight on harder in her honor."

Rataan stood there for a moment longer, something solemn in his eyes.

"Good," he said simply. Then he nonchalantly walked back past Faro.

"Carry on," the commander ordered dismissively, continuing on to return to the clan grounds. Faro hesitated for a moment, watching his leader leave. Then he turned and lumbered forward on his original path, his head hanging wearily.

The cold strike of lightning pierced between his shoulder blades, shot through his center heart, and plunged out his throat. A long, guttural moan howled forth from his chest as his heavy body fell forward onto the spear now embedded in the soil. He slowly sunk down onto it, his skull sliding down the pole toward the blade and his front legs collapsing. The shaft's end stuck up between his shoulders like a flag of conquest. Another gargling wail softly fell from his mouth, agape in dimming horror as his own weight pushed him deeper onto the blade. Thick, black blood poured from his maw and nostrils, sputtering and steaming as he choked on it. His once mighty form twitched and convulsed uncontrollably, yet his weakened front legs buckled beneath his chest and could not lift him off the spear. His back legs remained standing, quivering but paralyzed. As he drowned in the tar flooding his throat and seeping from his eyes, he silently begged the Mother to take him, to take him swiftly. Tears and blood clouded his vision of the ground before him, his face pinned to the sickly rotten mud as the spear held him in a forced bow. His final bow.

Through the blurry fog, he could make out gleaming golden claws stepping in front of his face.

17
WRAITH

Tahro watched little She'ri as it paced back and forth from one opening of the log to the other, studying each end. It seemed uneasy, so he followed along closely in case it slipped and fell — it wasn't the most graceful creature.

"She'ri?" he called curiously. It patted him on the shoulder dismissively as it paced.

He didn't know how to ask what it was doing in its native language and, for hardly the first time, he wished it was intelligent enough to pick up *his* language as well. Though, so far, it didn't even seem to be able to hear very much of his vocal range. Finally, She'ri stopped. Tahro could sense it taking deep breaths, seemingly in deep calculation. Then it reached out of the opening of the log, gingerly grasping a thin vine. It gave the vine a few tugs, then began wrapping it around its... torso, he guessed.

"What are you doing, little guy?"

She'ri appeared to have a compulsion to wear clothing, as even though it already wore several cloth garments, it wanted to be covered in vines as well. He was just beginning to wonder why its species hadn't evolved fur when he noticed it climbing out of the log.

"She'ri!" He gasped, and quickly snatched the little animal back into the safety of the hollow. It huffed, seemingly frustrated that he'd rescued it from suicide.

"No, Taro!" it squawked. *"Go down!"*

He only recognized two of those words, 'no' and 'Tahro.' It had finally learned his name, and from what he'd gathered, the first word had no real meaning — more of a general exclamation of sorts. She'ri then pointed with one of its small jointed fingers. Straight down into the vast drop below the log.

"Down," it said again. Pointing, the universal language. That he could work with. He pointed in the same general direction — straight below.

"Down?" he parroted, though he struggled with the 'ow' sound, it came out more like 'd-oh-n.'

"Yes!" She'ri chirped. *"Down."*

"No, She'ri, you can't jump. You will die," Tahro explained as he ushered She'ri away from the edge. If only he knew how to express the concept of mortality in its rudimentary native tongue. It sighed, and once again went for the lip of the hollow as it squeaked incomprehensibly. Tahro sighed too as he scooped it back from the fall, becoming increasingly frustrated with this creature's incessant desire to kill itself. She'ri rubbed its face, looking around studiously as it always seemed to.

It noticed a pocket in the wood of the log and curiously approached. It reached inside and pulled out a large handful of loose soil. Then She'ri spread the dirt on the bark floor and patted it down.

"Sherri," it tweeted. *"Ground... down."*

She'ri stood up and stepped on the dirt pile. It jumped up and down a few times, and Tahro stepped back as he feared that behavior might be some sort of intimidation tactic. Then it squatted and patted the dirt more, once again docile.

"Oh! You want to play in the dirt? Why didn't you say so?" Tahro asked. He grabbed She'ri by the satchel and tossed it onto his back. Of course, it was a wallowing creature; that would explain why it was covered in mud and grime when he found it. Perhaps it had something to do with the apparent instinct to cover its mangy skin.

No matter; Tahro hopped down to the next lower branch to begin their descent. He heard She'ri make a frightened yelp and felt it grab on tight to his hair — which he didn't appreciate very much but chose to allow. Down he climbed, hopping from limb to limb and clawing down stretches of tree trunk through the jungle canopy. He passed through the mist, through the many twisting layers of vines and leaves, each like their own unique world. Every once in a while, he checked back to make sure She'ri was still holding on tight. It always was.

Tahro hadn't wanted to leave his secret treehouse ever since he'd adopted She'ri. He was almost certain if he did, some other predator would find it while he was gone. That, and he was still stalling before he went home. He knew the longer he hid, the worse his punishment would be, but finding a new friend had been a fortunate distraction from his impending doom. Admittedly, he had been getting a little stir-crazy, and maybe a tiny bit homesick too. As he hopped down the twisting roots of the mammoth tree, he wondered if his parents would let him keep She'ri in their home.

Tahro landed on solid ground with a heavy thump. Pausing there for a moment, he scanned the tree line and sniffed the air. No unwelcome visitors, at least for the time being. He turned his head all the way around to check on the state of his little friend. He found himself looking directly into She'ri's beady brown eyes, which he'd decided was the most effective way to communicate with it, even beyond words. It seemed a little shaken up, sure; its frizzy mane was barely tied back with plumes of curls sticking up in every direction, leaves and twigs caught in the tangle. But She'ri was fine, and it told him with a quick pat on his shoulder and a few deep breaths.

"Down," he said definitively. She'ri nodded in confirmation as it caught its breath.

"Down."

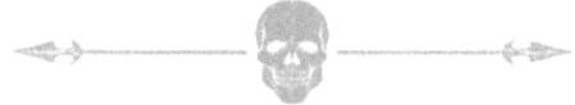

Riding on his back was a feeling she knew would never be recreated by anything else. It was cresting the summit of a mountain above the clouds, it was being swept down the rapids of a raging river, and it was being rocked in the immortal arms of an indescribable love. Sitting atop his shoulder filled her with a sense of power she almost didn't think herself worthy of as a mere human. It felt nearly godlike, marching so tall and wielding such danger below her. She simultaneously felt in control of the planet itself and at its entire mercy.

As they walked through the forest, Taro's giant steady paws stepping over logs and through the brush, Sherri watched the world around her not as an outside observer but as a tenant. She savored the gentle touch of leaves and grass stroking her legs, the even sway of her hips with his gait, and the sounds of the jungle that always seemed to hide when there were strangers around. But with Taro, they trekked as one single body, and she was no longer a stranger to the planet. She inhaled the cool crisp air and the mist around them; she let it welcome her home.

The sound of something else rose above the forest choir and soothed her tired ear. Something foreign to her senses, and yet somehow, she'd missed it dearly. A sweet song.

Taro was vibrating beneath her, and she glanced down. He now had his head raised up to the trees, his eyes closed, his ears relaxed, his behemoth maw slightly agape.

He was singing.

Sherri felt a rush of pieces falling into place — it was them. It had always been them. The sound mission control thought to be birds, the singing before the first attack, the singing before the specimen that chased her to the tunnel. It was the natives. It was obvious, then, as she observed him do it. It was orchestrated music, too deliberate to just be an animal call. As Sherri watched the mammoth being sing into the foggy air with a skilled voice like warm honey and children's laughter and gentle rain, she understood why it had stumped all her knowledge of the natural world. Because the music wasn't something at all. It was *someone*.

That realization consumed her racing mind, then spread through her pulsing chest. They had been trying so hard to sort the natives into the boxes their rudimentary human brains could harness. But they weren't things, they weren't beasts, they weren't data. Taro wasn't numbers and samples and theories; he was someone. He was her friend.

Sherri had been right to assume Taro would naturally take her near where they'd met; she was banking on him keeping to a regular territory. That would explain why he was immediately hostile with the other native; at the time, he may have seen her as 'his' prey. She still shuddered at that nightmarish memory; she'd never seen something so swiftly brutal and hoped she never would again.

She pushed the image from her head, trying to forget the violence her gentle giant friend was capable of. Instead, she focused on the hope that built inside her as they passed some of the trail markers she'd left for herself — cairns and vines tied around young trees. She could make it home.

Sherri entertained the idea that she might be able to steer him like a horse, and she reached down to grab one of the longer tassels of hair that hung from his neck. She gently pulled it to the left — no response. Then she tried pressing her heel into his side, just firm enough to possibly signal a direction to him. Still no reaction; he either didn't notice or didn't care. She briefly wondered if it would be degrading to try fashioning him some sort of bridle but postponed the idea for another day.

"Hey, Taro? I want to walk now," she said, giving his shoulder a quick pat, thinking he might stop on his own if she got his attention. She successfully piqued his interest, as he turned his head around one-hundred-and-eighty degrees like an owl to look at her — she hated when he did that and shuddered at the sight of it. But he didn't stop moving, simply moseying forward as he blinked and clicked at her.

Sherri sighed, then looked down at the ground moving below. He wasn't walking very fast, but it was still about a seven or eight-foot drop from his back, and it looked a whole lot farther.

She quickly took off her backpack, dropped it off his side to commit, then tucked and rolled onto her shoulder. It hurt significantly more than she thought it would, but she quickly jumped up and put her backpack on.

"*Ah-ah!*" She dodged Taro's massive open jaws as he tried to grab her. "No, Taro. I want to walk now. I don't want a ride, thank you."

Sherri just began walking in hopes he'd catch on. He did, trotting along beside her and picking flowers to tuck into his bag as he went. She searched for trail markers and familiar landmarks instead of flowers, though she'd much rather be looking for flowers. Stealing glances at Taro as he collected shiny rocks and colorful plants, she felt a deep kinship with the strange creature. She wondered what his uses for the objects were, if they were similar to hers. Maybe he was a botanist or a scientist of sorts in his own right.

Finally, Sherri spotted a familiar giant rock formation. She picked up the pace, jogging through the forest in the direction she knew the compound lay. Taro had no trouble keeping up, of course, shaking the ground as he meandered after her.

A miraculous golden wall of light peeked through the dark shelter of the jungle ahead — the tree line. Sherri almost broke into a run to meet it, but instead, she stopped in her tracks as she remembered.

Taro.

She turned around to face him as he trotted up and dropped a moss-covered boulder at her feet, winged creatures fleeing from the trees as the planet jolted beneath it.

"Thank you, Taro." She smiled warmly. "I... I can't take this, though," she explained as she pet his nose. Her smile began to fall as he leaned down into her touch.

"I need to go home now, buddy. I can't stay out here with you forever."

Taro studied her face intently, seeming to realize that she was trying to tell him something.

"She-ri," he responded plainly. She got the sense that he just wanted to feel like they were communicating, even if they didn't understand one another.

"I'm leaving for a while..." she started, then sighed at the perplexed look on his face. He sat down in front of her patiently, and his pupils rapidly dilated as he tried to figure out what she was saying, what she was doing. It made her heart ache.

Sherri reached up and gently stroked his cheek, desperately trying to think of some way to communicate with the beast. *Goodbye, but not forever*. It seemed an impossible concept to explain without a common language.

"I'll be back, I promise. I'll find you again, I'll find the tree again — I know you stay there. But I have a home too, Taro. And I have to go back to it. My people need me, and I... need them."

For once, his innocent, goofy face was serious and confused. So confused. She leaned up and kissed his nose, scratching under his chin.

"You have to stay here, okay? You go home and I go home. And then we'll meet up later." She took a few steps back, holding her hands out in front of her to signal for him to stay put. She hadn't prepared herself for how badly this part would hurt.

"Okay, Taro, bye. Can you say bye?" she cooed hoarsely. He cocked his head slightly, watching her every move.

"Bai," he chirped. With a sad smile, Sherri turned around to begin walking away. She heard familiar thumping footsteps behind her, then felt a rough tug on her backpack.

"*No*, Taro. No. I'll see you later, but you can't follow me," she turned back and explained as pain rose from her stomach. She took a few steps backward, and when he took a step forward to pursue, she placed a firm hand on his nose.

"*No!*" she barked as harshly as she could muster through the tears welling in her eyes and the sob stubbornly clawing its way up her throat. Sherri turned around to march for the meadow as Taro's ears drooped, before she could change her mind. She would go see him again soon, and then he'd understand the routine. He'd understand that she would come back.

That time, he didn't try to follow.

The difference between the jungle and the plains was like walking into a floodlight. The sunlight was blinding, the open sky endless and daunting.

Sherri trekked on through the oceans of tall grass and the cool wind untainted by the trees. The suns began to set behind her, bathing her sore back in soft heat and rays of gold. As the silver glint of the compound came into view across the vast field, she felt her posture slump. The weight of her adventure began to pull on the muscles in her legs and arms. The exhaustion of all that she'd seen stung her weary eyes and dragged at her eyelids.

Then a massive, ugly black stain on the planet's flesh came into view. It swept off to the side and dragged the grass in one direction like a giant had stroked the meadow with a black paintbrush. At first, she thought it was the blast mark of a grenade, until her boot sank into the wet ground and she realized the entire area was flooded with liquid. Her mind flashed to the image of Taro, biting the throat of the other native with an explosion of what looked like oil. Black blood.

Sherri's heart began to pound frantically as she examined the black smudge, and she now noted the torn-up ground, vicious blast marks, and rain of bullet casings around it. She studied the way it trailed off and flattened the grass. The whole area was still soaking wet; it had to have happened that day. It smelled rancid in a way that made Sherri lightheaded, and her stomach ached with the dread that something catastrophic had happened where she now stood. There was so much blood, it seemed like one of the beasts must have bled out. She cursed herself for standing there and thinking about it, knowing that a predator had just come through and dragged it away. She took a sample of blood and then hurriedly started back to the compound.

As she marched home, her pulse blared in her ears and questions rang around in her skull. *What happened? What the hell were they doing out here? Was this for nothing?*

She broke into a jog.

"Rebels," a firm, rugged voice said from closer than the rebels had expected. They'd been preoccupied, lounging beneath a canvas canopy and discussing the differences in their cultures. Smiley stood before them on the beach with two blacksmiths beside her, holding a colorful rolled carpet between them.

"Celesteal's blademasters took heed from your recent armed training sessions and have forged the following weapons for you. They are... unconventional, but apparently, they will fit your fighting styles well," the commander explained. She nodded at the smiths, who unrolled the carpet.

"For the winged one, the blademasters observed a favoring of the claws in combat. Your fighting prowess banks on the swiftness of your talons and the grace of your aerial maneuvers. To aid your natural tendencies and not disrupt your agility in flight, we've crafted specialized gauntlets tailored to your anatomy."

One of the assistants reached for Leida's arm, which she immediately retracted as she spit out a vicious hiss. Alvi quickly stepped in and took the gauntlets from the smith before the situation could escalate. Leida hesitated but slowly sat back to give Alvi her hands.

Alvi fastened the gauntlets on each paw, placing a lightweight scaling of thin silver with razor-sharp elongated claws over her natural ones. They gleamed like diamonds, so brightly it was difficult to look at them directly. Leather straps wrapped around her forearms, and she fidgeted uncomfortably as they were tightened. Leida tentatively went to set one paw down, only to pick it back up in reaction to the new sensation.

"They should retract with your born claws," Smiley added. Leida remained still for a moment, then hesitantly sheathed and unsheathed her claws, watching the hook-like silver extensions disappear and reappear into the gauntlet. Smiley continued.

"The blademaster who designed them, Synaos, has named them the 'Gauntlets of Xilai.' Should you keep them clean and polished, they'll also double as a diversion. Made from the most reflective metal on the planet, they will gleam brightly in use to blind your enemies. At least, that's the theory," the commander explained, her voice monotone from memorization. Leida said nothing for a while, retracting and extending the claws and staring at the glow of light. Finally, she spoke.

"Who is this Xilai?"

"Not who, what," Alvi said gently, fascination on her face. "The xilai are giant, magnificent creatures who live deep in the ocean. They don't swim with tails or fins, but with long wings like yours. To us, the name means 'gauntlets of those who fly.'"

"Like my name," she observed quietly, glancing at Kodo who gave her a small smile.

"For Alvi," Smiley began again.

"The blademasters observed your flexibility in combat; you move on land as you do in water. Using your tail as a fifth leg, you keep the enemy at bay and fight like you paddle when swimming. Because of this, the smith Kedrai has designed a tail blade for you."

The assistants began strapping a contraption to Alvi's tail, which she offered readily. Leather straps were fastened around the base of her tail fin, and rings were pierced through the skin to clamp around her spines. When she opened the fin, the contraption sprang out into two curved blades on either side of her tail, sharpened to lightweight razor edges.

Alvi waved it around gently, testing the extra weight as she opened and closed the contraption with her fin a few times. Then she thrashed her long tail like a whip, and with a whistle of wind and a flash of gold, the shaggy upward edge of Rykr's mane was shaved down into a straight line.

"*Al!*" Rykr snarled. The young woman just laughed hysterically.

"Oh, I like this," Alvi cackled.

Smiley quickly spoke over Rykr, interrupting before the bickering could continue.

"Kedrai has named it 'Whiplash.' Whiplash should be light and flexible enough to even improve your speed in the water, but you must exercise constant awareness of the posture of your fin at all times if you wish to avoid accidentally disemboweling yourself or your friends. And don't... sleep with it on."

"Got it." Alvi nodded quickly.

"Giving her that was a grave mistake," Rykr grumbled.

"For *you*, boy," Smiley growled, "the blademasters chose to take advantage of your large mouth and thick skull to craft you this."

Both of the blacksmith assistants worked together to hand him his weapon, one holding either side. He took it from them effortlessly — a bulky hammer, one side a flat base and the other like a sharpened fang. The handle was wrapped thick in leather to pad his teeth, and set in the flat end was a gilded bone that the metal had been poured around.

"The hammer's maker, Pyro, has named it 'Vyrja Varo' — Heavy Heart," Smiley noted.

Rykr nodded, testing the feel of the hammer and swinging it around a few times. His brows furrowed in concern.

"It feels odd... like it's moving by itself..." he said, dropping it to the ground head first, then immediately regretting the action as an explosion of fine sand shot through the area in every direction. Smiley shook the sand off her, her nose twitching in anger.

"There is a solid ball of iridium inside of it. It rolls with the movement of the hammer, increasing the momentum. You'll have to learn to be acutely conscious of the motion of your body, as it will react to every shift. If you want to harness its force, you must harness gentleness."

Smiley raised a brow at the mountain prince, looking him up and down as if unconvinced. He picked up the hammer once again, more carefully this time, and nodded at her in appreciation.

"We'll make you a back sheath for it, but the tailors will need to... measure you."

"I figured, thanks," he muttered. Finally, Smiley turned to Kodo.

"And you, behemoth... the blademasters spent much time considering how to arm you. You have adapted to rely on your brute strength alone. Any weapon you tried hindered instead of helped, and your height causes any wielded arm to affect your balance. After deliberation, the blacksmiths agreed it would be of most use to instead forge armor for you. Your offensive abilities won't be improved by a weapon, so your defensive capabilities should be built upon instead. The tailors have asked me to bring you down to the forge for sizing."

Kaishek spoke up before Kodo could.

"They truly believe he would not benefit from a weapon?" the old man asked, his face pinched.

"Our blademasters are the most renowned experts on weaponry and armed combat on the entire planet," Smiley growled slowly. "I do not question their decisions. I suggest you do not either."

Kaishek reluctantly stowed his apprehension, but began to inquire further about the armor before he was interrupted.

"I don't need it."

Everyone turned to Kodo. His tone grew less assertive with all eyes on him, but he continued.

"I appreciate the generosity from your blacksmiths. Really. But I don't need armor, and I don't need a weapon either. I know, and it sounds like the blademasters know, that anything they give me will just get in my way —"

"*Kodokuna*. Don't be a fool," Kaishek snapped. Kodo looked between him and Smiley, both staring daggers into him.

"I'm not," the young giant insisted. "I don't want anything to slow me down. I'm fast, I'm strong, and I'm not afraid of getting hurt. We all know that I came into this world a beast and a behemoth, so fine. I accept it. Nothing you give me will be better than what I was born with."

A growl rose in Kaishek's throat as the others stood speechless, but Kodo only nodded to Smiley in confirmation of what he had declared.

"Tell your smiths not to waste the metal and leather. Instead, train me to fight unarmed against my enemies' weapons. Deal?"

Smiley stared up at him in something other than distaste for once. Pride, maybe.

"So be it."

Every crew member was crowded around the living area, talking over one another in fear, confusion, and discord.

"One got in? *Two!?*"

"Are we in danger?"

"How did this happen?"

Like a school of fish caught in a fisherman's net, they panicked and struggled. Some were finally breaking into tears. Doctor Cuthbert wouldn't lift his face from his hands, as if he were hiding from the others.

In the back corner, Captain Short exchanged words with Master Sergeant Mendoza. The two men spoke quietly under the tumult of the room, Sergeant Crawford standing with them and following along as well. After a moment, Mendoza broke away and headed for the front of the crowd. He pulled a chair from the side of a nearby table and stepped on top of it, then put his fingers in his mouth and released a deafening whistle.

The frantic voices ceased. The man in uniform cleared his throat.

"Excuse me. If you'll give me a moment of your attention, I will do my best to explain what happened today."

His words projected throughout the room, though his tone sounded like it should have been spoken softly.

"As we know, the compound is surrounded by an electric fence that prevents anything from reaching the buildings. Unfortunately, that fence was not built around the terrosphere. It connects at the conjunction of hallway Delta. According to the compound manual, this is because the light radiation from the fence was believed to have an effect on the crops in the terrosphere."

The stocky man on the chair paused and took a short breath.

"Two natives managed to break through the shell earlier today while Doctor Cuthbert, Nurse Penham, and Nurse McNeil were out for some sunlight. Both Mia Penham and Caroline McNeil lost their lives in the incident."

The sergeant's throaty voice grew hoarse like he was losing it. Captain Short silently slipped out of the room and into a nearby hallway.

"I knew both women, not well, but enough to know they were good people," Mendoza continued, clasping his hands together at his waist. "McNeil was friendly, outgoing, and she made regular med checks that much more bearable. Penham never had much to say and avoided small talk like the plague, but she did a fine job of keeping us soldiers from getting too rowdy in the med bay. They will be missed.

"Eternal rest grant unto them, O Lord, and let perpetual light shine upon them. May their souls and the souls of all the faithful departed, through the mercy of God, rest in peace. Amen."

He put his head down for a moment, taking a breath while he gave a moment of silence for the two women. Then he continued.

"From this point forward, the terrosphere is closed. We will be sealing the door and abandoning all agricultural projects, and an update will be sent to mission control today.

"Now, there are no other gaps in the fence. During the incident, the door showed no signs of giving out under the force of the natives. So long as we keep that door shut and protected, we're safe inside. All you folks need to focus on is keeping your heads on your shoulders and doing the job you were sent here to do. For me and my people, that job is to protect all of you. We are fully committed to that objective. Are there any questions?"

Whether for a lack of questions, or an unwillingness to speak aloud, the crowd remained silent.

"That concludes today's briefing."

Mendoza put the chair back where he'd found it and headed to rejoin Crawford. The captain appeared to meet them as the group reconvened.

"From now on, I want two fully armed guards on that door at all times. Switch out every four hours," Short ordered. "Ma, you're on pairings. Everyone taps in for a shift, including myself and Greene when he's back on his feet. How's the leg?"

"Attached," Crawford replied.

"Out-fucking-standing," Short huffed in dry relief. "Dismissed."

The two sergeants quickly marched away to fulfill their duties, and the captain was left alone. He aimlessly wandered out of the commons once again, back down the empty side hallway as he pulled a cigarette from the pack in his pocket.

Sixteen.

He knew how many were alive and how many were dead from the carvings on the poker table, the abandoned desks in the lab, the empty seats in the commons. Short passed the armory entrance and lit his cigarette, then leaned back against the door as he took the first long drag. Twenty-six people had landed on the planet, and ten were dead. He chewed on that fact; he tasted it in his mouth like metallic blood and salty tears and bitter soot. His head weakly fell back to rest against the cold steel door, and stinging smoke plumed from his nostrils while the room on the other side whispered in his ear.

What have you done? What have you done? What have you done?

...

Marshall had no interest in weather. Four PhDs of varying disciplines; if he gave a damn about the weather, he would have gone to school for it.

But he'd never been so grateful for weather data. He needed something to do after running out of tests to perform and lab equipment to reorganize. The mind-numbing task of downloading, organizing, and uploading the meaningless weather data was a welcome distraction. He supposed he'd just send it back to mission control with a text file attached that said 'You'll have to analyze this yourselves, assholes, the in-house guy just died.' He zoned out for a moment, daydreaming about all the things he'd like to say to mission control. 'Remember when you told us to grow a pair and study the native life? Well, no one left alive is remotely qualified to do that, so... suck it.'

He wistfully considered actually doing it for a moment, wishing it wasn't too late to get himself fired. Then he slowly refocused as he came back from his daydream. His gaze wandered to one of his further monitors, the one he'd set to stream a live feed of the cameras he'd finally gotten around to setting up above the main door.

Marshall abruptly realized that he was actually watching something on the screen beyond the usual still scenery of the meadow past the fence. Something was moving out there. He leaned in close.

A figure. A human figure. Marching across the plains toward the compound. It was her.

Unmistakable. The wild blonde curls, the wide hips, the purposeful walk. He was watching Doctor Daniels, clear as day.

Marshall leaned back in his chair with a huff. He roughly stroked his face, briefly cursing the faint texture of stubble that seemed to grow back by lunch every day.

"Shit," he muttered under his breath. He hesitated for a moment, considering the possibility that he was hallucinating.

"Doctor Rosenquest," he called across the walkway.

"*Rosenquest,*" he hissed. Harrison looked over from his own desk with a start.

"What do you see on this screen?" Marshall asked as he turned the monitor to the other man. Harrison choked on his own saliva and coughed loudly.

"*Doctor Daniels!*" He gasped as he jumped out of his seat and stumbled out of the room, knocking over a few things on the way.

...

As the glorious suns went down behind her, light warmed her shoulders in a beaming shower and the sight of the compound looming ahead made her breaths shift to ragged gasps of emotion. The layer of grime on her face cracked when she broke into a grin as the fence disappeared and the door whirred open. The Rosenquest brothers fell out of the exit, shoving past one another to meet her in the meadow. She let herself fall into them with a hoarse chuckle as they both enveloped her in a hug.

"I'm okay, I'm okay," Sherri assured with a weary smile as Giovanni pulled her head under his chin while Harrison frantically checked her over for injuries.

"Get her inside," the captain ordered, stepping out of the doorway and scanning the area. The brothers guided their lost friend back toward the building, and Sherri felt like she might weep but couldn't quite identify why. As she walked through the doors, the plastic and metal and fluorescent lights welcomed her despite their eternal glare. Even Captain Short was a sight for sore eyes; she noticed that his stoic face was just a little softer than it usually was. Or maybe a little weaker.

As Sherri was led through the entryway, the common area, and toward the med bay, her heart began to sink. The air was different than she'd left it. Emptier, colder, and full of dread. She remembered the stain in the meadow, and she anxiously chewed on her dry lip as her fears began to spiral and her pulse began to race.

She found herself guided onto a hospital bed as Gio and Harrison were sent out of the room by an older woman in glasses. The med bay was calm and mostly vacant; Sherri hoped that was a good sign. God, she hoped that was a good sign. The only other patient was a young soldier lying on the bed next to hers, his leg in a cast.

"Corporal Greene," she quietly acknowledged. It seemed foreign speaking to another human being. It hadn't been more than a couple of days, yet she felt like she hadn't seen the man beside her in years. She felt like she hadn't seen *a man* in years.

"Living dead girl." He nodded at her, looking relatively unphased to see her. Sherri breathed shallowly for a moment, the building around her suddenly overwhelming compared to the quiet of the forest. How ironic, to find safety so uncomfortable. She already knew something had happened, something terrible;

she could see it in the rough state of the corporal and the tenseness of the doctor checking her vitals.

She finally looked back at Greene, and the words out of her mouth sounded distinctly unlike her. They were childlike and frightened.

"What happened?" she whispered.

"I broke my leg," he said nonchalantly. Then he finally looked over at her and hesitated before letting out a slow sigh.

"Went out to find a weather drone. Three people died. Two of mine, one of yours. Then we got back, and the sons of bitches broke into the greenhouse thing. People were out there, two died. Her people," he said, gesturing at the doctor who was patiently ignoring him.

Horror washed over Sherri as she hung onto his words, and the doctor laid a firm hand on her arm as her heartbeat quickened. *Weather drone — Carl*. All she could do was cover her mouth with her hand as helplessness hit her in the gut and emptied the breath from her chest. Five people dead, just today. Her breathing grew panicked and she wasn't even aware enough to be ashamed of it. It was all for nothing. Maybe if she'd been there. Maybe if she'd gotten back just a little sooner.

Maybe there was nothing she could have done at all.

She let her head fall back against the pillow as tears stung her eyes.

"Ysha hei, ysha hei,
The night eats the day,
A'taja ho, a'taja ho,
The blood of the young swallows the old,
The ground opens up and swallows the bold,
Ysha hei, ysha hei!"

The rebels looked up to see the Medicine Seer sauntering by, a swing in their crooked tail as they sang enthusiastically. At first, they limped right past the group of outsiders. Then the ancient shaman seemed to remember something, and backtracked to meet them, their head turning around after their body did.

"Oh! Someone has been seeking you, travelers..."

The rebels looked between one another.

"Who?" Kaishek asked.

"Me!" the Seer guffawed. The old king's face dropped in irritation as they cheekily grinned in his face.

"I bear a message," they continued forebodingly, growing serious.

"Spit it out," Kaishek groaned.

"Aye, and the spit of the lords will poison their swords!" the shaman exclaimed. "But words come with a price, they do, swords too. And so my presage you will not learn, should you not offer in return…"

"How wonderful, they rhyme now," Kaishek growled as his companions looked at each other in curiosity.

"What do you w—" Alvi was the first brave enough to ask.

"An answer!" Seer cried gleefully. "A low cost, everyone has one. And so I ask, and you answer, I ask: what rises like the suns, breathes like the lungs, and strengthens when it's spun?"

The young rebels furrowed their brows in deep thought, but only for a moment before Kaishek's sharp voice rang out.

"Oh, *Mother*, enough with the theatrics! Get to the point, old-timer!" he snapped with a snarl. Several fishermen on the docks and children in the wake froze and stared, and Alvi nervously waved at them. The shaman just snickered.

"Ah, you and me *do* share a love for the theatrical, Lost King," they sang slyly. Kaishek's face twitched in growing fury, and Alvi silently scooted herself between the two, giving the old king a threatening glare.

"Vaus-Kharax has requested I bring word from the river scouts," Seer finally explained, clearly disenchanted without an accompanying riddle. "The Ramys clan has built dams at the crossable points of the river, aye, and manned them with warriors — the pesky tunahk-dahn included. They say you will not be departing the territory that way, though you *will* soon have to depart."

A dark look fell over the rebels' faces. The Medicine Seer continued offhandedly.

"Smiley say you charming travelers will be slaughterstew upon first step from these borders, whether by Ramys from the west, or Kocea to the east. Ah — the queen did not ask I tell you that bit. And Smiley may not have said 'charming travelers,' either, but she did say slaughterstew!"

"Bastards." Kaishek, deep in thought, shook his head. "You four have drummed up quite a fuss with Ramys, haven't you?"

The old man was still not entirely sure how his young rebels got themselves in such bad standing with the forest nation, but he'd gathered it had something to do with a dead hunter and a headless tunahk.

"We did not cross the river to get here before," Leida reminded them. "We can fly over the gorge as we did last time."

"Fly over?" the Medicine Seer's lively eyes flashed with interest. Their question went unanswered as Kaishek continued.

"No. If they are surveying the river that closely, they're already monitoring the weak points of the surrounding region. If we try to cross the gorge as we did last time, we risk getting ambushed while separated. It could be a death sentence."

"We're trapped," Rykr growled, snorting through his flared nostrils.

"No," Kaishek insisted. "We just need to hit them hard and fast, then get around them before they know what's happened. Then we find somewhere to train and grow. We need a plan."

"Very exciting, yes, all very exciting," the Seer interjected. "But Alvi…"

"…Yes, Seer?" Alvi responded. It wasn't quite like the flamboyant shaman to begin a conversation with only a name, not some vague riddle or insulting proverb.

"Come with me, girl, lend an ear, aye?" they said warmly, nodding toward the opposite end of the shore as they began walking. Alvi glanced at her companions briefly, then trotted to catch up with the ancient ghaengste. They walked down the seaside for quite a while, leaving the other rebels to discuss.

"We should flee east and be done with Ramys for good," Kodo piped up.

"We can't just run," Rykr snapped. Kaishek spoke over them both, raising a hand to silence the younger men.

"If we go any further east, we will be under Kocea's shadow and at their mercy. None of you save for Leida are ready to fight sky dwellers. They will pick us off before we ever have time to prepare," the eldest rebel explained. "We will go toward Ramys, but we will strike quietly through their defenses and drive westward past them before they can organize."

"We've been training hard, but we're not ready to go up against Rataan-Leih and his warriors yet," Kodo argued, old fear in his dark eyes.

"No, you are not, which is why we will not stick around to meet the full force of the Ramys clan," the Lost King continued. "It is time for us to grow greater, to rise strong enough to rival their tyranny. It is time for us to form our own clan. The clan of the rebellion.

"But to do that, we must find somewhere safe and guarded, where we can train and flourish. We need to hold a territory of our own."

"Where?" Leida spoke up suddenly, her brows furrowed in deep focus. Kaishek nodded to her.

"That question is for you to answer, Leida. You know this land better than any of us, with your nomadic history. Can you lead us west?"

"I can lead us west." She nodded definitively. Kaishek looked around at the eyes of the rebels as Alvi returned to the group.

"Good. Then let's figure out how to get the hell out of here, shall we?"

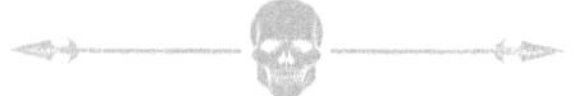

She looked fine. More than fine — she was in one piece. She was so covered in dirt, blood, and bruises that you could hardly see her skin, but compared to skeletons hanging in trees, she looked like a million bucks.

The captain watched her through the glass from across the common area as she lay there in the med bay getting checked over, and he almost didn't believe it. He wondered when he'd get the chance to ask how she'd survived, and he wondered if she'd even have an answer for him. Lucky. She was lucky.

But the others weren't. They'd gotten Daniels back by some miracle — he guessed the lord took pity on her for reasons beyond his understanding — but they'd lost Bridgeland. They were still down another asset. He'd still failed.

"Captain Short?"

A voice shook him from his thoughts, and he glanced over to see Private Zheng standing at attention.

"What is it, Private?"

"I came to ask if I could bring Doctor Daniels a uh — a plant I found outside yesterday. I thought it might raise her spirits." Zheng cleared his throat.

Short hesitated as if he may not have heard right.

"You picked up a plant while we were looking for a missing woman?"

"...Yes. Well, the missing woman was — is a botanist, so, I thought she might appreciate it," the private explained timidly. Short silently blinked down at him for another moment.

"Fine, but give her another half hour," he finally confirmed.

"And you don't have to ask me for permission to give flowers to civilian women, Private, that's your business," Short added, softening just slightly in amusement.

"Thank you, Captain," the young man said quickly as his face grew red and he stepped away. Short was once again left alone, watching the ghost in the med bay. He took a long, deep breath.

Seventeen.

...

Corporal Greene had finally fallen asleep, but not before verbally recounting the entirety of *Sons of Anarchy* seasons one-through-five in explicit, *explicit* detail. Thankful for some quiet time alone to gather her thoughts, Sherri focused on a timeline of her survey before she had a chance to focus on anything else.

She brought herself back to when she'd first left. All the samples she'd gathered, her first time alone in the jungle, all the new sounds, smells, and sights. Then the native that chased her and the fact that she'd been unable to scare it off. She compared her experience with Taro and the makeshift blowtorch and decided that the natives were too big or too smart to be scared off by anything — likely both. It was a very, very unfortunate conclusion, as they were also too fast to run from for long distances and too strong to effectively fight.

Fortunately, Taro had taught her much more than the first native had. He'd taught her that they were intelligent, marginally civilized, and most importantly, not inherently hostile. They just had to figure out which were hostile and which weren't. She was still working on that part.

Then there was the intriguing evidence that they not only possibly had names, but could be rudimentarily communicated with — although that was still a far-off dream. Sherri remembered something and quickly grabbed her journal to take note:

Ask Dr. Rosenquest
What is the evolutionary significance of jewelry? Collections?
How did early humans learn different languages/communicate?
Are names a universal marker of civilization?

Sherri closed her journal and put it back in her backpack. She had a seemingly infinite amount of work to do, an entire world of data she'd barely tapped, and another friend lost. But for the time being, the doctors wanted to monitor her, and she needed to eat something more than half-melted granola bars before she had any hope of forming organized thoughts. She felt heavy and slow, and the hospital bed began to feel less confining as her weight slowly gave in to it.

"Doctor Daniels?" a masculine voice whispered from the doorway.

"Yes?" Sherri replied, looking up to see a very young man with dark, soft eyes.

"I don't know if you remember me — I'm Private Zheng, I was in the search party looking for you yesterday and I picked up something I thought you might want to see — ma'am," he explained quickly. "But if this is a bad time..."

Sherri shook her head and sat up in the bed a little more, beckoning him over with a wave of her hand.

"No, no, let's see it." She did remember him — the smart one. Zheng approached with his ALICE pack in hand but hesitated just before he opened it. Sherri watched his face expectantly.

"Hey, I told Captain Short it's a plant, but it's... not a plant. So if he, I don't know, asks..." he muttered timidly, and a smile grew across Sherri's face.

"I'll corroborate," she assured with a wink. The private gave her a quick, thankful nod before reaching into his bag and pulling out a jar. Sherri's eyes widened.

The jar contained a small organism that Sherri might have described as an insect due to the fact that it was hovering around in its container. Only it looked more like a squid, with a soft translucent body and small tendrils attached to it. Its wings were less like wings and more like gliding flaps. It seemed to move impossibly, bumping around the jar aimlessly in a manner that was more floating than flying.

"Private Zheng, how did you... get this thing?" she whispered in amazement.

"I found it sitting on my pack and scooped it into the jar. With a stick, though, I didn't touch it."

"And you kept it alive all day?"

"Well, I tossed a couple of leaves in hoping maybe it would provide air and food, like on Earth... I don't know how well it worked, but he's still alive and the leaves are gone." Zheng shrugged. Sherri laughed softly and slowly turned the jar to follow the little creature as it floated.

"I'll make a real habitat to keep him comfortable. Why did you lie to Short?" she asked, looking up at the youngest soldier.

"I thought he might kill it if he knew it was an animal. Or make me put it outside."

Sherri chuckled more.

"You did the right thing, picking this little guy up for me. Thank you. Would it be alright to call you by your name instead of rank?"

"Oh, sure, it's Peter. Peter Zheng." He nodded quickly. Sherri looked up at him with a smile, her exhaustion slowly subsiding into a previously held hope.

"Thanks, Peter."

The tunahk's return to the Ramys grounds from their duties was gradual, scattered, and hopeless. They had been bearing a wound like nothing they'd ever experienced in the days after Io-Dahn's death.

The warriors had been destined to fight together from birth, raised together from childhood. They had not experienced the world outside of their bond. They had known nothing of heartbreak, they had known nothing of loss until now. And it gutted them deeper than any blade, any claw. It bled them dry.

But none more than Iago.

She didn't remember what tasks she'd done that day, or even what day it was. Her body trudged aimlessly back through the border gates, but her mind was somewhere else entirely. She hardly noticed the wall guards avert their gazes and hush their whispers, and she only realized that Mahrz and Teihnan were walking with her when she lazily veered to the side and bumped into them.

The others were already waiting in the tunahk courtyard except for Faro. For a moment, the nine warriors just stood there.

"Faro won't join us for dinner, anyway. We should go ahead." Lih was the first to speak as they listlessly began to shed their armor. It was true; Faro had hardly been spotted in the village at all lately.

"You don't know that. We should wait for him," Kjell argued with a cold glare.

"Is Rataan-Leih at home?" Mahrz asked as he scanned the surrounding territory, looking for the commander among the huts and bustling ghaengste preparing for dinner.

"We haven't seen him yet," Lih said. "Perhaps he is waiting until after the meal to receive the report."

There was an uneasy, freezing chill in the air, but no one was bold enough to call it out. Iago normally would have been the one to say what they were all thinking, but she just stared vacantly.

"Something is wrong," Raiz said abruptly, and the others perked in surprise as the man spoke only on rare occasions. The fact that he'd used his voice at all was a harrowing omen that something terrible had happened. That, and the figure trudging toward them in the distance.

"Great Mother..." Kjell choked out.

Rataan approached the congregation slowly, struggling to carry something on his back. He shuffled and limped, his head hung low in a quivering posture they'd never seen before in all the years he'd raised them. The object slumped over his back was larger than him, dark-colored, and indiscriminate until they noticed a long tail dragging on the ground. A steady trail of black blood smeared the ground in Rataan's wake — he was covered in it — and a massive paw flopped over his shoulder, completely limp.

"No... It can't be..."

All nine tunahk ran to meet the wounded commander; they swarmed around him and pulled the corpse from his back.

"No, no, *no, no, no —*"

"*Faro...*"

"*Please, Mother, no.*"

Rataan was covered in bloody wounds, gashes and bites and gouges. Slumped at the commander's golden claws, Faro's mauled body was barely recognizable. Most of his once mighty form had been crushed, his bones shattered. His skull was smashed to pulp and splintered pieces that were contained by his dented helmet. His muscles were flayed by claws, his ribs split by powerful blows. The only way they could be sure it was their brother was from the size of the body and the familiar markings across his pelt.

"I am sorry, children, I tried — we were outnumbered..." Rataan muttered hoarsely, staring down at the ground. Faro's mutilated carcass soon became damp with the tears of his tunahk siblings and warm with the heat from their tentative hands. Eleven chosen were now nine, each one of them no longer whole, their union now gutted by a spear driven through its belly. The beast had lost two legs.

"The rebels…" Rataan croaked as he caught his breath, "They did this. They grow strong, stronger, and I… I need you strong."

They stood in silence, every eye between them wrought with salty devastation from their tears. All but one.

Iago's single eye held no more tears; it was dry with hatred.

A crowd of Ramys citizens had begun to stare from a distance, whispering amongst each other about the number of tunahk and the fallen body in the center of the courtyard. Rataan spoke again, lifting his head in spite of the weakness from the blood loss and his trembling muscles.

"We have lost a brother and a sister, tunahk-dahn." His voice wavered at first, but slowly it rose. "Two great warriors, taken in the fight against the rebellion."

The remaining tunahk winced, agony striking through them with his words.

"But we will carry them with us, warriors, we will carry them on our shoulders and in our hearts. We will carry their names in our blades, so they may strike down the enemies in death that they could not in life. We will not let the loss of our brother and sister be in vain. You must stow your tears, warriors, save them. The last thing Faro-Dahn said to me, before the attack…" The commander faltered, his breath caught. His lip twitched as the power stubbornly came back into his tone.

"He told me, 'Io would not want us to mourn before we bring the rebels to justice. She would tell us to mourn while we fight.'

"So save your pain for the battlefield, warriors, save your tears for the storm. You may weep when your fangs meet flesh, when your tongues taste blood. You may cry when the giant has fallen, when every traitorous rebel has been slaughtered. We will mourn for our comrades when we have delivered what we owe to them.

"We will mourn when we have brought their killers to *justice*.

"Until then, we do not have the right to weep."

…

As the rebels entered the lunai chamber, escorted by the Celesteal tunahk-dahn, there was a sense of dissipating tension in the glittering cave. Like the shedding skin of a reptile, the first rain after a drought.

"I hear you seek an audience with me, rebels."

The queen lounged in her usual spot atop her pillar in the chamber. This time, Smiley laid atop it as well, bare of armor and gently grooming the queen.

It was a strange form of intimacy, to see the brutish ghaengste without her armor and weapons, expressing tender affection as opposed to harsh brutality. She stopped shortly after their entrance, however, and stared down upon the rebels with her threatening gaze as she always did. Leida stepped forward and nodded, wearing her gauntlets in an effort to get used to walking in them.

"We have come to tell you our plan," the sky woman announced.

"For what?"

"To leave your land."

"Good answer." Vaus-Kharax raised a brow. "So tell me, and I'll decide whether you are a quick and dirty distraction for the Ramys clan or a lasting ally to my people."

Kaishek stepped forward to stand beside Leida, but he slowly bowed his head.

"Permission to speak, my queen."

"Go ahead, ghost," Kharax granted in a dry tone, though her violet eyes gleamed with subtle amusement.

"Our intention is not only to be a distraction for the Ramys clan, and not only to be a lasting ally to the Celesteal nation. We seek to form a united rebel clan fierce enough to rival Ramys, and strong enough to fight alongside Celesteal in its trials," Kaishek said boldly, lifting his head as his voice echoed throughout the cave.

"We will leave your borders, journey across the valley, then find and hold a territory west of Ramys land. We will kill as many of their warriors as we can in their inevitable opposition and send a message loud enough to reach the sky above and the ocean below. When all is said and done, your people will have the position east of Ramys, and ours will have the position west. The Ramys clan will lose their advantage over this region, and in time, all people of the valley will be freed from their choking claws."

The queen watched him closely, then skimmed over the faces of each rebel. Her eyes narrowed.

"Prove it."

Kaishek nodded at her without breaking his fervent eye contact, then turned to Leida.

"Your scouts say the river crossings are guarded by Ramys warriors," Leida began. "I will create a diversion and lead them away from their posts and into the valley. They will not leave the river unguarded, but the tunahk-dahn will follow me and leave only a few warriors on the dams."

Alvi picked up where she left off.

"I will quietly take care of the remaining warriors on the dams from the river while Kaishek, Kodo, and Rykr wait hidden. The guards will be dead before they know what's happening, and the others will cross before we've alerted the rest of the jungle," Alvi explained quickly, then gestured to Rykr with a tip of her head.

"We'll stay low and sneak through the forest to meet Leida in the plains," he took over. "And take out any patrols we see along the way. As we move, we'll light flares to cover our movement with a smokescreen and hopefully keep some of the tunahk distracted after we've already made it out of the trees."

Rykr finished with a confident look and knocked the edge of his horn against Kodo's.

"Leida will hang in the air at a safe distance until we can meet her," Kodo jumped in. "When we get there, we'll take care of whichever tunahk she's pulled from the river stations and start pushing west. By then they'll have figured out what's happening, but the forest fire will keep them spread thin. We'll kill as many as we can, traveling through the valley — they're fast, but as long as we move fast enough to keep them from grouping up, we'll make it. Leida knows the land west of Fohs'il Ridge. We'll find somewhere safe there while we train and grow our numbers, and the Ramys clan won't push that far out of their land to look for us; at least not after we've thinned out the tunahk-dahn."

He finished, looking rather cocky and satisfied with himself, and they patiently awaited Kharax's reaction.

"You five look very pleased with yourselves for dead ghaengste walking," the queen said bluntly. "What makes you think their tunahk will be separated at all? And what makes you think you will stand a chance against them even if they are?"

"I know how they work, I used to live among them," Kodo explained. "The Ramys territory is vast, and there are only eleven tunahk-dahn. They're rarely assigned to the same post at a time, and if they are, it's in pairs. Our only problem is the harbinger — her name is Teihnan-Dahn. A thin warrior with black fur, she wears the calling horn around her neck. If we see her, we'll need to kill her before she can blow the horn, because she will call all eleven tunahk at the same time."

There was a hint of dread on his face when he explained the harbinger, and Kharax studied him closely. Then she glanced over them all.

"Very well. When is this plot taking place? The fish in the bay will run out if we have to feed the behemoth much longer." Her words were cold, but her gaze held just a trace of fondness. Kaishek was the one to speak up.

"Two more days to prepare and rest, if you'll have us that long."

The queen observed the room for a moment as if considering many different things. She gave a subtle nod.

"I look forward to hearing the stories, whether you live or die. But it will be a much better story if you live and Ramys blood runs dry. Good luck, rebels. I do not know if Matka has mercy for you. But for all of our sakes, I hope She does."

Even the barracks were slow and heavy like the air had turned into a thick fog. The normally rowdy soldiers were settling in for a quiet game of poker; Master Sergeant Mendoza had been left in charge as Crawford and the captain were taking guard duty. The guns were vaguely aware that Captain Short didn't have the patience to deal with them at the moment, and none could really blame him. Fortunately, they were mellowed by the turmoil of the day and hadn't caused too much trouble. Yet.

The room grew tense as Corporal Keenan came swaggering through the double doors, knocking over a rifle case on his way and not bothering to pick it up.

"*Hoooo boy*, y'all keep dying and I just might win a game one day." He snickered as he shoved around the cash in the center of the table to count it. Mendoza slapped his hand away.

"We lost people today, Keenan. Show some damn respect."

"Oh, cry me a *fucking river*," Keenan groaned as he reached up and jammed a pocket knife through the edge of the vent on the ceiling. He jerked the blade at an angle, and the vent popped open and swung down on its hinge.

"Get over it! They're alien shit now, you gonna bitch and whine over alien shit?" he continued as he reached up into the opened vent, pulling out a stowed bottle of whiskey.

"Sit down, Corporal," Mendoza warned, his eyes tired but dangerous. Keenan just walked around the table aimlessly.

"Why don't all you pussies go out there, shovel up the manure, and bury it with a little cross — we can have a *funeral!*" The marine cackled. "Wouldn't that be just fucking touching? I'm getting all tingly and horny just thinking about it."

"Shut the fuck up, Keenan. No one's listening to your bullshit," Corporal Greene barked from his bunk, his broken leg elevated and his arms folded behind his head. Keenan's gaze snapped over to look at the other corporal, and he took a step toward him.

"Did I strike a nerve, Greene? 'Cause your little boyfriend's a fucking piñata now, hanging from a tree out there with all his meat rotted off?" Keenan chortled, flicking open the whiskey bottle and taking a hearty swig. He laughed a little more, then his face contorted with rage and he slammed the bottle on the table with a loud bang, pointing directly at Greene.

"You fucking watch yourself, boy, if you wanna keep your brains in your skull and your cock between your legs."

"*I said that's enough, Corporal.* Sit down," Mendoza boomed, his rough voice startling the room. "I won't ask you again."

The master sergeant was still seated, but in his dark eyes was a deathly warning that it was in everyone's best interest he stayed that way. Keenan stared at him, his jaw tightly clenched and his bad eye twitching. Before Mendoza could rise, Keenan cracked into a loud, obnoxious guffaw. He grabbed a chair, straddled it backward, and grabbed the whiskey bottle to begin pouring drinks.

"No fun, no sense of humor around here." He chuckled. "Drink, lighten the fuck up a little, yeah? Shit."

He passed the glasses around as Mendoza watched him closely, vicious thunder in his normally kind eyes. Keenan took a few eager gulps of whiskey before putting a cigarette in his mouth and lighting it. He took a deep drag from the cigarette, then huffed smoke across the table as he sang loudly through the side of his mouth.

"Rich man lives in a castle, poor man lives by the sea,

But we cheers to a whiskey glass and a fat girl's ass *'cause that's home sweet home to me!*" Keenan howled and raised the bottle in the air enthusiastically before pouring it down his throat, the alcohol running down his chin and chest as his comrades weakly drank from their own glasses. They watched their cards with dead eyes and held them with scraped hands, playing the game with less and less interest than they used to. They prepared to do it all again tomorrow.

...

Sherri laid in bed on top of the covers, and it felt strikingly like lying on a raft stranded in the middle of the Pacific. Though she didn't know why, exactly; the bed was comfortable enough — at least compared to a hollow log. Her skin was sunburned but finally clean after a well-needed shower. Her muscles were sore, but her wounds were bandaged.

She was home, but so deeply homesick.

She missed Taro and she had no idea when she'd be able to visit him. She missed the Rosenquest brothers, who were in the room right next to hers. And she missed Roger and Carl, who she would never see again. She still couldn't quite wrap her head around that. Maybe she'd managed to convince herself that Roger was still sulking and avoiding her newest theories, and Carl would show up out of nowhere to say something unwelcomely logical. She hadn't known her fellow crew members for very long. But whether she admitted it or not, they were the entirety of her human world now. The compound was their Earth, and they were her village. Her family. How stupid and how stubborn she'd been, not to realize it until she'd left them. And how late she was.

Sherri's contemplative silence was interrupted by a knock. She was just preparing to face the Rosenquest brothers and once again assure them that she was fine, but she blinked in surprise upon opening the door.

It was Doctor Novak standing in the doorway. He almost looked as surprised to see her as she was to see him, and for a brief moment, she wondered if he had the wrong room.

"Hey," she said, quieter than she meant to, suddenly forced to get used to how tall he was all over again. He wasted no time explaining his presence, which she found out of character considering how much he normally loved to waste time.

"Hi. I need access to your research on the native plant respiration. I was working on a new carbon cycle theory in your absence but I'm missing some pieces, figured you could help me fill them in. When you have the chance, of course, I know you're probably recovering. But your test results would be helpful."

Sherri blinked up at him for a moment, catching up with his rushed words, but the aggressive focus on work was strangely comforting.

"Sure, yeah." She nodded. "My test results are in the left drawer of my desk and alphabetized. You had to come all the way to my room to ask me that? The drawers are labeled."

Her tone came out brasher than she intended. Marshall shrugged and leaned his shoulder against the door frame.

"I don't believe in snooping through a fellow researcher's findings without permission. If you did that to me, I'd kill you," he said in an almost eerily genuine tone. Sherri laughed, a more spirited laugh than she'd had in quite a while. He had a way of being funnier when he didn't mean to be than when he did.

"Normally I'd agree, but before today, didn't you think I was..." she started, but he finished her sentence for her.

"Dead? Yeah, I — we... did," he said, his voice becoming slower and quieter as he finished his sentence, like he was wishing he hadn't said anything but felt obligated to follow through. There was a brief silence between them as she studied his face, and he looked everywhere but at her. Marshall then seemed to snap himself out of his thoughts.

"But here you are," he said with his usual nonchalance, gesturing at her with an open hand.

"Here I am," Sherri replied with a small smile, but the words came out wistful. She found herself noticing a dusting of stubble on Marshall's face, the kind she'd only ever seen on him first thing in the morning. Maybe he hadn't shaved today, or maybe she was just noticing new things about his face because she hadn't seen it for a while. For people who had been stuck in a glorified ant farm for months, a couple of days away from one another seemed like an eternity. Sherri felt like she could see the subtle ways in which everyone had aged since she'd been gone. She caught Marshall studying her face, too, and she wondered if he was noticing the same little changes.

"Sherri..." It slipped out of Marshall's lips like a held breath, and she didn't give him the chance to realize he'd used her first name and correct himself. Sherri cupped his cheeks in her hands and pulled his face down for a slow, hungry kiss. The embrace of his lips was gentler than she'd known it to be, but just as desperate and passionate as it always was. As she leaned herself up into him, craning her neck to meet his face, her lips formed into a smile while pressed against his.

"What?" he whispered into her mouth. Sherri quietly chuckled in his breath, allowing her nose to fall into him as the rough texture of his chin tingled and tickled against her skin.

"You don't even shave for me anymore!" she teased in a hush as he smiled and fell into another deep kiss, and she grabbed him by the tie to pull him into her room.

18

PULSE

Business as usual.

It was strange, no doubt, but Sherri had yet to decide if it was a good strange or a bad strange. More likely, it was somewhere in between.

The squid-insect seemed to be doing fine; Sherri had transferred it to a tank full of native soil, vegetation, and water. She and Gio were calling it 'Henry,' which was apparently Harrison's middle name. Unfortunately, Sherri was strongly considering the possibility that it would make for more useful research as a cadaver and she was becoming increasingly convinced she'd have to euthanize and necropsy Henry soon.

She missed the terrosphere. She kept walking past the hallway, stealing glances at the door between the armed guards. All her samples abandoned, the research material that had gone into it, all the answers that would have come out of it, just gone.

But more than anything else, Sherri had been deliberating over what to tell the rest of the crew about her solo survey. She hadn't said much yet; she knew she'd have to be careful what details she disclosed and how she presented her findings. She needed them to know that the natives could be safely observed, only she had to explain it in such a way that it didn't paint her as clinically insane. She didn't see Short taking 'I know because I talked to one' as an answer. They couldn't know about Taro at all. He wasn't a sample, he wasn't a lab rat, and it was her responsibility to keep him sheltered from any possible harm that could come from their scientific objectives. That, and if Captain Short caught wind of a native with a habit of picking people up and running away with them, he'd try to kill him. No questions asked. So Taro would have to remain a secret, even from those she trusted.

Short was a problem of his own; Sherri heard about Master Sergeant Fischer's death, and about how she'd taken one of the natives down with her. She feared the incident had solidified to Short the mortality of the natives and given him hope that he could kill them. Sure, it was possible, but not without getting himself killed in the process. Sherri didn't know what she could do to stop him if he tried.

But she did know she'd have to talk to him. Talk to all of them. So, after lunch, she held a crew meeting.

"Excuse me." She cleared her throat, hoping she wouldn't have to stand on a bench like Short loved to do so much. Thankfully, most of her peers gave her their reluctant attention.

"As I'm sure everyone knows by now, I was briefly missing," she began, attempting to break the ice with a lighthearted tone. The attempt fell flat.

"I saw a lot, I learned a lot." She took a seat on top of an empty table. "I'll spare you the entire monologue, but the experience put a lot of things into perspective. The truth is, yes, the natives are dangerous. But they are not inherently deadly, as proven by the fact that I'm sitting here before you now. They *can* be safely studied. I know because I did it.

"But I think we need to level with each other here, right? All of us. We've been working at two different objectives for a while now, and it's cost lives on both sides. We need to get smarter, we need to come up with a better way to do this."

She took a deep breath, increasingly aware that her next words were not going to be well received.

"I recognize that due to recent events this may sound at best insensitive and at worst absolutely insane. But through my field observations, I have strong evidence that the natives are sentient and intelligent. I believe that they can possibly be reasoned with and communicated with. I know they're dangerous, and I know that so far, they've been our enemies. But what I learned out there is that it doesn't have to be that way. There are different ways to do this, *better* ways to do this. I don't expect you to believe me. But I'm imploring you to entertain every resource and theory we have before resorting to violence. Because put plainly, if it comes to violence... we won't win. We'll never win that fight."

The commons were quiet for several moments and Sherri glanced back at the research team's table in hope of some sort of reassurance. She was met with blank stares and furrowed brows. Several of the guns across the room burst into hysterical laughter but were immediately silenced by a forceful look from Captain Short.

"Can I talk to you in private, Doc?" the captain said, his perpetual glare boring into her.

"No, I think this should be a group discussion between everyone whose job here is related to the native life," she answered calmly. Short let out a sharp exhale.

"Fine. I believe you."

"What?"

"I believe they may be sentient, intelligent, shit — maybe they drink their coffee with milk and sugar. Not a god damn thing would surprise me at this point; the motherfuckers hung my men's bodies from trees. They didn't eat them, they strung them up to *rot*. I've looked them in the eyes, I've seen their sentience, their intelligence, whatever you want to call it."

Sherri blinked at him in shock, speechless for once. He continued.

"And you know what, Daniels? You're right that there's a better way to do this. Tanks and airstrikes. But we're just shit out of luck, aren't we? You said it yourself, we've got a job to do here, and it ain't up to you or me. I'll tell you what you're wrong about, though." The look in his stern eyes grew harsh and resentful.

"They are enemies, there's no changing that. Them or us, that's how it's got to be."

"You're wrong." Sherri shook her head in frustration.

"No, he's not," Doyle interjected. "And if by some miracle you're right about their intelligence, it makes them even more dangerous. We at least need to establish ourselves as an equal threat."

Sherri roughly pushed her stubborn hair back out of her face and against her head with a sharp sigh.

"You're an idiot, Doyle, we *aren't* an equal threat. We're not a threat at all!" She looked around the room desperately. "Will you people just listen to me? Do you think I didn't try that? We won't survive if we keep trying to fight this battle!"

"If I'm an idiot, you're fucking delusional," Doyle shot back.

"I'm trying to keep us *alive!*"

"Let's calm down here," Harrison spoke up uneasily.

"Don't tell me to calm down, Rosenquest," Sherri snapped as she caught sight of Captain Short dismissing his men and trying to leave.

"Short!" she called after him.

"I'm done with this," he called back. Sherri jumped off the table and pointed at the other researchers firmly.

"This discussion is *not* over," she insisted as she jogged after the captain.

"How did you and my mother even end up together?"

"Keep your voice down, boy. The people here don't need to know that."

"Sorry," Kodo said as he barely dodged an axe blow by ducking to the side. He chuckled proudly, still full of energy even after sparring all morning. Kaishek swung Y'xara again, the blades padded by a leather cover to avoid real injuries. Though Kodo wasn't convinced a layer of leather would do anything to stop accidental amputations if he got sloppy.

"Slowly and unwillingly," Kaishek finally answered, then immediately caught a hard tail-blow to the stomach. "-*Ngh*, good shot."

"What do you mean?"

"Well, at first I tried to kill her."

"What—?"

Kodo received the blunt end of the axe to his temple, wincing in pain and then abruptly headbutting the older man with his still-aching skull.

"*Ah f*— ow." Kaishek shook his head to rid himself of the blurry vision. "I was caught under a fallen tree. Iva happened across me, tried to free me, and I attacked her. She thought I was quite the curiosity, I guess, so she left me there and brought me just enough food and water to keep me alive until I was desperate enough to accept help."

The old man rolled away, dodging a strike from Kodo.

"Then, of course, as soon as I was free, I attacked her again. I failed again, considering my bones were crushed by the tree, and immediately blacked out. At that point I was such a uniquely pathetic sight, she took me home and nursed me back to health — you need to get quicker with that left parry."

"You were stuck under *a tree?*" Kodo howled, unable to stifle his explosive laughter. Kaishek whipped Kodo's feet out from under him, slamming him into the ground so hard it knocked the laughter out of his lungs.

"Mhm, yes, Iva found it very amusing as well," he said smugly, standing over Kodo as the young man wheezed. Kaishek's face slowly softened to something else, for a moment, something solemn. Then he heaved Kodo up to his feet with a labored grunt.

"Enough sparring for now, best not to waste our energy. It is almost time to go," the old man explained as he secured his axe back in his harness. Rykr and Leida approached from a walk down the shore.

"Where's Alvi?" Kodo asked.

"Catching up with her friends and family," Rykr replied, gesturing to a lagoon not far away where Alvi sat surrounded by other ocean women. She laughed and talked with them, reenacting the stories from her adventure while they helped groom the woven locs of her mane. Little girls ran around her as well, playing in the water and splashing each other as they giggled. Rykr watched with longing eyes for a moment.

"We should give her a minute before she has to say goodbye again," he finished softly.

"Rebels." Vaus-Kharax gracefully stepped through the shallow wake to meet them, Smiley dutifully escorting her as always.

"I hear you are leaving soon."

"Yes, we are preparing for our departure now." Kaishek nodded graciously. "We owe you great thanks, my queen. Not only for the weapons and the allyship, but for harboring us and providing a safe place to rest."

"Mh, we shall see if it was a waste of metal and fish," she said in her deep, proud voice.

"And we shall see if the metal and fish were worth a tongue," the Lost King teased with a challenging gleam. Smiley looked ready to sever the rest of the old man's tongue, only to be interrupted by the queen's jovial chuckle.

"You're not too bad, ghost," Kharax mused with a smile. "If you rebels survive your journey, send word back to me; we'll keep an eye out for red wings in the sky. I am sending you with provisions for the road as well — food and medicine. Mother knows you'll need it. And if you find yourselves in need of somewhere to rest again... well, just follow the water."

The rebels thanked her again, and Smiley too despite her rush to send them off. As a young ocean dweller came to strap side bags full of supplies onto Kodo, shaking in terror the entire time, Alvi returned to the group.

"Is it time to go?" she asked, faltering.

"You represent our people out there, Alvi," Vaus-Kharax said to her slowly.

"Prove them wrong." She winked. Alvi bowed her head to her queen with a quiet promise.

They left Celesteal the way they came, through the jawbone arch with ocean eyes watching their every step.

...

The trees welcomed them hungrily, and the darkness pulled them in as if it had desperately missed them. They crept through the underbrush as silently as they could, nearly on their elbows and bellies as they quietly made their way toward the river. The trek through the thick jungle was tedious and yet fleeted by too fast, they could hear the rushing water long before they could see it. It echoed through the trees like a beacon, reverberating through the area and drawing them in. They halted as soon as they saw the tops of constructed formations, made of wood and chain, and heard the howling roar of a waterfall.

"Alvi, scout ahead to see how many dams and how many warriors," Kaishek whispered to the smallest rebel. Alvi stalked forward, finding a window to peer through the leaves.

A raging waterfall, one of the many steps that carried the river as it gradually descended to the bottom of the gorge. At the summit of the cascade stood a wooden dam that kept the water high over the crossing points, with a chain mechanism that appeared to function as a drawbridge. Posted atop it, two warriors with the telltale symbols of the tunahk-dahn, and one other minor guard. Alvi slinked closer to look further up the river. There was another dam just past the first, smaller and less robust. On it, one more guard, but no tunahk. She crawled back to where the others waited and quietly reported what she saw.

"Alright, Leida, you need to draw those tunahk away. Keep it quiet, and keep it far away. If we make too much noise in this spot, we'll have them all over us," Kaishek whispered.

"I will scout further upstream first." Leida nodded, "To make sure there are no more near threats. Then follow the river back to the valley and lead them out of the trees."

"That's assuming the tunahk *will* break off to follow," Rykr said hesitantly.

"They will," Kodo assured. "They know what we look like, and they want us dead after what we did to Faro-Dahn and the twins. Trust me."

He barely finished his sentence as a whoosh of air blew past his head and they were startled by the sound of a wet *thunk*.

Y'xara was embedded in a Ramys patrol guard's skull, pinning them to the trunk of a tree as their head split open and blood poured from the cavity like a cracked barrel of wine. Kaishek let out a low growl as the rebels turned to look at him.

"Stay alert, even this side of the river is riddled with Ramys activity," the old man whispered sharply as he quietly stepped over to the stranger's corpse and ripped Y'xara out of their head. They fell to the ground in a bloody heap. Leida shuffled her wings, ready to take flight.

"Wait." Kodo stopped her.

"You're sure you'll be okay alone? Maybe splitting up isn't a good idea." His face suddenly pinched in fear as he seemed to comprehend for the first time that Leida was going off by herself.

"Yes," Leida whispered. "I can fly. I will stay out of reach until you meet me."

Kodo studied her calm face, his brow furrowed.

"I am very fast," Leida added.

"Yeah, you are," Kodo conceded with a short breath. "See you on the other side, okay?"

"Okay," Leida agreed, then took off into the trees with one silent wing beat. She left nothing but a cloud of dust and a swirling of leaves in her wake.

"Short, wait."

"No."

Sherri followed him down the hall, nearly jogging to keep up with his long strides.

"I'm trying to talk to you, *god damn it*," she snapped and cut in front of him, forcing him to either stop or run her over. He stopped, staring down at her warningly.

"We don't have anything else to talk about, Doc," he said.

"Just listen to me, for once, Short," Sherri pleaded. "They're smart, they're affectionate, they may be capable of empathy—"

He began to walk around her, and she followed along beside him stubbornly.

"They have personalities — interests! I can show you my notes! They're, they're like us—" The captain abruptly stopped and leaned down close to her face.

"*Bullshit,*" he snapped.

"It's true!" Sherri argued. "I've seen it."

She had to choose her words carefully, to deliberately reveal only what she thought was safe to share. Too much could put everyone at risk, too little could do the same.

"When I was out there... I saw what's possible. They have expressions, emotions, they communicate, and I really believe we could find a common ground. We just need to be safe, and be smart about it — if we're more deliberate about our contact and more cautious of our interactions I know we can coexist. I know it, Short. We don't have to keep going on like this, we don't have to treat this expedition like a war. We can learn about this planet safely if you'll just—"

"That's *enough*, Daniels," Short spat, nostrils flaring as he seethed.

"I don't give a fuck what you saw out there, I don't care about your notes, I don't care what you *think* could happen. I know what I've seen. Those fucking things will stop at nothing for blood, and I'm sick and fucking tired of sending good men out as fodder so you can run around the woods and try to domesticate the natives!"

"I am *not* trying to domesticate the natives!" Sherri exclaimed. "I'm trying to save your fucking men! And mine! Why can't you just *try* it my way?"

"Because your way will get us all fucking killed!"

"How do you know!?"

"Because they came in here!" Short roared. "Because they broke through the glass like it was nothing, and they slaughtered two innocent women who didn't sign up for all this. And they mauled that crazy old son of a bitch where he stood, he didn't even have a chance. And the motherfucker, it wouldn't even *fucking die* without killing Fischer. It was carved out like a god damn turkey, lord knows how it was even still standing, and it used the last breath it had to crush every bone in her body. You think it did that for hunger? Fuck no, that was *hate*. I saw in its eyes, those fuckers won't stop. They won't stop until we're all dead, or they're all dead."

Sherri stared up at him in horror and anguish, her stomach twisting at his words. Not because of their anger, their sorrow, or their violence. But because she could see in his face that he believed in them with everything he had. Her heart sank as she stared into his eyes, searching for something that was no longer there and that she hadn't been able to see when it was. He just watched her back.

Someone entered the hall behind them.

"We got a transmission from Houston," Marshall said, leaning out from around the corner. He looked between the two for a lingering second, then disappeared the way he came. They both rushed after him.

"RREP Wolf One,

The Planet 7355264Z weather data recordings were received and processed by NASA meteorologists, the results of which revealed a hydrologic cycle increasingly congruent with that of Earth. The further developments have set Planet 7355264Z apart from previous candidates for permanent human settlement and increased its value within the Salvation Initiative. In order to advance the RREP objective within the plan illustrated in the mission statement, any endemic threats present on 7355264Z will require neutralization. Furthermore, extensive samples of the indigenous water sources are needed to screen for possible bacterial and chemical contaminants to further establish the composite value of 7355264Z. The top priorities for the RREP crew from this point forward are as follows:

A.) Militia leadership is to formulate and assess means of neutralizing indigenous organisms, recording all results and forwarding them to mission control through detailed reports.

B.) Research team personnel are to collect and test a wide array of water sampled from every source encountered, chiefly subterranean sources.

Mission Control to Wolf One:

We thank you for your service to your nations and planet.

[message via Houston NASA Mission Control Center- RREP support terminal]"

Doyle paled as he read the message aloud, and by the time he'd finished, his wavering voice was barely more than a whisper. Sherri's blood ran cold. The compound itself seemed to slow and quiet down as it bore witness to the condemning words.

Sherri grew dizzy; she felt the sudden and intense need to sit down yet couldn't make herself do it. Her teeth ached like she'd been struck hard in the face, and two things became clear to her all at once:

She'd gotten herself into something very, very different than what she signed up for.

And she couldn't be complacent in it.

The crew went their separate ways without bothering to discuss the transmission's contents. Their orders were clear, and for once, it felt like there was nothing left to say.

She'd been so naive. *So damn naive.* Of course, she should've known this was how it would end. How else could it have ended? A tale as old as man himself, a pattern repeated by the century. Search, find, take, burn. Rinse and repeat.

Sherri's mind raced frantically as she paced back and forth in her room, clutching her fingers over her mouth as if scared that when she finally swallowed the truth, she'd choke on it. They never could have coexisted with the natives. Not because it wasn't possible, not because they were too violent or too intelligent or too different. Because it wouldn't have produced the proper results.

Fuck. What was I thinking?

Being scouted for the Remus-Romulus Expedition had been the most exciting moment of Sherri's entire life. It was supposed to be the crowning achievement of her career, the opportunity to do something truly and uniquely amazing with her life. She had been so obsessed with discovering what was out there, with feeling it in her own hands, that she'd never once stopped to consider what would happen when they found it. She had been so blinded by the glory, so consumed with her own ego, that she never bothered to think about what she was really working toward. And the answer was obvious. So, so obvious, and she was just a fool.

They would destroy it. There was no other outcome. They found a planet, a planet that had spent eons evolving and forming into the vast, magnificent, fertile world it was today. And she was actively responsible for convincing them it was *the* planet. Her research and her discoveries were proof of its sustainability. Her head spun with guilt and desperation; potent nausea flooded her throat. Her work made this possible. And she knew what came next.

Mission control would make them learn everything possible about the valuable ecosystem. Once the numbers had been crunched and they'd proven the planet was an ideal colony, they'd send a clean-up crew. If it couldn't be used in some way, it would be destroyed. Who could know what would've happened to the original RREP team at that point, who would care? They'd send armies, explosives, tanks, and airstrikes — just like the captain said. They'd cut off water and food sources, whatever they had to do. They would gut and defile every crevice of the rich world, and they would starve out every native creature that dared to call it home. Then they would bulldoze the entire planet, sow Kentucky bluegrass, and put up white picket fences over the graves of the innocents and the evidence of their evils.

And when Planet 7355264Z was bled of all it had to give, when it was burned and barren and pillaged, they'd find another. Rinse and repeat.

Leida scanned the jungle as she soared silently from tree to tree. It would have been easier to fly far above the canopy at much higher altitudes, and safer too. But she needed to confirm there were no lurking reinforcements and search for the perfect opportunity.

She found it.

Two ghaengste walked through the jungle brush below, both lightly armored and wielding blades. They spoke to one another, but Leida didn't listen to their words. She was focused on the red hue painted across their eyes — the mark of the tunahk. She silently leaped to a lower branch, moving carefully, quietly, and gently like one of the leaves that floated down from the trees. As she found a better scouting angle, the hair on her neck and shoulders stood on end. One of the warriors was a tall, slim, dark-pelted woman. Strung around her neck, a twisted and curved horn not unlike Leida's own. The harbinger, just like Kodo described.

...

"We should not be this far east," Lih hissed. "Rataan and Faro were ambushed by the western mines. We should be scouring that area for the rebels."

"Rataan-Leih said to patrol every corner. We will find them," Teihnan replied.

"I just..." Lih sighed, shaking their head. "I want them dead. I can't lose anyone else."

"I know," Teihnan whispered.

Both warriors stopped in their tracks as the wind changed, and a chilling scent hit their nostrils. Sky dweller.

Teihnan turned to Lih to confirm they sensed the same thing.

"Do you —"

A bright flash of light, a sickening *shhhink*, and a black splatter.

Teihnan stared at Lih with eyes wide and glazing over, still standing though her throat was slashed ear to ear. A thick pour of hot inky blood flowed out of her neck, a gushing waterfall of slick oil seeping down her chest and soaking the ground at her feet. The horn around her neck was gone. A guttural sob left Lih's lips before they could stop it.

"Teihnan!" Lih shrieked in agony as the dark woman went limp and crumpled into the growing pool of blood, and a red feather gently fluttered to the ground. Lih drew their blade from their back as scarlet wings launched through the canopy above. They tore their tearful gaze from Teihnan's hollow, dimming face and took off in a dead sprint, tearing through the jungle after the flying enemy.

...

One dead, but it was lucky. Leida knew that was their only opportunity to take a tunahk warrior off guard, and killing the others wouldn't be so easy. She swooped through the trees as fast as the wind itself, hearing the warrior behind her screaming death threats. It wasn't one of the three she'd met, and she wasn't sure if they had recognized who she was yet. She figured it didn't matter, considering she'd just slain their comrade in front of them. Leida barrel rolled and dipped through the branches with skill; a life on the run had her well prepared. But this time, she wasn't trying to get away. Before long, she shot over the dams and swooped southwest at the waterfall.

"Look up! They killed Teihnan!"

"Go!"

It was impossible to miss their cue. Leida came shooting through the air over the river like a meteor and brought with her a blazing trail of chaos.

She'd collected an extra warrior, who had vaulted over both dams and gotten the two tunahk at the checkpoint to join the chase. Leida soared away through the trees as quickly as she'd appeared, three Ramys tunahk-dahn in her wake scrambling through the branches and hungry for her blood. The other rebels reminded themselves that if she got into trouble, she could just take shelter in the sky.

Alvi moved swiftly as soon as the commotion began, and the others hardly noticed as she slipped away and made it to the riverbank. She disappeared into the depths before anyone had a chance to catch the slight ripple in the current.

Kaishek, Kodo, and Rykr were left to wait. They found a sheltered vantage point, though Kodo had to lay down entirely to be covered by the shrubs. The three men stared at the dams, the two remaining guards pacing along them and conversing amongst themselves over the gap between the bridges. It felt like an eternity, sitting there and watching as they waited for something bloody to happen. They listened in on the patrol.

"These wingbacks are getting out of control. It seems like they're venturing closer and closer to the walls," one said. Their comrade called back from the other dam.

"I suppose they're finally getting bored of sitting on their prissy feathered asses up on the cliffs and fucking themselv—"

A flash of gold burst out of the water and sliced directly through his chest and face. Alvi's tail, armed by Whiplash, cut through the flesh and bone in two nearly simultaneous explosions of black blood. Before the guard on the other dam even had a chance to react, a loose chain shot out of the turbulent water and wrapped around their ankles, yanking them into the depths. For an agonizingly long time, all was still. There was no noise except for the sounds of the jungle, the rushing waterfall, and the babbling river. It was almost peaceful. Then the water between the two dams began to run as black as night, an oily sheen atop it, and the rebels' chests clenched as they feared the worst. Alvi's head breached the surface near them with a cocky smirk.

"We don't have all day, boys!" she called into the trees with a whispered hush. Her companions finally rushed from their hiding spot to join her.

The tension in the lab reminded them all too much of the transmission following Roger's death. Only this time, the message from their contractors was not a vague threat, it was a haunting promise. The dwindling research team did the only thing they could do — try to distract themselves with the work that had become their inevitable downfall.

Doctor Doyle had hardly said a word. For once, he had no snarky comments, no insulting jabs. He was too deep in his own thoughts, mulling over mission control's words over and over again. They needed as many water samples as they could possibly get, and not only from trees or streams or morning dew. They needed groundwater. He would have to be the one to get those samples.

He'd known the day would come that he would have to go back out in the field. He was the resident water expert, and they had barely even breached the surface of the major water sources of 7355264Z. But Doyle had let himself get comfortable, too comfortable. Maybe he'd convinced himself that they would all just give up before he had to go back out there. But the day had come, and mission control was calling on him to rise to the occasion.

If any of them would have the gall to send back that fateful 'go fuck yourselves, you can't make me' message, it would be Doyle. But he couldn't find the will or the energy. He just found himself thinking about his wife on a rare occasion since he'd left; he hated the woman and she hated him. And yet, he couldn't help wishing to fight with her just one more time.

"Doyle," Marshall said, pulling him from his thoughts, though it took him a moment to actually look over.

"What?"

"Do you have an extra pen?"

"No."

"I don't believe you."

Doyle just stared at him blankly until Marshall let out a sigh and got up.

Marshall considered sending someone else to get the extra pens he'd stashed, or at least asking. But, unfortunately, he'd set them on the very top shelf of the supply closet for the specific reason of deterring other... shorter, curious coworkers. Not that Harrison or Giovanni couldn't reach if they tried, although Harrison did have a bum shoulder, but he'd rather not reveal the hiding place. Pens had become almost as expensive in their barter economy as condoms. Valuable commodities called for sacrifices, including getting off his ass and getting them himself.

Marshall casually opened the supply closet door and flicked on the lights, immediately taking the first step in, but it was his only step. He froze in place as his brain slowly comprehended what he was seeing.

There was a man hanging from the ceiling.

He was facing away from the door, slowly spinning in a sluggish, lazy circle. It took Marshall a moment to figure out who he was. Then he noticed the yellow tie. Doctor Cuthbert, one of the medical professionals. Marshall seemed to remember his first name being something with a 'W.' William, maybe. It didn't matter.

He was dead. It was clear as he completed his circle and turned to face the door; Cuthbert's belt was wrapped tight around his engorged neck and hung from the rafter. His swollen face was blotched ruby red and royal purple, his lips blued with asphyxiation and limply parted. His head just sort of dangled, cocked to the side loosely as the skin of his cheek brushed the leather of his belt.

Marshall didn't remember him being that old; Cuthbert's hair was gray and thinning, but he didn't think the doctor was much older than himself. Only his bulging face now looked ancient, as if it had already begun to wither away and decompose. The wrinkles around his eyes and forehead were carved deep, wrought with a poisonous shame and a hellish punishment. Cuthbert's scleras were completely red from the ruptured blood vessels; it made his gray irises contrast a milky, sickening, ghostly white. His eyes stared straight through Marshall, stared at nothing. Trained on empty space as though they'd stopped in the middle of something. Like a moving part of a machine that had been abruptly switched off, frozen in place prematurely. A trail of pale foam oozed down his chin from the corner of his mouth; there was just enough blood mixed into it that it was a rotten salmon pink. The already stuffy closet was filled with the thick, rancid smell of death, and it felt distinctly like standing in a coffin.

Marshall found himself surprised that freshly dead bodies apparently had such a potent scent, or maybe it was just his imagination.

Doctor Cuthbert didn't look pained, but he looked far from restful. Numb, maybe. Gone. There was nothing, no life, no soul, no person. In fact, it looked like it had never once contained a life, a soul, or a person at all. Unused. Nothing about it looked human, it was just an empty vessel now. So far from life.

A strong wave of nausea slammed into Marshall as vomit rushed up into the back of his throat, and he instinctively covered his mouth with his fist as he stumbled out and closed the door. He exhaled shakily, blinking hard and slow as he tried to figure out whether or not he was about to faint. His eyes stung and he realized he was closer to tears than unconsciousness, though that felt worse. He heard his name, but for a moment he assumed it was just in his head.

"Novak." Sherri approached, her brows slowly furrowing in concern. "Hey, you okay? You look a little —"

"I'm fine," Marshall said quickly, swallowing a mouthful of bile with a shiver and taking his hand away from his mouth. "I'm fine," he repeated more to himself than her. Sherri stared up at him.

"What happened?" she said slowly, her eyes cautiously wandering to the door behind him.

"Nothing, Daniels, let's go," he assured her, trying to guide her away. She didn't move.

"Let's go where? Novak, what's in the closet?" Sherri demanded with increasing distress evident on her face. Marshall reached out and held onto both her shoulders, looking between her eyes.

"Sherri," he said quietly but steadily. "We need to go get someone else. Okay?"

She stared up into his eyes with alarm. The word came out in a whisper as she stared intensely between his eyes, like she was afraid of what she might see anywhere else.

"Okay."

...

At first, he was going to send Keenan to go do it because he knew the marine wouldn't be bothered by it. But he also knew Keenan wouldn't treat the body with respect, so Short went in and cut it down himself. He did it alone.

Bearing the body on his shoulder was the burden of more than another life gone. It was the weight of the innocent nurses and the guilt that would haunt the captain for the rest of his life. The weight of every lost soul on board, alive and dead, and the end of their journey dragging closer every day. It was the weight of the sins they had committed, and the sins they would commit, and the sins of others long before them that they bore like the rest. Cuthbert chose his own retribution, but it was the same fate as them all.

They awaited their penance not with dread, nor with welcome. They awaited it like the passing of time itself, always far too much and always far too little.

Everything after that went by too fast to keep track of. The remaining medical team confirmed the time and cause of death, they had yet another crew meeting, yet another unmemorable memorial, and yet another moment of silence. It could have been survivor's guilt following the death of the two nurses, but it could have been anything or everything. No one could fault him, and they tried not to envy him. Hopelessness suffocated the closed-in walls and choked the winding halls of the compound.

Doyle insisted they go on a short water sample survey as soon as possible. He'd made it clear he intended to do the bare minimum of his duties to get mission control off his back, and he seemed to think that was best done before their manpower and ammunition decreased any further. Captain Short couldn't really blame him for that conclusion, and none of them tried very hard to talk him out of it. They reluctantly agreed to get in and get out, and Sherri begged Short not to go looking for a fight. At least not when they had a scientific objective. He conceded, but he knew it wouldn't last long. The transmission spelled it out in plain English — he and his men were to figure out how to kill the natives one way or another. He figured Doctor Daniels was going to get in his way at every turn, but his fate was just as sealed as Doyle's was.

They all had a job to do.

"You will need to eat eventually."
"I've eaten."

Rataan gave the woman beside him a look; he knew Iago hadn't been eating. He wouldn't be surprised if she eventually just wasted away into nothing, and at this point, he wasn't sure if he cared. Maybe she was just more dead weight.

"If you starve to death, you will never avenge Faro or Io," the commander said coldly.

"I will not *starve to death*," Iago hissed. "What are we doing, Rataan? We should have gone after the rebels immediately after the attack, and we should be sending troops to Kocea right now, scouring those dreaded cliffs for that fucking winged savage and burning the entire kingdom to the ground."

"Patience, girl," Rataan warned, but an outburst was better than weak silence, he supposed.

"That is not our call to make. The lunai are discussing counterstrikes as we speak," he continued. "But Io would not have had to be on that bridge in the first place if not for the rebels. They are just as much at fault. Focus your vengeance on the enemies who are here now."

Iago fell silent. Silence seemed to be her new natural state. Perhaps she'd inherited it from the quiet sister in her death. Iago had always been the loud, impulsive, violent twin. Now she emitted even more vitriolic hate, but it was a silent, sick hate. It did not fuel her like it once would have. It dragged her down like a sinking anchor, it leeched her strength like a parasite. Rataan had hoped she would use her hatred to avenge her lost sister and brother, but it seemed she was incapable of using it for anything except the chance she might die from it.

"Commander," Iago said, and Rataan was surprised to hear her speak without first being spoken to. He'd thought she lost that ability. He noticed she didn't call him by name, as she normally did.

"What?" he asked as they approached Lih and Teihnan's post to switch shifts.

"Take a breath," the warrior said plainly, and he realized she'd stopped walking. Rataan furrowed his brows and inhaled deeply.

Blood. Metal. Death.

Sky.

The commander picked up the pace, charging through the trees as Iago followed. He cleared a fallen log, and the smell became so potent that the metallic odor stung his nostrils and eyes. Then his paws splashed into a pool of blood. It was gigantic, filling the clearing with an ocean of black. Almost as much as one ghaengste had in their entire body. And in the center of it...

Teihnan.

Her throat was slit so deep that her head was only partially attached. Her eyes were frozen wide open, the pupils dilated into tiny crosses and glazed over with a milky film, her mouth slightly agape. At first glance, it looked as though her severed trachea hung out of her gaping neck wound. Further examination revealed that it was her long tongue, splayed out on the ground beyond her throat. Iago's face contorted to an agonized grimace, and she whined as she shook her head as if to reject the sight before her.

Rataan's lip curled in rage, and his golden claws unsheathed into the bloody soil.

"The calling horn is gone. They are going after the tunahk-dahn. Go get Sahga and Mahrz from the west border patrol, I will get Kei and Kjell from the dams. *Now!*"

He took off in a dead sprint down the river bank.

...

"How do they work?" Kodo asked as Alvi fished around in his side bags and pulled out the flares they'd been given at Celesteal. They were small, unsuspecting bundles packed in dried coral. Alvi handed one to Kodo, then one each to Rykr and Kaishek, and kept one for herself.

"They're glass inside, and when the glass breaks, it causes the reaction that starts the fire. So all you have to do is throw them against a tree," she explained as she hung hers on a braid in her hair for safekeeping. Kaishek observed his cautiously, then nodded in understanding.

"If we spread them out, hopefully the fire will grow large enough to distract the clan while we get clear of the trees and head west," the old man said. "We move quietly in a staggered diagonal formation as we make our way south to Leida. Set them off one by one as we get further away from the river and closer to the clan grounds. We start from the back and work forward so no one gets trapped or burned. Yes?"

The three younger rebels nodded.

"I'll take up the back of the formation because I move the slowest," Rykr clarified. "Then Kaishek, Alvi, and Kodo leads the way because he knows this area. Just don't leave us behind, big guy."

Kodo nodded with a smirk and tapped his horn against Rykr's.

"You got it. Let's go catch up with Leida before she hogs all the action, yeah?" The young man began to lead the group off the larger bridge and onto the opposite river bank. The roaring of the waterfall filled their ears and dampened their fur, and the mist that rose from it hid the intruder that appeared above. They didn't notice him until he called out.

"We've been expecting you, rebels!"

Rataan stood on a rock ledge above the river, shrouded in fog and fury. The gold of his fangs, eyes, scales, and claws gleamed bright and blinding through the thick mist. His scarlet mane blew in the wind and his face curled into a grin.

19
PRODIGAL

"Go," Kaishek ordered. "Go meet Leida. I will catch up."

The other rebels hesitated for a moment as the burning flames of Rataan's gaze rained down on them from above.

"And Rataan?" Rykr asked, the only one who had not taken his eyes away from the looming figure. The Ramys commander watched the rebels calmly, holding perfectly still.

"I will take care of the kaunek-leih. Now go," Kaishek answered in a rush, sharing a nod with his young companions. Kodo furrowed his brows, trying to catch his father's gaze. When he finally found the yellow of Kaishek's eyes, it was as if they were running from his own.

"What about you?" Kodo asked not in fear, not in distrust, but in the tone of a son unready to be away from his father's side. Kaishek's face hardened.

"Enough, go find Leida. I will meet you there." His rumbling voice was reassuring but his gaze flared in impatience.

"But—"

"*Go!*" he roared. "Now."

The Lost King took a sudden step toward the rebels as if attempting to scare them away. This time, they obeyed. Alvi led them, pulling Kodo along as they stepped off the bridge and into the jungle.

Kaishek turned to face the newcomer.

Rataan was now climbing down from his overlook, slowly stepping from rock to rock as he descended to the level of the dam where Kaishek stood. He observed the mountain king in flickering curiosity, studying him like a rare animal. Kaishek approached, his claws unsheathing and scraping along the wooden boards and through strewn chains at his feet like the rattling bones of ancient warriors.

"Rataan." His low boom echoed over the roaring of the waterfall as if it were called through a tunnel. The name tasted bitter like blood, a soldier's name.

"I am Kaishek." His name alone warned of the end and told of the future. A king's name.

"I've heard of you."

The new voice clanged like a sword against armor.

"What was it they called you? The Blood Prince? The Black Revenant?" Rataan spoke as he moved. Inquisitively, deliberately, but his eyes were wild and hungry.

"I have gone by many names, and I have been many things. Prince. King. Traitor," Kaishek said, beginning to turn at a slow pace as Rataan stalked nearer and they met in the center of the bridge. The man before him was younger and armored, though his exposed brown pelt was grizzled in healing wounds. Kaishek saw in him the hearts of a man who had seen battle but not learned from it. The hearts of a man who was still young enough to be angry.

"*Monster. Animal. Beast.* I remember the stories," Rataan spat disgustedly. "You are the tale we hear when we learn of the mountain savages. A feral king, a gluttonous barbarian, a mindless creature. Like the rest of your kind."

"And what are you now?" Rataan asked, a slight twitch to his lip. "Back from the dead with no kingdom to rule, now conspiring with rogue vermin. A *hona'dei.*"

The mountain king lifted his head, watching the commander closely.

"I am many things, yes, I have been many things. But I am no rogue, and I am no hona'dei. I belong to a clan.

"And I will readily reclaim my bloodstained titles in the name of protecting my people."

The old warriors circled each other slowly.

"Your people," Rataan echoed. "Is that what you call the pathetic band of rebel traitors? I will say I am surprised, savage or not, you were once royalty. *That* is the difference between you and me, Lost King, you have no honor. You lower yourself to the likes of renegades and fugitives, you bring shame upon your very bloodline. You repulse me."

Kaishek stopped circling. He raised his silver-bearded chin and stared into Rataan's furious golden gaze. His posture was strong but relaxed. He searched under Rataan's helmet almost listlessly.

"No, Rataan," the Lost King said coldly. "The difference between you and me...

"Is that I am the tale you are told when you are taught of savagery. But you?

"I've never heard any tales of you."

Kaishek unhinged his jaws and bellowed a vicious roar that shook the planet, the long fur on his shoulders bristling on end to form a spiky cape as he drew the axe from his back.

"You think you've heard of *savagery,* boy? *The only story told of you will be the day the Lost King split your fucking skull beneath his jaws."*

A ravenous cry exploded from Rataan's throat as rage invaded his eyes, and he flew at the mountain king.

Kaishek swung his axe with his entire might, but not for Rataan.

He brought the giant blade straight down into the dam below them, the boards erupting into splinters as the entire structure caved in the middle. Shrapnel shot in all directions and the shockwave that exploded from the center of the bridge sent Rataan flying backward away from the destruction. His gilded claws tore through the wood's surface as he skidded to a halt and pulled the spear from his back. Kaishek stood tall on the other side of the concave structure, water spraying through the damaged boards and chains as he stared at the commander. Rataan spit out a guttural rattling hiss and launched himself into the air at Kaishek.

Rataan was quicker; he dodged the deadly axe swings and crushing jaws and kept the other man at bay with his long spear. Kaishek refused the distance, driving forward into his enemy hungrily. His mammoth fangs begged for flesh and blood, his axe demanded contact.

The two aged beasts fought ferociously, horns and teeth and claws and blades tearing each other apart like two warring kingdoms. Their shrieks and roars echoed through the jungle and the waterfall began to run thick and dark with their shed blood as it dripped through the dam's remains.

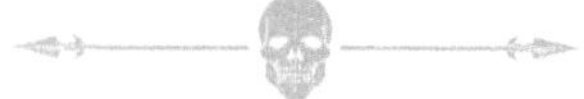

Nothing had been the same since Cuthbert's death and the last transmission. Nothing at all. But the remaining sixteen crew members certainly tried to pretend.

The usual survey team was reluctantly joined by Doyle, who looked like a man on death row. Harrison made attempts to comfort him but wasn't in much better shape himself. Both brothers had been permanently altered by what they'd witnessed on the last survey, and they didn't hide it as well as they thought.

Even Sherri paced and fidgeted uneasily as they prepared for departure, though not quite from nerves. In deep thought, she was debating how unethical it would be to sabotage Doyle's water samples. She hated the idea, she knew it was a bad one, but she'd already decided she had to covertly slow down the progress of the expedition in any way she could. It was all she could think to do, at least until she had some sort of plan. If Doyle's samples were the only collateral, she could live with that. But she couldn't shake the feeling that they wouldn't be.

"Crawford, Mendoza, Keenan, Carnahan, Zheng," Short counted heads. "Daniels, Rosenquest Co., and Doyle makes four squints. Ten heads total, lady and gentlemen. Let's get this over with and get the fuck out of there."

"Oo-rah!"

Sherri made a face as she looked around and realized for the first time that she was, in fact, the only 'lady' present. Although, she wasn't sure if the captain was labeling Carnahan a gentleman or just excluding them entirely. She shoved the distractions from her mind as the group stocked their backpacks, loaded their weapons, and tied their shoes in preparation for the survey. Sherri noticed Marshall leaning on the wall in his usual spot at the entrance to the hallway, seeing them off.

"Gonna be all alone today, try not to get into trouble," Sherri called over to him, though her tone was laced with bittersweetness at the vacancy of the once bustling compound.

"I'm thinking about throwing a party," Marshall replied nonchalantly.

"Oh yeah? Sorry to miss it," she teased, briefly forgetting about all the perils ahead.

"Mhm, med team and I have some pretty insane plans." He winked, though kept a straight face and cool demeanor like she might've believed he was serious if they weren't on an alien planet, or if he had any sort of friendship with the med team. She chuckled, unsure if he was being intentionally dorky or just sarcastic as usual, but his carelessness gave her comfort. She supposed it must have given him some too.

"I expect an invitation next time, okay?" Sherri said as she finished tying her boots and stood up.

"If you live to see it, sure." Marshall shrugged, but she could see on his face that was his way of saying 'be safe, see you soon.' She waved him off as the first whirrs and clicks of the door began to sound out through the hallway.

"I'll be there."

It was almost routine now, the blinding light, the gust of fresh wind, stepping single file down the stairs. But then they were faced with the daunting cloudless sky, its stars, its spectating planet, and they were reduced to an earlier stage of evolution. Put out in the open air and under the blazing suns, they were no longer humans on a mission. They were no longer scientists or soldiers. They were simply trespassers seeking asylum, victims seeking mercy, criminals seeking judgment. They were stripped bare to only what they sought and what they deserved.

For once, Sherri found herself studying something other than the vibrant world around her. Instead, her gaze kept wandering back to her own crew. She saw dead eyes, droplets of sweat, and shallow breathing. She silently cursed Short for insisting they take such a large team; she'd begged him to keep it small and quiet. If only she'd had more time to speak with him, more time to plan before they'd gotten that damned message. Maybe they could have finally met in the middle. Now, as she watched his tense jaw and twitching fingertips, she thought they might never get that chance.

Part of Sherri believed no matter what, the mission would fail. Part of her couldn't imagine the planet quivering at anything, surrendering to anyone. The ground beneath her felt solid in a way she could hardly understand, inherently unable to yield. But it didn't matter. She couldn't be complicit in its downfall, she wouldn't bear witness to its collapse. Perhaps that meant she would bear witness to her own downfall and the collapse of her friends in its place. And maybe that was a worthy sacrifice, but maybe it wasn't.

She was distracted from her dilemma as they were once again surrounded by the jungle, and she remembered how chilling it once was. Upon first entrance, all life hid away in the dreadful shadows, the forest silent and still, and it warned of terrible fates for those who did not kneel before its roots. It was not the world she'd gotten to know with Taro. It wasn't the world she'd been accepted into with open arms and a motherly womb. It was now the valley of the shadow of death, and as they walked through it, they did not fear its evil. They feared damnation for their own evil.

"Waterboy," Short called from the front of the group, his voice more hushed than Sherri had ever heard it before.

"What are we looking for?" He turned back to look at Doyle, who made a face at the phrase 'waterboy' when he realized the captain was talking to him.

"I need somewhere I can drill a borehole and siphon water out. The ground here is too hard. We should be looking for somewhere near a creek or a stream," Doyle explained in a slightly raised whisper. Short nodded, treading along slowly.

"Low voices, close formation, in and out. No wandering off. I'm talking to you, Daniels," the captain whispered to the group, not taking his eyes off the trees as he scanned. Sherri stepped on the back of his boot.

"In and out, I remember. I'll be good," she whispered back. She didn't expect him to believe her, but she desperately hoped that it would go as he planned. Whether the captain accepted it or not, Sherri wanted the same thing that he did — to get everyone back inside safely. At least, she hoped that was still all he wanted.

Unfortunately, what he wanted didn't matter. He had just been effectively ordered to hunt the natives, and in the time she'd known the man, Sherri knew one thing about him for sure: he would follow his orders, and he would complete his mission. So if they said hunt them, he was going to hunt them.

Her sureness in that fact was solidified by the whispers ahead.

"This is a shoot-on-sight operation, but we can't afford to waste rounds, you hear me? We don't need this jungle lit up like a god damn white neighborhood on Christmas, you shoot where it counts or you don't shoot at all. Head, neck, chest, stomach. Especially stomach. Everyone's got grenades, use them."

The sergeants on either side of him, Crawford and Mendoza, confirmed. He sent them to reiterate those instructions to the soldiers at the back of the pack as Sherri jogged up next to him.

"Hey. What the hell happened to not looking for a fight?" she hissed.

"I promised to peace-keep to the best of my ability, and I will," Short responded dryly.

"Shooting all the animals in the face on sight is not peacekeeping."

Short shook his head and finally looked down at her.

"Look, Doc, that's the best I can do. My men are instructed to only fire off a shot if they have to. In the case of seeing one of the damn things, that's a 'have to' basis, you understand? Get off my back and do your job."

Sherri bit back an insult, then calmed herself with a deep breath.

"Okay, just compromise with me here, dude —"

"Don't call me dude, I ain't your friend."

"Whatever. If you have to shoot on sight, fine. But how about shooting on *their* sight? Because if a native is minding its business and one of your trigger-happy toy soldiers *shoots it in the side of the head*, we're going to have a bloodbath where it maybe could have been avoided. Right?" Sherri looked up at him hopefully.

Short gritted his teeth and scowled intently at the horizon like he was fighting himself.

"But if one of them shows indication that *it* saw *us* and I open fire, you'll stay off my ass?"

Sherri pursed her lips but hesitantly nodded.

"Yeah."

The captain walked in silence for a few paces, and for a moment, Sherri thought he was just ignoring her in hopes she'd go away. She was about to remind him of her presence when he finally spoke.

"Fine. Deal."

Kodo, Alvi, and Rykr charged through the jungle silently, their noses close to the ground to keep from choking in the smoke. They were wise about their placement of the flares; the fire grew and spread like a virus as it ate through the forest around the Ramys clan. The towering water-filled cinceida trees resisted the fire well, but the lower canopy and shrubbery burned into a hot inferno. It brought a twinge of pain to Kodo's heart, seeing his homeland engulfed in bright emerald flame and black smoke. He reminded himself that after the destruction would come new life, and he held onto that knowledge tight. He clung to its truth.

"How the hell will Grandpa get through this to meet us in the plains?" Alvi called to her companions as they swiftly raced the flames.

"He'll find a way," Kodo answered, "but we need to get out of here, clan ghaengste will be here any minute to get this under control."

They scrambled through the brush; the smoke and roaring flames made it hard to see what was around them. But Kodo knew the area well, he kept his sense of direction as he led them south toward Leida.

Alvi's ear twitched and she cried out before she'd even turned around. *"Rykr!"*

Without hesitation, Rykr pulled his hammer from its sheath and spun around. He struck the figure behind him in the side with a crack so loud it rang out over the tumult of the fire.

"It's just a patrol, pick up the pace!" he called to his companions ahead as he dropped the hammer on the Ramys guard's head for good measure, leaving a slick mess on the grass in its place. He picked up the hammer and kept running.

"I can see the tree line," Kodo shouted over the growing raucous. "Go!"

He reached behind and picked up Alvi, setting her on his back as he rose to his full height and ran for the meadow. Rykr followed close behind, sprinting to keep up with the taller man.

They burst through the burning brush and into the open air, taking their first clean breaths with grateful heaves.

...

Rataan was losing.

He knew it; not even his pride could obscure the journey toward death. The mountain king was old, but he was strong. Stronger than Rataan had thought. The commander panted hard from the blood loss and the aching in his head, the blur in his eyes. His spear was gone now, half of it embedded in his opponent's side and the other half nowhere to be found. Kaishek was also slowing down, weakened from exhaustion and weighed down by his massive bulk; their battle had already drawn on longer than either warrior had the vigor for. But Rataan was weakening faster, too fast. He shouldn't have sent Iago away. He shouldn't have wounded himself so badly to feign an attack after he killed Faro-Dahn.

Kaishek lurched for the killing blow of his axe, but Rataan was quick despite his fatigue. He threw himself to the side, clumsily rolling hard onto his back, and the axe met wood instead of flesh. Rataan pulled the remaining strength from his muscles and frantically kicked out with both legs. Not at Kaishek — the axe.

Y'xara broke free from splintering wood and was slammed out of the hold of Kaishek's jaws. The weapon went soaring over the waterfall, and Kaishek just watched with heartbreak in his eyes as it disappeared into the mist below.

Rataan lurched for his neck, clamping down hard through the heavy fat and thick hair. Kaishek roared in pain and rage, his wooly layer of fur protected against the jaws of normal ghaengste, but Rataan's gilded fangs sank through his flesh like a heated dagger. Kaishek thrashed frantically, biting at anything in his reach — jaws clamped down on Rataan's horn. The old king began wrenching with all his strength to pull Rataan's sharpened fangs from his neck. Rataan howled through the mouthful of blood and flesh, but he refused to release. Instead, Kaishek slowly forced the horn straight from Rataan's skull as he pulled. It finally ripped free at the base, leaving behind a bloody hole of crumbling bone.

Rataan shrieked out a long, agonized wail but held on still, frothing and hissing in desperate fury. He violently thrashed his head like a hungry animal despite the blackness flooding down from the gouge in his skull. His ravaging fangs ripped and flayed Kaishek's flesh wide open. Then mammoth claws dug into Rataan's back to crush him in place down onto the wood surface, and the Lost King forced himself away. His flesh, fur, and skin were shredded into tatters as Rataan's bite was gored straight from his thick neck, and he roared in wounded torment as blood poured from the gaping wound. Kaishek was now unarmed and bleeding out profusely and rapidly, but his eyes glowed with fresh, hot rage. He lunged, headbutting Rataan in the side and throwing him clear across the bridge. Rataan tumbled to a halt, limp from fatigue and breathing shallowly as his ribs fractured in his body. Slowly, the commander forced himself to rise once again.

"You... will not make it out of this land alive." Rataan laughed, slurring through the thick ropes of blood that choked his throat. Kaishek's fur was now solid black, his white markings stained by the blood that covered his body. He wheezed as he slowly walked nearer to the commander.

"That's alright," the old king said on a sigh as if musing about the weather. "I have had a long story. Perhaps too long. My people will carry on without me."

Kaishek marched tiredly across the bridge toward where Rataan was barely keeping his footing.

"But you, Rataan," he called boldly through huffs, "I promised you a worthwhile tale."

Rataan's jaws frothed bloody saliva as he panted, his grotesque wounds oozing oily liquid on the ground below his quivering feet. His head hung in weakness, but his eyes burned with wrath. Still, he limped forward to meet the mountain king, his bloody claws shuffling through the chains on the ground, scraping the wood as he dragged himself nearer.

"Fighting to the last moment, I see," Kaishek growled, baring his bloodied saber fangs. "You'd rather die than accept a changing world."

"I will fight for the glory of the Ramys clan until my dying breath," Rataan hissed, spitting the thick blood from his throat and letting it drool down his chin. "Because I have *honor*, like my people."

"Because you are arrogant, and cowardly like your people," Kaishek heaved back, breathing in a few hungry gasps as his muscles clenched.

"And you will *die an arrogant coward*," the old king bellowed. He stood tall despite the gaping gouge in the muscle of his neck, the chunks of skin and fat that hung from it, and the hot slick of bloody sweat that covered him.

Then he rose to his hind legs and released a battle cry like an exploding sun as Rataan leaped.

Kaishek's jaws clamped down not on flesh, but something hard. Metal. His eyes caught a silver shine between Rataan's golden teeth.

It was already too late by the time he felt the chain loop around his throat. The king and the commander grappled backward over the waterfall.

Crack

Rataan desperately grabbed at the chain, but he was too weak. His body ached and gave out as his muscles surrendered. He flailed down the length, claws clumsily scratching at the lifeless form at the end to no avail. He fell into the raging water below.

This was not how it was supposed to end.

His lungs filled with water.

You haven't even seen your victory.

He fought to keep conscious.

You won, they must see that you won.

Swim, you idiot. You weak fool.

And then something grabbed him.

The river washed the blood from his fur, where his own had mixed with the blood of the mountains. The water cleansed him of the filth, it purified him as he emerged from the depths.

Rataan was pulled out of the rushing current, his limp body dragged onto the rocky shore. He coughed and sputtered, vomiting the water from his lungs onto the bank beside him. As he heaved for precious air, he managed to look upon his rescuers.

Raiz, Sahga, Mahrz, Garja. His warriors.

The commander's gaze finally cleared enough to focus on the ghaengste standing over him, but none looked back at him. They looked straight past him, up at the falls. Rataan shook with violent tremors as he forced his head up, tracking their gaze.

The Lost King hung dead by his broken neck at the end of the chain. Blood poured from his eyes, nose, and mouth as he slowly spun like a pendulum.

The forest slowly awakened as sunlight peeked through the canopy. It enveloped Sherri in an embrace of citrine and opal warmth as if it had missed her as much as she'd missed it. The tingling whispers of the trees softened, and the stinging threat in the cold air quietly dissipated. She savored the small gift as the planet took fleeting pity on them, giving them a moment to catch their breath and warm their shivering flesh. Captain Short didn't seem to feel the momentary mercy, or he refused to accept it. He kept his rifle ready; every once in a while, his trigger hand would hover just slightly apart from the cool metal, his fingers clenching and then splaying.

Sherri took her own samples as Doyle checked the ground condition, though silently tortured by the fact that she never intended the results of her tests to see the light of day. She couldn't let any more of her discoveries be weaponized against the planet she'd grown to care for like a friend. It was unnatural and lonely not to share her work, and yet she never once considered not working at all. But as she measured the guilt in her head, she felt a faint comfort from kindred scientists who had come long before her. The doctors, theorists, and academic pioneers throughout the history of mankind who were forced to grapple with the very same responsibility she had. To refuse to let their knowledge be abused, or their findings to fall into the wrong hands. Perhaps knowing when to hide was as much an integral part of being a scientist as the science itself.

"Harrison," she whispered as she remembered the questions left unanswered in her journal.

"Yes, Doctor?" he responded.

"When did jewelry become commonplace in human civilization and why?" she asked curiously, though still scanning the area. Harrison seemed all too enthused to answer but kept his voice low.

"Well, wearing adornments is a practice almost as old as civilization itself. In some societies, it predated clothing, even. Since the dawn of homo sapiens, we've decorated ourselves for many reasons — spiritual, hierarchical, sexual. You know, there's a theory that our attraction to shiny, sparkly things like diamonds and pearls stems from our attraction to light reflecting off of water? Though I

— did that rock just move?" Harrison stopped in his tracks, staring ahead with his heavy brows furrowed. His eyes held not fear, not yet, just quizzical interest.

"Short. Stop," Sherri whispered ahead to the captain. She hadn't seen what Harrison spotted, but she believed him all the same. Captain Short held out his hand to halt the entire group.

There was a sudden chorus of rifles clicking off their safety.

"Why are we stopped?" Doyle asked, and Giovanni looked at his brother and friend as if to ask the same thing.

"Which rock?" Sherri whispered up to Harrison, ignoring the question.

"Big boulder straight ahead, completely covered in moss, you can't miss it. There's another rock to the left of it, and a tall plume of grass."

"I see i— holy shit."

It moved, they all saw it. The soldiers raised their rifles in sync as the boulder slowly began to wiggle, then raised out of the ground slightly.

"Hold fire..." Short murmured to his men as the group stared ahead in silence. The boulder abruptly lifted from the soil, followed by the rock beside it and the plume of grass. Only the boulder had a face on its underside and twisted horns that ripped out of the ground, tangled in roots and moss.

As the creature slowly rose, they were struck by the magnitude of it. It was gigantic, the size of a small house, but even taller as it just kept rising. The first boulder was its head; it was further revealed to be covered in thick green fur with a shaggy beard and backward-curved tusks. The second rock with the pluming grass was a gigantic hump, an erect mohawk of long olive-colored fur trailing down it. It resembled a colossal bison, covered in moss and dirt and roots, with broad scales under its belly and heavily muscled legs that ended in wide paws. Small beady eyes glowed an iridescent white on the sides of its mighty skull, almost as if it were blind. After standing up to its full height, it pulled a long, thick tail almost indiscernible from a tree root out of the ground. With it, the flowers, grass, and shrubs that were growing on top of its shaggy fur were carried up above the ground, as if its hide were part of the planet's crust. It took a slow and lazy step forward.

Short's finger hung over his rifle's trigger, and the eyes of his subordinates glanced at it with each passing second. Every member of the team dripped in warm sweat despite the chilling breeze.

"*Do. Not. Shoot,*" Sherri hissed. "Either it doesn't see us or doesn't care."

The massive beast shuffled ahead into the trees with slow steps, paying no mind to the humans. As it gently shook its hide, shrugging off the remnants of its slumber, insects and winged creatures resembling bats fluttered out of its thick fur and into the canopy. Tiny luminescent particles floated up from the ground in wake of its footsteps, as thunderous as an earthquake yet gentle like a soft embrace.

Captain Short gradually lowered his weapon. The other soldiers reluctantly followed his lead.

They stood in frozen silence, watching as the titan wandered peacefully through the trees without so much as a second glance at them. Its heavy steps left behind a patient, tranquil weight, like a magnificent canyon carved over the course of centuries by a tiny stream. They might have believed it was a god or a deity — its ethereal gaze was all-knowing and its colossal form was as mysterious as the planet itself. The trunk-like tail dragged sluggishly through the soil, carving a long ditch as it trekked on. The small ecosystem growing along its spine softly jostled with each leisurely stride. A long, restful sigh so low it vibrated the entire atmosphere heaved from its gaping nostrils; a sleepy breath after lifetimes of carrying the jungle on its strong back and nurturing the seeds of creation. The planet stirred to welcome it into the morning, to thank the beast for its stewardship, and to sing with blissful revival. The suns shone through the canopy to warm its mossy hide; small animals hovered around it to guide its way.

The survey team stood there long after it left, their guts hollow in awe and their legs weak with the veiled instinct to kneel in the benevolent god's wake. It vanished in the giant winding trees as mysteriously as it had appeared, the only trace of its presence the deep track of its tail and the vast crater in the ground that bore testament to its slumber.

Eventually, they continued on.

...

"You *sure* you can't use this dirt?"

"Positive, it would break my boring pipe. It's not about the *dirt*, it's about what's *under* the dirt. Don't think about it too long, wouldn't want you hurting yourself."

Captain Short shot Doyle a warning look but walked on in silence as the oceanographer continued assessing the ground.

Sherri could barely hear the bickering of her teammates; she was still thinking about the moss bison. It was the embodiment of the world she'd grown to love so dearly, the world that Taro had invited her into. It filled her with ease, the sight of such a gigantic beast that regarded the world around it with such tenderness. She felt deeply fortunate to have witnessed the timid creature, and she entertained the idea that they'd been walking right on top of the native fauna this entire time. A rising hope began to form in her chest after hope had become a blessing she'd given up on. There was peace on this planet, true harmony and true mercy. They all saw it in the titan's serene gaze and its tranquil rest. In the gentle disregard it granted them, the greatest gift they could possibly beg for. Sherri was finally pulled from her thoughts by the feeling that she was being watched.

She looked around at the rest of the team. For the most part, they were all preoccupied. Her eyes landed on Short, and it occurred to her that maybe she had something to tell him.

"Thanks," she said as she walked past him. He glanced down at her from the corner of his eye.

"For not shooting that thing because I asked you not to. That was..." She trailed off as she attempted to verbalize her appreciation for him, but it was far from natural.

"That was surprisingly reasonable of you."

The captain made the most animated face of annoyance she'd ever seen him make.

"I pray for you, Daniels, you know that?" he replied. Sherri almost laughed, but instead just raised her hands in surrender.

"Sorry I said anything."

"Go away."

"I'm going!"

She shook her head with a soft chuckle but left him alone to go take some more samples. As she squatted down to pick up a small seed pod of some sort, she once again got the feeling of being watched. Only this time, it was so near and so intense it made her skin prickle. She slowly scanned the area around her. Her chest tightened as her gaze focused into the bushes ahead.

Bright emerald eyes, watching her with an unmistakable kinship.

Taro.

No.

Sherri's stomach lurched in horror. The captain was only paces away from her, and she was surrounded by soldiers fanned out through the brush. If any of them spotted him, she knew they would open fire. He was staring right at them, his pupils dilating rapidly in curiosity.

She stared, frozen, her eyes piercing into his, and she hoped he could somehow tell in her gaze that he wasn't safe. But he didn't fear them, why would he? He didn't understand enough English for her to tell him to leave. Her heart pounded out of her chest, she had to protect all of them. All of them. *Fuck, Daniels, think.*

A giant tawny paw stepped out of the brush tentatively. He was coming out.

No, no, no, he trusts me too much. She could see it in his gaze; he was timid but he thought there was no danger. He was just happy to see her. He was just happy to see friends. Tears welled in Sherri's eyes as she imagined the next few seconds — the call as soon as he was spotted, the bullets, the grenades. Would he defend himself? She knew it didn't matter. Someone she cared about would die, and more likely all of them.

The image cleared from her head all at once, and her body moved before her mind did. Desperation took over.

A soldier passed behind her, and she lurched up from the ground for his hip. She managed to grab the sidearm from his holster, and it took a split second for him to react without dropping his rifle from his hands. That was enough time.

Sherri turned and fired rapidly at the ground between her and Taro, squeezing the trigger as many times as she could as soil and mud exploded in front of her. Taro disappeared into the trees after the first shot, but she fired off two more before being roughly grabbed from behind. Her wrist was forcibly twisted until she dropped the weapon and she could hear people shouting at her, but she couldn't make out what they were saying. Her eyes were misty, her mind too as she stared at the spot where he'd been.

Please don't come back.

Captain Short's stern voice finally broke through the turmoil in her head.

"Look at me — *look at me, Daniels.*"

Sherri finally made contact with dark eyes, a silver fragment in one of them.

"What the fuck was that?" Short demanded, firmly holding onto both of her upper arms. There was something familiar about the feeling. She tore her gaze from his face to look around at all the wild eyes staring at her. Then she swallowed hard and told him the truth.

"I saw something in the bushes. I wanted to scare it off before you killed it," she said, forcing her tone to sound like that was a reasonable answer. Which she knew, on some level, it wasn't. The captain searched her face in pinched confusion.

"What happened to quick and quiet? You shouldn't even be out here, we're turning back."

He let go of her arms to roughly drag her away by the backpack and pointed at Crawford as he passed.

"You're brushing up on your hand-to-hand training when we get back. Letting a little god damn botanist disarm you, Jesus Christ."

He yanked Sherri along as he turned back the way they came, motioning for the others to follow. She shoved his hand off her bag to continue on her own.

"I can *walk*," Sherri snapped.

"You need a fucking psych eval," Short snapped back, but he let her walk by herself. Doyle protested as soon as he realized they were abandoning the survey.

"But my samples—!"

"Not this time, Doctor, now *let's go*," the captain ordered.

Iago coldly watched the old king's death; she lavished the sight of the hanging corpse and what it represented. It wasn't too late; she could smell that the other rebels were near. As she observed from the trees while her comrades fished their commander from the river, his words echoed in her head, *focus your vengeance on the enemies who are here now.*

And like the hellish incarnation of that very vengeance, the burning smell of smoke and soot stung her nostrils as a hot glow crackled to life behind her. Cries sounded out from beyond and within the blackening haze.

"Fire! Fire!"

"Tap the tree basins! Don't let it reach the border walls!"

Iago slowly turned around as jade flames consumed her homeland, casting an emerald sting over her face. Then she charged straight into the fire, straight through it, passing the clan border and the calls of her allies. She charged along the singed source trail, sparks and embers staining her white pelt black.

She charged for the meadow.

...

As Kodo, Alvi, and Rykr erupted out of the flaming trees and into the open plains, they spotted her immediately. The red wings and white body dancing through the air, soaring and rolling so fast the eye could barely track it, yet still clear as day.

Three tunahk were clustered below Leida, hurling blades and leaping off one another's backs to get blows in. She swooped down for the occasional slash or bite to keep them interested, but hung back as much as she could. The other three rebels tore through the field to join her.

Confusion briefly crossed Leida's face as she spotted her companions. Her momentary lapse in focus allowed for one tunahk to catch hold of her wing, dragging her to the ground. She didn't even get the chance to defend herself as Rykr immediately slammed into the warrior atop her and tackled them to the ground.

"Where is Kaishek?" she called out as Kodo helped her to her feet.

"It may take him a bit to catch up, that fire got out of control," Kodo replied, then ducked as she leaped over his shoulder to knock away the warrior that charged him from behind. The fight began.

The tunahk-dahn fought as one body, swift like the wind through the trees. The rebels began to realize if they were ever going to be worthy opponents, they would need to learn to fight together, not separately. Leida took to the skies, covering her friends from above, but there was too much for her eye to track all at once. Alvi took advantage of her small stature, dodging the blows of swords and dipping between legs — she fought the exhaustion more than anything. The tunahk were faster than Rykr, though they discovered the deadly power of his weapon immediately. They put distance between themselves and the hammer, swirling around him with their choreographed combat so gracefully he couldn't track them. Kodo was strong, and the tunahk knew it. They targeted him, and he was soon bloodied and covered in gashes, but he kept the tunahk occupied for his companions to take them off guard.

"I was expecting more from the famed tunahk-dahn — is this all you've got?" Kodo laughed over the clanking of teeth and blade and armor.

"Not even close," a new voice sneered from behind him, crippled into a raspy whistle by a partially collapsed trachea. Kodo turned to see Iago spectating the small battle, and his smile disappeared. Three tunahk, they'd had a chance.

There weren't enough warriors to focus on all of them at once, and they'd been using that small advantage to its fullest. But Iago made four against four. They only hoped Kaishek would make it to them soon.

Iago's ravenous eye found Alvi, who slid across the ground as she dodged a blow from one of the other tunahk.

"Oh, I've been *dreaming* of tearing your head off, you little bitch," Iago hissed savagely through a cracking wheeze. For a split second, Alvi didn't seem to believe the warrior was talking to her. Then a smirk crossed her face as it became apparent, for the first time, how gravely she'd wounded the fearsome warrior so long ago.

"You mean little old me?" Alvi mocked as she ducked under two charging tunahk, causing them to ram straight into one another. Kodo called out to where Iago stood, blinking as he recovered from a hard blow.

"What are you waiting for, Iago? We were hoping for a fair fight," the young giant teased arrogantly, snarling through a maw full of blood and broken teeth. Rykr mouthed the words 'shut up, dickhead' as he toppled to the ground, wrestling with one of the warriors. Iago looked relaxed for once, less erratic than she normally did. A twisted smile formed across her face.

"Let's hope you four can do better than just *fair*," she croaked back. "It was a fair fight between the commander and the old man, but Rataan-Leih *still snapped the bastard's fucking neck.*"

The battle halted, the rebels turning to stare at Iago in disbelief. For a moment, even the other tunahk stopped fighting, as if wondering if they'd heard her correctly.

"No," Kodo said, almost calmly, like he simply didn't believe it. Iago's lip curled over her sharpened fangs in a wicked grin.

"Oh, yes," she snarled. "The Lost King is *dead*. Hell of a fight, too, *whew!* You should've seen it."

The other tunahk took the opportunity to catch the rebels while they were vulnerable, attacking once again with even more ferocity. Leida, Alvi, and Rykr fought past their disbelief, their hopeless odds, their anguish, and their loss. They fought back even harder. All except for Kodo.

Kodo stood in the center of the chaos, completely still, unarmed and naked of armor. He saw Iago lunge for him, but he made no attempt to defend himself. He watched as Alvi and Leida intercepted her in midair to protect him in his stillness, and struggled to keep the warrior at bay. The battlefield raged around him like a desperate, starving hurricane, and he stood in the calm of the eye. Lost again. Orphaned again. For a short while, he felt nothing at all. He heard nothing, he smelled nothing, he tasted nothing. He could see his friends fighting for their lives, the tunahk fighting for theirs as well.

And then, he was found. Suddenly, violently, he felt again.

Rage.

His body no longer answered to his mind, but to the feral hunger in his gut and the fury in his hearts. He turned and reared, rising to his full height, standing over the entire battle as Kjell lunged for him. He could see the realization of his mistake in the tunahk's eyes. Kodo caught him by the throat in mid-air, then slammed him into the dusty ground so hard his skull shattered on impact and a gush of black exploded against the grass. The giant didn't let go, no, Kodo picked him up and then smashed the warrior's head into the planet again, again, again, until his brain was a gooey sludge on the firm soil. He bludgeoned the long-dead man's skull until there was no more of it to hold onto; it crumbled and dissolved between his teeth.

Sharpened claws raked down Kodo's flank, gouging deep bloody lesions in his back as a triple-headed dagger was plunged into the thick flesh of his shoulder. He rose again, standing above the plains not as a beast of beasts, or a barbarian of barbarians, but as a monster over men. He released a roar so guttural it scraped his throat raw and exploded through the entire valley. Then he slammed his colossal weight backward like a felled tree, he let himself drop onto the warrior clinging to his back. Her spine snapped in half, her vertebrae crushed to dust beneath him as her dagger drove into his shoulder up to the hilt. He didn't feel any pain.

Kodo stood up once again, turning to face the crushed corpse — Kei, the sister of Kjell. He picked the dead woman up by the tail like she was nothing, then hurled her at the enemy on top of Rykr. Lih was thrown far away into the grass by her comrade's carcass, and Rykr gave a quick nod at Kodo before jumping up to continue the fight. Iago broke free from her struggle with Alvi and Leida, and she lunged for Kodo again. His massive skull slammed into hers and sent her rolling away through the grass.

As Iago rolled to her feet through the blinding pain and blurred vision, she witnessed Rykr slam his hammer down on top of Lih's chest to hold them in place as Leida bit down on their neck and ripped their throat clean out.

She looked around as she rose, met by the seething eyes of the rebels and the corpses of three tunahk siblings. She was the last one standing.

Iago roared as she leaped into the air, swinging her sword gracefully with a shower of black as it made contact with Kodo's flank, slicing a deep gash across his side.

"I'll rip out *all three of your bleeding hearts and FUCKING FEAST ON THEM!*" she shrieked as she dodged a blow from Kodo's claws, then slid between his legs and swung her sword at the backs of his ankles. Her weapon met metal instead of flesh, and her eye widened at silver armored talons pinning her blade to the ground. The sword was flung to the side and it slid across the grass, shaving down the blades as it skidded away.

With a flash of white and silver, Leida struck Iago across her snarling face, the razor-sharp claws of her gauntlet cutting through the flesh effortlessly.

Iago's gashed-open face poured floods of inky liquid, covering her entire front in a waterfall of spurting black blood. She screamed in agony but lunged without hesitation, tackling the winged woman to the ground. Her jaws unhinged but before she could bite down, she was slammed off Leida by a strong blow from Alvi's tail, Whiplash slicing a deep cut into her torso.

Iago rolled through the grass, coughing and gasping for air as the rebels surrounded her. She was unarmed now, her white pelt soaked black with blood and soot, but her eye glowed with starving wrath. She laughed as she lunged again, digging her claws into Rykr's back and then leaping off him. She soared into Kodo with enough force to slam his mammoth form down to the ground with a gigantic explosion of soil and grass. As soon as he went down, Iago was again grappling frantically with Leida. She rolled and thrashed out of Leida's grip and caught her by the wing, throwing her into Alvi as both women went tumbling over one another.

Iago cackled and panted as the rebels rose to confront her again. She shook not with weakness, but with visceral, overflowing rage.

"I'm going to slaughter you," she said with a chuckle as they surrounded her. "I'm going to slaughter every single one of you! I'll paint the valley with your filthy fucking guts! *You want more!? I'll SKIN YOU ALIVE FOR ALL YOU'VE DONE! For the tunahk-dahn! For Faro! For Io!*"

Confusion flashed across Kodo's face, and he faltered in his approach. "What?"

"You don't remember?" Iago snarled, bloody saliva splattering from her jaws. "You don't remember all the blood on your claws, *giant?* You don't remember crushing Faro's skull, crippling him? You *don't remember* coming back to ambush him and Rataan-Leih to finish the job? Don't tell me you forgot breaking *every single fucking bone* in our brother's body, you're the only one who could have. Don't tell me you forgot him, or the huntress, or Teihnan, or *my sister,* or everything else you've taken from us."

A deep growl vibrated through Iago's teeth; her eye was crazed, blinded, and starved for revenge. Black smoke and glowing green flames began to engulf the jungle behind her, framing her in a smog of desperation. Kodo glanced at his companions to confirm the madness of the woman's words. They looked back at him with growing unease.

"I killed Jarao," Kodo said suddenly, boldly. "I did it. And I defeated Faro-Dahn. But I left him standing when we last met, I watched him walk away with you. I didn't kill him."

"*LIAR!*" Iago shrieked. "He was weak, and you shattered him to *nothing,* Rataan was there. I saw his mangled body with my own eye — and you're too *fucking cowardly to own up to it, you pathetic rats! ALL OF YOU!*"

Iago was circling now, her hair standing on end and her muscles rippling in fury. *Rataan was there.* The words made Kodo's blood run cold, and he began to realize all at once that this was no longer about the huntress. None of it was, and maybe it never had been.

Iago readied once again, and the forest flames burned hot behind her.

"I wouldn't own up to it if I'd finished off Faro-Dahn," Kodo called to her. "I'd be boasting about it."

At one time, not so long ago, Kodo had carried a deep shame for what he'd done to the huntress. And for what he'd done to the tunahk, and for horrors he hadn't even witnessed. But he wouldn't claim blood he didn't spill; he would no longer bear the shame that didn't belong to him. He took a step toward Iago, looking down at her.

"You just watched me kill every tunahk-dahn I've had the privilege to kill with your own eye. You know exactly whose blood is on my claws."

A deafening crack echoed through the valley. It sliced through their ear canals and blinded them. Then the world began to grow dark, and all five ghaengste turned to look at the rageful storm clouds swirling over the burning jungle.

Limping out from the flames of the tree line, the wounded commander and his remaining tunahk.

The suns shined proudly through the canopy of the ancient trees as they headed back to the compound, and the air whispered playfully with songs of bird-like creatures and crisp breeze. After all that had happened in the recent past, all the weight and the terror that had hurtled down upon them, just a little bit of warmth was paradise. It was one of those deceivingly beautiful days that made the tension melt off their shoulders and tempted the crew to hope for a better day ahead. They knew those kinds of days were dangerous, the kind that made them let their guard down. But they didn't.

It didn't matter.

One second, the captain was passing an extra magazine to Private Zheng, and the next second, the body of a man flew right past them and hit a tree so hard his skull exploded on impact.

Fifteen.

They hadn't even noticed Doyle lagging behind.

Captain Short had just begun to scream out orders to get the researchers back to the compound when a sound like an earthquake shot through the air, drowning his voice in the shockwave. A roaring shriek burst out so loud, several of the people closest to the source felt blood begin to flow from their ears as they doubled over and covered their heads. A tree taller than a building was toppled with a splintering crack, crashing to the ground and revealing something that made every crew member's stomach drop—

The devil itself rising out of hell.

Four natives clambered through the trees, toothy jaws agape and frothing with rabid hunger. Another hideous roar burst forth from one beast's unhinged maw; a second emitted a horrific hissing screech as bile bubbled down its bearded chin. A raging cyclone of bullets erupted, raining fire into the natives. One beast stood above the smaller trees and then slammed its mammoth feet into the planet, the force sending a nuclear shock through the chaos; the others ripped trees up from the ground and threw them at the scrambling humans. Through the deafening gunfire and demonic howls, Captain Short could barely be heard screaming orders.

"Stay back! Keep your fucking distance — CRAWFORD! Get up!" He charged forward and caught the back of his friend's coat. Sergeant Crawford had been knocked to the dirt in the uproar of the raging beasts. Crawford shrieked in guttural agony, and Short looked down to see that boiling liquid was eating through his disintegrating pants and legs with a smell like burning ammonia and decomposing flesh. The captain dragged the other soldier across the ground, yanking him to safety until the weight was abruptly ripped from his hand.

"NO!" Short turned back just in time to see the beast throw Crawford high into the air, then out of nowhere, another native lurched forward and skewered the falling soldier onto its massive horn. It charged on, pinning him to the bark of a tree as its horn drove through his gut. Crawford wailed in agony as his entire abdomen was bored through. It ripped the bull-like horn from his flesh, then caught him in its jaws before he even hit the ground and beat him against the tree until his body came apart.

Fourteen.

Short took off sprinting to the rest of his team as giant claws cut down Private Carnahan beside him, slicing their chest and stomach wide open. He could see them reach out to him after they hit the ground, but he knew as soon as their lungs spilled out of their ribcage it was a lost cause. His boots slipped around in the blood as he ran.

Thirteen.

Short scrambled back to the gunmen as one of the natives thrashed and whipped its tail into a tree. A barrage of needle-sharp splinters showered them as they ushered the research team out of the carnage.

Just as the crew began to scatter away through the trees, the planet began to shake and lurch beneath them. Two of the beasts reared on their hind legs, pounding their feet into the ground over and over again, knocking the humans to the dirt. They desperately crawled through the brush and dragged themselves across the dirt as the other two natives clawed through the trees after them.

Sergeant Mendoza was thrown in the mud and rolled to the side as one of the beasts lunged for him, its treacherous teeth burying into the ground where he'd been seconds before. Before it could dig its maw out of the soil and strike again, the fallen soldier grabbed a nearby branch. He slammed it deep into the native's double-pupiled eye. Mendoza twisted and gored the stick deeper while the demon shrieked, then flung its head up as black blood exploded from around the branch in its socket. It flailed and vomited up more boiling acid, spraying the area with the froth from its gnashing jaws. A splatter of hot saliva landed on Mendoza's arm while he scrambled to his feet, and he cried out in excruciating pain as it began to steam and fester. He stumbled back to the others through the blinding agony and fell into Captain Short's chest. Short caught the sergeant around the body, pulling him away from the battle as he barked orders.

"Cover fire! Cover fire! Zheng, *get them the fuck out of here! NOW!*" the captain roared as he tossed grenades to keep the natives at bay. Private Zheng guided the scientists away, pushing Giovanni and Sherri forward as they tore through the trees. The private turned to pull Harrison along right as one of the beasts hurled its body into a nearby tree, which split in half and came toppling down on top of the straggling archaeologist. He was trapped, but not dead.

"NO!" Giovanni screamed and ran back for his brother, but Short caught him by the arm and dragged him away with Keenan's help. The captain threw another load of grenades to put more distance between them and the natives when he saw Zheng sprint in the wrong direction—

Straight for Harrison.

"PRIVATE! Get your ass back here, you hear me!? *Zheng!*" Short screamed and started firing at the beasts to draw their focus while the young man ignored his orders.

"Get their attention!" the captain shouted as he and the remaining soldiers emptied magazine after magazine into the natives.

Zheng slid on his knees to the fallen tree, and Harrison shook his head as his face filled with horror.

"Just go!" the trapped man yelled at the young soldier. Zheng ignored him, tuning out the sounds of roaring, screaming, and gunfire as he pushed at the log.

"HEY! Heyyyy! Right here, you ugly motherfuckers, eyes on me!" Short cried out and waved his arms frantically at the natives, jumping up and down instead of firing as the others covered him.

Zheng shoved his rifle under the trunk, heaving down on the butt end with his entire weight, attempting to use it as a fulcrum to raise the tree.

"Come on!" Zheng yelled, and Harrison emitted a loud groan as he lifted with all the strength in his body. The tree began to move. Short was successfully distracting the natives now; he'd pulled a flare from his pack and lit it, waving it in their faces and screaming lewd insults.

"*Move it, Zheng!*" he urged between taunts.

The tree trunk rose just enough for Harrison to squeeze himself out, but the others couldn't keep the attention of all four natives.

One of the beasts lurched and tore Zheng's entire head off so swiftly that his body seemed to kneel there, upright, for an eternity.

"*PETER!!!*"

Twelve.

Zheng's headless body fell limp into the mud, and the native with the branch in its eye lunged for Short as he dropped the flare.

It was assaulted by an eruption of heavy gunfire directly down its throat; he pulled his rifle and shot into its open mouth with a rageful scream. It shrieked back at him in wrath and agony, its gaping maw overflowing with chunky black blood as its tongue and flesh were pulverized. The back of its head finally gave out under the relentless fire and exploded, a void bored from the soft palate of its throat through the crown of its skull. It finally fell as the captain was yanked away from the remaining three beasts by his rifle strap, still roaring at them in unbridled fury.

20
REPENTANCE

Aching legs. Burning throats. Pounding footsteps. The symphony of Planet 7355264Z raged on like an angry god. Ragged breaths ripping through lungs as they heaved with the cold wind of the jungle. Adrenaline sending blood shooting through stinging muscles like bullets. It was familiar now, the most familiar thing to the forsaken. Maybe the only familiar thing.

Twelve.

There were only twelve of them now. The other fourteen crew members were skeletons strung from trees, or bloodstains on the floor of the compound, or nothing but fertilizer for the very soil their feet were pounding against now. Twelve left alive.

And six left running for their lives in the forest.

"Go, GO!"

A roar like the sound of the sky falling.

"Don't look back!"

Booms like thunder, cracks like lightning, the splintering of wood.

"Where's Daniels?!"

Screams like the opening of the gates of hell.

The captain looked around wildly through the trees shooting past in blurs and the branches whipping his face.

"Daniels!" he yelled over a horrific rattling shriek.

"I'm here!"

He caught sight of blonde hair and tan skin. Short reached out and caught Sherri by her backpack as she ran past him, holding onto her as they drove forward together. He spotted Mendoza a few yards away through the trees, the other two assets with him. Keenan brought up the end of the small group, shooting wildly at the natives behind them and laughing hysterically.

"Corporal!" Short barked, tugging his rifle strap to usher him along as he lagged behind.

"I'll take up the back, you got her?" he asked, pushing Sherri to keep going and assuming Keenan would run ahead with her. Keenan didn't follow.

"Nope, but I got him!" the marine cried enthusiastically as one of the natives broke through the trees, and he unloaded a barrage of bullets into its face. Short almost instinctively grabbed Keenan and simply dragged him along. But he fought the urge away; he knew it would render them both vulnerable. *Fuck.* He reluctantly kept going, starting at a frantic jog.

"Keenan, we have to go!" he called back, picking up the pace and finally forcing himself into a full sprint.

"Keenan!!!" Short bellowed angrily into the wind, realizing the corporal wasn't going to follow. He made the mistake of looking back just in time to see Keenan take a violent blow to the head, the native's claws slicing through his skull in a grotesque explosion of red as the marine went down, his face nearly gone. The beast snatched his bloodied form by the leg and shook it around violently, then seemed to bite down too hard as the chunk of flesh in its mouth detached from the rest of Keenan's leg. The soldier was freed from the bite and thrown hard against a tree with a crack and a groan. The captain aimed his eyes forward and kept running, spotting Mendoza stop and try to turn back.

"Leave him, Sergeant!" Short yelled at the other man and roughly shoved him on through the trees as they heard a maniacal scream.

"LET'S GO, COCKSUCKER, YOU'RE COMING WITH ME!" Corporal Keenan's crazed roar mixed with the shrieking of the natives and filled the jungle as one dreadful sound.

"COME ONNNN!!!"

They heard him scream once more, a guttural howl that ripped through his throat and then was cut off by the unmistakable bang of a grenade explosion. The ground beneath them jolted and their ears rang as they stumbled to keep their footing. The sound of the carnage behind them pounded through the forest with wailing, hissing, and shrapnel whizzing past. Flesh splattered against the trees and stuck to their clothes.

Eleven.

They fought through the shrubs and winding branches, scrambling over fallen logs and breaking out of tangled vines. For a moment, while their ears were still clogged and ringing from the explosion, it seemed it might be over.

Then the smoke cleared and the tumult raged on; one of the natives burst between the conjunction of two trees and another jumped straight over the first. The third was nowhere to be seen, and one of the remaining beasts had a littering of bone shards and grenade shrapnel embedded in its flank. Still, they ravenously hunted the dwindling survivors as they tore through the foliage.

"Come on, man, you gotta keep up!" Captain Short called to Harrison over the thundering footsteps of the natives behind them. He clutched the older man's sleeve to keep him from lagging behind, yanking him along as they ran. Harrison reached out to his brother, refusing to lose track of him. Giovanni grabbed his hand and held on for dear life, catching his eyes for one fleeting moment as they dodged trees and low-hanging branches. Mendoza suddenly placed a firm hand on Giovanni's shoulder to ensure he didn't get separated from the researchers. Captain Short held tight to Harrison's sleeve but searched the brush to make sure Sherri was keeping up. She was still beside him, looking frantically around the leaves and limbs until she locked eyes with him. He reached out a hand, and she firmly grabbed hold of it.

The five survivors shoved between the trees, soaked in their own and one another's blood. They held tight to hands, shirts, backpacks, shoulders. Hanging onto one another for dear life like they'd known each other forever, they refused to be torn apart. They broke through the shrubs and branches in a haphazard chain, picking each other up as they fell. As they clawed toward the edge of the forest, the heaving of the natives' hungry breaths grew nearer.

Warm bodies burst into the meadow one after the other, finally clearing the tree line. They scrambled through the brushy field, pulling along their companions until each of them was desperately wading through the grass toward the compound. The natives broke through the trees just behind them.

Captain Short let go of Sherri's hand and Harrison's sleeve.

"Go!" he ordered as he stopped running and drew his rifle from his shoulder.

Sherri stopped in her tracks and grabbed a handful of his shirt, trying to pull him along.

"Short, you can't stop them!" she yelled at him, yanking at him to no avail. "They will kill you, *just come on!*"

"Daniels, GO!" he roared back, aiming at the nearest native's face as it charged. Sherri knew she should leave, she wanted to, but her hand wouldn't let go of him. She didn't know if she had it in her.

She didn't get the chance to decide.

Before Short could get a shot off, the charging native was rammed into the ground from the side, and a gigantic billow of soil exploded into the air from the crater where it landed.

A new native stood over it, thin and tawny. His massive claws planted firmly on its throat and his maw curled into a vicious snarl. Taro.

Sherri and Short were frozen in place, staring up at the monstrous spectacle as he released a guttural cry and lurched down to rip out the other beast's throat.

The third native tackled Taro from behind, throwing him to the ground as the first coughed and sputtered at its release.

"No," Sherri cried out in weak desperation before she could stop herself as she watched Taro grapple with the native, its claws raking across his hide in a bloody spray. Taro threw the other creature off and it skidded in the grass and soil like a crashing missile, but the other native was on him as soon as he rose. Tears filled Sherri's eyes as she stared in horror while he was overtaken by both beasts.

The attackers were wounded, but Taro was outnumbered. In mere seconds, the entire landscape was black and wet, and it was nearly impossible for human eyes to comprehend the brutality occurring. The cracking of bones and crushing power of jaws, giant scythe-like claws slashing through flesh. Inky blood splattered across the meadow and the ground quivered like it might crumble beneath them. Sherri's eyes desperately searched the battle for signs of where Taro stood, but someone pulled her away by the arm.

She let herself be dragged away from the carnage, whether out of weakness or the urge to flee, but the pressure was released as she was pushed toward the compound.

"Go home!" the captain yelled at her and began walking the wrong way. He switched out the magazine of his rifle and pulled a grenade from his belt as he marched straight toward the fighting natives.

"*NO!*" Sherri screamed and lurched at him. She grabbed the hand that held the explosive and wrestled it away from his mouth before he could clamp his teeth down on the pin. Short shoved her off him and kept on his warpath, his storming eyes refusing to meet hers.

"Short *don't! Let's go!*" Sherri desperately tried to grab hold of him, stop him, but he threw her into the grass. She climbed back to her feet and lunged again, wrestling with him for the grenade as he rushed nearer to the bloodbath.

"Don't do this, Short, please don't do this. Just let them fight," she cried, a tear falling from her eye as she said it, *let them fight*. Those words were bitter on her tongue and sour in her stomach. He pushed her away again as she cried — a pathetic, lost, childish sob. He charged ahead and aimed his rifle straight into the vicious battle, straight at Taro, and Sherri reached out for him in the only way she knew how.

She took off into the storm.

Sherri ran hard toward the warring monsters, the blood, the flesh, the hellish violence. She headed straight for the barbaric carnage, her face twisted into an agonized grimace. And Short reached for her back.

The captain chased after her, like she knew he would, like he always did. He grabbed on tight and dragged her away from the annihilation.

They ran to the compound hand in hand, away from the vicious shrieks of the battle behind them. Tears streamed down Sherri's face as she refused to let herself look back.

"This rebellion will die here, you know it as well as I do."

Rataan stood tall in the wind, the long end of his scarlet mane blowing in the powerful gusts like the flag of war.

He looked like he'd already been through a war; his reddish fur was singed from the fire and smeared in ebony blood, his muscular hide littered with gaping wounds. His visage reflected a standing corpse, like he shouldn't have been alive at all. Chunks of his flesh were missing, ugly black voids of tar in their place. One of his horns was ripped clean off his skull, leaving nothing but a gushing hole in the side of his head. He was wet from the river, yet it cleansed him no longer. He was bathed in oily black blood; it dripped down his fur like he'd been baptized in it. His muscles trembled in fatigue, but he stood tall.

Five tunahk warriors stood with him, and the rest of them lay dead on the ground.

Kjell's skull was decimated entirely, crushed into a chunky black pool in the grass as if it had exploded. Kei lay thrown away from the others, her body folded and bent in half by the clean break of her spine, blood seeping out of every orifice in her body. Lih's chest was caved in, the bones in their torso crushed and their throat ripped out as they sat curled in a bloodied heap. Teihnan was with neither group, but her fate was made devastatingly clear by her absence.

"It's not dead yet," Kodo called back to Rataan as the wind began to rip and howl, the sky darkening with storm clouds. Leida, Rykr, and Alvi stood close beside Kodo. They were beaten and bloodied, weak and exhausted. The sight of the five new enemies was a villainous laugh in their faces that they had so little fight left in them, and their opposition still had so much fight to give.

But they weren't dead yet.

"The Lost King is," Rataan hissed with a crooked toothy grin, gold-plated fangs gleaming.

"You'll join him soon, you fucking bastard," Kodo bellowed as the first drops of rain began to fall from the clouds.

"Not by your fangs. Not by a hona'dei," Rataan spat back. The four tunahk around Rataan readied their weapons and tensed for the attack, but Iago did not. Rataan stared at the one-eyed woman, the hot embers of his gaze searing into her.

"Iago," he hissed at the bloody woman in between the two groups.

She stood completely still, watching the chaos around her with a wild eye and an aimless, building fury. Rataan's words from earlier that day echoed in her head as the sky's gentle tears began to wash the blood from her face.

Io would not have had to be on that bridge in the first place if not for the rebels. They are just as much at fault. Focus your vengeance on the enemies who are here now.

But the rebels didn't kill Io. She died alone, caught vulnerable where she shouldn't have been. She died alone. Rataan sent her alone.

"It's your fault," Iago said, abruptly calm.

"What?" Rataan growled as rage invaded his face, and Iago's was consumed with the same.

"It's your fault they're dead!" Iago screamed at him, her calmness obliterated as bloody saliva sprayed from her jaws. Rataan opened his mouth, but she flared hot like the forest fire.

"YOU put Io on that fucking bridge! You put her there alone! She'd still be alive if you hadn't given her that impossible task!" she cried as the rain began coming down harder, washing the blackness from her fur. Rataan stepped toward her, his gaze warning.

"Watch your—"

"Who killed Faro!?" Iago shrieked. "Why didn't we go find them after the attack? Why didn't he smell like the rebels? *Who fucking attacked you, Rataan? Who killed our brother?"*

Her demands carried desperately into the howling gusts as her own tears mixed with the raindrops that pelted her face.

"It's your fault! IT'S YOUR FAULT MY SISTER IS DEAD! YOU—"

Rataan's spear soared through the air like lightning, cutting through the wind and the rain until it met its mark with a low *squelch*.

Iago's eye widened in horror at the red-pelted man in front of her. He fell to the ground.

Mahrz crumpled at her paws, Rataan's spear embedded deep through his gut. He panted shallowly, shaking as blood began rapidly pouring from his mouth and wound. Iago stared down at him in shock and confusion, and for a second, Rataan could only do the same.

Then all at once, the storm exploded to life with roaring thunder and cracking lightning. The fire in the forest was quenched in the downpour, hissing with steam as the trees were released from the choking flames.

Rataan belted out a deafening call that reverberated up through the rain, the thunder, the lightning. A long, drawn-out war cry that rang out loud in reckoning, filling the valley and carrying up through the trees and the mountains.

"This ends now!" he roared, charging forward and ripping the spear from Mahrz's flank as he lunged at Iago.

As soon as Sherri and Short crossed the barrier, the turquoise light began to crawl between the posts. Sherri immediately fell to her knees in the grass. Captain Short looked around at his people.

Daniels, Rosenquest, Rosenquest, Mendoza. Short.

Only five survivors and only one of his men had returned with him. He locked eyes with Sergeant Mendoza, and he could see that he was realizing the same thing. The other man's brows were furrowed tightly, his cheeks slightly sucked in like he was biting the insides. His arm was grotesquely marred, still bloody and festering, though he didn't seem to notice it. Short had to catch his tongue to keep himself from apologizing to the master sergeant.

"My god..."

Giovanni broke their wounded silence, his eyes wide in horror and awe as he stared through the fence. Harrison looked too, then Short and Mendoza.

"Fucking Christ," Short whispered under his breath, sucking in some air with the slightest flinch of his stoic face.

Sherri's eyes stayed trained on the grass, her stomach churning, and she thought she might vomit. She didn't dare look back; she couldn't bear to witness Taro's fate. But as a sound like a tsunami consumed the air of the meadow and echoed off the mountains above, she lost the battle with her better judgment.

She finally turned around, mouth falling agape as she stared through the clear blue glow of the fence.

Two more natives had joined the battle, larger than the original three. They had ripped the two attackers off Taro, and he'd limped out of the crossfire in miraculously decent shape. He was wounded, but intact, which was more than seemed possible. But he didn't run away; instead, he sat in the grass a few yards away from the fight panting and resting.

Sherri's eyes wandered back to the now even odds, which she quickly realized weren't even at all. The smaller of the original attackers was now missing its head entirely, and its stomach was split open with its giant organs spread across the grass like an oil spill. The two largest natives were now in the process of ripping the remaining enemy apart limb from limb.

The group watched in dizzy terror as the mighty creature was torn to shreds, destroyed and devoured. The only thing Sherri could compare it to was the sight of piranhas feasting on a carcass, so quick and so violent that human eyes could barely perceive it. Only, the carcass was a mammoth beast alive mere seconds before, and the piranhas were two even more monstrous titans that disemboweled and obliterated the creature not out of hunger, like the piranhas, and not for survival either.

They ripped it apart with hatred and roared in rage as they shredded its corpse to nothing but bloody tatters and splintering bones.

Sherri slowly backed up with the others as the door whirred open, but she was the last to turn around and step inside.

...

Walking through the compound doors was like walking into a mausoleum. No music playing faintly from inside the dorms, no lone shower or sink running nearby, no chattering or tapping footsteps or doors opening and closing. The seemingly ever-present hum of the microwave was absent, the constant tune of someone whistling was too.

As the survivors walked through the hallway and into the commons, they were greeted with silent gazes. One by one, the homebound crew members peeked out from their workstations to check how many had returned. First, the three remaining medical personnel peered out the windows of the med bay to check for wounded, their eyes weary. Then Corporal Greene and Private Wilkes took a quick glance around the corner of the hallway where they'd been posted; their faces dimmed with a stabbing pain as they realized only two of their comrades had returned. And Doctor Novak leaned in the doorway of the lab by himself. Waiting.

One by one, their eyes filled with desolate knowing.

Eleven.

They went their separate ways without a single word spoken.

Iago dodged, but barely. Rataan's spear sliced down her neck and shoulder as she rolled to the left and swung around, her tail striking the weakened man's side. Her own inertia sent her tumbling. She slid away from him as he was thrown in the opposite direction. The remaining three tunahk rushed to his side, lifting their severely wounded commander off the ground.

Iago skidded to a halt directly before Kodo's feet. Silver hooked talons grazed the flesh of her throat as they unsheathed.

Iago stared up at the rebels, her face now washed of inky blood and sobered by acceptance, tears mixing with the pelting shower of rain. Her eye closed, her face relaxed, and her fatigued muscles gave out as her head came to rest on the wet grass in a final yield.

"I'm coming, sister."

The sharp pointed claws were removed from her throat, and the killing blow never came. Iago's brows furrowed, then she reluctantly opened her eye to see all four rebels now looking down at her in cold judgment.

"Fight with us," Leida said, "or die here."

The sky woman's tone favored no option more than the other, and the young giant's dark eyes were completely different from the first time Iago had met him. The eyes of a new man entirely.

"But choose now," Leida finished, looking up at the horizon.

The remaining tunahk had helped Rataan to his feet, though his wounds were consuming his strength and stamina fast. Despite the lifeblood draining from his mangled body like sand through claws, his twisted grin was proud and triumphant as the sound of the beating rain was accompanied by the pounding of feet.

New Ramys warriors were flooding out of the trees like a landslide, the pouring storm dousing the confines of the fire and giving them passage into the valley. They followed Rataan's call, their cries echoing above the screaming wind and weeping rain.

"Fuck," Iago hissed as she forced herself to her feet, wrestling with her trembling limbs, weakened muscles, and bleeding wounds. The rebels weren't in much better shape, but she had nothing more to lose. She rose, staring into Rataan's eyes with a craze to match his own, refusing to bow once again.

"You always were the weak one, Iago," Rataan bellowed over the tumultuous rain. "You are *nothing* without your sister. A suitable death it will be, to die among strangers."

"I would rather die among strangers than fight beside a false leader. A false father. *You killed Mahrz!*" Iago screamed back, though she looked past him at the last three tunahk. Her gaze pleaded with them, but they remained frozen by his side.

"And I would kill anyone else that stood in the way of *justice. That stood in the way of the Ramys nation!*" the commander cried over the torrential downpour.

"What do you know of *justice?*" Kodo snapped.

"I know it will only be brought by wiping every single one of you savage creatures from the Mother's grace!" Rataan roared over the growing storm, drawing his spear once again and taking a stride toward Kodo.

Leida landed hard on the ground in between them, her blood-red wings outstretched and the hooked claws of her gauntlets sinking into the wet soil. Rataan snarled, insanity a kindled flame in his eyes.

"If it takes my *last breath*," he raged, staring at the winged woman, *"I will reap your heads for the lunai! I will cull your vile flesh from this land!"*

Leida lifted her chin into the rising wind, and her wild garnet mane was blown out of her face with a powerful gust. Her hidden eye was revealed, dead and milky white with a horrific gash through it. The grotesque scar formed a lightning-shaped web down her face, and in the blind eye was powerful thunder.

"It will," she promised.

The furious golden fire in Rataan's eyes flickered with disgust and cracking hysteria. He slowly backed away from the winged woman, step by step with his face now calming. The tunahk stepped with him, leaving a growing gap between them and the rebels.

"We shall see."

The Ramys reinforcements crested the hill with a sudden flood of battle cries.

"We're not going to make it out of this one, are we?" Alvi yelled over the tumult.

"Form a circle to protect our backs." Rykr raised his voice above the wind as he backed up, not taking his eyes off the approaching Ramys troop, still singed and faintly smoking. He and the other rebels moved into a circular formation, facing out and ready to fight.

"You can fly," Rykr said as Leida fell into the circle beside him. "You could get out of this. You could take Alvi and find shelter."

Leida briefly met his eyes, shaking her head firmly as the wind ripped at her feathers and hair.

"You are my shelter."

Iago was the last to fall in, completing the circle.

"Fuck!" the warrior snarled. "Why am I fighting with you? You people killed my siblings!" she roared at no one in particular as she stepped through the slain bodies of her comrades.

"You people killed my father," Kodo spat back. "We'll call it even."

"What?"

"They are here!" Leida cried out as the wave of reinforcements passed Rataan and charged for the rebels. They could hear the commander's laughter over the wind as the Ramys forces overtook them.

You can't stop them.

Doctor Daniels' words echoed in the captain's head over, and over, pounding with the headache that the ibuprofen from the med bay was doing jack-shit to fix.

You can't stop them.

He knew she was trying to save his life, trying to keep him from giving it up. But her words meant more than that.

Because she was right. Maybe he could have stopped one of them, maybe two, by giving his life and endless floods of ammunition like Fischer and Keenan had. But there would always be another one, lurking in the jungle or stalking the fence. It was their planet that he stood on, their domain. He and his men and the rest of the Remus crew were simply fleas on the back of the beast, and it would never spare them. No matter what Doctor Daniels said, no matter what she believed with her whole heart and soul, he could see it. He could see inside them; he had looked them in their double-pupiled eyes while they stuffed their bloody maws with the remains of his comrades. His friends. His family.

They were no creatures of god. They weren't animals, they weren't people. They were some disgusting, blurred conglomerate of the two that reflected the worst parts of each. They didn't kill for hunger or survival like wild animals, they didn't kill for religion or persecution like mankind. They killed because they could. Because they wanted to.

And he'd led his unit straight into their foaming jaws, following the orders of people that didn't give a damn whether they lived or died. He'd led his unit to their deaths for a doomed mission that could be completed in no other way.

His mind crawled back to Private Zheng. Back to Peter.

He'd turned nineteen shortly after landing, the kid couldn't even drink yet. The captain was plagued with a rush of memories of Zheng and all the things he'd never do.

You got a girlfriend back at home, Private?

No, Captain.

Why's that?

Why don't I have a girlfriend?

That's what I said.

I don't know, I kind of thought the girlfriend would come with the job. But I guess since I enlisted, I've spent most of my time in the most remote places known to man, with the least girls.

Short remembered his boyish laugh and hopeful eyes. The smile that always gave the sense he wasn't worried about much but was prepared for anything.

And the girl in your picture frame?

Just a friend, Captain.

Sure she is.

Hey, maybe when I come home a couple inches taller with a few more ribbons on my blues, we'll see.

Nineteen years old. Dead. And it was Short's fault, he'd written the letter that got him accepted for the expedition, he'd signed it like a death certificate. He had been asked to pick a private from his squadron, and he picked Zheng. He'd seen that he was strong, that he was smart, and that he was meant for better things than tents in the desert. And now he was dead. Captain Short would carry that with him for the rest of his life, he'd see it every time he looked in the mirror like it was carved into his flesh. Just like the nurses, their names were cut into his back, and those cuts reopened every time he laid down for bed. Their blood was on his hands, already soaked to the bone with red instead of black.

Short found his way to the armory again, as he always did. He looked around at the numbered rifle lockers as he turned around in a slow circle. Some were empty, the tenants somewhere out in the jungle they'd never be recovered from. Some were occupied, but the ownerless rifle inside was scuffed and damaged, stained with an oily sheen. His gaze finally rested on locker 01. His rifle.

It was detached and deeply sinful to look at it caged behind the mesh locker door instead of in his hands. It begged him to unlock the door, it begged him to load it, it begged him to avenge his fallen. He didn't save them, he couldn't protect them. He had already failed. Wrath bubbled over in his gut as the dusty room seemed to vibrate around him, and he breathed hard as his hands twitched with longing. The armory no longer whispered to him, it screamed at him and shoved his guilty face into images of giant burning carcasses and seas of black blood.

What's left? What's left? What's left?

...

Sherri ended up in the control room.

She was alive; she reminded herself of that over and over again. She was alive, Taro was alive. She tried to attach herself to that fact, cling to it with all she had left.

But so many people were dead. Her friends, her peers, shit, people she'd never even exchanged words with but her chest still ached for them. Good people, bad people, what did it matter? Their village crumbled around them, and Sherri's eyes burned with guilt and confusion and sorrow. They had lost so much, and still, mission control demanded more. They intended to bleed every artery of the expedition dry until there was nothing left, and they didn't care who died in the process. The crew was nothing to mission control, they were nothing in comparison to the very future of the human race.

Sherri grew sick to her stomach as she recalled her part in it all. She remembered her excitement to be a *settler*. She'd jumped at the opportunity to explore the new frontier, to be a part of something revolutionary. But it wasn't revolutionary, it was pathetic and filthy and wrong. The land they stood on was already owned, it wasn't theirs to settle. The haunting final transmission declared a hunger for Planet 7355264Z at any cost, it declared a proud desire to destroy what it already was and rebuild it as what they wanted it to be. As a new Earth, born from the annihilation of an entire world that had so much to lose. A world that was rich and old, and full of life and glory. A world with a fertile future that the selfish apostles of mankind could never understand. The expedition would never be considered complete until the planet was brought to its knees.

But it wouldn't be.

They would never force Planet 7355264Z to yield. They wouldn't exterminate the natives, they wouldn't defeat them, and they wouldn't even live long enough to try. In their hubris and their shameful lust to conquer what wasn't theirs to seek, they had become the conquered. They had been brought to their knees. They would die there, and it wasn't a matter of ammunition, or the will to survive, or a chance at redemption. The planet would eat them alive until there were no more.

That was okay.

Sherri stared at the last transmission from mission control pulled up on the computer monitor. It was wrought with arrogance, it promised that their mission would be achieved no matter how much blood was shed, no matter how many people died. But they were almost out of people. Sherri almost laughed through her tears, she could have smiled. They were *wrong*. They had already failed. It was over.

They were all going to die, and there was nothing anyone could do about it. Maybe mission control would send a new crew after another few decades of planning and building. Maybe they would try again after the Remus-Romulus Expedition Project was just a ghost in the archives. But their war was over before it had begun. Planet 7355264Z had won. The final eleven settlers would be eliminated in due time, they'd be remembered on Earth as heroes. They would die and be buried with the mission, and the universe would not weep for them. Their sins would not be forgiven, and whatever awaited them on the other side would not welcome them gently.

But there would be no dishonor in their end. It was the only redemption they had left.

A cup of pens fell over off the desk, clattering all over the floor, and Sherri was ripped from her thoughts. The entire compound began to vigorously tremble and shake under an invisible force. She leaped up from the chair and ran out of the control room into the commons.

The world rumbled violently as if the air itself were under siege. It wasn't the random thrashing destruction of an earthquake; there were no walls toppling, no dust flying into the air. It was an even vibration — steady, consistent, and deliberate. Sherri was met by her teammates evacuating the lab.

"What's going on?" she called frantically to Marshall as he rushed out of the lab, followed by the brothers.

"Earthquake?" he called back over the sound of the entire base creaking.

"No." Giovanni shook his head as he studied the ceiling beams. "Not an earthquake, there's a pattern. Do you feel that? A pulse."

The remainder of the crew clambered out from their individual corners of the compound.

"What the fuck is that!?" Captain Short yelled as he caught a flatscreen falling off the wall. The vibration was accompanied by a distant hum that grew in intensity. It got louder, angrier, yet it sounded far away and far above. Sherri looked around at her startled colleagues, then made a break for the door.

"Daniels!" Short barked as he set the TV down and ran after her. He was followed by Giovanni and Harrison, but none could make it to her before she typed in the code.

"We have to see what's happening!" Sherri insisted as she punched the enter button on the keypad. The hum from above became louder, louder, rumbling and roaring now as the inner mechanism of the door began whirring.

"God damn it," Short growled as they heard the clang of the outer layer. Another few whirrs and clangs, and the door began to slide open from the center.

They were met by a blinding flash of green lightning. Then the pitch darkness of a raging storm as the rumbling became a clearer moan, endless and victorious and commanding like the trumpets of the rapture.

Sherri plunged out of the door and into the pouring rain.

"It's— It's raining! There are clouds!" she cried over the deafening torrent in awe, lifting her face to the swirling atmosphere and allowing herself to be soaked in the downpour. Never a single cloud in the sky before, and now it was covered and blacked out completely. With every crack of flickering lightning, the silhouette of the looming planet above was visible through the angry billowing fog.

Sherri's companions began stepping out after her into the chilling wind and cutting shower. One by one, every single crew member stepped off the stairs and into the wet mud until each warm body was wading through the soaked grass in front of the door. They bathed in the icy pour, they were washed in forgiveness and christened in it.

Then the rumbling noise called out like the infinite song of a celestial whale, filling every trembling molecule of the universe. The humble eyes of the settlers traveled up to the endless rageful sky, as something pierced the dark sea of clouds like a silver lance.

A shuttle descended through the storm, mighty engines screaming over the apocalyptic monsoon. It slowly sank toward the surface of Planet 7355264Z. Painted on its metallic flank, a familiar insignia glinted in the glare of the lightning strikes. The heads of two wolves, a star and a planet in between them.

Romulus had arrived.

The storm raged like the fires of hell, and the battle did too.

It was nearly impossible to tell what was mud and what was blood; the rebels slipped around in the wetness that soaked the grass and fought desperately to keep the enemies at bay while staying tightly grouped together. The thunder and lightning shook the ground beneath them and clogged their ears, the flashing light against the pitch dark glared in their eyes and glinted off the weapons of the warriors.

Leida was flanked by two enemies at once. As her armored talons slashed through the throat of one, she was tackled and slammed to the ground by another. Her gauntlets raised to deflect the sword aimed at her face, but she struggled to fight it away. Leida snarled frantically, pulling every ounce of strength from her tired muscles to stop the blade from driving down with the warrior's weight, but her limbs threatened to give out.

Just before the sword pierced her skull, the enemy was slammed off her by Rykr's mighty hammer with a crack of bones and a thud of steel. He dropped the hammer to catch her by the wing and pull her out of the slippery mud, but his jaws released as he screamed in pain. A launched spear stuck out of the flesh of his shoulder, then another soared through the rain and pierced down into his brawny back.

"*No!*" Leida cried out, and her broad wings flapped open to shield him as they were assaulted by a shower of more and more javelins. They caught in her feathers, and an agonized sob escaped through her teeth while her wings were shredded by thrown spears. Rykr struggled to remain standing despite the wooden poles sticking out of his flesh like spines, but his legs could no longer hold his weight. He collapsed into the mud.

Iago fought viciously, still without her sword, but she was swarmed and outnumbered as their formation broke and the blood loss began to claim her energy. Kodo thrashed wildly as three warriors clawed onto his back and fought to down him, but he threw himself hard to the ground to roll them off his gored flank. As he struggled to rise again, covered in sweat and dark mud, his desperate eyes landed on Alvi. Her tail blade thrashed lethally as she sliced at enemies and slid out of the way of their blows, but her breaths were shallow with terror as more and more surrounded them. She caught Kodo's gaze, and for a moment, her amber eyes held a deep sorrow. The giant's exhausted, accepting face spoke silently to her, and she heard his unspoken words as clearly as the deafening cracks of lightning.

As long as it's here. As long as it's beside you.

Alvi shook her head stubbornly, refusing his acceptance, and her face hardened. She rolled away from the warriors near her, and then in one powerful leap, she landed on Kodo's back.

"Cover your ears!" Alvi screamed over the tumult, trying to find the eyes of her companions through the battle. *"Cover your ears!"* she roared as she stood up over Kodo's head, pressing her palms over his ears as hard as she could.

With no understanding of her order, and with all the trust in the world, the rebels did what she asked of them.

Leida, Rykr, and even Iago all stopped fighting and hit the ground. They allowed their enemies to overtake them as they gave up their arms and held their ears closed.

A shockwave exploded through the atmosphere.

Ravaging the valley, a low rumbling howl erupted and drowned out the rain, the thunder, the lightning, the roars, the clanking of armor and weapons. It consumed the air, it consumed the entire planet.

Black blood sprayed from the ears of the Ramys warriors overtaking the rebels, and they immediately toppled to the muddy wet ground, screaming in agony. Those nearest to Alvi went limp as they lost consciousness and the contents of their skulls boiled over.

Alvi stood tall over the valley with her jaws agape, her throat pulsing, and her eyes closed tight in focus. Her call invaded the plains, shaking the molecules in the atmosphere and vibrating through the skulls of the enemies as they noiselessly shrieked and their eardrums disintegrated in their heads.

Rataan's weakness finally overtook him as the noise pounded through his bones, and he crumpled to the grass at the other end of the field. The mighty commander, who should have been dead hours ago, now fell as his eyes rolled back into his head and he could stand no longer. His last three tunahk-dahn cried frantically to one another, calling for a retreat, but their voices made no sound over Alvi's deathly song. They worked together to drag their unconscious kaunek-leih to safety as the remaining warriors followed them. The dwindling forces stumbled away, falling over one another as they raced across the wet grass and muddy soil. They fled to the safety of the charred trees. To the end of the agony.

When the only Ramys ghaengste left in the valley were bodies on the ground, Alvi ceased her call.

She closed her mouth, then slowly uncovered Kodo's ears, gently checking them for damage. Gradually, cautiously, the other three companions opened their eyes and released their ears. Even slower yet, they rose from the mud.

The rain finally slowed as they stood in silence. It calmed as if submitting to Alvi's shocking will. The young ocean woman looked over the cloudy sky, and she wondered if somewhere, the Lost King was surprised too.

"What the fuck was that?" Iago demanded, the first to come out of their terrified stupor. Kodo turned his head to look at Alvi still sitting on his shoulder, timidly as if he wasn't sure she was the same Alvi he'd known before. Alvi looked over his frightened gaze, then at the rest of the eyes on her.

"They call it the siren's song." She cleared her throat, hesitating. "A rare ability I only learned how to do when we were at Celesteal."

Her words were rough and ragged as she explained, as if she'd torn her own voice apart. The other rebels watched her in shock and confusion.

"Why did you wait so long?" Leida asked sharply as she settled by Rykr's side and began to gingerly pull the spears from deep in his flesh. He growled in pain and lifted his head to bite at her, but his aggression gave his companions a grateful wash of relief.

"Because I didn't know if it would kill all of you." Alvi descended from Kodo's back. "I promise to explain more later, but we have to go."

Kodo helped Leida guide Rykr to his feet and hand him his hammer after packing his wounds. The rebels rose, exhausted, injured, and quivering as the rain finally slowed from a shower to a tender sprinkle. It pattered against their fur, gently repenetrating the heavy layer of mud, sweat, and blood. When Leida finished plucking the spearheads from her wings, they began limping west. But Leida stopped, turning back to the white figure that stood aimlessly behind them. Iago.

"You are strong," the wounded sky dweller called to Iago hoarsely, studying the other one-eyed woman.

"You could join us," she finished as she looked around at the other rebels, and they nodded hesitantly.

"Join the rebel clan?" Iago said, her lip lifting with distaste.

"The Isthmus clan," Kodo corrected with a wistful look. The rebels stood a little taller together, leaning on one another, watching the warrior.

Iago let out a slow breath and looked around the carnage in the meadow, the bodies of her comrades. Her brothers, her sisters. Her kin.

Then she leaned down and picked up a dropped Ramys dagger. The rebels tensed and stared at her, but the blade cut her own flesh instead of theirs. Iago jerked her head to the side, slicing the dagger across the scarification on her shoulder. The symbol of the tunahk-dahn. In its place, an ugly wound. The dagger dropped from her jaws.

"I have nothing left here," she said, her whistling voice tired and lost. "Damn it all. Where are we going?"

A small smile crossed Kodo's face.

"West," he said gently, gesturing with his head for Iago to follow. They limped after the westward horizon as the dark storm clouds finally receded, and the triumphant glow of the sunset warmed their weary backs. They headed for the sunrise.

GLOSSARY

GLOSSARY

1. **7355264Z:** The numerical moniker assigned by the RREP to the planet of the ghaengste.

2. **AHSUEI** *(AH-SHWAY)*: The name of a Matkan clan of mountain bandits.

3. **A'TAJA HO** *(AH-TASHA HO)*: "All over."

4. **BLADEMASTER** *(BLAYD-MAS-TER)*: The most skilled weapon smiths of the Celesteal clan.

5. **CAITO/CAITA** *(KYE-TOE/KYE-TUH)*: A healer or shaman. Caito: feminine derivative, Caita: masculine derivative.

6. **CELESTEAL** *(SELL-ESS-TEEL)*: The name of the ocean ghaengste clan.

7. **CINCEIDA** *(SIN-SAY-DUH)*: The giant hollow trees of Matka.

8. **THE COMPOUND:** The grounded form of "Salvation" Shuttle I and the base of operations for the RREP crew.

9. **EIDOLAN** *(AY-DOE-LON)*: The name of the mountain ghaengste clan.

10. **FOHS'IL** *(FOSS-EEL)*: The name of a ridge west of Ramys.

11. **GHAENGSTE** *(GAIN-ST)*: The dominant species of Matka; intelligent, cannibalistic, quadrupedal predators.

12. **GUTFYRE** *(GUTT-FIRE)*: The name of a Matkan tribe of venom-spitting forest bandits also known as "gutters."

13. **HAJVA** *(HAH-SH-VAH)*: A type of Matkan soup made with thinly shredded meat and vegetables.

14. **HONA'DEI** *(HO-NAH-DAY)*: A derogatory Matkan word meaning rogue, renegade, or exile.

15. **HYYECUT** *(HI-YE-KET)*: A Matkan species of medium-sized

herbivore.

16. **IESU'TALEI** *(YES-OO-TALL-AY)*: "Justice."

17. **IJGRA** *(EE-GRUH)*: A derogatory oceanic term for forest ghaengste meaning driftwood.

18. **JEL** *(HEL)*: The designated hunter/gatherers of a Matkan clan.

19. **KAUNEK-LEIH** *(CON-NEK LAY)*: The commander of the armed forces of a Matkan clan, or second-in-command under the lunai.

20. **KOCEA** *(KO-SAY-UH)*: The name of the sky ghaengste clan.

21. **KRAJFELL** *(KRAY-FELL)*: The name of a Ramys outpost.

22. **KRU'VAII** *(KREV-EYE)*: A Matkan species of pack predator.

23. **LEI'DA** *(LAY-DUH)*: "To fly," the phrase Kodo uses as Leida's name.

24. **LUNAI-VAUS** *(LOO-NYE VOSS)*: The leader of a Matkan nation.

25. **LA'AL MAIXAY** *(LUH-ALL MY-SHAY)*: "Until blood spills," the first half of the Ramys tunahk mantra.

26. **LA'AL MAIJEX** *(LUH-ALL MY-ESH)*: "Until blood rains," the second half of the Ramys tunahk mantra.

27. **MATKA** *(MAHT-KUH)*: The native word for the planet of the ghaengste.

28. **RAMYS** *(RAY-MISS)*: The name of the forest ghaengste clan.

29. **REIHGGUS** *(RAY-JUS)*: A Matkan species of giant herbivore.

30. **REMUS-ROMULUS EXPEDITION PROJECT**: The four year long mission to scout Dwarf Planet 7355264Z for human colonization, abbreviated as RREP.

31. **SALVATION INITIATIVE**: The united world program tasked with seeking a replacement Earth for humankind.

32. **SLAUGHTERSTEW** *(SLOT-TER-STOO)*: A type of Matkan stew typically made from the meat of multiple different ghaengste.

33. **SUNCHAENGE** *(SUNN-CHAYN-J)*: The period in the Matkan solar orbit when the secondary sun is replaced by the next in the cycle and there is a monsoon season across the planet.

34. **TERROSPHERE** *(TARE-OH-S-FEER)*: The giant dome-shaped greenhouse connected to the compound.

35. **TUNAHK-DAHN** *(TOO-NOCK DAWN)*: A special order of the most elite warriors in a Matkan clan, usually raised and trained by the kaunek-leih.

36. **VYRJA VARO** *(VEER-YUH VAR-OH)*: "Heavy Heart," the name of Rykr's hammer.

37. **WOLF ONE:** The first stage of the RREP consisting of the Remus crew and "Salvation" Shuttle I.

38. **WOLF TWO:** The second stage of the RREP consisting of the Romulus crew and "Salvation" Shuttle II.

39. **XILAI** *(SHILL-EYE)*: A Matkan species of giant winged fish.

40. **XINSEI** *(SHIN-SAY)*: The name of the pass that divides the southern mountain range in half.

41. **YSHA HEI** *(EE-SHUH HAY)*: "Mother war."

42. **Y'XARA** *(EE-SHAR-UH)*: "Fear of God," the name of Kaishek's axe.